HOPE REFORMED

The General Series

THE GENERAL SERIES
by David Drake

The Forge with S.M. Stirling
The Hammer with S.M. Stirling
The Anvil with S.M. Stirling
The Steel with S.M. Stirling
The Sword with S.M. Stirling
The Chosen with S.M. Stirling
The Reformer with S.M. Stirling
The Tyrant with Eric Flint
The Heretic with Tony Daniel
The Savior with Tony Daniel

OMNIBUS EDITIONS

Hope Reborn with S.M. Stirling
Hope Rearmed with S.M. Stirling
Hope Renewed with S.M. Stirling
Hope Reformed with S.M. Stirling and Eric Flint

HOPE REFORMED

The General Series

S.M. Stirling
Eric Flint
David Drake

HOPE REFORMED

This is a work of fiction. All the characters and events portrayed in this book are fictional, and any resemblance to real people or incidents is purely coincidental.

A Baen Books Original

Baen Publishing Enterprises
P.O. Box 1403
Riverdale, NY 10471
www.baen.com

ISBN: 978-1-4767-3690-7

Cover art by Kurt Miller

First Baen paperback printing, November 2014

Distributed by Simon & Schuster
1230 Avenue of the Americas
New York, NY 10020

Library of Congress Cataloging-in-Publication Data

Drake, David, 1945-
Hope Reformed / David Drake, S.M. Stirling, [Eric Flint]
pages cm. -- (The General series ; 4)
ISBN 978-1-4767-3690-7 (paperback)
1. Science fiction. I. Stirling, S. M. II. Flint, Eric. III. Title.
PS3554.R196H68 2014
813'.54--dc23

2014032805

Printed in the United States of America

10 9 8 7 6 5 4 3 2 1

CONTENTS

VII
THE REFORMER

David Drake
S. M. Stirling

To Marjorie Stirling

CHAPTER ONE

The High City of Solinga had been the core of the ancient town once; first a warlord's castle, then the seat of the city council. Three centuries ago, when Solinga was capital of the Emerald League, several million arnkets of the League's treasury had mysteriously found their way into a building program to turn it into a shrine to the city's gods—to the Gray-Eyed Lady of the Stars, first and foremost.

Money well stolen and spent, Adrian Gellert thought, as the procession mounted the broad flight of marble stairs that led to the plateau. Right hand tucked into the snowy folds of his robe, left hand holding the gold-capped scroll that marked him as a Scholar of the Grove, he kept to the slow hieratic pace suitable for a religious occasion. About him gulls swooped and shrieked; before him stood the cream-white marble pillars, the golden roofs, the great forty-foot statue of the Maiden holding Her bronze-tipped spear aloft to guide the mariners home. Behind him was the tarry workaday reality of Solinga smelling of fish and offal and sea salt, narrow crooked streets and whitewashed walls peeling to show the mud brick, tile roofs and only occasionally the walls and colonnades and courtyard gardens of the rich. But here, amid the scent of incense and the light silvery tones of hand bells, was the ideal the reality served.

We may have fallen from our forefathers' power, but this at least we can say—that we alone gave godlike things to the gods, he thought with a melancholy pride that edged out the anxiety and grief of his father's funeral.

The procession halted as a priest confronted them, a blue-edged fold of his blanketlike mantle over his head like a hood. "Why do you come to this holy place?"

"To render homage to the Goddess, in such seemly wise as is allowed to mortal men," Adrian's uncle said, speaking as the eldest adult male of the Gellert clan. Besides, he was paying for the ceremony. "In memory of Ektar Gellert, a free citizen of this city, that the Maiden may judge him kindly; and in the name of his sons, Esmond and Adrian Gellert, that She may watch over them in the trials of life."

"Come, then, and do worship."

The procession resumed; Adrian, his brother Esmond, uncles, cousins, grandfathers, hangers-on, with hired musicians following behind playing double-pipes and lyres. Pilgrims and priests and citizens making sacrifice parted before them. Their sandals scuffed across the pavement, slabs of white-veined green marble edged with gold. They passed the Plinth of Victories, a huge column set with the beaks of captured warships; past the black-basalt fane of Wodep the War God, the pink and gold marble of Etat the All-Father, and at last to the great raised rectangle of the Maiden's fane. It was a simple affair of giant white columns, each ending in a riot of golden acanthus leaves. The roof was copper-green tiles, and all around from pediment to architrave ran mosaic panels done in gold glass, lapis, amber and semiprecious stones. Some showed the Goddess giving Her gifts to men—fire, the plow, the olive, ships, the art of writing. Others were scenes from the Five Year Festival, the city's knights on their velipads, the Year Maidens bringing the great embroidered shawl, the athletes naked in their iron pride.

"Follow, then," the priest said.

Hot charcoal fires burned in a pair of tall tripods of fretted bronze. Gravely, Esmond and Adrian strode up the steps. Each took a silver bowl from the acolytes, pouring a stream of translucent grains into the white-glowing bed. Fragrant smoke rose, bitter and spicy.

The others drew up a fold of their mantles to cover their heads as the priest raised his hands; the Goddess' moon was visible over the horns of the roof, the other two moons being below the horizon at this hour. Adrian's uncle led the sacrifice forward, a white-feathered greatbeast with four gilded horns and a myrtle wreath around each. It came to the altar willingly enough—*drugged*, he thought: no sense in courting a bad omen—and collapsed almost soundlessly as the broadaxe flashed home with a wet, heavy thud on its neck.

Slowly, the tall ebony and silver doors of the temple slid open, rolling soundlessly on bronze bearings. Adrian's mind reflexively murmured three citations and an epic poem on the building of the Maiden's Temple; all of them described the effect, and all of them inaccurately as far as he knew. The cult image came forth on brass rails set into the marble of the pronacs floor, gliding with oil-bath smoothness. It was hidden in a tall cedarwood and silver shrine, emblazoned with the full moon on all sides. At a touch the sides sank down to reveal a rock. Black, slagged and metallic-looking in spots with a trace of rust, a metorite and very ancient.

Adrian Gellert had long since been trained in the precepts of the Grove; that God was Number and Form, and all the lesser images merely avatars or imaginings of men unable to conceive of the One. God did not need to Do, only to Be—but he still felt a trace of numinous awe as he extended his hand. And of course a gentleman showed respect for the ancient cults.

"Scholar of the Grove—"

Adrian held up the scroll in his left hand.

"Scholar of the Blade—"

His brother Esmond raised his sheathed sword.

"Receive the blessing of the Goddess, your patron."

Adrian closed his eyes and let the hand rest on the sacred rock. It was cool, cooler than it should have been, and—

Where am I? Where am I?

He thought he screamed the words, but he had no lungs. No eyes, for surely even the darkest night at the bottom of the silver mines of Flowerhill was brighter than this. He was nothing but Fear, adrift in a world of midnight. Stroke. Heart attack.

Compose yourself, he thought sharply. *Remember that anything that can happen, can happen to* you. *All men are initiates of the mysteries of death.*

That was the comfort of philosophy, but a little hard to remember when one was only twenty-one.

Light. He blinked . . . and saw a room around him. Furnished in an alien style, strange padded furniture, a fire burning in an enclosed brick space in one wall, tables and chairs of subtly foreign make. And a man standing there, a dark man with bowl-cut black hair. Odd clothes, something like those worn in the Western Isles, or even among the Southron barbarians; trousers, those marks of the savage, a curious tailored coat of blue with tails dangling behind. A curved sword and a holster with something rather like a carpenter's tool were lying on one table.

Either I have gone mad, or something very strange has happened, Adrian thought. He was conscious of his own terror, but it was distant, muted. He looked down at himself, and he was there again—not in the snowy draped robe of ceremony, but in an everyday tunic, with inkhorn and pen case slung from his belt.

"Adrian Gellert," the oddly-dressed man said; he spoke good Emerald, with a hint of a soft accent. "What is it that you desire?"

It was the manner of the Academy to teach with questions. He closed his lips on his own enquiries, on the fleeting ephemeral desires of every day, on the anxieties of his father's untimely death. That question had asked for *truth.* Perhaps there was truth in the old stories of Divine intervention in the lives of men.

"I want to *know,*" he blurted.

The dark man nodded.

"An excellent dinner. Many thanks, Samul," Esmond said, from his couch across the table.

Adrian nodded and murmured something. His brother-in-law Samul Mcson had been a catch for his sister Alzabeta. A catch of sorts; the Mcson family was important in the dye trade and had a fish-sauce works whose products were sold by name as far away as Vanbert, the Confederacy capital. He'd never liked the man, and the sneer on the heavy fleshy features showed the feeling was returned. Also there was honey-glaze sauce on the front of his robe, which was rose-colored silk from the Western Isles. *Probably brought back on one of Father's ships,* he thought, smiling and nodding at his surly relative by marriage.

The servants—Mcson retainers as well, since the Gellert retainers were dispersed—cleared away the fruits and pastries and cheeses; the dinner had been the traditional seven courses, from nuts to apples. Restrained, at least by Confederacy standards; the simple tastes of the antique Emeralds only survived in Cadet training and the Academy's dining halls. The broken meats and scraps would be distributed at the door to the city's poor, who gathered whenever the garlanded head of a greatbeast was hung over a door to mark a household that had made sacrifice.

Adrian dipped water into his wine and poured a small libation on the mats set out on the tile floor. He suppressed a stab of unphilosophic anger at his father for dying at such an inopportune time; the business had been going well enough, but the capital was all in goodwill, contacts and ongoing trade, and neither of the Gellert sons were inclined to take up the shipping business to the Western Isles. Their father wouldn't have heard of it, anyway; what had all his ignoble labor been for, if not to buy his sons the leisure to be scholars and athletes, gentlemen of Solinga, greatest of the Emerald cities? But he'd died too early. By themselves the physical assets were barely enough to cover the debts, dower their youngest sister and provide a modest but decent living for their mother. The younger Gellerts would have to cut short their education and find their own way in the world.

He looked around the room; two dozen guests reclining on the couches, some of them rented for the occasion. It was the men's summer dining room, open to the garden on one side, with old-fashioned murals of game and fish and fruit on the walls. Scents of rose and jasmine blew in from the darkness of the courtyard, and the sweet tinkle of water in a fountain. Most of the guests were older men, friends or business acquaintances of his father. Esmond lay on one elbow across from him, his mantle falling back, exposing the hard muscle of his chest and arm, tanned to the color of old beechwood. It made the corn-gold of his hair more vivid as it spilled down his back; a rare color for an Emerald, and the only thing besides blue eyes he and his brother had in common physically.

I'm weedy, in fact, Adrian thought. Short, at least, and only middling competent in the athletic part of the two-year course of Cadet training every well-born Solingian youth had to take when he turned eighteen. Once it had been preparation for military service, but that had ceased to be important long ago, in his great-grandfather's time, when the Confederacy's armies had conquered the Emerald lands.

The servants brought in another two jugs of wine, yard-high things with double looping handles and pointed bottoms. They splashed into the great bulbous mixer; light from the oil lamps flickered on the cheerful feasting scene painted across its ruddy pottery. Not much like tonight's memorial dinner; no flute-girls or dancers or acrobats here, since it wouldn't be seemly. His father hadn't hired such for most of his parties. *These things are for men with no conversation.* He smiled slightly, remembering the deep gravel voice and the face weathered by twenty years of sea weather and spray.

"Excuse me," he murmured. Three parts wine to one of water now, and the talk grew louder.

The garden was warm and still, starlight and two of the moons showing the brick pathways between beds of herbs and flowers. Not very large, only fifty paces on a side, but tall cypress trees stood around the perimeter wall, throwing pools of stygian blackness. The pool and fountain shone silver; he could see the mouths and tentacles of the ornamental swimmers breaking the surface, hoping for a few crumbs of bread as he passed. Down towards the end of the garden was a little pergola, an archway of withes covered in a flowering vine, with a stone seat beneath and a mask of the Goddess in Her aspect as patron of wisdom set in the wall behind.

The most private place in the house. Outside the womens' rooms, and from the noise coming from those, the female side of the party was getting more lively than the mens'. He'd often come to this bench to read, meditate and think.

"If you wish to speak—if you are more than the imaginings of my mind—then speak," he murmured.

it is not necessary to vocalize your thoughts, the cold, relentless voice in his head replied. It felt . . . heavy, as if it were packing more meaning into the forms than the words could properly carry. **merely articulate them internally.**

He did so, not an easy task . . . but then, he'd trained himself to read without speaking, or even moving his lips, an uncommon skill even among scholars.

Who are you?

We, the other voicc replied, the voice of the strange dark man. ***I am Raj Whitehall, and my . . . companion is Center. I'm . . . I was a man, on another world. Center is a computer.***

Despite the utter strangeness, Adrian's dark brows drew together at the last word. *Computer.* It wasn't one he was familiar with, but in the Scrolls of the Lady's Prophet there was a remote cognate . . .

A daemonic spirit? he thought. *Interesting. I thought those superstition. And you are a ghost, you say?*

A mental sigh. ***Not exactly. Let me start at the beginning. Human beings are not native to this world . . .***

An hour later he was sweating. "I . . . understand, I think," he muttered, and looked up at the starry sky.

Other worlds, whole worlds *attendant on the stars! The stars are suns!* It was more radical than even the speculations of the ancient Wisdom Lovers, the ones who'd spent their time trying to measure the sun or the shape of the earth, before modern philosophy turned to questions of language and virtue. The scale of timc involved staggered him; the vision of men coming to this world of Hafardine in great ships of the aether, falling out among themselves, tumbling down into savagery after wars fought with weapons that had eerie parallels to the most ancient legends.

"Why?" hc went on. "Why me?"

Because, lad, you're a man who wants to find out the truth of things, Raj's voice said. ***This world has gotten itself on a wrong road, and we need a man to set it right. So that, in due time, Hafardine may take its place within the Federation of Man.***

Adrian gave a shaky laugh. "Me, a world-bestrider like Nethan the Great?" he said. "You should have picked my brother Esmond; he's the warrior in our family, the one who burns to bring back the days of the Emerald League."

not a conqueror, the slow, heavy voice of the . . . machine? continued: **a teacher. although elements of collective violence may well be necessary to disturb the established order on this world.**

"What's wrong with the established order?" he said, curiously. "Apart from those vulgarian bumpkins from the south ruling the Emerald lands, that is."

observe:

The world vanished, as it had in the High City by the temple of the Maiden. Again he saw Hafardine as it had been just after the fall of the Federation's machine civilization. Little villages of farmers scattered through the valleys and plains of the figure-eight-shaped main continent and along the coasts of the islands; bands of hunters in the vast forests of the mountains and the southlands. Some of the villages grew. He gasped as he recognized the great cities of the Emeralds in their earliest days, their rise to greatness, the long struggle with the Lords of the Isles and the founding of the Emerald League. His heart beat faster as he saw Solinga in the days of her glory, as the deathless beauty of the High City rose from the dreams and hands of men. Then the long, terrible civil wars, city against city, the League against the Alliance. Solinga's defeat that solved nothing, and then the Confederation's armies moving in from the south.

observe. the world as it now exists.

A view from above, first. The Confederacy's wall across the narrow waist of the continent, separating the barbarian southlands from the land of cities and law to the north. The estates of the Confederacy's nobles expanding across valley and plain; Vanbert growing from a straggling shepherd's camp to a city far vaster than any in the Emerald lands. He could sense years passing.

the maximum-probability result of a continuation of present trends.

Images . . .

. . . armies clashed, both sides in the armor and equipment of the Confederacy. Behind them a city burned . . .

. . . a view down a street. It was the buzzing heat of noon, and nothing moved; a fine broad paved street, arrow-straight, obviously in the Confederacy's heartlands. A body lay in one gutter, the exposed skin purple and swollen. Flies buzzed around it. A handcart came slowly down the pavement, drawn by men with cloth masks around their faces and more of the swollen bodies piled high behind them.

"Bring out your dead!" one of the men called. "Bring out your dead!"

. . . men in shabby tunics and women in drab gowns gathering as a proclamation was read from a plinth in some anonymous farm town. The plump official droned on, and on, some sort of edict setting prices and wages: "*And the price of leather harness for a carriage velipad shall be no more than one hundred twenty-five New Arnkets, of which one in four shall be paid to meet the needs of the State, in cash or kind. Sandals shall be no more than . . .*"

. . . slaves worked on a hillside, dragging boxes of earth on ropes looped over their shoulders; he could see the cheap sleazy fabric of their tunics, hear them grunt as they tipped the earth into a deep gully that slashed across a sloping wheatfield. It began to rain, and muddy water torrented down the cut in the field, washing away the earth a hundred times faster than the slaves could hope to haul it back.

. . . Vanbert itself, capital of the Confederacy and the known world. But it was on fire, greasy black smoke rising to hide the outlines of temple and palace and tenement block. Down one street a noblewoman ran, the silks of her gown trailing behind her. Behind her rode a Southron, a barbarian in greasy furs, his long yellow braids swaying with the gallop of his velipad. He leaned sideways in the saddle, one arm out to scoop the fleeing woman up and a gap-toothed grin on his face. A priestess' necklace of amber and gold bounced on his bare, painted chest.

. . . Vanbert again, but it took a moment for his eyes to recognize it. Trees covered the ruins, *old* trees. A few small fields stood, among log longhouses. A woman scattered grain to chickens, and a lean bristly pig rooted along the outskirts of a fly-buzzing midden.

Adrian gasped as the vision released him. Raj's voice spoke in his mind: ***Your world is trapped in a cycle of war, empire, decline and war,*** he said. ***It could repeat itself indefinitely, the only difference that each cycle falls further and climbs less as the land itself becomes less fertile.***

this is what you must prevent, Center's passionless tones went on. **we have waited seven hundred years for a man such as you.**

"*Me?*" Adrian squeaked. "Why not my brother Esmond?"

this world does not require a warrior, Center said. **it needs . . . wisdom.**

"Philosophy?" Adrian asked, bewildered. "Rhetoric? Yes, they're the arts of civilization, but our thinkers and speakers are the finest that have ever lived. How can *I*—"

Raj cut him off. ***I'll explain; the concept wasn't very easy for me, either, back on Bellevue—back on the world where I was born,*** he said. ***It's called "technological progress."***

Adrian felt a familiar excitement; it was like the first time he grasped that this syllogism thing the lecturer was talking about *meant* something, or understood just *why* the angles of a right-angled triangle had to add up in a certain way—the feeling of real knowledge, like a conduit to the mind of God.

"Tell me," he whispered.

"Way!" the soldier's voice rang harsh and loud. "Make way!"

Adrian and Esmond reined their velipads to the side of the highway. It was a Confederation road, built a century ago to nail down the Confederacy's control of the coastal river valleys to the north. Twenty paces broad, ditched, and paved with hexagonal blocks of volcanic rock, built to last for the ages—Adrian had seen one undercut by a flash flood once, and it was five feet thick. A layer of fist-sized stones in lime mortar, a layer of sand, another of mortar with smaller rocks, then a layer of mortar and gravel, and then the paving blocks . . .

Hobnailed sandals crashed down in unison as the battalion came down the center of the roadway in a column of fours, legs moving like a single centipede. *There goes the thing that ended the glory of the*

Emerald cities, Adrian thought. Out of the corner of his eye Adrian could see Esmond's hands tightening on the reins, then relaxing with an effort of will, one going forward to stroke the feathery bronze-colored scales of his mount's neck. Their ancestors had fought in dense-packed squares, each man locking shields with his neighbor and thrusting with the long spear. The Confederates . . . Adrian focused on one soldier, conscious of a very slight feeling of pressure behind his eyes, more mental than physical. Raj was taking an interest.

The trooper was a typical Confederate peasant of the central territories, a little stockier and thicker-built than the average Emerald, a little lighter in complexion, his face a beak-nosed harshness closed in with the long effort of the march and wet with sweat. He wore a short-sleeved tunic of mail that hung to his knees, with doubling patches on the shoulders; beneath it was another tunic of scarlet wool. On his left shoulder hung a big curved oval shield with an iron boss; on the march it was covered by a canvas sheath, with the bearer's name and unit neatly stenciled on it. Clipped to the interior of the shield were three short thick javelins with barbed points, each weighted behind the point by a small lead ball. On his feet were thick-soled sandals studded on the bottoms by iron nails, and strapped up the calves over wool leggings. On his head was a round helmet with a shelflike projection over the eyes, hinged cheekguards and a lobster-tail flare at the rear protecting his neck.

A pack and rolled blanket were on his back, but beneath them rested the weapon that had cut the proud spearmen of the Emerald cities to so much bleeding meat. Ready to draw over the right shoulder jutted a three-foot length of hardwood, topped with a lead ball. In the sheath hidden by the pack was the business end, a broad two-foot blade that tapered to a razor point; in battle the man would throw his darts in volley with his companions, then pull the assegai free and close, shield up, blade poised for the underarm gutting stroke. The column gave off a peculiar smell, of sweat and leather and the olive oil rubbed on armor and weapons, a rank masculine odor.

The battalion's commander rode at the column's head beside the standard-bearer, on a high-stepping velipad. *He* wore a version of classic Emerald war gear, bronze breastplate cinched with a scarlet sash, long single-edged sword, bronze helmet with a flaunting scarlet plume running fore-and-aft like a cock's comb, kilt of leather strips. He rode easily, one hand on his hip, hawk-nosed face disdainful; beside him the standard swayed, an upright hand with gold wreaths below it to mark the unit's victories. The standard-bearer himself wore an antique hauberk of brass scales, and his face was hidden by the tanned head of a direbeast, eternally snarling defiance and hunger at the world.

"Useless bastard," Esmond muttered. "It's the noncoms make the Confederacy army what it is." He grinned suddenly; neither of the brothers had seen three years past twenty. "*Useful* bastards, those are."

Adrian nodded in agreement, looking at the weathered faces beneath the transverse helmet crests, marching along in ranks with the others.

Several centuries of collective experience there, Raj murmured at the back of his mind, scanning the veterans' faces. ***A lot of stored knowledge.***

"Reinforcements for the Ropen forts," Esmond said judiciously. "Islander raids out that way, I heard."

The last rank of soldiers tramped by, followed by a few plowbeast carts and pack-velipads; most of those were probably carrying the commander's dunnage. Merchants, travellers, pilgrims and peasants surged back into the roadway, the brothers with them; the travellers on foot mostly made way for the brothers, given their gentlemen's cloaks and the loaded pack-velipad behind them. They made way in their turn, for a courier, a noble lady in her palanquin borne by picked slaves who could trot longer than a velipad . . . although the armed outriders helped, there. They could smell the towns coming a fair distance before the road arrowed through them. Not from the sewage; Confederates were lavish builders of sewers and water systems.

"Another token," Esmond said, wrinkling his nose and glancing up.

The pole stood leaning slightly in a barren patch of sand by the side of the road, thc unevenness giving it a weird demihuman quality. The man hanging on it was suspended twenty feet in the air; the short crosspiece ran through the elbows of his bound hands so that his body slewed forward, twisting at the spike that nailed his feet to the wood. A leather-winged flyer landed, hooking onto the naked body with the small claws on its wings and the longer ones on its legs. The long snaky neck bent and twisted as the toothed jaws poised consideringly. When they lanced home and began to worry loose a titbit the man awoke and began to scream weakly, unable to thrash hard enough to disturb the feasting scavenger. His cousins had taken much of the meat off the bones of the next half-dozen.

"Savages," Esmond muttered. "Why not an axe across the neck, if a man needs killing?"

Adrian nodded, breathing through his mouth. "Probably to keep the rest in order," he said.

Most of the bodies had lead plates nailed beneath, inscribed with their crimes. RUNAWAY SLAVE was the most common, next to INCENDIARY. There were slaves everywhere, of course, but in the heartlands of the Confederacy they outnumbered the free men, sometimes by a considerable margin, the fruits of centuries of conquest.

The velipads were sniffing with interest, opening both pairs of eyes and pulling the rubbery lips back off the stubby ivory daggers of their omnivore teeth.

"Let's keep going," Adrian said. He glanced up; the sun was about a handsbreadth from the mountains on the west, turning their snowpeaks to blood-red. "We can stop with father's guest-friend in Kirsford."

"Better than fighting bedbugs in an inn," Esmond agreed.

For a moment Adrian let himself envy his brother. *Now,* there's *the picture of a hero from the age of greatness,* he thought. Chiseled straight-nosed, square-jawed features, six feet tall, broad shoulders tapering to a flat stomach and narrow waist, long legs, every muscle moving beneath the tanned skin like living bronze. *And he's not even stupid.* Not a Scholar of the Grove, but he'd read the chronicles of Themston on the Pelos War, and Epmon's work on the Art of Battle. Sunny-natured, too; and the gods had stinted him nothing, making him brave as well.

Soon Esmond was whistling through his teeth, a jaunty marching song popular among the Cadets of Solinga; their father's guest-friend proved to set a good table, and they set off early the next morning. The land rolled away before them, sloping to the great central basin that held Vanbert, the largest of all the valleys in the center of the northern lobe. Tall forests of broadspike and oak mantled the mountains and foothills; then came the lush level lands. It was more orderly than an Emerald countryside, lanced through with the straight tree-lined expanses of the Confederacy's military highways and gravelled secondary roads, every town laid out on a grid. Canals looped more gracefully, carrying water from dams in the mountain valleys and spreading it into irrigation channels. The fields were almost painfully green, where great blocks of fruit trees were not flowering; Adrian looked with interest at cherries and apples, rare on the subtropical northern coast.

No olives or citrus, he thought. *Must be too cold in the winter.*

Here and there a peasant cottage stood, often abandoned and falling down; on hills some distance back from the highway he could make out the groves and gardens of a gentleman's mansion. Four-horned greatbeasts grazed quietly in the meadows, or pulled plows turning the rich reddish earth; herds of baaing fleecers went clumped with shepherds and dogs guarding their brainless vulnerability. Once they passed a field of maize that must have been a hundred acres in a single stretch, with fifty or sixty leg-hobbled slaves weeding in long rows.

Esmond looked and made a *tsk* sound between his teeth. "I'll say this, when these Confederate magnates are *rich*, they're *rich*. How much did it take to get into the highest voting class in Solinga, back in the old days?"

"Four hundred bushels a year, or equivalent," Adrian said, reaching up and snatching a spray of blossom, putting it to his nose for a second before tucking it behind one ear.

"Four hundred lousy bushels," Esmond said, shaking his head. "By the way, you'd better not do that when we get to Vanbert."

"Why not?"

"Because only pansies wear flowers in their hair, among the

Confeds," Esmond grinned. "Pansies and girls. So unless you want to attract the attention of some rich old Councillor—other than as a teacher of rhetoric, I mean—"

Adrian laughed and punched his brother on the arm; it was like striking a tree. "You're the pretty one in the family," he said.

They passed the field, and rode under the arches of an aqueduct that ran over the road as it dipped into a shallow valley. Esmond's mouth tightened again as they glanced back along the length of it, where it disappeared into the heat-haze.

"Arrogant bastards," he muttered.

"And you'd better learn to control your tongue, or you may lose it, in Vanbert," Adrian said. "They don't take kindly to Emeralds who don't keep their place."

Traffic grew steadily thicker; by the time they were within a day's travel of Vanbert itself, they rarely managed more than a trot. *Everything comes to Vanbert,* Adrian quoted to himself. Most of it prosaic: long wagon trains of grain and jerked meat, herds on the hoof stopping traffic—one memorable half-day spent behind a flock of waddling geese ten thousand strong—salt fish, smoked sausage, vegetables, cheeses and butter and giant tuns of wine. Once a fast two-wheeled carriage, with *snow* packed inside its sawdust-insulated box chassis, passed in a clatter and clangor and cracking of whips. More whips over the shuffling coffles of slaves, walking chained neck and neck with hard-eyed mounted guards, most of those barbarians from the Southron territories. Wagons and pack trains and wheel-barrows and porters, salt and iron and copper, gold and reed-paper and spices, and more races and tongues than he'd thought existed. Once he even saw a man whose skin was *black*, striding along in an ankle-length robe of cotton, ignoring pointing and whispering and daring small boys who darted in to touch his skin to see if it was real.

"I keep expecting to see the city over the next rise," Esmond said, on the fifth week of their journey.

Adrian grinned. "We're *in* the city," he said. "Have been for hours."

Esmond gaped, then looked around. The truck-gardens of yesterday had given way to elegant suburban estates; most of the road was lined with high walls of brick and concrete, usually whitewashed, broken here and there by an elaborate gate of wrought iron and brass. Each gate had at least two direbeasts on chains guarding it, their heads all mouth and the great overlapping pairs of canines often tipped with bronze or steel. The human guardians in the gatehouses were sometimes chained to the walls by their ankles as well; it made the slogans set in tiles by the entrances—WELCOME or HAIL HOSPITALITY—seem a little hollow.

Of course, that means hospitality for their own kind, Adrian thought.

"What can you expect," he said, "from a people who have a word in their language that means 'kill every tenth person'? And who think their first ancestors were nursed by a direbeast."

There was no edge to Vanbert of the type they were familiar with, no wall marking the place where city gave way to country. Not even the fringe of grave-memorials that ringed an Emerald city, since Confederates burned their dead and kept the ashes with the living in little pots under their wax masks—something he'd always considered rather gruesome, but then as Bestmun said, "Custom was king in every land." The suburbs grew thicker, the traffic denser, and above them rose the famous eight hills; and *those* were only higher places among the buildings that carpeted the land for more than a day's journey in every direction. Virtually the only breaks in the spread of buildings were the small groves that surrounded temples—usually round with pointed roofs here, or domes on some of the more recent—or the courtyards of the very wealthy; even the drained swamplands that had once helped feed an earlier Vanbert were built over.

"Dull, though," Esmond said critically, as they led their velipads aside to let a wagon loaded with column drums pass. "Brick, little shops—nothing really magnificent."

"We just haven't seen that part yet," Adrian said.

The street they were on didn't look like much in truth. It was five-story, brick-and-concrete apartments, remarkable only for their size; between the arches on their ground floors were shops. Bakers' shops, or so he thought until he saw the lead chits the ragged-looking patrons exchanged for big round loaves. *Bread dole,* he thought sourly. *Our taxes at work.* Others were taverns, or little restaurants with soup kettles sunk into the stone of the counters, or tailors' shops, or cubicles where shoemakers fitted their customers and then worked with awl and waxed thread and tapping hammer while they waited. Or others selling sharp-smelling cheese, or hanging birds and rabbits, or anonymous lumps of flesh. The crowds might just as well have been from an Emerald city, save that their tunics covered both shoulders and that women wore less and walked more boldly.

And the size of the crowds. "A million people in Vanbert, they say," Adrian muttered. A thought struck him. "How in the name of the Lame Craftsman are we going to find this Redvers fellow?"

Esmond's face paled as he looked around. That wasn't a problem in Solinga—even if you didn't know the city, you could just take your bearings from the High City temple roofs or the docks. Nowhere was more than a half-hour walk from anywhere else within the walls, after all. Vanbert didn't even have the right-angled network of streets of the newer Confed towns, it was too ancient, and its roadways had been laid out as greatbeast tracks.

here is a map, Center said helpfully. **take the following turnings.**

"How did you suddenly become an expert on the streets of Vanbert?" Esmond asked an hour later.

Adrian grinned. "The Gods of Wisdom whisper in my ear," he said, looking up at the high blank wall of the mansion; only slits on the upper stories and an iron-strapped borkwood door faced the street, with a surly-looking ex-games fighter lounging by it, tapping his brass-bound club against the pavement to discourage loiterers.

They dismounted and walked towards the gate. "Let's go find our fortunes," Esmond said.

And change the world, Raj whispered.

"Yer'll hafta keep that higher, m'lady," the trainer said, the point of his spear touching lightly at the base of his pupil's throat.

Helga Demansk nodded curtly and raised the small round shield as they backed and circled. The sword in her hand was an old Emerald model, forged for her of Solinga steel, single-edged except for a handspan on the reverse back from the point, and about as long as her leg from mid-thigh to toes. The hilt was sawfish hide, good for a grip, even with the fingerless chamois leather gloves her father insisted she wear—if she was to have a personal trainer at all. A bell-shaped guard of pierced bronze protected her hand; that and the shield were her only burden save for a short tunic. The trainer wore a leather corselet and brass helmet with a faceguard; his spear was tipped with a mock head of hide, but Helga's sword was sharpened to a knife edge.

That didn't worry him. He'd been a games fighter for fifteen years, and lived to see retirement before he slowed down too much. The full-busted, auburn-haired good looks of the young woman across from him were more of a distraction than her sword, although she really wasn't bad. The looks could kill him just as dead as a blade, if he forgot himself—she *was* Justiciar Demansk's daughter, after all. You didn't survive the games that long without learning self-control, though, and he had a couple of very nice little servant girls attending to his needs. This post was a retired fighter's dream, and he wasn't about to risk it for a pair of titties, no matter how nice they looked heaving away there with the thin cotton sticking to them.

Both fighters moved, bare feet scuffing the packed sandy dirt of the training shed. The sun was hot outside, coming in shafts of white-gold light through the gaps between the timbers that upheld the roof. He feinted with a one-two, felt the shiver as the spear shaft was turned aside, beat the point of the sword out of line with his own weapon.

"That's right, missie!" he cried. "Keep 'em moving *together.*"

Really not bad at all. If she weren't a nobleman's daughter, she might actually do for the games—matching female pairs against each other was a staple sidelight of the more elaborate games these days, despite how some of the magistrates huffed and puffed about it. And she kept at it, too, the better part of a year now, back in Vanbert and on this country estate in the westlands.

"Faster—keep it smooth. Push at me, get inside the spear's point!"

It was the screams that alerted him. Far too many of them, long and high; and underneath, something else, a harsh guttural shouting. He froze, and if Helga hadn't pulled the blow the sword might have laid open his right arm. "What is it?" she said, stepping back and breathing hard.

"Pirates," he said shortly, tossing aside the practice weapon. There were real spears racked by the door; he took one in his shield hand, and a couple of javelins.

"How—"

"I know Islander." He'd known men who spoke it, in the games—slaves, mostly, and freedmen who'd done well. That was an Islander war cry, and they *were* within a day's march of the coast—closer, if you counted rivers, and an Islander galley could run far up into the shallows. "Let's *go*, woman!"

She quieted; he opened the door a crack and peered out. They were a couple of hundred yards or so from the main building, a big open house with tall windows sparkling with an extravagance of glass, colonnades that looked out to the gardens rather than inward to a courtyard like a townhouse. He could hear more screams now, and men's laughter, and see figures moving about . . . sparkles in the sun. Light from blade edges, and from the metal studs of light Islander-style armor, much like what he was wearing himself. A man with a tall fountain of plumes on his helmet seemed to be directing things as they dragged out armloads of loot from the house. Others were shepherding the house slaves into a clump, and some raiders were bringing out animals and carts from the business part of the plantation, down past a clump of cypress trees.

"This way," he hissed, the smell of his own sweat harsh in his nostrils.

They dodged out, climbed the fence of a disused corral, crossed it and ran across a meadow, heading for the shelter of an orange grove. *Damn,* the trainer thought. *I'll be set for life—rescue the Justiciar's daughter—*

The thud of velipad paws brought his head around. Four men riding fast after them; the pirates must have looted mounts near their landing and dashed inland, hoping to catch rich unguarded targets like this by surprise. One of them was raising a bow, the short horn-backed type the Islanders used, but he couldn't hit anything from velipadback.

"Keep running!" he screamed, and tossed one of the javelins up, caught it, let fly. "You stupid bitch!" he yelled in frustration, as he saw her taking up stance beside him, waving the sword and shouting some family battle cry.

The javelin caught a velipad between neck and shoulder. It went down, and the man on it rolled and tumbled, losing his bow. He was up at once, drawing the short curved sword at his belt; a stringy active-looking youth with a brown face and a gold ring in his hooked nose, black hair in a queue at his back. The trainer took a chance and ignored him for the moment it took to throw his second javelin; that slammed into a mounted man's shoulder with an audible thud. He twisted desperately to face the youth on foot, only to see him falling backward with a foot of Helga's sword coming out of his neck.

Not bad at all.

"*Will* you run, you dumb twat!" he yelled, backing up himself. "Thank the *gods*," he added in a snarl, as she finally obeyed.

The Islanders had gotten themselves untangled from their mounts, which were going berserk at the scent of so much blood, torn between appetite and fear. One promptly set on the pirate who'd stolen it, leaving the trainer facing two men; the third unwrapped a sling from around his head and reached for a pouch on his belt. The trainer charged, ducked under the swing of a sword and threw himself to the left, cracking the shaft of his spear on the man's knee, and then stabbing him hard through the spot where the latches of his leather corselet fastened into the side of his gut. There was a stink of shit as the point came out, infinitely familiar, and the pirate shrieked in quick shocked agony.

Move, move, move! the trainer screamed to himself. The armor was squeezing his ribs; he wasn't in shape for this sort of thing any more. *Go, go.* He got himself turned around just in time to knock a sword cut aside with his shieldboss, springing back to give himself distance to use the spear.

Crack.

The slung stone hit him over the breastbone. The edges of his world went gray, and the shield and spear dropped as his arms lost strength. The swordsman hacked at him twice, into the collarbone and then up into the side of his thigh from below. He fell to the ground, feeling himself yawning in reflex. There was time enough to see Helga dragged back, one leg limp from the stunning impact of a slingstone.

A pirate turned him over on his back with a foot. *What a complete fuckup,* he thought, watching the spearpoint rise over his face. *Guess I didn't make it out of the games alive after all.*

An impact, then blackness.

"I've got to admit, the Confederates outdo us in this, at least," Adrian said, lying back in the cool water.

Public baths in an Emerald city were usually small and utilitarian. This was a palace, and not a small one either. The main pool lay under a high dome, the tiles that coated its interior silvered to reflect light from the round windows that ran completely around the base. The walls below them were rose-pink and snow-white marble, with a ten-foot band of bas-relief murals below *that,* and the floors had fifteen different types of colored stone. Water arched from the mouths of fabulous bronze beasts into the pool; in halls leading off on three sides were steam rooms, hot tubs for soaking, rooms for scraping down and massage, exercise and workout rooms, small libraries . . .

It *was* rather noisy; someone was making the air hideous with song as he stood under a stream of water and rubbed himself with a sponge. He could hear the slap of hands on flesh from a massage table, the click of dice from a friendly game in a corner, the grunting of would-be athletes as they swung lead weights, the tremendous splash as someone did a belly flopper in another corner of the pool, the cries of a vendor with a tray of sausages and pickled artichokes.

"When you've got the whole world to loot, you can afford the best," Esmond said. "Shameless degenerates," he added.

Adrian smiled. Public baths in the Emerald lands didn't mix the sexes . . . and the women here weren't all whores, either. It certainly added to the scenery, he mused, watching a statuesque redhead go by in nothing but the towel draped over her shoulder.

"Come on, we'll get weak as girls if we just lie about like this," Esmond said.

His brother attracted more than his share of looks as they walked over to the steam room—mostly from women. The hot chamber was empty, the time being a little early—the baths really filled up after three o'clock in the afternoon, when free men knocked off work and came to meet their friends and spend a pleasant few hours before dinner. They said you could meet anyone from a Priestess of the Hearthfire to the Lord of the Western Isles in the Vanbert baths, and hear what the Council was going to do before the Councillors knew themselves.

"Don't sneer too much at Confederate wealth," Adrian said. "Since you're going to get your hands on some of it yourself . . . Three hundred arnkets a year, plus your keep, a room and a servant! You can easily save two hundred of that. With three thousand, you could open your own *salle d'armes* back in Solinga, or buy an olive grove or shares in ships."

Esmond made a restless gesture and tossed a dipperful of water on the hot rocks in the corner of the room. A smell of hot cedarwood went up from the chips mixed with the glowing stones, and the heat struck like a padded club.

"Here," the older brother said, tossing Adrian a blunted, curved bronze knife from a rack. "Do my back."

Adrian began scraping the smooth, rippling muscle. "It only costs a copper *dimeh* to get a slave to do it," he teased.

"They never get it right . . . harder."

"What's really bothering you, brother?"

The broad shoulders shrugged. "I don't know why in the Gods' names Wilder wants a trainer. He's middle-aged, fat, and sluggish."

"Maybe he wants a weapons trainer *because* he's middle-aged, fat and sluggish?" Adrian suggested. "He's certainly paying enough."

"To him, three hundred arnkets is like you or me buying a spiced bun in the street," Esmond said, and then shrugged. "I'm to get a bonus for working as a bodyguard, though—protecting him and his wife when they go out, and so forth. It's work with a sword at your belt, at least."

"Don't they usually hire old games fighters for that?" Adrian said, curious.

"I'm better than any of those broken-down masses of scar tissue," Esmond said scornfully.

"And a lot more decorative," Adrian grinned. "There—your turn now."

"*Decorative!*" Esmond said, in mock indignation. "Here—I'll show you how they scrape loudmouths down at the wrestling ground for the Five Year Games!"

He whirled and came at Adrian with his arms out, the wrestler's pose. Adrian fell into the same stance, and they circled on the hot planks. It ended as it always did, with the younger man facedown on the boards and slapping his free hand down on the floor in sign of surrender.

"Peace! Peace!"

"Peace is a suitable theme for a teacher of rhetoric," Esmond laughed, letting him up. "A rinsedown and a cold plunge, and then we'll have to get back—move our things out of the rooms and into the Redvers house. I managed to get you permission to use the library, by the way."

"Thank you, brother; I'll take advantage of that. But I won't be teaching cauliflower-eared ex-generals how to give speeches, nor their pimply sons."

Esmond paused. "You won't?"

"No, I'm going to go to work in the law courts."

"Clerking?" Esmond looked shocked. "That's slaves' work."

Adrian shook his head. "Pleading cases."

"But . . ." A puzzled frown. "That's illegal, only Confederate citizens can appear before the Vanbert courts."

Adrian tapped a finger along his nose and winked. "In theory. In fact, if you're formally reading the speech of some Citizen advocate, it's allowed."

"You won't get far in front of a Confederate jury," Esmond warned, shaking his head. "And think, brother. I don't doubt you're an expert on Solingian law, but this is Vanbert."

"Oh, I don't know, I've picked up a good deal," Adrian said. He shifted into the Confederacy's tongue: "And I'm fairly fluent, aren't I?"

The blue eyes went wide. "No accent at all!" he exclaimed. "How did you do *that* in four months?"

"Divine intervention," Adrian laughed, slapping him on the shoulder. "Let's go take that plunge."

CHAPTER TWO

The Redvers family had an extensive library in their townhouse; Adrian bowed a greeting to the Emerald slave who ran it. The man was wrinkled, bald, stooped, and dressed in a long robe uncomfortably like that of a Scholar of the Grove. His grandfather might well have *been* a Scholar, enslaved in one of the endless wars.

"Greetings, learned Salman," Adrian said.

His reply was a sniff and a quick shooing motion of the hand. Adrian walked past the simple slab desk where Salman worked, repairing and recopying and keeping every one of the six thousand or so scrolls in its proper niche. The library beyond was nearly as large as the Academy's, and far more sumptously fitted. The ten-foot-high racks were Southland curly maple, clasped and edged with gilded bronze, each bolt end wrought in the shape of a woodspirit's face. The scrolls lay in the familiar manner, each one in the hollow of a honeycomb in the rack, the same way that wine bottles were kept. These were mostly fine goatskin vellum, though, not the cheap reed paper. The twin winding rods were gordolna ivory, and the little listing tags that hung down on cords from each were ivory and gold, bearing the title of the scroll in elegant cursive silver inlay. The walls on either side were clear glass, large panes fully a foot on each edge in metal frames, and there were comfortable padded couches and marble-topped tables at intervals for the use of readers. There was a pleasant smell of well-cured vellum, ink, and furniture wax.

So much, so good, Adrian thought critically; suitable for a man of immense wealth and some pretension to culture. The statuary along the walls, one in each window bay, was far too much—just to begin with, most of it was loot from the Emerald cities, and from *temples* at that.

Only a Confederate Councillor would boast *of having loot from temples in his study.* The piece of Gellerix, the Goddess of Passion, was a case in point. Fine enough in one of Her temples, but a life-size marble depiction of the act of generation was scarcely conducive to philosophic calm in a place of learning.

Adrian shrugged, sighed, and walked around the statue to the row of legal case-scrolls he knew resided there. Then he stopped, turned on his heel and came again, coughing and clearing his throat.

Lady Tinia Redvers was composed and cool when he appeared for the second time, her long clinging silk gown—itself a violation of every sumptuary law the Confederacy Council had ever passed—draped as decorously as anything that sheer could be. She was a woman of about thirty-five, with a figure that would be plainly fat in another decade but was now on the ample side of superb, and a mass of black ringlets piled high on her head; she had the good taste to avoid more than a gold armring in the shape of a snake and ruby eardrops. The full-lipped features were amused as he bowed.

"Ah, the little Emerald . . . my bodyguard's brother, aren't you?"

"I have that honor, most excellent lady," Adrian said, straightening.

Esmond was standing by the couch now, at a creditable parade rest; he was dressed in a studded belt of black leather, a breechclout of the same, high-strapped sandals and a sword and dagger; the hilts were rich with gold and sapphires, but the edges were functional enough. His long blond hair was tousled, and there was a red mark at the base of his neck. Adrian lifted a brow a fractional inch, enough for a grin between the brothers. He lifted it a bit more at Esmond's look of well-hidden throttled fury.

"With you guarding us in the courts, and Esmondi's sword, my husband and I are *quite* safe," she said, and snapped her fingers.

Two maids in long plain gowns—plain Western Isle cotton that would have bought two good riding velipads—came from somewhere they'd been discreetly waiting. Lady Redvers swept away in a waft of lilac scent.

Adrian calmly walked along the row of scrolls and found *Smanton's Commentaries on Early Popular Assembly Edicts and Precedents Thereunto*, sat on the couch and began reading, scrolling left to right.

"Bit distracting, all that perfume," he said after a moment. "And are there foundation garments under that sheer silk? I find it hard to believe they stay up like that naturally."

He looked up sharply at his brother's growl. "Something's wrong," he said, a statement rather than a question.

"Of course something's wrong," Esmond growled, flushing and rubbing at his neck. "I didn't come here to be a he-whore, for one thing."

"No, you came to be a weapons trainer," Adrian said. "Maybe you can teach our esteemed patron to use his double chin to throttle his opponents."

"Wilder Redvers would fall down with an apoplexy if he ran three times around a training track, much less fought a bout in armor," Esmond said bitterly. "It's the *fashion* to have an Emerald weapons trainer, a victor of the Five Year Games. Next year it'll be philosophers, or dancing dogs. And his *wife*—"

Adrian grinned. "Come now, it's not as if she was eighty—and *bodyguard* is a perfectly respectable job here." Insofar as being anything but a wealthy Confederate citizen was respectable. "And Wilder Redvers would fall down dead if he had to do *that*, as well."

His smile died as Esmond looked around, making a careful sweep of the nearby parts of the library. "Brother, that isn't why I asked you to meet me here—*she* just happened in, damn it. You've got to listen to me. This is serious."

"*What* is serious?" Adrian said. "Beyond our patron's imminent bankruptcy, conviction for extortion and malfeasance in office, and cordial invitation from the Conciliary Court to open his veins in the bath? And *that's* the talk of the law courts, let me tell you."

"Because Redvers isn't going to sit and wait for the man with the dagger," Esmond said bluntly. "Listen." His voice dropped to a whisper. "This morning . . ."

"Admit the Emerald," a voice said from beyond the doorway.

The guards weren't Redvers family slaves, Esmond saw. They were Confed Army veterans, grizzled stocky men with legs and arms like knotted trees. Not the smooth athlete's muscle Esmond wore, but perfectly servicable . . . and the assegais that glittered in their hands had seen plenty of use.

"Sort of a tall, tow-haired one, looks like a pansy with a sword, sir?" one of the veterans said, grinning and leaning on his shield. "Give us a kiss, pretty boy."

"Admit him, I said, you oaf!"

"Shall we take his sword, sir?"

"Admit him!"

The veterans straightened to a braced attention. "Sir, yessir!" the other barked. They slapped the blades of their assegais across the bosses of their shields. "Pass, Emerald!"

Esmond straightened his shoulders and walked through the fretted-bronze doors. He'd never been in to Redvers private apartments; they were less gaudy than he'd expected . . . although that was probably his wife's taste. High coffered ceilings, decent murals—by an Emerald artist, of course—and geometric-pattern floors. Pillars gave out onto balconies overlooking a courtyard of rosebushes and palms, with fountains in the shape of seagods. A dozen silk-cushioned couches of silver-inlaid bronze surrounded a table with cherries, figs, and ewers of wine; a dozen Confederate nobles lounged at their ease. The only thing missing was the bodyslaves who should have been hovering behind the couches, ready to fill cups or fan away a fly or run an errand.

The Emerald brought a fist to his chest and bowed. "Lord," he said, suddenly conscious of his native accent. "You summoned me?"

His eyes flicked across the assembled nobility. A good ten or twelve million arnkets around the low table . . . but at least twice that in debts. Young Mark Silva, who'd managed to assemble the slowest stable of racing velipads in Vanbert, and bet the family estates on them. Johun Audsley, a famous general and famously bitter former associate of Ark Marcomann, an even more famous general who'd died in retirement and not left a thing to his right-hand man. Tows Annersun, who'd run for every elective office and managed to offend so many highly-placed people that he'd won none of them, despite a fortune in bribes and games and free wine . . . and his esteemed patron Wilder Redvers himself, ex-governor of Solinga Province for the Confederacy, extortionist and thug. A fleshy balding man just on the wrong side of fifty; muscled like a bull greatbeast when he was young, and now with a great sagging belly and wobbly undersides to his arms.

But not entirely a fool, Esmond reminded himself. He'd even been a competent general once, in the western wars a decade back.

He'd also spent every penny he'd wrung out of his province on trying to be elected Speaker of the Popular Assembly, one of the two magistrates who ruled the Confederacy, as much as anyone did. Virtually every well-established noble family in and around the city must have thrown their influence and clientage against him, for him to have lost after spending *that* kind of money.

And without the opportunities of a Speaker, he was doomed. If his creditors didn't get him, the lawsuits of the provincials would—they'd be able to attract more than enough patrons in the capital, anxious to bring Redvers down and feed on the estates that would go on the block.

"Do sit down, over there, Esmondi," Redvers said. "Pour me some wine, and yourself, my boy."

Little Esmond, the little Emerald, Esmond thought, grinding his teeth as he smiled and obeyed.

"We've brought you here to discuss a little matter of politics," the Confederate noble said.

Esmond managed not to choke on the wine. Politics were for Confederate citizens—*rich* Confederate citizens, if you went beyond the level of the dole-feeders selling their Popular Assembly votes. Vision took on the clarity of desperation, the same bright hopping focus he'd had before the Five Year Games. One or two . . . no, three of the guests weren't what they appeared. Purple-edged tunics and robes, yes, but those hard furtive eyes didn't have the lordly arrogance of the nobles beside them. *Gang bosses,* he thought. The type who could deliver a ward for a patron, or see that the other side's canvasers hurt bad or just disappeared. Some of them were as powerful as many Justiciars or generals . . .

The others murmured among themselves, nibbling on little pastries rich with nuts and creamed bananas, sipping at their wine. *And looking at* me, *Goddess be my shield.*

"My lord honors me beyond my worth," he said smoothly. *I may not be a rhetorician, but I've been listening to Adrian all my life.* "If my lord will open his mind to me, I will assuredly do my poor best to aid him."

Redvers nodded. "As you may know," he began, "I was recently cheated—foully cheated—of my legitimate election as Speaker of the Popular Assembly. By corruption! Unprecedented, extra-constitutional corruption! Interference from the Council!"

Esmond darted a quick look at Audsley. Audsley's mentor Marcomann had been the one who ended the last round of civil wars, and he'd restored the powers of the Council and restricted those of the Popular Assemblies . . . Audsley smiled and nodded.

"To cleanse the State, a fire is needed. Drastic measures! Only thus can justice, peace and good order be restored!"

Grave nods, glittering eyes.

"My lord, may the gods *themselves* aid your enterprise." Esmond shot to his feet, then went to one knee, drawing and offering his sword. "I see that a new age is about to dawn for the Confederacy!"

"Well, well, that's very handsome of you, Esmondi," Redvers said. "Each one of us has a part to play, you see. Councillor Audsley is collecting a sufficient force among Marcomann's veterans—many of them living in poverty, despite their many services to the State."

Having blown their loot and land grants on whores, dice and wine, Esmond thought. They'd come back from the Western provinces staggering under the gold . . . or rather the innumerable slaves they'd taken had staggered. Marcomann had used them to climb to the highest office. Usually the Confederacy had two Speakers, one for the

Popular Assembly and one for the Council; Marcomann had been Sole Speaker from the day his troops marched in and the proscriptions began to the utterly unexpected day of his retirement. He'd died in bed, too, which was a strong argument for the belief that the gods did intervene in human affairs.

"These other gentlemen will rise in arms on the appointed day. Some will seize the public buildings; others will start fires and riots to distract the City Companies. And you, my dear Esmondi . . ." Redvers smiled. "It struck me just now . . . there are so *many* foreigners in Vanbert these days. Emeralds especially; why, there are twenty or thirty Emeralds in *my* household, aren't there? And you're what passes for a great and famous man among them, aren't you?"

"I have some small influence, yes, my lord," Esmond said. A Five Year victor *did* have a fair number who knew his name. That wasn't exactly what Redvers was looking for, but Esmond had no intention of lessening his value. He'd already heard far too much to live if they suspected for an instant he wasn't with them or wasn't useful.

"And you'll be rewarded for it," Redvers nodded. "Why, even Confederate citizenship . . . perhaps the narrow stripe and a modest estate in the provinces." He beamed, the furrows beside his fleshy beak nose deepening. "All you must do is call on the Emeralds and whatnot to rise and kill the leading corruptionists on the appointed day. Won't *that* cause confusion!"

"My lord, it's brilliant," Esmond said, his voice hushed and sincere. "But please . . . pardon my ignorance . . . what will Councillor Ion Jeschonyk be doing? I've never seen the Speaker of the Council abroad in the streets without two dozen of his retainers, many of them army veterans or games fighters. And if *any* of the magistrates should escape and reach loyal garrisons . . . loyal to them, I mean . . ."

"Clever, these Emeralds," one of the men drawled.

"Well, my boy, all these things have been considered," Redvers said indulgently. "Indeed, mine is the hand—along with a few of my friends here—who will strike down the tyrant Jeschonyk. We'll call on him at home, you see, in the third hour of the morning, before his clients arrive to pay their respects. We'll stab him as he comes to greet us, and with him dead nobody will dare lift a hand against so many Fathers of the State. And Justiciar Demansk has twenty thousand men under arms not far from the capital, the levy for the coming Island campaign."

"Justiciar Demansk is of your party, my lord?" Esmond strove to put worshipful admiration in his tone. *Don't overdo it,* he warned himself. But then, dealing with these people it was nearly *impossible* to overdo it . . . on the other hand, the gang bosses were less likely to be taken in. If Demansk was with them, they actually had a chance to bring this off.

"Justiciar Demansk . . ." Redvers smiled, "is a man of ambition, shall we say, who has been . . . approached. So. What do you say, Esmondi my lad?"

Esmond stood and gave Redvers a salute, fist to chest. "Command me, lord, and success is ordained as if the gods themselves had spoken."

"Are you *serious*?" Adrian blurted, as his brother finished his tale, running his hands through his long curling hair.

"Deadly. Most probably simply *dead*," Esmond said.

Adrian stared at him, appalled. "Oh, Maiden of the Stars," he whispered. "They're all going to die."

"That doesn't bother me," Esmond said grimly. "You're right, incidentally. The only reason they haven't gone up the post—" in fact, most of them were of high enough social standing that they'd be offered the knife "—is that the Council and the Speakers are nearly as much a bunch of amateur buffoons as they are."

The tall form of his brother sank to a bench. "How in the name of the gods did we ever end up being subject to these people?"

"They had a better army," Adrian said absently, the eyes of his mind fixed inward. "And in those days they didn't fight among themselves as much as we did. You know the saying: two Emeralds—"

"—three factions and a civil war," Esmond said gloomily. "And the hell of it is, we're involved in this . . . this abortion. I wouldn't give them one chance in twenty. The Confederacy may be ruled from Vanbert, but it isn't a city-state or a monarchy. You can't just seize one man or a couple of buildings and rule, or parade a little bodyguard the way . . . what was his name, somebody the Tyrant, the one who came into town with a big girl dressed up as the Goddess, way back?"

"Petor Strattis," Adrian said. Strattis had been Boss of Solinga for twenty-three years back four centuries ago, and his reforms had laid the basis for the later democracy and the Emerald League. "Wait—let me think."

esmond gellert's appraisal is remarkably accurate, Center said, a slight tinge of surprise in the machine voice. **stochastic analysis indicates that the probability of a successful coup is in the range of 8% ±3.**

Raj's gray eyes opened inside Adrian's head. ***Remarkable young man, your brother,*** he said appraisingly. ***I'd have been very glad indeed to have him as a junior officer; he's got natural talent, and I think men would follow him. Hmm . . . that's something to consider. Center?***

correct. we must reevaluate long-term plans . . . however, esmond gellert's fundamental belief-structure offers impediments to his usefulness as a tool.

My brother isn't a tool! Adrian thought hotly. *He's a human being!*

Human beings can be the tools of mankind, Raj thought gently. ***There's no higher honor. Better to serve mankind than some politician's greed or a myth that turns to ashes full of dead children.***

Sorry, Adrian thought. *What can we do?*

Well, Redvers and his friends have one great merit, Raj mused. ***Two, actually. First, they're corrupt, amoral, shortsighted and utterly selfish. Responsible nobles wouldn't listen to you if you told them about earth-shaking innovations—they'd look beyond immediate advantage and realize that they could destabilize the system, and those of them who're loyal to anything besides themselves are loyal to the system here. Second, they're desperate. They'll grasp at straws, because it's a tubful of very bloody water for them if they lose.***

Adrian raised his head. "Did they give you any idea of the time of this . . . uprising?"

"Not immediately. They want to get Demansk on their side if they possibly can. Beyond that, at least a couple of months—I doubt if they know precisely themselves. Why? Do you think we can make it to the Western Isles before then?"

"No, I think I have an idea," Adrian said slowly. "But I need some time for it to work."

One of Lady Redvers' maids came back into the alcove where the brothers sat. "Oh, Esmond, I was so frightened—" she began, speaking a pure upper-class Emerald.

Then she saw Adrian, and froze. Esmond went defiantly to her side and took her hand. "Brother, this is Nanya. Formerly of a citizen family of Penburg."

Adrian bowed gravely; Penburg had been sacked after a revolt six years ago, while Wilder Redvers had been governor of Solinga Province. Every adult male sent to the pole, the rest sold into slavery. His eyebrow lifted: *Do you know the risks you're taking?* it signaled. If Lady Redvers found out . . . being flogged to death was the best Nanya could expect. Killing a free resident of Solinga like Esmond wouldn't be legal . . . but that wouldn't stop the lady, and she'd get away with it, too.

"And, when the gods allow, my wife," Esmond went on.

Nanya looked up at him with adoration, her large brown eyes going soft. Adrian closed his eyes. *Give me strength.*

We will, son, Raj's voice spoke silently.

Vanbert's law courts had grown with the city. The highest of them—the Assembly Courts of Appeal—were housed in a new marble complex not far from the Temple of the Dual God, on the Spring Hill. The building was in an exaggerated form of the classic Emerald style, adapted to the needs of Confederate legal institutions. Two square blocks on either side held long halls where advocates, clients and hangers-on could walk and speak and deal; they were plain as Emerald temples, surrounded by giant columns supporting a Confederate invention, a barrel-vaulted roof. That was coffered and gilded, and tall windows ran around the eaves just below it. Even on a cloudy winter's day like this the light diffused off the hammered gold leaf in a shadowless glow, lighting the pale marble of walls and column and floor.

Joining the two halls to make a square C-shape was a connecting bar, with a covered amphitheater in its center. Juries in Confederate cases were huge—in theory any citizen could sit, although the requirement for a purifying sacrifice excluded the poor—and they sat below the advocates and judges, like spectators at a games fight. Adrian had often thought that the comparison had merit on more levels than one; though more subtle, the clash of wit and quotation below was just as savage as sword and spear, or tusk and fang. The expressions on the jurors were similar too. Except that nobody was paid to attend the games, while jurors received a stipend, not counting bribes of money or patronage.

An important case could be almost as expensive as a municipal election.

Adrian gathered his plain white mantle around him and strode towards the low symbolic metal fence that surrounded the sun disk inlaid in mosaic on the floor of the court. The acoustics were wonderful; he could hear whispered conversations on the top benches, and even sleepy belches from the inevitable seedy hangers-on taking a nap.

A man with a ceremonial whip and axe stopped him at the entrance. "If you come to speak, proclaim your citizenship," he said in a bored voice; his equipment was meant to indicate the magistrates' power to punish and kill, but it had been a long time since they were used on the spot.

"I come not to speak, but to speak the words of another," Adrian said, pitching his voice in the way Center had trained him to do. The computer had also eliminated the last trace of the soft Emerald accent; now his voice had the slow, crisp vowels of a native Confederate—the upper-class city dialect, at that.

"Pass, then," the usher said.

Adrian advanced, his soft kidskin sandals noiseless, and made a deep bow before the panel of judges. They were all older men today, he saw, seamed hard faces with tufts of chinbeard and disapproving eyes.

"This seems to be in order," the senior magistrate said, examining the scroll which deputized Adrian to speak for a citizen advocate. "I suppose we have to let the little Emerald speak. I don't know what Vanbert is coming to. A girl costs more than a sword, a pretty boy more than a tract of land, a jug of imported fish sauce more than a good plow team, and they let foreigners speak in the courts of law where Confederate gentlemen once showed their mettle. They'll be allowing them into the army next. Go on, Emerald, go on."

His voice rolled heavy with disapproval. Adrian bowed again.

"We are faced," he began, "with a case which runs on all fours with the notable—"

He spoke easily, his voice conversational at first. That itself was daring—the usual mode was Oratorical, one hand outstretched, the other gripping the front fold of your mantle, right foot advanced, voice booming. He was using a rather daringly avant-garde style, at least for the introduction.

Center's prompting flowed through his mind. Precedent, allegory, snippets of verse, or the doggerel that passed for poetry in this land. He could feel the coldness of the jury turning, men leaning forward in interest.

"A pretty tissue of words to hide the plain truth," the other side's advocate said at last. "Yet *Dessin and Chrosis* clearly establishes that provincial corporate bodies have no standing for a petition *for and through* in this esteemed court. Citizens! Such appeals are *your* prerogative!"

An appeal to Confederate pride rarely fails, Adrian noted. He'd expected that.

"Citizens!" he replied. "Citizens . . . what pride, what glory, what power resides in that simple word. Citizens of the Confederacy of Vanbert! Yours is the power to bind and loose; yours the hand that wields the assegai of justice. It is beyond dispute. The esteemed advocate for the Smellton Tax Farmer's Syndicate is entirely correct. A mere assembly of provincials—without standing in this court—*cannot* assume the right to present a petition 'for and through' in strict form."

"Eh?" The chief magistrate's mouth moved, as if he was chewing toothlessly. "Are you conceding the case, Emerald? Is that what your 'principal'—" the scorn was back, this time for the legal fiction "—has set you to read?"

"By no means, excellent magistrates, do I concede. For indeed—" he moved into Formal Mode "—even as my humble self is but a mouthpiece for my principal, who *is* a citizen of the noble Confederacy, so this petition is launched in the name of the following indisputable citizens, their names on the ten-yearly roll: I speak of Jusin Sambert, Augin Melton—"

He rolled on, his voice booming up to the eaves. Faces along the rows of jurors' benches began to nod; heads leant together with murmurs of agreement.

"Justice! That strict Goddess with axe and flail in hand, terrible in aspect, unbending in righteousness, watches us even now!"

Adrian launched himself into the conclusion of his speech. When he halted, head bowed, hands outstretched, the jurors rose to their feet and applauded, the noise ringing back from the dome overhead. The mantled heads of the magistrates huddled together, mouths working beneath the sound.

"Petition accepted for examination," the senior said, looking down on Adrian from the high seat. "Jurors and panel of magistrates in accordance." Which virtually guaranteed that the petition would be reviewed favorably . . . which meant that the Smellton Tax Farmer's Syndicate would face a swingeing fine. "Dismissed."

Adrian left slowly, despite an overwhelming impulse to bolt for the hall and get a glass of lemonade, or watered wine; you needed a throat of brass and a bladder the size of a wine jug to work the courts. Instead he strolled, smiling and bowing and exchanging a few deferential words with some of the long-established advocates and their clients.

You can see how surprised they are, he thought ironically. *How does an Emerald do so well in a place where* real *men are supposed to shine?*

If ever the Confederacy was destroyed, he suspected it was going to be because somebody simply couldn't refuse the temptation to smash a lead-weighted fist into the face of that bland, complacent assumption of superiority. You could only swallow the sour bile at the back of your throat for so long.

"Ah, young Adrian," a voice said.

He felt the cold clutch of fear, the sort that makes the stomach clench and the scrotum try to draw itself up into the abdomen. *This is* exactly *what I had planned,* he told himself.

"My lord," he said, turning and bowing. Wilder Redvers in the life, his ample form looking impressive in the wrapped mantle of a Councillor, with the broad purple stripe along the edge.

"I heard the summation of your speech. Most impressive, most impressive—a Confederate advocate couldn't have done it any better. I can see that giving you the run of my library was a sound decision, yes, sound."

"My gratitude is eternal, my lord," Adrian said. He glanced around. "If I might beg a minute of your time?"

"Well . . . I suppose."

"Alone, my lord. It's a very sensitive matter."

The plump beak-nosed features changed. ***He suspects you know something,*** Raj cautioned. ***He's remembering that you're Esmond's brother.***

In the privacy of his mind Adrian nodded. *And I'd be dead inside the hour if he confirms his suspicion,* he thought. *Or even if he doesn't. Now to show myself useful.*

"As you may know, my lord, I've been putting together some notes for a history," he said. Redvers' face relaxed slightly; that was a traditional hobby for lawyers. "And I've come across some information in the most ancient chronicles that may be of importance to the State. Naturally, I didn't presume to judge such matters myself, but thought first of you—my patron, a citizen of standing and influence, one competent to judge such matters."

"My boy, I'm glad you show such wisdom and maturity," Redvers said softly. "To others may be given the art of speaking, of shaping marble so that it seems to live—but to the Confederacy alone is given the mandate of the Gods to rule, to spare the humble and subdue the proud," he said.

That would be more impressive if I didn't know you were quoting,

Adrian thought, the words dry under the hammer of his pulse. They reached one of the inset niches along the walls, this one holding a small chryselephantine statue of the God of War, flourishing an archaic spear, heroically nude, with his foot on a dead Southron barbarian.

"I have found a series of formulae known to a select few among the ancients," Adrian began. "Knowledge long since lost."

Redvers nodded; it was well-known to educated men that before the Age of Iron had been an Age of Gold, whose glories were forgotten.

"With devices based on these formulae, an army would be invincible—it could sweep aside forces many times its size. And the formulae are quite simple; within three months—" *Six months, but let's not get too realistic* "—given the resources and artificers needed, a force could be so equipped as to sweep the Western Isles, or the Southron barbarians . . . a great boon to the State, and of course undying fame and glory to the commander."

Redvers stood stock-still, his eyes hooded. "And you've come to your patron with this knowledge. Very proper, my boy; very proper."

He's going to buy it, Raj said, his mental voice almost as dispassionate as Center's.

probability of agreement 92% ±5, Center added.

"What on earth is the Emerald babbling about?" one of the nobles said pettishly. "Invincible weapons . . . what does he mean? A better catapult, something of that nature?"

The Redvers family was wealthy enough that their townhouse gardens had a secluded nook like this out of sight and most hearing from the main house. Adrian would much rather have conducted the trial somewhere outside the city . . . but Center had decided that Redvers was becoming quite dangerously impatient.

The stretch of lawn ahead of them held an oak tree and a circle of scarecrowlike dummies, each hung with the mail tunic and helmet of a Confed soldier. In front of them rested a simple jar, stoppered with a clay disk that was pierced for a wick of cotton that Adrian had soaked in the solution that Center showed him . . .

He shuddered at the vision, one from Raj's memories. A vision of what the explosion of a *shell* or *bomb* could do to men's bodies.

"The jar contains my mixture, my lords," Adrian said. "Surrounding it—"

"Get on with it, Emerald! We're not apothecaries, you know."

"Yes, my lord. If my lords will step behind this barricade . . ."

Adrian walked towards the jar, blinking at the bright sunlight, a lighted oil lamp in his hand. He held it by the loop at one end and touched the flame to the wick with the other. It started to sputter and fume with evil-smelling blue smoke, and he turned and walked—it was an effort not to run, but the nobles must be *impressed*—towards the thick pine logs of the barricade.

"See here," one said as he ducked gratefully behind the thick wood. "How are we supposed to see whatever-it-is if we're huddling behind here?"

He started to rise. Adrian clamped a hand on his shoulder and pulled him down again; sheer surprise helped him, since the Confederation nobleman couldn't *imagine* that an Emerald would lay hands on him.

"You—"

BWAAAAMMP.

The sound was louder than thunder, louder than anything Adrian had ever heard, loud enough to stab pain into his ears. He'd been expecting it. The other men there had not. Esmond's sword flashed out in a movement too fast to see except as a blur. One or two of the Confederate nobles threw themselves down with their hands over their ears; another turned and ran for the villa, tripping on a chair leg and lying sobbing and beating his hands against the ground. Most of them simply stood and stared at each other. Audsley, the ex-general, gathered himself, shook back his shoulders to settle his mantle, and walked around the edge of the barricade.

He stopped, staring at the forward part of the logs. Holes had been gouged into them; he ran his little finger into one, and pulled it back with a jerk.

"That's hot," he said. "What is it?"

"A ball of lead, like a sling-bullet, my lord," Adrian said. "Hurled by the daemonic force of the ancient formula's mixture. And that is a hundred feet from the bursting. If a man was closer . . ."

He smiled and spread his hands. Audsley and the others moved towards the place where the jar had rested. A knee-deep hole had been gouged in the soft black dirt, and bits of sod flung all over this corner of the garden. The front of the oak tree gleamed cream-white, the bark scarred and blasted away. Bits and pieces of the armor on the scarecrow stakes were scattered about; one helmet was embedded in the tree itself, three inches of the plume holder driven into the living wood. Audsley examined a mail shirt, putting a gingerly finger through a hole in the iron links.

"Well . . ." he said.

"Consider, my lord, catapults throwing dozens of such vessels into a tight formation of infantry," Adrian urged. "Still more into cavalry."

"Yes, I do see," Audsley said. A grin stole across his lined, weathered face. "Redvers, I thought you were wasting our time, but you weren't. Brilliant, man—brilliant!"

The nobles gathered around Wilder Redvers, slapping him on the back and laughing like men reprieved from death . . . which might well be what they were. Adrian turned, feeling the pressure of eyes on his back. Esmond was standing by the barricade, looking at the havoc the bomb had wrought and then at the sword still clenched in his hand.

"What exactly am I supposed to be doing out here?" Esmond asked, looking back over his shoulder. "You've got your infernal machines to tinker with, but I should be back in the city."

"Don't worry," Adrian said. "She's a lot safer with you *gone* than she is with you there."

Esmond nodded gloomily. "The question remains."

They were two days travel out of Vanbert's outskirts, and an hour's travel down a gravelled road that turned off the military highway west of the city. They'd been travelling on Redvers land that whole hour; past slave villages, wine presses, an alum mine, past fields where the yellow grain was mostly reaped and stooked, past pastures and orchards where green fruit swelled . . . and now they were turning into the paved laneway that led up to the villa of Wilder Redvers, one of many he owned. It was a handsome building, a simple rectangular block with a portico of pillars in front and the usual formal gardens behind; to the front was a stretch of close-cropped pasture dotted with trees, and the cypress-lined driveway.

"Two things," Adrian said. "First, most of the higher-level staff here are probably Emeralds. I need you to deal with them."

"Why? You're just as much an Emerald as me."

"But I'm not a victor of the Five Year Games, and I don't look like Nethan the Great returned," he said. "By the Goddess, brother, I think you're blushing."

That brought an unwilling crooked grin. "Besides that," Adrian went on, "somebody's going to have to command the unit that actually uses this stuff . . . and the guards that make sure nobody spears us while we're doing it."

Esmond glanced over at him. "Nonsense. Redvers will never let a bunch of foreigners get their hands on something like this."

"Redvers will," Adrian said. "When he sees what *they* make of it."

He nodded to the left of the manor house. The pasture there had probably been for the master's riding velipads; right now it was covered with leather tents in neat rows, each just the right size for a squad of eight men.

"Marcomann's veterans, joining Audsley," Esmond said. "Must be about three battalions there . . . say, fifteen hundred men."

"And there isn't one single one of them who's going to admit that he has *anything* to learn about fighting from a foreigner," Adrian said. "Trust me."

And my unseen advisors, he added. *Never forget them.*

"This little thing is supposed to *kill* somebody?" the soldier guffawed.

The hilt of his assegai jerked as his thick shoulders moved; he was in full fig: mailcoat, dagger, stabbing-spear, shield across his back, helmet with transverse plume. There was a fair bit of gray in the stubble on his square chin and in the thick hair on his scarred forearms, but he moved easily under all that weight of iron and wood and leather. This was one of Audsley's elite, a hundred-commander in Marcomann's wars; there wasn't enough equipment to kit out all the volunteers gathering on the Redvers estate.

"Yes, sir," Adrian nodded. "You light this"—he pointed at the fuse where it came out of the little wine jar—"throw it, and drop flat. Believe me, it's dangerous."

The hamlike hand tossed the bomb up and down. "If words were blades, you Emeralds would rule the world," he laughed. "I've defeated plenty of Emeralds in my time, from the North Range to the sea—talking less, and hitting harder." He shrugged. "Oh, well, the general says we've got to try this stuff, so by the cleft of Gellerix we will. Hand me that striker."

A little way off a baker's dozen of soldiers stood, leaning casually on their shields; Adrian saw one of them reach down into the calf-high grass and pull a stem to chew.

Adrian smiled and handed over the flint-and-steel, taking a few steps backward. The soldier grinned at that, and worked the scissorslike action. Sparks shot out, and on the third try the fuse caught in a sputter of blue smoke.

"Funny smelling," the soldier said with mild interest, holding it up.

"Please throw it now, sir," Adrian said calmly, backing off another few steps. "Right out there in the pasture, towards the crabapple tree, if it please you."

"Maybe it doesn't," the veteran said. "Don't get your loincloth in a twist, Emerald."

The thick-muscled arm arched back and whipped forward and the jar soared out, trailing smoke. Adrian's movements had put him behind a low swelling in the ground; he went down on his belly with prudent speed. Dew soaked into the front of his tunic, chill on his skin. As he'd expected, the veteran remained upright. He did bring his shield around, peering curiously over the rim.

Crack. The sound of the grenade exploding was a malignant snap; he knew what it would look like, too—a red snapping spark and puff of grayish-black smoke. This time he was far too close for that, and his face was pressed firmly into the grass and clover. Something hit the ground with a heavy thump; he looked up to see the soldier on his back, hands clapped to his face and blood leaking out between them. Then he went limp, with a final drum of heels on the turf. Over by the spectators, another was shrieking endlessly, louder than a wounded velipad.

Adrian moved over to the dead man. He'd felt like smiling, until he saw what was left of his face.

"Idiot! I ought to have you poled right now. Do you have any idea of how valuable four trained soldiers are?"

Adrian and Esmond bowed low, their heads level with General Audsley's foot where it rested in the steel loop of the stirrup. The big hairy saucer feet of his velipad moved on the grass before them, each with its seven blunt claws. The cinnamon-and-musk scent of the animal was strong in their nostrils, and the naked tail with its tuft of fur swung angrily as the beast sensed its rider's mood.

"Most excellent lord," Adrian said softly. "I fully realize it, and my apologies are most abject. Using these devices is more a matter of the mechanic arts than real soldiering. Could I—once more—humbly beg that men more suitable for such lowly occupations be assigned to them? Freedmen, even slaves, would be more suitable."

"Arm *slaves*?" Audsley said, quick anger in his voice. It had been only two generations since the Great Revolt; Audsley's father had been a young officer when Justiciar Carlos poled six thousand of the rebel survivors of the last battle along the road from Vanbert to Capeson.

"*Freed* slaves," Adrian said. "And perhaps . . . there are foreigners among the slingers recruited by the great Confed Army as light troops, are there not? Some of those would be most suitable. If I might consult with my lord Redvers . . ."

Audsley scowled; Redvers was providing far too much of the money to be offended lightly. "See to it, then. And keep them out of the way of real soldiers!"

He wrenched the velipad's mouth around, bringing a blubber of protest and a waving of the big round ears. Esmond stood silently until he was out of earshot.

"For every insult, for every slight, I'll see a Confed liver," he said at last.

Adrian nodded. "We've actually got some prospect of that, now," he said. "As long as we can get what I need."

"I don't know whether it was the Gods or the daemons who told you where to find the formula for this stuff," Esmond said roughly. "But *by* the Gods, you'll get what you need."

"It's quite simple," Esmond said to his audience of four. "This is our chance."

"Our chance for *what*?" the assistant steward of the estate said.

He was an Emerald freedman; his nominal superior was a one-legged Confed veteran who hadn't been sober past breakfast for ten years. They were meeting in his office, a pleasant room with plastered walls carrying scrolls and dozens of the wax-covered tablets of folding wood used for taking temporary notes; a latticework window opened onto the kitchen gardens. His fingers played with an abacus on the desk as he leaned forward and spoke, twitching nervously. A slave girl came in with a tray of cups and jugs of wine and water. The steward motioned her away impatiently and poured himself.

Esmond rose and stood facing them. He was wearing Emerald light-infantry armor, a tunic of three-ply greatbeast hide boiled in wax and vinegar and fastened with bronze studs, armguards of the same and high-strapped sandals.

"There's going to be another civil war among the Confeds," he said.

The steward blanched. So did the head stockman, the superintendent of field workers, and the woman who directed the household staff proper.

"We can't stop it; we can't stay out of it," Esmond went on. "You all know what my brother has brought here."

"Death," the stockman muttered.

"We're *all* initiates of the mysteries of death," Esmond said. "But in this case, an awful lot of Confeds are going to die."

"So? There have been civil wars before—Penburg rose during one of them. The wars end, and then the Confeds stamp on anyone who rebelled like a boot on ants."

Esmond nodded. "That might have happened without my brother," he said easily. "Why do you think we're helping with this idiot coup?"

"Because your patron told you to," the steward said.

"Velipad shit. We could have lifted a few thousand arnkets and headed for the Isles—our father traded there, and we have contacts in Chalice. This madness of Redvers would have been over in a few months, and all his properties would have been forfeit to the State."

He watched them shudder at that. Sale at auction, families split up . . . and freedmen were always suspect when a man was put on trial for treason. Their testimony was taken from the rack, or with burning splinters put under their nails.

"With my brother to even things out, the war will go on for a long time," Esmond continued. "Many things could happen. For example, one side or the other could get so desperate that they offer concessions to the Emerald cities . . . they might even withdraw, leaving at least nominal independence like the Roper League has. Or they might weaken each other so much that the provinces can revolt and *win*. Or at least if Redvers and Audsley win, we personally stand to be rewarded."

The steward looked at his subordinates. "Well, it's worth a hearing, at least . . ." he muttered. "Tell us more. What exactly does your brother need? We've all heard the explosions and heard the rumors."

Adrian held the handkerchief to his nose. It was soaked in vinegar, but even so the stink from the bottom of the manure pile was overwhelming; there was a row of piles in back of the barns for the master's racing velipeds. He didn't envy the field slaves who were set to the task, even if they were shambling dull-eyed brutes.

A few years in that underground prison they keep them in would do that to most men, Raj pointed out.

Sorry, Adrian thought.

"Don't you ever put the manure out on the fields?" he asked the chief stockman.

The stockman was from the Isles, a short brown-skinned man, wrinkled but still agile. There was a strong gutteral accent to his Confed. "Not very much of it," he said. "Place is too big to make it worthwhile, too much trouble to haul it out to the distant fields. Sometimes if it gets in the way we dump it in the river."

"Stop!" Adrian said.

He walked over to the base of the pile. "Here," he said, pointing.

Gray crystals like granulated sugar carpeted the ground. "That's what we want, those crystals—the saltpeter. Scrape it up and put it in the barrels."

"Here, now, sir, you're a gentleman—you can't do that!"

The carpenter's voice was shocked and reproving.

Adrian smiled. "I'm afraid I have to," he said sympathetically.

The tub was an old wine vat, big enough to hold several hundred gallons. They'd set it up at a shed half a mile from the house, in case of accidents. Slaves were rigging a simple machine over it: a pivot on the beam above, with a hanging pole inside the barrel turning paddles. The power was furnished by ten more slaves, each pushing on a long sweep set into the pole at its top, near where it turned on the iron bolt set into the roof beam.

Adrian pulled his head back and dusted his hands; there were blisters on them, and a few splinters. He was surprised by how little that bothered him, as he pulled one free with his teeth. Not the pain; any Scholar of the Grove was expected to master the body's needs. It was the *disgrace*, the manual labor.

"My father captained his own ship, when he got started," he said by way of explanation.

Although he did it so that his sons wouldn't *have to do it,* he thought. Only leisure could give a man the freedom to cultivate his mind, or shape his body as an athlete . . . and there was no slavemaster like an empty belly. That was why all the best philosophers were agreed that manual labor and its necessities were essentially degrading. Bestmun had held that labor should be delegated to those whose natures fitted them for slavery . . . of course, in his day Emeralds had rarely been enslaved.

"Now here's how you do it," he went on. "You take *three* of those barrels—" he pointed to the ones that held the saltpeter, boiled and dried and reground "—and two of those—" the finely powdered sulfur; there was a hot spring on this estate "—and *one* of those with the charcoal dust, and you put them in. Three and two and one, three and two and one, until the big tun is two-thirds full. And all the time you're doing that, the paddles have to be kept going."

He turned and put his face close to the carpenter's. "And I'll be coming back now and then to *check* that you're doing it right, and the master will be *very, very angry* if I tell him that you're not. Understand?"

The carpenter nodded; he was as jumpy as a cat around a diretooth. Most of the estate slaves were, these days, with all the soldiers on hand. None of the troopers cared much about preserving Wilder Redvers' propery.

"And they *still* don't do things properly unless you stand over them," Adrian said in frustration.

Why should they? Raj replied.

A vision flashed into Adrian's head; a steam engine, that's what it's called . . . on Raj's native Bellevue. A mass of metal tubes and wheels and parts, wrecked and fused. A man with a whip was beating another man, nearly naked and with an iron collar around his neck.

A slave has a positive incentive to damage things, unless he's a coward or unusually well-managed. And simple carelessness is bad enough.

The velipad was an estate animal, and knew the laneways better than his rider. Any landholding of this size had its artisans; Redvers had his in a series of workshops not far from the cottages that housed the home-farm segment of the plantation's workforce. Adrian pulled up and tapped his toes on the elbows of his velipad; the animal crouched to the ground, and the young man stepped off. The smell of hot metal came from within the bronzesmith's forge. Experiment had shown that bombs launched from a catapult tended to disintegrate if they were housed in clay pots of practicable thickness. Redvers had grumbled at the expense of sheet bronze, until they showed him a few survivors of the effects of a finely-divided mist of gunpowder meeting open flame.

The problem was, the bronzesmith had trouble grasping the concept of turning out large numbers of uniform containers without ornamentation or excess effort.

Why not? Raj said again. ***This man turns out fine work because it gives him pleasure. He's not particularly concerned with Redvers' political ambitions, or with anyone else's convenience. Why should he churn out things that don't give him satisfaction? He won't be paid any more if he does.***

Adrian sighed again. Raj and Center were putting him through a course of study a good deal less agreeable than the Grove's lectures on the Good and the Beautiful . . . but their concept of the Just Order was a good deal more empirically grounded.

He checked half a step. "I'll give him a bonus!" he said. "Under the table, of course." Redvers' funds would stretch to that.

You're learning, son. You're learning.

"*Ufff!*"

The other man grunted as his back struck the hard-packed dirt of the corral. Esmond stepped back panting; he had a graze under his right eye that was seeping blood, and his left thumb had been painfully wrenched. The six men who'd offered to take their new employer on were in considerably worse shape, though some of them had shown a thoroughgoing mastery of informal all-in style.

"Any more fools among those looking for a job?" he asked.

There were thirty men grouped around the entrance to the corral. All Emeralds; none too young—most of them had a few years on him—and all fairly hard-bitten. Many of them wore sailors' knitted caps with tassels, and the Goddess only knew how they'd ended up so far from the sea. Sailing on merchantmen going foreign was the main way an Emerald could learn the use of arms these days, that and signing on with one or another of the Lords of the Isles as a mercenary . . . or as a pirate, not that there was much difference in that part of the world. A few did a hitch with the auxiliary light-armed slingers of the Confed forces.

"Good," he said, when no more volunteers stepped forward. He reached out his right hand, and his servant tossed a spear into it; the old Emerald pattern, six feet long with a narrow sharp-bladed stabbing head. "Now let's see who can use a sticker. Then we'll go on to javelin, sling, sword and knife."

The testing process lasted all afternoon, while the hot summer sun baked strong-smelling sap out of the eucalyptus trees that shaded the pasture beyond the corral. When he was finished Esmond's eyes looked twice as brilliant, staring blue out of the mask of reddish dust streaked with runnels of sweat. He gasped as he shoved his head into the bucket of water resting on the coping of the well, then poured the rest down his neck and tossed the bucket in for another load.

"Rejoice," he said dryly as his brother came up, a look of intense concentration on his face and a staff-sling in his hands. "Managed to bonk yourself on the back of the head again?"

"No, I think I'm getting the hang of it," he said seriously, his thin, intelligent face warming. "It's not that complicated once you grasp the basic theory."

Esmond snorted. "Weapons are something you have to learn with your skin and muscle and bone, not with your head," he said.

"Oh, I don't know," Adrian said mildly. "Knowing the basic principles always makes things easier to learn. Here, I'll show you."

The sling the younger Emerald held was a weapon popular because of its simplicity and compactness, but it needed as much skill to handle as a bow. There was a wooden handle four feet long, two silk cords of about a yard each—leather would have done, but not as well in damp weather—and a chamois pouch for the ammunition. Esmond blinked in slight alarm as his brother dropped an almond-shaped lead bullet into the pouch and let gravity draw the cords taut. Adrian's arms were well enough muscled, in a lean whipcord fashion; he'd be able to sling the bullet hard. Where it went was another question, and Esmond's fingers tightened on the single handgrip of the small round buckler he was carrying in his left hand.

"That tree," Adrian said. "Just below the forked branch." He whipped the sling in a single 360-degree circle before he released the free cord.

The gum tree in question was a hundred and fifty feet away. It quivered and there was a hard *thock*; the bullet itself travelled too swiftly to be seen, except as an arching blur. A scrap of bark detached itself, and fell, exposing the lozenge-shaped hole in the pale wood of the eucalyptus.

Esmond blinked again. *Dead center.*

"Not bad, little brother, not bad at all," he said. "I wouldn't like one of those to hit my head." *Because it would spatter my brains for yards.*

"Oh, it's not so hard. As I said, I understand the principle . . . and when I throw, it's as if spirits were showing me where the shot will fall. I'll be—we'll be—throwing grenades," he went on. "They'll be more effective than lead bullets."

"We just might make it," Esmond said, with a slow smile.

"If Demansk comes in with his fourteen regiments," Adrian said seriously. "I'd say . . ."

He turned his head to one side, as if listening; Esmond noticed because it was a habit he'd picked up since they came to Vanbert.

"That the chances are about fifty-fifty if we—our esteemed patron and his friends—enlist Demansk. Fifty-fifty for a prolonged war rather than immediate disaster, that is."

"Without him, fucking zip," Esmond said.

"Oh, not quite that bad. About one in twelve, really."

"Where's the master?" the steward bleated.

"Under house arrest, you fool. I have fifty men with me. Food and wine for them, and send messengers to the battalion commanders to meet me here immediately."

Johun Audsley's face was set like a death mask carved in bronze. It turned with the mechanical precision of a catapult on a turntable as Esmond bowed and saluted:

"My lord, what's the situation?"

"Who the daemons are . . . oh, the Emerald with the toys. Well, boy, someone blabbed. Tows Annersun, at a guess—he never could keep his mouth shut while he was dipping his wick. Now the Speaker knows everything."

"Councillor Annersun told Speaker Jeschonyk?" Esmond said.

"No, you idiot, but he was sleeping with the man's daughter, and *she* told him. He moved fast, I'll give the old bastard that . . . stop wasting my time and get your Emeralds and their toys ready, for what they're worth."

"My lord!" Esmond saluted.

The Confed ignored him, sweeping past with his entourage; they all had the look of men who'd ridden far and fast, and several wore bandages that were seeping red.

Esmond stood frozen on the stairs for a full three minutes. *Amazing how many things you can think of at once,* he thought. On an impersonal level: disaster for the conspiracy. Jeschonyk alive, and most of the Council. They'd be mobilizing this minute, no matter what other parts of the plan had come off on short notice. Audsley had nearly twenty thousand men here and on neighboring estates, but less than a third of them were fully equipped, and their organization was poor. And . . .

Nanya. Left alone in the Redvers' townhouse, with the magistrate's guards, probably a force from the City Companies too. If the Speaker decided Redvers was too dangerous to live, they'd make a sweep of his household as well—

Esmond turned on his heel, clattering down the staircase and out through the service wing. His men were barracked in what had been spare housemaid's quarters; they looked up as he burst in, most of them sacked out on their straw pallets. Hands froze as they worked on gear, sharpened a sword blade, clattered dice ready to throw.

"Jusha!" he roared. "Full kit, get your mounts, I want first company ready to move in fifteen minutes with one led remount per man. Full satchels of grenades, and five packhorses with spares. Canteens, but no food or bedding—we're going straight into the fight from a fast route march. *Move!*"

He'd had the training of these men for four months now. The long room dissolved into chaos, a chaos from which order grew. He walked to his own room, a boarded-off cubby, and hauled down what he needed; a bucket of javelins slung over his shoulder, his helmet, war gloves with brass and lead covers over the knuckles. And a map of Vanbert; they might have to take an indirect route out.

"Ready, sir."

"Then let's ride," he said, striding out to the entrance and vaulting into the saddle with a hand on the pommel, ignoring the weight of weapons and leather hauberk. His hand rose and chopped forward. "Follow me!"

"No, no, no!"

Adrian Gellert turned and slammed the flat of his palm into the wall of the shed. The slaves looked up from pouring powder into small bronze kegs, then whipped their heads back to their work. The last four months had taught the survivors that handling powder was *not* something to do with half a mind. The sharp peppery-sulfur smell of the explosive filled the air inside the barn.

"No, no, tell me my brother's not as stupid as the hero of a street-epic!"

Adrian stopped, controlled his breathing and pressing his hands to his face. *Suicide,* he thought. *He can't possibly cut his way into Vanbert—riots, chaos, street fighting—and get out with Nanya.*

probability of success 35%, ±7, Center said.

Surprise flashed through Adrian's mind. Raj's mental voice cut in: ***If you're going to stage a raid into a major city, riot and insurrection make it a lot easier.***

A vision floated through Adrian's consciousness: East Residence, the capital of Raj's native land on Bellevue. Blue-uniformed troops fought from behind a barricade against rioters, volley-firing in silent puffs of off-white smoke. Men screamed and writhed and lay and bled before the improvised breastwork . . . and behind the soldiers a gang of thieves calmly loaded furniture and bolts of cloth and tableware from a mansion into a waiting cart.

"I've got to help him," Adrian said. "He's being an idiot, but he's my brother . . . how much does *that* improve the chances?"

There was a long silence in his head; he was conscious, somehow, of Raj and Center speaking at a level and speed beyond his comprehension.

Tell him, Raj said at last.

probability of successful rescue attempt increases to 53%, ±5, with your participation and full support from raj whitehall and myself, Center said. **however, this is an unnecessary risk to you, our operative, and does not advance the prime objective to any significant degree.**

That was a long speech, from Center. Raj's voice held a flash of amusement: ***Center's learned to trust me when it comes to judging men. You're going to do it, son—I would, if I were you and I were alive—and we might as well give you all the help we can.***

Adrian nodded, startling the slave with the funnel again, and walked out into the bright morning light. "Fered," he said. "Gather the slingers. I need their help."

CHAPTER THREE

There was an eerie familiarity to the streets of Vanbert, full of mobs and the bitter smell of smoke from things not meant to burn. *Like the visions,* he thought.

scenarios, Center corrected. **multisensory holographic neural-input simulations of probable outcomes calculated by stochastic analysis.**

As you say, Adrian thought. *Visions.* Raj chuckled softly at the corner of his mind.

That was the only humorous thing in Vanbert this day. Adrian's mounted grenadiers—a hundred men, freedmen new and old—looked military enough with their slings and shortswords to fend off ordinary mobs, even though they were obviously mostly Emeralds. Many of the mobs out today weren't in the least ordinary. He threw up a hand and the column halted with a ragged bunching in the mouth of an alleyway.

"Down with Jeschonyk!" the men in ragged tunics shouted as they ran past. "Down with Jeschonyk! Long live Speaker Redvers! *Long live Bull Redvers! Death to Jeschonyk!*"

The rioters weren't armed, technically speaking, although many of the belt knives they waved were considerably longer than was convenient for cutting your food. Some waved torches, others iron spits and pokers, or clubs made from pieces of furniture and the limbs of ornamental trees. A number were pausing now and then to pry up cobbles from the street; and there were *thousands* of these people. Here and there was a man with a sling draped around his neck; a fair number of the Confed Army's light-armed slingers were recruited from the urban poor. A spray of outrunners went before the rioters, pounding on the shuttered windows of shops. Every now and then a crash and a scream would echo back, a counterpoint to the snarling rumble of the mob. Adrian craned his neck. A hundred yards back was a wagon, full of skins of wine. Men in the livery of a noble's house slaves were handing them out to grasping hands, with a dozen guards in full armor to keep the distribution quasi-orderly.

He turned his head the other way as there was a check in the surging trot of the mob. A line of men from the City Companies stood there, two deep. Their right arms rocked backward at a barked command from a noncom, marked by the transverse red crest on his helmet.

"Throw!"

A curled tuba blatted to emphasize the order. Darts flew up, then down into the front ranks of the mob. The barbed points were designed to punch through shields and armor, and they were driven by lead weights behind the head and the throwers' strong arms. The front rank of the rioters shattered like a glass jar struck by a mallet, men falling dead or screaming and pulling at the whetted iron in their bodies. The slingers among them might have helped break that thin line of armed men, but they were too crowded to use their weapons.

On the other hand, that mob doesn't have any cohesion to lose, Raj observed. ***Only the ones in front, the ones who can see what's happening, can be frightened enough to run; and they don't have room to run.***

"Throw. Throw. Throw."

Scores of the men packed into the head of the mob were down. Others were throwing a rain of cobblestones, but those simply boomed on the big hemispherical shields. A snapped order, and the rear ranks of the City Companies raised theirs to make a roof. The javelins were gone; another rasp of command, and every man's right hand snapped up behind his left shoulder. A long slither, and the assegais came free, glinting bright and long.

The street was only twenty feet across. The City troops could advance almost shield to shield, stabbing. Confed armies had beat bigger odds, killing undisciplined barbarians until their arms grew too tired, and here the mob had no room to use its numbers against the flanks or rear.

"Jeffa," Adrian said, pitching his voice to carry over the roar of the mob. *Rhetorical training's some good after all,* he thought, licking dry lips. The snarl of the crowd touched something older and deeper than any training, something down at the base of his spine and in the scrotum. It felt warm and loose and weak, the touch of fear.

"Four throws and a lighter," he said, touching his mount's forelegs. The animal crouched with a blubbering snarl of uneasiness.

Adrian stepped forward, his men behind him. There was a short bubble of clear space in front of the alleyway, but that wouldn't last when the bulk of the crowd realized what was going on and tried to escape. There were enough of them that anything in their way would end up as another greasy smear on the filthy pavement of the alley.

"Ready . . ."

He unclipped his own staff-sling and put a grenade in the pouch, the fuse hanging free. The other four slingers imitated him, spreading out so that their weapons wouldn't foul each other.

"Target is formation of troops," he said again, feeling a mild distant astonishment that his voice was firm and calm.

"Light."

The lighter went from man to man, touching his coil of quickmatch to the fuses. The fuses sputtered and bled blue smoke, but they were more reliable than the first they'd tried.

"*Cast.*"

He whipped the staff around his head with both hands and loosed at the quiet tone in his inner ear that was Center's judgement of the aimpoint. All *he* had to do was get the staff moving in the right plane. The cord flew free, and the grenades arched out. His headed towards the noncom commanding the blocking force, and exploded precisely at chest level. The others were within a second and a half of it, and only one shattered on the ground before it burst. That produced an effect he hadn't seen before, a sort of exploding fiery mist up to waist height.

The front rank of the mob was as panicked as the surviving soldiers; those were running—or limping or crawling—away from the blasts as fast as they could. The front rank of the mob *couldn't* run, although some tried to, turning and pushing at the solid mass of humanity behind them. Some of them were knocked over and trampled as the packed throng went forward, joining the City Companies soldiers as stains on the pavement. He saw a few of the more thoughtful picking up shields, helmets and assegais as they passed the bodies.

Adrian turned and looked at his slingers; they were grinning, laughing, slapping each other on the back. One was dancing the *kodax*, prancing and snapping his fingers.

"Shut up!" he said, his voice the crack of a whip. They did, falling silent and shuffling their feet, the mounted ones looking down at their saddlehorns. "Now we've seen what our weapons can do. Let's get moving."

"Sir, if you go, I'll follow you. I can't say how many of the men will, though."

Esmond looked at Jusha. His second-in-command was a grizzled middle-aged man, shorter than his commander but thicker through the shoulders, with a seaman's rolling gait and a scar that drew his upper lip off one yellowed dogtooth.

Esmond nodded silently, then looked back at the Redvers townhouse across the road. There were City Companies men outside the front entrance, blocking the street both ways, and the scouts said there were another hundred around the rear walls and wagon entrance. Magistrate's guards, too; not real soldiers—even the City Companies weren't *real* soldiers, though there were plenty of paid-off veterans in their ranks—but still armed men. *Say two hundred, two hundred and fifty in all,* he thought. *More than half of them inside, and the place was designed to be held against attack.* It was all blank exterior wall, three stories high here and ten feet even where it surrounded nothing but interior courtyard-garden. The narrow windows on the third floor here would serve the purpose of a fort's arrow slits quite well.

Esmond swallowed salt sweat. "Here's what we'll do," he said. "It'd be suicide just trying to storm the place—too many of them, they've got the position. So we'll tie them down with a diversionary attack; grenades first. Then I'll go in with a satchel of grenades, and toss them against the door."

That was set back into the wall facing the street, making a little alcove.

"One will be lit. You've seen what the stuff can do. Then when the door's blown in, we throw more grenades through and go in on their heels—by the ashy banks of hell, man, it'll be like spearing stunned fish."

Jusha looked at him. "Hope you can get something from her that you can't buy for half an arnket any day," he sighed. "All right, sir; we ate your salt and took your weapons. Let's get ready."

"Didn't work, did it, brother?" Adrian said.

"No. What's *wrong* with the bloody things?" Esmond said, glaring across the street.

They were crouching behind the stone counter of a soup shop across from the Redvers mansion. Adrian could smell the bean stew still bubbling in the big vats, and the heat of the charcoal fire was almost painful on his knees and belly. Absently he tore a small loaf of bread in half and reached over the greasy marble to dip it in the soup.

"There's nothing wrong with the grenades," Adrian said. "You just weren't using them properly. The force of an explosion propagates along the line of least resistance."

Esmond was staring at him with tightly-held anger. "I recognize every one of those words," he said. "But they don't make any sense."

"The power of the grenades goes where it's easiest. Out into the open air, not into the solid door. You've got to put the explosion in a confined space for it to do much against doors or walls."

"Oh," Esmond said.

There were bodies lying in the street in front of the soot-stained walls of the great house; mostly magistrates' guards and men of the City Companies, but a few of Esmond's Emerald mercenaries, too. They'd been killed by darts hurled from the narrow third-story windows. Adrian's jaws worked mechanically as he examined the scene; Center drew diagrams over it in green lines, with notes on distances and trajectories.

"The street's a long javelin cast, even from a height," he said thoughtfully. "But it's possible for good slingmen. That bronze grill over the main door, that gives into the hallway, doesn't it?"

"Yes."

"All right, here's what we do."

Esmond looked at him again; not angry, but with a sort of wondering curiosity. *Uh-oh,* Adrian thought. *By the Maiden's Spear, I've started sounding like Raj.*

It *was* comforting to know he had an experienced general living in his head, when it came to things like this. Adrian had read a good deal of history during his time in the Academy of the Grove, but it was Esmond who'd been interested in things military.

"Jeffa," he went on. "The four best men. Target is the third-story windows; on my command, not before. The next two sections are to lob grenades right over the roof—see if they can land them on the other side of the ridge tree, and let them roll down into the courtyard. Brother, you get your men ready—we won't have much time."

He waited while the messages were passed down to the clumps of men concealed behind shop windows and planters; this side of the street was a mansion much like the Redvers', but like many wealthy men the owner had let out cubicles along the streetfront for stores. A minute later a hissed word came back.

"They poured boiling water on my men," Esmond said in a cold tone, his eyes fixed on the enemy. "They're going to regret that." There was an angry red weal down his left arm.

Good man, your brother, Raj said. ***He's got a lot to think about, but he isn't forgetting his command.***

"That they are, brother," Adrian said. "They're going to regret it extremely." His voice rose higher. "On the three . . . one . . . two . . . *three.*"

The slingers dashed out into the street. Javelins and darts arched down from the windows, but they skittered sparking across the paving stones. One or two stuck in the cracks between blocks, humming like malignant wasps. Adrian lit the fuse to his first grenade from a helper's torch, swung . . .

now.

Hours of practice had connected Center's machine voice to his own fingers. The cast was sideways, up at a slant. The clay jar spun through one of the gaps in the bronze grillwork over the main door of the Redvers mansion, and exploded just before it reached the wooden shutter inside.

Crack. Then *crack . . . crack . . . crack . . .* as three more arched into windows on the third story of the facade. The bleeding trunk of a man collapsed out of one slit opening, trailing tattered arms and a runnel of blood down the smoke-dimmed whitewash. The second gave only screams, but the third added a gout of flame.

"Must have had a pot of boiling oil over a fire," Adrian muttered. Louder: "Again!"

More grenades arched out, for the windows, and a dozen or more over the rooftree. His own snapped into the bulged framework of the bronze grill, and blasted a corner of it out in a shower of wood splinters and metal fragments that pinged and whined off the wall and the street. His next went through the gap, and a hollow roar told him it had exploded in the hallway within.

"Again . . . all right, let's go for it!"

Esmond and scores of his men joined him. They flattened against the wall, but no darts or boiling water or oil cascaded down from the windows above. Adrian lit another grenade and tossed it overhand through the shattered grill; it was one of the red-banded kind, the ones with lead balls packed into the double shell outside the powder. He could feel them slamming into the teak of the door's interior.

Crossed spears tossed Esmond up. He gripped the stonework edges that had held the grill, looked within.

"All clear," he said, and swung himself through feetfirst with an athlete's impossible grace. They heard him swear mildly on the other side, as he wrenched at the warped bar, and then the doors were open.

Adrian looked through and swallowed. Men must have been packed in here pretty densely, when the first grenade came through. More had been trying to drag away the wounded, when that last one he'd thrown had landed among them.

Esmond stood with blood splashed up to his knees, like a statue of Wodep the War God poised with shield and sword. His face held a stony unconcern.

"This way," he said, pointing.

The main staircase to the second floor ran up from the other side of the vestibule courtyard. In ancient times there would have been an open light well over the pool, letting in water for domestic use. Here it was a skylight, and the pool was ornamental . . . less so now, since a grenade had evidently landed in it, and the colorful swimmers were pasted across the columns and mosaics. A wounded man had crawled as far as the staircase, and was making a messy time of dying. Black smoke poured down the landing.

"Oh, Maiden shield us, the place is on fire," Adrian blurted.

"Well, what did you expect?" Esmond said harshly. "Let's go."

"Wait." Adrian ripped a strip of cloth off the bottom of his tunic and dipped it in the water of the ornamental pool before tying it around his nose.

"Good idea," Esmond said, following suit along with the rest. "Half of you hand over your grenades and follow us," he went on to the men. "The rest of you, keep a sharp lookout on the street for enemy reinforcements."

The water smelled rankly bad, but it was welcome as they forced their way up into the furnace heat of the second story. The fire had started along the streetfront, and the doors in that direction were belching gouts of fire. It was running fast into the northwest corner of the building, though, running along the tinder-dry cedar rafters and the laths of the plasterwork that made up most of the big house's interior partitions. *And the paint in the murals, that's linseed oil,* Adrian reminded himself. *And the tapestries . . . Maiden shield us!*

They crouched and went down the connecting corridor around the central courtyard, towards the suite of Redvers' wife, where her personal servants would be. Halfway down it was an improvised barricade of furniture, with the gasping, coughing forms of half a dozen City Company troopers behind it.

"We can—" he began. His brother ignored him.

"*Nanya!*" he shouted, like a battle cry, and leapt.

Adrian followed, sword in one sweating hand and buckler in the other. *This isn't my proper work*— he thought.

His brother struck. Adrian's eyes went wide; he felt Raj's surprise at the back of his mind as well. The sword moved, blurring with its speed, and a spray of red droplets followed it in an arching spatter across the pale stucco of the walls. A man screamed, looking at the stump of an arm taken off at the elbow. Another slammed backward as the edge of Adrian's sword ploughed into his forehead and then fell in a spastic quivering heap. As he wrenched the weapon free, Esmond kicked another in the crotch, then broke his bent-over neck with a downward blow of the shield rim. Adrian struck at a man backing away with his face slack in horror and the assegai loose in his hand. The City Companies trooper wailed and fled, clutching a gashed forearm. He looked up to see Esmond driving the remaining two Confeds before him down the corridor. As he watched, one went over backward at a slam from Esmond's brass-faced shield. Esmond leapt high, came down on the man's ribcage with both heels, managed to spring free in time to turn a final assegai thrust with his shield. Then the sword sprang out like a kermitoid's licking tongue. The Confed gaped down at the blade through his torso, then slid backward as his face went slack.

"Nanya!" Esmond screamed again, and dashed forward.

Adrian followed, stopping only long enough to snatch up a canteen and rip a piece of cloth free. He wet it and held it across his mouth and nose as Esmond ran through gathering smoke and heat towards the family quarters. The door there was locked. Esmond's sword went straight into it; the steel snapped as he twisted, but so did the mechanism of the lock.

Adrian was close behind. He saw what his brother did, as the door swung back in a belch of flame that singed their eyebrows. The women were huddled in the center of the room, clutching each other, some of them still conscious. They had time to see the men in the doorway before a flaming beam and mass of plaster fell across them.

"Nanya!" Esmond screamed a last time, foam on his lips.

Adrian had to hit him three times across the back of the head with his shield rim before Esmond slumped; then he put his hands under his brother's arms and dragged him backward, cold with fear that he'd struck too hard.

But he'd *had* to hit him. Nothing but unconsciousness was going to stop Esmond from plunging into that room, and the very *gods* themselves couldn't bring him alive out of it.

CHAPTER FOUR

Dust. Whenever Adrian remembered the retreat to the west, it was the dust that came back, the acrid taste of it in his mouth and clogging his nose. After a while he got the knack of sleeping while he rode, nodding along in a half-doze. Shouting woke him.

He rubbed a hand over his face, smearing reddish dust and sweat. Esmond was standing in the stirrups, looking forward.

"Messenger just came in," he said, with a little more life in his voice than there had been over the past week. There was still something missing from it. . . .

Youth, lad, Raj said. ***That comes to us all. He's just had it removed faster and more painfully than most.***

"And there go the cavalry," Esmond went on.

The velipadsmen were riding at the head of the column, where they could spread out to screen the infantry. Adrian blinked gummy eyes as he watched them fan out into the low rolling hills ahead; they were Southron barbarians, mostly, mercenaries serving for pay and adventure under Confed officers. *Screen* . . . he thought, watching their velipads trot into the ripe standing wheat like boats breasting a sea of living bronze—*Damn, I'm thinking in hexameter*—if the cavalry were being sent out to screen the main force, then the Emerald light infantry would too.

One of Audsley's tribunes rode up, fingers plucking nervously at the crimson sash that circled his muscled cuirass.

"Deploy," he said, pointing westward with his staff of office. "The enemy is approaching from the west in strength. No more than three miles distant."

"Three miles?" Esmond said sharply. "To their cavalry screen, or to their main body? How many? Who commands?"

The legate looked down his well-bred nose; he was about their age, a young spark of the nobility following his patron to war, and unused to such a tone from a mere Emerald mercenary.

"Justiciar Demansk commands," he drawled. "But that needn't concern you, Emerald; you won't be treating with him yourself, you know."

He reined his velipad about and clapped heels to it. Esmond snorted. "If Justiciar Demansk was ever involved in this—and I beg leave to doubt—he's certainly going to prove his loyalty to the State *now*. With our blood and bones."

probability 97%, ±2, Center said helpfully in the back of Adrian's mind. **probability approaches unity as closely as stochastic analysis permits.**

I could die here, he knew sharply. Suddenly he could see and smell and feel more vividly than ever in his life; the smell of trampled barley and dust, the heavy shamble of a half-armed Audsley "volunteer" a hundred paces back, the song of a shrikewing . . .

probability 52%, ±3, Center said. **as you were warned.**

"All men are initiates of the mysteries of death," he whispered.

"Death, *hell*," Esmond said, grinning through sweat-caked dust. He raised himself in the stirrups and called to his men: "*Those* poor sorry ignorant bastards are going to be doing the dying, aren't they, lads?"

The men cheered him. "Deploy, and remember the training! They've got nothing like our thunderbolts—or our guts. Deploy!"

Justiciar Demansk grunted as he looked up from the folding map table set on the little ridge. Trampled barley stems were glassy and a little slippery under his hobnailed sandals, and he was sweating under the bronze back-and-breast that tradition mandated for a general officer.

"Here they come, the fools," he muttered.

Audsley had been a competent commander once; how could he have gotten himself into this position? *Good Confed troopers are going to die because Audsley and his friends can't pay their debts,* he thought. *Meanwhile the Islanders raid the coasts and the barbarians stir in the southlands. What a waste.* Granted that the State was like a knot of vipers these days, all old good ways breaking down, but this . . .

This was a ratfuck waiting to happen, he thought coldly. One day—not too long from now—a strong man was going to have to seize the reins, or everything would melt down as the generals fought over the bones of the Confederation like crabs in a bucket. Either one strong man emerged to end the endless rivalries, or it would go on until the Southrons and the Islanders fought each other to see who picked the bones of civilization. *But Audsley is not that man.*

Am I? ran through his mind, and he pushed the thought away with a mental effort. Even if he was, this wasn't the time. Not yet.

His head swiveled from side to side, the silk neckerchief that kept his skin from rasping on the edges of his back-and-breast sodden with the heat and chafing him.

Ten thousand men, he thought. Two brigades of regular infantry, somewhat understrength; call that six thousand all up. The core of his force, and they waited in formation with ox-stolid patience. Companies deployed in lines three deep, each battalion with a company in reserve; the men were kneeling with their shields leaned against their shoulders. The helmet crests ruffled in the wind; here and there an underofficer walked down the lines checking on lacings and positions. *And three battalions as general reserve,* he thought. That ought to be enough. He could feel the regulars, ready to his hand like a familiar tool that a man grasps by instinct in the dark.

A thousand cavalry. Mercenaries, Southrons under Confed officers. They lacked any semblance of the strict order and silence of his infantry brigades. There was a general uniformity of equipment—mail shirts, kite-shaped shields, helmets, lances and long swords—but within that every man suited himself. They had some discipline, of course, more than any barbarian warband, which wasn't saying much. And he had to admit that they were highly skilled individual fighters, sons of the Southron warrior class for the most part. *Audsley doesn't have any cavalry at all.*

Forward of the main line his light forces were deploying, skirmishers with javelin, sling, bow, buckler and assegai. They didn't have the staying power of the heavy infantry, but with any luck they'd handle this battle alone.

He narrowed his eyes. Audsley had a core of men in regular formation, looking fairly well equipped—one full brigade's worth, say four or five thousand men. They'd be veterans, but not drilled much recently, and it was a scratch outfit. On the flanks shambled more of his supporters, *not* properly equipped and in no particular order; eight or nine thousand of them, but they were meat for the blade. Out in front were what looked like mercenary light infantry.

"Grind me away these rabble," he said, in a voice harsh with distaste and impatience. "Loose the velipads!"

Let the Southrons earn their pay, he thought. Every rebel they killed was one less to menace his precious trained men . . . a*nd every Southron who dies is one less to raid over the border a few years down the road.*

Gallopers spurted away from the command group. A few minutes later the cavalry on either flank began to trot forward, moving into open order. The Confed officers dressed their ranks, and then dust spurted as the trot turned into a canter and then a slow hand gallop. Lanceheads came down in a rippling wave.

"Here come the even-more-barbarous barbarians," Esmond said, his voice full of confidence. "God of the Shades, accept our sacrifice—even if it does have fleas."

Adrian didn't join the chuckle that ran through those of the Emeralds who could hear his brother; it rippled down the loose formation as men repeated it to their neighbors. His own mouth was dry as he watched the line of bright points boiling out of the dust . . .

Intimidating, isn't it? Raj's voice whispered. A vison ran through his mind: another battlefield, and *thousands* of men riding the giant dogs he'd seen before. Men in steel helmets and breastplates, big bearded yellow-haired men with fifteen-foot lances, some of them with great wings sweeping up from the backplates of their armor. The howling of men and mounts and the earth-shaking thunder of paws filled his mind.

Ahead—ahead and to the right of Raj's viewpoint—men in blue uniforms and bowl helmets bent over the curious chariotlike device Raj called a cannon.

"Juicy target," one of them said, grinning and spitting through brown irregular teeth. He stood aside and gripped a cord that ran to the rear of the cannon. "Nine hundred meters, shrapnel shell . . . fire!"

Adrian blinked and nodded, smiling internally. A few of his slingers gave him odd looks, but it was only to be expected that a man who made miracles would be . . . odd, occasionally.

"Fuses ready!" The fuse men whirled the rods that held the slowmatch, and trails of bitter blue smoke cut through the air. "Light!"

Each touched the slowmatch to the fuse of a grenade, and the cords sputtered into life. There was a gingerly care to the gestures that put the round brown pottery shapes into the pockets of the slings; the fuses were supposed to be seven-second, but they weren't entirely reliable yet.

"Targets—"

The slingers raised their staff-slings, eyes picking out spots in the onrushing formations. The snarling fangs of the velipads were clearly visible now, and the shouting contorted faces behind the bar visors of the helmets.

"Loose!"

The slings had yard-long wooden handles, and the silk cords at their ends were as long again. Each man swept staff and cords around in a full circle that put the strength of their shoulders and torso into the cast, not simply their arms. The one-pound bomblets didn't have the blurring speed a lead shot did; those almond-shaped bits of metal could punch through a shield and kill the man behind it through a cuirass. The grenades *did* snap out quickly enough to make men look up and raise their shields.

Crack. Crack. Crackcrackcrackcrack—

Vicious red snapping sparks, faint in the midday sun, visible only against the puffs of dirty gray-black smoke. The velipads reared and whistle-screamed at the noise and the unfamiliar sulfur stink. What couldn't be seen or heard were the fragments of hard ceramic and lead shot that smashed out too fast for the eye to catch, and the shockwaves of the grenades. Then men and beasts screamed as fragments gouged into flesh. The order of the charge disappeared into sudden chaos. An armored man and heavy war-velipad weighed over a ton; at a full gallop they *couldn't* turn swiftly, or overleap the writhing heap of mangled flesh that suddenly appeared at the footclaws of the mount. The riders' efforts to turn their beasts simply added to the chaos as clawed feet skidded out from under the torquing weight that hindered them. Worse, the lancers further back in the formation could see nothing within the dust cloud ahead of them, and spurred their velipads forward.

And the second volley of grenades burst over the heads of the milling, thrashing mass. More velipads went down, to add to the bone-breaking weights rolling and kicking in the tangled barrier of flesh. Another volley, and another . . .

"They're running, by the Maiden!" Esmond shouted.

"That they are," Adrian replied, grinning, slapping him on his corseleted shoulder. He carefully avoided looking at the killing ground before him.

"D . . . ddd . . . demonic thunder !" the courier stuttered, his face the color of the whey that dripped from the pans when the dairywoman squeezed the curds to make cheese.

"Control yourself!" Justiciar Demansk snapped, shading his eyes with a hand; when that proved inadequate he swung up onto his velipad and stood in the stirrups.

Something had happened to his cavalry, and that was a fact. There was a huge cloud of dust; extraordinary noises were coming out of it . . . and so were Southron mercenaries, some of them lashing their velipads, others lumbering on foot, all of them in utter screaming witless panic.

"Runner," he said. "If those imbeciles attempt to interfere with the formation, give them a volley of darts."

An order which his regular infantry would follow with zeal and enthusiasm. Nobody liked Southrons.

Demansk's eyes scanned as much of the battlefield as he could see. "And a general order," he went on. "The enemy has some sort of incendiary weapon." The pirates of the Isles used those, naphtha and seabeast oil and quicklime, compounds that would burn even under water. "Remind the officers that it can't do more than kill them."

One could get away with a good deal in the Confederacy, in these degenerate days. Even his own class was not safe from the rot anymore. But running away in battle wasn't among the pardonable offenses, thank the gods.

"Here it comes," Adrian said, licking dry lips.

look for a line of retreat, Center's passionless voice said.

What?

Do it, lad. This is a disaster waiting to happen, Raj confirmed.

"Esmond," Adrian whispered. "We should be preparing a line of retreat."

His brother looked back at him, his eyes sapphires in his dust-caked face. "Adrian," he said, "there are times when I think the Gray-Eyed gave *you* the general's gifts. All right, let's see."

He thought for a moment, called a pair of his underofficers, gave low-voiced instructions. They trotted off to the rear.

The Emeralds were on the right of the rebel position, at the junction between Audsley's brigade of fully-equipped troops and the shapeless clot of the volunteers. The dust had died down a little, and out of it Demansk's army came marching. Light sparkled and rippled down their line, sunlight off the points of the darts they held in their right hands, off helmet crests and standards and the gray gleam of oiled links of mail.

"My, aren't they pretty," Esmond said.

Adrian found himself joining in the chuckle that ran down the ranks of the Emeralds. *I wonder if the rest of them are as nervous as I am,* he thought.

Most of them, Raj murmured. ***The ones who aren't are stupid, overconfident, or very experienced.***

Adrian licked his lips, tasted the sweat running down his face from the light helmet, and spoke: "Pick your targets. Aim for officers and standards—standards, and the ones with the transverse helmet crests. Wait for it, wait for it."

"Now!"

The slingers were loosing as fast as their loaders could put lighted grenades into the pockets of their weapons. The projectiles arched out towards the first line of Confed regulars, and eyes went up nervously under the helmet brims. Horns screamed harsh bronze music, and the whole formation speeded up into a trot—not a solid line, but a sinuous bronze-and-steel snake that advanced in pounding unison, keeping its alignment across the slight irregularities of the barley fields.

Crack. Crack. Crackcrackcrackcrack—

The bombs exploded, and a two-hundred-yard stretch of the Confed line vanished in smoke and malignant red snaps. Screams sounded louder than the explosions, as sharp metal and ceramic sliced into human flesh.

. . . and out of the smoke marched the survivors, still moving at the same steady trot. Men double-timed up from the second and third ranks, and the whole formation rippled and closed as the gaps were plugged and the replacements effortlessly fell into alignment. Adrian could hear the harsh clipped commands of the officers and file closers, but no screams apart from the wounded men—and not all of those.

"Shit," Esmond swore feelingly. Then louder: "What a target! Give 'em more, lads."

Adrian whipped his own staff-sling around his head, aiming for a standard in the fourth rank of the nearest Confed battalion borne by a man with the tanned head of a direbeast over his helmet. The bomb flew faultlessly, exploding at waist level before the standard-bearer had time to do more than flinch. Smoke kindly hid what happened next, but he could see the pole with the upright gilded hand totter backwards and fall. Then the standard rose again; a trooper had scooped it up, bracing it on his hip as he trotted forward.

Esmond's head was whipping back and forth as he tried to keep the whole field under observation. He fell back half a dozen steps.

"The battalion in front of us is edging right," he yelled to his brother. "But any second now—"

"*Vanbert! Vanbert!*"

The shout was loud, and the rebel regulars to their left closed formation and raised their shields in a sudden bristling of vermillion-dyed leather and brass, turning their formation into some huge scaled dragon. The volunteers to the Emerald's right tried to do the same—most of them had shields, at least—but lacked the instinctive cohesion of real fighting units.

Ahead the attackers' formation rippled as well. Adrian felt the small hairs along his spine as he realized why; the whole front line was leading with the left foot, getting ready to—

"*VANBERT! VANBERT!*" the front-line troopers roared, pivoting forward as their throwing arms flashed up.

The sound of seven thousand men shouting in unison was like a blow to the gut. The whistle as seven thousand arms launched their lead-weighted darts made Adrian's testicles try to draw themselves up into his gut.

Heads up, lad, Raj's voice said, cool and steady at the back of his brain.

Not many of the volley struck the Emeralds—the grenades had cleared too much of the front line opposite them. Men went down, here and there; others cursed and flung aside their shields as the barbed heads with the ball of lead behind the points stuck and could not be removed. To their left, the volley struck the raised shields of Audsley's brigade, most of them glancing from the curved surfaces or the metal facing, some rattling off mail, some punching into flesh.

"That's torn it," Esmond said.

He was looking to the right, where the volley had ripped into the shapeless clot of half-armed volunteers. What happened there was like a glass jar falling on rock, only what it spilled was redder than any wine. Few of the volunteers wore armor, and none had the tight shield-to-shield formation that was the only hope of stopping most of the missiles.

"*VANBERT! VANBERT!*"

Another volley, and the Confed trumpets sounded again, a complex rising-falling note. The battalions facing the volunteers drew their assegais with a long rasping slither and began to double-time forward.

"It's time," Esmond said; his face was white about the lips—with rage, Adrian realized, and the effort of will it took to order retreat rather than stay here and die killing Confeds. He nodded to their right, where the scythe of Demansk's wing was about to rip into the edge of the unravelling rebels.

"You're right, brother," Adrian said. He raised his voice. "One more volley to discourage them, men, and we'll leave the Confeds to each other."

The bombs punched out, as accurate as the first round. Other men were helping the wounded who were still mobile, or giving the mercy stroke to the helpless. Adrian swallowed a bubble of pride; his mercenaries and freedmen and general rabble were steady with the many-headed beast almost within arm's length of them.

Esmond's light infantry spread to cover the grenadiers, hefting their javelins.

"Give them a shaft, then we go!"

Esmond turned, hefted his javelin and threw with a skill that made it seem effortless. It ended in the face of a Confed underofficer; the fan-crested helmet snapped back, and the volley that followed made them waver for an instant. The Emeralds turned and trotted away in a compact body, heading to the rear and to the west—behind the still-solid ranks of Audsley's brigade.

The same mounted galloper as before drew rein before them; Adrian could smell the rank omnivore breath of the velipad as it came up on its haunches, pawing the air before it with great blunt claws.

"Where do you think you're going?" the young Confed nobleman cried. "Back to your posts, you Emerald scum—"

Thunk.

Esmond's javelin punched through the light cuirass of linen and bronze scale with a sound like an axe hitting wood. The Confed goggled, and then his eyes slid down to the slim ashwood shaft in his gut. He slid free of the saddle with the same expression of bewildered indignation, as if he could not *believe* that a mere Emerald mercenary had dared to raise a hand against him.

"For every slight, for every insult, I will send a dozen of them to the Shades," Esmond muttered as he caught the velipad and swung into the saddle with effortless grace. "For Nanya, not all their lives are enough."

Adrian swallowed at the sound of his brother's voice, even now. There was a huge rasping slither behind them as Audsley's men drew their assegais in turn, then a banging clatter like all the smiths' shops in the world as the fight came to close quarters. He risked a glance over his left shoulder; the volunteers were going down like greatbeasts under a sacrificer's axe, but there were so many of them that it would take some time . . . and the dust and confusion were immense. Without Center to sketch images across his vision it would have all been a mass of steel and shouting and blood, patternless, Chaos and Old Night come again.

"When Demansk's men get through with the rabble, they'll curve in to take Audsley's regulars from the rear," he called up to Esmond. "If we get out of the bag in time . . ."

"Exactly," Esmond said, like an apparition of Wodep the War God on the restive velipad, his armor splashed with blood.

Me too, Adrian realized, daubing at himself. *Me too.*

"Strike sail," Adrian said.

The skipper of the *Wave Strider* shrugged. "Lay aloft!" he shouted. "Strike sail!"

The ship they'd hijacked was much like the ones their father had run out of Solinga for most of their lives: a hundred feet long and forty at the broadest part of the hull, fully decked, with one tall mast and a single large square sail. Adrian didn't think his father would ever have tolerated the skirt of weed that showed green against the blue water all around, or bilges that stank badly enough to overpower even the iodine smell of the sea. The swan's head that curled above them on the quarterdeck was standard, but the blue and gold paint was chipped and faded. For all that, the hull was watertight and they'd made good time from the west-coast port of Preble. Adrian licked dry lips, squinting out over the white-flecked blue of the Western Ocean; they hadn't had time to ship extra water or supplies, and with two hundred men aboard they were down to a cupful a day—green, slimy, sweeter-tasting than any wine.

The big yard came down with a rattle, and a curse from the Emerald mercenaries on deck who had to scramble out of the way. With the sail down, Adrian had a better view of the craft that was approaching them.

It was no merchantman. The hull was low and long and snake-slender, with glaring eyes and snarling teeth painted above a bronze ram that flashed out of the water with every forward bound. Outriggers held seats for oarsmen who would drive two banks of long oars when the mast was down. Right now it was rigged for cruising, the mast up and a sail painted the same blue-gray as the hull bent to it. Two light catapults stood manned near the bows, ready to throw rocks or jugs full of clingfire; two ballistae flanked the quarterdeck, with giant javelins ready to hurl. The knot of men by the steering oar was bright with plumes and gold and blowing cloaks dyed in the famous purple of the western islands. And the flag above them had the stylized cresting wave of the Lords of the Isles.

The other ship's sail came down like magic, neatly furled—a heavy crew, a warship's crew. Esmond came up beside his brother, shading his eyes with a palm. As he did, the oars flashed out of the other ship's sides and struck the water all together like the limbs of a centipede, slashing creamy froth from the waves. The slender hull jerked forward, then turned to present its ram to the merchantman's side in a smooth curve, turned by the oars as well as the twin steering oars; they could hear the *clack . . . clack . . . clack* of the hortator's mallets on the log that served as drum.

"Bireme," Esmond said. "Twenty marines, hundred and twenty oarsmen, thirty sailors. They can't be far from home. Royal ship too, I think, not a freebooter. Very well-trained crew."

Adrian nodded, although being a royal ship wasn't always much of a distinction, with Islanders. Any king's ship would turn pirate if the opportunity offered.

One of the officers on the warship's quarterdeck raised a speaking trumpet. He hailed them in Confed, accented but understandable.

"Ahoy there! What ship?"

"*Wave Strider*, out of Preble," the captain said. "Bound for Chalice."

"What cargo?"

The voice sounded suspicious; there were far too many armed men on the merchantman's deck, but she was equally obviously no pirate or longshore raider. That would make her cautious. Even a successful ramming run might leave the warship vulnerable to boarding; a little bad luck, a ram caught in the wounded ship's timbers, and the *Wave Strider*'s men could swarm aboard. That was how Confed ships had beat the Kingdom's fleets despite the Islanders' seamanship, grappling and turning naval battles into land fights.

Adrian stepped forward, speaking in the tongue of the Isles; he could feel Esmond stiffen in surprise. Which was natural enough, since as far as he knew Adrian spoke only a few words.

"Our cargo is brave men," he said. "Come to serve King Casull IV, Lord of the Isles, Supreme Autocrat, Chosen of the Sun God and Lemare of the Sea, against the thieves and tyrants of Vanbert. We are Adrian and Esmond Gellert, of Solinga."

The ships were close enough now that Adrian could see the officer's eyes go wide in a swarthy, hook-nosed face. The plume at the forefront of his turban nodded as he turned and spoke urgently with some others.

"They've heard of us, and not just through Father," Esmond murmured at his ear.

"Now the question is whether they want to get in good with the Confeds or poke them in the eye," Adrian murmured back.

The gorgeously-dressed officer turned back, sun breaking off the gilded scales of his armor. "The King, may he live forever, must hear of this," he said. "You will transfer to Slasher."

"Esteemed sir, we will remain with our men," Esmond said, in slower and more heavily accented Islander. "But we are very eager to lay our fates at the feet of the King, to whom the gods have given a great realm."

There was a moment of tension as stares met. The plumes nodded again as the Islander captain nodded. "Very well. Make what sail you can."

"Enter," King Casull said.

The audience chamber was small and informal, one wall an openwork lattice of carved marble looking down over the city of Chalice. For the rest it held a mosaic of sea monsters—most of them quite real, as Casull had learned in his years as a skipper and admiral, before the previous King had met an untimely end in the last war with the Confeds—an ebony table inlaid with mother-of-pearl, embroidered cushions, a tray of dried fruit and pitchers of wine and water. A girl in a diaphanous gown knelt in one corner, strumming a *jitar*, and two guards stood by the entrance, the points of their huge curved slashing-swords resting on the floor before their boots and their hands ready on the hilts. A stick of incense burned in a fretted brass tray, melding with the scent of the flowers in the gardens outside, and the tarry reek of the harbor below.

Two men came through the door with a eunuch chamberlain following, in robes even more gorgeous than theirs.

"O King, live forever!" all three cried as they prostrated themselves on the floor.

The silver aigrettes at the front of the two merchants' turbans clicked on the tessellated marble of the floor, as did the ruby in the eunuch's turban. *A palace chamberlain might lack stones, but not the opportunity to acquire precious stones.* Casull smiled slightly to himself at his own pun and made a gesture with one hand. Another girl rose with silent grace and moved to pour thick sweet wine into tiny cups carved from the gemlike teeth of the *salpesk*.

"Rise, my friends," he said genially. His father had once told him that even if you had to kill a man, it cost nothing to be polite. "Speak. Your King would hear your tale."

The merchants rose and sat cross-legged on cushions, raising the cups the slave handed them in a two-handed gesture of respect before sipping appreciatively. Both were middle-aged men with gray in their curled, oiled beards. *Enri and Pyhar Lowisson,* Casull reminded himself. *Brothers.* Their father had been a fish farmer, but the sons had made a fortune in trade . . . and in raiding, during the chaos of the wars with the Confeds. They'd served ably in Casull's own campaigns against islands that had fallen away from the Kingdom while his predecessor was occupied on the mainland, too.

"Know, O King, that we have long traded with Solinga," Enri said; he was the elder of the two.

Casull nodded. "Dried fish, textiles and spices for wine, grain and jerked meat," he said. "With sidelines in zinc ore, bar iron and general handicrafts."

The merchants blinked and bowed their heads in respect. "Go on," the King said.

"We have dealt, over the years, with one Zeke Gellert of Solinga," Enri went on. "He died last year, but we exchanged *tesserae* with him some time ago."

Casull nodded again, silent. He'd found that was more effective than talking, often enough. Tesserae were tokens—usually ivory—exchanged between guest-friends in the Emerald countries. The token was broken in half; when the other half was presented, the guest-friend was obliged to offer help and shelter to the man who brought it, and the obligation was hereditary. Or so Emeralds generally thought; Islanders were more . . . flexible. Still, it would harm the Lowissons' reputation in the Emerald lands if they turned away their guest-friend's heirs.

Enri moistened his lips and sipped delicately at the wine. "Well, O King, Adrian and Esmond Gellert have come to Chalice, claiming hospitality of us . . . and wishing an introduction to the King's self."

He hesitated, and the King spoke. "The Adrian and Esmond Gellert who took part in Audsley's rebellion in the Confed territories, yes," he said. "They are outlaws in the Confederacy—not the first time exiles from the mainland have sought the Isles."

Although no other exiles have been preceded by such rumors, he thought. Weapons like the lightning of the gods, thunder and fire that left men torn to shreds . . . *There may be something to it,* he thought.

Still, less than rumor paints, or Audsley would have made himself master in Vanbert.

The conversation wound on, intricate and indirect; the three might all be self-made men, but they'd aquired polish as well as wealth and power on their journey up the slippery pole of rank. The Isles weren't like the mainland, where a man's life was fixed at his birth. Here a sailor or a peasant might end his days with a palace and a harem, if he had the luck and the *nous*; but equally, the pit of failure yawned before his steps all his days, and his rivals' knives were always sharp and ready.

Casull smiled and nodded. *Yes, you wish to share in any favor that may befall the Gellerts,* he thought. *Yes, equally, you wish to avoid the blame for any failure, if they are nothing but boasters. Yes, these desires conflict—for if you wait too long, you will surely lose. A beautiful dilemma.*

At the end, he clapped his hands. "We will grant these Emeralds the favor of an audience," he said. "Talk is cheap, and stolen goods are never sold at a loss."

His gaze sought the city that tumbled down the slopes from the palace to its circular harbor. *And I need any help I can get,* he thought. The Isles were far from united, and when they were the Confeds would still outweigh him by thirty to one. Skill and distance had kept the Islands independent, but . . . what was that old saying? Ah, yes.

Quantity has a quality all its own. He would seize any advantage that came his way with both hands, preparing for the inevitable struggle.

CHAPTER FIVE

Impressive, Adrian thought, pausing in his restless pacing and looking up the slope of the volcano.

The mansion of their father's guest-friend was down by the docks—the Lowissons liked to keep in touch with the sources of their wealth. Like most buildings in Chalice it was made of stone blocks, like volcanic tufa plastered over and whitewashed or painted, with a flat roof where the inhabitants could sleep during the hot summers . . . or pace while they awaited the word of the King. Other buildings stretched up the steep slope, along roads cobblestoned or paved or deep in mud, narrow and twisting except for the Processional Way that led from the docks to the great blocky temple of Lemare, the Sea Goddess. The buildings lay like the dice of gods themselves, tumbled over the slopes in blocks of brilliant white, emerald green, purple and blue and crimson; they turned blank walls to the streets, centering around a myriad of courtyards large and small. A wall might hide anything; the mansion of a merchant prince, a teeming tenement house, the workshops of artisans. Over some one could see the tips of trees swaying, and within could be beautiful gardens and fountains of carved jade splashing cool water . . . or flapping laundry and shrilling children.

The streets were crowded themselves, with near-naked porters bent double under huge loads, with chains of the Island dwarf velipads under similar burdens, with water sellers and sweetmeat sellers and storytellers, rich merchants in jewels and silk, swaggering crewmen from pirate galleys with curved swords at their sides and horn-backed bows slung over their shoulders, priests with their heads shaven and painted in zigzag stripes . . . Here a wealthy courtesan went by in her litter borne on the shoulders of four brawny slaves, crooning and feeding nuts between her teeth to a gaudy-feathered bird; there a scholar paused to buy a cup of watered wine, while his students gathered behind and broke into arm-waving argument, using the scrolls they carried to gesture—or to rap each other over the head. . . .

Chalice took in three-quarters of the circumference of the ancient volcanic crater that made up its harbor and gave it its name; the knife ridges above made a city wall unnecessary. The great expanse of the caldera was thick with ships, galleys spider-walking to the naval base on the north shore, fishing smacks, the lines of buoys that marked the outlines of fish farms. Above the buildings reared the slopes of other volcanos; the Peak of the Sun God highest of all, topped with eternal snows and trickling a long plume of smoke into azure heavens. The lower slopes were terraced for orchards of pomegranate, mangosteen, orange, fig; the upper bore dense green forest, the source of valuable hardwoods and ship timber.

Adrian turned back to his brother . . . and stopped a moment, shocked. *Esmond looks* older, he thought. *Thirty, at least.* There were deep grooves from the corners of his mouth to his nose, and his blue gaze was blank as he waited.

What can you say? he thought. The School of the Grove taught that the love of women was a weakness, disturbing the equilibrium that a wise man constantly sought. He didn't think that was what Esmond's grief needed to hear; and he'd obviously loved Nanya with exactly the sort of grand obsessive passion that Bestmun had denounced, the sort that had set a thousand ships to sailing and brought the wrath of the Gods down on the city of Windhaven in the ancient epics. *The problem is, he'd say it was worth it, even with the pain,* Adrian decided. *Thank the gods I'm free* of that, *at least.* It would have been more wholehearted if he'd been able to deny an element of wistful envy . . .

His host saved him the embarassment of speech. "Come," he said, smiling. "The King will hear you, most fortunate of men."

Adrian's eyes went to the volcano for a moment. The slopes of such mountains bore soil of marvelous richness . . . but anything a man grew there might be destroyed by fire and ash at any moment.

We never said it would be easy, lad, Raj said.

Adrian took a deep breath and bowed in his turn. "The King does us honor," he began.

"The King does us honor," Adrian said again as they sat awkwardly, unused to the cross-legged position.

"The King is finished with ceremony," Casull said, leaning back against the pile of cushions. "I can see men beating their heads on the floor of the throne room any time of the day—men with something interesting to say are much rarer, and I prefer not to have important news bellowed out in open *durbar*. Even the Confederacy can find the occasional able spy."

The day had turned warm; the King was glad enough of the peacock-feather fans stirring a little air across his face, and the fine mist from the fountain in the courtyard. The palace of the Kings of the Isles was a warren that had grown by accretion over four centuries, every new monarch adding something and few tearing anything down. This chamber was open at both ends, slender pillars with coral capitals giving onto the corridor and a terrace that looked over the outer gardens; the through breeze made it tolerable on these hot rainy-season afternoons. From the raised platform where he sat Casull could see past the Emeralds to the city, and to the black thunderclouds piling up on the eastern horizon.

Luridly appropriate, he thought.

"The . . . grenade, did you call it? The grenade was very impressive. At sea, such weapons could be decisive—at least for the first few times, when the enemy were unused to them, and had none themselves."

He spoke Emerald, the cultured version of Solinga's gentlefolk, not the patois of the sea. The younger Emerald's Islander was impressively fluent, but it wouldn't do to let him think he was dealing with a boor, a mere jumped-up pirate chief. Casull's mental eyes narrowed as he appraised this Adrian Gellert; outwardly he was very much a young Scholar of the Grove, but there was something else . . . *Harder than one might expect,* he thought. *And more perceptive—he misses nothing.*

The brother was more outwardly formidable. A fighting man, Casull judged, and not just an athlete. The reports from the mainland, and from the spies among the barkeeps, whores and gamblers who'd had contact with the mercenary troop the Gellerts had brought with them, all said he had the *baraka*, the gift of inspiring men in battle. Wits besides; and he certainly *looked* like an incarnation of Wodep, the ancient War God of the mainlanders.

The younger Emerald bowed. "O King, the grenades are the *least* of what can be done with the new . . . new *principle* involved in these explosive weapons."

Casull raised his eyebrows. The Emerald word meant *underlying cause*, and he didn't quite see how it applied.

"Speak on," he said mildly, quelling a restless stir by his son Tenny. *Let the boy learn patience; that's not the least of a ruler's virtues.*

"If my lord the King would deign to look at these—the first is what is called a cannon, for hurling iron balls and giant grenades; to smash ships, or batter down the walls of a fort . . ."

Two hours later Casull leaned back again. "Interesting indeed," he said. His eyes turned to Esmond. "And you, young sir, what have you to say?"

Esmond smiled, a gesture that did not reach the cold blue eyes. "My brother is the scholar," he said. "What I do is fight. I've managed to kill a fair number of Confeds, over the past six months. I intend to kill a good many more." His fist tightened on his knee; the scars and burns across the back showed white against his tanned skin. "For every slight, for every humiliation they've inflicted on me and my city, I shall take recompense in blood—and they owe me a debt beyond that. When the last trooper dies in the burning ruins of

Vanbert and the Confederacy is a memory, then *perhaps* I'll consider the account settled."

Casull nodded thoughtfully; he'd seen hatred before, but none more bitter. *Pity,* he thought. A man that eaten with hate turned inward on himself; his luck might be strong, but it would run too swiftly, carrying out the current of his life. *But I can use him.*

He clapped his hands. "Hear the commands of the King!" he said, his tone slightly formal. The *wakil* leaned forward, pen poised over a sheet of reed-paper.

"It is the command of the King that the noble warrior Esmond Gellert's-son of Solinga, be taken into the forces of the King, to command the Sea Striker regiment; he shall rank as a Commander of Five Hundred—which is about what they'll come to, with the men he brought with him. The usual pay and plunder-shares."

Esmond bowed again, and this time his smile was more genuine.

Casull turned his eyes back to the younger man. "You shall have a chance to demonstrate your new weapons," he said. "It is the command of the King that Adrian Gellert be accepted into the Court with the rank of Scholar-Advisor, with the usual pay and perquisites. For the purpose of building his weapons, he may exert the royal prerogative of eminent domain, acquiring land, and requiring artisans and merchants to furnish the materials he needs . . . saltpeter, you said? And the metals. He may use a royal estate to be designated hereafter, and royal vessels, within reason. All goods and labor to be paid for at fair market prices, of course."

A King of the Isles was theoretically absolute; in practice there were always enough claimants that a monarch who angered enough of the powerful merchants and ship owners would find that the despotism was tempered by assassination and leavened by coup d'etat. He certainly wasn't going to risk that for this Emerald's untried notions. The potential payoff was certainly huge, though.

"Ah . . ." Adrian looked uncertain. "My lord King, this work will require considerable funds," he said. "Even for demonstration purposes. How . . ."

Casull smiled at Enri and Pyhar Lowisson. "Your patrons will, of course—out of patriotic duty as well—loan you the funds at a reasonable rate of interest. No more than fifteen percent, annual, compounded."

The two Islander merchants winced; that was the rate for a bottomry loan, with no premium for risk.

"If the weapons are satisfactory, I will reward you richly; and they shall have the interest doubled from the royal treasury, as well as my favor, of course."

He beamed at the Emeralds and the two Islanders as well. Unspoken went the fact that if the weapons *failed* to satisfy they would get nothing, and the Lowissons could try as best they could to get satisfaction from their penniless guests.

Casull clapped his hands. "This audience is at an end!"

"By the Dog," the mercenary officer said. "Has the King sent us a pretty boy for a party?"

"The King has sent me here to command," Esmond said. "Name and rank."

The mercenary turned crimson. "I'm Donnuld Grayn, and I command here now that Stenson's dead, by the Dog!"

Esmond rested his hands on his sword belt and looked the man up and down. By his accent he came from Cable, ancient enemy of the Solingians—not that that mattered much, these days—and by his looks, scars upon scars, he'd been in this profession most of his thirty-odd years. And from the look of his bloodshot eyes . . .

"Are you usually drunk this early?" he said. "Or are you just naturally stupid?"

"Ahhhh," the man said eagerly, his hand falling towards his sword hilt. "I'll see your liver and lights for that, you mincing Solingian basta—"

The growl broke into a yelp as Esmond's thumb and forefinger closed on his nose and gave it a powerful, exactly calculated twist. As he'd expected, the mercenary forgot all about his steel and lashed out with a knobby fist.

Esmond's own hand slapped it aside, and his right sank its knuckles into his opponent's gut with the savage precision of the palaestra. As the man doubled over, the Solingian stepped to one side and slammed another blow with the edge of a palm behind his ear. The mercenary dropped to the ground like a puppet with its strings cut and lay wheezing at the victor's feet.

The victor looked up; there were a crowd of Strikers looking on, together with some of the camp followers and children that crowded the barracks. Some were smiling, some glaring, most wavering between the two.

"You!" Esmond said. "Name and rank, soldier."

The man stiffened. "Eward, sir—file closer, second company."

"Eward, get Captain Grayn to his quarters—he needs to sleep it off. Trumpeter," he went on, "sound *fall in.*"

That took far too long, and he had to detail some of his own men to push the noncombatants out of the way. When it was finished there were about four hundred men standing on the pounded clay of the parade ground; it was surrounded on three sides by barracks, and on the fourth by a wall. Esmond paced down the ranks of the sweating, bewildered men, pausing now and then.

Not bad, he thought. About half-and-half javelineers and slingers. They all had linen corselets with thin iron plates sewn between the layers of cloth, shortswords, and light open-face bowl helmets. Most of them looked to be in reasonable condition, and King Casull certainly wouldn't be wasting his silver on deadbeats. From what he'd heard, a lot of them would be men who'd left the Emerald cities for reasons of health, or on their relatives' urgent advice; but war and the Confederacy had left a lot of broken men in the southern lands.

"All right," he said at last, standing in front of them with his left hand resting on his hilt and the cloak thrown back from his shoulder. "My name is Esmond Gellert."

A slight murmur. He noted it without the pleasure it might have brought him a few months ago. He'd always been proud of the fame he'd won as a competitor in the Pan-Emerald Games—if not for undying fame, why would men go through the rigors of the palaestra? Now it was like his appearance, something he noted with cold objectivity, a tool to be used. *And some of them will have heard about the war on the mainland, too.*

"You know—or you should, if you're paying any attention to

anything besides booze, dice and pussy—that there's war coming. Probably with the Confeds." Another low murmur. "I've fought them myself, not too long ago; so have these men with me." He indicated his own followers with a toss of his head. "They're tough, yes, but they're not ten feet tall, and they bleed as red as any man when you stick 'em. The King wants this unit ready to fight, and by the Gods, it will be—or we'll all die trying."

He nodded at the last murmur. No use saying anything more; they'd be waiting to see if he was real, or all mouth.

"For starters, we're going on a little route march. Fall out in campaign order in twenty minutes. Dismissed!"

"Faugh, this stinks," Enri Lowisson said.

"Think of it as the smell of money," Adrian said, chuckling with delight.

The cave was halfway up the side of Gunnung Daberville, the main volcanic peak that loomed over the port of Chalice. From the entrance you could see down past jungle and orchard to the city itself, the bastioned wall, the near-circle of the drowned caldera that made up the harbor, and over miles of sail-speckled water beyond. It was what lay within that interested him, however, down into the depths of the fumarole that twisted like a frozen intestine into the depths of the mountain.

Thirty feet overhead the ceiling of the cavern was not of the same pockmarked gray-green rock as the rest of the cave. It was brown instead, lumpy . . . and it *moved* as the chitterwings nesting there for the day stirred uneasily at the light and heat of the party's torches. A soft pattering left gloppy white stains on the floor, adding to a layer that was probably four feet deep at least. That was the source of the rancid, ammonia-harsh stink that had several of the party breathing through pieces of their tunics.

"The stuff we need, the saltpeter, will be concentrated in the lower levels of this," he said, kicking at the hard dried surface of the chitterwing dung that covered the ground. "We'll dig it out, cart it down lower, then leach out the saltpeter in a system of trays and sluices."

"That will cost," Enri warned.

He looked backward, and Adrian nodded. The way down was near-as-no-matter roadless; if it had been easier, farmers would have come to dig the dung out for fertilizer, as they had with several caves lower down. The chitterwings went out in huge flocks at night, to feed at sea on tiny phosphorescent fish. At dawn they returned, to sleep, and to breed and nest in season—most of the females had tiny young clinging to their belly fur with miniature claws right now.

"It'll be worth it; there's more here than we'll need in a generation." He looked downslope as well, and suddenly a tracery of drawings was overlaid on it.

so, Center said. **and so.**

Adrian started and came back to himself, conscious of the curious stares Enri and his men were giving him.

"There's a way to make it easier," he said. "See how this ridge curves away down to the foothills?"

"Building a road?" Enri said. He shook his head. "I don't think that's practical."

"No, what we'll do is build a trackway," Adrian said. The words tumbled over themselves at the series of silent *clicks* just behind his eyes; suddenly Center's drawing made *sense*. In fact the principle . . . *Why haven't we thought of this before?* he wondered. *It would make so much easier.*

The problem was he knew the answer to that. "*Thought was not to be sullied with the base, contemptible concerns of men whose lives were warped away from virtue by cramping labor . . ." Which, in effect, means anyone who isn't an absentee landlord*; not something that would have come to him before Raj and Center took up residence in the rear of his mind, but it was his own thought.

"We'll lay down two rails of hard wood, spiked to cross-ties," he said. "Carts will run down it, on flanged wheels. When they're empty, they can be hauled up easily."

Enri winced. "Oh, that will *cost*. Sawyers, carpenters, the metal for spikes, all that cordage . . ."

"No, it'll turn a profit," Adrian said. "What we extract will still leave the sludge good for fertilizer, and think of what that fetches in the gardens around the city."

Enri brightened. "And, of course, the King will pay . . . eventually."

"Interesting!" the blacksmith said.

Well, thank the Gray-Eyed Lady for that! Adrian thought to himself. *At least I'm not getting "but such a thing was never done in the days of our fathers" so often here.*

The smithy occupied the lower story of a house near the docks, with the quarters of the smith's two wives, his children, the two apprentices and the three slaves to the rear, on the other side of the courtyard. It held a large circular brick hearth built up to about waist height, the bellows behind that, and a variety of anvils. The front entrance could be closed by a grillwork that was now hauled up, a little like a portcullis; the walls held workbenches, racked tools, vises and clamps, and more anvils of different shapes and sizes. It was ferociously hot—the smith wore only a rag-twist loincloth under his leather apron and gloves, and the slave working the bellows less than that. The smells were of hot oil from the quenching bath, burning charcoal, scorched metal, sweat.

"Interesting, the Lame One curse me if it isn't," the smith said. "This tube you want, now, it's to be sixty inches long?"

"Sixty inches long, and an inch and a quarter on the inside. I thought you could twist the bar around an iron mandrel, red-hot, and then hammer-weld it."

"Hmmm."

The smith went over to a workbench and brought back a sword. It was nearly complete except for the fitting of the hilt and guard; a curved weapon with a flared tip, more than a yard long, the type of slashing-scimitar that the Royal bodyguards carried. Adrian whistled admiration as he peered more closely at the metal; it had the rippled pattern work of a blade made from rods of iron and steel twisted together, heated, hammered, doubled back, hammered again . . . and repeated time after time until there were thousands of laminations in the metal.

"Look," the smith said.

He braced the point of the blade against the floor, placed his foot against it, and heaved. Muscle stood out like cable under the wet brown skin of his massive, ropy arms and broad shoulders. The blade bent nearly double . . . and then sprang back with a quivering whine when he released it.

"That's good steel," Adrian said sincerely; tough and flexible both.

The smith gave him a quizzical look, out of a face that looked as if it had been pounded from rough iron itself, with one of the sledges that stood all around the big room.

"You're not the common run of fine Emerald gentlemen," he said. "Never a one of them I've met who thought *how* a thing was made."

Adrian smiled. "I have unusual friends," he said. "Can you do what I ask?"

"Oh, certainly: Lame One be my witness. The thing is, friend, it'll take *time*. Three weeks to make a good sword blade—not counting grinding, polishing, and fitting; I contract those out. I'm not one for fine work with brass and ivory, anyway . . . say the same for one of these . . . what was the word?"

"Arquebus barrels," Adrian said helpfully.

"One of these tubes, then. And it'll cost what a good sword blade does, too."

"If I paid you extra, to take on more labor, could you do more?"

A decisive shake of the head. "No, sir. Guild rules." At Adrian's expression he went on: "But see here, sir, I like gold and silver as much as the next man, and I like to do something new now and then. What I *can* do is contract out. There are dozens of mastersmiths in the Brotherhood; not many as good as I am, if I do say so myself, but nearly. And there are plenty of journeymen we *could* hire away from their regular work, and who could do the simpler parts. Say . . . thirty in three weeks, with as much again every week after that. It'll go faster once we're used to it."

Adrian sighed. "Well, if that's all that can be done . . ."

the artisan is not being entirely truthful, Center pointed out. An image of his face sprang up, with pointers indicating temperature variations and the dilation of his pupils. **mendacity factor of 27%, ±7. i suspect that he is merely establishing an initial bargaining position.**

Oh, Adrian thought. He was the son of a merchant, but most of his life had been spent among the Scholars of the Grove. *What should I do?*

Well, I wasn't a trader either, Raj's mental voice said, amused. ***But I did do a fair bit of dickering with sutlers. I'd suggest you say that's not enough to make the project worthwhile. He'll scream and modify his terms; then point out that he and his friends will be able to sell the muskets elsewhere, too . . .***

"What is this, a flowerpot?" the brassfounder said.

"No, it's a weapon," Adrian replied, biting back the first words that came to mind. "The one the King has commanded me to build," he added.

"May the King live forever!" the artisan said, without taking his eyes off the model Adrian had had carved from soft wood.

The Emerald's hands trembled slightly as he pulled on it. Not enough sleep, he thought to himself as the model split down the middle.

"This is a—" He paused, frustrated. *What's "cross-sectional view" in Islander?* he thought.

Lad, there's no word for it. There's no word for it in your language either, Raj said.

"—what it would look like if it was cut down the middle?" Adrian said. *Have I changed so much in a year?*

He shook aside the obscure sense of instability that lay like a lump of cold millet porridge below his breastbone for a moment. The reasonable man did not doubt that he himself *was*, the School of the Grove taught.

The brassfounder was in a bigger way of business than any of the smiths; he was a merchant, as well as the manager of a workshop. Iron was much more common than copper, vastly more common than tin. You had to have long-distance contacts to deal in bronze. Hence the warehouse attached to his house, and the courtyard with its ruddy tile and fountain, that Islander symbol of status. The man's turban was of plain cotton, though, and the eyes below it were shrewd and dark.

"Like a tube closed at one end, then," he said, tracing the model. "You know, this trick might be useful for making preliminary models of castings of many types . . . and the metal outside the tube grows much thicker towards the closed end. What's this, though?"

"It's a thin hole going from the outside—this depression—into the tube at the breech end. The closed end," he added, at the man's frown.

"Hmmm. Well, with bronze, it would be simpler to *drill* that afterwards. And what are these little solid tubes at right angles to the main one for?"

"You'll find out," Adrian said, smiling slightly.

Good. We don't want too much getting out too early, and I'd be surprised if some of these people aren't for sale, Raj said.

Or all of them, Adrian replied.

"Well, you make pumps with close-fitting pistons, don't you?" he said.

"Of course, honored sir," the metalworker said. "By lapping—you use the piston head to do the last little bit of boring out, covering it with *naxium*—emery is your Emerald word, I think. That will give you a very close fit."

"Well, then, that's how we'll make this engine work," he said, forcing cheerfulness into his voice.

"Yes, but I really don't think it can be done with iron," the metalworker replied. "Iron is too hard—and too hard to cast, honored sir. By the Sun God, I speak the truth."

Adrian sighed and let his head drop into his hands. *My back hurts,* he thought; he was never, never going to get used to sitting cross-legged on cushions.

"All right," he said. "We'll start off by using bronze for the pistons. We want two, to begin with, six inches in bore and four feet long. But the piston rods will have to be made of iron—wrought iron."

"Hmm-auhm," the Islander—his name was Marzel, a plump little man with a snuff-colored turban—said.

He picked up the model Adrian had had made by standing over a toycrafter. It showed a single upright cylinder, with a piston rod coming out of its top. The rod connected to one end of a beam; the beam was pivoted in the middle, and the other end had a second rod that worked a crank, that in turn moved a wheel with paddles.

"I've seen wheels like this used to move grindstones," Marzel said. "This is the same thing in reverse, isn't it?"

Gray-Eyed Lady, thank You, Adrian thought. *Finally, someone who* understands *what I'm talking about!*

"Exactly!" he said aloud. "The steam pushes the piston, the piston pushes the beam up and down, the crank turns that into around and around, and the wheel pushes the ship—one on each side."

"Hmmm-auhm," Marzel mused again. "You know, honored sir, one could use this to move a grindstone, too."

A hecatomb of oxen to you, Lady of Wisdom. Aloud: "Yes, it could—think of it as a way of transforming firewood into work, the way a man or a velipad converts *food* into work."

Marzel laughed aloud. "Ah, you have a divine wit, honored sir!" He returned to the model. "So, let me see if I have grasped this. The steam goes through these valves *here*, at each end of the cylinder. As the piston moves, it uncovers these two rows of outlets here at the middle of the cylinder, letting the steam escape."

At Adrian's nod, the artificer turned back to the plans, tracing lines across the reed-paper with a finger and then referring back to the model.

"Honored sir," he said at last, "I love this thing you have designed—so clever, you Emeralds! Yes, I love the thought of making it. But I am not sure that it *can* be made, in the world of real things. In the . . . how do you Emeralds say it? In the world of Pure Forms, yes, this will work as you say. But it has so many valves, so much piping, so many *joints*, you see. Holding water in such a thing, for say the fountains and curious metal beasts in the Garden of Curiosities in the King's Palace, that is difficult. Holding hot steam . . . can fittings be made precisely enough? Even with the finest craftsmen? And these parts will be *large*."

Adrian nodded in respect for the man's honesty; and his courage, expressing doubts here in the palace rather than telling the royal favorite whatever he wanted to hear.

"I am certain that if any man can do it, Marzel Therdu, you can," he said. "And I am certain that it *can* be done." He spread his hands and smiled. "And my head answers for it, if it cannot, not yours."

Marzel rose and made the gesture of respect, bowing with palms pressed together. "Perhaps . . . Perhaps we would be well advised to try first a *model* of this thing, this . . . hot water mover?"

"Steam engine."

"Steam engine, then. Not a toy model, although that was useful. A *working* model, enough to drive a small launch, of the type rowed by ten men?"

probability of success of steam ram project has increased to 61% ±7, Center said. **as always, stochastic analysis cannot fully compensate for human variability.**

Adrian smiled; if that had been a human voice speaking aloud, and not a supernatural machine whispering at the back of his mind, he'd have sworn there was a rasp of exasperation in it—rather the way one of the professors of Political Theory in the Academy had spoken of the Confederacy of Vanbert's Constitution; it should not work, but it *did*.

"I think you are right, Marzel," he said. "If you could bring me the costed estimates, in . . ."

"Three days time, honored sir."

"Three days, that would be excellent."

They parted with the usual flowery Islander protestations of mutual esteem; this time they were sincere. As the Islander left, Adrian rose to circle the ship model on the table once more. It showed a craft halfway between a galley and a merchant ship, perhaps five times longer than it was wide. The bow ended in a ram shaped like a cold chisel, and there were neither oars nor sail. Instead two great bladed wheels revolved on either side, and the hull was covered over wholly by a turtlelike deck. Octagons covered that in turn like the scales of some great serpent, marking where the hand-hammered iron plates would go. The upper curve was broken by two smokestacks, one to the left and one to the right; between them was a low circular deckhouse, with slits all around for vision.

Esmond rose from the corner where he had been sitting silently. "Brother," he said gently. "Will this really *work*?"

"I don't know," Adrian said. "I *think* it will. The gunpowder worked . . ."

"Yes." Esmond paused. "I know I haven't been much help to you . . . much help since Vanbert," he said hesitantly.

Adrian turned and gripped his shoulders. "Oh, no—just saved my life half a dozen times in the retreat, got us all out alive, got us a ship, rushed around like Wodep would if he had enough sense to listen to the Gray-Eyed . . ."

"Brother, I'm worried about you," the taller of the Gellerts said bluntly. "I don't . . . I've known you all my life. Yes, you're the smarter of us, and yes, you're a Scholar the Grove could be proud of—but all these, these *things* you've been coming up with since Father died . . ."

"These *things* are our only chance of revenge on the Confederacy," Adrian said, with a peculiar inward wrench. *I cannot tell the truth even to my brother, who is not only the brother of my blood but the brother of my heart,* he knew. First, Esmond would simply be horrified that his brother had gone mad. And even if he *believed*, would he *understand*? The concepts had been hard enough for Adrian, and he had two disembodied intelligences speaking directly to him.

He thrust aside certain fears that had come to him in the night, now and then. *What if I am truly mad? What if these are demons, such as the ancient stories tell of?*

Esmond's face hardened. "You're right," he said. "I thank the *gods* that you've stumbled on these things." A smile. "Forgive my weakness."

"I'd forgive you far more than a concern for me, Esmond."

The cry was a huge shout, like a battle trumpet. Adrian Gellert shot out of the low soft bed as if he had been yanked out with cords, not fully conscious until he realized he was standing barefoot on cold marble with the dagger he kept under the pillow naked in his hand.

Nothing, he thought. Nothing but the night sounds of Chalice, insects, birds, the soft whisper of water in the fountain that plashed in the courtyard below, a watchman calling out as his iron-tipped staff clacked on paving stones.

Then a woman screamed; that was close, just down the corridor. Adrian was out the door of his bedroom in seconds, feet skidding on the slick stones of the floor. One of the Lowissons' guards was there not long after him, likewise in nothing but his drawers, looking foolish with his shaved head showing—no time to don the turban—but a curved sword ready in his hand. Adrian ignored him, plunging into his brother's room. The door rebounded off his shoulder and crashed against the jamb and Adrian's gaze skittered about. The room was dark—even the nightlight in the lamp by the bed had gone out. Then it grew a bright greenish cast, as Center amplified the light that was reaching his retinas. Even then Adrian's skin crawled with the revulsion that brought, but there was no time for anything but business now.

Esmond Gellert was sitting up in bed, his muscular chest heaving and sheening with sweat. His eyes were wide and staring, and cloth ripped in the hand that held a pillow. An Islander woman crouched naked against the far wall, sobbing.

"He was asleep!" she cried, looking blindly to the door. "I did my best, I swear!"

"Go," Adrian said gently in her language, rising from his crouch and letting the dagger fall along one leg. "Go, now. This is not your fault."

She scuttled out, scooping up clothing as she went. Adrian moved over to the bedside. "Esmond," he said sharply. "Esmond, it's me. What's the matter?"

His elder brother shook himself like a dog coming out of a river. "A dream," he muttered softly. "It must have been a dream. My oath, what a dream . . ."

"What dream, Esmond?" Adrian said carefully.

"Nanya," he said. "The fire . . ." His face changed, writhing. "They'll *burn*."

"Who will burn?"

"Vanbert. The Confeds. *All* of them. They're going to burn, *burn*."

"Esmond, it's late. Do you think you can sleep now?"

Esmond shook himself again, and something like humanness returned to his eyes. "What . . . oh, sorry, brother. Bit of a bad dream. Yes, it's going to be a long day."

"The man will be impaled, otherwise," Casull said. "He is a criminal."

Adrian sighed; it was not something he wanted to do, but on the other hand . . . well, *he'd* rather be shot than have a sharpened wooden stake up the anus, if he had to choose.

King Casull was present, and his eldest son Tenny—a twenty-year-old version of his father, except that there was a trace of softness around the jaw, of petulance in the set of his mouth. There were a scattering of Islander admirals as well, ships' captains, mercenary officers, and an interested score or so of Adrian's own Emerald slingers. Three of them were serving as the arquebus' crew. Adrian squinted against the bright sunlight; the first target was floating on a barge twenty yards away, tied to a stake and with a Confed infantry shield set up before him. Royal guardsmen kept the crowds well away from this section of the naval dockyards.

"These have two-man crews," Adrian went on. "They load . . . thus."

He nodded to his men. The weapon was clamped into a tripod with a pivot joint. The gunner pushed on the butt, and the weapon spun around. He seized and held the muzzle, while the loader bit open a paper cartridge and rammed it and the eight-ounce lead ball down the long barrel. Then he spun it again, taking a horn from his belt.

"You see, lord King, the small pan on the right side? That is where the fine-ground *priming powder* goes. Then this hammer with the piece of flint in its jaws goes back . . ."

"Ah, yes," Casull said. "A flint-and-steel—the sort travellers use."

"Yes, lord King. The flint strikes this portion of the L-shaped steel, pushing it back from over the pan—the sparks fall down onto the powder—the powder burns, the flame goes through a small hole into the barrel and ignites the main charge."

He raised his voice a little. "Gentlemen, there will be a loud crack, a little like thunder."

There were alert nods, dark eyes bright with interest. *You know,* he thought, *this Kingdom of the Isles would seem to be a better place to start "progress" than the mainland. They're a lot less . . . hidebound, I think you'd say.*

no, Center said. There was more than the usual heavy certainty to its communication. **this culture is too intellectually amorphous.**

Adrian felt a familiar baffled frustration. Raj cut in: ***Sure, they'll take and use anything that looks useful. But they're pure pragmatists. Your Emerald philosophers have gotten themselves into a trap—staring up their own arses and trying to find first causes in words, in language. But at least they*** **think** ***about the structure of things; so do the Confeds, when they think at all—they caught it from you. The Islanders just aren't interested; to them, everything you've shown is just a wonderful new trick, to be thrown into the grab bag.***

accurate, if loosely phrased, Center said.

Hmmm, Adrian thought. This time he felt the wonderful tension-before-release mental sensation of *almost* grasping a concept; it was like sex just before orgasm, only better. *But they have a lot of . . . what was that phrase? Social mobility?*

correct, Center said. **if anything, an excessive amount.**

Sure, you can get ahead, here, Raj said. ***But you can't*** **stay** ***ahead. Everything here turns on the fall of the dice; the ruler's favor, a lucky pirate raid. This place is as unstable as water, while the mainland's set in granite. You can carve granite into a new shape, though; water will just run through your fingers.***

Adrian shook himself back to the world of phenomena; the mental conversation had only taken a few seconds, but he was attracting looks. Most of them were tolerantly amused; the Scholars of the Grove had a solid reputation for otherworldly abstraction.

If only they knew, he thought to himself. Aloud: "*Fire!*"

The gunner carefully squeezed the trigger. There was a *chick-shsss* as the hammer came down and the priming caught in a little sideways puff of fire and dirty-white smoke. Then: *Bdannggg* as the arquebus fired; the cloud of smoke from the main charge was enough to hide the target from Adrian's eyes for a second. Esmond gave a silent whistle of relief beside him; the bullet hadn't missed. Casull's eyebrows went up as well, and the Islander grandees were laughing and slapping Adrian on the back; eight ounces of high-velocity lead had smashed a hole the size of a fist through the Confed shield, through metal facing and plywood and tough leather, and then removed the entire top of the target's head in a spatter of pink-gray froth and whitish bone fragments.

Adrian swallowed. "So, you see, my lord King," he said. "Many such arquebusiers could sweep the decks of an enemy ship, beyond the effective range of archers."

"But not beyond the range of catapults and ballistae," Casull said. "Still, a dreadful weapon, yes. These . . . arquebuses? Arquebuses, yes—they can fire faster than catapults, and we can put more of them on a ship. The Confed marines have always been our problem, the Sun God roast their balls; we're better seamen, but as often as not they swarm aboard and take the ship that rams them."

"Lord King, I'm just getting started," Adrian said with a grin. "Next is a much larger version of the arquebus, for use against ships and fortresses."

The King's dark eyebrows looked as if they were trying to crawl into his widow's peak. "Show me!" he commanded.

"This is the weapon," Adrian said, signalling. A half-dozen of his men dragged it over; a bronze tube seven feet long, mounted on a low four-wheeled carriage of glossy hardwood. "I call it a *cannon.*"

The barge teams in the military harbor were busy again; this time they towed out a small and extremely elderly galley. It was listing, and the dockyard workers had stripped it of most of its fittings; they anchored it to a buoy two hundred yards out in the harbor.

Meanwhile Adrian's men were busy around the gun. Adrian gave Casull a running commentary: "First, as you see, lord King, a linen bag full of the *gunpowder* is pushed down the hollow—the barrel. A wad of felt goes in next, to hold it in place."

The crew shoved the bag home with a long pole, grunting in unison as they slammed it down. "Now the gunner runs a long steel needle through the *touch-hole*, to pierce the bag, and fills the touch-hole and this little pan on top of the gun with *priming powder*—finely ground."

"And here is what the cannon will hurl," he said. The team paused for a second to let the King see what they were doing.

"A bronze ball?" Casull said. "Wouldn't stone do just as well, and be much cheaper?"

"We will use stone balls to strike fortress walls," Adrian said. Cast iron would have been better still, but the only furnaces capable of making it were in Vanbert, and not many of them. All the ironworks in the Islands were what Center called *Catalan forges*, turning out wrought iron.

"But this is a *shell*, lord King," Adrian amplified.

"You mean it's hollow?"

"My lord sees as clearly as the eye of the Sun God. It is filled with the gunpowder, and this"—he pointed to a wooden plug in the side of the metal ball, with a length of cord through it—"is the *fuse*. It is a length of cord soaked in saltpeter; when the cannon fires, the main charge lights it. Then in ten seconds, the cord burns through to the charge in the middle."

While they spoke the crew had been fixing the cannon's tackle to bollards sunk in the stone of the dock, and aiming it with handspikes and main force. The gunner glared down the barrel with its simple notch-and-blade sights, then stepped back and adusted the wedge under the breech of the cannon that controlled its elevation.

"If my lord wishes, he may fire the first shot," Adrian said, bowing. "If it please my lord King, please stand well to one side—the cannon will move backward rapidly when it is fired. And," he went on, raising his voice for the assembled dignitaries, "this time the noise will be *much* louder."

Casull was grinning like a shark as he brought the length of slowmatch at the end of the long stick down on the little pile of fine powder. It caught with a long *sssshshshshs*, and an appreciable fraction of a second later . . .

BAMMMMM!

This time some of the Islander magnates took startled steps back, mouthing curses or prayers. The gun leapt back until the breeching ropes brought it up with a twang, belching a cloud of smoke shot through with a knife blade of red fire. The wind had picked up, and the smoke swept to one side in good time to see splinters and chunks of frame pinwheeling up from the target galley. Then three seconds later there was another *crack*, muffled by the wood the shell was embedded in. A quarter of the light galley's side exploded outward; when the smoke cleared from *that*, it was already listing to one side . . . and burning.

Casull gave a whoop and hiked up his robe in one hand, snapping his fingers and hopping through the first steps of a bawdy *kodax* dance; one could see he'd been a sailor long before he was King. His son stood blinking, red spots on pale cheeks; the buccaneer admirals and mercenary commanders were swearing, spitting, thumping each other on the back.

The King stopped first, pausing to turn and shake a fist to the east. "Now see who goes to the bottom, you turnip-eating peasants!" he shouted.

Then he turned to Adrian, eyes snapping. "What else have you for me, O Worker of Wonders?"

Adrian smiled thinly; the problem with getting the reputation for being a magician was that he had to live up to it, and when they expected him to be infallible . . . Esmond was looking hungrily at the burning galley and a slow, deep smile was spreading over his face.

"There are two other types of shot the cannon can fire, lord King," he said. "Solid stone balls, heavy basalt or granite. Those will pound down the walls of forts, as catapults might, but since they strike much harder from further away, they do it quicker. The other is *case-shot*. It's a leather bag full of lead balls, like the arquebus fires, but a hundred of them. Imagine them flung out in a spray, into a dense formation of men—a Confed infantry battalion, or a section of marines about to board."

Casull nodded hungrily. Esmond, from his expression, was imagining precisely that.

"Why didn't you make these for the Confed nobles you were working for?" the monarch asked.

"First, lord, I didn't have time. Second, they didn't take me seriously enough to give me what I needed. These cannon take a lot of bronze, and bronze is expensive—this one twenty-four pounder takes more than two *tons* of bronze."

Casull grunted as if belly-punched, losing a little of his joy. "That *is* something to think on," he said. "Not just the money, but the bronze itself—there isn't all that much around, we'll have to import . . ." He clapped Adrian on the shoulder again. "Still and all, you've done all that you promised and more. And there is still another wonder to lay the world at my feet?"

Hardly ambitious at all, all of a sudden, isn't he? Raj observed.

Adrian nodded—to both the entities he was communicating with. "Yes, my King. The next is a small taste of what a full-scale steam-propelled ship will be . . ."

He heard a *chuff . . . chuff . . . chuff* . . . sound. The twelve oar launch he'd converted came into view. Murmurs arose from the Islander chiefs; they *understood* the sea and ships. He could see them pointing out the rudder and tiller arrangement he'd rigged, debating its merits, and then there were louder murmurs as they realized that the launch was heading directly into the wind at seven knots, throwing back white water from both sides of its prow as well as the wheels that thrashed the harbor surface to foam on either side. Black smoke puffed in balls from the tall smokestack secured like a mast with staywires to fore and aft.

"Think of a full-sized ship, my lord," Adrian said. "Her decks covered over with a timber shell and iron plates, and with an iron-backed ram. No vulnerable oars, impossible to board, free of wind, tide and current . . ."

Casull was a fighting man who'd spent most of a long life waging war at sea, or preparing to.

"Tell me more," he said, breathing hard.

CHAPTER SIX

"Pity you didn't get an opportunity to try out your new toys at sea," Esmond said.

"This will do," Adrian said.

The archipelago ruled—ruled more or less; from which they collected protection money, at least—by the Directors of Vase was considerably smaller than the one centered on Chalice. Few of the islands in it had enough area to grow crops, and they were low-lying and therefore dry, covered in open forest and scrub rather than jungle. To balance that there were mines, the fishing in the shallow waters round about was excellent, and they were a very convenient location for raids on the mainland. Vase was the largest, and the only one which looked like giving the Royal forces any sustained resistance.

"I can see why," Adrian said, bracing a hand against the mast of the transport, where it ran through the maintop. He'd been at sea long enough now to sway naturally with the motion of the ship, exaggerated by the sixty-foot height of the mast. They were both used to the bilge stink and the cramped quarters by now as well, and the unmerciful heat of the reflected sun that had tanned them both several shades darker.

"This is a tough nut," he said to his brother.

Esmond grunted agreement. "Harbor shaped like a U," he murmured, half to himself. "Steep rocky ground all around—absolute bitch getting men up those, never mind the walls at the top. Let's see . . . harbor wall just back from the docks, looks like it started out as a row of stone warehouses. Streets—tenement blocks, mansions, whatever, all bad—then the citadel itself on that low ridge."

Esmond squinted carefully, then looked down at the map King Casull's spies had provided. "Now, that's interesting," he said.

"What is?"

"This shows a ruined tower back of the rear wall of the citadel—unoccupied. Careless of them."

Adrian peered over his brother's armored shoulder. "That commands the citadel walls?" he said.

"Looks like. It's a thousand yards from the rear wall of the citadel, say a quarter-mile from the inner face of the works facing the harbor," he said. "Hmmm. Well out of bow and slingshot, of course, and you couldn't mount a useful number of torsion machines there."

He looked up, and for a moment his grin made him look young again, the youth who'd stood to be crowned at the Five Year Games. "But they don't know about your toys, do they?"

Smart lad, your brother, Raj said. ***He's got a real eye for the ground. That's extremely important—nobody fights battles on a tabletop, and a rise of six feet can be crucial.***

"No, they don't," Adrian said, smiling back. *Oh, shit,* he thought to himself.

King Casull looked up at the burning fortress at the outer harbor mouth of Vase. It was a low massive blocky building, set cunningly into the rocky crags and scree, well placed to rain down arrows and burning oil and naphtha on any force trying to scramble up the gravel and boulder-littered slopes to its gates. That had helped it not at all when the shells from Adrian Gellert's mortar landed behind the battlements. A thick column of greasy black smoke rose, heavy with the scent of things that should not burn, a smell he was intimately familiar with comprised of old timber, paint, leather, cloth, wine, cooking oil, human flesh.

"How do you advise we assault the town and citadel, General Gellert?" he asked.

"If it please my lord the King," Esmond said, "we'll send in the *gunboats* now."

Those were waiting beside the royal galley, keeping station with occasional strokes of their oars. Ten of those to a side, with two men on each; the single cannon fired forward, over the bows; a long inclined wooden slide reached backward to nearly amidships, letting the weapon run in when it was fired or be lashed over the center of gravity when the gunboat was at sea. The crews waved respectfully as they saw the royal eyes fall on them.

"And we'll send the troop transports close behind. The cannon will fire solid shot until they've battered down a gate, or a suitable breach in a wall."

Casull nodded; it was often better to break down a wall, if you could—the rubble provided a natural ramp for assault troops, and gates usually had nasty dogleg irregularities and unpleasant surprises waiting for a storming party.

"That will give us the town," Esmond said. "But the guns are large—getting them up to the inner edge of the Directors' citadel, that will be difficult. Most of it's within bowshot of the walls, and all of it's within range of the boltcasters."

He nodded towards Vase. Two tall semicircular towers rose from the edges of the citadel facing the town. That was a curve itself; the whole inner complex where the ruler resided was shaped like an irregular wedge of pie, with the palace and keep occupying the outer, narrow tip.

"Well, my lord King," Esmond said. "My brother and I have thought up something that may distract the men on the battlements quite considerably."

"Here you are, sir," the transport captain said.

Adrian nodded, modeling his expression on the one Esmond used. *Firm, confident, in charge, but not hostile or remote,* he told himself.

Men were going ashore in relays; the little semicircle of beach was too small to take the ship, or more than a few score at a time. *Three hundred men* didn't seem like too many, until he saw them all together like this. A hundred of the Sea Strikers had gone ashore first: Esmond's security detachment—light infantry with sword, buckler and javelin. The two hundred arquebusiers and grenade slingers were following more slowly, burdened with their heavy weapons and ammunition. Adrian heard a thump and a volley of curses from the netting on the side of the ship where men climbed down into the boats. *Long, clumsy* and *heavy,* he amended to himself.

Beyond the little cove rose stony hills covered in thorny scrub . . . and beyond those, the ruined tower where he was supposed to "amuse" the enemy and keep them from hindering the main assault. Adrian shook the captain's hand, adjusted his satchel of grenades, and swung over the bulwark himself.

"Feet here, sir," one of the Emerald slingers said cheerfully.

"What's that *sound*?"

"Ninety-*nine*, one *hundred*," Helga Demansk said, completing the series of sit-ups.

"Oh, *stop* that, Helga and come look," Keffrine said.

The woman who'd once been the pampered daughter of a Confederation Justiciar unhooked her feet from the back of the chair and padded over to the high barred window. If she stood on tiptoe, she could see some of the rooftops of Vase, down from the citadel. If she sprang up and gripped the bars, she could see a good deal more. She did, jumping nearly her own height and holding herself up easily, shaking tawny hair out of her eyes and peering against the bright light of morning reflecting off sea and roof tile.

"Oh, you're so *strong*," Keffrine said, batting her eyes upward. "Don't you think you should have a back rub, after all that exercise, though?"

"Can it, Keffie," Helga replied with a half-amused, half-exasperated twist of her lips. "I'm not that desperate yet."

"I can wait," the younger girl grinned. "Nobody's going anywhere."

Helga suppressed a shudder at that; even when the Director died, nobody in the hareem would go anywhere but into retirement . . . which meant they'd be shut up together until the last of them died of old age, and they'd never see another entire male until the day they did die—not even a loathsome toad like the Director. She pushed her mind back into the present, recoiling from the waste of years that stretched ahead. It could be worse; not so many generations ago, the hareem of an Islander magnate accompanied him to the tomb, with a cup of hemlock if they were lucky.

I wonder what that noise is? Helga thought. And: *Sky-Father Almighty, I'm* tired *of waiting.*

She hadn't thought that being sold into the hareem of a pirate chief would be tedious—other things, but not that. The Director of Vase was an old, fat, worried, overworked pirate chief, though, with the fifty concubines that custom and prestige demanded. After the brutality of the pirate crew—exactly according to legend—and the transit here, she'd thought that a deliverance . . . for the first four months in this velvet-cushioned, lavender-scented prison where nothing, absolutely nothing ever happened. There was a pool, where she could swim about six paces; there were a few chess sets and card decks; there were no books at all—it would never occur to an Islander chief that a woman would want to *read*. After a full year, only keeping up her training regimen and pretending she was going to escape had preserved her sanity and kept her from strangling someone at the seven hundredth repetition of the same inane gossip, the same shrill giggling at the same stupid jokes, the same fatuous cow-eyed flirting, the same . . .

Being summoned to the Director's quarters at least meant she got *out* for an evening, even if under guard. Usually the old heap of lard couldn't do anything anyway.

"Smoke from the harbor," Helga said meditatively. "And I think I can hear . . . yes, that's an alarm drum."

There was a section of garden and wall below the window, just visible. A dozen men trotted through it; archers, in brass-scale hauberks and spiked helmets, led by an officer with his saber drawn.

The young Confed woman released the bars and dropped back, her lips shaping a soundless whistle.

"War, I think," she said. "Wasn't there a rumor that the Director was having trouble with the King in Chalice?"

Keffrine nodded eagerly, blond bangs swinging around her ears and releasing a strong waft of verbena. Helga wrinkled her nose a little; she still didn't like the way Islander women slathered themselves with scent. That and cosmetics were the main pastimes here, along with intrigue and love affairs; one couldn't even dress up much, since tradition mandated hareem occupants wear filmy trousers and spangled halter tops.

"Isn't it *exciting*?" Keffrine squealed.

Helga sighed. *Well, what can you expect.* Keffrine was a gift from Sub-Director Deneuve, and born in *his* hareem. This sort of environment was all she'd ever known. *And I thought* I'd *led a sheltered life.*

"It may get more exciting than you'd like," Helga said. "Come on, we'd better go talk to the Eldest Sister."

The old bat was a harridan of the first order, but she'd been here since the Director was sixteen, and he *told* her things. If anyone knew . . .

"Yes, let's!" Keffrine grabbed her hand and pulled her out into the corridor, past arches and mosaics, into the main circular room where a dozen or so of the others lounged on couches, nibbled snacks, or paddled languidly in the pool about the carved youth whose seashell spouted warm scented water. The light from above was filtered through a fretwork stone dome.

Helga felt her heart beat faster. *More exciting than they'd care for,* she thought. *But any change is an opportunity. I've been here far, far too long.*

Keffrine was really starting to look tempting, for instance.

Far, far too long.

"Oh, what a beautiful, beautiful position," Simun wheezed.

Adrian nodded, breathless himself despite being twenty years younger and less burdened. The tower was ruined in the sense that some of the internal floors had collapsed, fire or rot destroying the beams. The central spiral staircase was stone, though, and still reasonably sound. So was the uppermost floor, and the crenellations were still waist-high. That would give the arquebusiers cover and excellent rests for their weapons; they were setting up now, with a little amiable squabbling for the best shooting spots. The infantry from the Sea Strikers had taken up ground around the tower's base, blending in to the maquis-covered slopes. The air had a slight brimstone smell from the black powder in grenades and cartridge boxes, and a wild spicy scent of crushed herbs from the ground around. It was warm now, and insects buzzed through the flowers; fliers darted by snapping at them.

Vase was laid out before them like a relief map, too—he could see men hurrying in and out of the two towers that anchored the citadel's harborward wall, others massing on the wall itself, still more movement in the narrow twisting streets beyond. Overhead the sky was a hot white-blue; he could even see the banners snapping on the gunboats in the harbor beyond, and the foam where the measured centipede stroke of their oars churned up the water. As he watched, a puff of smoke came from the lead craft. A measurable time later the flat deep *thudump* reached his ears, like a very large door slamming far away. A slightly louder explosion came from among the warcraft packed along the docks in front of the sea wall; they were firing shell initially, then. Smoke and fragments vomited up over the harbor defenses, and a slender galley began to burn and sink at its moorings, spine snapped. It couldn't sink far, in water only six feet deep under its keel, but that served to put the fire mostly out.

By the time the fourth round had hit, the remaining crews were scrambling ashore, tiny as ants as they swarmed through the sally ports next to the main gates.

"Ah, already spooked from the forts at the outer harbor, sor," Simun chuckled. "Ah, this is a fight how I loik it, sor," the middle-aged mercenary went on. "No risk, none of that there nasty hand-to-hand stuff."

Adrian smiled in turn. *Odd,* he thought. This man and he had as little in common as two beings of the same species, gender and nationality could, yet in a way they'd become good friends . . .

Comes of risking your lives together, son, Raj thought, amused. ***One of the things that, unfortunately, makes war possible.***

"Sort of a commentary on humankind, I suppose," Adrian muttered.

"What was thot, sor?"

"Just regretting you weren't a beautiful woman, underofficer," he said briskly.

Simun chuckled. "Well, then I'd be out of place here, eh, sor? Place for everything, yis, yis." He looked at the minarets, domes, gardens of the palace citadel ahead of them. "Though they say hareem girls smells tasty enough, yis. Hey, sor, you oughtn't to be doing that, now!"

Adrian ignored the hand that anchored the back of his weapons belt as he leaned over the crumbling sawtooth outer wall of the tower. "Simun," he said sharply. "Take a look there—do you see a mark in the ground there, leading from the tower to the citadel wall?"

The noncom respectfully but firmly pulled him back, then leaned over and peered himself. "Hmmm, now that you point it out sor, so I do, indeed. Old wall, mebbe? Hard to see why, though—just the one—tis not a walled way to this here tower, that would make sense, though . . ."

Adrian craned his neck. The line through the scrub was irregular, as much a trace-mark in the vegetation as anything, an absence of the low thorny scrub trees in the middle and a thicker line of them on either side.

He froze as Center's icy presence seized his eyes. For a moment the world became a maze of lines and points and moving dots, a glimpse of something too vast and alien for him to comprehend. Then it settled down to a schematic—clear white lines outlining the trace through the slope, and a cross-diagram beside it showing a tunnel with an arched stone roof.

covered way, sunken to escape detection. The machine intelligence sounded inhumanly confident . . . but then, it always did, even when confessing a rare error. **since the tower went out of regular use, the initial covering of soil has partly eroded from the upper surface of the ceiling.**

"Yes, by the Gray-Eyed Lady!" Adrian said.

Simun was looking at him with mingled alarm and expectation—the Gray-Eyed was also a Goddess of War; more precisely, of stratagem and ploy, as opposed to Wodep's straightforward violence. Adrian knew that the Emerald mercenaries they'd brought with them thought he communed with Her regularly; Esmond's new troops were picking up the superstition rapidly.

"That's a tunnel—a covered way into the citadel," Adrian said.

"Oh, *ho*!" Simun said. "First in, first pickings . . . no, sor, though, even Islanders, they wouldn't leave it open—not when this here place ain't garrisoned, no, no."

"We'll take a look," Adrian said. "Can't hurt."

Simun nodded. *Yes, I know Esmond set you as my watchdog,* Adrian thought without resentment—after all, he *was* the younger brother, and not trained to war. On the other hand, curiosity was an Emerald characteristic; where it concerned his trade, even a professional like Simun had his fair share.

"Oll right, sor, but me'n the squad, we goes along."

"No argument."

"The city of Vase is under attack," the Eldest Sister said calmly.

A chorus of squeals and giggles died down into uncertain murmurs as the figure beside the head of the hareem stepped forward—it was an entire man, one of the few Helga had seen since she passed through the door. A soldier, one of the Director's personal guard, slave soldiers bought in infancy and raised in the household; armored from head to foot in black-laquered splint mail, with a broad splayed nasal bar on his helmet that hid his face. He rested the point of his huge curved sword on the carpet and folded his hands on the hilt.

"Do not worry!" the stout, robed, middle-aged woman said. "In all things, we will accompany our lord."

Helga was standing well to the back, among the junior and childless members of the hareem—even then she took a moment to thank the Mother Goddess for *that* mercy. Although there was a rumor that all the pregnancies recently were the result of the Director sending in his younger brother under cover of darkness. . . . She was standing shoulder-to-shoulder with Keffrine, and felt the other girl suddenly begin to tremble. Helga decided that she didn't need to hear the rest of the Eldest Sister's speech.

"What is it?" she whispered sharply in her ear, then gave her arm a pinch to shock her out of the wide-eyed stare. "Keffrine, what is it?"

"Wuh—wuh—"

"*Keffrine!*"

A few others glanced at her reprovingly as her voice rose a little. That seemed to bring Keffrine back to herself a little; she dropped her eyes and whispered.

"They think we muh-muh-might *lose*," she said.

"What?"

"What the Eldest Sister said, about accompanying our lord."

"What, into exile? Ransom—"

The guileless blue eyes turned to her, and tears slid down the lovely cheeks.

"No. The Director's honor can't let other men touch his women. They'll cu-cu-cut our th-th—"

Quietly, hopelessly, Keffrine began to sob; she wasn't the only one, either.

Cut our throats, Helga Demansk realized; that was the end of the sentence. In more ways than one.

The plug at the end of the tunnel took on the flat, greenish-silvery look that Adrian's vision always did when Center was amplifying the available light. Something about extrapolating from partial data. . . . He shoved away the neck-tensing eeriness and instead tapped on the concrete and rubble with the hilt of his dagger, pressing his ear to listen. Only a dull clink came back through the ear pushed against the porous roughness, but Center spoke with mountainous certainty:

the blocking segment is from five to eight and a half feet in thickness. beyond it the tunnel resumes with the same dimensions.

A picture formed in his mind; the covered passageway on the other side of the block, and then a wooden door beyond that—thick with dust and cobwebs.

How do you do *that?* he asked.

echolocation, Center answered. **your auditory sensors receive much information of which you are not conscious. by calculating the time and angle of sound reflected through and beyond the solid material, i can infer the shapes and relationships of objects.**

Oh. Like most of Center's explanations, that raised more questions than it answered—sound could bounce? *Anyway . . .*

one ten-pound cask of powder emplaced at the base will clear the obstacle, Center said. **possibility of collapse of tunnel ceiling is 27% ±7.**

"Can't hurt, then," Adrian mused.

Sure you want to do this, lad? Raj asked. ***It isn't your proper line of work, really.***

Adrian nodded. *My* brother *is out there, under the walls,* he replied firmly, swallowing through the dryness of his mouth and acutely conscious of the smell of wet stone and his own sweat.

"Simun," he said. "Get someone with a pick up here—two men with picks, and one with a prybar. And a barrel of powder, and—" he consulted his unseen friends "—ten feet of quickmatch. Now!"

The distant thudding sounds were closer now, louder; like nothing so much as thunder. Beneath it Helga Demansk thought she could hear something far less uncanny than thunder from a clear blue sky; a snarling clamor of voices, and the harsh metal-on-metal sound of battle, with an undertone of the flat banging thumps that blades made on shields. The concubines were kneeling silently in rows according to seniority; several more of the black-armored Director's guardsmen had come in. One of them was pale-faced and had a bandage around his forearm; another was limping. The sunlight crawled past under the dappled shade of the dome, the water splashed in the pool, all infinitely familiar sights gilded with a nearly supernatural film of horror now.

Another man came in, the metal heel-plates of his military boots loud on tile and marble, muffled where he traversed colorful rugs. He looked at the guard commander standing above the Eldest Sister, swallowed, and gave a jerky nod.

"It is time," the commander said harshly.

"It is time," the older woman said calmly. "I shall go first, to show my sisters that there is nothing to fear."

She raised her chin. The soldier shook his shoulders back and raised the blade; sunlight broke off the bright edge as he took careful aim and swung with a huffing grunt of effort.

There was a wet cleaving sound. Blood splashed backward over the gilt mosaics of the wall, over young fleecebeasts gamboling in a spring meadow. Keffrine gave a breathless little scream.

"Time to get moving," Helga muttered to herself, and took one last deep breath.

"All right," Adrian said to the worried arquebusier. "I'm leaving you the twenty best shots, with all the loaded weapons to hand. They should be able to keep up a respectable fire for half an hour or so, and that's all that we'll need."

The man nodded, saluted, and trotted away back up the stairs. Adrian looked at the other men near him: Simun; Tohmus, the commander of the Sea Striker detachment; the rest of his gunmen, now holding their cutlasses and targets.

"Everyone!" he said. "Be prepared for a very loud—"

THACRACK!

Smoke and debris vomited out of the mouth of the tunnel into the basement of the tower, shrouding its dimness and peppering them all with grit and small fragments of rock.

Adrian spoke again, his voice tinny in his own ears after the monstrous blow of the explosion in the tunnel's confined space. "Simun, Tohmus, no crowding. I'll go first."

He plunged in, coughing, waving a futile hand in front of himself. The breeze was strong from the seaward, from the blocked end of the passageway—previously blocked now—smelling of patchouli oil and flowers under the sulfur stink of the powder. The plug was scattered in toe-stubbing chunks for a hundred yards back from where it had spanned the tunnel, bits of it having bounced off the curves in the walls. Beyond it was the chamber Center's eerie sound-vision had shown, but the doors beyond were splinters hanging from twisted hinges. Ahead was a long sloping corridor, then a staircase with sunlight filtering down from above.

And barrels on either side; one was smashed, and the rich fruity odor of wine filled the confined space. Above the casks hung hams in nets, bunches of herbs, sacks of fruit . . .

"Gellerix's *cunt*," whispered Simun, beside him. "Anrew, Mattas, you pick six reliable men and *guard* this, you hear me?" To Adrian: "Sorry, sor—don't want to tempt the lads mor'n's right. And sor? Might be an idea to draw yor sword now."

Adrian did, gripping the little brass-rimmed buckler with his left hand. He peered around. "Storerooms . . ."

Center strobed one of the lateral corridors giving off the big arch-roofed cellar. There was an ironbound door set into the wall there, with a massive lock—rare and expensive.

"Simun, put that under guard too—I think it'll bear investigation. We'll keep going straight up," he said, indicating the stairwell.

Keffrine was still sobbing, her eyes squeezed shut and tears leaking out from under them. Helga waited . . .

. . . and a dozen women broke and bolted as the soldiers approached the front row. *Eldest probably knew they would,* ran through her; that was probably why she'd gone first, to spare herself seeing the indignity. The gathering dissolved into a chaos of running women and harassed, determined guardsmen. Blades began to flash, not in the orderly execution planned but in a frenzy, men slashing at figures that ran by or trembled and pled.

Helga moved herself; sideways, to where a tall fretted-brass brazier sent a coil of incense upwards. She gripped it by the base and heaved, toppling the man-high structure against the wall. Glowing embers scattered into gauzy hangings, and flames began to lick upward.

"Fire!" she screamed in Islander. "Fire!"

A guardsman had been approaching, blade in hand. He looked aside—no sailor or town dweller but had a healthy dread of uncontrolled flame—and when he looked back he met the second brazier full in the face as she swung it two-handed. Brass met flesh and bone with a loud *thock*. Helga scooped up the falling sword; it was a different shape from the ones she was used to, and too heavy, but that didn't stop her short efficient jab up under his chin.

"Come *on*," she shouted to Keffrine, and grabbed her by one hand. Trailing the sobbing girl, she bolted for the exit to the basement storerooms.

"Keep the men well in hand," Adrian said.

Screams were coming from the room at the head of the stairs. *Women's* screams, but also men's shouts, and the distinctive, unpleasant sound of steel driving into flesh.

"Let's *go*!"

The noises ahead were loud enough that it was several heartbeats before anyone noticed the enemy surging up through the passageway. Adrian had time to check his rush a step in sheer astonishment at the sight before him; a room floridly overdecorated even by Islander standards, full of running, screaming women—*dying* women—and soldiers in black-lacquered armor trying to butcher them all. Dozens down on the floor, wounded or dead; a nauseating mixture of smells: perfume, flowers, blood, shit . . .

And right in front of him, one of the women *fighting* a pair of soldiers. An auburn-haired woman, one he'd swear was Confed-born, not an Islander. Not doing badly at all, either—

She beat aside a thrust, both hands on the hilt of the long saber. The other soldier lunged as well, at a smaller blond woman by the first one's side, and the point of his blade slammed out her back. The redhead screamed and slashed him across the face, blood and a spark where the blade grated off the nasal bar of the killer's helmet.

"*Get* the hell out of the way—sir!" someone shouted in Adrian's ear.

Men poured past him. He leapt forward himself, batted the saber of the man fighting the redhead aside and lunged with his own basket-hilted, Emerald-style sword. The black-armored man vanished in the melee; a second later Adrian saw him toppling into the fountain pool in the center of the room with a javelin through his neck. The fighting was brief, three mercenaries against an Islander here, four there—overwhelming numbers. The screaming didn't stop, and now he saw his own men chasing the women. They obviously didn't have butchery on their minds, but—

"You!" he said. One had grabbed the auburn-haired woman—girl—from behind, hands over her breasts. "You! Release that woman!"

"Wait yer turn—" the mercenary began.

Get them in hand now, or you never will, Raj said.

"Right."

Adrian took two steps forward and smashed the hilt of his sword into the would-be rapist's face. Bone crumbled under the blow, with a tooth-grating yielding feeling. He had time to see the woman's face go slack with surprise, and then he tossed her his sword to clear his hand.

He hooked a grenade out of his pouch, the ceramic cool and pebbly under his fingers. His other hand whipped the slowmatch from its covered metal holder on his belt, twirled it to make the lit end glow brightly, touched off the fuse. He waited three seconds, and then tossed it gently underhand into the pool.

THUDUMP.

Water—and bits of the dead man dangling over the fountain—sprayed through the room. The water prevented the fragments from being deadly . . . or not very deadly.

Silence fell in the echoing aftermath of the explosion. Adrian held the slowmatch next to the fuse of another grenade.

"If discipline is not restored immediately," he said, half-surprised at the calmness of his own voice under the enormous reined-in tension, "I am going to light this grenade and drop it in the pouch."

"We'd all be killed!" one of the Sea Strikers wailed.

"That's the idea." Adrian nodded. "We have a battle to fight, and it's *that* way. Anyone have a problem with that?"

"No, sir."

There was a general chorus of agreement, and men who'd seized women released them, forming up and heading for the doors.

"Simun."

The little mercenary came up, limping and pressing the tail of his tunic against a slash wound along one thigh—a vulnerable point in light-infantry armor, protected only by the studded leather strips of the military kilt.

"Simun, get some of the walking wounded together. Police this area, get the surgeon working . . . oh, he is."

The man had half a dozen of the more seriously wounded lying on improvised pallets, and twice that number of the hareem's occupants. Some of the hale ones were tearing up sheets to help him.

"Anyway, keep things under control."

Simun nodded. "Good choice, sor," he said. "Cut like this, Gellerix 'erself couldn't tempt me."

"I'll be with the unit," Adrian went on. "See you when it's over."

"I'm coming too."

Adrian looked around, startled, and met level green eyes. The auburn-haired girl offered him his sword; she'd taken a similar weapon from one of the dead, and a small buckler. The filmy hareem costume was plastered to her, mostly with blood, and there were smudges of it across her face where she'd bound back the russet-colored hair with a strip of cloth.

"Miss—"

"Fuck that," she said. She was speaking Emerald, with a slight Confed accent—upper-class Confed, he realized. "I'm a . . . soldier's daughter, and I've been here an Almighty Allfather-cursed *year*, and I'm going to *kill* some of these Islander bastards."

"Soldier's daughter?" Adrian said.

"Name's Helga. My father . . . fought with Justiciar Demansk's armies."

Things clicked behind Adrian's upraised eyebrows. ***She's really not bad with a sword,*** Raj mentioned.

That meant she *wasn't* what she'd implied, the daughter of some long-service Confed trooper. Women of that class didn't train with the sword—certainly not in the classic Emerald style. Some rich young women did; it had been quite the craze for the last couple of years, much to the scandal of the conservative nobility. A few had even appeared in the Vanbert Games, first-blood matches, until a reforming Justiciar had outlawed the practice. *Noblewoman,* he thought.

observe, Center said.

A grid formed over her face, countour lines sprang out. Justiciar Demansk's face appeared beside it, and arrows sprang out to mark points of resemblance.

allowing for gender, probability of close genetic relationship is 97%, ±1, Center said. **as near unity as a hasty analysis permits.**

And Demansk . . . one of his daughters *was taken in a pirate raid, and not ransomed,* Adrian thought. Demansk had several sons, but that was the only daughter he'd ever heard of . . .

The analysis had taken half a dozen seconds. "All right, Miss Helga," he said crisply. "You may rest assured of my protection." The courtly phrase seemed oddly out of place in this room of gilding and blood. "But keep close to me and don't get in the way."

"I won't," she said. The sword moved easily in her hand; it was the standard Emerald style, single-edged and with a handguard of bronze strips. "This may get in some other people's way, though."

"They've stopped retreating, sir," Donnuld Grayn panted.

"That's obvious," Esmond said, taking a bite out of the skin of the orange in his hand and tossing another to his second-in-command.

He squeezed the juice into his mouth, pitched the husk aside, and swished his hand in an ornamental fountain before drying it on the skirt of his tunic. The noise of combat grew in the courtyard ahead, and far and faint came the distinctive sound of one of Adrian's grenades. Esmond's grin grew; from the barely-glimpsed tower came another slow, aimed arquebus round. There was a shriek behind him—somewhere on the battlements that he'd bypassed when he took his men straight through the breach in the wall. Amazing what an entire oxcart full of gunpowder run into the ditch in front of the wall would do. The dry moat just focused the hellpowder's power on the stone.

Little brother's been busy, he thought, taking up his sword and buckler again, and pulling down the helmet he'd pushed up on his forehead. Trickles of tepid sweat ran down from the sponge lining, and the world shrank to a T-shaped slit of brightness . . . and he felt *alive.* Alive in a way he hadn't, except in combat, since Nanya died.

"Well, what are you lot waiting for?" he said as he came through into the next courtyard.

The Palace of the Directors of Vase was built to the same general plan as the King's house in Chalice, but it was older—older, and less centrally planned, having grown slowly over centuries. Essentially it was a series of interlocking courtyards, sometimes separated by narrow service alleys, and sometimes as much as three stories tall. Some were elaborate with fountains and mosaics, others workaday storehouses, warehouses, workshops, guard barracks. The one through the arched gate ahead was one of the fancy ones, which was all to the good—the tall fountain in the middle would provide his troops with clean water, once they'd taken it.

"Keep *down*, sir," an officer said.

The men here were, behind the pillars of the arcade that lined the courtyard, moving only in short dashes between points covered by the stone. The movement got thicker as the hundred or so reinforcements he'd brought with him filed in among the stalled assault point element.

"They've got archers over there," the officer continued. *Maklin, that's his name,* Esmond thought. He'd made a point of learning all the officers' names, at least. "They're good, and they're not moving for shit."

Esmond nodded thoughtfully, looking at a couple of bodies out in the open. The black-fletched shafts were driven right through them, scale-reinforced leather corselets or not. From the angle, they'd been hit by men on the second-story balconies fifty yards to the east. Spearheads twinkled among the ground-story columns, ready to receive anyone who'd run the gauntlet of arrowfire across the open space. Many Islander archers used recurved bows, backed with strips from the mouthparts of sea monsters. They had a *heavy* punch, in expert hands.

"We need to get them distracted," he said. "Maklin, get twenty-five men down to each end of this arcade." The arches and pillars ran around all four sides of the courtyard. "Have them work towards the enemy, from pillar to pillar. Donnuld, back out and up, onto the second story—give those fucking bowmen something to think about besides sniping. Take a company."

Esmond waited with a cat's patience while the orders were obeyed. His mind and body felt light, tight, strong; it *was* like the Games, in a way.

"All right, men," he said when he heard the rising panic in the voices from the second story, across the way. An archer leaned far out to shoot at a man dodging from one pillar to the next; while he aimed and drew, a javelin sank into his back, and the body arched out to fall, *thump*, in the courtyard below.

"All right," he said again, raising his voice. "What are you waiting for, the enemy to send you enough arrows to open an archery shop? *Follow me!*"

With the last word he was sprinting out, dodging and jinking, as if this were the running-in-armor event at the Games. *There are times,* he thought, as a bodkin-pointed shaft chipped marble by his right ankle, *when straight up the middle is the only way to go.*

With a roar like the sea striking rocks, the troopers behind him surged out of cover on his heels. He kept well ahead of them until they were almost in contact. A volley of thrown spears came at him; he batted one out of the air with his shield as he curved around the fountain. Then he checked his pace, another, and the Strikers struck the line of Islander spears together.

One slammed forward, aimed for his belly. He swayed aside, his body moving in a single smooth curve, and then punched the boss of his small round shield into the face behind it. Bone crackled; he ignored the wounded man and turned his run into a lunge. The long sword in his right hand slipped into a throat; he twisted and jerked it free against the constriction of spasming muscle. Blood sprayed in an arc like water coming out of a hose as the man turned in a half circle before he fell. A saber slashed at him, motion caught out of the corner of his eye; Esmond swept his shield around in a circle, moving it without putting it in front of his face and blocking his vision. The steel struck and sparked on the studs in the surface of the leather, wrenching painfully at the wrist of his left hand. Esmond stabbed low automatically, stepped forward, beat a spear aside with his sword and let the blade and shaft slide up his sword and punched the man behind it in the face with the guard.

"To me, Strikers!" he shouted. "Push 'em, push 'em!"

They *were* pushing them, in a heaving, thrashing confusion that swayed backward a step, another step, another, shouting snarling point-bearded faces and spearpoints, curved swords, knives. Men locked chest-to-chest, no room to dodge now, naked extreme violence, blows given and taken. Then they were under the shade of the arcade's pillars, then past it, and suddenly the combat broke into knots of men that spilled out into a big room—an audience hall, like Casull's back in Chalice.

"Rally, rally!" he called.

Beside him a signaler pulled a horn from his belt and blew the call. The chaos gradually sifted itself into order, men coalescing with their comrades, small bands being overrun, until there were again two distinct bodies of troops. His grew, as more men filtered in, and the Vase troops retreated to stand in a clump around the high throne with its backing of peacock-inlay feathers. Some of them, he noted with glee, were standing guard at the *rear* entrances to the room. Adrian was there, right enough. *How in Wodep's name did he get over the wall? Think about that later.*

Donnuld Grayn came panting up with his company; a couple of them were waving inlaid bows and pear-patterned quivers, or carrying silver-sheathed daggers on their belts.

"Got those fucking archers," Grayn wheezed. "Couldn't bear on us much, up there—good idea. Some sort of Director's Guard, I think—lot of 'em were Southrons, war slaves, maybe."

Esmond nodded. "We're through the rind and near the kernel. Let's see how determined this lot are."

"Not too much, I hope," the Cable officer said, rubbing his hands on his kilt to dry them. "Wodep bugger me blind, I've never seen anything like some of the rooms here—Director's palace, all right, a looter's delight."

"Let's get the fight finished first," Esmond said. "Surrender!" he called to the defenders.

A roar of obscene abuse returned, and a scatter of throwing axes, javelins and arrows; men snapped up shields around him as he ducked, and he could hear things clattering off them. One man backed into him involuntarily as a shaft went into his shield with a solid *whack*, the point showing through the tough layers of greatbeast hide and metal facing.

"Where's your leader, then?" Esmond called, straightening again. "Let him come out and face me—if he dares!"

The Emerald was distantly aware of a commotion at his back—Casull's name came through, but the King could wait. A man in his early middle years stepped forward from the crowd of Vase troops, a bloodied saber in one hand and a hacked buckler in the other.

"I am Franzois Clossaw, Director of Vase by right of blood," he called, wiping at a cut on one cheek with the back of a gauntleted hand.

His armor was plain but rich, and looked nicked and battered as the man himself; he had mustaches curled up into points like horns and a pointed beard, but the point had been slashed off at some time today, leaving him looking a little frayed at the edges. *Hmmm,* Esmond thought. According to reports, the Director of Vase was about seventy, and nearly twice this one's weight.

"I thought Antwoin Clossaw was Director," Esmond said in a conversational tone.

"My brother is dead, killed by your coward's weapons of magic. Until the Syndics of Vase can meet and settle the succession, I am Director—and no foreigner shall sit on the throne of Vase while I live!"

"That can be altered," Esmond purred. "I am General Esmond Gellert, commander of the Sea Striker regiment of Emerald Free Companions"—a little more elegant-sounding than *hired killers*—"and thrice victor of the Five Year Games, free citizen of Solinga. Let this be settled here and now."

Franzois swallowed, looked to either side. His men were apparently ready enough to make a last stand . . . but understandably not wildly enthusiastic about it.

"You guarantee the lives of my men if I lose?" he said.

Esmond nodded, and went on at the beginnings of a rumble behind him: "I can't guarantee the lives or estates of your nobles," he said. "That is in the hand of my lord, King Casull of the Isles—of *all* the Isles." The rumble turned to a purr. "But for your common soldiers, yes. Amnesty, and employment for those who'll swear allegiance. They fought quite well, all things considered."

"And if I win, we get safe passage to the harbor."

"Yes," Esmond said. "I so order my underofficers, in the sight of the Gray-Eyed Lady and by my own honor." That would be a hard promise for Casull to break; the regiment would be seriously pissed off if he did. The rumble was back, but he ignored it as he strode out.

"May I see your face?" Franzois said.

Esmond pushed his helmet back, letting the light fall on his features. The Islander smiled.

"Very much the Emerald hero," he said, taking a quick swig from a leather bottle one of his companions handed him. "My great-great—no matter—one of my ancestors fought against the Solingians at the Narrow Straits. He recorded that it wasn't a very good idea."

"My ancestors fought in the League Wars too," Esmond said politely. He took the time to lean his sword against his hip and carefully dry hand and hilt. "Both sides came off with credit, but the Fates spin the thread of every war."

He pulled the helmet back down and brought up sword and buckler, the small shield under his chin and sword advanced. Franzois nodded and took his own stance, slashing-sword up and back, leading with his shield. Esmond watched the way he held his weapons, the movements of his feet, the set of the thick blocky shoulders.

Fast heavy man, he thought; *that was rare, and dangerous. Sword's seen a lot of use.*

"Watch *out*, for Allfather's sake!" Helga shouted to Adrian.

The billhook crashed across the surface of her buckler. There was vicious weight and an urgent desire to kill behind the blow from the darkened alcove ahead, nothing like training back on the estate. Her left arm went numb for an instant, then gave a burning throb of pain that agonized from wrist and elbow right up into the shoulder. The weapon—a big straight razor on a six-foot pole, with a spike on top and a hook behind—slammed into the stucco of the courtyard wall, raining lime plaster and brick chips on her, leaving the billman bent over with the staggering surprise of *not* having his momentum stopped by his target. She stepped forward in a passing lunge, drilled reflex, sword out, her whole body taking off from the left foot and slamming forward behind point and arm, right foot coming down and knee flexing to add distance to the stroke. The soft heavy resistance as the point went in over the Vasean's collarbone was still an unpleasant surprise; so was the grating of steel on bone somewhere in the man's body.

So was the backstroke with the butt of the weapon, the iron ferrule thumping painfully into her thigh.

"Ow! *Pigfucker!*" she yelped, twisting and yanking to get her own weapon free.

The blood that splashed over her simply added to the drying, sticky mat that covered her from throat to shins; she'd learned to ignore the smell . . . mostly. With a grunt she braced a foot on the still-twitching body and pulled. There were ugly popping, rending sounds as she did, more felt through the hilt than heard through the ears.

"Don't you ever look where you're going?" she snapped at . . . *Adrian Gellert*, she remembered.

Confed folk wisdom had it that Emeralds had no bottom, no real guts; she'd seen enough today to make her seriously doubt that. It also held that Emerald wisdom lovers would step into a well while looking at the stars, and if Adrian was typical, *that* was pretty much true, at least. Her mouth twisted wryly as she fought to get her breath back. She'd had fantasies of rescue, of course; usually her father, or some handsome well-born young tribune in a crested helmet and figured back-and-breast. This slender young Emerald with the dreamy blue eyes and his air of listening to voices nobody else heard was a bit of a contrast, with his rumpled hair showing around his open-face helmet and bits of the iron plates wearing through the leather of his jack.

Well, he's certainly good to have around, she thought, looking out of the corner of her eye at the mercenary troopers crowding forward for the rush into the next courtyard.

Although *they* mostly weren't looking at her like a dog at a porkchop anymore. A couple of them crowed laughter at the sight of her tugging her blade out of the Islander.

"Good work, missy," one grinned. "The lord here needs someone to look after him."

She flushed and turned away at the laughter. "What *is* that stuff?" she asked, nodding at the satchel of round jarlike things at his side, each with its little tail of cord.

"I call them *grenades*," Adrian said absently—that seemed to be his usual manner of speech—and patted them. "They've got a powder inside that I found in certain . . . ancient records, very ancient. It has a number of uses."

"Like those thunder sounds we heard earlier?" she asked.

He looked at her, the absent-mindedness blinking away, and passed her the canteen someone had handed to him. She accepted it and took a pull; the wine that cut the water was nearly vinegar, but it was welcome in the gummy dryness of her mouth.

"Yes, as a matter of fact," he said; it was a second before she noticed he'd switched from his Solingian-accented Scholar's Emerald to a pellucidly pure dialect of patrician-class Vanbert Confed. "It *explodes*—that is, generates a lot of rapidly expanding gas—and pushes away whatever's around it. In the grenades, that pushes fragments of the casing out much faster than an arrow or a sling-bullet. If you put some in a bronze tube sealed at one end, it'll push out a *big* metal or stone bullet—big enough to smash ships or knock down gates and walls."

Helga whistled silently. "Now, won't *that* be useful," she said. "My father's men . . . men of my father's company, that is . . . would call it cheating, though. Not fighting fair."

Adrian shrugged. "I don't like fighting," he said simply. That made her blink again; not many men she knew would admit that—actual *men*, that is. The Emerald went on: "When I do have to fight, I fight to win. Fair fights are for idiots and Con— I mean, for those who are strong enough to be sure they'll win anyway."

Helga nodded slowly. "You know, that makes a lot of sense," she said, and felt herself obscurely pleased at the look in the Emerald's hazel eyes. "Of course, I'm a woman, and we can't afford some of the idiocies men get involved with."

"I see your point," Adrian said, and heaved himself away from the wall he'd been leaning against. "Now, I think there's a fight we—or I, at least—*do* have to engage in calling out."

The noise of combat had died down ahead; she cocked her head. "That's two men fighting," she said. "Odd, almost like a duel." With a quick urchin grin at the Emerald. "And you saved my life, but it looks to me like you need someone by you to return the favor—often."

"That's right, missy," one of the troops said.

"Hear her, lord," another chimed in.

Adrian straightened. "Let's get moving," he said. "Your munificent pay doesn't come for propping up walls." His eyes scanned around, and took on a hint of that distant look again. "This way leads to the throne room. Up one more flight, left, and that's the anteroom—they were probably going to try and get out right this way."

"How does he *know* that?" Helga whispered aside to a man with another satchel of grenades as the commander turned and walked briskly towards the landing at the base of a flight of stairs.

"You'll find Lord Adrian knows most anything he wants," the man said with unshakeable confidence. "The Gray-Eyed Lady speaks to him, y'see."

Helga felt her eyes go wide.

Esmond went into a stop-thrust, then recovered smoothly, turning it into a feint as Franzois beat it aside with his buckler and cut, backhand, forehand, boring in with a stamp-stamp-stamp and a whirling pattern that made a silver X of his sword.

Right, let's see you keep that *up,* the Emerald thought grimly as he backed. Normally he didn't think much of the Islander school of swordplay; all edge and dash and no science. Director-for-a-couple-of-hours Franzois was as good a master of that style as he'd come across, though, and thoroughly accustomed to using it against the more point-oriented Emerald blade-way.

He waited, point hovering, backing with an economical shuffle and his feet at right angles. Clang-ting-*clang*, and the saber knocked against his buckler, rang on his blade, shed itself from that with a long *scring* sound and deflected off his helmet and a shoulder piece with bruising force and there was the sting of a slight cut on his upper shoulder.

Good steel, he thought absently—to be that shaving-sharp after a long day's work. They had good smiths here in the Isles.

Franzois' face was a deeper purple now, his mouth open below the splayed nasal of his helmet. Esmond waited, backed once more . . . then *lunged*, with all the dense muscle of his weight behind it, the springing power of his rear leg, and a wrist locked to put it all behind the punching tip of the sword.

The Islander stopped, blade still raised for another slash. It came down and faltered weakly as Esmond's point ripped free of his inner thigh. From the sudden arterial rush of blood, he'd cut the big vein there. The Emerald stepped back and raised his sword again in salute.

"That was a brave man," he murmured as the body kicked and voided, the usual undignified business of dying.

"Esmond! Esmond!"

He jerked his head up suddenly. The chant had begun during the fight, but there was no room for it in the diamond-hard focus of a death duel. The men were yelling it, pumping fists and weapons in the air.

"*Esmond! Esmond!*"

The roar echoed back from the walls of the great room, bouncing back in confused waves of sound as the last of the defenders were disarmed and marched off. Not only his own Strikers were shouting it, but the Royal troops as well—only the knot of noblemen around King Casull weren't, and many of them were waving swords in salute as well. Even the King was, and smiling; there was a cut on his face, and blood on his sword—Casull was a fighting man whose praise you'd respect, and Esmond felt a sudden lurch as the truth of it rammed home.

Well, dip me in shit! he thought. *I not only won, I won big with the big boss looking on.* The news would be all over the Royal army and fleet by sundown, too.

Esmond bent, pulling off Franzois' helm. There was a purple-gold circlet around the dead man's brow; he paused a minute to hold the eyelids shut and close the staring gaze, then rose with the symbol of Vase's sovereignty raised high. The chanting gradually slowed, stopped, left a silence full of rustles and creaks and clanks as armed men shifted their feet and murmured to each other.

With sword and buckler in his right hand and the circlet in his left, Esmond paced across the throne room to where Casull stood. He went to one knee and held both forward.

"My lord King," he said, in slow, clear, carrying tones. "Vase is yours!"

Another roaring cheer. Cries of "Casull!" and "Esmond!" were mixed, together with "Hot damn!" and "Loot! Loot!"

Casull took the circlet, a wry smile on his face; he winked slightly as their eyes met.

"Well, you're a showman, as well as a fighting man," he murmured as he accepted the symbol of sovereignty. "Maybe you'll find a realm of your own someday; a man who's actor and fighter both is born to rule."

He straightened, took Esmond's sword and rapped him sharply on each armored shoulder.

"With swords such as yours, my throne is secure!" he cried. *From everyone but the people carrying those swords,* went unspoken between them—warning and mutual recognition at once. "Let the farmer-clods of the Confederation interfere if they dare—let all men take note that what we have, we hold, we and our valorous nobles and troops. Rise, Excellent Esmond Gellert!"

Esmond's eyes widened slightly, and his men redoubled their cheers. *Well, there's a step up,* he thought; he'd just gone from outland mercenary captain to the lowest level of Islander nobility. *Mind you, what the King gave, the King could take away;* and from the smolderingly jealous looks of the courtiers gathered about him, he'd also acquired a set of instant enemies. Casull's wry smile as Esmond rose—for an instant, until he noticed the added pain of the stiffening face cut—told the Emerald that the King was perfectly aware of *that*, too.

Casull paced across the room and up the dais to the Throne of Vase, turning to take the salute from the warriors who filled the great room to overflowing now.

"Hail to our lord King—King of all the Isles!" Esmond cried.

Helga Demansk watched the end of the duel wide-eyed, especially when Esmond Gellert pulled off his helmet after his victory. *Oh, momma!* she thought, glancing aside at Adrian. Yes, there was a family resemblance there, but . . . *Well, if the old stories about Emerald philosophers are true, I suppose the ones about the Five Year Games winners can be too.* Maybe even stories about god-fathered heroes, although like anyone with a modern education she tended to believe—consciously, at least—that the old gods were aspects of the One, Who needed only to Be, not to do.

Looking at Esmond Gellert, it was easy to remember things her nurse had told her, and old tales in books. The other Emerald was a big man, but with none of the beefy solidity she was used to in soldiers, or athletes, for that matter. He moved like a big golden cat, and his features might have been chiseled by a Solingian sculptor of the lost golden age right after the League Wars.

But there was something . . . something *missing* there. A liveliness that was in his brother's eyes, even when they were abstracted. It grew as the flush of combat faded from his face, leaving it even more like a statue—painted marble, with a deadness behind. Except that marble did not conceal an ocean of pain. . . .

Stop being fanciful, she told herself. *Concentrate.* Adrian had said she was under his protection, and oddly enough she believed him. But *Adrian* might need protection. Would the King protect him? Could his brother? She stepped back a pace, hating the necessity but wishing for a cloak, too.

"Adrian!" Esmond said, stepping forward and shouldering nobles and ranking officers aside. A little life returned to the carved planes of his face. "Brother! By the *shades*, how did you get here?"

"Found an old access tunnel to that tower," Adrian said, flushing with pleasure himself and clasping forearms. "Blasted out the plug with some hellpowder, and went looking for trouble—and found you, eventually."

Esmond laughed. "I *thought* it was something like that. The Vaseans were retreating in pretty good order—stood up to the guns pretty well, even your sniping at their backs—and then they went to pieces."

"Men will, when they're attacked from the rear," Adrian said. "You managed to cover yourself with well-earned glory, I see."

Esmond laughed again; the sound was a little hoarse, as if he didn't do it very often. He caught the smaller man by the shoulder and pushed him forward unwilling, until they were before the throne. Helga slipped forward unobtrusively, absently knocking a questing hand aside with the rim of her buckler on its wrist bone, and ignoring the indignant yelp that followed.

"My lord King," Esmond said; not shouting, but pitched in a public-speaking mode copied from his brother's rhetorical training, and found useful on the battlefield as well—much likelier to attract attention than the usual roar, as conversation built up in the throne room.

"My lord King," he went on, grinning. "Here is my brother, Adrian Gellert, who has served you well—not only the devices which battered down the walls and gates of Vase, but by taking the citadel from behind through a secret passage and blocking the escape of Director Franzois."

Casull looked aside from a consultation with one of his admirals who'd brought him a tally of ships captured intact.

"Then he has served me well," the king said graciously, waving aside a surgeon who was trying to suture the slash on his cheek. "If the Director's heir—a pretender to this throne—had escaped, this victory wouldn't be complete."

He gave Esmond a slight, hard stare at that; if the Director had won the fight, Casull might well have had to let him go . . . which would have had much the same result, with the added disadvantage of the sort of colorful story likely to attract free-lances who valued a lucky commander.

"You'll not find me ungrateful," Casull went on.

"My lord King," Adrian said. "Forgive me if I claim your gratitude so early, but there's a favor I *would* like to claim."

Casull's eyebrows went up; it was slightly boorish to take him up on his offer so early. "Ask," he said.

Adrian reached behind himself without looking around; Helga squeaked slightly as his hand closed on her shoulder and pulled her forward. The fingers were slender but unexpectedly strong, warm through the cooling blood on the fabric of her halter.

"My way here came through the Director's—the *ex*-Director's hareem," he said. "I'd have this woman assigned to me, if Your Majesty would be so kind."

Helga swallowed. *Hell, it's* got *to be better than the hareem,* she thought. Women in the Emerald lands were closer-kept than in the upper classes of the Confederacy, but vastly better than in the Isles . . . and Adrian hadn't made the slightest objection when she took a sword and came along for some payback. He'd even *thanked* her for probably saving his life—it would have driven most men she knew crazy, to owe a woman that.

Although he has eyes in the back of his head, for a man who isn't paying much attention, she thought, puzzled for a moment. His brother Esmond, you could *sense* that he saw with his skin, like a cat. Adrian, he gave off a feeling you could walk right up to him and bash him on the head; only you couldn't, he'd start and look up and be ready for it, from what she'd seen. As if someone was talking to him, and paying attention when he wasn't.

The King's words brought her back to her own personal reality with a thump.

"That's a little irregular, but since they're Royal spoils . . ." he said. Then he looked at Helga and laughed. "I see the former Director wasn't averse to a little perversion—that one looks like a boy with tits, or a field woman . . . no, those are acrobat's muscles, I suppose. Well, she'll be athletic, if you like that sort of thing. But what by the Sun God is she doing with that sword?"

The King's voice was amused, a little contemptuous. Adrian's was blankly polite when he replied: "Killing Vasean soldiers, mostly, my lord King. Five . . ." His head went to one side. "No, six, with two probables, O King. Probably saved my life, as well."

The King laughed uproariously. "We can't deprive our master artificer of his *body*guard, then," he said. "By all means—"

"Excuse me, my Royal Cousin," one of the nobles said. A tall slender brown-haired man, he'd had time to shed his armor, but the padded leather doublet underneath was rank with sweat. "If I might?"

Casull nodded uncertainly, and the Islander noble came two steps down from the dais, giving Helga a slow head-to-toe.

"As you say, rather perverse . . . but interestingly. By ancient law," he went on, giving Adrian a cool glance, "officers chose personal spoils by rank—and I believe I outrank this outlander."

Casull's lips pursed in annoyance. He glanced around the circle of courtiers, and saw many nods and chuckles. *Of course,* Helga thought. An outlander, raised high so suddenly, was bound to arouse resentment—any Islander court was a snakepit at the best of times. And Adrian, unlike his brother, hadn't just pulled off a spectacular Wodep-like feat of public heroism.

"Unless," the noble said, "he'd like to fight me for her? No? I didn't think so." The noble had several skull-and-bones earrings, and he moved like . . . *Like Adrian's brother Esmond,* Helga thought. *No! I will* not *go back into another Islander hareem! No!*

The Islander stepped forward, and she tensed.

"Actually," Adrian said mildly, "I *do* object, and if necessary, I *will* fight you. But I appeal to our lord the King, whose wishes you are quite obviously contravening, my lord . . . Sawtre, isn't it?"

Sawtre grinned, flushing and letting his hand drop to his sword. "Interfering in the affairs of *real* men, little Emerald manure strainer? Better to get back to your toys. We should all consider the consequences of our decisions, shouldn't we? You are what you do, after all. And we *know* what you are."

Adrian swallowed, shaking his head once and then again—*as if,* Helga thought under the rush of relief at his words and then horror at his prospects in a duel with this trained killer, *he was talking to someone again . . . and disagreeing with them.*

"I think you're forgetting something, my lord," Esmond said quietly.

"Yes?"

"Forgetting that if you harm my brother, in any way whatsoever, I'll kill you and piss on your grave," Esmond said, smiling himself. His eyes had taken on the same febrile brilliance they'd had during the duel with Director Franzois, and Sawtre checked for a moment.

"You don't dare, Emerald," he said softly.

"You'd be surprised what I dare," Esmond replied, his voice equally calm.

Behind him the men of the Strikers tensed, and exchanged glances with Sawtre's fighting tail. Those men began drifting towards their lord; one of them dashed out, to collect others of their band who were lifting their share in the sack of the palace.

"Excuse me," Helga said loudly. Sawtre's eyes did not waver. Helga tapped the edge of her buckler against her sword. "*Excuse me. You, the asshole in the arming doublet!*"

That brought amazed snickers from the crowd around the throne; even Casull, half-risen in annoyance and gathering apprehension at the sudden prospect of a battle royal before his eyes, turned to look at her.

The nobleman flicked her an annoyed glance. "Be silent, woman, or you'll get a worse beating than you would otherwise."

"Oh, *excuse* me, my mighty Islander Pirate Lord dumber-than-dogshit, but you're *forgetting* something."

"*What?*"

There was a slack amazement on Sawtre's hard face; he could not *believe* that this was happening to him, this public defiance by a woman. His hand went to his belt. Not to the hilt of his sword, as it had a moment before, but to the thonged crop that hung there.

"Forgetting *this*," Helga said, and thrust underarm.

Lord Sawtre's face went slack with an amazement even more complete than before. Even then, his hand began a movement towards his sword, struck the hilt, began to draw. *Hey, really good reflexes,* Helga thought—it helped keep her mind off the fact that she had just probably condemned herself to death. *I'd rather* be *dead,* she thought, at the thick wet butcher's-cleaver sound as the blade went in from below, just above the man's left hip. Sawtre's mouth and eyes went into identical Os of shock as she dropped her buckler, put both hands on the hilt, and ripped the blade upward with a twisting wrench of arms and shoulders and back.

It came free with a hard shit-stink following it, and the Islander noble dropped to his knees and clutched at the pink-and-red intestines spilling into his lap.

"*Be silent*, woman, you said?" Helga said, her voice breathy with exertion. "Try being silent about *this*, you velipad's ass."

The sword went up, and her right foot curled up and then slammed down to add emphasis as the blade fell—spattering red drops even before it struck the man's neck, and with white shreds of fat sticking in nicks in the steel. Sawtre flopped boneless to the ground, and blood spilled down, crimson against the marble white and malachite green of the steps.

For a long moment there was absolute silence; Adrian was staring at her and looking—again as if he was talking to someone. His brother was staring at her too, seeing her as a person for the first time rather than a symbol his brother was willing to fight for, and his eyes were wide with an expert's appreciation of what she'd just done. King Casull was frozen in a different set of calculations. His voice cut across the beginnings of a murmur:

"Well, it seems he *was* silent about that," he observed, leaning back in the throne and resting his bearded chin on the knuckles of one hand. "And you know—I've thought Sawtre was a velipad's arse myself, for a good long while now."

He chuckled, then threw back his head and laughed outright. Some of the courtiers chimed in immediately, and others took it up, until the whole room was roaring.

Allfather of Vanbert, Greatest and Best—what a bunch of pirates! Even after a year in the Isles, she forgot sometimes. . . .

Helga felt her shoulders begin to shake with reaction. Adrian laid his hand on her back again, gently—cautiously—but firmly.

"And now, if my lord King will excuse me," he said.

"By all means, my Iron Limper," Casull said, referring to the lame smith of the gods. "Keep the vixen, if you want her. I'd say not to turn your back, but—" he gave another shout of laughter "—that didn't do Lord Sawtre here any good, did it?"

He raised a hand and shouted over the court's merriment. "And now, my lords and gentlemen, we have a city to sack!"

"An' here's to lord Adrian, the favored of the Gray-Eyed, victory-lucky, best lord a fightin' man could follow!" Simun shouted, raising his cup.

The arquebusiers of the Lightning Band—they'd come up with the title on their own—raised a deafening cheer. Adrian smiled and nodded; it was rather like having a pack of pet direbeasts: alarming at times, but it certainly beat having them against you. The long palace hall was full of them, and of servants and women—the latter volunteers, or mostly, considering their alternatives—and the smells of food and wine and hastily washed mercenary rubbed with scented oil, and incense from braziers, perfumed lanterns, garlands. . . . Light flickered on hard battered faces, on ranks of bundles of plunder stacked against the walls, neatly wrapped in canvas and inked with their owners' names, and on the unit's equipment. They were ready to move out in the morning.

"Here's to his brother, who's Wodep come again," Simun said loyally. "Yer can't go wrong with leaders who're favored of the gods—smart, too."

"Long live lord Adrian, who taught us to wield the lightnings!" someone else yelled.

"Long live lord Adrian, who's brought us to a place where we can swim in gold!"

That brought a *really* enthusiastic cheer. The wine cellar they'd gone through had turned out to be a subtreasury or something, probably the ready funds for the management of the Director's hareem. Strictly speaking it should have gone into the general pot, but everyone had agreed that that would be taking the rules to a ridiculous extreme. It had come out to about a year's pay for every man in the unit, not counting what they'd picked up elsewhere the rest of the day.

"And now I'll leave you to your well-earned feasting," Adrian said.

There was another good-natured cheer. They didn't resent him not taking part in the celebration; they'd come to take a certain pride in the oddity of a Scholar of the Grove commanding them, now that nobody could doubt he had balls enough despite it. It had worked; it was lucky; and if it wasn't broke, they weren't going to try and fix it.

"Won't be a gentleman's symposium, no, sir," Simun said. He leered cheerfully. "Watch out for 'er sword before you show 'er yours, too, sir!"

He left the chamber in a roar of bawdy advice, flushing and smiling a little. His own chambers had probably been a royal guard captain's rooms, up a flight of stairs, with half a flat roof as well, enclosed by a head-high wall except where a low balustrade overlooked the courtyard-drillyard, and set with plants in pots, tumbles of blossoming vine falling down to the brown tiles. The scent of the flowers was faint and cool, after the heat and smells of the main hall; the walls blocked out flames and sound from the rest of Vase, leaving only the stars above, many and bright.

"Ah—" he caught himself before he said *Lady Demansk*; the Gray-Eyed knew he didn't want Helga to know he knew *that*. "Freewoman Helga." There, at least he'd gotten across that he regarded her as a free citizen of the Confederacy, not a slave who'd changed owners. She nodded, taking note of the title, and he went on: "I've had some things gathered up for you, and you can have that chamber by the stairwell; we'll be leaving tomorrow."

"Well, yes, I'd sort of wondered about that," Helga said, stepping forward into the puddle of yellow light a brass globe full of oil with a cotton wick cast on the tiles.

She was wearing a clean tunic—man's clothing, but there was no doubt at all about the gender of the body within it. A garland of white-and-purple flowers crowned the long auburn curls that fell past her shoulders; it was hard to remember her turning the billhook meant for him, bathed in blood . . . *And fairly easy, too. All the gods witness, I was terrified.* Not half as terrified as he'd been challenging Sawtre, of course.

Adrian cleared his throat, glad of the night dimness. A voice drifted up the stairwell, followed by a tremendous shout of laughter, and then the jaunty notes of a *kordax* on the lyre. A line of torch-bearing men stamped out into the courtyard of this building, mostly leaning on their companions—women of the town, or boys in a few instances—and began weaving in a chain dance around the fountain and back into the hall. They were singing something, something with his name in it, but between distance, drink and the blur of voices far from used to singing in unison, he couldn't make it out.

Interesting, Adrian thought with a distant scholar's part of his mind. He'd never actually seen a victory *komos* before, although the old epics were full of them. This wasn't much like the descriptions the poets gave; they left out the bits about men who stopped to throw up, or just fell down paralytically drunk.

I suspect that this is more like what they were really like, even in the War of the Thousand Ships, he mused.

"Ah, um." *Oh, Gellerix, that's lame,* he thought and found his voice. "I'm definitely not going to force myself on you, Freewoman Helga," he said.

Helga smiled. "That's extremely gentlemanly of you," she said, with a polite nod and toss of her head. It wouldn't have been out of place at a dinner party at Audsley's house in Vanbert, except that most of his wife's acquaintances didn't have that much style. "But I assure you that force isn't required."

"Ah, um." *Oh, Gellerix.* "Ah, you really don't have to feel any sense of obligation, Freewoman Helga," he managed to choke out.

"You do *like* women, don't you, Adrian?"

Adrian felt a chuckle rising at her expression of sudden worry. "Well, yes. Don't believe everything you hear about Emeralds, my—ummmph."

"You're exactly the right height," Helga said as she broke the kiss. "Two and one-half inches taller than me. . . . Look, Adrian, I'm not a virgin, my marital prospects are crap anyway, I've been locked up with sixty women for a year and I *don't* like girls . . . and I *do* like you. You're a fascinating man. You're also not someone my father picked, either—*I* like you, I said." Her smile grew. "Am I making myself clear?"

"Abundantly," he said, and scooped her up with an arm under the shoulders and another under the knees.

CHAPTER SEVEN

"Preble," King Casull said.

His pointer tapped down on the map table. The greatbeast hide there showed an island covered in buildings, shaped like a peach pit with a stretch of blue water down the middle. Puff-cheeked wind spirits were drawn to represent the prevailing winds, and a line eastward showed the mainland coast. A few men stood around it: his heir, Tenny; Esmond; Adrian; and the Grand Admiral of the Isles, a half-brother of Casull who'd supported him in his thrust for the crown and had no sons of his own. A cooling evening breeze blew curtains aside to reveal the harbor of Chalice, crammed with shipping, a tarry reek penetrating even this far above the harbor. It was growing dark, but a flicker of red showed on the underside of the clouds that hung in the deep-purple sky—reflection of the lava in the craters above the city.

"We held Preble under my predecessor, Casull III, may his spirit rest with the Sun God," Casull went on. "Justiciar Marcomann took it away from us, along with the old mainland possessions of the Kings of the Isles. It's barely half a mile from shore—you can see the old city, Sor, here—but it's a magnificent naval base and does a heavy trade. According to my spies, who are many there, there's only a small Confed garrison there, barely a battalion."

Silence fell around the table. The Crown Prince cleared his throat. "A strong party loyal to the Kings of the Isles has risen in Preble," he said. "They have extended an invitation to me, to come and free them from the tyrants of the mainland, and then to rule them as men are meant to be ruled."

"And not to pay the Confed tribute anymore," Casull added. "It's heavy; they don't really understand sea trade . . . farmers, really."

Adrian nodded in unison with Esmond. ***No doubt a little gold from Chalice was spread around to get that Royalist party going,*** Raj said. ***But yes, on the whole, it looks like a good opportunity to test the Confeds.***

probability of initial success is 77%, ±10, Center interjected. **high degree of uncertainty indicates several factors, principally—**

We'll discuss that later, Adrian thought firmly. Aloud: "My lord King, perhaps we can take Preble," he said. "Can we hold it?"

Tenny's lower lip stuck out slightly. Adrian cursed himself silently; he should have framed that a little more tactfully. Casull nodded.

"That *is* the question," he said. "Normally, no. The island is too close to the mainland, to the Confed armies, and to their fleet. The fleet's laid up in ordinary"—meaning stripped and hauled up in boat-sheds—"but they can put it to sea fairly quickly."

"As sailors, they'd make good cowherds," Tenny observed. His father frowned.

"True, but don't underestimate their numbers, or their discipline, or the way their infantry fights once they get on your deck—previous Kings of the Isles have done that, to their cost." Casull III, for instance, had paid with his life for doing exactly that. "With 'zieur Adrian's new weapons, we *may* have a chance of holding it."

Adrian traced the narrow strait with a finger. "What's the depth, here, my lord King?"

"Ah, you see the problem. Shallow—full of shifting sandbars. Impossible to interdict with warships, but fine for shallow-draft barges carrying assault troops."

"They might try a causeway, then," Adrian said thoughtfully. "If they could round up enough peasants to dig."

Casull winced slightly. "That would be even worse. Damn them, they're always trying to turn sea into land."

"By the Lord of the Trident, they'll regret it this time," Esmond said confidently. "Most of Adrian's new weapons have the range to turn the straits into *hell* for them."

"So we'll put them into the hands of the Shades." Tenny chuckled, licking his lips. "And I will be King in Preble."

"Under me," Casull added dryly, and the Prince looked down. Patricide was an ancient tradition in the Isles. "By sending you, my son, I assure the men of Preble that they are to be free subjects, not a possession to be squeezed."

"What about the city militia?" Esmond said. "There ought to be . . . what, eight, ten thousand of them? In a city that size."

Casull nodded. "They will not be involved initially," he said. "Not if our plan goes as expected. Then they will have no *choice* but to fall in with us, and fight for us."

"Certainly, if the Confed thinks they were disloyal," Esmond said. "I take it, my lord, that the Strikers are to be the spearhead of this enterprise?" He bowed to Tenny. "Under your valiant son's direction."

"Of course," Casull beamed. "And your brother will be with you, to see to the emplacement of the new weapons to defend our new city. We will follow with the fleet."

The two Emeralds smiled and bowed to the King of the Isles. Adrian needed no voices from beyond the world to know exactly what the King was thinking: if the throw of the dice failed, he was out only one replaceable son and some Emerald mercenaries; if it succeeded, he had one of the richest cities in the Western Sea.

That's how a King has to think, lad, Raj said. Adrian had an image of gray eyes, weary and amused. ***I never had to be* that*, for which I thank the Spirit of Man of the Stars.***

"When do we strike?" Esmond asked.

"As soon as may be. With the fleet gathered, Confed spies will swarm here like flies to velipad shit, and this is a logical step. I will feed them a dozen contradictory stories—that way even if they learn the truth, it may drown in a storm of plausible lies—but better still to strike before they decide to reinforce all their coastal garrisons."

Esmond nodded. "Then if my lords will permit, my brother and I will withdraw, to make our preparations. The Strikers will be ready to sail within three days."

"My Lightning Band within a week," Adrian said. "I will need time to modify some equipment and gather others."

"You gave her *what*?" Esmond laughed, cracking a nut in his palm.

"Well, it was what she wanted," Adrian said defensively.

"Flowers, a hare, jewels—but you gave her a *sword*?"

"Well, the one she had wasn't really very good quality," Adrian explained.

He was tired; they both were, with the load of work they'd been doing. A light meal stood between their couches on a low table: cured fish, olives, oil, bread for dipping, watered wine. The room was plain whitewash with a pattern of leaves in blue around the upper edges, and a door gave out onto a garden full of lilacs. It might almost have been in Solinga, even the smell of the sea was familiar, if it weren't for a subtle wrongness in the noises, an undersmell of strange spices and rank lushness to the familiar reek of a port. Another table at the end of the room was littered with wax-covered board diptychs, scrolls, and scraps of reed-paper, models.

Esmond pulled a piece off a long loaf of bread. "Well," he said, with malice aforethought and a brother's cruelty, "it was a good enough sword to gut Lord Sawtre very effectively. If you finally had to take up with a woman regularly, and with a Confed woman, you at least picked one with some unusual talents." He laughed. "At least she's not Audsley's wife—or Justiciar Demansk's daughter."

His brother might not be a Scholar of the Grove, with an ageless machine and an ancient general's ghost at the back of his mind, but he was an Emerald and no fool—which was to say, a keen observer.

"*Wait* a minute!" Esmond said, half-rising. "Shit among the Shades, she *is* Demansk's daughter—the one captured by pirates."

"*Shut up!*" Adrian barked.

Shocked, Esmond fell silent for a moment. Adrian rarely spoke roughly; this time he fought for a visible instant to control his temper, something rare enough to make his brother's eyes go wide.

"You will *not* speak of that again," he said coldly.

"But why?" Esmond said.

"Because I don't want her to think I'm using her as some sort of angle against her father—which I'm not, by the way, and won't be."

Esmond's blue eyes blinked in bewilderment. "But why, brother if—oh, no. *Don't* tell me you've been scratched by one of Gellerix's cats and caught a fever!"

That was the slang term for being hit by love; any sensible Emerald regarded it as a form of infectious madness sent by the gods to plague mankind with suffering—the divinities could be remarkably petty and cruel, sometimes.

Adrian looked down and toyed with a dried fig. "That's one way to put it. You might also say that I like and respect her," he snapped.

"Adrian, my brother, please—think." Esmond stopped for a moment, and snorted. "Here I am, stealing your lines, like an actor . . . but really, think, brother. At least there's no question of marr—oh, Gellerix!" he broke off at Adrian's expression.

"Esmond, have you any conception of how *dull* most women's conversation is?" he snapped. "How dull most women *are*? It's not their fault, the gods know, most of them shut up all the time and uneducated, but—"

He stopped at Esmond's expression of bafflement. *Your Nanya was like a trembling dove,* he thought with kindly exasperation. *And the gods know, the Wodep in your soul would make that seem the sum of all womanhood to you. Me, I'm differently made, my brother.*

"She's—"

A dangerous glance passed between them, and an unspoken message: *You don't call her* used goods *and I won't say anything about Nanya, that's about it,* Adrian thought.

"Adrian," Esmond said slowly. "Demansk's daughter is going to be a Confed—not just by origins, she'll have been *brought up* on their old stories, walked past the death masks of Demansks who were Justiciars and Speakers back to when Vanbert was a mud-and-wattle village. How do you think she's going to feel when she finds out you're fighting to bring the Confederacy of Vanbert to the ground?"

I should remind myself how smart Esmond is occasionally, Adrian thought, wincing. His brother didn't have the temperament for a Scholar, but he had at least as much raw brainpower as his younger sibling, and a tremendous ability to focus.

"That's . . . for the time it has to be faced," he said slowly. "Look, Esmond . . . can't I have a few days? Just a few?"

"Of course," Esmond said. His eyes grew slightly haunted. "I know how brief that can be."

Feet clattered outside, and voices rang; one a high clear soprano. Helga Demansk swept in, wearing women's dress this time, a long blue robe with a fold of her mantle over her hair. That was tied back with a ribbon, and twisted into plaits.

"Adrian!" she said, handing her shopping basket to a maid. "It fits! Oh, hello, Esmond."

"Helga," he said, half-rising and bowing his head. "What fits?"

"The cuirass and helmet," she said. "They do good metalwork here, I've got to admit, even if they are pirate dogs." Adrian winced slightly, and looked around. "Oh, don't worry, Adrian," she went on. "They're *proud* of being pirates."

"But not dogs," he said.

"Are you going to tell me yet where this new expedition is headed?" she said, a green gleam in her eye. "Casull will have all the islands soon, at this rate."

"Are you so eager to slay men, lady?" Esmond asked.

This time Helga looked aside slightly. "Well, no," she said. "Not really. But it's . . . exciting, you know what I mean?"

"Unfortunately I do," Esmond agreed.

Helga reached into the basket. "*And* look at what I found," she went on more brightly. "A copy of the *War of the Thousand Ships.* I kept myself sane partly by reciting big chunks of it from memory, but it's been so long since I had anything to *read.*"

Esmond laughed. "You and my brother were made for each other by the gods, lady. Even when we were running for our lives, two pack-velipads full of scrolls followed us."

Helga chuckled, but scowled slightly. "That idiot Audsley got a lot of good men killed, from what I hear," she said. "Damned traitor . . . and of course he got his head handed to him when he met . . . Justiciar Demansk. Demansk is a *real* general, and he has the interests of the State at heart."

correct, Center said. **which is why with a high probability he would be hostile to our innovations. however, it would be advisable to gain a fuller psychostatistical profile of him—the subject helga demansk would be a valuable source of data.**

Shut the hell up, Adrian thought. He could feel Raj agreeing with him, an eerie nonverbal communication, like some ghostly equivalent of seeing expression on a man's face.

"Sorry," Helga went on after a moment. "Sometimes I forget you're Emeralds."

"Emeralds and Confeds are near-as-no-matter blood brothers here in the Isles," Adrian said lightly—which was true in one sense, and an outright lie in another.

Helga met his eyes and smiled, and worries seemed to dissolve themselves in time sweeter than honey. After a moment Esmond cleared his throat and stood.

"Well, I can tell when I'm the third wheel on a chariot," he said. "Tomorrow, then, brother."

"We're getting sort of close to the mainland, aren't we?" Helga said.

"That *is* the mainland," Adrian replied.

The galley had been under sail alone, one squat square sail driving the lean hull eastwards. Adrian stood on the quarterdeck, with his arm and cloak around the woman beside him; he'd been still, because if he was still all he need see was the frosted arch of stars above, the ghostly arcs of the moons, the smells of salt water and sweat and tar and the mingling of jasmine and clean healthy woman that was Helga. If he did not think, his mind need not crack and bleed. . . .

"Sir . . ." began the ship's captain; he was Casull's man, and they were not authorized to be anywhere but on the approaches to Preble.

"Shut up, you," Simun said.

The Islander skipper looked at him, and at the scores of Adrian's arquebusiers sprawled about the galley's deck, sleeping wrapped in their cloaks, throwing dice in the hollow of an upturned buckler, chewing hardtack and dried fruit, or simply sitting patiently on their haunches. His crew numbered roughly the same, though all but fifteen of them were oarsmen and sailors, tough hardy men and handy in a fight, but no match for soldiers with swords and light body armor. And from the flat dispassionate stare of the little underofficer, they'd be perfectly happy to slit his throat, throw the crews' bodies after his, and turn pirate if this Emerald gave the word. They were *his* men, not the King's.

"Your orders, sir?" he said to Adrian.

"Beach the ship lightly," he said, then looked ahead. "There's shallow shelving water and soft sand there—just touch her."

The captain shivered and made a covert sign with his fingers. Those eyes . . . *They're not like those of other men. As if demons or spirits—or gods?—were looking out of them. Telling him things, that's what the tales say. He's not canny.*

He turned to give his orders to the steersmen and sailing master. The sail and yard came down with a muted thump and were furled; below the oarsmen stirred in sleepy protest. There was a yelp or two as the bosun's rope-end persuaders swung, and then the oars came rattling out, poised, dipped down into the dark star-reflecting water and bit. The ship turned towards the black line of the shore, where low waves and white foam and pale sand made a line in the night. It was calm water, and the ship was a raider, built for 'longshore work. Behind him the sorcerer was talking with his woman in Confed, a language the captain knew only a few words of.

"Adrian," Helga said. "What's going on?"

The Emerald drew a deep breath. "I didn't tell you where we were bound," he said. "Because I didn't want to spoil things more than . . . earlier than I had to."

"You're bound to attack Confederacy territory," she said, her voice quiet and level as her eyes.

"Yes," Adrian said.

"Preble? It's the logical target and weakly held."

Adrian felt a knife twist deeper. *This woman has brains,* he thought. Some of the Scholars of the Grove held that the only true love was between man and youth, because only then could there be a meeting of minds and not merely of bodies. He'd admitted the theoretical force of the argument, but not anymore, not anymore. . . .

"Yes."

"Adrian . . ." She stepped closer and put a hand on his shoulder. He could barely feel it through the shoulderpiece of his corselet, but a heat seemed to gather beneath.

"Adrian, don't do it. You'll be killed, you can't understand even if you win at first, the Confederacy *always* comes back in the end, please, don't throw yourself away—"

She's thinking of me, he realized with a glow of wonder. He shook his head and went on:

"I've . . . got to back my brother. And I'm not going to ask you to fight against your country . . . possibly against your father's own troops."

Shock turned Helga's face white. "You knew?"

"You favor him. And I knew about the raid." His hand came down on hers, where it rested on the bronze of the armor. "Helga . . . I didn't give a damn. Don't now."

She looked at him for a long slow moment. "I believe you," she said. "And you're not sending me back now as a gift to him?"

His mouth quirked. "Your father is notoriously patriotic. Who was that ancient Confed general, the one who executed his own sons when they proposed surrender . . . ?"

"Louis deVille," she said automatically. "That was in the war of King Peter."

The one who came up with the phrase Petric Victory, a scholar's corner of Adrian's mind remembered. That was long before the Confed conquest of the Emerald lands, when an Emerald—or half-Emerald—general could still invade there himself. But he'd won no concessions, although he'd carried half a dozen bloody fields against the nascent Confederation's army. The problem was that they could replace the men, and he couldn't.

"Well, if deVille was ready to sacrifice his sons, I think your father—much though he must love you—will sacrifice a daughter for Preble. I'm not going to be buying any favors from him with you."

Her eyes searched his. "How well you must know him," she said. "Is there nothing you don't know?"

"I don't know how to come by what I want most in the world and still keep my honor," he said.

The tears that glittered in her eyes stayed unshed; he'd found the one argument that would weigh heaviest with someone raised in the household of a Confed noble of antique virtue. *The fact that it's the miserable truth is sort of a bonus, I suppose.*

The cry from the bow was soft but carrying. "She shelves."

"Avast oars!" the captain called. "Brace for grounding!"

Adrian and Helga did, with an arm around each other as well as a grip on the rigging. The ship surged softly, and half a dozen crewmen dropped over the bow to hold her steady; the water was to their waists. For all its length and wicked bronze-sheathed ram the galley was absurdly light, a racing shell of thin pine planking.

The man and woman walked to the bow, hand-in-hand, in silence. Adrian vaulted over into the cold water, caught Helga by the waist and lifted her down. She was a solid armful, with the light corselet on her and the rest of her kit. Arquebusiers of the Lightning Band handed down the servant he'd bought her in Chalice, and a light duffel.

"There's enough here to see you safely to Grand Harbor, and the Confed garrison there," he said, tucking a soft heavy purse of chamois leather into her belt pouch. "And . . ."

"And?" she asked, chin up.

"And I may not be the Confederacy's enemy forever," he said in a rush. "When—if—that happens, may I come to call?"

She smiled with a courage that wrenched at his heart. "Yes," she said. "I will so petition my father." A moment's urchin grin. "I told you what my marriage prospects are, didn't I?" Solemnly: "Stay alive, Adrian."

"I'll do my best. Yes, best I go. Gods go with you."

He watched the two figures walk up the beach, towards the tree-lined trail a hundred yards inland; it shone white in the moonlight, a wanderer's ribbon across the moor that bordered the sea here. Then he turned and accepted a hand; others boosted him back to the deck. He stood there, unspeaking, while the crew pushed off and the oars bit, backing water and turning the galley's prow to the west.

Esmond Gellert decided that the waiting was the hardest part.

The *Briny Kettle* was no warship, no sleek galley lavishly equipped with oars. She was a tub, a merchantman that carried grain and fish and oil and general cargo along the western coasts, out to the Islands, down south to the barbarian country. The only oars she had were half a dozen sweeps on a side, used only for working in and out of awkward ports. For the rest she was a deep-bellied teardrop, with a swan's head curving up over the quarterdeck and steering oars at the rear, one tall mast in the center, and bluff-cheeked bows up front. At five hundred tons she was quite large, and that and her high sides and substantial crew, plus a couple of dart-casters, was usually enough to discourage pirates. Longshore raiding paid better anyway, usually.

"Yeah, waiting's the worst," Donnuld Grayn said.

Esmond started slightly. "Hell, I didn't know I was talking."

The older mercenary grinned gap-toothed, and offered a skin of well-watered wine—one part to three. "This business, you spend most of the time being bored, and a few minutes out of every hour shitting yourself," he said philosophically. "When you're not being seasick, that is . . . this tub pitches worse than a galley."

The *Briny Kettle* carried no cargo but armed men; five hundred of them, packed like cured fish below decks, or lying flat on deck to ride concealed from anyone else—anyone, for instance, like the inspector in the little customs galley that was coming alongside. Its dozen oars easily matched the long slow rocking-horse pitch of the merchantman, avoiding the bows where a creamy V of white water pointed towards the low dark bulk of the city ahead. Reddish lights glimmered on the water from some of the lights there, and from masthead lanterns on the clustering ships docked to it, and from sentries pacing on the high crenellated walls.

"You're late, Sharlz," the official called out, holding up a lantern.

That glittered on the water, on his bald scalp and big-nosed face and on the gold hoop in one ear. He was an Islander himself, not a Confed—Preble was officially a free city in alliance with the Confederacy, although the Confed prefect here would have a lot more say than the council of magnates.

"Tide and wind and a woman's mind, Juluk," the captain said, scratching at his hairy chest where the open shirt showed a mat of grizzled hair; he was a very tall man, enormously tall for an Islander, and his nose was a beak that made even the customs officer's look moderate.

"Where from, this trip, and what cargo?"

"Chalice. Ornamental stone, fig brandy, dried tentacle fish and hot peppers, indigo in cakes, conqueror root, and coffee," he replied calmly.

"Ah. Any sign the King in the Isles is getting stroppy?"

"Not that I saw—but I keep my head out of such things."

"Well, good for you," the customs man said. "Keep it under seal until tomorrow, eh?"

"You eat shit too, Juluk—am I going to start breaking bulk in the middle of the night?"

"I could come aboard and inspect now, Sharlz."

Captain Thicelt unhooked a purse from his belt and tossed it across the gap that the customs boat's crew kept open with fending oars. "The usual sweetener—and you don't need to share it with your boss, out here."

"Not all of it," Juluk said, weighing it. "Sail on."

They came to the entrance of the narrow canal that split Preble from north to south—a natural channel between two skerries, when this had been a dwelling place of fliers and seabeasts, rather than men. A semicircle marked the harbor, wharves and jetties three-deep with ships, some as large as theirs, others of all sizes down to fishing smacks. Their masts made a lifeless, leafless tracery against the sky, an angular forest that creaked and rustled and swayed. Light died as ships and buildings dimmed moons and stars, and the clean smell of the sea gave way to the ever-present stink of a major port. Plops and rustlings came from the water, and once a pair of huge silvery eyes glinted—the scavengers that feasted on the filth, and inconvenient bodies, and drunks who fell off gangways at night.

"Strike sail," the captain of the *Briny Kettle* said, and turned to Esmond. The Emerald could see the sheen of sweat on his face by the dim reflected lights of lanterns and sky, and smell it. "Out sweeps to the canal entrance . . . All yours from here on, excellent sir General."

Esmond clapped him on the shoulder. "Good work," he said. "You've earned what the King pays you—and more besides. Don't forget to come and see me about it after the city's ours."

A grin split the tall Islander's face. "That I'm not shy about, you'll find, excellent sir."

Even this late at night dock-wallopers were ready with a team of heavy greatbeasts. They caught the cable the sailors threw, hitched their team, and began hauling the ship through the sea gates and into the town.

Paved roadways lined both sides of the canal, from one half-moon harbor to the other; behind them warehouses loomed, linked until they formed seawalls of their own, preventing any enemy from storming into the city from this open water. Heavy iron grills closed the occasional roadway that led deeper into the town; iron chains could close the canal at need, as well.

Men were waiting halfway down the length of the canal, men with shuttered lanterns that they blinked briefly. They surrounded the laborers, and Esmond caught a gleam in their hands—probably long knives in one, and gold in the other. He knew which he'd have taken if he was a sleepy municipal slave on night watch at the harbor. They backed away, followed by their bewildered greatbeasts, and more lines flew to the roadway. Willing hands grasped them, drew them tight. Timber crunched against stone.

"For the King and the gods," a voice called softly.

"For Prince Tenny and liberty," Esmond replied.

He vaulted easily from the rail to the pavement four feet below. "General Esmond Gellert, with the Prince's troops. You're ready?"

"Enry Sharbonow, Suffete of Preble. Ready and more than ready. This way."

Esmond turned. "Disembark according to plan," he called. "No shouting, and I'll geld the first man that breaks ranks!"

Except him, of course, he thought sourly, as Prince Tenny jumped ashore in a swirl of purple cloak and clash of silvered armor—plumed spired helmet, back-and-breast, engraved armguards . . . The half-dozen friends-cum-hangers-on he had with him were just as gorgeous, or had been before some of them got seasick. Tenny, to give him credit, didn't look nervous as some of them did, either. *Brave, or too stupid to understand the risks, or both,* Esmond thought.

The Prebleans went to one knee before the Prince. He smiled and signaled them to rise. "Be at ease, my friends," he said, in a trained orator's voice. "Soon the night of Confed tyranny will be lifted—as the sun rises, so will a new, independent city of Preble."

Several of the Preblean conspirators seemed inclined to answer the Prince's speech with ones of their own. Esmond was relieved to see that Enry wasn't one of them.

"Your Highness, welcome to your loyal city," he said. "This way, please—the garrison doesn't patrol, but they're not blind and *somebody* will alert them if we don't move quickly."

The Strikers had formed up rapidly, and with as little noise as five hundred armored men could when moving on flagstones in the dark. Esmond fell in at their head, beside the banner and the commander's runners. Donnuld Grayn grinned at him out of the side of his mouth.

"Think the Prince'll screw things up really bad?" he said, *sotto voce.*

"Hopefully, not until we've taken the town," Esmond said. "By the way, I wasn't joking about taking the balls of anyone who starts chasing coin or skirt."

Grayn nodded. "You'll have to take 'em off the man dead, after I'm through with him," he said. "Probably will be one or two idiots—keeping hired soldiers in line in an enemy town, at night, ain't going to be easy."

"This *isn't* an enemy town. It's supposed to be *our* town, and we're taking it from the Confeds."

Grayn's grin grew wide. "That's not a distinction your average trooper is real interested in," he said. "But they'll understand my boot up their backside—and don't worry, sir, they're not going to upset a good thing. You've won us a couple of hard fights now; if you say paint ourselves green and hop around like kermitoids, most of the men'll do it."

"They've got the gates *open*?" Donnuld said incredulously.

"Wouldn't have believed it either, if I hadn't seen it myself," Esmond said.

Enry Sharbonow coughed discreetly; he was a discreet man, middle-aged and slim, with a pointed beard and a small gold ring through his nose; the cutlass at his side looked to have seen some use, though.

"We arranged a party for the commandant and his officers," he said. "As proof of our loyalty to the Confederation, you might say. They're all away at the Town Guildhall right now. And we sent in a wagonload of wine and roast pigs and fairly high-priced girls so the men could have a good time too. Some of the girls are getting a bonus, and they saw to the door."

"Brilliant." Esmond grinned. "I hope you'll do as much for my men."

"Oh, of course, excellent sir," Enry said. "And we won't spike the wine with cane spirit, either."

Esmond laughed aloud. Colorless and tasteless, but if you tried to drink it like wine . . .

"All right," he said, unfolding a square of reed-paper. "Donnuld, Makin, as far as I can see there's nothing to prevent us going straight in the front gate. The barracks are in a square around a paved court with a well, the usual arrangement; Confed regulars on these two sides, this is the command block, and here's where the light infantry are stationed. Half of the men are out in the square, eating and boozing, and half are back in their barracks screwing their brains out, or vice versa. They've been at it for a couple of hours, more or less. Makin, you bottle up the light infantry. We'll try and get them to surrender. Donnuld, you take care of the men in the square. I'll secure the barracks and the headquarters."

It was no use trying to get Confed regulars to give up, unless they bashed their heads in first. That was one of the reasons Confed armies usually inflicted heavier losses than they suffered, even when they lost—they rarely ran away, and it was in rout and pursuit that the real killing was done. One could spear a running man in the back while chasing him, but he couldn't fight back.

He looked up at the Preblean conspirator. "What about the commandant and his staff?"

"Oh," Enry said, "I don't think you need worry, excellent sir."

Esmond winced mentally; the wine servers stepping up behind men relaxed and unwary, only this time with curved daggers in their hands, instead of flasks. That had happened to the commanders of a famous Emerald mercenary unit serving in Chalice, just after the Alliance Wars, although the men had mostly been able to fight their way out—quite an epic. In a way it was fortunate, reminding him of the thin crust he walked, over an active volcano. He was never safe here, never . . . and it was no consolation that the local magnates played the same game among themselves. They were Islanders; they *liked* it.

It was strange. He hadn't really been *happy* since Nanya died; but it wasn't like he was *numb*. He could still feel some things just as well; he could be afraid, anxious, angry . . . hatred was stronger than ever. It was as if some *section* of his psyche had been cauterized.

And I can still fight, he thought. And now he could fight Confeds, not just Islander pirates. *I was wrong. I can still be happy . . . in a way.*

He drew his sword. "Walking pace," he said. Men running were more alarming than men walking. "Follow me."

Esmond turned the corner, walking lightly on the slimed cobbles. The streets here were narrow between banks of four-storied tenement houses, canyons of darkness with only a narrow slit of stars and moons above. The bright lights from the Confed garrision buildings were almost blinding by comparison, although the broad square of light there was narrowing quickly.

"Shit—charge!" Esmond yelled.

So much for being subtle. The doors were still open, but they were swinging closed; a section of frowsy-looking Confed regulars was doing it, under the direction of a noncom, a brick-built bristle-headed graying man with legs and arms like gnarled, scar-slashed tree trunks. He was wearing a scarlet dress tunic rather than armor and transverse-crested helmet, but there was no mistaking exactly what he was—and drunk or sober, he wasn't going to leave that door open. It was sixty yards between the alley where the Strikers had been waiting and the barracks gate . . . they'd have plenty of time to drop the bar in place before the first Emerald mercenaries reached them. It wouldn't save them—the force had grappling hooks and ropes and the wall was low—but it would turn the battle into a bloody dogfight.

Esmond's body reacted with automatic reflex, turning his run sideways as the javelin went back over his right shoulder. One skipping sidestep, two, and arm and back and shoulder moved with the smooth inevitability of a machine. The javelin disappeared, arching up into the night. He'd practiced throwing at the mark, stationary and moving hoops, nearly every day of his life since he went into the boys' palaestra at six.

The Confed noncom looked up at the whistle of cloven air just before the long narrow steel head of the throwing spear punched into his throat above his breastbone. Eight inches of it disappeared, and the point crunched into his spine between the shoulderblades. He toppled like a cut tree, with only a single galvanic jerk as his heels came off the ground.

That paralyzed the men pushing at the door for a crucial two seconds; few of them had the noncom's experience, and they'd all been drinking wine much more potent than they thought it was. Time enough for twenty or thirty other Strikers to throw; they weren't Five Year Games victors, but they were closer, and there were a lot of them. Falling bodies knocked the gates wide again, and the Strikers burst through, roaring.

The courtyard had been set with trestle tables and lighted with tall iron tripods holding baskets of burning pinewood. Most of the Confed soldiers were sprawled about the picked-clean remnants of the pigs, bowls and cups in their hands, some of them with women in their laps, others watching a convoluted act involving four nude dancers and a very large trained snake. It took them gaping seconds to react, and none of them had weapons other than their eating knives at hand when hundreds of fully-armed alert soldiers poured through.

The first rank of Strikers launched their javelins and drew their swords; the second rank threw over their comrades' heads and plunged after them. Confed soldiers were dying—not only soldiers, Esmond vaulted over a whore in spangles and body paint, whimpering and pulling at the spear through her gut—and others were running, probably for their weapons. Some tried to make stands, grappling with the Emeralds or snatching up stools and eating utensils.

Esmond plunged through the chaos, over flagstones slippery with wine, spilled food, already wet with blood. Sword and buckler moved in clear, precise arcs; he seemed to be wading through honey, in a strange amber world in which everyone else moved very slowly, and he had more than enough time to do whatever was necessary. A solid wedge of men were following him, shields up and swords out. . . . A scrim of bodies marked the entrance to the barracks, men trying to get in, others trying to get out with snatched-up shields and assegais. The one in front of him stumbled and went down with a spear in his back, and then Esmond was facing an armed man at last.

The big shield with the crossed thunderbolts of Allfather of Vanbert on it—Allfather Greatest and Best—punched at him. The tip of the assegai glittered, held low and point-up for the gutting stroke. Esmond spun to the side, light on his feet as a dancer, hooking his buckler around the far edge of the oval shield and wrenching sideways to pin the Confed's spear arm against the frame of the door. His sword hilt went up high, like a beast fighter dispatching a greatbeast in the Vanbert arena after he'd teased it with the cape. The point punched down, in over the collarbone—unnecessary, the man hadn't had time to don his mail shirt, but you didn't think in a fight, you reacted on drilled reflex.

A wrench and jerk and the Confed went down. Esmond's foot and point snapped forward in a longe-lunge, skewered a thigh, pulled out with a twist to open the artery. He slammed his shoulder into another hastily-raised shield, and he was through the door. A Striker crowded through behind him, and in the dim light of the oil lamps he could see swarming confusion within, whores running and shrieking and the more sensible ones hiding under cots, men ripping weapons down from racks or stumbling in drunken bewilderment and getting in the way of their more sober comrades . . . and more of *his* men coming in the tall open windows. Barracks didn't run to glazing, but you wanted plenty of ventilation in this climate.

"*Strikers!*" he shouted. "*Strikers to me! Down Vanbert! Down Vanbert!*"

The Strikers were mercenaries, yes. They were also Emeralds almost to a man, and if there was one battle cry in all the world Emeralds could agree on, it was *that.*

Half an hour later, Esmond tucked his helmet under one arm and walked into the shrine room of the Confed headquarters, stepping over the bodies of the knot of men who'd died on its threshold. The slash on his thigh would make the leg stiffen in a little while, but for now he ignored it as he lifted out the ebony pole, with its golden wreath and hand and campaign-ribbons. He carried it himself onto the colonnaded porch that overlooked the courtyard, and the assembled Strikers roared his name as he held it high.

"Men!" he shouted, when the noise had died down a little. "So much for the invincible Confederacy!"

Another roar, with heartfelt emotion behind it this time. "Strikers," he went on. "We're soldiers loyal to our salt. But we're Emeralds, too. This—" he waved the standard "—has fouled the land of the Hundred Cities far too long. This war is against the Confederacy." A hush, then. "You know the gods favor my brother and me."

Nods. *Or at least, my brother's productively crazy . . . hands of the Shades, maybe the gods* do *talk to him. Something does.*

"The gods foretell the fate of the Confederacy—they tire of it. Vanbert shall *burn*!"

Wild cheers, and Donnuld Grayn looking at him with a raised eyebrow—the expression looked a little odd on the scarred, beaten-iron face.

"And think of the loot stacked up *there*," the mercenary shouted.

This time the cheers split the night.

((•)) ((•)) ((•))

"Where the hell were you?" Esmond asked.

"I had an errand to run," Adrian said, walking down the gangway.

Esmond peered behind him. "Where's Helga?"

"As I said, I had an errand," Adrian said, and forced a smile. "Look, let's forget about it, okay? Business."

"Certainly, brother," Esmond said. "This is Enry Sharbonow, Suttete of Preble, Chief Minister to the sovereign, Prince Tenny of Preble."

Adrian bowed, returning the Preblean magnate's more elaborate salute. "Everything went well? Where's the Prince?"

The northern dock of Preble was busy enough, although most of it seemed to be ships loading for departure—Adrian could see an entire household, from a portly robed merchant to veiled wives and a dozen children to skinny porters under huge bundles wrapped in rugs. They were scuttling up the gangplank of a freighter, and they were far from the only ones he could see. There was a smell of smoke in the air, as well.

"Things got a little out of hand," Esmond said. "There aren't many Confed civilians left in town, either. We're letting some of the non-Prebleans leave."

Enry spread his hands. "The Confeds are not—were not—popular here," he said.

Adrian nodded. They never were; the first thing that happened in a country taken under Confed "protection" was a tribute levy, and then officials to collect it. The Confed Council didn't like hiring bureaucrats much: too many opportunities for political patronage with implications at home. They put tribute and tax collection up for competitive bidding; that might not have been so bad, if it weren't for the fact that the successful bidders had no fixed fee. The winning syndicate made its profit by collecting whatever it could above the amount it had paid for the contract, with the Confed army to see that nobody objected. Then Confed merchants swarmed in, to buy up goods and property at knock-down prices as the locals frantically tried to raise cash, and Confed bankers to loan at fifty percent interest, compounded, to those who *couldn't* raise the cash. If anyone defaulted on the loan, they'd sell every stick and rag he had, and march him off to the auction block, and he'd find himself hoeing beans on some Confed Councillor's estate outside Vanbert.

The nod was general; everyone knew how the system worked. "Funny," Adrian said. "The Confed peasants go into the army, because they can't compete with the big slave-worked estates . . . then they go out and get the Councillors the money and slaves they need to set up the estates in the first palace."

"Nice work if you can get it," Donnuld Grayn said. "Meantime the civvies ran down and killed maybe a thousand of 'em last night, once word got around we'd taken out the garrison." He smiled, a nasty expression. "Sort of commits 'em, don't it? What's that Confed saying?"

" 'I am a Confed citizen; let kings tremble,' " Adrian said. "They're *not* going to be happy at a massacre."

Enry Sharbonow shrugged. "I put my arse above the stake when I enlisted in Prince Tenny's cause," he said. "Now everyone else in town is in the same boat."

"Where's Prince Tenny?" Adrian asked.

Enry coughed discreetly; it seemed to be his favorite expression. "He is occupied with setting up the Royal household," he said. "In his mercy, he has decided to take into his hareem the now-protectorless females of the Confed commandant and his officers, or some of them."

Adrian winced slightly. ***One of the drawbacks of this business,*** Raj said at the back of his mind, ***is that you usually end up working for some son of a bitch. Politics attracts them.***

"Well, we've got business to attend to," Adrian said. "I suppose I should start setting up the artillery?"

"Too right," Esmond said. "I don't think the Confeds are going to wait long to try a counterattack—some refugees will have made it out, over the wall and swimming if no other way."

"Sir!" One of the Strikers came up, panting. "Lord Esmond, Confed troops are putting out in small craft from the shore—barges, some ladders."

Enry made a small, appalled sound. Esmond nodded. "Numbers?"

"Fifteen hundred, sir."

The blond Emerald slapped Enry on the back. "Not to worry. That's the local commander, trying it on in case this is just some sort of pirate raid. Your militia ought to be able to see them off; there's seven or eight thousand of them."

"If they turn out," Enry said, taking a deep breath.

"Wait for it," Adrian said.

"Sor," Simun whispered back, "why don't we have the arquebuses up here? They're such *lovely* targets!"

technological surprise, Center whispered. **you may define this as—**

"Because we don't want them to know about the arquebuses until we really need them," Adrian said.

"They'll have heard."

"That's not the same thing as seeing something for yourself."

The landward edge of Preble had a narrow strip of sand studded with crags and boulders below the city wall, which was big ashlar blocks, enclosing a concrete and rubble core. It was crowded with men now, crouching down below the crenellations or behind the tarpaulin-covered torsion catapults. They were keeping surprisingly quiet, for civilians; nervously fingering bows, spears and slings, but not talking much. Esmond's Strikers probably had something to do with that; they'd kicked and clubbed a few noisy ones into unconsciousness to begin with.

Adrian turned his eyes from the mass of robed figures, from gleams of starlight and moonlight on eyes, teeth, the edge of a blade, out to the sea. The Confed flotilla was led by two light war galleys, each towing a string of barges; for the rest there were fishing boats, small coastal traders, a merchantman or two. They were crowded with men as well, probably the local coastal garrison; this area had been taken away from the Islanders by Marcomann only a decade or so ago, and it still resented Confed rule.

He turned to his brother. "Wasn't there a military colony around here?"

Esmond nodded. "Paid-off Marcomann veterans," he said.

"Allied Rights settlement. I wouldn't be surprised if the governor had mobilized them."

Adrian nodded in turn; that was what a military colony was for, after all. They'd be ready enough, too; a successful revolt would let locals who'd had their land confiscated to make farms for the ex-soldiers get their own back, literally and metaphorically.

The ships were close enough to hear the rhythmic grunting of the oarsmen under the creak of rigging and wood. Adrian peered into the darkness, and suddenly it took on a flat silvery-green light.

"They've got ladders on those galleys," he said. "And on the barges—ladders with iron hooks on the ends. And what look like modified catapults. I'd say they're rigged to throw grapnels with rope ladders attached."

Esmond grunted. "Standard operating procedure," he said. "Looks like the local commander really is going to chance the walls being lightly held." He cocked a sardonic eye at the militiamen. "Enry has earned his corn—I hope King Casull is paying him generously. He's had agents out all day, pointing out to the locals exactly what'll happen to them if the Confeds retake a city where six or seven hundred Confed citizens were massacred."

"Forward, sons of the Emerald! You fight for your homes and families, for the ashes of your fathers and the temples of your gods!"

The poet had said that about the League Wars, when the Emerald cities had turned back the Kings of the Isles. It was just as true here. In the open field, all the determination in the world wouldn't have stopped the Confed's armor and discipline; but fighting behind a wall, all the militiamen really needed to do was not run away.

"Ready," Esmond said. "Ready . . ."

The barges were coming forward, awkwardly, the oarsmen too cramped to pull efficiently. The square raftlike craft dipped at the bows, as armored men crowded forward with the ladders.

"Now!" He stood, waving a torch—three times, back and forth.

Brass trumpets rang along the wall. The men of Preble—sailors, craftsmen, shopkeepers—stood and shot. Arrows hissed out towards the Confed troops in a dark blurring rush, hard to see in the faint light, but appallingly thick. Flights of javelins followed, not very well thrown but very numerous, and sling-bullets, rocks, cobblestones. The Confed troops roared anger and surprise, with a chorus of screams from wounded men under it. Shields snapped up in tortoise formation, overlapping. At this distance some arrows drove right through the thick leather and plywood; rocks broke arms beneath them, crushed helmets. The catapults on the wall and its towers fired their four-foot arrows, pinning men together three in a row. A rock hurler sent a fifty-pound lump of granite skimming over the quarterdeck of one of the galleys, taking off the head of the captain as neatly as an axe and crushing the steersman against the tiller.

"Damn, they're still coming," Esmond said.

Men picked up the ladders of the fallen and ran them forward; others set the points of assegais against oarsmen's backs, to encourage them to keep rowing. Others beached their craft and jumped ashore, whirling grappling irons. A ladder thumped home against the crenellations of the wall, and then another. Men toppled off the rungs, and others replaced them; archers and slingers were replying from the invasion craft, concentrating their weaker fire on the crucial space around the heads of the ladders.

Four militamen came hurrying past Adrian, their rag-wrapped hands on the carrying handles of a huge bronze pot that had been bubbling quietly over a charcoal brazier. Adrian swallowed at the familiar scent of hot olive oil.

They reached the parapet and heaved the cauldron up, poured. The screams from below were unearthly loud and shrill, as the boiling oil ran over men's faces and through the links of their mail shirts. He could see Confed troopers throwing themselves into the ocean and drowning as they tried to extinguish the clinging agony.

"All right, Lightning Band," he called in a high carrying voice. "Let's see them off."

Adrian stepped up to the parapet, taking a grenade out of his satchel and lighting the fuse. One of the galleys was not far away below, more Confed troopers clambering over the pile of dead men in the bows to reach the grapnel-throwing catapult. Adrian waited a second for the fuse to catch fairly and then lobbed it overhand, an easy throw. The sputtering red spark of the fuse arched through the night; the clump of men suddenly turned white as faces went up to see what was coming at them.

With malignant, unplanned precision the grenade burst just above head-height, sending fragments slicing into the faces. Men scattered, screaming. Other red sparks were arching out from the wall, lobbed by hand or thrown with the sling at craft still trying to come up to the wall. Adrian threw two more; one rolled under the quarterdeck of the galley, and when it burst, pine planks shattered and began to burn. Several others of the invasion flotilla were burning as well, lighting the surface of water dotted with the heads of swimmers and men clinging to bits of wreckage—those must be oarsmen and sailors; anyone who went over the side in sixty pounds of armor wasn't coming ashore unless he walked along the bottom.

"Go back, you fool! Get your men out of here!" Esmond was shouting as he threw another javelin. "Order a retreat, gods condemn you!"

Adrian listened to the voices at the rear of his mind. "Their commander is probably dead," he said grimly. "There's nobody to order a retreat, and his underofficers are operating on their last instructions—press the attack."

"Wodep!" Esmond said. His eyes on the carnage below were full of a horrified pleasure. Adrian could read the thoughts on the shadowed face: *They're Confeds. But they're brave men, too.*

Even Confed discipline could take only so much. One by one the barges and fishing boats backed away, set sail or began to thrash the surface of the narrow channel with frantic oars. On a few of the craft fighting broke out, men who wanted to live in frantic close-quarter struggles with those determined to follow their orders regardless. Neither of the galleys was going anywhere; they were both outlines of yellow flame on the dark water, with men going up like torches or jumping overside. Some climbed the masts, scrambling frantically higher as the flames licked at their heels, screaming as the rigging burned through and the pine poles toppled over towards the water. Some of the water was burning too, pools of olive oil flickering with sullen orange-red.

"Gray-Eyed Lady," Adrian whispered.

The screams from below were drowned by the cheers of the militia, dancing and shrieking their relief and incredulous joy at beating back the Confed attack. They capered along the parapet, shaking fists and weapons, some lifting their robes and waggling and slapping their buttocks at the retreating enemy. The narrow strip of beach and rock below the walls was black with a carpet of men, a carpet that still crawled and moaned slightly. Adrian looked up at the stars for relief from the sight, and started.

"It's a full hour," he said wonderingly. "I'd thought fifteen minutes, thirty at the outside."

"Time flies when you're havin' fun," Simun said beside him, shaking and blowing on a hand scorched by a fuse that burned too fast. "We ought to get some men down the wall, sor—salvage them mail shirts 'n helmets. Better than some of our lads have—better than almost anything the milita here got. Must be seven, eight hundred we could get at."

"I suppose so," Adrian said quietly, looking down. *If you can accomplish the work, you should be able to look at the results,* he told himself.

"Victory!" Enry Sharbonow said, coming by with a train of servants carrying wineskins. "Oh, excellent sir, honorable sir—here, have a drink."

Adrian took a flask, swallowing rough red wine, unwatered.

"A great victory," the Preblean said.

Esmond lowered his own skin, looking around at the cheering milita; his own men were cheerful enough, but much quieter as they leaned against the parapet and watched the Confeds flee.

"I'd call it more of a skirmish," he said. "Come and tell me about our victory in a month or two."

CHAPTER EIGHT

"Sun-stabbed by spears of *brazen* light," Speaker Emeritus Jeschonyk said. "*Brazen*, you see. Not *bronze light*."

One of his aides frowned. "That would be an irregular use of the pluperfect, though, wouldn't it?"

A babble of controversy erupted in the hot beige gloom of the command tent. Justiciar Demansk cleared his throat.

"Speaker," he said. Eyes turned towards him. "I think it's a dialect form, actually—Windrush Plain Emerald, archaic, of course." It would have to be; the poem they were discussing was eight hundred years old, an epic on the Thousand Ships War. Bits and pieces of it might go *back* to the Thousand Ships War, half a millennium before the poet. "In any case, Speaker, I think that at the moment we have more pressing, if banausic, concerns."

"By all means, Justiciar," the Speaker sighed, willing to listen to reason. He was a square-faced square-shouldered man, dressed in the purple-edged wrapped robe of his office, in his sixties, not a soldier recently himself, but still vigorous. "What do you recommend?"

When Demansk ducked outside the tent, one of his aides fell into step beside him. The man was a hundred-commander technically, but also First Spear of Demansk's First Regiment, the highest slot that a promoted ranker could reach. Within, it sounded as if they'd gone back to the irregular pluperfect. *Sometimes I wish we'd never let the Emeralds civilize us,* Demansk thought. *Particularly, I wish they'd never taught us literary criticism.* Rhetoric might be the foundation of civility—everyone agreed on that—but it did get in the way, sometimes.

"Get 'em to discuss business, sir?" he said, his voice still slightly rough with the accent of a peasant from the eastern valleys.

"More or less. We're putting in an attack as soon as we can get a causeway built. It's only half a mile, and shallow water. Meanwhile we'll get the fleet in Grand Harbor operational."

The promoted ranker shrugged mail-clad shoulders. "You get my men on solid ground next to the enemy and we'll thrash the wogs as soon as we get stuck into 'em, sir," he said. "But by the belly of Gellerix, we can't walk on water—or swim in armor, either. Not half a mile, not a hundred fucking yards, sir."

They reached the gate and took the salute of the watch platoon; Demansk trotted easily up the rough log stairs to the top of the openwork wooden tower, the left of the pair that flanked the gate. From there he could see out to Preble—the Speaker's camp was on the shore opposite the fortified island. One of the small ships the local commander had used in his abortive attempt to retake the city was still burning on a sandbank directly below the city walls. *Not encouraging.*

The camp itself *was*. Jeschonyk had brought four brigades, twenty thousand citizen troops, regulars, and nearly as many auxiliaries—slingers and archers and light infantry, of course; cavalry wasn't going to be much use here and he'd mobilized only enough for patrolling and foraging. The camp was a huge version of the usual marching fortress that a Confed force erected every night; a giant square cut into the soft loam of the coastal plain, with a ditch twelve feet deep and ten feet wide all around the perimeter. The earth from the ditch had been heaped up into a wall all around the interior, and on top of that were stakes pegged and fastened with woven willow. Each wall had a gate in the middle, flanked by log towers and guarded by a full company. Sentries patrolled the perimeter, and the rest of the men were hard at work. Four broad streets met in a central square for the command tent and unit standard shrines, and working parties were grading them, laying a pavement of cobbles and pounding it down, cutting drainage ditches along a gridwork throughout the camp. Orderly rows of leather tents were up, the standard eight-man issue for each squad; picket lines set out for the draught animals; deep latrines dug; even a bathhouse erected. Smiths and leatherworkers and armorers were already hard at work, repairing equipment and preparing for the siege works.

Demansk felt a surge of pride; this whole great city, this expression of human will and intelligence and capacity for order and civilization, was the casual daily accomplishment of a Confed army. If they were ordered to move, they'd take it all down before breakfast muster—no use presenting an enemy with a fortress—and do the same again the next evening after a full day's march. And if they were here for a couple of months, it would be a city in truth—paved streets, sewers, stone buildings.

Then he turned and looked at Preble. *I hate sieges.* Sieges were an elaborate form of frontal attack, which was a good way to waste men at the best of times. With a siege, all the Confed army's advantages of flexiblity and articulation were lost. Against an Emerald phalanx . . . well, you didn't have to run up against the pikepoints. Draw them onto broken ground, have small parties work in along their flanks, disrupt them—then they were yours. Islanders were like quicksilver; if you could get them to stand still for a moment, a hammer blow spattered them, no staying power. But behind a stone wall, even a townsman with a spear could become a hero. You had to go straight at him, and climbing a ladder left you virtually defenseless.

If we can get the causeway close, we can batter the wall down with catapults. The problem with that was that the defenders could shore it up, or build a secondary wall within while you were battering—ready to mousetrap you as you charged in over the rubble. *Or we could undermine, use sappers . . . The butcher's bill is still going to be fearsome. And if it takes too long, we'll get disease, sure as the gods made the grapes ripen, we'll have disease.* That *really* frightened him. He'd seen dysentery go through armies like the Sword of Wodep too many times.

"Sir!"

An aide came trotting up. "Sir, Justiciar Demansk—we've got a . . . a person, sir, who claims to have urgent news."

Demansk's eyebrows went up towards the receding line of his close-cropped grizzled hair. "A *person*?" he said.

"Claims to be a relative of yours, sir." The aide's aristocratic features curled slightly in disdain. "On the off chance that they might have some information I didn't have them whipped out of the camp, sir."

The Justiciar lowered the hand he'd been shading his eyes with as he peered towards Preble. "By all means, let's see this . . . person . . ." he said.

Anything that could distract me from this would be welcome. Even a dancing ape.

A small slight man came trotting up the log stairs of the tower, with an Islander woman at his heels. *No, wait a minute,* he thought. He looked at bare legs and arms, at the way the stranger walked. *That's not a man, it's a woman in armor.* What looked like Emerald light-infantry kit, bowl helmet with cheekguards, linen corselet with brass shoulderpieces and probably iron scales between the layers of cloth. A trooper was carrying a sword and shield and pair of light javelins behind them, puffing along. . . .

This *was* out of the ordinary. Then the stranger took off her helmet, and long tawny-auburn hair fell free, nearly to her waist.

Demansk's eyes went wide. "Helga!" he said . . . almost sputterings.

"Father!"

"What are they doing?" Enry Sharbonow said, squinting.

"They're getting ready to build a causeway," Esmond said. He pointed. "See, they've got a good hard-surfaced road right down to the water's edge. They've almost certainly got local pilots and fishermen who can tell them exactly what the shoals are like. Now they're starting. See those lines of log pilings, a hundred yards apart? Those mark the edges. Between them, they've got working parties, their troops and whatever civilians they can round up, unloading those oxcarts full of rock—boulders, up to sixty pounds. See how they're passing them hand to hand? They'll pile those up until they get above the surface, compact them, then cover with a layer of smaller rock. By the time it's safely above high-tide level, they'll have a section of first-class paved road."

Enry swallowed. A little beyond him Prince Tenny lounged with elaborate unconcern, nibbling on a honeyed fig and fingering a set of healing scratches along one side of his bearded face.

"And those wooden things they're building, a little further back?"

"Well, that's a little far to see, but I'd say they're probably siege engines. Catapults, of course, heavy ones. Siege towers—wooden fort towers on wheels, covered in hides or possibly metal plates, so they can roll them up to our walls and climb protected. Solophonic ladders—big counterweighted things like a covered bridge on a pivot, sort of the same thing. Fire raisers. Metal-shod battering rams under heavy roofs, also on wheels, for forcing a breach. When they get the causeway close enough, they'll use the catapults and archers to keep our heads down while they complete it—batter a hole in the wall, if they can. If they can't, they'll roll the Solophons and siege towers up to the wall and storm it, while the battering rams knock sections of it down and make ramps for their assault troops."

Enry's natural olive skin had gone very pale, a sort of doughy white color. "What are we going to *do*?" he said.

Esmond took a fig from the silver tray being held up for Tenny, popped it into his mouth and chewed with relish. "Oh, there are a few tricks we can try," he said cheerfully, and cocked an eye at the sky. "No moons tonight."

"You shouldn't be here," Esmond hissed into the darkness.

"Neither should you," Adrian said.

"Sirs, with respect, shut the fuck up," Donnuld Grayn said, pausing as he tightened the strap on a greave. "We're getting close."

We shouldn't, Esmond thought. *Typical Confed arrogance.* When they sat down to besiege a place, they expected the defenders to sit tight and cower, waiting for inevitable doom, so what point was there in taking elaborate precautions?

At least, that was what the Preblean scouts had said, swimming in after sculling across the strait on inflated sheepskins. None of them had been caught, so either the Confeds were extremely confident or fiendishly clever at misdirection.

Esmond showed teeth, white in the darkness against skin covered with burnt cork. *Now,* fiendishly clever *is something that might be applied to an Emerald, or even an Islander. But to a Confed? No, no* . . . systematic, *yes.* Methodical, *yes. But fiendishly clever? Rarely.*

"I'll show them fiendish," he whispered, chuckling, and looked back along the boat.

It was about thirty feet long, the Preblean sailors at the muffled oars, the men his own Strikers with some of Adrian's specialists for luck. That dampened his mood, slightly. He might have known that Adrian wouldn't send his men along and not go himself; he wasn't a professional, but he thought like one, sometimes—as if soldiers' ghosts were whispering in his ear.

That checked him for a moment. *I suppose I* am *a professional now,* he thought. Not an athlete or a weapons trainer, but a general. *But not a mercenary. I have a cause.*

"Row off," the Preblean at the tiller oar said softly. "Row soft, all . . . raise oars and let her glide. *Not* raise it upright, Rawl, you stupid bastard; ten lashes for that."

The high timber wall of the causeway's edge loomed ahead of them. The Confeds had driven the logs into the sand and mud of the channel bed at an angle, slanting outwards. That made it easier to climb as the boat came alongside; he leapt, got a grip, swarmed upwards. Rope nooses flew up from his and the other boats, but Esmond ignored them as he poised crouching at the top. According to the scouts' reports, the sentry ought to be . . .

There. Pacing stolidly along, and no more than fifteen paces away, now. *Have to get him to turn around.*

"Hey, you Confed donkey fucker," Esmond said, in a conversational tone. "Did you know that your mother used to suck my dad's dick, and for free?"

Thc Confed soldier whirled at the sound, gaping. Esmond's arm whipped forward; it was an awkward position to throw from, but a clout shot at this distance—there were fires in iron baskets further in towards the shore. Iron crunched through the mail shirt the trooper wore, and he pitched over backwards. Esmond dropped four feet to the surface of the causeway; this section was half-complete, and loose rock shifted and crunched under the hobnails of his sandals.

The sentries died, quickly and with relative quiet. Men were forming up around him; others were coating the logs that ran along both sides of the causeway with oil and tallow brought along in leather sacks. More were handing up small wooden barrels from the boats.

"Ready, General," Donnuld panted.

"Follow me."

The Strikers followed. Behind them were Preblean archers; he'd picked them himself, from men with good sea-beast hornbows and plenty of experience. Forward . . . *Yes. They really didn't fortify their construction yard.*

Siege engines reared about him in the dark, like monstrous beasts in a child's nightmare. More sentries died, but a few survived long enough to sound an alarm. They'd have to work quickly.

Adrian and his men ran to the larger engines, the siege towers and heavy catapults. The kegs of gunpowder went underneath them, hastily buried. Esmond let his nose guide him to stacks of timber, mostly fresh-cut pine oozing sap.

"Right here, boys," he called.

Covered firepots were brought out, torches lit and whipped into flame. Esmond thrust one under a stack of four-by-six timbers and shouted glee as the wood began to catch. Others of his men were kicking over barrels and pots of pitch and tar, throwing long coils of rope onto growing blazes; the archers were sending fire-arrows buzzing about, into piles of cordage and wood further in, into tents and heaps of sailcloth and fodder. Esmond was whirling another torch around his head when a lead-weighted dart whipped by his ear close enough for him to feel the draft, going *thunk* into a timber and whining with a malignant buzz like an enormous, very pissed-off bee.

"Fall in!" he called. Beside him the signaler sounded his horn, and the bannerman waved the flag. "Fall in! Everyone else back to the boats!"

The Strikers formed up at the head of the causeway—most of them, at least, and anyone too hopped up or too stupid to remember the signals he'd gone over at great length deserved what was going to happen to them. Happy arsonists ran by, climbing the wooden edges of the causeway and sliding down to the boats or into the water, whooping. The Confeds were reacting at last, though; he could see blocks of them working their way through the burning equipment, and the fires were making this area as bright as day.

"Discourage them," he said to the Preblean in charge of the archers. The man nodded and turned to his own command: "Loose!"

The archers drew to the ear, thumbrings around the strings of their powerful composite bows. A cloud of yardlong shafts whickered out, vanishing from sight into the darkness and smoke above, then whipping back down into the gathering Confed ranks. A dozen men went down, silent or jerking or screaming and ripping at the barbed shafts in their flesh. More shrugged aside slight wounds, or started when armor or shields deflected the steel raining down out of the night.

"Keep it up," Esmond said, teeth showing. "Pour it on!"

The Confed noncoms were hustling their sleepy men into battle order, shoving, bellowing orders. The formation began to shake itself out into the dreaded double line of the Confederation, shields up, darts rocking back ready on thick muscular peasant arms. Here and there a man fell as an arrow or slingstone went home, and the formation rippled as it closed up to maintain the precise one-yard gap between each soldier. In a minute, that living wall would begin to walk . . .

Except that in less than a minute . . .

BWAMMMP.

"Yes!" Esmond shouted.

Dirt, flame and splintered wood vomited up from beneath one of the siege towers. Shattered along one side it began to sway, leaned drunkenly, and then fell—four stories of heavy timber, crashing down across the back of the Confed formation.

About three hundred of them, Esmond thought. *But—*

BWAMMMP.

The other siege tower writhed as half a dozen ten-pound kegs of powder went off beneath it; this one disintegrated where it stood, showering the wavering Confed troops with heavy bone-cracking lumps and baulks of timber.

"*Charge!*" Esmond shouted.

The trumpeter sounded it, but the Strikers were already running forward, howling. A cloud of javelins surged out before them, and the archers fired over their heads. When they struck the Confeds, they struck in a solid line abreast, struck men whose formation had already been shaken. A rippling series of explosions shook their nerve even more, as catapults leapt into the air in fragments and rained down out of the dark.

"Wodep's thunderbolts!" a Confed trooper bawled, and threw down his shield.

The noncom behind him killed the man before he'd taken his second panic-stricken step, but then the Emeralds were upon them. Esmond threw at point-blank range, and the javelin crunched through the Confed's face to knock his helmet off as the point met the inside rear with an audible *clank*. He punched his buckler into another face, stabbed a throat, brought the buckler around to break the wrist that held an assegai and then stab downward into a thigh. The Confeds shattered the way a clay winejug might when dropped on solid stone . . . and spattered red in the same way, too.

"Rally!" Esmond shouted, and the trumpeter blew it again and again. Some of the men were reluctant; one or two were so victory-drunk that they careened off into the darkness. "Rally!"

"Fall back to the boats," he went on.

"Feels good to see their backs, by Wodep," Donnuld said, as they jogged back.

Behind them the Confed siege works and timber stores were fully involved, a cone of bright orange flame rising into the spark-shot night and underlighting its own black cloud of smoke. *Glorious, glorious destruction,* Esmond thought, feeling the savage heat of it on his face.

They reached the edge of the causeway, slid down into the boats.

Esmond took a torch and tossed it at the oil-soaked wood as they left; flames ran across the timbers in a sheet of orange-red, adding to the hellish symphony of flames.

"It won't be as easy the next time," he said, chuckling. "But I think we'll come up with some way to annoy them."

He started as Adrian nodded beside him. "We haven't shown them most of our surprises yet," he said. "*Technological* surprise."

"What's technology?" Esmond asked, curious.

"That's what the Confeds are about to find out, brother."

"What am I going to do with you?" Demansk asked his daughter.

She lounged back in the camp chair and sipped from her clay cup. "Velipad piss . . . well, you're not going to marry me off, not after all this."

Demansk flushed and hit the table with a fist, making the jug bounce. "You don't speak to your father like that, missy!" he growled, his voice filling the tent like a direbeast's warning. "And a tent is not a place to discuss family matters at this volume."

They were both speaking Emerald, but so could any Confed citizen with any pretensions to education. The ranker guards outside probably couldn't, and there probably wasn't anyone else within earshot . . . probably.

"Sorry, Father," Helga said, dropping her eyes. "I'm just trying to put the best possible face on it."

Demansk sighed and rubbed a hand over the gray-and-brown stubble on his chin. Small insects were coming through the laced opening of his tent and immolating themselves in the oil lamps with small *spppt* sounds and a disagreeable smell; the scent triggered old memories of camps, running back to his earliest manhood. Helga had been conceived in a tent like this, to his second wife; she'd accompanied him on several campaigns down around the southern border, when he'd been one of the senior officers overseeing the building of the wall against the barbarians.

"Your mother was a lot like you," he said heavily. "Perhaps if she'd lived . . . maybe that's why I've indulged you so. Too much, probably."

He sighed again; with commendable self-command, Helga held her piece. "Oh, we could patch up some sort of match. . . ."

"You'd have to pay heavily, and I wouldn't be getting any prize, Father. I'd rather be a spinster. It isn't as if you don't have grandchildren already, and besides . . ."

"Besides, there's this pirate," Demansk said dryly.

"He's not a pirate!"

"Mercenary, then," Demansk said, with a slight wry smile. "Emerald rebel, surely."

"Redvers was the rebel, and he was Adrian Gellert's patron," Helga said reasonably. "A client has to follow his patron, doesn't he?"

"Well, that's the tradition." Demansk gestured at the wine jug, and Helga poured for them both again, adding dippers of water from the bigger clay vase by the door. "I think sometimes it would be better for the State if it wasn't."

Helga chuckled. "Father, you're not rebelling against the Customs of the Ancestors yourself, now?"

"Our Ancestors were a bunch of pig farmers," Demansk said bluntly. "My grandfather used to be out every day, weeding the fields beside his slaves. Times have changed; Audsley's rebellion, Marcomann's dictatorship, the proscriptions . . . things are falling apart." His gaze sharpened. "And evidently my daughter has been driven mad by a scratch from one of the cats that draws Gellerix's chariot, and has become besotted with a rebel."

Helga shook her head. "Adrian's not . . . not really a rebel. His brother, Esmond, yes—Esmond would bring the whole Confederacy down in ruins, and everyone in it, I think, if he could. Adrian's more . . . reasonable."

"Reasonable and learned," Demansk said, keeping his voice casual. "He's the one that came up with this damnable hellpowder stuff, isn't he?"

Helga laughed ruefully. "You know, Father, the reason Adrian put me ashore was that he didn't want me to be forced to betray the Confederacy. And here you are, trying to worm *his* secrets out of me! I'm between the mad velipad and the direbeast."

"If you don't want to talk about it . . . I suppose I *do* owe this man something for getting you out of Vase, and for putting you ashore."

"There's not much for me to say," Helga said. "I don't know how the hellpowder is made—Adrian didn't tell me, and it's a close-kept secret. So are the other weapons."

"Other weapons?" Demansk said sharply.

"There were all sorts of rumors, and I *saw* what happened in Vase—the city wall pounded to rubble, and the gates of the citadel smashed like kindling."

"Hmmm." Demansk rubbed his chin again. "I suppose . . . larger barrels of hellpowder thrown by catapults? That *could* get nasty, very nasty, especially in siege operations, or at sea—and here we're faced with both!" He slammed a fist into the arm of the folding camp chair, hard enough to make the tough wood and leather creak. "I spend my whole life learning the trade of war—not leaving it to the underofficers, but really *learning* it, the way Marcomann did, damn his soul to the Ash Fields—and this whippersnapper of an Emerald turns it upside down, all at once. A *philosopher*, a rhetorician!"

"Father . . . I don't think Adrian really *is* a rhetorician, not anymore. He studied rhetoric, and he's very good at it . . . but what he mostly seems to be interested in now is . . . is the . . . way the world's put together."

Demansk's eyebrows shot up. "A *natural* philosopher? Hmmm. There haven't been any of those since the League Wars! If this hellpowder is what comes of it, I'm glad there hasn't been. Still, the wine's out of the jug now, no use trying to put it back." His shrewd green eyes fastened on his daughter's face. "Just what do you think this Adrian fellow will do, facing us now."

"Facing *you* now," Helga snorted. "Jeschonyk couldn't find . . . what's the soldier's expression?"

Couldn't find his dick with both hands and a hooker to help, Demansk thought automatically. Still, however much of a tomboy she was, there were things you didn't say to a daughter.

"Couldn't find his arse with both hands on a dark night," he chuckled aloud. "Not quite fair. He has enough sense to leave details to experts, and he *listens* . . . occasionally. But he's set in his ways even for a man of his generation. And I asked you a question, missy."

Helga's chin went up. "Adrian will do what you least expect, and when you least expect it," she said proudly. "His brother's a good soldier and a demon with a sword but Adrian . . . thinks about things."

Demansk shuddered, a little theatrically. "Allfather Greatest and Best, this business is bad enough without *scholarship*," he said, and then cocked an eye. "Rumor has it that the gods talk to your Adrian."

He hid his surprise when Helga looked distinctly uneasy; she was as skeptical as any young noble—the way the younger generation openly said things that were whispered in his younger days shocked him, now and then. In his grandfather's day they'd been killing matters.

"I'm . . . not altogether sure about that," Helga said. "Sometimes . . . sometimes I'd catch him murmuring to *somebody*. Somebody who wasn't there."

Demansk grunted. "Perhaps he's mad, then."

"I don't think so, Father. Madmen hear voices, but if Adrian's listening, it's to someone who tells him things that are *true*. Or at least very useful."

That's a point, a distinct point, Demansk thought.

He was lifting the cup to his lips when the alarm sounded out across the camp.

CHAPTER NINE

"This time they're being cautious," Esmond said, bracing his feet automatically against the pitch and roll of the ship.

"How so?" Adrian said curiously, peering towards the shore, where the causeway swarmed with workers and troops, like a human anthill.

"They're putting in a wall with a parapet and fighting platform along the edge of the causeway as it goes out, see? And they've got their building yard completely surrounded with a ditch-and-stockade, *and* they've brought out those two fighting towers—they'll push them out as the causeway proceeds. The catapults on them outrange anything a ship can mount, and they've got archers packed tight in there too. They can shoot from shelter."

"Hmmm," Adrian said. "*Not* good, brother."

similar situations tend to produce similar solutions, Center said.

Meaning what?

Center tends to get a little oracular now and then, son, Raj thought with a chuckle.

Well, that's appropriate.

What he—or it—means is that this isn't the first time these tactical conditions have come up. Back on Bellevue, I got a

reputation for originality partly because Center kept feeding me things that other generals had done, back on Earth before spaceflight. I've studied more since Center and I have been . . . together. There was a man named Alexander . . .

"Adrian? *Adrian?*"

Adrian shook himself, stopped squinting at the eye-hurting brightness of water on the purple-blue sea, and looked at his brother.

"Sorry."

"I know Scholars of the Grove are supposed to be detached, but we have a *problem* here." A scowl of frustration. "Or are you still mooning over that Confed girl?"

"Yes, but that doesn't mean I can't think of practical matters," Adrian said, slightly annoyed.

I've been getting that detached *business since I was fourteen,* he thought. One of the earlier Scholars had had the same problem from his family, and had cornered the olive-oil market for a year, just to prove a philosopher could also outthink ordinary men in ordinary affairs.

"Don't think of it as a *problem,*" Adrian went on aloud, with a smile he knew was a little smug. "Think of it as an *opportunity.*"

He began to speak. Esmond's eyes narrowed, then went wide. When he'd finished, the older Gellert spoke:

"Well, I will be damned to pushing a boulder up a hill for all eternity. That *just* might work—and it's a little longer before we have to let them know about the rest of your surprises. Captain!"

Sharlz Thicelt hurried over. "Sir?" he said.

Esmond looked up, frowning a little—there were few men taller than he—and spoke:

"What are the prevailing winds like here, this time of year?"

"My General, they vary. Usually from the northwest, particularly in the afternoons—an onshore breeze, very tricky. It dies at night and backs in the morning, though. Of course, the Sun God alone can predict the weather on any given day; at times there are strong offshore winds, particularly if we get a summer thunderstorm, and—"

"Thank you very much, Captain Thicelt," Esmond said hastily;

the Islander loved the sound of his own voice—something of a national failing in the Islands as well as the Emerald cities. "That may be very useful. Very useful indeed."

"Odd," Justiciar Demansk said, shading his eyes with one hand. "Those look like merchantmen."

The causeway had made two hundred yards progress, and the siege towers were half that distance from shore. Already the inner surface looked like a paved city street, flanked by fortress walls; attempts at hit-and-run sniping hadn't been more than a nuisance. *And we've sunk one of their galleys.* That had been the stone throwers on the siege towers. Nine stories of height made a considerable difference in one's range; when they got out to Preble, the tops would overlook the city wall by a good fifteen feet, and the archers and machines there could sweep the parapets bare for the infantry. Thousands of workers hauled handcarts and carried baskets of broken rock out to the water, and the sound of it dropping into the waves was like continuous surf. Masons worked behind them, setting up the defense parapet, and where it hadn't reached yet the workers were protected by mantlets—heavy wooden shields on wheeled frames. All was order, and rapid progress. At this rate, they'd be out to Preble in less than a month. And the troops would be *royally* pissed at having to work this hard for this long—it was worse than road-building detail, itself always unpopular. Added to what had happened there during the uprising, and the fact that Jeschonyk didn't even intend to try and keep the men in hand, and it was going to be a very nasty sack.

Demansk felt a *little* sorry for the inhabitants of the island city. The Confed occupation had been enough to drive anyone to distraction . . . although not, in his opinion, to suicide. Which was what came of massacring Confederation citizens; the ones spared for the mines would be the lucky ones. Jeschonyk was talking about a special Games for the captured adults; a Games Without Issue, pairs forced to fight to the death and then the winners matched with each other, with one survivor left to be poled.

He took an orange out of the helmet he had balanced on one knee and began to peel it with methodical care. *We've really got to do something about provincial government,* he thought. Every time there was a political crisis at home there was a revolt *somewhere*, and it was all because of the tax-farming system. *They're our subjects, we've got to stop treating the provinces like a hunting ground.* As it was, a provincial governor *had* to extort to the limit, to stand off the lawsuits that would be launched when he retired; for that matter, anyone who crossed swords with the tax-farming syndicates would be sued into bankruptcy or exile.

The Preblean flotilla was approaching the causeway from the northwest, with the sun behind them and to their right, and the wind directly astern. *Hmmm,* he thought. *Four galleys, and they're each pulling a merchantman. Could they be trying an assault?*

No, they weren't insane, or that desperate yet. He had a full brigade of troops ready to hand, with more to draw on—the working details had their equipment stacked and he'd drilled them in moving rapidly to kit out and fall in.

"Then what *are* they doing?" he asked.

Helga's got me spooked, with her tales of that damned Emerald she took up with, he thought sourly. *This is the modern age, not the plain before the walls of Windhaven during the Thousand Ships War. The gods do not don mortal disguise to fight in mortal quarrels, if they ever did.*

Still . . . "First Spear," he said. "Get your outfit standing to."

"Yessir!"

That would be done competently, he knew. He squinted again, then stiffened as the rebel flotilla came into closer sight, just outside catapult range from the siege towers. The galleys were casting off their tows, turning, their oars going to double-stroke; heading away, then halting and backing water, their sterns to the causeway. The tubby deep-hulled merchantmen were sheeting home their big square sails, though. Heading straight for the causeway . . .

No. Their crews were diving overside, climbing into small boats and rowing like Shadesholm back towards the galleys. One paused, just close enough to see, and pumped a hand with an outstreched finger towards the Confed forces. The four ships came on with the tillers of their dual steering oars lashed and the wind steady on their quarters, faster now, little curves of white foam at their bluff bows. And smoke, smoke curling up from under their deck hatches.

"Messenger!" Demansk barked. "The towers are to open fire on the ships—rocks. Knock down their masts, or sink them—immediately. I'll have the rank off the commander who lets them get through. *Move!*"

Demansk was a man who rarely raised his voice. The man ran as if the three-headed hound of the Shadow Lord were at his heels, and the Justiciar ground his teeth in fury.

Emeralds, he thought. No discipline; he'd fought them from Rope to Solinga, talking less and hitting harder. But they were . . .

"Sneaky. And these Gellerts, they're sneaky even for *Emeralds.*"

The tendrils of fire licking up from the hatchways of the ships were growing even as he watched, pale in the bright sunlight, but full of promise and black smoke.

"Burn, you Confed bastards!" Esmond whooped.

Beside him on the raised stern of the galley, with his head on the curling seabeast stemhead, Adrian winced slightly. A rock from one of the tower catapults splashed into the water a hundred yards astern; either someone there was getting vindictive or they were *really* bad shots. More fifty-pound rocks were striking the fireships sailing in at six knots towards the Confed siege tower, knocking bits off their railing, making holes in the sails, some of them crashing through decks or striking masts. The holes in the deck simply gave the fires spreading belowdecks among the barrels of pitch and tar and sulfur and oil and tallow more air, miniature volcanoes shooting up after each hit. One ship's mast did fall over; the high stern of the merchantman was still enough to keep it drifting steadily before the wind towards the tower, although it turned broadside on.

"Haven't a prayer of sinking them," he said.

You could sink an ordinary galley by catapult fire, if you were lucky. They were lightly built, racing shells of fragile pine, quickly made and quickly worn out. Freighters had oak frames and much thicker hull planks and frames. They were built to take strains and last; many sailed for thirty or forty years before they had to be broken up. The only real way to sink one was to ram it, or burn it . . . and these weren't going to burn to the waterline until long after they hit the causeway.

"They're bringing up men with oars," Esmond said.

Adrian could see them too; someone had been bright enough to rig a pump, to keep them covered with water. They'd never be able to stand the heat, even so. Probably.

"We'd better discourage that," he said. "Captain Sharlz, if you could bring us broadside on?" He turned and looked down onto the gangway of the galley: "Simun! Six arquebus teams—target the men trying to fend off."

"Sir, yessir!" the underofficer shouted back, as the galley heeled and turned in its own length, oars churning and then going to a steady slow stroke to keep the craft on station.

Puduff. Puduff. Puduff . . . Sulfur-stinking smoke drifted back to the poop. Men fired, stepped back for their loading teams, stepped forward again, intent on their work. The first six rounds brought one man down—good practice, at this extreme range. The four-ounce balls and seven-foot barrels gave the arquebusiers more range than any torsion catapult, though.

"Bastards don't know what's hitting them," Esmond chuckled.

That they don't, Raj added. ***There's no reason for them to associate a bang and a puff of smoke with someone getting killed. But they'll learn.***

They did, as more of the men getting ready to fend off the fireships went down. Confed troopers trotted up, raising their big oval shields to hold off whatever it was that was killing their comrades. Adrian could see the bronze thunderbolts on their facings glitter as they raised them; another row behind held them overhead, making a tortoise as they would for plunging arrow fire. Habit, but it was also habit that kept them so steady. Even when the first soldiers went down; the arquebus balls knocked men back, punctured shields, smashed through the links of mail.

This time Esmond winced; Adrian sensed he wasn't altogether happy at seeing personal courage and skill and strength made as nothing by a machine striking from twice bowshot.

" 'Strong-Arm! How the glory of man is extinguished!' " the elder Gellert murmured; a king of Rope had made that cry from the heart, the first time he saw a bolt from the newly-invented catapult.

"Progress," Adrian replied. Then: "Cease fire!"

The first of the fireships would ground not ten yards from its target. The Islander sailors had done their work well.

"Ungh."

A man not two paces from Justiciar Demansk went down, grunting like someone who'd been gut-punched. Unlike a gut-punched boxer he wasn't going to get up, not from the amount of blood that welled out around his clutching fingers. *Better he bleeds to death now,* Demansk thought with a veteran's ruthless compassion. *I'd rather, than go slow from the green rot.* A puncture down in the gut *always* mortified. He could smell shit among the blood-stink, even from here.

"That went right through his shield," he said aloud.

"Fuckin' right it did," his First Spear said. "Sir, you've got to get *out* of here! You get killed, who's going to command this ratfuck? I can't, and them bastards in the command tent, most of 'em *can't.*"

Demansk shook his head. Jeschonyk actually had half a dozen reasonably experienced advisors—one good thing about the past twenty years of Confederation history was that the upper classes were full of men who'd seen red on the field. He turned in exasperation, keeping his voice low:

"I can't expect the men to hold steady under this if I don't—"

Ptannggg. Another trooper went down in front of him, a hole punched through his shield. Justiciar Demansk found himself on the rough stones of the causeway as well, blinking up at the First Spear's horrified face.

"Where's the velipad that kicked me?" he muttered.

His hand went to where the pain was, the left side of his torso, and then he jerked it away from metal burning hot. When he looked down there was a trough along his flank, ploughed into the thick cast bronze of his breast-and-back muscled cuirass. Lead was splashed across it.

"The Justiciar's dead! The commander's dead!" someone was wailing.

That pulled him out of his dazed wonder. He took a deep breath; there was a shooting pain in his ribs, but nothing desperate, no blood on his breath or grating of bone ends.

"I am *not*!" he said. "Get me up, gods condemn you!"

Hands pulled him up; he walked up and down behind the ranked troops, letting them see him.

Some way of making hellpowder throw *things,* he realized. *Throw them farther than a torsion catapult can, and too fast to see. That's what those puffs of smoke on the galley are.*

Another thought brought his eyes wide, appalled. "First Spear!" he snapped. "Get those men with the oars away from there."

"Let it ground, sir?" he asked, puzzled.

"We can't stop it." Still less push it around the front of the causeway, to drift harmlessly downwind. Somebody out there—those *damned* Gellerts—had probably timed this very carefully. "Have the battalion retreat—get everyone else out behind us. Walking retreat, shield-wall formation, but be damned quick about it. Move!"

He turned himself and began to walk to the rear. He'd been campaigning most of his fifty years; there was nothing in him of the need to prove his courage that had driven a young tribune to lunacy, so long ago. And the First Spear was partly right; nobody else was going to do this job better, if he couldn't.

"They're bugging out," Esmond said, disappointment in his voice. "Someone got a rush of thought to the head."

Adrian nodded tightly; he wasn't grieved that fewer men would be burned alive. The first of the fireships was almost in contact with the sandbank the causeway was being built on . . . almost . . .

"There!" he said.

The comandeered merchantman touched, lurched forward and then stopped dead. With a long slow crackling audible even over the growing roar of the fire, the mast toppled forward, to lie with its burning sail over the rock of the causeway. It fell towards the tower, but did not quite touch it—men were leaning out of the upper works of the siege tower, reckless of arquebus bullets, and pouring water down the layers of thick green hides that made up its outer skin. Any moment now . . .

BUDDUFFF.

The force of the explosion was muffled by the hull of the ship, and the weight of combustibles lying above it. That confinement increased the force, as well. The burning deck of the fireship vanished in a spectactular volcano of flame, burning planks, beams, and dozens of barrels of flammables; many of them had ruptured in the hull as well, and added their sticky, fast-burning contents to the cone of flame that leapt upwards. It wasn't aimed at anything in particular, but the breeze bent it south and eastwards . . . and most of it fell across the wall of the siege tower. Buckets of water became utter irrelevancies, and so did the layers of hide—they dried out and began to burn almost immediately. When the explosion cleared, the whole flank of the tower was already burning, and smoke was pouring out of the arrow slits and catapult ports all along the other side of it. Men jumped too, men with their hair and clothes aflame. A few were running from the other side, but not many could have made it down the ladders. The tower was a chimney now, sucking in air from the bottom and blasting it out the top and every opening along the sides, the thick timbers and internal bracing adding to the holocaust.

The next three fireships drifted into the red heart of the flames and exploded almost immediately. Adrian felt a huge soft pillow of hot air strike his face, making him fling up a hand as his eyeballs dried. When he blinked them clear the first tower was falling onto the flaming pillar of the second, nine stories of burning timber avalanching down unstoppably. The second tower cracked, shedding men and planks and hides; part of it hit the shallow water beyond, but the thick stump of it remained to burn with the whole of the first. Pieces of flaming wood flew through the air for hundreds of yards, well into the walled camp where the Confeds had crammed their carpentry supplies and naval stores. Fires started there, too; he could hear trumpets and drums as officers tried to organize fire-fighting parties. It would be difficult, though—the way to the nearest water supply was thoroughly blocked by the conflagration on the causeway.

There, stone would be beginning to crack as it glowed white-hot. Esmond was laughing, and the crews of the galleys were joining in—even the rowers were grinning through their oar ports on the outriggers, and the soldiers and sailors on deck were dancing, snapping their fingers and making obscene gestures towards the shore.

"A thousand men lost, there," Esmond said, slapping his hand exultantly on his swordhilt. "A thousand men, and a month's work, and all those materials. Lovely."

Even against the wind, Adrian thought he could catch a whiff of the smell. He gagged slightly and nodded.

"That will set them back a little," he said. "But I think we're going to be real, real unpopular over there now."

"Well, then," Esmond said, clapping him on the back. "We'll just have to continue closing the door in their face, won't we?"

"It's called a 'trebuchet,' " Adrian said to the carpenters and blacksmiths and shipwrights. "And it's a form of catapult."

He was standing on a platform of rammed rubble behind the city wall, the section nearest to the Confed's causeway. Everyone had been up there, and seen the redoubled efforts—this time the blocking wall along the sides was like a small city's, and the towers pressed forward to the edge of construction were squat monsters sheathed in plates of beaten iron and brass, glittering like malignant serpents in the bright sunlight.

The craftsmen crowded around to look at the man-tall model he'd built. It had two heavy tripods, linked by an iron axle. Pivoting on that was a beam, anchored about one-third of the way along its height. The short end of the beam held a box full of rocks, itself pivoting on an iron bar driven through the outermost part of the beam; the long end had a leather sling on its end, holding a fist-sized ball of rock.

"How does it work?" one carpenter asked after a minute, baffled. "There's no twisted sinew, no bow neither—how does it throw things?" He made a sign with one hand. "More of your hellpowder sorcery?"

Adrian smiled soothingly. "No, this is pretty straightforward," he said. "I'll show you. Simun."

The underofficer motioned two arquebusiers forward. The other hundred were on the wall, happily potting men through the wooden shields that the Confeds moved forward to protect the working parties. They'd doubled and redoubled the thickness of planks on those, until they could barely move them over the uneven ground of the forward working surface, but the odd ball still penetrated. More still hit men *behind* the row of shields, or on exposed limbs, or struck the working parties that tried to move the mantlets forward. Other gunmen waited patiently for one of the trapdoors on the siege towers to open and spit a catapult dart at the city. They were just within extreme range . . . extreme catapult range, that was. The arquebuses were comfortably within *their* range, and a dozen fired every time the Confeds made the attempt. Men died within the tower, but that was secondary—a four-ounce ball travelling at nine hundred feet per second did unpleasant things to a torsion catapult's frame and fixings whenever it struck.

Simun chuckled, looking over his shoulder, then signed to the two men. They hauled on ropes running through a block and tackle, and the long arm of the miniature trebuchet came down until he could slip an iron hook into a ring driven into the wood just above the sling. The load in that now rested, just touching the ground.

"Here, sor," he said, handing a lanyard to Adrian.

"So, we pull this—"

Thwack.

The heavy basket of rocks pulled the short arm of the trebuchet down. The long arm moved more quickly, leverage driving it. The sling added to the momentum, and the rock blurred across the fifty yards to the wall in a streak of vicious speed. It cracked into the granite facing hard enough to spall off a foot-square flake. The craftsmen and sapper officers gave long, admiring whistles.

"The thing is," Adrian went on, resting a hand on the model, "that we can build this as big as we can get timbers for—and Prince Tenny and the Syndics have authorized us to demolish buildings, even temples. We're a shipbuilding city, here, so we've got plenty of men used to working to these scales, and with heavy cables and pulleys. We'll need winches to pull down the throwing arm, but when it's ready we can throw really *big* weights; we can throw them on a high arc, to lob over the wall, and we can throw them all the way to shore, or nearly—dropping them right on the Confeds' heads."

A circle of beatific grins broke out as the image slowly sank into the consciousness of the onlookers.

"Shark-Toothed Sea Lord," one said, awed. "Like it was raining boulders, eh, lord? But how do we aim it?"

"We can move the whole frame around for direction," he said. "That won't be easy, but we can do it if we're careful how we build the underlying platform and if we apply plenty of manpower. For distance, we just fire ranging shots, adding or subtracting rocks from the basket on the short arm—that's where the impetus comes from, you see. We store up . . ." He halted; the Islander he was using had no word that precisely corresponded to "force." "We store up the ability to throw by hauling up the basket, you see. Then when it comes down, all that, ah, *strength*, is transferred to whatever we're throwing all at once. By altering the weight, we alter the strength—as a man does when he's throwing a rock by hand."

A few seemed to grasp what he was driving at. There were blank looks from the others, and he removed his hat and sighed. Sweat ran down his forehead and stung in his eyes; it was hot, and the stone buildings everywhere around reflected the heat.

"We can do it," he said. Center had filled his mind's eye with images of what the trebuchet could accomplish, and precise step-by-step instructions in making it. "And when we do, it'll ruin the Confeds' whole *day*."

Men on the wall looked down, grinning reflexively at the laughter around Adrian. It spread spontaneously along the parapet, until the wall was ringing with cheers. Morale in Preble was *very* good.

"Enjoy it while you can," Adrian muttered below his breath.

Out there, the resources of the Confederacy would be moving, moving—slow at first, like an avalanche did. But very heavy in the end.

((•)) ((•)) ((•))

Experience had shown that the base of the causeway was safe from the weapons on Preble's wall . . . and if you stayed low, from the ones on the galleys harassing the quarter-mile length. Justiciar Demansk stood, scowling and watching the stone stream forward, the dead and wounded trickle back. A solid line of guards was detailed to check that nobody came back without a real wound; they leaned on their shields, stolid and bored and glad they weren't out at the sharp end right now. The smell of sweat was heavy on the air, the smell of velipad and greatbeast dung, the dusty odor of cracked rock and the salt-silt of the shore.

At least we're getting plenty of time to drill the new recruits, he thought. That was the one good thing about siege operations, even this gods-cursed one. He ground his teeth as he watched the sails of a convoy of merchantmen appear on the horizon. Preble would be eating well; intelligence said they had six months' supplies, *and* they could import grain—from the Southern continent, through the freeport at Marange. As long as they had money, and they had plenty of that, too. Melting down the Temple treasuries, from what he'd heard; when that was done, there was always the King of the Isles.

"We're certainly not going to starve them out as long as they hold the seas," he said. "So, how do the men feel, First Spear?"

"Pissed off and scared, sir," he replied promptly. "They want to get stuck into those damned rebels out there, but they're starting to think that every time it *looks* as if we're getting anywhere, the fuckers come up with another trick. Sir."

Demansk nodded sourly. *I can't think of anything else they could do,* he mused.

They'd planted iron-tipped stakes in the shallow water a hundred yards out from both sides of the causeway, using conscripted local sponge divers. *No more fireships, thank the gods.*

The *arquebuses*—spies and prisoners had brought the name back from Preble—could punch through shields, but not walls or reinforced mantlets, or the iron plates on thick timber of the new siege towers. The trickle of casualties from the towers was getting worse as they got closer to Preble, and so was the continuous sniping from galleys ranging along the causeway, but the Confederation had a big army. Soon enough they'd be within effective catapult range, and a little after that of archery. The Confed army had a lot of mercenary archers, too. The new towers were an absolute bitch to move, they were so heavy they'd had to use iron-plated wheels under them, but as a side benefit they ought to be fairly immune to battering rocks from catapults, as well.

"What am I missing?" he muttered.

"Sir! Heads up!"

Demansk felt his eyes go wide with surprise as he saw the tumbling dot rising from behind the walls that fringed the peachpit shape of the island city. *I'm getting to absolutely* hate *feeling that expression on my face,* he thought angrily. It was a rock, obviously. And equally obviously it was *huge*, a quarter of a ton, far heavier than anything a catapult could throw—could have thrown, before the gods condemned him to this nightmare operation. Once more he felt the ground shifting below his feet, as the certainties of a lifetime—of uncounted lifetimes, back to the times of the heroes—crumbled.

The boulder dropped into the water with an enormous splash, a hundred yards short of the left-hand, southern tower side of the causeway. The water was shallow enough there that the tip of it remained sticking up above the water. Men began pelting back, their mouths open Os of fright—conscripted local workers, he noted with somber pride, not Confed soldiers.

"First Spear, evacuate the causeway," he said heavily. "Everything but enough men in the towers to stand off a fast attempt at a landing."

Wouldn't it look lovely on his record if he pulled everyone out, and a commando set the towers on fire *again*? But he wasn't going to waste more troops, not if this got as nasty as it might.

The evacuation was orderly enough; five minutes later men were filing past him in columns, profanely shepherded along by his troops, and they were taking their baskets and hammers with them, their carts and beasts and timbers. One of the surveyors was jittering around the edge of the circle of Demansk's personal guards, probably come to complain about the interruption to his work.

"Heads up!"

Another quarter-ton boulder. This one grew with remorseless

speed, dropping down from the sky like an anvil thrown by the gods from heaven, like the dim legends of the end of the Golden Age before history. Demansk traced its curve with his eye and sighed.

CRACK. It hit the forward left corner of the southernmost of the pair of towers. Iron plates sprayed out as the bolts and spikes that held them to the wooden frame sheered off. Fragments of rock and iron and wood sprayed across the forward end of the causeway, knocking down a few men not yet withdrawn; he could see the sudden red gush of arterial blood, imagine it running pink into the sea, and the sudden frenzy of sea life there—scavengers had gathered from all over, and swimming had become much less popular.

"Get the men out of the towers," he said.

"Sir—"

"They're going to pound them into splinters and there's not a fucking thing we can do. Get them out!"

Luckily, whatever-it-was out there on Preble seemed to take a long time to load—not as long as he would need to get the ultraheavy siege towers out of the way, but at least five to eight minutes between rocks. The archers and artillerists in the towers were pouring back in disciplined but hasty streams, jog-trotting past him, when the third rock struck the tower halfway up its length. The whole squat wide-based mass rocked backward, and the projectile didn't shatter or rebound. Demansk winced; that meant it had broken right through the surface, even though it had struck at a glancing angle as it fell from on high. *Like the fist of a god,* he thought.

In fifteen minutes the towers were empty; and the southern one was leaning like a drunken man, and he could see daylight through the frame. Half a dozen more shots, and it was a toppled wreck. *A hundred thousand arnkets,* he thought. That much in materials alone; metals were expensive, on that scale. Not to mention the man-hours that had gone into it . . .

More waiting, a half-hour, and then a boulder skimmed the northern tower's top and cracked into deadly splinters on the causeway behind it. The next one fell with malignant precision right on the roof, and he could hear the crack of rending wood as it slammed down the center of the tower. Five of the huge rocks served to send it toppling backward, with a chorus of groaning, rending, slamming sounds like the end of the world. When the dust cleared he could see it lying prone, the hole the first rock had made in the roof like an eye in the sagging rectangle of immensely thick timbers that made up the frame.

Another pause, and another tumbling dot from Preble. As it grew, he could see that it was trailing . . . not flame, but blue smoke. *Like . . . like one of the* grenades, *but so much* bigger. *Which means . . .*

"Down!" he shouted, diving for the ground; his repaired back-and-breast gouged at him as he landed on the paving stones. "Down, you idiot!"

He reached out, grabbed the thick muscular boot-clad ankles of the First Spear and yanked, pulling him level. Then the world went out in thunder and pain.

"There's a bloody *hole* in the causeway where that big iron barrel of hellpowder landed!" Esmond said enthusiastically.

a crater, Center whispered pedantically at the back of Adrian's mind. There where times when the god-spirit-machine reminded him of a particularly literal-minded instructor of rhetoric he'd studied under in the Grove.

The Gellerts were sitting on chairs brought up to the wall's parapet, with a table laden with watered wine, olives, fish, ham, bread and fruit. Esmond was tearing into the food with methodical speed, his eyes glued to the shore and the Confederation works.

"Yes, as long as the gunpowder holds out we can batter it to pieces faster than they can rebuild it," Adrian said.

Esmond nodded, smiling. "It's a pity we can't reach their camp that way—perhaps we could mount one of the trebuchets on a ship? A big merchantman, say—take out the mast, put the trebuchet on the center."

"Accuracy would go to the Shades," Adrian said, surprised and impressed. Esmond was starting to think in terms of the potential of the new devices.

Weapons technology diffuses faster than anything else, Raj said, his mental voice somehow tired and amused at the same time. ***Medicine and new ways of growing crops may get ignored as outlandish nonsense, but come up with a better way of cracking skulls and they'll fall all over themselves to get their hands on it.***

"But pretty soon," Adrian said, "it's going to occur to the Confeds that nothing we've shown them is much good against moving targets—like ships, for instance."

Esmond's smile turned to a scowl. "King Casull will support us with the royal fleet," he said.

The brothers' eyes met. *We hope,* went unspoken between them.

" . . . save the arm," someone was saying.

Justiciar Demansk's eyes blinked open. There were two physicians hovering over him, and Helga. He looked down; his left arm was immobilized with bandages and splints, and just beginning to deliver a ferocious ache. For the rest he felt the usual sick headache-nausea you got from being knocked out, and bruises, wrenches and sprains. *About like a bad riding accident,* he decided, and pushed the body's complaints away with a trained effort of will. The scents of canvas and the sharp smell of medicine made him want to vomit, but that passed as well.

A few curt questions settled that he wasn't badly damaged—his First Spear had taken a bad head wound, been trepanned, and they were unsure whether he would live; now, *that* hurt.

When the doctors were gone at last, Demansk let his daughter raise his head and bring a cup to his lips. A distant sound like thunder made him jerk a little and spill the water on the thin sheet.

"More?" he said.

Helga nodded; the tent was dim, and it made her eyes seem to glow green at him. "More. The causeway is in ruins."

"Not to mention the reputation of everyone concerned with this fiasco," he said, laying his hand down on the pillow. "You know, this young man of yours—"

"Scarcely mine, Father!"

"—this Adrian Gellert, he threatens the whole course of things as they are. Starting with the Confederacy."

She snorted. "Oh, come now, Father. We'll take Preble, eventually."

"We may, but it's going to be very expensive. Why do you think the world is the Confederacy and some outlying regions now, instead of a tangle of little cities and valley kingdoms, the way it used to be?"

"Because we've got a better army, of course. And the gods favor us, supposedly."

"The two often go together," Demansk said dryly, not returning her smile. For one thing, it hurt too much. "But one reason is that cities don't hold out for years, the way they did back during the League Wars, or even the wars of the Alliance. The Confederacy can take most towns in a month or less. Your . . . this Freeman Gellert has made sieges a lot more expensive again, all of a sudden. If these *innovations*—" the word had sinister connotations of decay and evil, in Emerald and the Confederation's tongue as well "—spread."

Helga laid a cold cloth on his forehead, and he held back a groan of relief. "Always thinking of the welfare of the State, eh, Father?"

"If a Demansk doesn't, who will?"

She nodded. "But Father, what's to prevent *us* from using these . . . new devices?" He noted that she avoided the word he'd used. "A city's a big concentrated stationary target. From what I've seen and heard, hellpowder would be hell on fortifications."

He blinked, startled. "You know," he said, "there may be something to that . . . I've been sort of focused on getting into Preble *against* the Emerald's toys." He thought for a moment. "That bears considering, girl. It certainly does."

CHAPTER TEN

"All hail to the King! O King, live forever! All abase themselves before King Casull IV, King of the Isles, Overlord of the Western Seas!"

The leather-lunged herald cried out the call as the flagship of the Royal fleet dropped anchor. The vermillion-painted oars of the quinquereme pulled in all together, the crew trained to the precision of dancers. Behind it the hundred and twenty hulls of the Isles' war fleet—not counting a score or more of transports and storeships—closed in, not quite as precisely, but with a heartening display of fine seamanship.

Especially heartening when you compare it to the Confed fleet's, Adrian thought, as he went to his knees along with all the other thousands of onlookers. Watching the Confed quinqueremes wallowing into their temporary harbor down the coast had been reassuring, especially when a couple fouled each other in the entranceway, breaking oars and killing rowers. Reassuring, until one saw how many there were.

Standing near Prince Tenny with the high command he had the luxury of kneeling and pressing his forehead to a soft carpet instead of hard slimy cobbles, at least. He still came upright as quickly as he could, looking hungrily at the low turtle-backed shape with the covered wheels on either side that followed along behind a quinquereme, the tow rope coming free of the blue-green water now and then in a shower of spray. That was *his* particular baby. The warships made a formidable bulk, even in the magnificent circular harbor at the northern edge of Preble, and even with all the merchant shipping that had crowded in to take advantage of wartime prices when it became obvious the city wasn't going to fall quickly. The docks were black with people, or gray and red depending on the color of turbans and veils. So were the flat roofs of the houses that rose in a three-quarter circle above the water.

Casull came ashore glittering like a serpent in armor washed with silver and gold; the nobles and household troops around him were only a little less gorgeous. The trident banner of the Isles floated above him, and over the gaudy, metal-shining mass of ships and troops behind him. The citizens of Preble cheered themselves hoarse, throwing dried rose petals before Casull's feet. Priests in white robes and spotted leoger-hide cloaks sprayed scented water and intoned prayers; as the King set foot on land, the knives of sacrificers flashed and greatbeasts and woolbeasts died on altars.

"So," the King said at last, when the processions and sacrifices and speeches were over. He took off the tall spired helmet with its scarlet and green plumes. "I hate that polluted thing—even heavier and hotter than a war helm, when the sun's out."

Adrian smiled politely. The meeting was small: he, Esmond, Sharlz Thicelt, Enry Sharbonow, the admiral of the Royal fleet, a few aides and Prince Tenny, sitting on cushions amid blue tendrils of incense smoke from fretted gold censers.

Casull went on, looking around the round chamber walled in rose marble where the Syndics of Preble had once met: "They do themselves well here—I'm surprised some enterprising Confed didn't have it shipped to Vanbert!" The smile hardened. "I've heard good things of how the defense has gone here, under my son."

Tenny bowed, smirking.

Esmond bowed and spoke. "Lord King, live forever. Under the Prince's inspired leadership, we've smashed their attempt to build a causeway out to Preble, and we've inflicted heavy casualties—several thousand men, as opposed to a few score on our side. Even Justiciar

Demansk, second-in-command of the Confed forces opposite us, was badly injured. However, the Confed fleet is now nearly ready to take to sea. The city can't hold if the Confeds command the seas around it."

Casull nodded, leaning forward on his cushions. "The map," he snapped.

"My lord." The admiral in turn snapped his fingers, and a young aide who looked like his son, and probably was, brought it forward. "Speaker Jeschonyk has built an artificial harbor here, about a mile up the coast—out of trebuchet range. He sank two rows of merchantmen laden with rocks out into the sea, built wooden forts at the outer edges, and is basing his ships there. A hundred and thirty fighting keels, about the same number as ours."

"Hmmm," the King said. His finger traced down the map. "This town, Speyer, it's got a good harbor, I think—why not there?"

Thicelt bowed his head; he had an aigrette of diamonds and feathers at the clasp of his turban now.

"O lord King, the currents and waves are unfavorable—it's a bad row for a warship, the crews would be exhausted by the time they reached here."

"While ours would be rested." Casull nodded; that was the sort of calculation that any sea commander had to make. You couldn't keep the masts up on a ship that expected to see action anytime soon. "Besides which . . . wasn't Speyer ruled from here?"

"Yes, O King," Sharbonow said. *His* turban clasp was even more ornate than Thicelt's, and his cloth-of-gold jacket and red silk cummerbund were sewn with small black and steel-gray pearls. "And many families here have kin there. Marcomann's troops stormed Speyer, and they were not gentle. I have many spies active there, men zealous in your interest and full of hatred for the Confeds."

"So." Casull's finger returned to the improvised Confed harbor. "As many ships as ours, but many more quinqueremes—we're better sailors, but they can overmatch us in a boarding action. If they can drive off my Royal fleet, then they can isolate Preble and, in the end, retake it. If we can eliminate their fleet as a consideration, then Preble is ours and we can drive them to distraction by raiding along the coast, and cost them heavily by interdicting their commerce."

The shrewd dark eyes raked the brothers. "You, sons of Gellert. I am staking a great deal on your innovations." He used the Emerald word, with its connotations of the unnatural and perverse.

"Lord King," Adrian said softly. "We have advantages they do not suspect. A great victory here will surely render the Kingdom of the Isles safe from Confed aggression for many years."

"And a great *defeat* here could see the Confeds in Chalice within *this* year," Casull said, and then forced himself to relax. "We must trust to our seamanship, and to your weapons."

"I said, it's working well!" the new-minted engineer bawled in Adrian Gellert's ear.

The steam galley *Wodep's Fist*—the crew called it *Wodep's Prick*, from the shape of the ram at the bows—lay quivering with life in the great harbor of Preble. Adrian was quivering with shock at the heat, experienced before but forgotten; he understood why the crew mostly worked stripped to their loincloths, despite the risk of being pitched against rough timber or red-hot metal. Decorum required him to wear at least a linen tunic, and it was already a sopping rag plastered to his skin. The great arched interior of the revolutionary craft was dim, red-lit by reflected flames from the boilers, full of sweat-gleaming near-naked figures, like something from the fate of wicked shades. Most of the interior was taken up by the riveted iron tube of the boiler, hissing and leaking steam now from half a dozen places.

That floated in muggy clouds around the rest of the machinery. At either side stood a cylinder of cast bronze, as thick through as a small woman's waist, fixed at the bottom to thick timbers and joined to the boiler by pipes wrapped in crude linen lagging. From the top of each cylinder protruded an iron rod, joined to one end of a beam; the beam pivoted on an axle fixed to the hull, and the other end had still another rod that worked a crank running out through the hull. Like melancholy monsters run mad, the grasshopper beams worked up and down, up and down, with a smooth mechanical regularity like nothing Adrian had ever seen before.

He coughed. The air was thick with moisture, with the lard used as lubricant on the working surfaces, with the odors of sweat and scorched metal and wafts of soot where the twin stacks leaked smoke. Behind the boiler men were working in a frenzy, passing lengths of log to throw into the firebrick-lined pit beneath it; behind them others stood ready at the ropes and tackle that controlled the tiller, hitched to the world's first sternpost rudder.

"I say it's a wonder it's working at all," Adrian bawled back cheerfully.

He set hands to the ladder that ran up between the smokestacks, and gasped with relief as he came up into the square blockhouse that protruded four feet up through the turtleback deck of the *Wodep's Fist*. Narrow slits lined it on all four sides, and looking through them he could see Preble spread out around him—as black and gray and blue with heads and faces as it had been for King Casull's arrival yesterday. Now people flocked to see the latest wonder of the wonder-worker Adrian Gellert, their savior. . . .

And I do wish they wouldn't call *me that,* he thought. He could see King Casull's eyes narrow every time some fool yelled it out in the street, and Prince Tenny's reaction was even worse.

He took a cork out of one of the speaking tubes, whistled sharply through it, and shouted into the funnel: "Left full rudder!"

An answering whistle came, and he grabbed for handholds as the *Wodep* heeled sharply. One of the paddles came nearly out of the water, and Adrian winced as the piston rod on that side danced wildly up and down for a moment, then again at the crunch as the paddle bit solid water once again. The fabric of the ship groaned, and he could hear water sloshing around in the boiler. A thought struck him, and he bent to peer down and check on the safety valve. *Good.* Back in Chalice some enthusiastic soul had fastened it down once, to make the engine go faster.

"Pass the word!" he called, and shouted into the three speaking tubes. "We're going on a ramming run!"

More cheers, which made him shake his head in bemused wonder. Just sailing this thing on the straight and level was bad enough. . . .

"Do you see her?" he asked the Islander skipper.

"Yes, lord. That's the *Icebird's Claw*. Sun God, but my father served in her!"

The skipper was a young man; that might even be true. The galley lay drifting in the slow harbor eddy, its scarlet and blue paint chipped and faded, a low slender shape on the water a thousand yards away. Nobody was aboard but a crew of hastily trained criminals to man the catapults, promised their freedom if they put on a good show and impalement if they didn't.

"Helm forward," Adrian commanded. "All ahead full, but wait for my command on the reversing levers. *Go!*"

The paddles beat faster, throwing foam up higher than the command blockhouse. Occasional droplets came through the vision slits, welcome coolness even when they stung the eyes. Water broke aside from the ram, and washed up the deck as far as the triangular-board wave breaker he'd rigged to keep the bow from digging in too deeply; he didn't want to think what might happen to this wallowing tub in any sort of sea. The forward motion built, like nothing he'd ever felt at sea before, even under oars—there was a blind purposeful waddle to it, a *mechanical* feeling. The galley grew, larger and larger. It was vastly lighter than the *Wodep*, but longer and higher at the gunwales. A dart arched out from the catapult, and another; distance made them seem to start slow and accelerate as they neared. They glanced harmlessly from the octagonal iron plates, with nothing but banging and sparks to show for it. Adrian ducked as one seemed to be coming straight for his eyes, but it caromed off the blockhouse as well. Closer, and he could see the empty oar ports of the trireme, the white faces of the men winching the catapults back.

Bang! Bang! More bolts skittering off the armor. They were aimed forward of the galley's midships, at a thirty-degree angle.

"Brace for impact!" Adrian shouted into the speaking tube. A man began pounding on a bell with an iron bar, loud enough to be heard even over the monstrous *CHUFFF . . . CHUFFF . . .* of the cylinders.

"Reverse engines!" he cried again, and wrapped his arm through a cloth-padded iron loop bolted to the timbers of the blockhouse interior.

Closer and closer, the sudden lurch as the paddles reversed, but far too late to do more than begin to slow the ram. Then . . .

BOOOMM. The hull of the galley thundered like a giant drum, then cried out in a shrieking of snapping planks and timbers. Adrian was wrenched forward with a violence that almost pulled his arm out of its socket, and banged his head hard enough to bring blinding tears to his eyes, despite the padded leather helmet he wore. Somewhere there were screams of agony; men with broken bones, or those thrown against scalding metal and losing skin and flesh. When Adrian blinked his eyes clear and looked out the vision slit, he whooped nonetheless.

The galley was sinking, and fast. The *Wodep* hadn't just punched a hole in its side; the glancing blow had ripped ten yards of planking free of the slender strakes, and cracked most of those. Galleys *had* to be built lightly, if they were to be rowed at all; the *Wodep* was a massive lump of oak and iron by comparison, and when the two came together at high speed it was like a crockery pot striking pavement. As he watched, the other ship heeled over, raised its bow high and went straight down like a stylus punched into a watermelon.

"Left ten, paddles ahead one quarter—and well done, well done!" he shouted into the speaking tube.

The skipper yelled delight also, and pounded him on the shoulder. "With this ship, and you in command, sir, we'll sweep the Confeds back to the peasant pigstyes where they belong."

Adrian's grin left his face. "Rejoice," he said. "You're to have the honor of serving under the direct command of Prince Tenny, son to our overlord King Casull."

"Oh, shit," the man mumbled, staring at Adrian with dismay and then clapping a hand over his mouth.

"You really don't want to say that," Adrian murmured.

"Ah—thank you, sir. Yes," he went on, in a louder tone. "The Prince will lead us to glory!"

Well, he can't go far wrong, with a good crew and this ship, Adrian thought.

Don't count on it, lad, Raj thought grimly. ***You haven't seen as***

many high-ranking nitwits pull defeat from the jaws of victory as I have.

probability—

"Don't tell me," Adrian muttered. "There isn't a damned thing I can do about it anyway."

He looked eastward. There the Confederacy fleet was making ready for battle; according to intelligence, Justiciar Demansk was leading one squadron. Helga was still with him . . . and maybe *he* could make her keep to shore. Adrian was painfully conscious of the fact that he couldn't imagine stopping her from doing something she wanted to do, whether as husband, father, or god incarnate with a thunderbolt in his hand.

CHAPTER ELEVEN

"Well, thank the *gods*, sir," the coastland skipper of the galley blurted, his nasal singsong accent strong under fairly fluent Confed.

"Yes?" Justiciar Demansk replied, raising an eyebrow. "I merely said you should adjust the rowing pace as you saw fit."

"I was thanking the gods I'd gotten one who understands a ship isn't commanded from the same end as a velipod. Sir. *Thank* you, sir. I don't mind the risk of getting killed, it goes with this trade, but I'd rather not lose my ship because some damnfool landsman won't *listen*. Thank you again, sir."

Demansk nodded frostily and turned his attention elsewhere. The Confederacy's Grand Fleet of the West was making as good time as he could expect . . . when everyone was supposed to keep station so close their oars were almost touching. Speaker Emeritus Jeschonyk thought that that would reduce the risk of the fleet being disordered; as long as they kept to the holy line, the faster, lighter Islander vessels wouldn't be able to nip in with ram-and-run attacks.

It's won naval battles for us before, Demansk thought sourly, shifting his injured left arm to test it. A little pain, not too bad—not nearly as disagreeable as making Helga stay on shore had been; in the end he'd had to point out that coming might mean watching her precious Emerald die.

I just don't like the implications of this formation. We're conceding that the enemy are better than we are. That was true, on salt water; he still didn't like admitting it. The Confed fleet was fighting the way Emerald phalanxes had, in the old days; shield to shield, all spears out. It had a lot of punch—one of Demansk's ancestors had written in his memoirs that seeing four thousand men come over the brow of a hill in perfect alignment was the most frightening thing he'd ever seen in his life—but it lacked flexibility. That was how the Confed armies had *beaten* the Emeralds, using small units under independent command to work around flanks and into gaps, coming to close quarters with the stabbing assegai.

"At least it's calm," he muttered, and the sailing master nodded again. A calm sea was like fighting on a flat, even field—everything in plain sight, no surprises, no broken ground to disorder the formations. If he *had* to fight in a phalanx, that was the best place to do it.

Thing is, I just don't like fighting a battle this way, relying on brute strength and massive ignorance, he thought. It was . . . uncraftsmanlike.

He had to admit that the fleet made an imposing sight. The working parties that had gotten them ready for sea hadn't stinted on paint and gilding, either. The hulls and upperworks were almost as bright as the helmet plumes and armor of the officers, lacking only the fierce glint that the sun broke off edged steel. Each craft had a figurehead in the form of a snarling direbeast; there was a remote mythological connection, to the legendary pair who'd supposedly been raised by one and founded Vanbert. He was surprised that the Confederation made so much of that myth, sometimes—the rest of it wasn't at all creditable, involving fratricide, kidnapping, woman-stealing and general mayhem. But then, Vanbert had been founded by a bunch of bandit fleecebeast herders, if you read between the lines.

"We've come a long way," he said to himself, watching the vermillion-painted oars flashing in unison, churning the wine-purple sea to foam, the bronze beaks lunging forward and splitting V's of white to either side. The oarsmen knew their business, hired men mostly, with some conscripted fishermen from the coastal villages.

They were used to the shattering labor, but not really to working in teams; there had only been a month or so to train them.

Ahead, the Islander fleet was matching them stroke for stroke—backward, southwest, away from the shore, on a course that would take them out past Preble if it went on long enough; he could see the walls and stubby towers in the ocean beyond them. Demansk's squadron was second in from the left, landward flank of the fleet, and that section had come a little forward; it gave him a good view down to the massive quinqueremes of the center, where Jeschonyk's personal banner flew. The ability of the Islander fleet to back water as fast as the Confeds were advancing was dauntingly impressive, in its way—they weren't charging, but the pace wasn't leisurely, by any manner of means.

He stared ahead and to his right. *King Casull's banner there—standard formation, like ours, quinqueremes in the center, triremes on the flanks.* The great ships rode the ocean like floating wooden walls, each with two banks of huge five-man oars swinging with ponderous force. Casull's capital ships looked a little different, with low wooden forts on their forward decks, spanning the gangways along either flank. *Hmmmm. That must make them a little more sluggish,* he thought. *I wonder why they're doing that? Usually they stay as nimble as they can. And what's that column of black smoke from behind the flagship?*

He sincerely hoped it wasn't some sort of incendiary trick. He was getting thoroughly sick of those. He also hoped Jeschonyk wasn't just going to mirror their movement until the Confederacy fleet had been drawn well out to sea. Right now, the left flank at least was secure, anchored on the land. Out in deep water, the Islanders might get up to any amount of devilment.

A messenger galley came racing down the line of ships, flying Jeschonyk's banner and pulling just under their sterns; orders from the command, then. It was a light shell, undecked, with no ram—and a mast still stepped, although it hadn't set any sail. A galley always unstepped and stowed its mast before action, of course; the shock of ramming would send it overboard, otherwise. Demansk took the sailing master's speaking trumpet and stepped to the rail.

"This is Justiciar Demansk!" he shouted as the light craft came within hailing distance. His voice was a hoarse bull roar, roughened by a lifetime of cutting through the clamor of battle. "What orders?"

In theory, the officer commanding the racing shell shouldn't have told him anything. In reality, a Justiciar was hard to refuse.

"The left-flank squadron is to move forward and cover the causeway, while we resume construction," he shouted. "All other ships to maintain station."

"Carry on!" Demansk said aloud. *Oh, shit.*

"What in the Shades are they doing?" Esmond muttered from the quarterdeck of the ship he'd named *Nanya's Revenge.*

"Not what they should," Adrian said. "But then, neither are we."

correct, Center said. Center and Raj had agreed—they didn't, always—that Casull should put his gun-equipped ships out to the left, seaward, and use them to crumple the Confed line inward. That would throw them into disorder, and then the more agile Islander vessels could strike at the flanks of maneuvering quinqueremes. Instead, Casull was playing it safe, keeping all the heavy ships, the ones with the cannon, and the steam ram with him in the center.

Usually a mistake, when you're the weaker party but have better quality troops, Raj noted clinically. ***That's when you have to throw double or nothing, and hope to win big. If you fight a battle of attrition, it usually ends up with the last battalion making the difference.***

"We've been here most of the day," Esmond fretted. "And done damn-all but back up. They're not going to follow us out to sea, and even with summer it's going to get dark in five, six hours. We should—wait a minute, they're not just getting out of line, they're moving."

Ten triremes of the Confed fleet's landward wing *were* moving, their oarsmen stretching out in a stroke . . . stroke . . . stroke . . . pace that they could keep up for an hour or so, but that wouldn't exhaust them the way ramming speed did. Their smaller line was ragged as it drew away from the main body, but not impossibly so.

They're heading for the causeway, Raj thought. ***Probably the***

Confed commander got nervous and decided he had to* do *something. A mistake. Anything that opens this battle up is to our advantage.

"They're heading along the coast, south to the causeway," Adrian said. "Esmond, they're going to cover the causeway—start getting it repaired. We can't let them do that."

"We certainly can't," Esmond said; he'd put too much work and risk and blood into turning that into a disaster for the Confeds. "I'll send a dispatch to the King."

Adrian caught his arm. "No *time*," he said. "We're in the perfect position to intercept them, here on the right flank. If we wait, they'll be past us and we'll have a stern chase."

Esmond hesitated, looking around. He was in command of the right, the landward anchor of the Islander line, six triremes manned entirely by Emeralds—most of their people had some seagoing experience, after all. Adrian's arquebusiers were on board too, and the Strikers were working in their flexible light-infantry armor. It made the ships a bit heavier, but it would give any Confed that tried boarding a nasty surprise, and they were still faster and more agile than any but the very best of the enemy vessels.

"Six to ten . . ." he mused. Then, decisively: "We'll do it. Signal *follow me* and *prepare to engage*." To the helmsmen at the steering oars: "Come about. Oarmaster, take us up to cruising speed."

Esmond's *Revenge* heeled, turning in almost its own length, then came level on a course that would intercept the ten Confed vessels, bouncing forward with a surge that made most on the quarterdeck grab for rail or rigging. "Half a mile," he mused. "Flank speed!"

"All-father Greatest and Best," Justiciar Demansk said. "They're going to be massacred."

The Confed triremes were strung out almost in a line, as close to the shore as they could and not be in the surf. Demansk was no seaman, but he could see the mistake *there*—the commanders were landsmen like him, and they thought of the shore as safety. Instead it was a trap waiting to kill them on their left hand, while the Islander squadrons' rams—

No, not Islanders, by the gods! he thought. A banner was flying from the quarterdeck of the leading enemy ship, and it had the silver owl of Solinga on it! *Not royal ships. Mercenaries.* That must be Esmond Gellert, the man who'd vowed to see Vanbert burn.

Justiciar Demansk lowered his head a little, unconscious of the movement, like an old battered greatbeast, lord of the herd, snuffling the air and shaking his battered horns. *We'll see about that, bucko,* he thought.

A quick glance showed him that his squadron overlapped the landward end of the Islander fleet now; the ships there were opening out their spacing to compensate for the squadron that had peeled off, moving with dancer's grace. Still, they'd be thinner—probably wouldn't try anything, not for a while.

And while Esmond-burn-the-Confeds Gellert takes the detached squadron in their *flank, I can take* him *in his,* he mused.

"Signal," he said. "Squadron will form on me, and advance to the attack. Flank speed!"

"They're coming after us," Esmond said, pounding one fist lightly on the rail. "Damn! That's more initiative than I'd have expected from a Confed commander, and as tight a formation as they've been keeping."

"They're certainly making a hash of it, though," Adrian said, watching two of the Confed triremes fall afoul of each other, oars clashing. Confusion followed, until enough oars could be remanned to push the vessels apart. "They'll be late to the party."

Esmond shook his head, looking right to the Confed squadron that was his prey, and left to the other arrowing in to the rescue. "Or waddling to the rescue," he said. "They might as well be barges, but we can't let ourselves get trapped between them." He swore again, vicious disappointment in his tone.

"No, wait!" Adrian said, pointing seaward. "Look!"

There where the massive quinqueremes faced each other, something was happening. A snarling cheer ran down the Islander line, and a drumbeat signal from ship to ship. Signalers with flags relayed it.

"*General Attack*, by the Gray-Eyed Lady of Solinga," Esmond swore, but happily this time. His head whipped back towards the Confed line. The squadron that had lunged out to protect its comrades had halted. No, they were backing water! Probably recalled by their high command, to meet the Islander charge.

"Steady as she goes!" he shouted exultantly, looking ahead to the ten Confed ships. "Their arses are *ours*!"

"Ram, sir?" the helmsman said.

"By no means," Esmond laughed. "Bring us parallel, just out of dart-caster range."

He grinned like a direbeast, and Adrian nodded agreement. The enemy ships grew nearer with the always-surprising speed of meetings at sea, where you could be alongside one minute and hull-down when you looked back. Suddenly the ant-tiny figures along the enemy rail were men, and human limbs could be seen through the oar ports of the outriggers as their rowers strained and heaved to a quickening beat of the hortator's mallets.

Adrian winced mentally, imagining being down there . . . never knowing when a dart, or fire, or the bone-crushing blow of an enemy's ram was going to come through. Solinga had been a democracy for a long time after the League Wars—a democracy as far as freeborn male citizens were concerned, at least—and the main claim of the lower classes to equality with the farmers who provided their own armor was that it was the poor freemen who rowed the City's ships to battle. The Scholars of the Grove had always held that a specious argument, a sign of the City's decline. Now he was inclined to agree with the rowers.

His voice was steady as he spoke: "Aim for their catapults. The catapults only until further orders."

"Sor, yessor," Simun said, looking up from the port rail. The long weapons were leveled now, men kneeling with a hand over the lock to keep spray out of the priming powder, their barrels out over the uniform centipede motion of the oars. "Catapults it is, sor."

"Signaler, pass it along!"

Turning southward, the Emerald-manned ships were a line parallel to the coast, coming up on the Confed ships from the rear, with Esmond's in the lead. Four minutes of straining effort brought it level with the foremost Confed. Water was creaming up along the ram, curling down the side, and the ship had a slight rocking-horse motion as it clove the low swell.

"Open fire!"

Baaammmm.

Twenty arquebuses fired as one. The Confed ship had three catapults a side, two dart-casters and a stone-thrower, on pivot mounts. The stone-thrower fired, as the man standing behind it yanked the release-cord—not voluntarily, but as he was thrown backwards by a four-ounce lead ball smashing through his body and out the other side, to kill the man behind him as well. The rock fell halfway between the ships, a moment's unnoticed fleck of foam against the green-blue of the shallows.

Baamm. Baaam. Baaam. Over and over again, the long jet of dirt-colored smoke. The smell swept aft, sulfur and rotten eggs and the flint-on-steel scent underneath it. Less than half the shots struck the enemy ship, and less than half of those landed around the catapults, but enough did. He saw splinters flying from the machines and the deck they were mounted on; a throwing arm snapped forward as a holding line was cut; another pinwheeled up as a ball sliced through the twisted greatbeast sinew that powered it.

"They're out of action," Adrian said.

Esmond nodded, still smiling that disquieting smile. "Steersman, close us in—long arrow-shot."

Adrian turned to Simun. "Take out their archers and slingers."

Those had been crowding to the rail as the Emerald-manned ships approached, with the twenty or so Confed regulars standing behind them—as much to keep them to their tasks as to back them up; the missile troops were hirelings or noncitizen allied levies. A flight of arrows winged out, and fell a little beyond the foam lashed up by the galley's port oars.

"Fire!"

Baaammmm.

This time the target was bigger. Four men flew backwards, dead or dying—the heavy balls of the three-man arquebus would rip a limb completely off or turn a torso into a draining sack of ruptured flesh and shattered bone.

Baaam. Baaam. Baaam.

One of the arquebusiers whooped exultantly. "This is like gaffing fish out of a garden pond!" he shouted, and fired again.

Esmond nodded; he was looking back along the line. The other ships of his squadron were keeping pace and repeating his tactics; a little slower, perhaps, without Adrian to keep their arquebusiers on-target, but getting the job done.

When he turned back to look at the closest ship, the slingers and archers had vanished. He saw one take a running leap over the landward side of his vessel, and come up again swimming overarm—no Confed landsman *there*. Another tried the same, to fall overside with a Confed regular's assegai through his back. More were leaping down the hatchways, and the steady pace of the enemy vessel's oars went ragged as the missile troops threw themselves down on the lower gangway between the benches, anywhere to get away from the crushing, invisible death of the lead balls.

"Steersman! Close in!" he shouted exultantly.

The Confed marines threw their futile darts and waited behind raised shields—all but the last; he threw his down and ran, howling, until he splashed overside. *He* wasn't going anywhere but to the bottom, not with fifty pounds of armor on him. Esmond's ship was barely beyond oar's length from its opponent now.

"Adrian!"

His brother nodded. "Gunmen!" he called. "Targets of opportunity—grenadiers, prepare to throw." There was the slightest trace of a sigh in his voice. "Throw!"

His own grenade arched out with four others. Three struck; one straight down a hatchway, as if guided by Wodep's hand. The explosions were quieter than arquebus fire over this distance, but they scythed the trireme's decks free; the remaining sailors were over the side and swimming like eels, those not lying silent or thrashing and screaming. The arquebusiers were firing straight into the oarbanks now, through the ports or through the light planking of the deck; the massed shrilling of the oarsmen was deafeningly loud. And . . .

"Sor!" Simun shouted from the gangway. "She's afire, my lords! Burnin'!"

Another look back along the line of ships showed two more in flames; one was grappled alongside a galley of his, and taken; another two were adrift, their oars limp as their entire crews swam for it. That left four unengaged, and *they'd* turned for the shore, hoping to beach their ships—at a guess, the Confed marines aboard had "insisted" on that with their assegais pressed to the helmsmens' kidneys, and others guarding the hatchways to keep the oarsmen at their tasks.

"Well enough," he laughed. "We can tow them off when they're beached. Bit of a present for the King!" He turned, shading his eyes with a hand. "I wonder how that's going?"

"Speaker Jeschonyk!"

The Speaker Emeritus of the Council of Vanbert was in a small boat, with an aide and two men rowing. He looked up at Demansk.

"My flagship is gone," he said. "There."

Demansk looked up as hands pulled the commander onto the trireme's quarterdeck. The Speaker's great quinquereme was wallowing, its starboard oars broken. From beyond it came a shape like nothing Demansk had ever seen by land or by sea, like a great turtle with two tubes belching smoke from the uppermost part of its . . . deck, he supposed it should be called . . . and a small square structure just before them. Wheels thrashed the water on either side, churning up more foam than a quinquereme's oars, and driving it forward as fast as a trireme at ramming speed. It gleamed like wet iron . . . it *was* iron.

"But iron can't float!" he heard himself say.

"It is iron," Jeschonyk said bitterly from beside him; he started slightly. "Arrows bounce off it, catapult bolts do no damage—it sheared off the starboard oars of my ship *and* the one next to it in line, and—"

The iron ship was turning, a wide circle, much wider than a galley. After a moment it lay a hundred yards off, pointing at the command quinquereme's stern; the ram that split the water ahead of it as it gathered speed was *entirely* comprehensible, unlike the rest of it. Demansk could hear a mysterious *chuff* . . . *chuff* . . . from it as it made its run, like the panting of some monstrous beast.

"A monstreme?" he said, bewildered. "A galley propelled by monsters?"

The wheels reversed and whipped froth mast-high as the ram slid into the quinquereme's stern with a smashing crunch of timbers. The weird vessel backed off smoothly, and the quinquereme settled by the stern as water rushed into the huge rift. Its deck boiled with men as the hundreds of oarsmen ran screaming on deck, brushing aside the marines posted at the hatchway and throwing themselves into the water like fleas from a dying dog, heads turning the water black.

"What makes it *move*?" Jeschonyk cried, bewildered.

"At a guess, sir, it has something to do with fire—look at the smoke coming out of those two tubes."

Demansk thought that that was the most likely *logical* explanation. He sympathized with the half-dozen vessels he saw beating a hasty retreat northwards, although he'd see their commanders poled and their crews decimated if he survived this. His gut was showing him pictures of monstrous clawed feet pounding a treadmill inside that iron weirdness, and huge fanged mouths gasping out *chuff* . . . *chuff* . . . Jeschonyk was flinching in time with it, nerve shattered.

A thunder-loud noise rippled across the water, overriding the clash of timbers and the screams of thousands of men in pain and fear of death. A billow of smoke rose from the odd square structure on the forecastle of an Islander quinquereme. Less than a second later, a fountain of splinters and body parts rose from a Confed vessel. More jets of smoke, and the prow of the Confed vessel dissolved in a shower of smoke and wreckage; when it cleared water was already running over the decking. Square fins rose out of the water and swam closer, waiting. Demansk could feel the blank black eyes and hungry mouths beneath them. That was normal, at least. They always got scavengers around a battlefield, land or sea.

Then the *Islander* vessel's forepeak vanished in an explosion even louder, and left a huge bite out of the structure—enough to shatter the upper part of its hull as well.

"Whatever that thunder-weapon is, it isn't always reliable," Demansk said aloud. "They smote themselves, by the gods!"

He looked around. "You! Escort the Speaker below!" There was a cubbyhole of a captain's cabin on a trireme. "Sailing master!"

"Sir?"

"Take a look at that . . . thing. Doesn't it look to you as if those wheels are *pushing* it through the water?"

"Sir . . . I've never seen anything like it in all my life, and I've been at sea since I was six. Yes, that's as likely as anything."

The iron ship had just rammed another Confed quinquereme. This time it hung up for a moment, ram caught by a pinch of its victim's shattered timbers. Brave men leapt down from the quinquereme to its deck . . . and over into the sea, as their hobnailed sandals slipped and slid helplessly down the sloping iron. Demansk could see one man striking sparks as he windmilled for an instant and then went over with a splash.

"Lay me a course to ram it right in the center of the port wheel. Hundred-commander!"

The underofficer in command of the ship's Confed marines came up at a run. His face might have been carved from granite, but it was wet with sweat and rigid with tension under the transverse-crested helmet.

"Sir!"

"Have your men take off their marching sandals—I want 'em barefoot."

"Sir?" The man had been obviously, prayerfully thankful for orders; now he looked as if he feared the Justiciar might have joined the day's madness.

"Look at that thing. No, don't stare, just *look*. It's obviously timber, plated over with iron like a scale cuirass. Hobnails won't grip. Feet will! There are men inside, and I intend to kill those men."

"Yes, *sir*!"

The man strode off, bawling at his command. Demansk caught a strong whiff of the smoke boiling out of the iron ship as his trireme heeled and turned; honest woodsmoke, right enough.

If there are *men inside, and not monsters*—he thrust an image of claws on treadmills aside—*then they have to be steering from that little boxlike thing in front of the tubes. So they can't have a very good view, looking through slits like a close-helmet, and with all that smoke.*

He gave a quick, unaccustomed prayer to Wodep and Allfather Greatest and Best that he was right. His life and the Confederacy's western provinces both depended on it.

"Ramming speed!" he ordered. The iron ship was swelling with frightful suddenness.

"That's discouraging them," Esmond said.

Another Confed trooper on the beach staggered three steps backward and dropped, arms flung wide and shield spinning away. An arquebusier beside one of the *Revenge*'s steering oars chuckled and stepped back, letting his assistant and loader work. They moved in a coordinated dance, automatic now, grinning past the powder smuts that turned their faces into the masks of pantomime devils. Esmond's galley rose and fell with the surf, but the gunmen on it and the rest of his squadron were keeping the hundred-odd Confed troopers on shore from interfering.

"Line's hitched!" a sailor said, climbing over the stern naked and glistening wet.

Esmond nodded. "Take her out."

The oars had been poised, waiting. Now they dipped, driving deep; there was a unanimous heaving grunt from below, and again, and again . . .

"She floats!" the steersman said, letting his oar pivot down into water deep enough for it. "We've got her off!"

Esmond looked about with pride; five of his six ships were towing captives, the enemy ships coming after them oarless and sternfirst, the traditional sign of victory at sea. The other five triremes of the Confed squadron were burning hulks, or sunk. One was sticking out of the waves, its bronze beak planted firmly in the sandy mud of the shallow coastal waters. Wreckage floated past with the tide . . .

. . . an awful *lot* of wreckage. Esmond looked seaward, losing the diamond focus of commanding his own small section of the battle, and shaped a soundless whistle.

"Wodep!" he blurted.

The neat lines had vanished—he looked up at the sun and blinked astonishment—in only an hour. Instead there was a melee that stretched from here to the edge of sight, and almost to within catapult range of Preble's walls. Galleys were burning and sinking everywhere he looked; as he watched, a Confed quinquereme went nosedown and slid under the waves, shedding what looked like a coating of black fur at this distance, and that he knew was men clinging desperately to a life that sank beneath them. A little further off an Islander capital ship fired its four cannon directly into the deck of a Confed trireme, shattering the marines clumped to board into an abattoir mass of blood and torn meat, and punching through the deck into the crowded oar benches beneath. Even as it did a Confed quinquereme ranged up along its other side, and the boarding ramps slung up by ropes crashed down to link the ships, driving their iron beaks into the lower deck of the Islander vessel. Marines launched a volley of their weighted darts, and then swarmed across like implacable warrior ants. Here, there, a confusion no eye could take in. . . .

"Where's the ram?" Adrian was half-shouting, his eyes wild. "What has that donkey-fucking idiot done with my *ship*?"

"Allfather!" Demansk snapped.

The shock of impact threw him to his hands and knees on the deck, driving bits of armor into his flesh. He pulled himself upright again, watching with savage glee as the deck of the enemy vessel surged backward and the wheel beat itself to flinders on the bronze-sheathed timber of his ship's ram. Splinters rained back, as dangerous as flying knives, but he ignored them. Then the remnants of the wheel froze, and an odd muffled screaming sound came from within the . . . *Iron Monstreme*, Demansk thought. The monster-chuffing breath ceased abruptly.

"Follow me!" he roared. "Whatever it is, we hurt it! Now we finish it off!"

The boarding ramp fell. The iron spike penetrated at least a little, and Demansk ran down it. The iron plates felt strange beneath his bare feet, but skin gripped—the only problem was that it was just short of painfully hot. He crouched, holding his round officer's shield out for balance, and ran up the low curve towards the square blockhouse forward of the smoke cylinders. He could hear men following him, and one despairing scream as somebody slipped and slid into the water on his way to the bottom, and then they were crouched around the blockhouse. It was iron plates on timber, the same as the rest of the strange construction, but *steam* was leaking out of the slits—oddly like a bathhouse.

A hatchway on top of the blockhouse opened, and a man stumbled up and out, wavering, pawing at his crimson face. A dart landed in his gut with a wet *thwack* that was all too clear at this range.

"Prisoners!" Demansk shouted. "I want prisoners!"

Men clambered on to the roof of the blockhouse, and one of them gave Demansk a hand. The hatchway proved to be about the size of an ordinary door, but the space beyond was a ghostly mass of steam and vague thrashing figures.

Like an orgy in the steam room, Demansk thought, dazed. Whatever he'd been expecting, it wasn't *this*.

"We surrender!" a voice coughed, hoarse and rough, an Islander accent. "Let us out, for the love of the Mother!"

"Come out with your hands empty," Demansk called down.

A man came up, showing empty palms; one side of his face was a huge blister. "Spare us, lord! Mercy!"

"Who are you?" Demansk barked. "And what *is* this thing?"

Even as he spoke, he realized the futility of the question. Whatever this was, it probably couldn't be explained by a wounded man at assegai-point.

"Sharlz Thicelt," the man said. "Water, lord?" Demansk nodded, and a man handed over a canteen. The Islander drank, gasped, coughed, drank again. "I'm skipper of the *Wodep's Fist*—or was."

He spat some of the water on the corpse of the first man who left the hatchway, and tore off his turban in a gesture of pure rage, revealing a long shaven skull. The gold hoops in his ears bounced with the vehemence of his motion as he threw the turban after the spittle. Demansk thought that if the footing had been better, he'd have run over and kicked the corpse as well.

"And that *was* Prince Tenny, may the Sun God reincarnate him as the blind bastard of a pox-ridden half-arnket whore. The gods-forsaken little sodomite lost us the battle."

"Lord King!" Adrian said.

The King of the Isles was still wearing his gilded armor, hacked and battered and blood-splashed. That took some courage, in a small launch. There was no need to ask what had happened to the flagship; it was not a thousand yards off, with two battered but still floating Confed quinqueremes lashed to either side.

Casull stalked to the quarterdeck, his eyes travelling over the chaos that reigned on this stretch of reddened ocean. "I do not abide by a plan that has failed," he grated. "We'll retreat." He looked at the *Revenge*'s steersman. "Set course for the nearest ship still in our hands. We'll have to arrange a rearguard, if we're to get to Preble in one piece."

He looked at Esmond then. "Where is my son?"

Esmond met his eyes. "Lord King, the enemy holds the *Wodep's Fist.* Beyond that, I do not know."

Casull sighed, his eyes dull. "If he lives, we'll hear before sunset; demands for ransom, enough to leave the kingdom poor. If not . . . if not, we'll drink his spirit home to the Sun."

CHAPTER TWELVE

The King's eyes were alive and bitter by the time the sun had been down two hours; they were bloodshot and a little inclined to wander, as he lay on the cushions downing cup after cup of unwatered wine, but his voice was only slightly slurred. The air of the chamber was thick with incense, with attar of roses and patchouli oil from the courtesans who danced and sang and drank with men on their cushions, with the smells of wine and sweat and ointment on bandaged wounds. Light flickered from the lamps on the gilded plaster of the ceiling, worked in sea monsters and figures from legend, and on the pale stone of the walls and their lapis inlay of flowers and trees.

"A toast!" the King of the Isles said, glaring at the Emeralds where they sat halfway down the great municipal banqueting hall of Preble. The dull roar of conversation died, except for snatches of drunken song from those too far gone to care. "A toast to my son, the shining warrior, Prince Tenny!"

"*Prince Tenny!*" the hall roared back.

Casull threw the cup to one side, and the priceless Vanbert glassware shattered. A servant shoved another into his hand.

"And another toast! To the bastard son of a whore, Esmond Gellert, who lost the battle by running amok without orders!"

Esmond stood, graceful and tall in a plain tunic and swordbelt. His hand fell unconsciously to the place where a hilt would have been, if men could feast armed before the King. The guardsmen leaning on their great scimitars tensed slightly; a fighting man like the Emerald was never entirely disarmed. Before he could speak, Adrian rose beside him, bowing:

"O King, your kingdom's heart bleeds with you in your honorable grief for Prince Tenny, fallen like so many others on this day of sorrow!" he said, the trained rhetor's voice filling the chamber without straining. "Yet even in grief, a King remembers justice!"

The red-veined eyes turned on him. "You speak of justice, bumboy?" he grated.

"Indeed, Lord King," Adrian cut in, smoothly enough that it did not seem to be an interruption—one art both the Grove's school of rhetoric and the lawcourts of Vanbert taught. "It would not be just to punish the only squadron commander in your fleet who today sank his own numbers in Confed vessels, and brought as many more behind him, towing them in victory to lay at your feet."

That brought Casull to a halt for a second, his mouth open. Adrian swallowed, his own so dry that he was insanely tempted to stop for a drink; his temples pounded, and his body dragged with the weariness of the day's fighting. He flogged his brain into functioning, as merciless to himself as he'd been throwing grenades into the oar decks of Confed galleys.

"And indeed, he did so on my urging," he went on. Casull's eyes narrowed. "Not that I, a mere artificer, would have dared to put my word against the King's! May the King live forever! We are as dust beneath his feet. No, my own wisdom is only wise enough to know that I should never interfere in such matters. Yet before the word of the shining Prince Tenny, the hero and heir, what could I do but obey?"

"What is this?" Casull said, visibly trying to gather his wits. He didn't need to be sober for the sort of temper-fit he'd had in mind, or to give the necessary orders afterwards. He hadn't expected to be engaging in the *elenchos* of the Grove.

"In this very harbor, while I showed him the ship *Wodep's Fist*,

Prince Tenny commanded me on pain of his utmost wrath that any Confed movement towards Preble must be stopped—since the Royal garrison would be on shipboard for the great battle. Thus I saw Confed ships break away towards Preble, and thus I laid the commands of the Prince upon my brother. What could he do but obey, my lord King? What could I do? We were as dust beneath his feet. And see the wisdom of the Prince's commands; the walls of Preble stand, a strong base for our next attack!"

"Next?" Casull roared, shaking a fist. "You want me to lose my *whole* fleet, and see the Confeds sacking Chalice? Are you in their pay?"

"Ah, my lord pleases to jest! See how I laugh, taken by his wit! My lord will have noticed today, that our triremes—those that carried, as I advised, many arquebusiers, rather than spreading them about in small numbers—could devastate the slower Confed ships from a range that neither catapult nor bow could match. Thus were five sunk, and five captured, with hardly any loss. Next time—"

"Get out! I've had my belly full of your lies, and my son is dead, and I must beg the Confed commander for his body. Get out, before I kill you!"

"The King commands," Adrian said, bowing again.

"What *are* these things?" Helga asked, fascinated, touching one gingerly but trying to make it seem as if it was to steady herself against the gentle rocking of the anchored ship.

Demansk frowned at his daughter, but it wasn't really a formal occasion where it was grossly improper for a woman to speak. Most of the Confed force's commanders were asleep in their tents, and so were most of the surviving men. Only a few aides and some troopers to hold torches were with him on the deck of the captured Islander quinquereme.

He peered at the bronze shape that lay on a carriage of oak with four small wheels, amid a cat's-cradle of ropes and pulleys. A smell hung about it, of hot metal and sulfur. *Death farts from the Lord of the Shades,* he thought sardonically.

"It's like those arquebuses, only much bigger," he said. "Look, there are the stone balls it threw—or those sacks of lead ones.

Hellpowder down the muzzle, the ball or bag on top, set fire to it, and out it goes—smashing ships and men." He shook his head. "This changes the whole face of war, forever, do you understand?" His anger was distant, muffled. "We can't keep it secret, now—not with the Islanders still having more. If they use these things, we must too, and . . ." His voice stopped with an enormous yawn.

"And you can curse Adrian more tomorrow, Father," she said. "I still think you weren't recovered enough for a battle—even if you *did* destroy the iron ram all by yourself."

Pride glowed through the sarcasm of her words, and Demansk felt himself swelling a little. Well, it *was* something of a feat . . . perhaps enough for a triumph in Vanbert? Perhaps even the Speaker's chair; there was so much that cried out to be done, to make safe the State.

And I'm out on my feet and getting delirious, he told himself severely. "Back to camp."

The captured quinqueremes were with the surviving capital ships of the Confed fleet, tied up to bollards at their bows, sterns out into the artificial harbor. They couldn't be drawn up like the dozens of triremes beached on either side, but they were secure enough here. *More than secure,* Demansk thought. The rock-filled merchantmen that made up the breakwaters reached well out into the ocean, defining a rectangle five hundred feet by a thousand; out at the entrance, two wooden forts rested on two large cargo carriers each. Flaming baskets of wood reached out on poles, to show the boom of chain-linked logs that sealed the entrance against raiders. The forts had archers and slingers and catapults, and they were well within range of each other. Shoreward were the dockyards and the whole Confed camp, still sixteen thousand regulars and as many auxiliaries—they'd even had time to run up timber barracks and housing, while the fleet was being made ready.

He glared out towards the dim lights of Preble, just visible on the southwestern horizon. The battle had been about even, which made it a Confed victory—and next time they'd have had time to study the new weapons, come up with countertactics of their own, *and* they'd still have the weight of men and metal on their side. Next time . . .

(((•))) (((•))) (((•)))

"The King was angry," Adrian said judiciously.

Esmond drank and wiped his mouth. "The King was ripshit," he said. "The King may have us all impaled before morning, if he doesn't pass out first—he may regret it when he sobers up, but that won't help *us*."

probability of execution in the next 6 hours is 67%, ±7, Center said helpfully.

To be fair, Raj said judiciously, ***Casull really doesn't understand the new weapons. He's a fair to good commander with what he does understand.***

Adrian looked around the small rooftop platform; he and Esmond, and their seconds-in-command, plus a scattering of Striker officers . . . Nobody was looking too cheerful. *Frankly, I doubt anyone here is in the mood to be particularly fair,* he thought.

"We're the only ones who kick Confed ass, and we're in line to be buggered by the Oakman," Donnuld Grayn said. "Ain't no justice in this world, not if you're a hired soldier. Fuck all Islanders, anyway. If *Lord Gellert*'d been in command today, we'd be drinking Jeschonyk's wine." He grinned with a friendly malice. "And Lord Adrian here would be back diddling Demansk's daughter."

Adrian flushed. How *that* news had gotten out, the Gray-Eyed alone knew. Although letting it do so was more in Gellerix's line, if you listened to the old stories.

"Esmond would have done better," he agreed neutrally.

Because he'd listen to you, Raj said. ***I think that left to himself, he'd make a battle plan and then use the new weapons in it, not build the plan around their capacities. Of course, he doesn't have Center to lean on. He's a better than middling commander, with the weapons mix you have here—very good indeed.***

There were times when the sheer *objectivity* of his invisible companions could get a little wearing, even to a Scholar of the Grove who'd striven for detachment all his days. All things in moderation, even moderation.

And we want the new weapons to make a difference, he observed.

correct, Center said. **to break this planet from its stasis, the**

innovations must be shown to be decisively superior. it must be shown that the future is qualitatively different from, and superior to, the past—an essential shift in overall paradigm.

"The question before us now," Adrian said aloud, reverting automatically to the *elenchos* of the Grove, "is what course of action can *save* us from being . . . ah, buggered by the Oakman."

"Well, we could bring the whole Confed fleet back for the King to roast prawns over," Esmond said morosely. "*And* all the captured ships, and all their cannon and hellpowder."

"Gunpowder," Adrian corrected automatically, and then froze. He was conscious of the others looking at him, but within his skull there was a blinding light; it was not unlike the near-orgasmic ecstasy of having an insight, but multiplied by three and with the resonances of three separate personalities added in.

"Wait, wait!" he said, holding up a hand. "Look, it's a longshot, but it beats being impaled. Here's what we'll do—"

When the words stopped tumbling forth, the other four men were staring at him with the stars reflecting in their wide eyes.

"Suicide," Esmond whispered.

"Oh, no," Adrian said. The thought of what he proposed to do stopped him for a moment, and his smile was a trifle ghastly. *All men are initiates of the mysteries of death,* he reminded himself sternly. "Waiting here for the King to decide we're to blame for his son getting killed, *that's* suicidal. This is just risky."

Grayn rubbed his chin. "Couldn't we just run off and take up piracy?" he said.

"That's slow suicide, with all the people we'd have pissed off at us," Adrian snapped back. "Confeds *and* the King of the Isles after our asses? I don't think so."

The mercenary nodded. Adrian looked at Simun. The grizzled little man shrugged. "Well, you're the lord, sir, so whatever you order's fine with us." He sighed and heaved himself erect. "Better go get the men ready, before they're too deep in the jug or dipping their wicks—makes a man grumpy if you interrupt him, and sleepy if you don't. Been a long day . . ."

His voice trailed off as he trotted down the stairs. Grayn was staring at the stars. "Getting out of the harbor, that might be a bitch," he said thoughtfully. "Got the chain boom up."

It was Esmond's turn to smile. "And we've got squads with the militia in the towers either side of the harbor mouth," he said. "Prince Tenny, bless him, didn't rearrange that—and I suppose the King hasn't had time to look into details."

"So, all we've got to worry about is the Confeds," Grayn said, rising and gathering up sword and helmet, and fastening the clasps of his armor. "All twenty-fucking-thousand of them, and a couple of hundred of us. Wodep, I should have stayed home and farmed olives with my brothers."

"Wish I was going with you," Esmond whispered as Adrian put his foot on the rope ladder over the side of the *Revenge*.

Whispering was unnecessary; they were well beyond hearing distance from the Confed harbor, far enough away that its watchfires were simply a dim glow in the distance, a glimmer that might have been phantom lights chasing each other across a man's closed eyelids.

"I'm glad you're not," Adrian said. "There has to be *somebody* out there to haul my ass out of the crack, big brother." Seriously: "May the Gray-Eyed Lady of Wisdom hold Her shield above you tonight, brother."

"And over you—you're her favorite." Then he snorted laughter.

"What's funny?"

"King Casull. He'll *just* be getting the news we've deserted!"

Adrian grinned back at him and dropped the last foot into the launch. There was a glimmer of white, a slow chopping *shssshhhh* as the trireme and its companions pulled away northward and west, looping out from the coast.

"Let's get going, then," Adrian said, when the ships had vanished in the moonless dark. He turned his head, and a glowing arrow painted itself across his vision.

"Yessor," Simun agreed; he and a nephew were acting as Adrian's loaders and rowers tonight, at his gentle insistence—he *was* a fisherman's son, as he pointed out, and as at home in small boats as any.

"All right," the older man went on to his relative. "Now lay out—row dry, ye dickhead, and row soft, or this oar'll cob you. Show no white on yor blade when it cuts the water, now. Row soft."

The soft glow grew ahead of them as they angled in to the northeast. A half-hour, and Simun and his nephew were breathing soft and deep; he could smell their sweat in the warm summer night. A touch of mist lay on the water, low curls of it; that was helpful. It was quiet enough that the occasional *plop* of a jumping fish was distinct and sharp through the darkness. Now square shapes cut the night, blotted outlines against the frosting of stars on the eastern horizon.

Adrian's vision brightened with Center's passionless certainty. Now he could see the fire-baskets out on poles from the wooden forts at each end of the artificial harbor, and diffuse fire glow from the vast Confed camp beyond. And smell it, the rank odor of so many men crammed together. The fires above the water had died down to dull glows.

Careless, he thought. They should be kept bright with pine knots the night through.

They've had a hard day too, lad, Raj said. ***It's hard keeping men up to the mark when they're that exhausted. Although you're right; I'd have the rank-tabs off any officer I caught letting this happen.***

"We're coming up on the boom," Adrian said softly from where he knelt in the bows of the small boat. "About a thousand yards. It's just barely awash. Big logs."

"Eyes like a cat, sor," Simun grunted, looking over his shoulder as he rowed. "Suppose it comes of bein' favored of the gods, like."

"Rest easy," Adrian said, clambering between them into the stern of the boat and carrying the big net of clay jars with him; that tilted its prow up, nearly out of the water. "All right—fast as you can!"

"Row!" Simun called softly to his nephew. "Fast now, boy, stretch out—*rapppiipai! Rapppippipai!*"

The two men leaned into their oars, rising and falling with breathy grunts of effort. Adrian waited, poised, while the towers loomed on either side like the gates of the land of the Shades—only the giant three-headed hound was lacking, and there were watchdogs enough in the towers, and in the camp behind. *I* am *insane,* went through him. *This has all been a delusion, and I'm completely fucking insane—*

Center's vision showed him the floating barrier of logs ahead. He waited; then the boat's keel ground on the rough wood with an ugly crackling, crunching sound.

"Forward!" he called, and leapt into the bows, using the shock of impact to power his jump.

The two at the oars followed him, and the stern came out of the water. The boat teetered, wavered . . . and then slid forward with a splash that sounded to Adrian's ears like the launching of a quinquereme down a slipway, with a flute and drum corps in accompaniment. Even his own breathing was like a bellows, and he slowed it with an effort of will, hissing the others to silence. The boat drifted, the oars loose on the thongs that secured them to the muffled oarlocks. Simun scrambled back on his hands and knees, swearing softly and checking the bottom of the boat with his fingers for the welling leaks that might show a cracked strake.

Nothing; no shouts, no blazing lights. The towers were looking for bigger fish . . . if they were looking at all, and not just dozing. Adrian sat for a moment controlling his breathing, feeling the slowing of a heart whose pounding shook his chest.

"All *right,*" Simun said, his voice low and fierce. "We *did* it, sor!"

"'Well begun, half done; half done, not begun,'" Adrian said, quoting an old Emerald folk saying. The founder of the Grove had been fond of it, too; it was *whispered* that he'd been a stonecutter and the son of a peasant himself. "This way."

The artificial harbor was as rectangular as men could make it, in the Confed style. They hadn't straightened the beach at the inner end, though; that was a half-moon, turning the whole affair into a U-shape. The low irregular line of the rock-filled ships loomed on either side, five hundred feet apart, with waves breaking on the outer sides and throwing a little white foam over the bulwarks. This arrangement would never survive a series of winter gales, but it only needed to last as long as the siege of Preble . . . and there at the base of the U were the ships.

Center's lightening of the darkness intensified; Adrian felt as if an invisible line were being wound tighter and tighter around his forehead. Then it eased, and a strobing arrow marked their course.

the four captured quinqueremes, Center pointed out.

Adrian looked up. "It's after midnight," he said. "Nobody'll be around."

"Deck watches, sor," Simun pointed out, nodding towards a dim lantern on the stern of one of the Confed vessels.

"But nobody on the captured ships, not yet. Take us in, but keep as near the middle as you can; beach her right next to the left-hand quinquereme of those four. When these"—he tapped the clay jugs—"start going off, things are likely to get a bit hairy, so be ready to push off when I get back."

"Bit hairy, sor." Simun chuckled softly. "Take yor time, but by Gellerix' cunt, don't linger, eh?"

The oars bit, and Adrian—slowly, cautiously—loaded one of the jugs into his staff-sling. The jugs held a mixture of fish oil, sulfur, naphtha oil that oozed out of rocks, and quicklime. Experiment had shown they'd burn like the heart of a forge fire and couldn't be put out. They were also fairly fragile.

"Coming up on the shore," he said. The darkness grew more absolute, as they ghosted into the shade of the captured quinquereme; it had the faint sewer stench a rowing vessel always did, even if the bilges were pumped regularly. "Lay on your oars."

The two men did, and Adrian hopped over the side. His sandals grated on pebbles and sand, and he reached back in for the sack of what Center, for some reason, called *molotovs*.

"Back in a minute," he said casually, and walked up the beach.

The rams of the quinqueremes almost glowed with Center's unearthly vision, serrated bronze catching faint starlight. Off somewhere a man's voice raised in song, then ended in a squall—probably a wakened sleeper hitting him, Adrian thought distantly. He walked casually: if you looked as if you belonged, you'd shed a casual glance—people saw what they expected to see. Turning, he took his stance and aimed. *Left to right,* he thought.

Swing, swing, *throw*.

The jug arched out, wobbling a little as the liquid within shifted. It struck the first quinquereme right on the forecastle, on the timber square added to bear the weight of the guns. *Crash.* Not very loud, but distinct amid the wave lap and insect buzz of the night. A flicker of light, as the air found the quicklime. *Crash.* One more, to make sure. *Crash. Crash. Crash. Crash. Crash. Crash . . .*

Fire on every one of the four captured ships. Enough to brighten this stretch of beach quite perceptibly; paint and rope and dry pinewood caught easily. Now all he could do was pray.

probability of optimal outcome 51% ±3, Center supplied hopefully. **in this instance, "optimal" requires the survival of adrian gellert.**

I'll still pray, Adrian thought, jogging back to the boat.

"*Good* to see ye, sor," Simun panted.

They shoved off and began rowing, not so quickly as to attract attention . . . he hoped.

"Uh-oh."

A horn winded through the night, and then an alarm drum. With the gathering light from the burning ships, the harbor looked much smaller than it had in darkness. Much smaller, and the fire baskets on the entrance forts suddenly blazed, as they were swung in and then out again with a fresh load of pine knots. The huts nearest the beach held the deck crews of the Confed warships; men were swarming down to the shore, wading out and climbing up the sides of their vessels. Already officers were beginning to warp them away from the burning ships—excess caution, really. They were close, but not that close, and without rigging or sails aloft it would take more than heat and sparks to set them alight. Confeds *might* have been able to extinguish the fires on the captured ships if they'd gone straight there, Adrian mused—anything to distract his mind from what might happen, and what he couldn't do a thing about. They had no chance at all once they'd finished seeing to their own ships, but trained reflex was stronger than thought in an emergency. It had to be.

Flames licked higher from the prows of the ex-Islander warships. Adrian suddenly felt like a bug on a plate, his head whipping to and fro as he tried to see in all directions at once. Simun and his nephew were cursing in antiphonal harmony as they dug their oars in madly, like the chorus at a Goat Song festival play. Men were crowding onto the parapets of the wooden forts—archers. A six-oared launch put out from one of them, and the officer in the bows was pointing at *him*. More and more men ran down to the shore, and the growing buzz from the Confed camp was like some great beast awakening, grumpy and angry from its winter sleep . . . and growling.

Sisst. A flight of arrows came slanting down out of the dark, into the water off the skiff's bow. *Sissst.* Closer now, and the raiders' own efforts were driving them further into range. The light grew ever brighter, as well. He could see quite plainly now, for several hundred yards; see the crew manhandling a catapult around on the tower top, a dart-thrower that could skewer a man at a thousand feet, much less the four hundred that separated his own tinglingly vulnerable body from it.

His head whipped back to shore. There were other small craft there; men were shouting and pointing at Adrian's skiff, and launching the boats. *All men are initiates of the mysteries of death,* he repeated to himself. And: *Helga. Damn it . . .*

The world ended.

"What's *that*?" Donnuld Grayn gasped.

"That is my brother," Esmond said, throwing up a hand and shouting.

He needed to do both. The Strikers had been creeping up toward the Confed encampment in the dark, their ships lightly beached behind them to the north. For a moment the night turned bright as day, a huge globe of fire rising to silhouette the rear of the camp's wall where the magazines of the captured Islander quinquerimes had exploded. Streaks and ribbons of fire shot up from it, and huge burning timbers pinwheeled through the sky. When they fell, whatever they landed on burned as well; the other ships in the harbor, the long sheds above the shoreline crammed full of pitch and tar, turpentine and rope and boards and sails, the warehouses of olive oil and grain, the rough pine barracks the Confeds had raised . . .

One of the wooden towers along the landward wall was blazing, too; a twenty-foot baulk of pine flaming like a torch had dropped out of the sky on it. Men swarmed along the parapet, frantically tearing at the burning wood and dashing futile buckets on it.

"Fire!" Esmond called, startled out of his wonderment. "Fire, and save your lord!"

The arquebuses of Adrian's men began to bark with a methodical eagerness. And on the wall of the Confed fortress, men began to die.

Oh, shit, Adrian thought, as he pulled himself up.

His ears hurt, and his head when he shook it to clear his vision of the spots strobing across it. When it did clear, a grin spread over his mouth despite the pain. Half the harbor was burning, and half the camp beyond—and most of the men there were *far* too occupied to be concerned with the small boat they'd spotted a moment before. *Make that three-quarters,* he thought, as another Confed vessel began to blaze out of control, and its deck crew scrambled ashore or over the side.

Sisssht. More arrows plowed into the water around the boat; this time two stuck in the thwarts, humming like bees.

"I'd be afraid if I had the time," Adrian said quietly. Louder: "Row for the north bank of the harbor—that ship there!"

He pointed to one of the sunken merchantmen, just within sling range of the north tower. Then he stood, trying to compensate for the pitch and roll of the little skiff with his knees, sling dangling from his hand. The enemy launch was quite close now, close enough to see the firelight glitter ruddily on the spears of the men between the rowers.

Swing. Swing. *Throw*.

His hand moved in blank obedience to Center's direction, fingers releasing the thong when the red dot blinked. The firebomb—*molotov*—arched out with a steady, inevitable trajectory. He could hear it shatter against the breastplate of the officer in the launch, and hear the man's scream as the flames took him even more clearly. Luck—Adrian's, not the man's in the launch—pitched him forward into the arms of his men, to spatter fire among them, lighting hair and tunics and the wood of the craft with impartial ferocity.

"Row, gods condemn you!" Adrian roared to Simun and his nephew.

The towers had seen what was happening, and worse, where he was going. He felt at the burlap sack; three more *molotovs*. Arrows fell around them, and more stuck quivering in the wood of the skiff. One passed by his ear, close enough for the feathers to sting; two inches left, and the last sound he ever would have heard would have been that one crunching into his brain.

Shock of impact; the prow of the boat was level with the railing of the sunken rock-filled merchant ship. The wood was splintery under his hands as he vaulted aboard, the deck wet and unstable underneath his feet. Two ships down, a party from the tower was clambering towards him, shields up and assegais out. Their faces were red with the light of the burning camp; he must be a black outline to them, a figure out of darkness and night.

"Behind you!" he screamed at them. "Your tower's burning too, you velipad fuckers!"

Swing. Swing. *Throw*.

The *molotov* whipped out, not at the soldiers but at the wooden fortress behind them. Heads followed it, and saw where it left a streak of red fire on the wood.

Swing. Swing. *Throw*. A sharp pain in his leg, above the knee, and the limb threatened to buckle. The pain was distant, and he ignored it. Ignored the weakness, forcing the muscle rigid. Swing. Swing. *Throw*. A last crackle against the wood of the tower.

One of the troopers clambering towards him bawled in panic and threw away his shield, leaping into the sea; not *quite* total madness, since he hadn't had time to don his mail shirt. He struck out for the other side of the harbor with a clumsy threshing stroke. As if that had been the first rock of an avalanche, men began to throw themselves out of the tower into the water.

Adrian felt a great tension drain, and his strength along with it. The leg gave under him, and he found himself somehow seated on the deck, staring without belief at the black-fletched arrow through the fleshy part of his thigh. Then the pain struck, and he bit his lip to hold back a moan.

Simun was bending over him. "Not serious, sir. Head's right through, clean. Here, I'll break it off and pull this out—"

"*Nnnghg!*"

"There we go, m'lord, right as rain when I tie it up—"

"Uncle."

Simun looked up, and saw the last two Confed troopers clambering onto the prow of the merchantman. "Well, fuck me, some people don't know when they're not welcome," he said, scooping up Adrian's staff-sling. He scrabbled in his own belt pouch, came out with a lead bullet the size of a small plum, and dropped it into the cup.

Crack. The first Confed pitched backward, with an oval hole in his forehead and his eyes bulging with hydrostatic shock from the blow that had homogenized his brain.

Simun dropped the sling and drew his sword, unhooking the small buckler from his belt. "Spread out, Davad," he told his nephew.

The two Emeralds did, and the Confed began backing up—he had shield, helmet and assegai, but not his mail shirt.

"And hurry up," Simun said, moving forward, light on his feet. "We've got to get the boat over this whore of a hulk and out to where Lord Esmond's waiting for us. The commander ought to get to the surgeon, too."

CHAPTER THIRTEEN

"Why do I feel as if this is a noose?" Esmond muttered under his breath as he backed away from King Casull with the chain of gold and emeralds bouncing on his chest.

The mutter might have gone unheard in the screaming roar of the crowd, if Center had not been filtering Adrian's perceptions. *I wish you could make the leg hurt less,* he thought. To his brother: "It well might be, if we're not careful."

The King of the Isles was all benevolence as he waved from the dais on the harborfront to the crowds, spreading an arm to indicate the Gellerts. Adrian didn't miss the slight narrowing of eyes as the cheers mounted into hysterical abandon. The Gellerts were far *too* popular now, with the Confed fleet in ashes and all but a precautionary garrison retreating eastward. Far too popular, and far too likely to be candidates to rule Preble themselves. The populace certainly wouldn't object; the problem would be to keep them from deifying Esmond and Adrian both, and sacrificing to them. After months with the horrors of a Confed sack hanging over the city, it wasn't surprising.

Nor safe, from Casull's point of view, Adrian thought, as the sons of the Syndics of Preble—who'd vied for the honor—picked up the poles of the carrying chair, to take him to the state banquet. *And I don't think he's the type to forget Tenny, either.*

"In a week," he said to his brother—they were close in the sedan chair, "he'll have convinced himself we deliberately set Tenny up, so we could seize Preble ourselves and set up as kings."

Esmond's eyes narrowed. "It's what he'd have done himself," he pointed out. Adrian nodded; King Casull IV was no son of Casull III, after all—he'd started out as an ambitious general. "In fact," Esmond went on, "it's not a half-bad idea. We could cause the Confederacy no *end* of grief here, running things."

Adrian looked around in alarm, fast enough to draw a fresh throb of pain from his bandaged leg. It was healing so quickly as to be near miraculous in this hot climate—Center had had some hints about spirits of wine—but it was a serious wound.

"No, don't worry, little brother," Esmond said. "We couldn't get away with it—not between Casull and the Confeds. The Confeds might take us on as client-kings, but that's out of the question, of course." His smile became a little strange. "Their camp burned, but Vanbert still stands . . . and Nanya's not avenged yet."

Adrian swallowed and looked away. "Well, there's an idea I've had," he said. *I and my friends.* "It would get us away from Chalice, which Casull would like; it'll cause the Confeds a lot of grief, which we'll both like—" *though you more than me, brother,* he thought sadly. Center's merciless visions left a man little of the loyalties he'd been brought up with. "—and I think it might *really* change things."

"As long as it's a change the Confeds hate, I'm for it," Esmond said, waving to a bevy of hareem beauties leaning out of a window and throwing dried flower petals. The sons of the Syndics were making heavy weather of the crowds on the way to the Town Hall, even with a squad of Esmond's Strikers going before them with active spear butts. "Tell me more."

"O King, live forever, your favor has been lavished on us like the Sun's light on the fields," Adrian said, gagging slightly on his own fulsomeness. It didn't sound quite so bad in Islander, but he could see why his ancestors had fought so hard in the League Wars to keep the Islanders out of the Emerald cities. "We wrack our brains for a means whereby we may repay a tenth, a thousandth of the kindness you have shown our unworthy, outland selves."

When you're dealing with an autarch, lay it on with a trowel, lad, Raj's voice said. ***At least, when he's got the jump on you. Part of the cost of doing business.***

Despite the riches and titles King Casull had showered on the Gellerts—he had little choice, with the greatest Islander victory over the Confeds in five generations dropped in his lap—it was notable that the Gellerts were no longer invited to small informal audiences. This one was in the Syndic's Hall of Preble; besides the guards who lined the wall behind the throne there were a brace before the dais as well, and a quartet of hard-faced Islander admirals—or pirate chiefs, if you looked at it from another angle—flanking the King.

"I'm sure you'll find a way," Casull said, leaning his bearded chin on a fist and the elbow on an arm of the throne. The aigrette of peacock feathers and diamonds nodded over a face more lined and gray than it had been when the Gellerts first saw him. "Do go on."

"O King, the Isles are strong at sea. The Confederation is strong on land; not least because of the endless number of their fighting men. This is the Isle's most insoluable problem, because while the Confed's numbers may learn skill, the Isles cannot bring forth a half a million peasants to draft into an army."

"Yes, yes." An impatient gesture of the hand.

"Would it not then follow—" Adrian caught himself falling back into the cadence of a Grove lecture, and gave himself a mental shake "—be sensible, I mean, to make alliance with the only other power which commands manpower on the same scale?"

Casull's brows rose. "Now you really *do* interest me! What power is left in the civilized world, beyond the Isles and a few little scraps, and Confed client kingdoms and puppets?"

"No *civilized* kingdom, lord King."

Adrian waited, sweating, while the lights went on behind the King's dark eyes. Inwardly, he asked once more: *Are we really going to serve civilization by arming* barbarians? *We call the Islanders that, but the Southrons—they're fucking* savages, *no mincing words.*

given a continuation of present trends, civilization on the

northern continent will fall; the probability is as close to unity as stochastic analysis allows, Center thought remorselessly. A vision unrolled before Adrian's eyes, one he had seen before—the gap-toothed grin of a Southron horseman as he pursued a silk-clad woman down a street in burning Vanbert. Adrian blinked it away with a shudder; his own mind had painted Helga's face on her.

One of the admirals snorted laughter. "The Southrons? They'd have trouble organizing an orgy in a whorehouse. They're fierce and numerous, yes, but the Confeds slaughter them like pigs in a pen, when it comes to open battle."

Adrian inclined his head. "My lord is acute," he said. "Yet the ignorant may learn . . . and I have some things to teach them, I think."

"Ah," King Casull said, sitting up. "You wish me to send you to Marange." The great, sprawling anarchic freeport that was the closest thing to a capital the southern continent had, and its only city. "Much might be done in Marange. The Southron lands are rich in men . . . and timber."

"But not in seamen," Adrian said. *Well, I knew Casull wasn't any kind of fool,* he thought. "As Your Majesty knows, the Gray-Eyed Lady herself couldn't teach the Southrons to sail a piece of soap across a bathtub."

An unwilling smile bent the monarch's lips; Adrian could hear a muffled snort from Esmond, where he stood at parade rest behind his brother with his helmet tucked under one arm.

"But fighting on land, that's another matter. Yes, most of them are brainless yokels, and a century of defeats wouldn't teach them not to run at the nearest foe like a greatbeast bull in musth running at a gate," he went on. "Yet have not emissaries from some of their chiefs come here to the Isles, speaking of alliance?"

"Yes, from Chief of Chiefs Norrys," Casull said absently; most of his attention was turned inward, to his own thoughts. "Or rather, from his kinsman, Chief Prelotta. Prelotta spent five years in Vanbert as hostage for a treaty, if I recall correctly."

Adrian nodded enthusiastically. Exposing a barbarian to civilization might convert him . . . or it could just teach him technique, sharpen his appetite, and show him where the really *good* loot was. In either case, it usually made him more dangerous.

"Yes," Casull said. "I will speak the truth; despite your services to me, the thought of my son comes between me and happiness when I see your faces. But this . . . yes, we must think upon it." He rose. "You may go."

Adrian and his brother knelt, rose, and backed out of the presence; Casull was already deep in conversation with his advisors.

"Phew!" Esmond said, in the corridor outside. "I'm getting nervous at these audiences—as Grayn would put it, my arse feels the shadow of the Oakman every time the King looks our way. I suppose that's why you came up with this crazy stunt."

"I haven't gotten us killed," Adrian pointed out. His brother's hand clapped down on his shoulder.

"Yet," he said. A cruel smile lit the handsome face. "But together we've gotten an entire *shitload* of Confeds killed—and this scheme sounds as if it'll be even better. The Confederacy can be wounded at sea, but to kill it you have to go ashore."

Adrian shivered slightly as he followed his brother's tall form out into the brightness of the courtyard.

"Men," the elder Gellert said to the waiting officers and noncoms. "Looks like we're going on a trip."

EPILOGUE

Helga Demansk turned in the saddle to look back at the wreckage of the Confed camp. Anger warred with pride as she looked at the ribs of the burned ships, stranded like the blackened remains of dead sea dragons on the shore. A brisk autumn wind brought the smell of the sea and soot to the rear of the Confederation column where the Justiciar and his daughter rode. She dabbed at her mouth with the back of one hand; she'd been ill, a little, lately. It was a cool brisk day, and waves were breaking high over the lines of rock-laden ships; in a month of storms they'd be driftwood and scattered stones on the beach. In two years, only mounds beneath the grass would show that men had ever come to make war here. For now there was a forlorn look to the empty barracks and the neat gridwork of roads, the lines of raw dirt where the earth walls had been spaded back into the ditches.

"Quite a mess," she said. Spies from Preble had brought word of who was responsible; and that the Gellerts had left, none knew where. "But Adrian won't be bothering us here anymore."

Her father worked his wounded arm, testing the healing. "My dear, I'm afraid we haven't heard the end of either of the Gellerts," he said. "If not here, then elsewhere." He raised the arm in salute, as one should to a capable enemy. It cost nothing to be polite, even when duty required that one kill a man; he went on:

"Still, it was a first-rate job of work. Maybe the gods *are* whispering in that young Emerald's ear." Another snort of laughter. "Maybe he's a god in disguise, as the old stories tell of—and this *was* like the War of the Thousand Ships."

His daughter's grin grew wider, and she ducked her head towards her saddlebow. *In that case, Father dear, I suspect you're going to be grandfather to a demigod.* It was better to laugh than cry.

She looked out to sea. And she suspected her father was right; sooner rather than later, they *would* be hearing from Adrian again.

Helga Demansk decided she was rather looking forward to that.

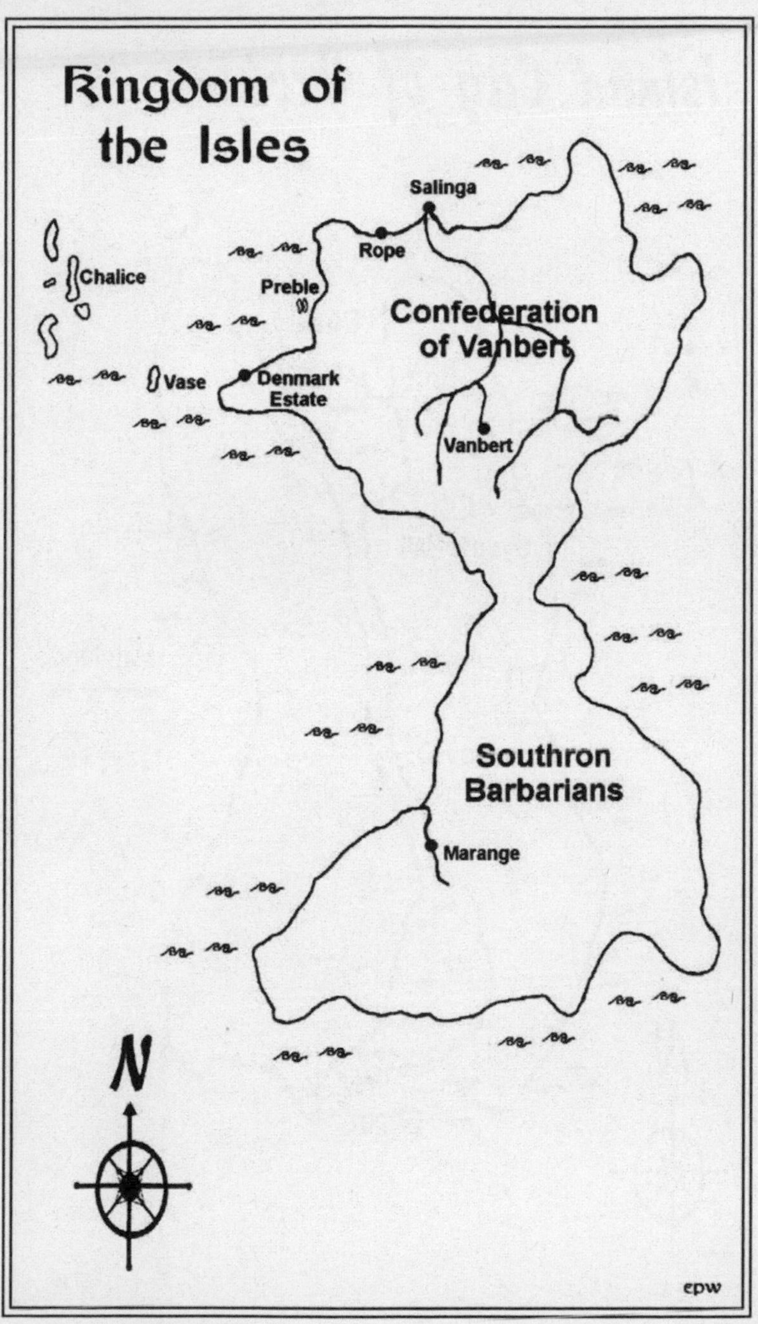
Kingdom of the Isles
Salinga
Rope
Chalice
Preble
Confederation of Vanbert
Vase
Denmark Estate
Vanbert
Southron Barbarians
Marange
N
epw

Island City of Preble

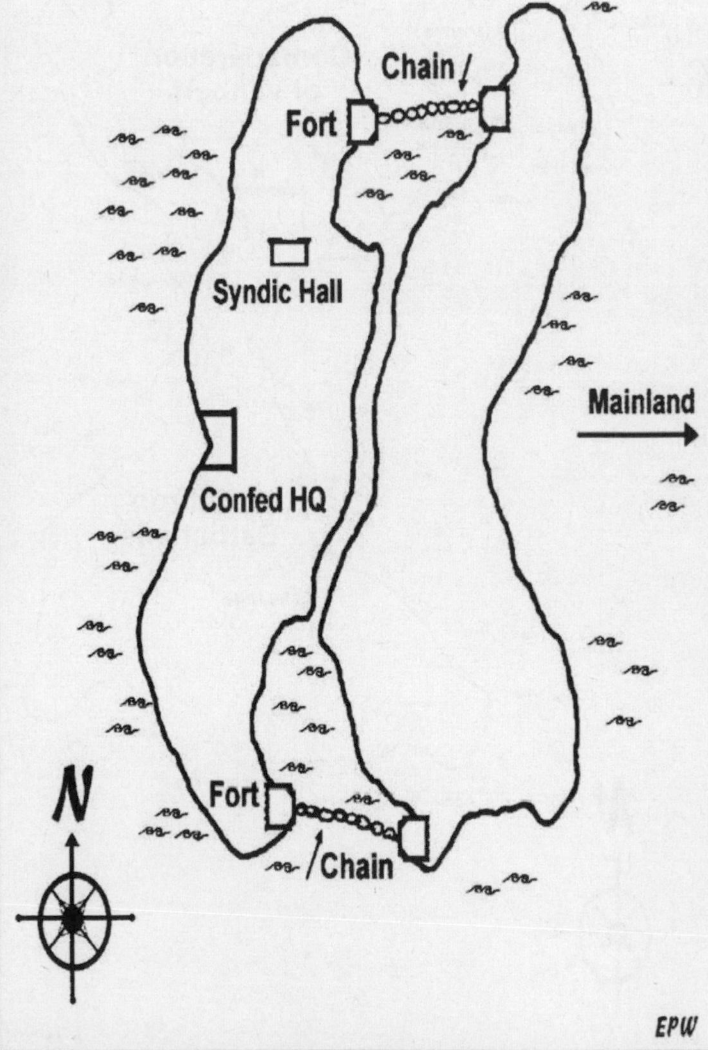

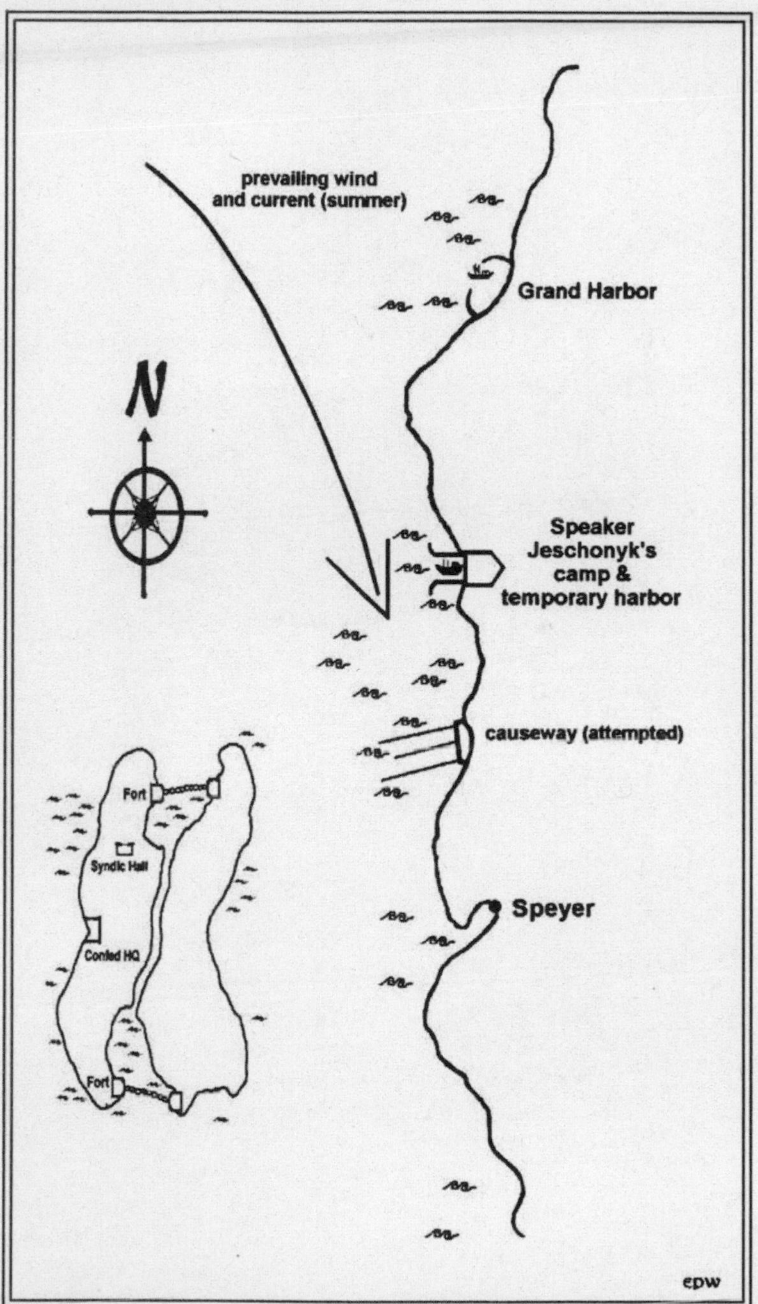
prevailing wind
and current (summer)
Grand Harbor
N
Speaker
Jeschonyk's
camp &
temporary harbor
causeway (attempted)
Fort
Syndic Hall
Confed HQ
Fort
Speyer
epw

VIII
THE TYRANT

David Drake
Eric Flint

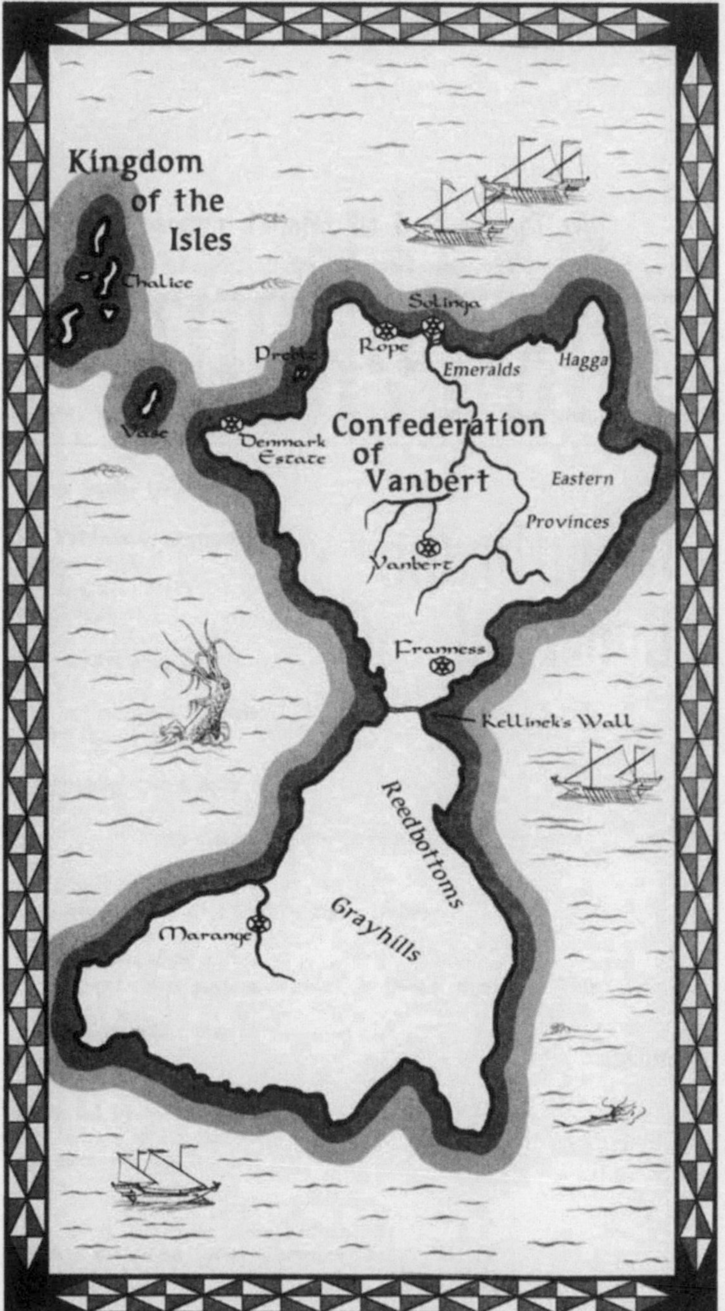

Kingdom of the Isles
Chalice
Vase
Preble
Rope
Solinga
Emeralds
Hagga
Denmark Estate
Confederation of Vanbert
Eastern Provinces
Vanbert
Franness
Kellinek's Wall
Reedbottoms
Grayhills
Marange

To Torgny, and to Frieda's memory

PART I
THE TRIUMVIR

CHAPTER ONE

When Verice Demansk had been six years old, his grandfather had taken him one day on a tour of the statuary in the gardens of the family's estate. The tour had finished in front of the statue of the All-Father.

"Whatever else you do," the old man had told him sternly, "make sure it will meet the approval of this god. The others—gods of love and war, the harvest, whatever—must always be respected also, of course. But, in the end, this god will be the judge."

Demansk was now a middle-aged man himself, with his own august presence, beard turning gray, long string of honors to his name, and bearing the title of Justiciar of the Confederation. His grandfather had died many years earlier. But, staring up again at the statue on a summer day, he could remember that moment perfectly. And he understood, finally, why his feet seemed to have brought him, without his even being aware of where he was walking, before this statue in the gardens.

He stared up at the painted marble face of the god for perhaps three minutes. Then, sighing softly, made his final decision.

Treason.

Another man would have called it something else. "The good of the nation," "the needs of the hour," whatever. Some wormy turn of phrase. But Verice Demansk would not. First, because he had never been given to euphemisms, nor to lying. Secondly—more important—because if he didn't think he was honest he wouldn't have made the decision to become a traitor in the first place.

"In this, as in many things," he said softly to himself, "evil is wasted on the wicked. Only the virtuous can truly plumb its depths, because only they have the necessary strength of conviction."

He recognized the thought as a modification of one of Prithney's *Dialogues.* And he found himself wondering, for a moment, what comment the father of his own grandchild might make about it. All Emeralds were prone to flights of philosophic fancy anyway, but Adrian Gellert was even a graduate of the Grove. A genuine Emerald scholar—a breed which Demansk had always thought was about as far removed as possible from the hard-headed practical way of thinking of such men as himself.

He mused on the contrast between grandfather and father, for a moment, still standing before the statue of the All-Father.

Demansk was a Justiciar of the Confederacy of Vanbert, the great nation which ruled half the world. Adrian Gellert had been born in Solinga, once the capital city—insofar as that term wasn't laughable—of the Emerald League, the collection of squabbling and quarreling city-states clustered on the north coast of the single great continent of the planet Hafardine.

The single great continent we know *of,* Demansk corrected himself. Emerald scholars had long since convinced their Vanbert conquerors that the world was round—and so, who was to say what lands might exist somewhere across the great Ocean?

The Confederation had conquered the Emeralds half a century ago. Demansk's own grandfather, in fact, had led the army which forced Solinga itself to capitulate.

And what would he think now, I wonder?

Demansk could still remember the old man vividly. Fierce old man, as accustomed—unlike modern noblemen—to working with pigs and leading farmhands in their labor as he was with the Council chamber and army maneuvers. And, though this was perhaps fancy,

Demansk thought he could remember his grandfather muttering, after the conquest was over, that no good would come of it. "*Damn Emeralds! Put three of them in a room, you've got eight opinions on any subject under the sun. They think too much! That's a disease, boy, nothing else. And it's contagious, so be careful. Stay away from the bastards.*"

His lips quirked a bit. "Well, I tried, Grandfather," he whispered softly. "But . . ."

In this, too, he would be honest. It was always tempting to blame others for one's ills. But, in truth, the rot within the Confederacy of Vanbert was not of Emerald origin. If anything, he suspected, the Emeralds might be part of the solution.

One Emerald, anyway. Adrian Gellert, the father of Demansk's grandchild.

No, Demansk knew full well the Confederation was rotting from within, and the rot had no alien source. Simple greed, and sloth, and envy, and corruption—all homegrown. Like gout of the spirit. Inevitable, perhaps, a disease brought upon itself by a nation which had grown too powerful too quickly. Or, to use a more homely simile, the stomach-ache of a reckless child after stuffing himself at the dinner table.

Demansk's jaws tightened. He had just selected himself to be the purge, after all. And, here also, he would not hide behind simile and metaphor. His purge would be far more brutal than that of a parent forcing too much food out of a child. Blood, not vomit—though there would be plenty of that, too—would be the product of his labor.

That thought set his feet moving again, and he found himself wandering through the gardens anew. With the self-awareness that had always been part of him, Demansk understood within a short time where his feet were leading him.

Soon enough, he was there, standing before it. The statue of Wodep, painted in red. He stared up at the image, for a moment, his own green eyes meeting the black-painted eyes of the savage-looking idol. Then, lowered his head.

Not in hesitation or fear, simply in thought. He had never cared much for that statue. Odd, perhaps, given his undoubted skill at the god's art. But Demansk had never been an enthusiast of battle, much less a lover. That was why, he sometimes thought, he was so good at it.

No, his head was simply lowered in thought. Having decided upon treason, it remained to implement it. And some of that implementation would involve the clash of armies in the field. Some, not all—Demansk allowed himself the hope that much of it might be accomplished using less ferocious means.

But, as his thoughts of the coming campaign followed their own steps, he soon relinquished the hope. True, some of it would involve political maneuver. As ruthless as war, perhaps, though not as bloody. But some of it . . .

He could see no way around it. At the heart of Vanbert's rot lay the great landed estates. (His own numbered among them, he reminded himself.) They had, like a cancer, destroyed Vanbert's yeomanry and replaced it with a huge caste of slave laborers. Conquered foreigners, for the most part.

Demansk would do what he could to make the revolution as painless as possible. But he had no illusions. The overseers on his own estate were mild, by Vanbert standards. Demansk saw to it. But even his own slaves would be prone to violence when the yoke was lifted. The slaves on many of the great estates would explode like a volcano.

It would be . . . bloody. The more so because Demansk would not hesitate, as other would-be reformers had done, when the time came. When a new slave rebellion erupted, he would yoke it to his purpose. But doing so would require letting the thing burn itself out.

His head still lowered, he lifted his eyes beneath thick eyebrows and looked up at the statue again. *It's not as if the All-Father hadn't warned us. Some crimes can only be purged with blood. The lash repaid by the hammer, or the hoe sharpened to an edge.*

The statue's eyes, painted solid black like those of a monster, gazed back at him pitilessly. He could almost hear the god's imperious demand: "Do what you must! Be what you must! But give it a true name. Whatever else, do not lie to yourself."

And what am I? wondered Demansk. *What am I to become?*

"The reformer." He shook his head. Demansk was not a reformer, because "reform" was now impossible. The Confederacy of Vanbert could not be fixed, the way a broken machine is mended. The whole thing needed to be torn apart—wrecked completely—and built on different principles.

He would be . . . what, then?

A revolutionary, perhaps.

But that term fitted him poorly. He was no slave, leading a slave revolt. Demansk was one of the most powerful men in the whole Confederation, after all—and one of the richest. Hardly someone who could call himself a "revolutionary" and keep a straight face.

Other terms flitted through Demansk's mind.

"The usurper." No, that implied a man simply driven by personal ambition. Whatever his other existing sins and crimes-to-be, Demansk could honestly say that he did not act from motives of personal gain.

"The redeemer." He snorted. He was not trying to save men's souls, nor purify the "spirit" of the nation. He was simply trying to save it from sliding completely over the edge into an abyss of ruin and corruption.

For a moment, then, he felt a trace of humor and chuckled a bit. His plans hinged, to a great extent, on that mysterious young Emerald by the name of Adrian Gellert. A Scholar of the Grove turned into a designer of incredible new weaponry, and possessed, it seemed, of some unearthly spirit. But Emeralds were fishermen as well as philosophers, and they had an old saying about the problem with catching a shark. Who's going to remove the hook? A good hook is valuable, but . . .

Demansk dismissed the whimsy. Emerald fishermen had long since solved that quandary. *Make damn sure the shark is dead, that's how.*

He would do the same. With blood and fire and iron, and a pitilessness which even Wodep could admire.

So, standing before the statue of Vanbert's god of battle, Demansk named himself. It was a simple name, and one which ignored all motives and intents. A name which simply *described,* and named the man by his deeds.

Good enough. Even, in its own way, satisfying. Demansk would destroy Vanbert as it was, and use Emerald subtlety and wizardry in the doing. But, in the end, the great Confederation would be shattered by one of its own true sons, using a true and simple name which any pig farmer could understand.

The Tyrant.

CHAPTER TWO

He was done then, with resolution. There remained the—not small!—matter of implementation. Again, his feet began moving, and he allowed them to lead him.

When Demansk realized where he was going, his lips quirked again. But, this time, into something resembling a genuine smile.

Say what the Emeralds would about Number and Form and all of their other fancy notions. Demansk, born and bred a lord of Vanbert, was a firm believer in the practical wisdom of feet. Calloused feet, ensconced in sturdy sandals, walking on solid and well-placed flagstones. There was a truth you could depend on.

His feet took him to a third statue, this one the statue of the Gray-Eyed Lady. The statue was nestled in a corner of a patio in the garden. This part of the garden, unlike the rest, was shaggy and unkempt.

As he neared the patio, Demansk could hear the object of his search humming a soft tune. He had had little doubt that she would be there. She usually was, this time of day.

So, when he entered the patio, he took the time to examine the surroundings rather than the young woman who sat on a bench near the statue. Those surroundings fit the woman. It was she herself, after all, who had strictly forbidden the estate's gardeners to do their usual work here. Rather to their quiet outrage, Demansk suspected. As was often true with servants, the gardeners tended to be even more devoted to established custom and practices than their masters.

He scanned the patio slowly. In the corner opposite the statue, a smoke tree had been allowed to grow unchecked. The "tree" was more in the way of a huge bush, and it had taken advantage of its liberty to spread exuberant branches in all directions. Yet, despite the luxuriance of its growth, the open nature of the plant itself allowed enough sunlight through for a multitude of smaller plants to thrive within its shelter. Some of them not so small, Demansk noted. One of the hostas bid fair to become a giant itself. And if the astilbes were groaning under the smoke tree's yoke, their abundant flowers certainly did not indicate so.

Demansk looked to his right. All along that side of the square a row of lilies—more a phalanx than a row—were crowding their enormous flowers into the square. It was a riot of color against a mass of green. With, still visible, the stalks of the irises which had sent forth their own glorious phalanx earlier in the year thrusting above the lilies.

His eyes flicked from a shaggy spirea to a triumphant sedum of some sort to a mound of lamb's ears; then, from another hosta to a nearby bed of marigolds. Demansk himself found the odor of those flowers a bit too acrid, but he knew that the mistress of the patio favored them. Enough so, in fact, that she relaxed her usual non-vigilance and kept the surrounding plants sufficiently trimmed to allow the low-growing marigolds their own needed share of sunlight.

Marigolds. It did not surprise Demansk, when he thought about it, that his daughter Helga treasured them. She was much like they, when all was said and done. Beautiful . . . and a bit acrid.

There had been times when Demansk had regretted that harsh edge to his daughter. Despite his official august status, Demansk shared very little of the hauteur of the average Vanbert nobleman. So, where most such would have—did, in fact, those who knew her—found his daughter outrageous, he simply found her annoying. At times, at least.

But . . . he had always loved her, and deeply. More so, though he would never have admitted it to anyone, than any of his three sons.

And he had realized, from the time she was a little girl, that his daughter was a marigold. A sun-lover, who would die in the shade.

Watching Helga now, from his position in the corner, Demansk suddenly understood that he had tended to his own daughter much as she had attended to her garden. Violating custom and tradition, true; but giving her the room she had needed to grow strong. And the air, and the sunlight.

He took some comfort from that knowledge, for a moment. Once he stepped into that patio, he would set in motion a train of events that would pile a mountain of sins and crimes onto his name. The marigold herself would be the instrument for many of them. But, whatever else, Demansk would be able to go to the afterlife pointing to that vigorous flower.

This too, gods, was my doing. Damn me if you will.

By now, of course, his daughter had noticed him. Demansk could see her examining him out of the side of her eyes. She would have detected him long before he arrived, in fact. She was as alert as any skirmisher in Demansk's legions, and would have made a better sentry than most.

But she said nothing, allowing her father the same room he had always allowed her. That was her way, and it was one of the many reasons Demansk treasured her. She simply returned her eyes to the infant suckling at her breast, and resumed humming her little tune.

Tune? Demansk had to suppress a laugh. It was a medley, actually. A ridiculous pastiche of three songs: an Emerald hymn, usually sung at religious festivals; a semi-obscene ballad popular among the seamen and pirates of the Western Isles; and one of the marching songs of the Vanbert legions.

He began to stride into the patio, but was immediately forced to slow down and concentrate on where he put his feet. A good half of the patio's worn flagstones were overgrown by a medley of ground-covering plants even more exuberantly jumbled together than the "tune" his daughter was humming. Aggressive vinca warred with carpet bugle; red phlox with yet another variety of sedum. In the shadier spots, silver beacon valiantly held its own.

In truth, the plants were all hardy—all the plants in Helga's part of the garden were—and could have withstood his sandaled passage easily enough. But Demansk took a subtle pleasure in avoiding destruction, as he marched toward it.

"You don't have to be so prissy, Father," Helga murmured, smiling faintly. "They'll survive."

For a moment, Demansk felt his facial muscles struggling between a scowl and a smile.

As usual, the smile won.

"In the good old days," he muttered, "girls wouldn't have dreamed of being so disrespectful to their fathers. Who"—his voice grew stern—"ruled their families with a rod of iron."

Helga's own smile widened. "Oh, please. In the 'good old days,' our illustrious forefathers were illiterate pig farmers. Standing on a dirt floor under a thatch roof, clad in rags, piglets nosing their bare feet—pissing on them, often enough—and bellowing their patriarchal majesty to a huddle of wrinkled women and filthy children. What I never understood is where they got the rod of iron in the first place." Slyly, looking up at her father under lowered eyelids: "Must have stolen it, since the beggars were certainly too poor to buy it."

Demansk grinned. " 'Stole it'? Well, I suppose. 'Plundered it' would be more accurate."

He lowered himself onto the bench next to her and added: "Say whatever else you will about those illiterate pig farmers, they were the toughest beggars the world's ever seen."

"True enough," she admitted. "Although you don't have to be so smug about it."

"And why not?" he shrugged. "Would anyone else have done a better job of ruling the world? Would you have preferred the pirates of the Isles, or the endlessly bickering Emeralds? Or the barbarians of the south?"

His daughter made no riposte. In truth, she had no disagreement with him on the subject, and they both knew it.

Demansk's gaze fell on his grandson's face. The boy had done with suckling, now, and his eyes were studying his grandfather in the vaguely unfocused and wondering way of infants.

Bright blue eyes, quite unlike the green eyes Demansk shared with his daughter—much less the brown eyes which were normal for those of Vanbert stock. And already the fuzz on the infant's head showed signs of the corn-gold splendor it would become.

Demansk cleared his throat. "Speaking of Emeralds . . . There doesn't seem to be much doubt who sired him."

Helga snorted softly. "There is no doubt at *all*, Father."

When her green eyes came up again, they came level and even. No lowered lids, now; not even a pretense of daughterly modesty or demureness.

"There have been only three men who have had carnal knowledge of me. Counting, as the first of those, the pack of pirates who gang-raped me after I was kidnapped." The shrug which rippled her muscular shoulders would have awed the demigod who, legend had it, held up the world. A titan, dismissing flies. "I know neither their names nor do I remember their faces. Nor do I care."

Her right hand, as well shaped and sinewy as her shoulders, caressed her baby's cheek. "Then there was the Director of Vase, into whose hareem I was sold by the pirates and remained for a year. A fat old man, who managed to get an erection—so to speak—exactly twice on the occasions he summoned me." Another snort, this one derisive. "And then, I'm quite certain, faked an orgasm after a minute or so, once he felt he'd maintained his manly reputation."

Despite himself, Demansk couldn't quite suppress a chuckle. Helga's lips twitched wryly in response. And, for a moment, Demansk was as awed by that little smile as the demi-god would have been at the shrug.

No woman he had ever known—no *man* he had ever known—could match his daughter's calm acceptance of life and its woes. It was not that she was blind, or stupid, or naïve. Simply that she had the strength to regiment horror and misery, and turn them to her own purposes instead of being broken by them.

"And then there was Adrian Gellert," Helga continued, the flat tone in her voice replaced by lilting warmth, "who was neither old, nor fat, nor—trust me, Father—had the slightest difficulty with any of the business." Smugly: "Nor, I am *quite* certain, faked anything."

She hefted her baby and held him up before her. "This child is

Adrian Gellert's and no other. You can be as sure of that as the sunrise. He was born much too late to have been one of the pirates', that's certain. And as for the old fat Director of Vase—"

Her soft laugh bordered on a giggle. "*Look* at your grandchild, Father! Even if that old toad could have managed it, do you think his son would look like *this*?" Her eyes were almost glowing. Some of that glow, of course, was because of the child. But most of it, Demansk knew, was because of the memory of the father. "He has Adrian's eyes, his hair—even that whimsical smile."

Demansk sighed. His face, he knew, was stiff as a board.

Helga studied him for a moment. "I have always been blunt, Father. Why should that disturb you now? It happened. You know it, and I know it. So why should we pretend, or try to cover my shameful past with vague phrases?"

He shook his head abruptly. "It's not that. It's . . ." His voice trailed off. For all his own quite-famous bluntness and directness, Demansk simply could not say what needed to be said. He had never been able to say it; not once, in all the months since Adrian Gellert had returned Helga safely to her family.

"Oh," murmured Helga. "*That.*" Her own face was as stiff and rigid as his own.

"Father, please. Do not insult me. For all my occasional sarcasm on the subject of our 'illustrious forefathers' and the 'grandeur of the Confederacy,' I *am* a daughter of Vanbert. In the bone, and the blood, and the flesh. And, for damn sure, in the spirit."

She plumped the baby back firmly on her lap. "I knew from the moment the pirates seized me that you would refuse to pay the ransom. I would have been furious if you had. The rest of Vanbert may have grown soft and corrupt, but not *Demansk*. Not us! Sophisticated we have become, and literate—and why not? But we, if no other family, are the true Vanbert breed."

Her green eyes were like two emeralds, as hard and unyielding as they were beautiful. "We do not pay ransom to pirates. We suffer their cruelties, if we must. And then, when the time comes, we wreak our vengeance. And our vengeance, and our memory, is a thing of terror to our enemies."

Demansk swallowed, fighting back tears. He had known, of course, what would be the fate of his virgin daughter once he refused the pirates' demand for ransom. Ravished, first, by the entire crew. Then sold into a lifetime of slavery. But—

He, too, was *Vanbert.* Of the old and true breed, undiluted and pure, for all the magnificence of his library and the glorious trappings of his villas and mansions. However far removed Demansk was in most respects from those ancient pig farmers, in one respect at least nothing at all had changed. He was *tough.*

The soft feel of his daughter's hand on his cheek startled him. He had been lost there, for a moment, without his usual soldier's alertness for motion.

For all their feminine slimness, the fingers were strong. And tough. They moved through the short gray-and-brown bristles as easily as a sharp scythe through wheat. As easily as the fingers of a pig farmer's daughter did whatever work was necessary. Without flinching, without complaint.

"Stop it." Her voice surprised him as much as the touch. The curt command was warm, almost humorous. "It wasn't that bad, Father. Really. A few horrible days, at the beginning. Then—honestly—even worse was the year's tedium that followed in the hareem. I was bored almost to the point of insanity."

Again, that demigoddess shrug. "Father, if I had been a son of yours, I would have been expected to serve in the legions. And would have done so, of course, and gladly. Eagerly, in fact. The chances are quite good that, at some point or other, I would have been wounded in a battle. Possibly killed."

A strong slim finger poked at the cloth covering his midriff, right above a scar. Then again on his lower thigh, where ridged flesh peeked beneath the tunic. And again, tracing the old wound which trailed down his left arm.

"So tell me, Father. When you received these wounds, were you in pain? Was your mind dazed with shock, for a time? Did you whimper—or rather, grind your teeth to keep from whimpering? Did you curse your fate? Did some part of your soul shriek outrage and protest at the universe?"

By then, Demansk was laughing. Softly, but aloud. "Oh, gods—yes! It was all *so* unfair. I was quite indignant."

Helga's laughter matched his own. And, for the thousandth time in his life, Demansk felt himself almost drowning in adoration of his daughter. Adoration—and pride. *This too, gods, was my doing. Damn me if you will.*

"So why should it be any different for me?" Helga demanded. "Is rape any worse than a blade tearing into your body? In some ways, yes, I suppose. It's more humiliating, certainly."

"Don't be so sure of that," grunted Demansk. His hand rubbed the scar over his belly. Some part of his mind, idly, was pleased to note the absence of fat. The muscle there was perhaps not as hard as it had been in his youth. But it still felt like a board, at least, if not a bar of iron.

"I got this scar because the man I was matched against in my first battle was vastly better at mayhem than I was. At that young age, anyway. He toyed with me, even—dammit! In the middle of a battle!—*taunted me*, played with me. Then took me down at his leisure, leering the whole time."

He found himself gritting his teeth at the memory. Then, realizing what he was doing, barked a laugh. "Gods, he was good! I felt like a virgin in the hands of a rapist, I swear I did. I can remember my cheek slamming into the ground and the feel of his sandal stamping over me as he went on to his next victim. I was in a daze for . . . some time, while everything around me was a blur of noise and confusion and pain. The only clear thought I can remember was that I realized how Errena must have felt after Wodep took her in his beast form. Used, humiliated, discarded like so much trash. As if all that was left of her was the bones tossed into the litter, after her flesh was eaten."

They were silent for a moment. Then Helga said, "Yes. And my—let's call it a 'wound'—didn't take months to recover from, as yours did." She eyed that portion of Demansk's midriff skeptically. "You're lucky, at that, you survived at all. If the blade had penetrated your bowels, you'd have spent weeks dying in agony."

"True enough," said Demansk. He took a deep breath. "All right, daughter of mine. I thank you—bless you—for understanding."

Seeing the way Helga's figure eased into relaxation, Demansk realized that she had misinterpreted the purpose of his visit. Again, he cleared his throat.

"But that's not actually why I came to talk to you. Although I'm certainly glad we did. There is something else. Something . . . greater." His lips twisted bitterly. "If 'great' isn't an obscene word to use, given the subject."

His daughter's level and even gaze was back. All humor was gone.

"Oh," she said. "*That.*"

Silence, for an instant. Then, as suddenly as a burst of sunlight erupting through a cloud bank: "And it's about time!" she cried gaily. Again, she hefted the baby up before her eyes; jiggling him in a parody of the stern and vigorous way a mother shakes a sassy brat.

"See? I *told* you! Don't ever underestimate your grandpa again!"

The baby's mouth gaped open in glee at his mother's exuberance. His wide-open eyes, as bright in their blue as they were vague in their focus, fairly shone in protest at such an outrageous accusation. *Me? A few months old? Doubt my grandpa? Nonsense, Mother! YOU were the one—*

Demansk was laughing again, and not softly. His daughter's eyes moved to him, a skeptic's sideways scrutiny.

"Not that he didn't take a ridiculous amount of time to come to his decision," she murmured darkly. "No better than an old pig farmer, fretting over whether he should fix the fence." Her voice fell into a quaver. "*Maybe tomorrer . . . my bones ache today . . . some more soup, first . . . build up my strength . . .*"

For a time, the little patio in the garden was given over to a family's gaiety. The laughter of a father and a daughter; and the innocent, confident, unknowing glee of an infant.

When it died away, Helga's face was suffused by sadness.

"You'll need to start by establishing your reputation. Well, not that exactly. Establishing it on an even higher pedestal than it is now. And, in the process, gaining the unquestioned loyalty of a major army."

She sighed. "Which means, of course, leading a campaign against the Southron barbarians. The same ones Adrian and his brother have been stirring up against us these past few months."

Demansk started to interrupt, but Helga waved him down. "Please, Father! *Daughter of Vanbert.* We do what we must." He could see her fighting back the tears. "If you can manage not to kill him, I would . . . appreciate that. Immensely. But you must do what you must."

And so, in the end, Demansk was able to restore the proper relationship between Vanbert father—patriarch unquestioned—and his impudent female offspring.

"Idiot girl," he growled. "Do *not* think you can teach strategy to your father. Spirit and courage, yes; maneuvers, no." He grinned. "Not even close."

He came to his feet like a young man, almost springing. "Idiot!" he repeated. "No, I think we'll leave your precious Adrian alone for a bit. He and his ferocious brother Esmond both. Let them stir up the Southrons and gather the forces of barbarism against us. All the better. When the time comes, that will turn the last lock."

Helga's eyes were as wide as her son's, and just as vaguely focused. Demansk was delighted to see how the wise father had left the cocksure daughter fumbling in the mist.

"Ha! Lecture your father on strategy, now, would you? No, no, girl. Adrian's for a later time. For the moment—I'm off to the Isles."

His own humor faded, replaced by an odd combination of emotions. Cold fury, overlaying a much deeper core of affection.

"I'll get your vengeance on your pirates, Daughter," he said softly, icily. "And then . . ."

Warmth began to return to his voice. "We'll see about Adrian Gellert. He's playing his own very intricate game, be sure of it. When the time comes, I won't be surprised to see him playing with the son he's never met."

He barked another laugh. "Actually, he'll be doing *that* soon enough! But, I think—not sure, nothing in this world ever is—that the time will come when he'll be doing so in a mansion of his own—his and yours—instead of a barbarian campsite."

By now, he had left Helga completely behind. She was no longer fumbling in the mist; her eyes were as blank as a blind woman's.

"As they should be," stated Demansk, with all the satisfaction of a pig farmer ruling his domain. He had a hard time to keep from giggling himself. But, a kindly father as well as a stern patriarch, he took pity on her.

"Haven't you figured it out yet, silly girl? I need to maneuver *with* Adrian Gellert, not against him. But to do that I need to send him an envoy. Someone from the Confederacy of Vanbert he can trust."

Helga's mouth formed a perfect "O."

Her father clucked his tongue. "Odd, really. She's normally rather bright."

O.

"Not as bright as her father, of course."

O.

"Which is as it should—"

He got no further. Helga had the baby down on the bench and was clutching her father. Not even clutching him so much as jiggling him up and down, as if he were an infant himself. It was a wonderful moment for him, one of the best in his life.

Not perfect, true. There was still the dull, aching sadness of knowing that it would all be swept away, soon enough, by the coming time of blood and iron, fire and fury.

CHAPTER THREE

It was a strange place. Even after all this time, and the familiarity of the many hours Adrian Gellert had spent here, the place still seemed . . . foreign.

I never got used to it either, really, came one of the two "spirits" which had created that strangeness. *Even after years had passed. And I only had to share my brain with one other, not two.*

Adrian shook his head slightly. Then, through the slight haze of the "trance"—as if he were seeing it on another's face rather than feeling it on his own—sensed his lips curling into a little smile. *It's not sharing my "brain" that's the problem, Raj. I wasn't using a lot of it anyway. It's that I'm always a little confused whose soul is working at the moment.*

i do not have a soul. Center's statement, as always, came so firm and certain that it reminded Adrian of a level plain. A sheet of granite, covered with only the thinnest soil. No hills, no gullies—no mountains, certainly, nor valleys—gave that "voice" any relief at all. Sometimes it was tiring; and it was always a bit annoying.

He sensed Raj Whitehall chuckling. "Sensed" it, only, because in the end Raj was as disembodied as Center himself. But Whitehall, at least, had once been a human being.

He annoyed me a little, too, back in the days long ago when I

was alive and he was my adviser. Damn know-it-all. And what's worse is that you can't really trust that knowledge—as he's the first to point out.

of course.

Center's "voice" had no emotional flavor or penumbra. It was always a bit of a shock, that. There was never the little moment of preparation that a human gave another when he was about to speak—a smile, perhaps; or a scowl, or a tilt of the eyebrow. Just . . . that flat, level voice. Blowing in as suddenly as a wind off the plain slams open an unlatched door, startling the occupant of the house within.

stochastic analysis deals with probabilities, not certainties. certainties do not exist, outside the fantasies of philosophers. neither do souls, as an objective reality subject to stochastic analysis. you humans have souls simply as referent points to yourselves.

Adrian wondered, for a moment, what his former teachers at the Grove would have said to that. Many of them, he suspected, would have agreed. With the proposition concerning certainty, at least, if not the rest. Privately, of course. In public, no professional philosopher would admit to any doubts on any subject in creation.

The thought was whimsical, not harsh. Whatever their faults, those teachers had shaped his mind. And, on balance, shaped it well. So, at least, he thought.

And so do we, lad, said Raj softly. ***Or we wouldn't have selected you for your mission in the first place.***

Ah, yes. "The Mission."

Raj Whitehall and Center had come to Adrian two years earlier, manifesting themselves in his mind in a manner which Adrian never really had understood clearly. They were incorporeal "beings." Projections, essentially, from a reality which existed on another planet. Center made reference to something he called "software" to explain it, but Adrian found the explanation too confusing to follow.

On that planet, Raj's home world of Bellevue, Whitehall had stumbled across Center by accident. Center was a battle computer, created by the now-long-gone Federation of Man which had once ruled the stars. It had, miraculously, survived the great wars which destroyed the Federation. Wars, and a Federation, which were now so ancient that they had been completely forgotten on those planets which had not been destroyed outright.

Between them, centuries earlier, Raj and Center had transformed Bellevue and set it back on a track which would, eventually, lead toward the reconstruction of the Federation of Man. Since then, they—or, rather, their recorded mentalities projected onto other worlds—had been attempting to duplicate their success elsewhere. On Hafardine, they had chosen Adrian Gellert as the instrument for that mission. And he had, not without some trepidation, agreed to the project.

Through the slight trance-haze of his vision when he was "communing" with the two intelligences which shared his mind, Adrian's gaze moved slowly across the landscape before him.

The heat and moisture struck him first—even physically, for all that his senses were somewhat shielded by the trance-haze. The southern half of the continent was mostly sub-tropical in climate, verging on full tropics in the southernmost regions. In the summer, as now, hot and humid.

Rain fell almost every day, this time of year, at least for a few hours. It had taken Adrian and his brother Esmond some time to grow accustomed to that. The Southrons seemed to take their semiaquatic existence for granted. But the Gellerts came from the northern half of the continent, whose climate was mild and generally dry. According to Center, much like places on Old Earth called "Greece" and "Italy."

His eyes fell on a woman walking past at the base of the slope on which Adrian had pitched his tent. She was apparently returning to her own tent, somewhere in the sprawling mass of barbarians who had gathered here outside the port city of Marange for their great annual conclave. A clay-covered reed basket was balanced atop her head, presumably carrying water drawn from the nearby Blood River.

Adrian sensed a little smile on his face. No woman of the north, not even a prostitute, would have paraded about publicly in such a costume—bare from the waist up, and with nothing more than a string loincloth elsewhere. Watching her heavy buttocks sway as she waddled past, he sensed the smile widen. *Certainly not a woman with such a dumpy figure.*

The men wore even less. Nothing more than what Adrian thought of as a codpiece. Not even in battle, often enough. The warriors of most Southron tribes tended to scorn armor, other than whatever protection was provided by the quivers which held their arrows and, of course, the great velocipad-hide shields they favored. They considered armor effeminate and cowardly. Going into battle stark naked, covered only with wild and extravagant paint, was by no means uncommon.

The semi-nudity of the Southrons was natural enough, given the climate. At first, Adrian had assumed it was because of the heat. But after experiencing the constant rainfall, he and his brother had shed most of their own clothing. Skin dried quickly, once the rain stopped. The humidity was bad enough without being covered in soaked garments.

If he hadn't been in the trance-haze, he would have sighed then. In truth, he detested the south—the barbarism of its inhabitants even more than the climate. What made it worse was that Adrian could not simply relegate the Southrons to the status of "barbarians" and then ignore their crudities, much as a man ignores the toiletry of animals.

Adrian could see past the surface, in a way that most civilized people could not. The Southrons were not "barbarians," really. At bottom, they were people not much different from Adrian himself. The same intelligence—capacity for it, at least; the same emotions—mixed slightly differently, perhaps, but the same for all that. Hopes, fears, yearnings—all the same.

They were simply people, mired in centuries of barbarism. But it was still aggravating, for all that he understood the phenomenon.

"The Mission." It had driven him to this place, whether he liked it or not. And, whether he liked it or not, had presented him with the Southrons as the raw material for his next work. Did a blacksmith "like" iron? It was irrelevant whether he did or not. Without iron, he had no work.

You'd have made a good general, came a thought from Raj. Adrian began to shape a witty denial, but let it go. Perhaps Raj was right. Whitehall had been a general himself, after all, when he had been alive. A great one, from what Adrian could tell, who had completed this same "mission" on his own planet extraordinarily well. So perhaps he knew whereof he spoke.

And that, too, was irrelevant. Raj and Center had not chosen Adrian for his martial prowess. There was no shortage of *that* on Hafardine, for a certainty. His brother Esmond provided enough of that for both of them—and, north of the narrow isthmus where the great Confederacy of Vanbert held sway over half the continent, there was already a man whose grim talents at war had become famous.

The thought of Demansk triggered Center. **he will make his first move soon. if he has not already done so. probability 89%, ±3 for the former; 46%, ±10 for the latter. the variables there are larger.**

The humor which bubbled up within Adrian was great enough to momentarily shatter the trance-haze. He burst into open laughter, even feeling the hammer of wet heat coming down on him.

You're so wrong, you all-knowing damn machine. Demansk has already moved, be sure of it.

He waited for Raj's input, wondering what it might be. It was an odd trio they made. A thinking machine called a "computer," the recorded "spirit" of a long-dead general, and he himself—a living man still in his youth.

As a rule, Raj sided with Center in their little three-way debates and discussions. But, not always.

This time, he simply asked a question.

Why are you so sure of that, lad? I would think he'd wait a bit longer. I would, in his position. Unless he understands what you're about, and he has no way—

The disembodied voice broke off suddenly. A moment later, Adrian sensed a ghostly chuckle echo in his mind.

I'd forgotten. It's been so long since I was a man myself. Adrian caught a momentary glimpse of a beautiful, patrician face, cheek pressed into a pillow and smiling. Raj Whitehall's wife Suzette, he knew. Now long dead herself.

There was no aura of sadness about the memory. Just . . . nostalgia? Hard to say.

Do you miss her? he asked.

Somehow he could sense a wry shrug, though he could not see it. ***It's hard to explain, Adrian. My own existence has been in what you call the trance-haze for centuries now. I am no longer really human, even in mind much less in body. Not a computer, of course, like Center. Something . . . else. I don't know what to call it. An angel, except that would be ludicrous. A spirit, let's say. My only real emotion left is serenity.*** The thought hardened, as a general's thoughts could do so easily. ***Not that I shall ever forget her.***

Center interrupted. **the two of you are prattling again.**

Oh, be still, retorted Raj. ***There are things you do not understand well, if at all. This is one of them.***

There was a momentary pause. Then, in a tone which *almost* had a tone—irritation, frustration—Center said: **that business. love interferes greatly with stochastic analysis. nothing else produces such wide variables. not even religious fanaticism, of which I suspect love is a disguised variant.**

The trance-haze was back, so Adrian only sensed himself grinning. It was too bad. He would have enjoyed feeling the strain on his cheek muscles directly. It was a very wide grin.

Sourpuss, what you are. Demansk will have moved already, because he KNOWS there is one envoy he can send whom I will trust.

He too deals with variables, Raj chimed in. ***And here is one he can ignore. Adrian's right, Center. Demansk will have begun the thing.***

Adrian knew that the silence which followed was Center, calculating the probabilities. At moments like this, the computer's incredible speed of logical manipulation was both awe-inspiring and . . . sometimes a bit ridiculous. The computer would factor in everything, matching cause against cause, effect against effect, then rematching them again, over and over, until—within seconds!—it would arrive at a conclusion which, now and then at least, was blindingly obvious to flesh and blood.

you are correct, came the pronouncement. **probability is now 94%, ± 2. which means we must move more quickly ourselves.**

It was Adrian's eyes which saw the milling, chaotic mass of

Southron warriors teeming in the great encampment below; Raj Whitehall's spirit which put words to the observation.

What a frigging, unholy mess. We've got our work cut out for us.

But Adrian was not really paying attention any longer. The trance-haze was breaking, now, shattering into little slivers. His own thoughts were plunging down through every vein and artery in his body, down into his groin. He felt so warm and wet himself that the surrounding air seemed almost frigid.

Another face was vivid in his mind. Also pressed into a pillow, but facing up not sideways. This face, though beautiful as well, was not patrician in the least. Certainly not at that moment of memory, when the auburn hair was tangled, sweaty at the roots; and the mouth was open, hissing wordless cries of ecstasy.

His breath was coming short. His own mouth was no longer closed.

Your brother's coming, with some chieftains in tow. You'd better get that erection under control, lad, or things'll get awkward. These Southrons, y'know, don't share your decadent Emerald tastes. They're likely to misinterpret your state of mind.

Laughter broke passion's rush. So, when Esmond and the chieftains strode up to the tent, Adrian was able to greet them with nothing more than a hand outstretched. But still, during the time which followed, his mind only followed the conversation at its edges.

There was room, really, for just a single thought at the center of it. A different sort of trance-haze had seized him.

She's coming back to me. I know she is.

For the first time, then, he was finally able to let go that rein of honor which had driven him to return her to her family, long months before. Almost a year, now. Let it go, cast it aside—and, with it, all restraint. He had never loved a woman before, and had never allowed himself—quite—to love this one.

Soon enough, he knew, Center and Raj would be back, pouring caution and cunning strategy into his mind. But on *this* subject, at least, he would listen no longer. He had satisfied honor once. Once was enough, for a lifetime.

CHAPTER FOUR

"Interesting idea," drawled Ion Jeschonyk. The elderly Speaker Emeritus lifted himself up on an elbow and swiveled his head toward the man lying on a couch directly opposite Demansk. "What do you think, Justiciar Tomsien?"

Tomsien was staring at Demansk, his dark brown eyes shaded by a heavy, lowered brow. Abruptly, he lurched on the couch and came to a full, upright sitting position. He planted thick hands on thick knees and leaned forward. A full but rather solid belly bulged within the expensive fabric of his robes.

"Interesting," he echoed. "But . . ." His brow was now gathered in a massive frown. "It's not that I don't trust you, Demansk—at least as much as I trust anyone in these rotten modern times." Demansk nodded his head in acknowledgement of the praise, as faint as it might be. "But," continued Tomsien, "I don't understand why you're proposing it. What I mean is—"

"What does *he* get out of it," finished Jeschonyk. The old politician smiled wryly. "Good question. Your answer, Justiciar?"

Demansk shrugged. "Personally, you mean? About what I said. Greatly increased power, obviously. With that will come the usual riches."

Tomsien was shaking his head before he had even finished. "I can't say I like you all that much, Demansk, but you've never seemed especially ambitious to me. And, as rich as you are already, I can't believe you care much about that business either. So stick with the 'good of the Confederacy' explanation. That's actually believable, coming from you."

The heavyset Justiciar was still obviously dissatisfied. "But *nobody* is that altruistic. There's *got* to be some personal angle to this you haven't told us. And before I agree to anything, I want to know what it is."

"Me too," chimed in Jeschonyk.

Demansk was now sitting upright himself; and, like Tomsien, had his hands planted firmly on his knees. He leaned back a bit and studied the ceiling. As could be expected in the villa of a man as wealthy as Jeschonyk, the frescoes were magnificent. Although Demansk thought depicting the legend of Wodep and the forest nymphs in such exquisite detail was in questionable taste for a room devoted to anything other than orgies.

Of course, by all accounts, orgies were likely to take place anywhere in one of Jeschonyk's residences. For all his advanced age and long-standing reputation for political sagacity, the Speaker Emeritus was one of Vanbert's more notorious lechers. His frequent thunderous denunciations of "modern decadence" in the Council chamber had never stopped him from indulging his own private vice.

Demansk's thoughts were not particularly condemnatory, however. Lechery was a harmless enough vice, as such things went. And this much could be said of Jeschonyk—the man had never, unlike many Speakers, plundered the public treasury for his own gain.

He lowered his eyes and gave the other men in the chamber a stony gaze. "I have not explained the *specifics* of my proposal yet. Forming what I'm calling a 'triumvirate' will bring needed stability to the Confederacy—and, no small thing, keep that greedy pig Albrecht from getting his hands on the Speakership again. Which—you both know this as well as I do—he's been spending enough money to pull off if he's not stopped soon."

Mention of Albrecht, as Demansk expected, caused the aura of vague suspicion in the room to change. Or shift, rather, from his own person. Whatever else, the three men in that chamber had one thing in common: a thorough detestation of Drav Albrecht, the current Speaker of the Assembly and, several years back, the Speaker of the Council. Even by the standards of the modern day, Albrecht took corruption to new heights. Not even the traitor Redvers had been—quite—so mindlessly avaricious.

Demansk took advantage of the momentary "meeting of minds" to drive on. "But that's just the beginning. Stabilizing the political situation in the Confederacy is pointless if we don't *use* that stability to solve some long-standing problems. The worst of which, in my opinion, lies beyond our own borders. Say better: the worst of which is caused by the fact that our borders don't reach far enough."

Jeschonyk and Tomsien froze. With one exceptional episode, Vanbert had ceased being an expansionist power decades ago. And that one exception had been under Sole Speaker Marcomann, who had used his conquest of the western provinces of the northern half of the continent to set himself up as—in fact if not in name—the dictator of the Confederacy. He had been the last man to hold the Speakership of both the Council and the Assembly simultaneously—an ambition which all the men in that room knew was held by Albrecht. If Albrecht obtained his goal, however, it would be by the profligate use of bribery. Which, in the end, was not as dangerous as the means of sheer military power which Marcomann had used.

Demansk's lips twisted into a grimace. Technically, the expression might be called a "smile." But there was no humor in it.

"Relax," he commanded. "I am as well aware as you are of the dangers involved. Which is why my proposal, I believe, accomplishes three salutary goals. It locks out Albrecht, it keeps any of *us* from becoming a dictator . . . and it allows me the chance to accomplish a personal goal which is rather dear to my heart. Vengeance."

Not surprisingly, it was Jeschonyk who first understood. Tomsien was . . . not stupid, no; but not quick-witted, either.

"Ah," murmured the old Speaker Emeritus. "I see."

"I *don't*," said Tomsien crossly.

Jeschonyk waved a languid hand. "Demansk will allow you to

command the southern provinces, facing the barbarians with most of our army. Since I'm too damn old anyway to take the field any longer—Preble was it, for me—I'll remain here in the capital exercising political control. Which frees *him* up to put paid to the stinking Islesmen altogether."

Tomsien's eyes widened. It took him longer to see a point, perhaps, but he was quite intelligent enough—experienced enough, at least—to see the implications once he did.

The real threat of a new dictator would come from whichever Confederate official could conquer large new territories on the *continent.* That alone would provide them with the land grants needed to cement the loyalty of a large enough army. The Western Isles, even all of them put together, did not allow for that even if conquered. The Isles were, and always had been, places for traders and fishermen and pirates. There simply wasn't enough acreage to create a large new layer of propertied men who could serve as the base of support for a dictatorship.

That was not the least of the reasons, of course, that the pirates of the Isles had been tolerated for so long. Yes, they were a pestiferous nuisance. But they posed no real threat to the Confederacy—and there simply wasn't enough to be gained by their conquest to make the effort seem worth it.

Unless . . . the man who led that effort had a serious personal grudge to settle.

Tomsien's eyes grew heavy-lidded, as he studied his fellow Justiciar. Demansk could practically read his thoughts.

What an idiot. She's just a woman, after all, even if she is his daughter. And for that he's willing to give me the lion's share of the army?

Demansk waited. Tomsien was not someone who could be rushed into a decision, anyway. And Demansk was quite sure that Tomsien had heard tales of Demansk's unseemly toleration of his daughter's outlandish ways.

He dotes on her. Always has, the fool. Odd, really, for such a man to have such a weakness. Almost effeminate, for all his skill at war.

When he needed to be, Tomsien could be decisive. "Done!" he barked. "As long as you give me the southern provinces—*and* a personal assurance."

Demansk frowned. "My word has never—"

"Damn your 'word,' Demansk!" snapped Tomsien. "Don't play the honorable old-style Vanbert nobleman with *me.* It's a rotten world today—rotten through and through—and you know it as well as I do. Facts are facts. I want a personal *assurance.* Something a lot more tangible than words."

Demansk ran fingers through his beard. "I see. Very well. My son Olver—"

"No! Your *oldest* son, Demansk. Barrett it'll be or there's no deal."

"He's already married," protested Demansk. But the tone of the words was mild.

Tomsien's grimace was not quite a sneer. Not quite. "Have him put her aside. He'll do it, don't think he won't. And the courts certainly won't be an obstacle—not after our 'triumvirate' is in place."

Jeschonyk chimed in. "Your daughter-in-law's family aren't all that well placed, Demansk. They'll say nothing, if they're slipped some quiet bribes."

Demansk had expected this moment to come. So he was a bit surprised at how difficult it was to keep his rage from showing. It helped that he understood the reason. Tomsien, for all his slow way of thinking, had clearly assessed Demansk's oldest son quite accurately.

Barrett was . . . not the son that Demansk wished he were. His daughter, the youngest of his four children, seemed to have gotten twice her share of Demansk honor—and all of it taken from the oldest. Barrett Demansk was a typical scion of the modern nobility. Ambitious, greedy, and—Demansk didn't doubt it any more than Tomsien—would be quite willing to discard a wife who had already borne him a child in order to make a more advantageous match.

"Which of your daughters?" he grated.

Tomsien shrugged. "Any of the three. Take your pick. It doesn't matter to me."

Demansk left that problem for a later time. He would allow Barrett to make the choice, in any event. His son would choose unwisely, and that too would further Demansk's scheme.

He took a moment to bid farewell to a piece of his own honor. Then:

"Done," he said softly. "But, now that I've given you the personal assurance you insisted upon, I will demand myself that I be given *complete* authority over all Confederate naval forces. Every ship, every crew—and whatever else I need to crush the King of the Isles. I *will* have my vengeance."

Tomsien's hand was too thick to wave languidly, but the fat Justiciar came as close as possible. Now that he had settled the deal in a manner very favorable to himself, he was quite willing to concede the crumbs from the table.

"Whatever you need," he agreed. "So long, of course, as you don't touch my armies, and don't try to extract resources from the southern provinces."

Demansk shrugged irritably. "I wouldn't do it anyway. I *am* principally motivated by my concerns for the Confederacy, Tomsien, whether you believe it or not. You'll be needing those armies and resources yourself, soon enough. Don't doubt for a moment that the Southrons will begin raiding again, as soon as they hear that we've committed a major expedition to conquering the Western Isles."

Tomsien said nothing. Indeed, he looked away, as if in momentary fear that Demansk might be able to read his thoughts.

Pointless, that. Demansk could read them easily enough. Tomsien was calculating the future. After he broke the Southron probes and launched his own offensive into the southern half of the continent. With its wide rich lands . . . And two partners in a triumvirate, one of them old and the other possessed only of naval power. Who was to say that there might not be another dictatorship? Marcomann had done very well for himself, when all was said and done, even if he'd left something of a mess behind him when he died.

Demansk watched as Tomsien, eyes turned away, made the same calculations concerning the future that he had made of his daughters.

Any of them. Take your pick. It doesn't matter to me. The havoc he might wreak in the lives of others was irrelevant, so long as it worked to his advantage.

Three hours later, when the day was almost done, Tomsien left the villa. Demansk remained behind in the chamber for a few minutes. Something in Jeschonyk's expression had made clear that the Speaker Emeritus wanted a few last private words.

"And now that he's gone, Verice, tell me what you're *really* planning."

Demansk was a bit startled. Jeschonyk hadn't addressed him by his first name in years.

The old man chuckled. "And please—spare me the speeches about the needs of the Confederacy. Not that I doubt you, mind. But *nobody* is that disinterested."

Demansk frowned. "I don't see where my motives really matter, Ion. You sat through this entire meeting, even if Tomsien and I did most of the talking and the bargaining. You know as well as I do that he came out of it with the most. I'd think you'd be worrying more about him than me."

"Cut it out, Verice. The thing about Marcomann, you see—people forget this because of his brutality—is that he was *smart*. Without his wits, all his land grants and his armies wouldn't have meant anything. Tomsien's simply not in that league. You are."

It was probably futile, but Demansk decided to try a ferocious scowl. "Dammit, I gave what amounts to a hostage to Tomsien! My eldest son. You know as well as I do that he'll make sure Barrett lives within his reach."

For the first time in hours, Jeschonyk lifted himself up out of the languid, half-reclining position of a true nobleman. He sat up straight and stared at Demansk. Then, sighed heavily and looked away.

"The gods help us, you *are* motivated by nothing more than principle." His old shoulders seem to shiver a little. "Most dangerous thing in the world, that. Bloodiest, for sure."

Jeschonyk's eyes came back to him. "A 'hostage'? And so what? Tomsien's incapable of understanding the thing, because his own daughters are nothing more to him than bargaining counters. But you—"

It was Demansk's turn to look away. Corrupt those old eyes might be, but they were still wise.

"You refused to pay ransom for her, now didn't you?"

Demansk rose abruptly from his couch. "I don't see any point to this."

Jeschonyk made a little rueful gesture. "You're probably right. Just do me a favor, when the time comes?"

Demansk stared down at him. Jeschonyk chuckled again. It was a very harsh sounding chuckle. "Remember that I am *not* incorruptible, when it comes down to it. So there's really no need for knifework. A little stipend will do the trick."

He glanced at the ceiling. "Well . . . not *that* little. I do have appearances to keep up. And I'm sure you wouldn't deprive an old man of the chance to find his own preferred way of dying. At my age—tired heart, all that—a healthy young girl is likely to work better than a sword anyway. Especially several at once."

Demansk studied the ceiling. The frescoes really were phenomenally well painted. And phenomenally detailed.

"Done," he said softly. Turned, and left.

CHAPTER FIVE

When Demansk left Jeschonyk's villa, it was still before sundown. The villa was on the northern outskirts of the capital city of Vanbert. Demansk realized that he still had time to make another visit before he left the next day on his journey back to his own estates. Which meant that an issue he'd postponed in his mind had to be settled.

After passing through the gate of the villa, he hesitated. The soldier holding his velipad—one of Demansk's personal household troops, not a regular—began bringing the mount up to him. Then, hesitated himself, when he realized the Justiciar was irresolute about something.

Some part of Demansk's brain was mildly amused at the way the soldier's jaw seemed to sag a little. Demansk was famous among his troops for his decisiveness. As well as notorious for it. Seasoned veterans appreciated the trait, on campaign and especially in a battle; generally detested it, at all other times.

He could see the Knecht villa from here, he realized. Given that it was the largest and most splendid villa in the Confederation, perched atop the most prestigious hill in the city, that was not entirely surprising.

"Just do it," he said to himself firmly. "Druzla's shade will never forgive me if I don't."

He took the reins from the soldier, who was the sergeant of the Justiciar's little escort, and nodded toward the distant villa. "We're headed there."

"Ah, yes, sir. Ah—" The soldier, as was true of all the men in his squad, was not very familiar with the capital. In fact, to the best of Demansk's knowledge, this was his first visit to Vanbert. Like all provincials, he was feeling overwhelmed by the place. With a population of a million residents, the city was six times larger than any other in the world.

"Don't worry, Sergeant, I know the way." Demansk smiled. "Just pretend you're riding ahead of me."

"Ah, thank you, sir." The sergeant scurried to his velipad. By the time he'd mounted, Demansk had already started trotting off.

It had been years since Demansk had visited the Knecht villa, and in times past he'd always approached it from another direction—the southeast, where he and Druzla had maintained a large villa of their own in the capital. After his wife died, Demansk had maintained the place—having a prestigious villa in the capital was a necessity for prominent noblemen of the Confederacy—but had henceforth spent little time in the capital.

Druzla had loved Vanbert, with its endless rounds of salon discussions, artistic pursuits and dramatic diversions. So Demansk and his wife had visited the city often, and their villa had become in fact as well as in theory their second home. Demansk had been quite willing to indulge his wife's tastes, even if he didn't particularly share them.

As he moved toward it, down one of the spacious boulevards which graced the richest parts of the city, Demansk studied his destination. The Knecht villa was magnificent, not simply grandiose, and the setting sun illuminated it beautifully. Toman Knecht had employed the finest architects to design it, the best craftsmen to build it—and had then spent a large fortune to fill it with what was, without question, the finest and largest collection of art in the world.

Given the size of his fortune, after all, Toman Knecht could afford to do so. He was thought at the time to be the richest man in the world—even *after* he built and accoutered the villa—and probably was. Nor, since Toman's death five years earlier, was there any sign that his family's wealth had declined. His widow, Arsule, shared all of Toman's extravagant tastes, true; but she also shared—even exceeded—his uncanny ability to amass and retain the wealth which made it possible. And she employed a financial adviser who was immensely capable, as Demansk well knew. His name was Prit Sallivar, and he was Demansk's own financier as well.

Demansk sighed. That was part of the knot he was trying to untangle—or cut in half, to be precise.

Prit Sallivar, along with many others, occupied a gray area in Confederate society. Vanbert's expansion had, over the past two centuries, produced a rather large class of wealthy men risen from the gentry—risen *far* above the gentry, measured simply in terms of money. But they were not part of the aristocracy, a fact which was driven home to them whenever, as the expression went, they "acted above their class." Some of them could, given time and the expenditure of half their fortune, leverage their way into the nobility. Albrecht's own grandfather had done so; effectively buying his grandsons—if not himself or his own sons—a seat in the Council by marrying a widow whose splendid title had been turned into a hollow shell by her former husband's profligacy.

Yes, some did. And, as was the way of things, typically became the most ferocious defenders of aristocratic privilege thereafter. But most did not. There simply weren't enough eligible marriage prospects; and, while the Council's Registrar could usually be bribed, he did *not* come cheaply. "Buy a Registration" was another popular slang expression in the Confederacy, used whenever someone referred to a financial enterprise that was either beyond one's wildest fancy or, if it wasn't, would be flat-out ruinous.

Prit Sallivar himself had never bothered with the business. Though he resented the constant little humiliations visited upon him, he had never seen the logic of wasting his wealth in order to obtain a title. He simply kept his social contacts in the aristocracy—outside of business, where any number of noblemen were willing to allow him entry through the back door of their villas—to that relatively small layer of the nobility which had a relaxed attitude about "one's station in life."

Demansk himself was one such. But another—and by far the most prominent—was Arsule Knecht. In this, if not in their shared enthusiasm for art, she and her former husband were diametrically opposite. Toman had employed the best financiers in the Confederacy, Prit Sallivar among them, and had then treated them much like he treated his servants. After his death, Arsule had swung open the *front* door of their mansion, and invited them in.

Demansk had never attended the salons and soirees and art exhibitions for which Arsule Knecht had become famous—"notorious" was a better word, at least among the aristocracy. His own wife Druzla had been one of Arsule's best friends, and would undoubtedly have enjoyed them. But Druzla had died two years before Toman, and Demansk had turned down all the subsequent invitations. Politely, but firmly. He didn't much enjoy such things himself and since his own prestige in Vanbert society rested on the "traditional virtues," he saw no point in eroding that position simply out of sentimentality.

"Traditional virtues," he muttered under his breath. "I'm the toughest pig farmer in the land, and I can steal anybody's pigs—and do it in broad daylight, which makes me a nobleman instead of a thief."

Gods, I've gotten cynical. He could remember a time when he hadn't been. A time when he'd spent months, as a boy, eagerly trotting alongside his beloved grandfather as the fierce old man went about his business. Which, needless to say, was the business of managing an estate in the countryside—except, in time of war, when the farmer turned into a soldier. And led his huge armies with the same skill and intentness that he managed his huge farm.

In truth, Verice Demansk had been brought up more by his grandfather than his father. His own father had been . . . of a different sort. "More modern," as he would say, on the rare occasions when he tore himself away from the endless squabbling and scheming in the Council to pay a brief visit to the ancestral estate.

In one thing, at least, Demansk's grandfather and father had shared the same attitude: neither of them had had much use for gentrymen, especially ones who were stinking rich. Outside of war, at least, where the grandfather prized their talents. The father, having spent as little time in the army as necessary for a man of his station, had even less use for them than that.

And here I am—in three generations!—scurrying to find their favor.

He suppressed the sour sentiment. True, with the exception of a few like Prit Sallivar, Demansk found the upper crust of the gentry even more distasteful than the aristocracy. Petty beyond belief; grasping; narrow; pompous—their pretensions at being patrons of the arts were rarely matched by any corresponding good taste—bah! There was practically no vice, certainly of the venal sort, of which they were not guilty.

The fact remained that, if Demansk's plans were to come to fruition, he would need to have that class of men in his camp. Squarely in the middle of it, too, not consigned to the outer ranks. He was about to launch a project never attempted in history—barely even conceived, in truth. A dictatorship built on money instead of land, and not even money gained by bribery and tax-gouging.

Demansk and his little escort reached the outer gates of the villa. A squad of Knecht household soldiers trotted out to greet them—as well as, of course, to determine their bona fides.

"Tell Lady Knecht that Verice Demansk would enjoy a moment of her time," he growled. Then, after the squad leader dispatched a man to convey the message, grit his teeth.

And why'd you have to be so curt about it? Stop lying, Verice. It's not the guard's fault if the prospect of seeing Arsule again—gods, what's it been now? ten years?—makes you edgy.

Arsule herself came down to the gate to let him in. Demansk was not surprised. The woman had so much energy that she'd been rumored to trot into her own kitchens to make herself lunch.

He had no difficulty recognizing her as she strode down the wide entryway leading from the mansion to the gate. First, because the mansion had been designed to take full advantage of Vanbert's typically splendid sunsets; second, because she was tall; third, because she *strode* instead of ambled in the accepted style; and fourth, because—

Looks just about the same. Except for that streak of white hair.

Demansk almost laughed. Any other noblewoman in the Confederacy would have covered that streak with dye. Arsule . . . didn't bother.

It's rather striking, actually. I'd forgotten that her hair was really black.

She was at the gate, and coming through. Now that she was close, Demansk could see that there were a few lines in her face which hadn't been there the last time he saw her. Not creases caused by worry or anguish, simply the inevitable effects of aging. Still, she looked much as he remembered her: heftily built, a narrow face which seemed to belong on a more slender woman, close-set dark eyes peering over a long nose.

The ensemble was odd. Taken feature by feature, Arsule was not really that attractive a woman. But, somehow, the whole worked together. Partly that was due to her vibrant personality. But most of it, Demansk thought, was because the personality infused the form shrouding it—which exemplified the word *matron*—with a kind of animal vitality. Arsule Knecht was one of those middle-aged women whom no one described as "good-looking"; but who, at the same time, most middle-aged men—certainly Demansk—found their eyes drawn toward.

"By the gods! It *is* you! I thought someone was playing a joke."

She stepped forward, hands outstretched. "Welcome, Verice! It's been so many years."

He took the hands and bowed over them. Then, kissed the knuckles in the approved style. Noticing, not for the first time, how slender and long the fingers were. As if they, like the face, belonged on a woman with much less in the way of a bosom and hips.

"Ha! Precious few times you ever did *that*. Haven't you become the proper fellow!"

Before he could say anything, Arsule had him by the elbow and was practically marching him toward the mansion. Talking without surcease all the way—in that, too, she hadn't changed.

"I've got quite a crowd here tonight, delighted to show you off—and why did you *really* come, Verice, don't tell me any lies!—but first you must see my new collection of sculptures, which really aren't sculptures exactly because they're carved from wood, they're icons made by Southrons, believe it or not—wonderful work and how do savages manage *that,* I wonder?—some new religious cult of theirs called the 'Young Word'—which, by the way, from what I can tell has some interesting twists to it, at least it's not the same old 'god of this, goddess of that' business—does *everybody* have to mimic *everything?*—Prit's here, by the way—"

That bit of news relieved Demansk. He'd wanted to have a word with Sallivar before he left the capital, and this way he wouldn't need to use part of the morrow for the purpose.

"—and so is Kall Oppricht—"

Another happy coincidence. Oppricht was one of the few Councillors whom Demansk thought he could trust completely. But he hadn't seen the man in well over a year. Tonight wouldn't be the time to broach anything substantive, but he could certainly make a discreet arrangement to have Oppricht talk to Sallivar after Demansk returned to his estate.

They'd reached the door of the mansion. Demansk felt like he'd been marching through mud. He'd forgotten just how exhausting it could be to listen to Arsule Knecht when she prattled.

"—but I've been prattling again, haven't I? And I don't imagine you've come to appreciate that any more than you did in years gone by." She grinned at him. "Poor Verice. But it was your own fault, you know. That 'proper virtue' of yours never gave Druzla a chance to prattle herself."

"The two of you made up for it, as I recall." He didn't *quite* growl the words.

"Oh, stop growling. It's not as if we ever had you cornered, except in the baths. Any other time, and you disappeared while Druzla and I enjoyed a *real* conversation."

That forced a smile from him. "True enough." She began motioning one of the servants to open the door. "A moment, Arsule—please, before you drag me into the mob."

She gave him a quick glance. Then, with another motion, ordered the servant to remain at his post; and drew Demansk off to the side where they could speak without being overheard.

"All right, what is it? I knew there was something other than a social call." Her close-set eyes were almost crossed. "No lies, Verice. If you came here to get my support for another Marcomann—that being you, of course—my answer is 'maybe.' It depends what kind of Marcomann we're talking about."

"Ah—" Damn the woman. I'd forgotten how smart she was, under all that jabber. Good thing for her, too—anyone else who spent money as fast as she does would be bankrupt within five years. Prit tells me her fortune has actually grown since Toman died. She's as shrewd about collecting estates as she is about collecting sculptures.

"Ah—"

"Never mind." As always, Arsule's patience for pauses in a conversation was nil. "I suppose we don't have time tonight for any lengthy discourses, anyway."

She cocked her head sideways in another mannerism Demansk remembered. It was almost histrionic, like everything about Arsule. And, again, the effect was odd. In almost any other woman, the gesture would seem a silly affectation. But, somehow, she managed to make it seem natural, as people with oversized personalities sometimes can.

"Prit'll be part of your scheme, of course. So I can get the details later from him—whatever I need to know, at least, which I *trust* you'll keep to a minimum."

He managed a smile which, he suspected, looked more sickly than anything else.

"Ha! 'You can count on it, lady.' " Her grin reappeared. The fact that it was coming at him sideways didn't make it any less effective. At moments like this, Demansk admitted, Arsule Knecht was a *very* attractive woman. For all the times she'd annoyed him, during her many visits—and vice versa—to his wife, Demansk could remember other times when he'd been forced to keep a casual demeanor around her. In the baths, especially. Clothed, draped in thick and expensive fabrics, her body just seemed heavy. Nude . . . the proper word was *lush.*

One good thing about Arsule, though. At least you never had to grope for the right words. She'd charge right in and provide them for you.

"But you don't really have Marcomann's lusts, do you? In fact, I've never been sure you had any real lusts at all. Oh, stop frowning. I'm not casting aspersions on your manhood—Druzla never complained, that's for sure." The grin seemed to widen, though it was a bit hard to tell seeing it at a near vertical angle. "You didn't *really* think women don't talk about such things, did you?"

"Ah—"

"Oh, stop pretending. I'm sure Druzla told you that I satisfied my own lusts with a sculptor, here and there, seeing as how my husband was spending too much time with his whores to do the job properly."

Well, yes, she did. Half in disapproval, and half in amusement. Arsule's carnal lusts seemed to be just as exuberant as her artistic ones.

She leaned a bit closer. "It's odd, though. Since Toman died—he *did* get killed in a whorehouse brawl, you know, the rumor's quite accurate—I've led quite the proper widow's life. I suspect I was mostly just retaliating. Well, almost. There was one sculptor, a couple of years ago, for about a month—"

"Arsule!" Despite everything, Demansk was still enough of an old-style Vanbert nobleman to feel a little shocked. Not by her history itself, so much as her ready willingness to talk about it.

"Oh, stop pretending to be shocked. Verice, the only difference between me and half the rich bitches in this city is that at least I picked my lovers for their *other* talents. Never been a single gigolo—not one—who wormed himself into *my* bed."

That was probably true, he thought. In this as in everything, Arsule Knecht would make the world fit her tastes, not the other way around.

"Enough," she proclaimed, the grin fading into a smile. "I dare not test the famous Demansk virtue any further, I can tell. All right,

Verice. I'll listen to whatever you have Prit say to me. Truth is, I suspect I'll agree—*but*!"

There was no smile now, and her face came back level. "One condition—tonight. The high priest of the Temple of Jassine is here, and I *insist* that you speak with him."

Demansk couldn't prevent the grimace. Jassine was the goddess of mercy, and her temples provided whatever there was in the Confederation by way of poverty relief. Which . . .

Wasn't much.

"They're getting overwhelmed, Verice," she said softly. "Every year, it gets worse and worse."

"Yes, Arsule, I know. But—"

Now, she *was* cross-eyed. "Oh, stop it! Do you think I'm an idiot? Obviously, if you're to be a new Marcomann you'll be spending your own money like water on other things. I don't want your *money*, Demansk, I want your *mind*." For a moment—miraculously—there was a pause. She even seemed to swallow a bit. Then, very softly: "Most of all, I suppose, I want your soul. I trust you, Verice Demansk, believe it or not. Druzla would never have married a monster in the first place, much less spent two happy decades with him. If I didn't, I wouldn't even consider this. But you must *promise* me you'll think about what the high priest has to tell you."

That much he could do. *Think*, yes—even if no answer came.

"Done," he said.

An instant later, she was sweeping him through the door. "Everyone—look who's here! Verice, this is my latest protégé—Gaorg's the most brilliant dramatist, the evening's devoted to him, in fact—have you seen his latest tragedy?—no, of course not—don't mind him, Gaorg, he's not really a boor he just pretends very well—"

CHAPTER SIX

As Demansk's velipad approached the little house, he felt a certain awkwardness coming over him. Almost shame, truth be told. He had always *meant* to visit the First Spear after the man retired, but . . .

In the months since the siege of Preble where the First Spear sustained his career-ending injury, something always seemed more pressing. It was not as if Demansk and the First Spear had been personally close. He didn't even know the man's name.

Still, there had been a certain bond forged between them, in those days of savage struggle against the Islanders armed with Gellert's bizarre and frightening new weaponry. And Demansk was acutely aware of the fact that his grandfather *would* have known the First Spear's name—that of every First Spear in his regiments, in fact—and *would* have visited the man, long before this.

And wouldn't have had an ulterior motive for doing it, either.

Perhaps to assuage his own feelings of guilt, Demansk's first words were blunt and honest.

"I'm afraid I came for a reason, First Spear. Though I should have come earlier, for which I apologize."

The former First Spear of Demansk's First Regiment lowered his head, his heavy-jawed face flushing a bit with embarrassment. The motion brought the man's scalp into Demansk's view. He was pleased to see that the wound seemed to have healed well enough, even if the scarring was heavy and the coarse black hair almost nonexistent in its vicinity.

"You needn't, sir," mumbled the First Spear. "I hadn't expected you to."

Demansk suppressed a sigh. No, the man wouldn't have expected it. But his own grandfather would have. There was a time when Vanbert bonds had run deep.

He couldn't repress a second sigh entirely. The First Spear, he knew, came from the eastern provinces of the Confederacy. At one time, he would have retired there, settling in for a comfortable old age among his own folk. Now—

Demansk's eyes scanned the flat terrain which surrounded the house. Flat, and just a bit arid. Typical of the farmland available in the recently conquered western provinces. The farmland in the east was better, but most of it had long since been gobbled up by the expanding slave-operated great estates of Vanbert's aristocracy. So, when the chirurgeons informed Demansk that his First Spear would survive the wound but would never be able to serve in battle again, Demansk had given him this land out of his own great estates.

"Any of your kinfolk nearby?" he asked abruptly.

The First Spear, obviously relieved to have the awkward apology behind them, raised his head and smiled. "Yes, sir. Quite a few." He pointed a thick finger to the north. "A good chunk of my clan lives up that way. When I told them—"

He hesitated for a moment. Then: "Well, sir, it's like this. I guess you told your land manager for the area to run easy on the prices, for me and mine. So a goodly number of my kinfolk moved here from back home. Got a little village up there now and everything. Even our own temple. Nothing fancy, of course."

Demansk felt his feelings of guilt ease. He'd forgotten that he'd given those instructions. Eyeing the still-muscular figure of the First Spear, he found himself smiling faintly. Between Demansk's instructions and, he had no doubt at all, the veiled threats of the First

Spear and his clansmen, the land manager had clearly decided not to apply the usual gouging tactics.

He heard a little noise behind the First Spear's shoulder and lifted his eyes. The figure of a young woman had appeared in the doorway of the house, with an infant cradled in her arms.

Demansk chuckled. "I see you didn't waste any time."

The First Spear turned his head. The smile which came to his lips seemed at odds with the blocky, brutal-looking face.

"Saw no reason to, sir. That's Ilset, the daughter of my second cousin Polter. I'd had my eye on her since she was no more than eight years old. Always made it a point to visit whenever I went home between campaigns." He tapped the scar on his head. "By the time this happened, she was already sixteen. So's as soon as I could move about I got home quick before someone else could sneak in ahead of me. Polter was willing, since I wasn't asking for much in the way of a dowry."

He jerked his head to the north. "As it happens, Polter wound up moving out here too. Things in the east are . . . not good, anymore." For a moment, his face darkened. "A free farmer doesn't stand a chance there, these days."

The young woman—not much more than a girl, really—gave Demansk a timid smile. He returned it quite cheerfully.

Better and better, he thought, giving her lush figure a quick and discreet inspection. Helga will need a wet nurse anyway, and if the First Spear's willing . . .

He cleared his throat. "As I said, I didn't really come here on a simple visit, First Spear. I need to ask you if you'd be willing to come back into my service again." Hastily: "Not as a troop leader, mind. Not exactly, anyway. I wouldn't expect you to do any actual fighting."

The First Spear winced and rubbed the scar on his scalp. " 'Fraid I can't. Fight, I mean. I can do most anything else—didn't even seem to lose any of my wits. But the chirurgeon told me that my skull's not up to any more blows. Kill me straight up, he said."

His dark eyes studied Demansk for a moment. Then, he turned his head again and looked at his new wife. "I dunno, sir," he mumbled. "I wouldn't mind, myself. Been kind of bored, to tell you the truth. But Ilset's not really old enough to run the farm on her own, and . . ." He swallowed. "Truth is, I'd miss her something terrible."

The last remarked warmed Demansk—and, perhaps oddly, reassured him. The one uncertainty he'd had in coming here was the First Spear's temperament. As a troop leader, the man had been superb. It was no accident that he'd risen to the highest slot a ranker could be promoted to. But the inevitable social distance between someone like him and a noble Justiciar in the modern Confederacy had made his actual personality an unknown factor to Demansk.

What pleased him was not so much that the man obviously doted on his wife. That was not really uncommon, for all the officially patriarchal nature of Confederate society. It was the fact that he was so readily able and willing to *admit* it. That spoke both to the First Spear's deep self-confidence as well as his lack of concern for long-standing custom.

Both of which he's going to need, thought Demansk, if he agrees to my assignment.

"That's not a problem," he said. "As it happens, I'd prefer it if your wife accompanied you anyway." He rushed ahead, forestalling the next objection. "And you needn't worry about the farm. I'll buy it back from you for twice what you paid for it—including extra for improvements—and I'll set aside a large retirement bonus for when the assignment's done."

Honesty forced him to add: "Though I can't tell you how soon that would be. Several years, most likely."

Again, the First Spear's dark eyes studied Demansk. Then, without taking his eyes from the Justiciar, he turned his head a bit and growled: "Go back into the house, Ilset. And close the door."

She obeyed promptly. Clearly enough, however much the First Spear doted on his wife, he retained the usual authority of a Confederate husband in his own family.

After he heard the door close, he took a long, slow breath. "Begging your pardon, sir—I realize it's not really my place to ask—but . . . how dangerous is this assignment really going to be, if I take it? Not for me, but for my kinfolk."

Demansk was impressed by the man's intelligence. All high-ranking troopers, of course, were adept in the skills of war. But most of them gave little thought, if any, to the complexities of political maneuver.

Demansk didn't answer immediately. He examined the house, for a moment. A typical yeoman farmer's dwelling, thatch roof over mudbrick construction. A bit larger and better made than most. There were panes in the two small windows in addition to the shutters, even if they were made of the cloudy glass which was all anyone except noblemen could afford.

His eyes ranged to the north, as if trying to study the unseen village where the First Spear's kinfolk lived. He was fairly certain he'd see much the same thing. A small settlement of freemen, who had managed to carve out a decent life for themselves amidst the steady decay of the Confederacy of Vanbert.

"It's possible they could all be impaled," he stated curtly, "if the worst happens. Not likely, but I can't rule it out. They'd certainly be stripped of their lands and sold into slavery."

Having gotten it out, he added a bit hastily: "But that's if the very worst happens. Which, to be honest, is not all that likely. If for no other reason, simply because things will be such a ratfuck mess that nobody will really know any longer who did what to whom. Your kinfolk would be more or less invisible in the fog."

The First Spear chuckled. "Like that, huh? 'Interesting times,' as they say." He gave the house his own quick examination. "And what if things turn out well?"

"They'll all be sitting pretty," said Demansk. "Good glass in the windows—and houses a lot bigger than this." He almost added: *with slaves to keep them clean*, but didn't. If Demansk's plans worked out, there wouldn't be any slaves left in the first place.

Whatever happened, Demansk had already decided, he would remain honest with this man. Partly because it would be foolish not to, but mostly because stubbornness did not allow it. His grandfather, full of the virtues of the Vanbert of old, would not have lied to his First Spear. Demansk, even as he destroyed that old regime, would retain at least that much.

The First Spear was silent, for a moment. He worked his jaws slightly, as his eyes moved slowly across his farmland. The crops were filling out well, now. It would be a good season.

"And who knows about the next?" he murmured. His thick chest swelled with another deep breath. Then: "What the hell. 'Interesting times' it is. No way around it, so far as I can see. May as well try to ride a wave as duck from it, since there's nowhere to hide anyway."

He gave Demansk a shrewd look. "Is there, sir?"

The Justiciar shrugged. "Not that I can see."

The First Spear nodded. "You'd make a better new Marcomann than anyone else, that I know of. That *is* what we're talking about."

The last sentence came as a flat statement, not a question. Demansk was reassured. He found himself also reassessing his plans for the man. He hadn't expected such political acumen from a former First Spear. After this initial assignment was done . . .

"Can you read?" he asked abruptly. "Well, I mean."

The First Spear shrugged. "Enough to get by, sir. I wouldn't call it 'well.' I'm no scholar, that's for sure."

"I'll have you taught. By Helga herself, at first. She'll have plenty of time on your voyage."

The First Spear's eyed widened. Demansk chuckled.

"Yes, that's your first assignment. I'll have others for you when it's done, First Spear. But, first, you've got to see to it that my daughter gets to Marange safely." His own jaws tightened. "I'll not see her fall into the hands of pirates again, and I've got no way to get her there except by sea."

The First Spear's jaws were working again. Demansk remembered the habit, from old campaigns. The man was chewing on a problem.

"I'm no seaman myself, sir. But you can hire such, easily enough. The trick is having the right escort."

His head swiveled, looking north. Demansk's gaze followed, and he felt his own eyes widen.

I hadn't considered—

The First Spear verbalized the notion. "Why not use my kinfolk, sir? *All* of them. It'd cost you some, sure, buying out all the farms. But you'd have to pay loose mercenaries near as much, if you wanted to have good men you can trust. And you *still* couldn't be sure there weren't any traitors in the bunch. My clansmen, now, them I can vouch for."

Demansk was already captivated by the idea. "How many fighting men, First Spear? And how many people, in total?"

The First Spear rasped a little laugh. "They're *all* soldiers, sir. Or, if they're too young, training for it already. Nothing else for a freeman to do, in the east. Can't make a go of farming without a retirement bonus to get you started." The heavy jaws worked some more, as he did his calculations. "Thirty-two men with experience, another dozen or so good lads ready to learn. Two first spears and seven file closers amongst 'em. Eight of the men are too old or crippled to fight in the ranks—me being one of them. But there's always other jobs need to be done, anyway. Quarter-mastering and such."

The jaws worked back and forth. "Say, give me a few weeks to organize 'em, and you've got a third of a hundred from my own kin. All fighters, I'm counting, complete with gear and kit. They can make the core, if you need a full hundred. We can get the rest, easily enough. There's plenty of retired and out-of-regiment men hereabouts, most of whom aren't finding that it's all that easy to work a farm. If you let me and my kinfolk pick them, we can get ones to be trusted."

Demansk was doing his own calculations. He needed to get Helga off as soon as possible, before the sailing season ended. That meant, at the latest, two months from now.

"You'll have to be ready to leave in six weeks," he said firmly.

The First Spear sloped his shoulders. It was not a gesture of despair; simply one of a man prepared to do whatever work was needed.

"I'm to be First Spear again, then?"

Demansk shook his head. "No. You'll stay out of combat. I need you to oversee the business—and give my daughter the advice and counsel she'll need.

"As far as possible," he added, remembering her headstrong attitude. The First Spear smiled. Clearly enough, he'd heard stories of Helga Demansk's temperament.

"You pick the First Spear," said Demansk. "I've got a different title for you. A new one." He'd given this some thought. "You're a 'Special Attendant' for Verice Demansk. The first of several, I suspect. The pay is a lot better, I might add."

The former First Spear pursed his lips. "And what exactly is the authority of such a . . . 'Special Attendant'?"

"Whatever it becomes," replied Demansk flatly. "I'll have a new title myself pretty soon. 'Triumvir.' "

The new Special Attendant nodded his head. "Good move that, sir, if you'll permit me saying so. Always defeat 'em in detail, when you can."

A smile came to Demansk's face. He suspected it was not a cheery expression, though. Several species of carnivores smiled also, at times. But his new subordinate's perspicacity pleased him, and besides—carnivores who smiled hunted in packs.

"I'll need to be off now, Special Attendant. I'll send money to you, as soon as you figure out how much you'll need for everything."

They had been standing in front of the house the whole time. The Special Attendant had the reins of Demansk's velipad in his fist, since he'd politely helped him dismount when he arrived. He held them out and Demansk took them back.

As he turned away, preparing to mount, a sudden thought came to him. His face flushed a bit.

"Special Attendant, what is your *name*?"

The man's actual grin, when it finally came, was surprisingly light-hearted. "It's to be the old times again, damn me if it won't!" he exclaimed cheerily. "Jessep, sir. Jessep Yunkers."

Demansk's escort was waiting for him in the tavern of a village nearby. He'd left them there so no one would know exactly where he had gone. The village, Demansk realized as he returned to it, was not the one Jessep had mentioned. Which was just as well, he decided. If spies started retracing his steps, they wouldn't find much here.

The officer in charge of the escort was a responsible man, so he had kept his men from drinking too much. The party was back on the road within minutes.

"One more stop before we're home," Demansk told him. Since

there would be no way to keep this stop secret—and no need to, for that matter—he added: "Trae's villa. The new one, on the other side of the river."

The new "villa" of Demansk's youngest son Trae was a peculiar sort of thing. The mansion which served as the actual dwelling was standard enough, if a bit on the small side for a scion of such a wealthy family. But the adjoining buildings along the riverside—all of them newly constructed—were not something you'd find on most Confederate noblemen's estates.

Not on any, qualified Demansk to himself, as he dismounted in front of the largest new building. Trae called it a "workshop." The fact that he'd even *call* it that was enough to demonstrate the young man's eccentricity. Modern Vanbert noblemen did not engage in such disreputable activity as "work."

Before he entered the workshop, Demansk walked over to the riverbank and studied the river. Trae's estates were on the northern bank of the estuary of the Wantrell. Demansk could see his own great villa in the distance, perched on a small hill across the river.

Here, very close to the sea, the river was almost a mile wide. And . . .

Deep enough, Demansk decided. We'll need to build a dock. But Helga's ship, even as big a one as I'll get her, can make moorage here.

He turned away and studied the workshop. There was nothing to see, really, other than a small door on the side and two great swinging waterdoors in the middle which opened directly on an inlet to the riverside. There were plenty of windows, but all of them began ten feet off the ground—above eye level, except for someone with a ladder.

And there wouldn't be anything to see, anyway, even if someone did use a ladder. Demansk noted, with approval, the frosty glass which filled all the windows. His son Trae was absent-minded, in some ways, but there was nothing at all wrong with his brains. The interior of the workshop would be better lit than most buildings, during daytime at least, but would be impossible to spy on easily.

He went over to the small door and gave it a tug. Locked, as he'd expected—and hoped. He gave the door a vigorous pounding with his fist.

The man who opened the door was the one Demansk had come to see. The *other* one, rather, in addition to his son.

The foreign face was blank with astonishment. "Justiciar!" the man exclaimed. "We hadn't expected—"

"Good," grunted Demansk, passing through the door. When he entered the workshop, his eyes fell on the object at its center. Impossible to look anywhere else, really. Even floating in its berth, the thing filled most of the building's interior.

It was the steam ram which Adrian Gellert had designed for the King of the Isles. The device had caused much grief to the Confederates in the first period of the siege of Preble, before Demansk had managed to capture the bizarre thing.

Capture it from—

His eyes moved away from the ship and fell on the man who had opened the door. Sharlz Thicelt, he noted, had given up his turban and was now wearing the garb of a Confederate freeman instead of an Islesman. But the tall former captain of the steam ram still had his head shaved, and still had heavy gold hoops dangling from his ears.

Demansk decided he approved of that small display of stubbornness. In an odd way, it spoke to a certain integrity in the former Islander naval captain.

That integrity would be needed. "Islander naval captain" was a term whose distinction from "pirate chieftain" could only be parsed by an Emerald philosopher. Demansk was now facing the old quandary: *How do you know that the bandit you're hiring is an honest man?*

Something of his thoughts must have shown. Thicelt's thick lips twisted, and he held up his wrists. "Your son will speak well of me, I think. At least, he removed the manacles weeks ago."

Trae had come up by then, a tool of some kind in his hand. A tool! Demansk noted. *Good thing no one knows, or the whole family would be disgraced in Vanbert's upper crust.*

"He's not a bad pirate, as these things go," said Demansk's youngest offspring cheerfully.

Demansk saw no reason to dilly-dally around the business. "But will he *stay* bought?" he demanded.

Sharlz Thicelt's expressive lips shifted into a different kind of smile. Still wry; but also, somehow, philosophical.

"Depends on the price," he said, just as bluntly. "If it's a fair one, yes; try and chisel me, you'll live to regret it." He shrugged. "Not a polite way of putting it, of course. But . . . there it is."

Demansk bestowed upon him the carnivore smile. "I dare say you'll have no complaint about the *price.* Though you might find the risk involved a bit on the steep side."

Thicelt's whole face was expressive. The smile vanished, the brows lowered, the cheeks thinned. The man was on the verge of taking insult. Whatever else anyone said about the pirates of the Isles, no one accused them of cowardice.

Demansk headed it off. "I'm not talking about *simple* risks, Sharlz Thicelt." He waved his hand in a dismissive gesture. "Boarding operations, battle—that sort of thing. I'm talking about the kind of risks that might leave you, someday, immured in a dark cellar. Dying slowly on a stake, with no one knowing you are even there except your executioners."

Thicelt's face cleared. "Ah. *Politics.*" He ran a long-fingered hand over his shaven skull. Then the wry smile returned. "And why not? Any common pirate can rob and plunder and rape and kill. It takes a great pirate to do *politics.*"

He squared his shoulders and tapped his chest with a finger. "Here, Justiciar Demansk, you see a great pirate. One of the best! So. What are to be my new responsibilities?"

"I'm not sure yet, as far as the long term goes. In the short term, I need a captain for a sea voyage." He matched the wry smile with one of his own. "I do know your new title, on the other hand. *Special Attendant.*"

"'Special Attendant.'" Thicelt rolled the odd words around in his mouth. "'Special Attendant.' It has a nice vague sound to it. Splendid! Vague titles are a damnation for a workman; a boon, for the overseer."

"Exactly," said Demansk. "And for the overseer's master."

He looked at his son, pointing at the steam ram. "And?"

Trae shrugged. "We can run it easily enough, Father, as well as fire the cannons. The damage has all been repaired. I think I understand how everything works—even, more or less, *why* it works. But I hope you're not planning to use it for your mysterious 'sea voyage.' I wouldn't trust this tub in open waters for more than a few hours, and then only in fine weather. Even Sharlz wouldn't."

The former pirate captain scowled. "A 'tub,' as you say. The damn thing gave me nothing but grief, except in battle. Where"—he grinned at Demansk—"it was a terror to my enemies until that unspeakable imbecile Prince Tenny insisted on taking command."

Having been one of Thicelt's enemies in that sea battle, Demansk couldn't help but agree. The infernal steam ram, with its armored shell and its cannons, had wreaked havoc among Demansk's own ships. But Prince Tenny, the oldest son of King Casull of the Isles, had been aboard the ram. He had forced Thicelt to abandon the captain's cunning tactics and try to mix it up directly with the Confederate forces.

The Confederate navy was notoriously clumsy, with none of the superb seamanship of the Islanders. But no one in their right mind ever tried to "mix it up directly" with Confederate naval forces. Those forces consisted mainly of marines, who were the world's experts at turning a sea battle into a land battle. Demansk himself had led the boarding operation which captured the steam ram—and its captain, in the bargain.

Prince Tenny had been killed in the course of that boarding operation, with a dart through his guts. Demansk could still remember Sharlz Thicelt spitting on the corpse with fury.

"I've got other plans for the steam ram," said Demansk. "You'll have a good seagoing vessel for your voyage, Special Attendant Thicelt, have no fear of that. In fact, your very first assignment is to select the ship in the first place. I'll give you the money to buy it." Again, he waved his hand. "I'll expect you not to skim more than a modest sum off the top."

Thicelt grinned. "And then?"

Demansk hooked his thumb at the ram. "If it's working, does it need you to captain it?"

Thicelt shook his head. "Any good captain can manage the thing, with some training."

"Good. Because what I really need is an *admiral.*"

All the good cheer left Thicelt's face. He studied Demansk very carefully. Then: "An honest pirate, as I said. So I will not lie. The 'price' involves costs as well as rewards. There is only one reason you would need an 'admiral,' and that is to conquer the Isles." The man's long face grew longer still. "I have family on those Isles, Justiciar Demansk. Political loyalties are nothing to me. Family . . . is a different thing. People get hurt in conquests. Killed and ravished and maimed. Their property taken and themselves sold into slavery."

Demansk nodded. "I wouldn't expect your loyalty under such conditions. Nor would I even want it, to be honest." He reached out a hand and seized the taller man by the shoulder. "I can promise you this, Sharlz Thicelt. If you let me know where your family lives—and especially if you can get word to them ahead of time—I will see to their safety and well-being."

He dropped the hand and shrugged. "I can't promise that none of their properties would be damaged or taken. In war . . ."

"Who knows?" Thicelt completed the thought. "Property can always be replaced. Especially when one of the family members is a 'Special Attendant.' "

He nodded his head. The gesture had a very formal aura. "It is done, Justiciar Demansk. A bargain, and an honest one."

"And what about me, Father?" asked Trae. "What do you plan for me?" His youthful face was creased with confusion. "And what *is* all this business about, anyway?"

Demansk spent the rest of the evening explaining. Trae and Thicelt were his only companions through that long discussion, and Demansk decided to allow Thicelt to remain for all of it. He had known from the beginning that he was taking a risk by employing Thicelt. He had done so because he *needed* the finest admiral he could get his hands on. And he was quite certain that the canny King of the Isles had chosen his very best captain to command the steam ram.

Still, it was a risk. With what he learned in the course of that evening's discussion, Thicelt could sell the information to any one of Demansk's enemies—and come out of the sale a rich man as well as a free one.

But risks have to be taken, at times. And Demansk had always been of the philosophy that there was no point in postponing them. Eventually, he would have had to tell Thicelt, anyway. And there was simply no way to keep under close guard a man whom he intended to load with so much power and authority as well as responsibility. So . . . may as well find out quickly.

By the end of the evening, however, Demansk's lurking fears were allayed. Thicelt, clearly enough, was the kind of man who enjoyed a genuine challenge. No one simply seeking to gain information for a later betrayal would have pitched into the discussion and the planning so eagerly—not to mention advancing so many excellent suggestions himself. Demansk suspected that the man's insistence on his piratical nature was due more to Islander custom than anything else. A role, as it were, rather than the man himself.

As a servant led him to the sleeping chamber where he would spend the night, after the discussion was over, Demansk found himself thinking about that "role." Not so much Thicelt's alone, as those of millions of men. When all was said and done, what Demansk planned to carry out was a gigantic "mixing of roles."

All of the Confederacy's decay, he thought, *could in the end be reduced to that*. The great realm forged by Vanbert had settled into layers, like sludge rotting in a pool. It was time to "mix it up." Break classes as well as nations, and churn new life into the mix.

And so it begins, he thought, as he lay down on the couch and closed his eyes. Verice Demansk, the head of one of Vanbert's oldest and most illustrious families, was already "mixing it up." It was not an accident, he now realized, that outside of his immediate family the first recruits to his conspiracy were a former peasant and a pirate.

He chewed on the thought for a while. Then, fell to sleep much more easily than he would have suspected. And why not? His own ancestors had been peasants; and pirates, too, for that matter. "Land pirates," of course. Vanberts were not natural seamen.

CHAPTER SEVEN

"I can't stay long," he told Helga. "I've got to get back to the capital in time for the Council session, and I've got to visit the siege of Preble along the way."

Helga looked down at the baby nestled in her lap. "Are you listening?" she demanded. "No, you're sleeping—lazy little sot! When your grandfather's giving you such excellent lessons in duplicity!

"This is lesson Number 64, too," she added, clucking her tongue with motherly distress. " 'How To Appear Deeply Concerned By Grave Matters of State.' You'll never be a successful politician without it."

Demansk's lips quirked. As much as Helga's tongue often annoyed him, he had long ago decided that, on balance, it probably also helped keep him sane. Unseemly as her sarcasm might be—her own father!—it was usually right on target.

Certainly in this instance. Demansk really had no legitimate reason to visit the Confederate forces maintaining the siege of Preble. Jeschonyk's enemies, with Speaker of the Assembly Albrecht leading the pack, had bayed for his dismissal after the initial disasters at Preble the previous year, and his replacement by Albrecht himself. Demansk had been dismissed from his command along with Jeschonyk. Partly because he was seen as Jeschonyk's loyal subordinate, which, in truth, he had been. But mostly because Albrecht wanted no independent top officer on his staff to share the credit for breaking Preble's rebellion—especially not one as famously competent as Demansk. Albrecht wanted no one beside him when he rode in the chariot at the triumph. Or even whispers that someone *should* have been riding beside him.

Neither Demansk nor Jeschonyk had made more than a token protest. Jeschonyk, because the old man had become weary in the course of the strenuous siege; Demansk, because his mind had already begun turning to a much more ambitious goal than breaking a single city's rebellion. A goal, and a scheme, which being forced to remain at the site of a long siege would severely hamper—as Albrecht was about to discover himself.

"That's the one good old custom, if nothing else," he said, "which still remains intact." He bestowed a stern look upon his sleeping grandson and wagged his finger. "Don't forget it, lad! The commander of an army on campaign *must* remain in the field with his troops until the victory is won.

"Which," he added cheerily, "is still a long way down the road at Preble. Ha! That arrogant bastard!" Somewhere in Demansk's soul, Albrecht's derisive remarks of the year before still rankled. "He's found out, hasn't he now, just how tough a siege can be against a determined opponent."

The unheeding, sleeping babe was now subjected to finger-wagging from his mother. "And don't think you'll be able to bribe your way out of it, either, you little rascal! Desertion is desertion. No amount of bribes will keep you from the executioner's blade. Not even if you've got Albrecht's fortune. Forget the blade, for that matter. Nobleman or not, you'll be fit onto a commoner's stake."

She raised her head and studied her father, seated upright on a stool across from her. The room they were in, where Demansk had found her upon his return, was Helga's weaving room. Other than the loom and the small divan on which she was perched, the only piece of furniture available had been her knitting stool. But Helga's father, unlike many such men in the elite of the Confederacy, had not hesitated to use it. Stools not much different, after all—except for the lack of fancy carving and inlaid precious stones—had been his customary seating while on campaign.

"Trae?" she asked.

"He's in. All the way, and with full knowledge. So is that tame pirate of his, Sharlz Thicelt."

Helga frowned. Demansk knew that she was less willing than he was to trust *any* Islander. Which, given her own personal experiences with the breed, was hardly surprising. But Demansk, in this if not in most things, was more broad-minded than his daughter. And he understood, in a way that she did not and probably never would, the manner in which the concept of "manhood" worked its way through the peculiar customs and habits of the Islesmen.

They were an odd folk, to Confederates—as notorious for their double-dealing in politics as they were for their brigandage.

Well, not that exactly, Demansk admitted. *Confederate politics can be just as treacherous. It's the way the Islesmen acknowledge it openly, as if treason were simply a wager rather than a sin. The way they deride an executed schemer for his lack of wits rather than his lack of morals.*

He thought about it for a moment. *And I can't honestly say, any longer, that their way is worse than ours. At least they're not hypocrites.*

He had waited enough time to allow Helga to make any open protest, but she hadn't. Rebellious the girl might be, but she was still smart enough not to quarrel with her father over matters of tactics.

"That's that, then," he said. "You'll be getting a new subordinate of your own, by the way. Jessep Yunkers. He'll be in command of your escort." Demansk conveniently skipped over the awkwardness of explaining that the name would mean nothing to her, since it had meant nothing to him either until a few days ago. "I don't believe you ever met him. Before he got badly injured at Preble, he was the First Spear of my First Regiment. A very good man."

There was no frown of disapproval now, on his daughter's brow. As was true of Demansk himself, Helga was partial to the breed of sturdy peasants who produced the Confederacy's non-commissioned officers. They were the backbone of Vanbert military power, and she knew it as well as he did.

"I'll want to keep Lortz," she said. Her tone made clear that she was prepared for argument.

But Demansk gave her none. He had decided that Helga's insistence on personal combat training was probably just as well. If nothing else, it kept her in superb physical condition. And . . . it might someday save her life.

Lortz was the former gladiator whom Helga had hired almost as soon as she returned from captivity. She had kept him busy even during the last trimester of her pregnancy, teaching her such skills as knife-throwing which her swollen belly still permitted. And she had resumed her regular training a mere week after giving birth.

He eyed his daughter's figure, so evident even under the modest garment she was wearing. "Modest" in its cut, at least. Demansk wasn't entirely happy with the sheerness of the thing, but—that was the modern style, after all, especially in summer. And this much he would admit: however modern the style of the garment, the muscles beneath the fabric were as hard as those of any peasant ancestress of the family.

"He'll insist on bringing his, ah, servants with him," Helga added, her lips curling at the euphemism for Lortz's two concubines. "But there should be room. I'll need to find a wet nurse anyway, so they can be company for her."

"I've already found you a wet nurse. Jessep's wife Ilset." He nodded toward the infant in her lap. "They have a baby themselves; just about his age, as it happens."

"A soldier's wife? Good. That'll be handy." She gave her father a sly look. "And I'll bet your entire fortune she's full-breasted. A retired First Spear of the First Regiment—especially with the bonuses you pass out—would have had every peasant family in his province trotting out their daughters for inspection."

Demansk grinned. "Ilset's good-looking, no doubt about it. And, as you guessed, not slender. Precious few soldiers share the taste of aristocratic aesthetes for willowy women. Not Jessep, that's for sure."

He planted his hands on his knees and thrust to his feet. "Now that it's definite, you should start making your preparations. It'll be a few weeks still, though, so you needn't rush anything. Sharlz will need time to find and outfit a ship, and Jessep the same in order to pull the escort together."

"There's really not much that I need to do in the way of preparation. A few days, no more." She chucked the baby softly under his chin. "And he'll need even less. Logistics is simple at his age. Where the tits go, he goes."

"True enough," chuckled Demansk. After a moment, the humor faded. "You'll probably need to comfort Lissel a bit, once the news hits. Which probably won't take long," he added sourly, "knowing Barrett. I'll be seeing him on my way to Preble."

" 'Probably?' " jeered Helga. "No 'probable' about it, Father. The minute Barrett learns he's got a better offer in the making, he'll march into Lissel's rooms and tell her to start packing. You watch—you'll probably even still be there when it happens."

Demansk didn't argue the point. His eldest son was . . . not a man he much liked.

Helga was scowling now. "And Lissel will come here straight off, wailing like a babe herself. I'll keep two laundresses busy for a week, just washing the tear-soaked linens."

Her father grimaced. "Do you really think she'll be that upset? It never struck me that there was much affection in the marriage."

"Heh. There isn't *any,* Father. And what's that got to do with anything? Lissel is a sweet enough girl, but she's got the brains of a . . . oh, hell, even pigs are smarter. She's a Vanbert gentry daughter, through and through. Never had an original thought in her brain. For someone of her class, a marriage to a Demansk meant a major leap in status. Being divorced will devastate her. It's got nothing to do with *Barrett.*"

Demansk sighed. "I'll see to it she's well taken care of. Financially, I mean."

Helga shrugged. "She'll survive. And, within a year, be deluged with other marriage proposals. From other gentry, of course, not real noblemen. The combination of her former marital status and a big dowry will be irresistible to that lot." A moment later, grudgingly, she added: "Well, some of them."

Demansk thought his daughter was being a bit uncharitable. He had a higher opinion of the gentry than she did. He'd had more contact with them, for one thing, and on this subject Helga's own unthinking prejudices were peeking through. Whatever the gentry's faults as a class, Demansk had found many of them to be quite admirable as individuals.

The upper class of the Confederacy fell, broadly speaking, into three categories:

At the top, the real nobility of the ancient, great families. All of whom were giant landowners and either stinking rich or up to their eyeballs in debt. This class provided the Confederacy with all of its Council members and speakers and, usually, with the Speaker of the Assembly. The Demansk family was part of that elite, and ranked high even in their midst.

Off to the side, so to speak, were the wealthy merchants, tax farmers, and usurers. Many of them originated from the gentry, but were no longer considered truly part of it. Not in theory, at least, even if in practice they often served the gentry as its "upper crust." These families could sometimes be as wealthy as the nobility but, of course, they shared none of the nobility's social glamour and respectability—except to the degree that, by forging a marriage between one of their own and a noble family far enough in debt to accept the offer, they could lever their way into the genuine aristocracy. Through the back door, of course. But, after two or three generations, no one remembered. Nowadays, at least.

Finally, forming the great base of Vanbert's ruling class, came the gentry. Respectable folk, of course—landowners rather than merchants. A number of them were even quite wealthy in their own right. And they provided most of the officers for the Confederacy's army, below the very top ranks.

Personally, Demansk thought the old Vanbert virtues could be found in that class more often than in the actual aristocracy. Certainly more than among the merchants and usurers. Gentrymen were invariably courageous in battle and often made capable, if usually unimaginative, officers.

But, while he thought Helga was being a *bit* uncharitable, he understood her sentiments well enough. The gentry was even more notorious for its endless and obsessive bickering than the nobility. With some exceptions—always regarded as eccentric—they treasured and gloated over every small increase in status like misers over gold; schemed for it constantly; and took any reverse, no matter how small, as if it were the world's worst natural disaster.

There was a popular legend—which Demansk suspected was probably true—that five gentry families died to the last person in the city of Ghust when the volcano erupted. They were on the outskirts of the disaster, and had plenty of time to flee. But they spent so much time quarreling over which of their carriages should get precedence in the escape that the cloud of gas and ashes overtook them in mid-squabble.

Demansk turned his head and examined the loom in the corner. It pleased him, even though he knew it was an excuse, to liken what he was doing to a weaver's work instead of a butcher's. Though the main color in the cloth he was weaving would be red—blood red—it was still work which would leave something other than ruin at its completion.

Maybe, he admitted. *If I do the work extremely well, and the Goddess of Luck favors me.*

The gentry, and its attitudes, would play a very big role in that weaving. Demansk was gambling that, when the time came, he could use their ambition and avarice to overcome their natural conservatism. With enough of them, at least, to enable him to hold power while he set about shredding the established ways of the Confederacy.

It would not be easy. The gentry, on their own farms, did not depend on slave labor to the degree that the aristocracy did on the great estates. Emancipation would hurt them economically, to be sure, especially at first. But the more capable and energetic families would also be able to take advantage of the chaos of the transition. Forming alliances with money-lenders and merchants; investing in manufacture—which would now have a large pool of former slave labor to draw on; carving out careers in a suddenly opened and merit-based government apparatus.

On the other hand . . . if they didn't *need* slaves, the gentry treasured their status as slave-holders all the more for it. It gave them the illusion of being noblemen themselves, at least in part.

Avarice against habit; ambition against custom; cold realism against unthinking conservatism. Those were the forces Demansk would manipulate, one against the other, until he had created the fabric he wanted. Or, in the failing, wreck the loom entirely.

"Stop being gloomy, Father," Helga said. As so often, daughter read father's mood to perfection. "It'll work. As well as anything does, anyway." She gave the loom a skeptical glance. "That's just a *construct,* you know. Something made; a thing with clear parts and sides and limits. The real world's a lot messier."

The baby woke up, and started bawling immediately. "Like this creature here," she added, good cheer mixed with exasperation. "Gobbling like a pig at one end and shitting even worse at the other. About as pretty as a hogpen." She silenced the infant in the time-honored way; wails were replaced by the soft sounds of suckling. "But he *works,* after all. And in the meantime, he's just so *cute.*"

Demansk's eyes almost goggled. Whatever other metaphor or simile or euphemism he had ever used to describe his project to himself, the word *cute* had never so much as crossed his mind.

Helga smiled. "It's just like the poet said, Father. 'Only the blood of women runs truly cold.' "

She nodded toward the door. "And now, you'd best be off. You've got hot-blooded man's work to do."

CHAPTER EIGHT

This was the only time Adrian Gellert was really thankful for the trance-haze. Dealing with his brother Esmond directly, without the shielding buffer which two other minds sharing his brain gave him, was . . . painful.

When did it happen? he asked, almost plaintively.

He could sense, if not see, Raj's shoulders rising and falling in a shrug. The sensation was purely one created by his own imagination. He'd never met Raj Whitehall in the flesh. What he knew of him, even the man's appearance, came solely from glimpses which he got from Raj himself. And those were filtered already, because they were Raj's images of himself when he had still been made of flesh and blood. As if a man knew a friend—closer in many ways than any friend he'd ever had—only from seeing him reflected in a mirror.

Who can say? There's never a moment for something like this. Any more than you can say there is a moment when poison kills a man. Hate's a toxin as corrosive and deadly as arsenic, if you take too much of it. And Esmond's been guzzling at that well for a long time now.

Sadly, Adrian stared down at the whimpering creature huddled in a corner of Esmond's tent. From the hair color and what little else Adrian could discern about the battered figure, he thought he came from the northern part of the continent. A "Confederate" in name, even if he was most likely a peasant rather than a true Vanbert. That would be enough to serve as a focus for Esmond's rage.

Adrian estimated thc boy was not more than twelve years old. It was hard to be sure, though, because his face was pulpy and bruised and the scrawny body was emaciated from hunger. The manacles on his thin wrists and ankles were quite unnecessary. The boy was obviously so weak he could not even crawl, much less stand. Adrian was not sure he would even be alive the next day.

"We'll see about that," he growled, dropping to one knee next to the child. He reached out his hand and lightly shook a shoulder. There was no response except a soft moan.

Moving as gently as he could, Adrian gave the boy a quick examination. The touch of his fingers brought forth more moans and whimpers. Every part of the child's body seemed bruised or lacerated. A few of the wounds were even still bleeding, although Adrian was relieved to see that none of them seemed to have ruptured any internal organs. At least, there was no blood or fluid leaking from any orifice.

He's got a broken arm and maybe some broken ribs. But he's not bleeding internally, I don't think. And it doesn't look as if Esmond raped him.

Probably not, agreed Raj. ***Esmond's lusts have gotten much darker than that.***

Adrian shook his head. Not in disagreement, simply in sorrow. He could remember a time—remember it well—when he had treasured his older brother. A time when Esmond Gellert's soul had seemed as bronzed-perfect as his superb athlete's body.

But that time was gone, now. Had been for . . . at least a year. The death of Esmond's lover Nanya had been the trigger for the change. Or so, at least, Esmond claimed himself on the few occasions when he was willing to talk about the transformation in his character.

Adrian had his doubts. True, Esmond had been besotted with the woman. But many men were besotted with women, and didn't react to their deaths in such a manner. Adrian thought the truth sat at a square angle, so to speak. He thought that Esmond's rage against anything Confederate had not been caused by Nanya's death so much as the fact that Esmond had not been able to prevent it.

Adrian had been standing at Esmond's side when it happened. Watching, along with his brother, the great roof beam in the burning mansion of the traitor Redvers when it collapsed onto Nanya and the other women of the household. They had come *so* close to saving her from the disaster. But—not close enough.

And so, Adrian suspected, Esmond had deflected his own feelings of guilt and failure onto Vanbert, which he'd already resented deeply for its conquest and exploitation of the Emeralds. Fueling his hatred and rage the same way Adrian's firebombs had fueled the conflagration which took Nanya's life. Firebombs which Esmond himself had been willing and eager to use in the battle, after all.

You're likely right, came Raj's words into his mind. ***But who's to say? The human mind is a complicated thing, and doesn't lend itself well to your scholarly methods.***

Center spoke for the first time since they'd entered Esmond's tent. **that is true. nothing in stochastic analysis has such great variables as what you call "psychology." which is a suspect term to begin with, since it presupposes a "psyche" which may well not exist anyway. so far as i can determine, all that actually exists are electrochemical reactions.**

Before Adrian could mentally mutter some curses on Center's typically detached analysis, Center pressed on.

but it is all irrelevant to our purpose. this is very dangerous, what you are doing. the slave belongs to esmond. under both confederate and southron custom, he may do with such as he wishes. in practice if not in legal theory.

Adrian did not argue the point, although he could have. In fact, many Vanbert slaveowners *did* follow the law when it came to the treatment of their slaves, which forbade physical cruelty for anything other than specified offenses. Many of them even obeyed the spirit of the law, not simply the letter. And while Southron custom was not congealed in any written legal codes, the barbarian tribes were actually more lenient toward their slaves. If nothing else, they did not transmit slave status onto the offspring of slaves. Within a few generations most slaves had become incorporated into their Southron tribes. Incorporated at the bottom of the social pyramid, to be sure, but incorporated nonetheless.

Still, it was a pointless argument. There were more than enough violations of law and custom regarding the treatment of slaves, in all parts of the continent and the Islands, to make the likelihood of a transgressor being punished fairly remote. Especially one who, like Esmond, had achieved high status.

Which he certainly had, in the short time since he and Adrian had planted themselves among the Southrons. In every respect except his skill at handling velipads, Esmond was the southern barbarian's "ideal type." Those few who might have doubted, early on, did so no longer—for the simple reason that they were dead. Honor duels were an established custom, even a hallowed one, among the barbarians. Four warriors, putting too much credence in the tales of effeminate Emeralds, had challenged Esmond within the first two months of their arrival. He'd killed all of them, and each time with a display of martial prowess which had dazzled the onlookers. Leaving aside Esmond's skill with weapons, the body which wielded that skill was that of the near-perfect athlete who had once emerged the victor from the Five Year Games of the Emeralds.

So, Adrian did not bother to argue with Center. He didn't really need to, after all. Center, like Raj, shared Adrian's mind. But neither of them had any control over Adrian's body—or his will. In that respect, at least, none of Center's incomprehensible prattle about "synapses" and "neurons" matched reality nearly as well as the teachings of the scholars in the Grove who had trained Adrian.

Mind was Mind and Matter was Matter, there was an end to it—and Adrian, *not* Center, controlled the matter that was his body.

He scooped the boy up in his arms and lifted him. Then, turned his head to the barbarian who had taken him to Esmond's tent. The old man was one of Adrian's spies. Spies whom he had hired, initially, to keep an eye on his new Southron "allies"—but had then found it necessary to keep an eye on his own brother. This oldster had been the one who had told Adrian of the tortures Esmond was inflicting on a new slave.

The man was very agitated by now, practically dancing on his feet.

"Hurry—hurry—young master!" he hissed. "Your brother will return soon. If he finds us—"

Adrian saw no point in arguing that point, either. The spy's worry was too shortsighted, for one thing. It had been midmorning when Adrian entered the tent. Leaving now, still before noon, they would be seen by dozens of the barbarians who teemed in the great annual meeting ground outside Marange. There was no way Esmond would not find out who took the boy. By the end of the day; probably even before nightfall.

Esmond would be . . . enraged. Furious enough that he might even attack his own brother. He would certainly seek vengeance on the spy.

As he stalked through the tent flap held open by the spy, carrying the boy's body quite easily for all his own short stature, Adrian paused a moment and said: "Take the gold in the pouch at my belt. There's enough there to reach your village—it's on the other side of the continent, I believe—and leave a goodly bonus for you. Take it and leave immediately."

He heard the spy whisper some kind of thanks, in a dialect he could not really understand. A few quick fingers working at the pouch—no tyro at theft, either, this spy—and the old man seemed to vanish.

Well done, said Raj. With some humor: ***That's an expensive bonus, but still a smart move. Your other spies will know what happened, and trust you for it. Half of them are probably watching right now.***

Adrian hadn't thought in those terms—he'd simply felt himself responsible for his employee's welfare. Not for the first time, Adrian was reminded that Raj Whitehall, unlike himself, was a master tactician.

He didn't doubt for a moment Raj's assessment of what his own spies were doing. As he threaded his way through the crowds spilling in the spaces between the multitude of tents and huts which made up the barbarian encampment, Adrian was almost amused to see how many eyes followed his progress. There were times, in his more sour moments, when Adrian wondered how the Southrons even managed to stay alive. They didn't seem to do very much except quarrel—with words and weapons both—and spy on each other ceaselessly.

that's the men, commented Center. **the women do most of the daily work. that's always been one of the problems pastoralism poses for civilization. herders have too much time on their hands, at least part of the year. so they make mischief all out of proportion to their numbers.**

It doesn't help any that their skills are so readily adapted to war, added Raj. ***Riding, hunting, the lot. Even their diet makes for easier logistics.***

It was true enough. On two occasions since he'd arrived in Marange, at the invitation of important chieftains, Adrian had accompanied Southron tribesmen in their treasured great hunts. He'd always known the Southrons were skilled cavalrymen and weapons handlers, however undisciplined they might be in battle. What he hadn't realized was how adept they were at living off the land. Vanbert or Emerald noblemen, when they went hunting, took a huge caravan with them laden with supplies. A Southron, even a chieftain, took nothing more than what he could carry on his own mount and a pack animal.

He reached his own tent, stooped through the entrance, and set the boy down on a thick pile of rugs toward one side. Then, commanded one of his three slaves to fetch a healer. The healer, he knew, would be what civilized people would call a "witch doctor." But since his arrival, Adrian had actually been rather impressed with the skill and knowledge of the old women. Strip aside the florid incantations and rather grotesque dancing they insisted upon, and the herbal remedies and poultices were often quite effective.

And now, we wait for Esmond.

This is going to be hairy, predicted Raj. **you are insane,** tossed in Center for good measure.

Adrian said nothing. His soul was at peace for the first time in many months. The rupture with his brother had been inevitable; so, best it be done with. The pain of prolonging it was simply unbearable.

(((•))) (((•))) (((•)))

Esmond was, indeed, in a rage—and a very public one. He stormed into Adrian's tent followed by all nine of the major chieftains of the Southrons. None of whom, it immediately became clear, had come to take sides. They were simply curious to see how the more mysterious of the pair of mysterious noble brothers from fabled Solinga would handle such a matter.

Adrian was not surprised. Since he'd arrived, he'd been trying to convince the fractious chieftains to unite their forces and allow him to arm them with powerful new weaponry. But the barbarians, as conservative as such folk always are, had been none too eager to listen to the advice. The only reason they listened at all was because of the many reports which had come to them of the role which Adrian and Esmond had played, as top subordinates of the King of the Isles, in breaking the first Confederate assault on the island of Preble.

The Southrons, like almost everyone else, had expected the mighty Vanbert empire to give short shrift to that rebellion. But here it was, a year later, and Preble still stood unvanquished. And the two men who had been most responsible for the Confederate defeat, by the accounts of all spies and rumor-sellers, had come to the lands of the Southrons to offer the same assistance.

Now the two men—brothers, to boot—had come to an open clash. And so the nine chief leaders of the barbarian tribes wanted to see how Adrian would handle it. They already knew, of course, how Esmond would handle it. By fury and force.

Fury and force, the barbarians understood. They were wondering if the other brother knew something else that might be useful to them.

Seeing where Esmond was headed within the first ten seconds of his bellowing accusations, Adrian cut to the quick. He had no choice. Give Esmond another ten seconds of rage and he would be drawing his sword.

"You're challenging me, then. So be it." Coldly, calmly: "I have the choice of weapons and ground, of course. Tomorrow morning, dawn. On the great meadow north of the town. Slings and bullets are the weapon—although you can bring a sword along if you wish. I won't need one. We'll start at three hundred yards and close."

That was the first time in over a year that Adrian had ever seen Esmond shocked into silence. His brother loomed over him, his head reaching a good six inches above Adrian's. Six feet tall, Esmond was, taller than almost any barbarian. Wearing the Southron-style loincloth which he'd assumed within days after their arrival, Esmond's superb physique was on full display. Wide shoulders, thick-muscled arms, tapered waist and steel-flat belly, long and powerful legs. Even his feet, bare except for twine-held Southron sandals, seemed more like a direbeast's than a man's. Every inch of him exuded *power.*

Now, he was silent. Somewhere, buried deep in the festering pool of hatred which Esmond's soul had become, what was left of the *brother* must have finally realized what his hatred had brought him to. Adrian wasn't certain, but he thought for a moment that a cry of appeal seemed to flash in Esmond's blue eyes. And he watched his lips, hoping to see the words coming out of them which might end this before the damage was irreparable.

It was a vain hope, though, as Adrian well knew. He shared his brother's blue eyes and corn-gold hair, and not much else. Once, true, they had shared laughter and comradeship. But even in his best days Esmond had possessed little of his smaller and younger brother's capacity for self-examination. And what little he once had was long gone now.

So, in the end—which took but three seconds—the only words which came out were: "Tomorrow, then. Dawn. I will kill you."

He turned on his heel, moving as easily as a direbeast, and strode out of the tent. Within seconds, all the chieftains had followed except one.

Adrian studied him. Prelotta was his name, and he was the chief of the Reedbottom tribe. The Reedbottoms held no great stature in the barbarians' informal but elaborate way of ranking the various tribes and clans, so Adrian had had no real contact with him previously. The land of the Reedbottoms was in the marshy lowlands of the northeast, where disease and parasites took too great a toll for velipads to be of much use. So the Reedbottoms, unlike any of the other Southron tribes, were mainly agriculturalists. They fought on foot, to the disdain of other tribes—even if, Adrian suspected from subtle signs he had detected, none of the other tribes was all that eager to wage war on them. Apparently the Reedbottoms were ferocious on their own chosen ground, where cavalry tactics were not well adapted. And Adrian had heard that they used some of the huge beasts they favored as draft animals quite effectively in battle.

Am I the only one thinking I've been an idiot? came Raj's soft "voice."

Center sounded almost sour; as close, at least, to having an emotion in his tone as Adrian could remember. **i overlooked them also. we have been too preoccupied with diplomacy. they would make far better raw material than the normal run of Southrons. the probability is 79% ± 4.**

"You wish?" asked Adrian politely.

Prelotta was rather young for a tribal chieftain. Not more than forty, Adrian guessed. It was a bit hard to tell, however, because Reedbottom customs favored even heavier ceremonial cicatrices and tattoos than other tribes. Prelotta's face was like that of a carved wooden mask, the cheeks drawn tight by scars and the brow almost completely obscured by elaborate designs. The light brown hair atop his head was arranged in a wild and heavily pomaded style which not even the most decadent Vanbert noblewoman would have dared to show in public.

"I am curious," he said in his nasal northeastern dialect. "Slings are a weapon not favored much by the Sons of Assan. Although we Reedbottoms use them, often enough." His hideous disfigured face twisted a bit. "But, then, that is perhaps one of the reasons we are often called the Nephew of Assan."

The "Sons of Assan" was the term that the Southron tribes used to refer to themselves. Assan being not actually a member of their pantheon of gods, as Adrian could remember being told by Emerald scholars in the long ago, so much as a vague ancestral spirit. A bit similar, in a way, to one of the race of giants which the Emerald legends claimed had been the parents of the gods themselves.

"Nephew" of Assan, is it? Well, at least he seems to have a sense of humor. That's a start.

And not a small one.

Adrian's own face twisted into a wry smile. He spread his arms and looked down upon himself. Like Esmond, he too had yielded to the climate and was wearing a loincloth. "You've seen my brother. Would *you* match this body against his with hand weapons?"

Prelotta spent a moment examining him. Then: "Your shoulders are actually very wide for a man with your slender frame. And while your arms don't have your brother's muscle, they don't look weak either. A good body for a slinger, that—provided, of course, you have the skill."

Despite the heavy dialect, Adrian was impressed by the man's diction. That was another myth of northerners, he'd found since coming here. The Southrons were thought to speak almost like animals. But Adrian had found that, despite their barbarism, the Southrons were actually prone to verbal pyrotechnics and frequent poesy. In their own way, their speech was just as flowery as that of any effete Emerald scholar or pompous Confederate official—annoyingly so, if you had to listen to hours of speeches by tribal chieftains in council.

So he was struck by the clarity of Prelotta's words, even more than his easy use of them. Prelotta's native tongue, of course, was quite different from the lingua franca which all the tribes used when they conversed with each other.

There didn't seem to be any answer expected, however, so he said nothing. After a moment, Prelotta nodded politely and left.

The duel lasted less than two minutes. Esmond charged immediately, as Adrian had known he would. He evaded Adrian's first missile easily enough. Cast when Esmond was still over a hundred yards away, his athletic brother had enough time to see the blurring lead bullet and lunge aside.

No matter. Adrian had known Esmond would dodge it. He'd cast the missile simply to rattle his brother. It was one thing for Esmond to be aware that Adrian's skill with a sling seemed supernatural. It was another for him—even with his incredible reflexes—to barely manage to duck one of those lead bullets thrown at such a distance.

"Supernatural" was perhaps as good a word as any. Center's visual acuity gave Adrian a degree of accuracy which was far greater than that of any normal slinger, even an expert one. "Visual acuity" didn't adequately describe it, really. Center's inhuman capability to translate what Adrian saw through his own eyes gave Adrian the kind of near-perfect aim which the computer itself thought of in terms which Adrian barely understood. "Range finding" was obvious, but how such a term as *azimuth* applied was a mystery.

The rest came from Adrian himself. Prelotta had seen the truth of it, where most people—even Adrian himself, more often than not—saw only the reedy scholar's build. He was five and a half feet tall, true, and wiry rather than muscular. But brute strength was actually not necessary for the task of sending a lead bullet flying through the air at a speed which would break bones and shatter skulls. Good muscles and quick reflexes were enough for that—provided the bullets hit where you aimed them.

The second cast brought Esmond down, at seventy yards. Adrian's brother made the mistake of pausing for a moment to sling his own bullet, which went wild; Adrian's bullet hit Esmond's thigh like a sledgehammer.

A less muscular man than Esmond would have been taken out of the fight entirely by that hit. A small enough man would have suffered a broken bone. Esmond managed to lunge back on his feet, hobbling, frantically fitting another bullet to the sling pouch.

Don't kill him, cautioned Raj. ***We'll need him, for a time. Then, sensing Adrian's mute cry of hurt and protest: I'm sorry, lad. I'm just telling the truth.***

Adrian said nothing. There was nothing to say. He fit another bullet to the sling, dodged easily the bullet his brother sent his way, and brought Esmond down for good.

Just as Raj had wanted—not killing him. With Adrian's accuracy, killing could be avoided. But not even a real demigod could have withstood the strike of that bullet on the chest.

A weaker and less powerful man than Esmond would have been

killed outright. Esmond himself would spend weeks at rest, letting the broken sternum heal. Cursing all the while, as he discovered—every time he tried to do something as simple as lift a cup—that every bone in a human body above the waist is ultimately held together by spine and sternum.

The boy died the next day. Apparently he had suffered internal injuries from Esmond's beatings, after all. Or, perhaps, his spirit had simply no longer been able to face life's torture.

Adrian never knew his name.

It wasn't all for nothing, said Raj. ***Your status is phenomenal, now, especially among the Reedbottoms.***

All Adrian could do was stare at the walls of his tent. Until finally, hours later, he gave out the cry which had been building since the first moment Raj and Center entered his mind:

Is everything just a maneuver?

He would spend the rest of his life pondering a ghost's answer. Never really knowing if he agreed or not.

Yes, everything is a maneuver. No, it's not* just *a maneuver.

CHAPTER NINE

Over the centuries, as the twelve villages which formed the original core of Vanbert had expanded to conquer half the world, the edifices of the Confederacy's government had undergone their own massive expansion. Whether torn down and rebuilt, or swollen by modification and accretion, the complex of buildings and plazas had become something of a monstrosity itself.

So, at least, thought Demansk, as he worked his way across the Forum of the Virtuous Matrons toward the still-distant but imposing Council Hall. "Threaded his way" was perhaps a better description. The Forum was filled with a huge crowd, as always after rumors spread of a major oncoming shift in political power in the Council. Most of the mob were simply curious. A large number were street vendors. Still others were taking advantage of the traditional custom of allowing unlimited speech in the Forum to harangue the crowd from jury-rigged speakers' pedestals. Others—

His sons were walking just behind him. He heard Olver whisper to the others: "Careful now; keep an eye out. Some of these fellows are not loitering."

Demansk, as befitted his aloof dignity as a Justiciar, ignored the whisper. He ignored as well the temptation to place his hand on the battle-ax hanging from his waist. At the moment, the temptation was hard to resist. There *were* a lot of suspicious-looking men here and there in the crowd, under whose robes might be concealed any number of weapons.

The ax was a ceremonial weapon; sized more like a hatchet than an ax. Because of his status as a Justiciar, Demansk was allowed an ax rather than the long knife permitted to simple Councillors. But where most members of the Council carried elaborately carved and inlaid "weapons"—some of them even with silver blades—Demansk's ax of office was perfectly functional. The blade was good steel, and sharpened to a working edge.

Still, he resisted the impulse. Dignity, manifesting itself among other ways in an apparent indifference to danger, was an essential ingredient for the "public aura" of a central Vanbert official. It was for that same reason that Demansk was unaccompanied by any bodyguards. His sons would have to do for that.

Which, when all was said and done, made the task of any would-be assassins quite difficult. All three of Demansk's sons were strong and healthy men. His two oldest, Barrett and Olver, were also experienced soldiers. The youngest, Trae, had only limited experience in battle—a single skirmish against the pirate raid which had resulted in his sister's abduction. But, perhaps oddly given his fascination with gadgetry and natural philosophy, Trae was actually the most athletic of the three. And if his combat experience was slight, the young man had never stinted on his training.

So Demansk was not surprised to see the subtle but careful way in which his sons shielded him as he made his way through the crowd. Nor was he surprised at the manner in which each of the three handled the task of moving people aside. Barrett, brusquely and rudely—he'd knocked down an old woman some fifty paces back; Olver, with his usual stolid firmness; Trae, as often as not, with a smile and a jest.

Another jest now, as he lifted (quite easily) a rather portly matron by the armpits and set her to one side. "Madame, you tempt me too much in my progress! For shame—here in the Forum!"

The matron's squawk of protest choked off into a giggle. She waved the fan vigorously in front of her face, and returned Trae's humor with gleaming eyes which were quite inappropriate for her respectable status. Despite himself, Demansk couldn't entirely force down a smile.

The Forum of the Virtuous Matrons was named after one of the many episodes in Vanbert's early history. The matrons of a small Vanbert village had committed suicide rather than be ravished by a band of raiders from a nearby tribe who had overcome their husbands on the field of battle.

So, at least, according to legend. Demansk had his doubts. The "field of battle" would have been a small meadow, filled for a time by sweaty, shouting pig farmers struggling with sweaty and shouting shepherds. As for the rest, who was to say?

It hardly mattered. Truth or legend, this much was certain: that small tribe of shepherds had been annihilated shortly thereafter. Even in the semi-mythical ancient days, the folk who would become Vanbert had been ruthless with their enemies. Ruthless, yet, in an odd sort of way, not given to holding grudges once their purpose was accomplished. The male shepherds would have been massacred, the women turned into concubines. But the offspring born of those women thereafter would have been, within not more than two generations, accepted without thought as part of the growing Confederacy. Just as would any bastards born of ravished Vanbert women less "virtuous" than the matrons of myth.

Demansk chewed on that thought as he threaded his way toward the Council Hall. Even as he destroyed the Vanbert that was, he realized, he would be bringing back to life *some* of its ancient ways. Become an empire, Vanbert had begun to hold grudges. Say better, had justified greed with the name of "grudge." Conquered folk now were enslaved, and remained in slavery—generation succeeding generation. A nation born of pig farmers copulating in huts, with little care for the origins of their offspring, had become an empire whose aristocracy was obsessed with "good blood."

His grandfather, he remembered, had not been much impressed with the newer strains of purebred pigs. Dogs, either. "Mongrels are always best," he could remember the old man telling him. "They may not be as fat or as pretty, but they'll last. And there's nothing wrong with chewing tough meat, anyway. Good for your jaws."

(((•))) (((•))) (((•)))

A whisper from Barrett broke his train of thought. "Won't be any trouble today, I don't think. Everybody's still wondering which way things will shake down."

There was an edge of excessive eagerness in his voice that irritated Demansk. But he let no sign of it show on his face.

Barrett was too ambitious. He had been so from at least the age of twelve. And it was an ambition unleavened by any kind of deeper thought. Where solemn Olver had carefully studied the writings of Jasprem and the speeches of Acclide and Lurth—if not the Emerald philosophers whom young Trae cherished—Barrett had never seen any need to add wisdom to intelligence.

Just as Helga had predicted, Barrett had already sent away his wife and prepared divorce proceedings. He was, as the Emerald sage Howark would have put it, entirely a "man of the senses."

So be it. That, too, Demansk would use ruthlessly.

They'd finally reached the short flight of wide marble stairs that led up to the Council Hall. A squad of soldiers kept the people thronging in the Forum from spilling onto the stairs. The stair and the hall itself were reserved for Councillors and their invited guests. The squad leader recognized Demansk at a glance and gave him a tiny nod.

Now that he was through the mob, Demansk felt he could let the pose of august dignity slip a bit. So he took the stairs in his accustomed vigorous stride instead of the leisurely amble which he'd been restricting himself to.

A moment later, he and his sons had passed under the great pillared archway leading into the antechamber of the hall. It was cooler inside, if a bit stuffy. The antechamber, lacking any of the large windows which allowed light into the great central room where the Council met for its deliberations, was rather dark. The faces of the ponderous statues of mythic heroes from Vanbert's past which lined the walls of the antechamber seemed even gloomier than usual.

But Demansk paid the statues little attention. He strode across the antechamber to the wide doorway leading into the chamber. The bronze doors had been flung open, as always when the Council was in official session. The two Council members who held the office of

Watchmen stood on either side of the doorway, full-sized battle-axes held in their hands.

Demansk suppressed a smile. The post of "Watchman" was a matter of ritual honor. By a tradition now at least two centuries old, it was given to the most elderly of the Councillors. Neither of these men, nor both put together—potbellied little Kirn and cadaverous Undreth—could have prevented a determined and energetic ten-year-old boy from entering the hall.

The two Watchmen shuffled aside as he came to the doorway. Undreth wheezed a welcome; Kirn, a longtime partisan of Albrecht, satisfied himself with a moue of distaste. To the first, Demansk responded with a polite nod; to the other, not so much as a glance of appraisal. Kirn was a meaningless enemy. His vote was a given, and, for the rest—

Once he was past, where Kirn could not see his face, Demansk's lip curled. There was an old saying, very popular among Vanbert's lower classes: *a nobleman's trough is his grave.* Kirn, in particular, was notorious for his gluttony. He would be dead anyway, soon enough, from natural causes.

The floor of the chamber was marble, inlaid with large copper and silver medallions. Each of the medallions recorded the name of a victorious battle or siege. A good two thirds of the floor was spackled with the things. Pausing for a moment to scan the Councillors assembling on the tiered stone benches which encircled the floor everywhere except the entrance, Demansk reminded himself of those medallions. Whatever else could be said of today's Vanbert, there was nothing false or illusory about those victories.

Workmen had already prepared a spot for the next. Quite some time ago, now. Demansk's lip curled further, into a gesture of open derision rather than simple humor. *Preble,* that medallion would read—whenever Albrecht finally managed to reduce it.

His open sneer, and the source of it, had already been noticed by at least a dozen other Councillors. However dull-witted they might be in many respects, Councillors were hypersensitive to political nuances. A number of them grinned; several scowled; several more looked away, feigning indifference.

Albrecht, as the old saying went, had truly hoisted himself on his own assegai. The year before, he had taken advantage of the stunning defeats which Adrian Gellert had inflicted on the Vanbert besiegers of the rebel island to have Jeschonyk and Demansk removed from command—heaping a mass of contumely on the first and a fair portion on the other. And he had also taken the occasion to get himself appointed the new commander of the besieging forces.

A necessity, that, if Albrecht's ambitions were to go any further. The Confederacy might be corrupt, but the rot still only went so far. No Councillor, even in modern times, could hope to attain the Speakership without a modicum of martial glory to his name. Albrecht had been famous for his political maneuvering, not his skills on the field of war. He'd seized the opportunity to have himself elected the commander of the siege precisely in order to remedy that flaw.

Demansk's sneer was now a thing of pure histrionics. He allowed the assembling Councillors to get a full taste of it, while he himself kept his eyes visibly on the spot long-since prepared for the missing medallion of triumph.

Albrecht had discovered, the hard way, that it was much easier to deride besiegers than to surpass them. A year had gone by, and Preble was still in rebel hands. Even after Adrian Gellert and his brother Esmond left the service of the King of the Isles to go to the southern half of the continent, the islanders had been able to keep fending off the Confederate forces.

Albrecht had been handicapped, of course. Needless to say, both Jeschonyk and Demansk himself had used their influence to keep Albrecht from getting the massive resources he needed to end the siege quickly. Jeschonyk simply out of political revenge, Demansk because—even then—he had begun seeing that he might someday need to overthrow the existing order.

The chamber was almost full, now. Only a handful of Councillors were scurrying to take their seats. Demansk left off his sneer and strode to his own accustomed place, on the lowest tier of benches reserved for the Confederacy's ten Justiciars.

When he sat down, he made the ninth present. The tenth was

not there, and would not be. Justiciar Albrecht was far away, staring at the island of Preble from a Confederate rampart. And, Demansk had no doubt at all, gnashing his teeth in fury and frustration.

Albrecht's many supporters, of course, would do what they could to advance their patron's interests at this emergency meeting of the Council. But without Albrecht himself there, to guide them with his political cunning and his seemingly bottomless coffers, they would have a much more difficult time of it.

Their difficulty began almost immediately. Speaker Chollat rose and made the ritual speech which opened a session of the Council. Fortunately, old custom held here still—the speech was mercifully brief. As brief as possible, in fact, which was Chollat's subtle way of indicating his continued neutrality. Chollat was, essentially, a prestigious non-entity. He had been elected Speaker of the Council the year before simply as a compromise between the factions—a position he apparently intended to retain.

No sooner had Chollat finished than one of Albrecht's principal supporters was on his feet. "I urge the Council to declare this session invalid!" he boomed. Quaryn was a big man, tall as well as fat. His voice was positively stentorian.

Speaker Chollat, still standing on the floor of the chamber, opened his mouth to protest at such an abrupt—almost rude—demand for a ruling. But Quaryn overrode whatever he was going to say.

"No debate! An urge for invalidation takes precedence!"

True enough. Demansk glanced toward Jeschonyk. He and Tomsien had agreed to allow the old Speaker Emeritus to be the "gray eminence" of their projected Triumvirate. The purely political maneuvering in the Confederacy's capital was Jeschonyk's domain—and specialty.

Judging from the cheerful smile on the Speaker Emeritus' face as he rose—almost a predatory grin—Demansk relaxed. Whatever his personal vices and limits as a field commander, no one had ever accused Jeschonyk of lacking skills in the endless maneuvers of Vanbert politics.

"Agreed!" shouted Jeschonyk. "No debate! I call for an immediate vote!"

Demansk could see Quaryn's heavy jaws tighten. Clearly enough, Albrecht's man had wanted some squabbling over procedure in the hopes that confusion might fray the ranks of his enemies. The quick and ready willingness of Jeschonyk to move straight to a procedural vote was the old man's own way of clashing assegai against assegai. He was signaling his confidence in victory to the triumvirate's supporters.

Sure enough. The vote rolled in quickly, even following Quaryn's insistence on an individual count of the voices.

For continuing the session: eighty-seven.

For declaring it invalid: fifty-eight.

It was as clear a procedural victory as any in recent Council history. And Jeschonyk used the boost of confidence to keep the tide surging.

It was late in the afternoon before Demansk rose to speak. By then, it was clear, a majority of the Councillors leaned in favor of establishing a new Triumvirate to supercede—temporarily—the authority of the Speakership. Their motives varied, from personal greed and ambition to simply wanting to be on what they perceived as the winning side.

Their concerns varied as well. Many, of course, really didn't care in the least about the troubles ailing the Confederation. But many did, and those concerns ranged from the fear of a slave revolt, to further depredations from the pirates of the Isles and the Southron barbarians.

A handful even thought in terms of the more long-term health of the Confederacy. Not many, to be sure, but some. Demansk made a note to seek them out for private discussions in the weeks to come. He intended to break the power of the aristocracy, but he had no desire to shed more blood than was necessary—and knew as well that the political skills of the noblemen would be needed in the years ahead. Those of them, at least, who could be won over to supporting the new regime.

Still, although the tide was running heavily in favor of Jeschonyk's proposal, at least half of the Councillors were still wavering. Their fear, of course, was of the rise of a new Marcomann. And almost all of them had a single target for those fears: Demansk himself.

He alone, really, presented the possible danger. Jeschonyk was too old, and not enough of a military commander, to make a creditable dictator. As for Tomsien . . .

Ambitious enough, yes; wealthy enough, yes; and few doubted he was unscrupulous enough. But although Tomsien had a respectable record in terms of military experience and command, it was nothing compared to Demansk's. Among modern leaders of the Confederacy, only Demansk had the aura of Marcomann about him. Not simply the record of success in the field, but—what was even more dangerous—a proven capacity to gain the loyalty and allegiance of the ranks of the army.

So, late in the day, Demansk decided it was time to seize the greatbeast directly and wrestle it to the ground. He stood up, indicating his desire to address the Council. But then, unlike many of his predecessors that day, waited politely for Speaker Chollat to call upon him before speaking. The man who would be tyrant understood perfectly well that politeness and outward modesty were weapons as sharp-edged as any others.

"Justiciar Demansk has the floor," said Chollat.

Demansk stepped into the center of the Chamber. Then, his left hand on hip and his right extended, as was accepted oratorical demeanor, he began his speech.

A very short speech, it would be. Taking a greatbeast by the horns and bringing it down could either be done quickly—or not at all.

"You fear another Marcomann!" he boomed.

Then, he waited. So far that day, no one had posed the fear openly. Circumlocution and euphemism had been the style of oratory and public debate for two decades now. That, too, was a legacy of Marcomann, under whose iron rule few had dared to speak clearly and openly.

Demansk had a reputation for bluntness. Almost to the point of crudeness. A simple soldier, whose skill on the battlefield and in campaign maneuvers was not matched by its political equivalent.

Over the years, Demansk had cultivated that reputation simply because it allowed him to avoid the tedium of endless babble. Now he found it useful for another purpose. Simplicity, like modesty and decorum, was another blade.

"And so do I," he added, loudly enough to be heard throughout the Chamber, but not in the booming tone of his opening statement.

"And so do I." Two strides forward, a half turn; right hand on hip; now the left extended dramatically. "We all know I am the danger."

A polite nod toward Jeschonyk. "The Speaker Emeritus being famous for his prudence and sagacity." A deeper nod, almost a bow, toward Tomsien. "And Justiciar Tomsien for his steadiness."

Steadiness, he thought to himself. Now there's a euphemism worthy of the best politician. Translation: Tomsien would cheerfully undermine the Confederacy and take the power, if he could. But his are the methods of a rising river, allowing time to levee the banks. Only I pose the danger of a tidal wave.

"And so did the three of us ponder the matter."

Half turn, one stride; pause; quarter turn; left hand back on hip, right hand extended hip-high, index finger pointing dramatically at . . . not much of anything, except marble, but it was nicely done and in the customary style.

"Thus did we agree to allot the portions of power wisely. To Jeschonyk, whose age if nothing else will serve as a check to ambition, goes the direct authority over the state. An equal among three in name, he will exercise the power here in the capital." Now he straightened his back, both hands on hips akimbo—the classic pose for announcing a surprising development.

"We furthermore agreed—and I hereby request that it be included as a provision in the establishment of the Triumvirate—that both Justiciar Tomsien and I be banned by law from entering the city so long as we retain our posts as *junior* Triumvirs."

The crowd of Councillors was relaxing visibly. Jeschonyk was a familiar figure. Alone in the capital . . . he could be reasoned with, persuaded—bribed, if need be.

Demansk spread his hands wide and took a half step back—then leaned forward. *A more surprising development still.* Even the legendary orator Hyrthel, who was said to have perfected the stance, could not have done it better.

"Tomsien will then be given the army. Command over all forces except those assigned to naval duty—as well, of course, as household troops permitted to Councillors by law."

He thought that was a nice touch, the last. Very few Councillors, Demansk himself being one of the exceptions, maintained a body of household troops as large as the law permitted. Doing so was extremely expensive, if nothing else. But by reminding them of their *rights*—whether they chose to exercise them or not—he was subtly reassuring the Councillors.

All eyes were now fixed on him. He turned about, took three strides, and resumed the standard pose: left hand on hip, right hand extended and raised slightly above his head. "And I, you wonder? I ask one thing alone—that I be given command of the naval forces. *All of them* . . ." He paused for a moment, then added a bit slyly: "except, of course, those which Justiciar Albrecht might need for his *continued* campaign against Preble."

He let it sink in, for a moment. That latest would further confuse and demoralize Albrecht's now half-routed supporters. Obviously speaking on behalf of all three of the proposed new Triumvirs, Demansk was making it clear that there would be no reprisals against Albrecht—or, by implications, his supporters.

Not immediately, at least. In the longer term, who was to say? But all the men in the Council Hall were experienced maneuverers. "The long run" . . . was later. Today they were looking at a major political defeat, and Demansk had just shown the rats the hole in the corner. He could see the benches stirring as men began whispering new offers and deals to each other.

It was time to drive home the spike. "I repeat: a*ll naval forces—as well as whatever auxiliary support is needed for them.* Never before in Vanbert's history has this been done. And do it we must—if I am to lead the expedition which will finally rid us of the pirates of the Isles. For I propose to conquer the Western Isles, and make them a new province of our Confederation."

That statement brought instant silence to the chamber. He could practically see the thoughts racing through the heads of the Councillors.

On the one hand:

Giving Demansk authority over all naval forces would give him considerable military might. The more so when all the possible implications of "whatever auxiliary support is needed" was added onto the balance.

On the other hand:

The Councillors, like all Confederates, thought in terms of armies, nor navies. Navies were simply not capable of conquering half a continent. Not even though a Vanbert navy was really more of an army on ships than a "navy" in the way that islanders thought of it.

It simply didn't matter. Every Councillor knew the basic arithmetic, if not the exact figures. Give Demansk every ship in the Confederate fleet, including the ones besieging Preble—even build as many new ones to add to it—and there *still* wasn't room on those wooden seagoing forts for more than . . .

At most, one fourth of the Confederation's forces. In practice, given the need to maintain the siege at Preble—and still under Albrecht's command—Demansk simply wouldn't have the forces available to impose himself as a dictator.

All that was needed was the final indirection. Demansk took a sudden step forward—almost a lunge—and extended both arms directly before him, hands clenched into fists. *A mighty resolve made.* "I will give you the Islands, fellows of the Council. *And I will have my family's vengeance.*"

The last sentence was practically snarled. Which, in truth, took no histrionic effort at all. Vengeance was indeed something Demansk would obtain. In passing, to be sure. But given his reputation for simplicity . . .

What might come after never crossed the Councillors' minds. It was plain to see, as each face grew slightly slack with easing tension. Some so slack as to almost indicate derision. Every man in the Council knew that Demansk's daughter was being held in seclusion on his estates. Shamed, once, by her violation; twice over, by bearing a pirate's bastard.

They had it all now. The assurance of divided power; the most dangerous to be given the smallest spear—and now, even his personal motive, as far as possible from the grandiose dreams of a would-be dictator.

Quaryn himself led the hail which rose from the floor, calling for an immediate vote. Hands stretched wide; left hand in a fist, right extended wide—all in classic style. A pity that he stumbled slightly rising to his feet, true; but the Council was as inclined to be charitable toward small lapses in that moment as was the new Triumvirate itself.

Afterward, of course, the new dispensation took not long to manifest itself. As he strode down the steps of the hall, being almost assaulted by the roar of the crowd in the Forum—the professional rumor-spreaders were already at work—thirty men trotted forward to join his sons at his side.

There would be no pretense of indifference here. The men were all veterans of Demansk's First Regiment, and they took up positions all around him and his heirs. Shields up; assegais ready. No potential assassin was allowed to get within twenty feet of the new Triumvir as he passed across the Forum.

Somewhere along the way, Demansk reminded himself that small errors needed to be corrected along with great ones. He commanded his new First Spear to his side.

When the man trotted up, Demansk considered him a moment. Cut from the same cloth as Jessep Yunkers, obviously. Perhaps not as intelligent, but thoroughly capable at his trade.

"First Spear," he said, "what is your *name*?"

CHAPTER TEN

"I'd feel better about this if you were part of a convoy," said Demansk. He stared out from the headland at the western ocean. It might just have been his overactive imagination, but the waters seemed to be already turning gray with the change of seasons. The last convoy of the summer had left a week earlier.

"The skies are clear," said Helga. "We'll reach Marange well before the first big storm hits. We're only in the early part of autumn."

"Still—"

"Come on, Father." She shifted the baby into the crook of her left arm and pointed to the ship moored at the pier below. "Sharlz Thicelt may be a pirate, but—like all pirates—he knows his ships. That thing must have cost you a small fortune."

Demansk scowled down at the vessel. As a matter of fact, it *had* cost him a small fortune. Thicelt had selected the finest "one and a half" he could find in the ports of the western Confederacy. The "one and a half"—technically called a *demibireme*—was a bastard design. In essence, it was a fast, two-banked galley, adapted for both sailing and fighting. The adaptations, which allowed for the quick removal of the second bank of oars as battle approached, required a great deal of expensive detail work. Demibiremes were therefore a rarity. They were only used for precious cargo—and were highly treasured prizes for pirates, for whose depredations the design was perfectly adapted.

It was the latter factor, not the expense, which was really causing Demansk to scowl. Granted, the demibireme was the ideal ship to get his daughter to Marange quickly and give her the best chance of escaping pirates. It was also sure to draw the attention of every pirate ship which spotted her.

Helga was having no difficulty following his train of thought. "Relax," she insisted. "That ship is more than seaworthy enough to stay out of sight of land, except for—"

"Every other night," growled Demansk. "Prevailing winds be damned, Thicelt still has to make landfall often enough to determine where he is. Pirates are rife all down the middle portions of the coast, in the no-man's-land between the Confederacy and the powerful Southron tribes of the interior. You know that as well as I do. If you have the bad luck to encounter a pirate nest . . ."

She shrugged. "We'll just move out to sea again. Even if the winds aren't favorable, that ship can be rowed almost as fast as a war galley."

Demansk left off the argument, but kept scowling. Helga was exaggerating the capability of a demibireme under oars. True, it could be rowed much more quickly than a normal merchant ship. It still couldn't hope to match the speed of a light galley, packed full with pirates at the oars. The only real chance it had was to stay far enough ahead of a pirate to exhaust the pursuers. Rowing was brutally hard work, especially at pursuit speed.

But the chance of *this* demibireme being able to exhaust an enemy crew in a long chase was . . . almost nonexistent. Most demibiremes carried very light cargoes. Gold, gems, jewels, spices, fine linens, the like. *This* demibireme would be carrying—

"And here they come!" said Helga gaily. "Come on, Father. Don't tell me *that* sight doesn't cheer you up."

Despite himself, Demansk couldn't help smiling. The sight did cheer him up, after all. As well equipped and disciplined a hundred as he'd ever seen, trotting down the long pier toward the waiting ship. Their thick-soled sandals, studded with iron nails, hammered the heavy planking in unison. Left, right, left, right, moving in the quick but orderly manner of experienced troopers.

Not all of them were experienced, of course. Demansk couldn't see much, at this distance, of the faces beneath the helmets. Confederate helmets, unlike Emerald ones, left the nose uncovered. But the cheek flanges, combined with the jutting forehead protector and the lobster-tail flare at the rear, still left the soldiers' features obscure. Probably a good half, judging from what Demansk could determine, were youngsters newly signed up.

But it hardly mattered. The eastern provinces, with their impoverished yeomanry, had been the traditional recruiting ground for the Confederate army for at least two centuries. Every one of those "newbies" would have been training under the supervision of veteran male relatives since they were eight years old. And, in this hundred even more than most, they were going into combat surrounded by their experienced older brothers, fathers, cousins, uncles and neighbors. What was trotting down the pier below him was as capable and veteran a unit as Demansk had ever seen. To all intents and purposes, that was the hundred his old First Spear had come from.

His eyes scanned the pier and found the man he was looking for. Jessep Yunkers himself, still technically a civilian, was following the soldiers with a group of about forty men wrestling heavy handcarts up the steps leading to the pier's entrance. Seeing those carts—and the man giving the orders to their handlers—Demansk's scowl returned in force.

"Come *on*, Father." Helga's tone was just a razor's edge short of a snap. Still most unsuitable, for a daughter addressing her august father. "You've got no more chance of keeping Trae behind than you do restraining a charging greatbeast with your bare hands. He *is* a son of Demansk, and since you've kept him out of the army he's not going to pass up this chance of getting properly blooded. You know it as well as I do."

Demansk tightened his jaws, but made no reply—for the simple reason that he *couldn't*. However much his youngest son was given to thumbing his nose at tradition, in this at least he was forged on the ancient anvil. Trae, like any scion of Vanbert's aristocracy worthy of the name, *would* earn his spear. And since, for his own purposes, Demansk had insisted on keeping him out of the army proper . . .

"Besides," Helga added, "*I'm* certainly happy to have him along. Especially since he's the only one who really knows how to use those gadgets."

Gadgets. Most of the troopers had now filed aboard the ship, and the handcarts were halfway down the pier. Close enough that Demansk could see their contents clearly.

The lead carts were filled with heavy two-man arquebuses and their tripods. The trailing carts, with ammunition for the weapons. Trae had wanted to bring one of the bombards along also, but the experienced seaman Sharlz Thicelt had convinced the eager young nobleman that the thin planks and lightly-built hull of the ship wouldn't be able to withstand the recoil.

The strange new weapons had been designed by Adrian Gellert and used by the King of the Isles against the Confederacy the year before. Some of the weapons in the cart below, Demansk imagined, had been captured during the fighting. But most of them—perhaps all of them—had been built by Trae's artisans in his workshop, using Gellert's design as the model. If no Vanbert natural philosopher would have ever dreamed of inventing the things in the first place, Vanbert's metalworkers and apothecaries were perfectly capable of duplicating them once shown how they worked.

In fact, Trae claimed that his own arquebuses and firepowder were superior to the originals. Demansk didn't doubt the claim. Trae had destroyed more than a few workbenches in his experiments to improve the weapons' performance. Fortunately, he hadn't killed anyone in the process. Not *quite.* But several of Trae's workmen, as well as Trae himself, would carry scars and burn marks to their graves.

Demansk took a deep breath. Then, forced the smile back onto his face. "Ah, well. The gods' will is whatever it will be." He put his hand on his daughter's shoulder and gave it a little squeeze. "Luck be with you, child. And my blessing."

He gave the shoulder another squeeze, this one more in the way of an assessment than a reassurance.

"You might want to leave off on the exercise," he said drily. "I'm not sure your Adrian fellow is going to be all that fond of a woman whose shoulders are wider and more muscular than his are."

The jibe bounced off Helga like a pebble. She just chuckled and replied: "Oh, his shoulders are quite wide enough, even if he isn't a legendary athlete like his brother. But then, I forget—you haven't actually met him, have you?"

Demansk shook his head. "Not really. I ran into his brains at a distance, you might say." His tone was a bit rueful. "He's an ingenious bastard, I'll give him that. I just hope his mind turns as readily to other things as it does to figuring out new methods of mayhem."

"I think he'd much rather be putting his mind to work at other things, Father. His brother Esmond, now . . . he's a hater, that one. Half-consumed by it already, when I knew him, and probably eaten up completely by now. But Adrian's a different sort. I think—"

She hesitated; then, softly: "We'll find out, soon enough. But I think he'd rather be Vanbert's friend than our enemy, if he can just see a way to do it . . ."

Her voice trailed off, as she groped for the right word.

" 'Properly,' let's call it," said her father. "That's a nice neutral sort of term."

He gave her shoulder another squeeze, this one full of affection. More in the way of a hug, really. "And now you'd best get down there yourself. The ship will be ready to sail soon."

When Helga came aboard the ship, her attention was drawn to the stern by Trae's cursing. Despite the volume of his voice, the profanity seemed spoken more in enthusiasm than actual anger.

"Not *that* way, you fucking whoresons! It's a *clamp,* now, not a tripod! Are you blind as well as bastards?"

Still cradling the baby, Helga moved toward the stern, working her way around the benches and equipment spread over the entire deck. The soldiers of her escort were settling into their positions, none too quickly and with a great deal of awkwardness and uncertainty. Their own confused milling was as great an obstacle to her progress as their gear.

As a rule, soldiers coming aboard a naval vessel were able to settle in easily enough. The soldiers doubled as rowers on the upper bank when the ship was not in combat. Even in sea battles, at least in the early stages, they remained on the benches. It was only when a boarding operation was about to begin that the soldiers abandoned their oars for their assegais.

But on *this* trip, the soldiers were unneeded at the oars. Thicelt had hired a complete crew of rowers. The task of Helga's escort, in case of pirate attack, was to remain hidden and out of sight until—and if—a boarding attempt needed to be repelled. The factor of surprise, added to the already ferocious skills of Confederate infantrymen, should be enough to break most pirate attacks.

Of course, that also meant that the none-too-spacious vessel was even more crowded than warships usually were. The soldiers, cursing almost as loudly as Trae, were trying to figure out where they could fit their own bodies as well as their gear. Not even Vanbert infantrymen could sleep standing up, after all. And this would be a long voyage, even with the prevailing winds in their favor.

Eventually, Helga worked her way through the press and came onto the cleared space at the very stern of the ship. "Cleared" in a manner of speaking. Trae's assistants—special squad, it would be better to say—had managed to keep the regular soldiery from spilling into the area. But between their own numbers and the ship's crew, the population density was only relatively lighter than that amidships.

Trae was hunched at the stern rail, apparently showing one of his aides how to do the job properly.

"We hinged the third leg, see? On board ship, the tripod doubles as a clamp. Slide it down over the rail . . . till it nestles solidly . . . then . . . *The gods damn this fucking thing!*" Trae's voice faded into mumbling as Helga neared him. "There, that's it. A bit tricky, that's all, getting the screw to engage. Now . . . tighten it down, like this. Right-over turn to tighten, just like a screw pump."

The man standing next to him, watching, murmured something. Trae's half-cheerful/half-exasperated cursing came back at full volume.

"*Never seen a screw pump?*" The young nobleman lifted his head and gave all of his nearby special squad members a glare. "None of you, from the ox-dumb looks on your faces! Fucking peasants! *Fat* peasants, that's the problem! Lounging about in the shade while the women do all the work. What little work there is on your rich bottomlands."

His squad members were fighting grins. Obviously, they'd had enough experience with Trae to know the difference between his genuine anger and this half pretense. Judging from their appearance, Helga thought all of them were the same type of easterners who filled the ranks of the soldiery proper.

"I'm an idiot!" bellowed Trae. "I should havc engaged nothing but those barbarians from the Gya desert! *They* know how a pump works, even if they are a lot of savages. Gotta have pumps in those drylands."

He turned back and demonstrated again, using exaggerated hand gestures. "Like this, see? Hand turning to the right. You *do* know the difference between left and right? *Please! O gods, I beg you!*"

Helga was close enough to look over his shoulder. She could now see clearly what Trae was doing. He'd fit one of the arquebus tripods over the rail and, using what struck her as an excessively elaborate screw dcvice, had clamped the hinged third leg on the wood. The tripod would now provide a solid and steady rest for one of the heavy two-man arquebuses, even in tossing seas.

"That's a stupid arrangement," she said. Her own voice was not much softer than Trae's. "Much too complicated. It would have been a lot easier to just leave the tripod alone, drill a hole in one of the legs, and screw *in* to the wood instead of trying to clamp around it."

Trae straightened to his full height, twisted, and glared down at her with outrage. Helga gave him a sweet smile. "You said it yourself. Women do all the work. That's what makes us smarter, too."

And with that, she turned and ambled away, a little chorus of chuckles following. None from Trac, of course.

She spent the next hour or so getting her own quarters ready. The "quarters" in question consisted of a section of the hold which had been set aside for the women accompanying the expedition.

These were Ilset Yunkers, the wives of the four senior noncoms of the hundred, and Lortz's two concubines. Ilset was, by a considerable margin, the youngest of the seven women. And Helga suspected she was probably the only one who was legally a "wife" to begin with. The other four had the appearance of campaign concubines. Veterans themselves, in a manner of speaking. Lortz's women didn't even make a pretense of being anything else.

No others had been allowed to bring female companionship. The soldiers hadn't complained. The veterans were quite confident in their ability to obtain camp followers wherever they went, and the youngsters took their cue from them. Even, Helga had no doubt, looked forward eagerly to that new rite of passage. Southron women, like Islanders, were notorious among Confederates for their loose and passionate ways—which Helga herself found rather amusing, since her experience in an Islander hareem had taught her that foreigners had exactly the same view of Vanbert women. So much seemed ingrained in human nature. The *others* were always brutes and swindlers, if male; sluts and carriers of disease, if female.

Since Ilset would be the wet nurse for Helga's baby, she and Demansk's daughter shared the most "luxurious" part of the arrangement. The "luxury" amounted to nothing more than a few extra cushions and a thicker cloth to separate them from the rest of the womens' quarters—which, in turn, were separated from the goods in the hold by nothing more than a cloth in the first place. The only reason it took an hour to get her quarters prepared was simply the cramped nature of the space itself. Even something as simple as rearranging a cushion seemed to take forever. Early on, Helga and Ilset agreed that it would be best to set up another partition between them, seeing as how Jessep would be spending his nights with his wife. So Helga's quarters got reduced in size even further.

But, eventually, it was done, just as Helga felt the ship begin to move away from the pier. Coming through the thin planking of the deck above her head—"above" only when she crouched; standing erect, she'd crash her head into it—she could hear the beat of the hortator's mallets pounding the drum which kept the rowers at their rhythm. The "drum" had a distinctive sound. It was a hollow box, actually, rather than the more typical drums which would be used to give signals in a fleet.

She was tempted to go back on deck. To get some fresh air, if nothing else. She resisted the impulse. The women's quarters were already heavy with odor, true enough, but Helga knew that by the end of the voyage the air down here would be well-nigh fetid. The men at their work above wouldn't appreciate having her underfoot; not in the least. And she'd rather save her trespasses on their territory for a later time, when she'd *really* need fresh air.

She leaned back against one of the cushions and gave Ilset a friendly smile. Jessep's young wife gave her a shy smile in return, but it was very short-lived. They were already catching the first waves of the open sea, and the motion was apparently beginning to bother the girl. Helga found herself wondering if Ilset had ever been on a ship before.

Apparently not, judging from the girl's reaction not five minutes later. Helga managed to get Ilset's head over a bucket soon enough to catch most of it.

Most, but not all. Helga sighed and began rummaging for an old cloth in her belongings. Finding none—she never got seasick herself and hadn't thought to prepare for the problem—she stuck her head through the opening in the cloth which separated her and Ilset from the other women.

"Do any of you—"

One of the women, grinning, was already handing her a rag. Ilset had not been quiet in her distress.

"Bound to happen," said the woman, grinning widely. Helga could see that she was missing a fair number of her teeth. An attractive enough woman, otherwise. Helga thought her buxom build was probably matched by a buxom temperament, and was cheered by the thought.

"It's going to stink down here something awful," she probed.

"Beats dying," came the immediate response, as the woman passed the test with flying colors. "Even if the poor girl thinks she'd rather be dead right now."

"We'll get along," predicted Helga. "What's your name?"

"Polla, ma'am. Polla"—there came a slight hesitation, just a hint—"Hissell. He's the new First Spear. Can I give you a hand?"

"Pfaw! Just to wipe up some puke? Do I *look* like a prissy noblewoman?"

Polla's grin was now matched by all the other women. "Not exactly, ma'am," said one of them. "A noblewoman, yes. Prissy, no."

Helga grinned herself, ducked back into her quarters, and went to work with the rag. Soon enough, she was half wishing she'd taken Polla up on her offer. But she knew that a small amount of inconvenience was well worth gaining the allegiance and trust of the women of her escort.

Women do all the real work. That makes us smarter.

After nightfall, Trae came into her quarters. Mumbling apologies to the women in the outer quarters, as he groped his way through the half darkness—all that their one little oil lamp allowed—he eventually stumbled through the curtain.

"Uck! Stinks!" he muttered, waving his hand in front of his face. Then, seeing Ilset's wan face in the flickering light shed by Helga's own lamp, his usual good humor returned.

"Be at ease, young lady. I assure you—from bitter experience—that you'll get over it. Eventually."

He turned to face Helga. "You were right, but don't brag about it more than two days. Or I'll sneak down here and piss in your gruel. It *would* have been easier to design it your way."

The word "gruel" seemed to distress Ilset. She turned her face away and fought down a gag.

"Cheer up!" boomed Trae. "Always eat gruel on your first sea voyage. Easy down, easy up."

Ilset immediately proved his point. Scowling, Helga handed Trae a rag.

"All right, loudmouth. Your turn."

CHAPTER ELEVEN

The first significant opposition came in Solinga, the capital of the northern province which had once been the independent league of Emerald city-states. Which was perhaps fitting in an ironic sort of way, thought Demansk. The Emeralds themselves figured prominently in his plans for the future—and the opposition came from the Confederate governor of the province.

It was almost as if the man understood that Demansk brought his own ruin in his train. Which, indeed, he did. If Demansk was successful, the status of the Emeralds would undergo a dramatic improvement. Not least of all, because Demansk would eradicate the long-standing evil of the Confederacy's system of tax collection—which, in practice if not in theory, relied on men like Governor Willech to make it work.

Willech, lounging on a couch across the room from Demansk, was a small and wiry man. Hard-faced, tight-featured, and surprisingly fit for a man who made his fortune with abacus and weighing scales rather than a plow or a sword. True, he resembled the popular image of a "tax shark." But Demansk thought it would have been more appropriate if Willech had sported a large, sleek, tapered and finned body—with a wide and whiskered face consisting mostly of jaws and teeth. Just like the breed of sea predators whom the Emeralds, using an ancient word whose original meaning was long lost, called a "shark."

"I'm afraid I can't agree to that, Justiciar Demansk." Willech's words, like his face, were clipped and hard. "One regiment, certainly; perhaps two. But *four*? That would leave me only two regiments in the entire province. Riot and rebellion would be the certain result."

Demansk did not reply immediately. He returned the little man's stare with a hard stare of his own, allowing Willech time to let his hidden uncertainty mount. And his fears.

Willech had been one of the main creditors of the traitor Redvers, who had led the Confederacy's most recent attempted coup d'etat because the only way he and his cohorts had seen to avert bankruptcy was to usurp state power and repudiate their debts. Demansk had played the key role in crushing that insurrection. And while most people would assume that such men as Willech would be grateful to him for it, the reality was much more complicated.

True, had Redvers and his co-conspirators achieved their aim, Willech would have been ruined—and, most likely, murdered in the bargain. On the other hand . . .

Redvers' property, as was traditionally the penalty for treason, had been confiscated by the Confederate government. And while *some* of the money obtained from liquidating what few assets Redvers still had left had been handed over to the creditors, most of it had disappeared into the coffers of the officials charged with overseeing the liquidation. Officials who were every bit as greedy and corrupt as Redvers himself—and Willech—if not as impecunious.

Demansk fought down a harsh grin. He didn't doubt for a moment that Willech assumed that *he* had swindled a fair share of the Redvers estate. Which, as it happened, was not true. Demansk was one of the few officials in the Confederate government who relied on the workings of his own estates for his fortune.

That, and the merchant establishments and manufactories which Demansk had begun investing in several years earlier, once he came to realize that agriculture alone was a risky basis for maintaining a family fortune. Of course, he'd been careful to use an elaborate network of "cutouts" for the purpose. Partly to protect his investments against his many enemies in the officialdom, but mostly because Vanbert custom did not allow a nobleman to engage in anything as low and disreputable as manufacturing and trade.

Unless, of course, it was the trade in slaves arising from conquest. Over the years, Demansk had augmented his fortune considerably from that particular trade. Like any successful military commander, slaves were part of his booty. But, even as a young man, it had struck him odd that the most savage and bestial of all forms of trade should be the only one acceptable to the Confederate elite. Looking back on it from the perspective of middle age, he thought it was that experience which first began sowing the seeds of doubt in his mind as to the health of his own society.

He decided he'd allowed enough time to lapse in these idle ruminations. When he spoke, his voice was even more clipped and hard than Willech's.

"That's *Triumvir* Demansk, Governor Willech, and I trust I won't have to remind you of it again. The penalties for disrespect to state officials are severe." *As in mutilation for a first offense,* he left unspoken. Even though, in practice, a nobleman like Willech would rarely suffer that penalty—not for a first offense—it remained a possibility. More than a few of the noblemen who had been distantly connected with the Redvers rebellion were walking around today with their left arms ending at their wrists rather than their fingertips.

"As for the danger of rebellion," he continued harshly, "that is your problem, not mine. I am charged with the task of conquering the Western Isles—a martial feat which has never been accomplished in the history of the Confederacy. You, on the other hand, are charged with the simple task of maintaining public order in a province—something which any competent governor can manage easily with a bit of thought and effort."

He rose to his feet. Unlike Willech, he had been sitting erect on his couch, and could thus rise easily and quickly. An old soldier's habit, that. "I will also remind you that, not so many years ago, *I* was the governor of this very province. And I managed to keep order, with no difficulty at all, using only two regiments."

Willech's face was like a nut, now, hard and wrinkled. Demansk gave him a smile which ended just short of a sneer.

"Of course, I used those troops to check the worst depredations of the tax farmers. Instead of using them to enforce outright robbery. I dare say you'll have the same success, if you adopt my methods."

Willech's face, as impossible as it seemed, tightened even further. But he said nothing.

What was there to say? Since becoming governor of the province three years earlier, Willech had attempted to extricate himself from his bad loans by squeezing the Emeralds mercilessly. It was an open secret that Governor Willech was taking a cut from every tax farmer in the northern province. That was illegal, under Confederate law. But, for several generations now, Demansk had been one of the few governors to obey that law. The main attraction to becoming a governor nowadays, in fact, was that the post allowed just such chicanery. The modern Vanbert aristocracy, most of whose members couldn't tell one end of a pig from the other, raised taxes the same way their ancestors raised swine.

Not even that, really. No swineherd was stupid enough to think that the way to get rich was to starve his pigs.

Demansk realized that Willech was going to remain silent. Not saying anything was, ultimately, the last resort the governor had. If he said "no," he would be in open rebellion. Demansk had enough of his own troops in Solinga now to crush all six of Willech's regiments—even assuming they would obey the Governor, which was highly doubtful. And if he said "yes," he would be officially acquiescing to Demansk's demand.

Demansk decided he could live with the silence. By the time Willech could even begin to figure out a way to circumvent Demansk's plans, it would be too late anyway. Unlike the Governor, the Triumvir *was* popular with the army. And he knew already which four regiments he was going to select. The best, naturally, with the best officers. The commanders of three of those four regiments were former protégés of his, in fact, and he'd already spoken to them privately.

So, matching silence with silence, he turned on his heel and marched out of the Governor's private audience chamber. He even closed the door himself on his way out, before a slave could do so. Partly, because he thought a formal display of politeness was to his advantage. Mostly, because he wanted to test the door a bit—in case it proved necessary to come back through it at the head of a squad of soldiers.

Which, he suspected, would happen very soon. Demansk had plans for Willech's money as well as his soldiers. And unless he was badly mistaken, the Governor would part with the latter far more readily than the former.

The docks were swarming by the time Demansk got there. Not with soldiers, or sailors, but with Emerald workmen drawn by the rumors sweeping the city of a massive new shipbuilding project. Governor Willech's tax farmers had, in a few short years, impoverished half the artisanry of the northern province—along with most of its fishermen and all of its peasants. Most of the workmen teeming on the piers and in the harbor taverns were shipwrights and other skilled craftsmen; or fishermen, whose trade was closely related. But many of them were simply farmers who had abandoned their land, with nothing to sell except a strong back and pair of hands.

Demansk surveyed the scene from the flat top of the building he had sequestered as his temporary headquarters. The building was typical of the better-built edifices of the Emerald country. Mudbrick and wood, true, where Confederates would have used stone. But in the sunny and dry Emerald climate, mudbrick and wood covered with paint was a perfectly durable building material. Especially given the excellence of Emerald tile-making, still the best in the world.

As he stood atop the tiled roof, three stories above street level and with a good view of the city's great harbor, Demansk allowed no trace of satisfaction to show on his face. For the project he had in mind, he would need a lot of strong backs and willing hands. Not simply to make the gigantic fleet he planned to build, but to man the oars on those ships afterward. Demansk took no pleasure in the poverty and misery of others, but he would not hesitate to use it for his purpose. If nothing else, he could assuage his feelings of guilt by remembering that, in the end, he would use the depredations of men like Willech to break them.

The *immediate* goal of his projected fleet, of course, was the conquest of the Western Isles. But Demansk thought he could show the world a new trick in the old repertoire of dictators. Since he planned, among other things, to use the shipbuilding campaign to create a great industrial center in Solinga, he would demonstrate that workmen could form as effective a mass base as small landholders.

Give a poor and desperate man a *stake* in the world—any kind of stake—and a stake which depended upon a tyrant's shield for its shelter . . .

"How many, do you think?" he asked Olver. His son, at Demansk's command, had taken charge of the Triumvir's temporary headquarters while Demansk was visiting the Governor. He was now standing beside his father on the roof of the building, staring down at the mob in the streets below.

"The gods only know," he muttered. "You wouldn't believe how deeply Willech's gouged these people. I just found out he even started taxing the Grove a few months ago."

Despite himself, Demansk was startled. For all their frequently derisive remarks about effete Emerald philosophers, the Confederate aristocracy had long since adopted much of Emerald culture for their own. Every Vanbert nobleman, and most noblewomen, were fluent in the language of the northern province. Demansk was by no means uncommon in having read most of the Emeralds' great poetry, and seen most of their famous dramas. He'd even read a respectable amount of their most important philosophical works.

The Grove, the traditional academy for training Emerald scholars, was thus almost as venerated an institution among Vanberts as it was for the Emeralds themselves—even if not more than a handful of young Confederate noblemen had ever attended the school. The Grove had enjoyed a tax-free status for . . .

"Since we conquered them," he murmured. "Whatever our other mistakes, we always had enough sense to incorporate the gods of our defeated enemies into our own pantheon—and we never meddled with their most hallowed shrines."

"Willech's an *idiot*," hissed Olver.

Demansk nodded sternly. He left unspoken the words running through his mind: *And a most useful one. I couldn't have asked for anything better.*

Demansk thought that Olver already suspected most of his father's ambitions. But his second-oldest son had always been a self-contained and solemn fellow. A very . . . *proper* sort of man. Demansk had no doubt at all of Olver's loyalty. But he saw no point in shredding what few illusions—or, perhaps, euphemisms—Olver preferred to maintain over what they were doing. Where Demansk's daughter and youngest son could be, and had been, drawn directly into his conspiracy, it would always suit Olver better to be left at arm's length from it. Still within reach, of course, just . . . an arm's distance away.

Good enough. Here, too, Demansk would do what was needed.

"I'd like you to take charge of organizing the actual naval project," he said. "Not the technical side of it, of course. You'll be able to find plenty of Emerald master shipbuilders for that. But there'll still be enough work to keep you busy."

Olver smiled. "To say the least. I don't expect I'll be getting much sleep for the next few months." He hesitated; then: "I'll need money, Father. A *lot* of money. So much, in fact . . ."

He let the thought trail off. Demansk could finish it with no difficulty. So much money that we'll bankrupt the family as well as empty the coffers the Council sent with us.

Those coffers were full, and there were a lot of them. But Demansk had never specified exactly *how* he planned to conquer the isles. And so the Council, having nothing to go on but the memory of great naval expeditions of the past, had allotted what seemed to be a suitable portion—and a very large one at that—of the Confederacy's standby war chest.

They'd assumed, Demansk knew, that he intended a long campaign. Two years, maybe three, in the preparations. And then five to ten years in the doing. The oceanic equivalent of a siege, along the lines of what Albrecht was doing at Preble.

Demansk intended to surprise the world here as well. For his long-term purposes, he needed a quick and crushing victory over the Islanders. Partly, that was because he needed to sidestep the inevitable economic exhaustion of a long campaign—which would be absolutely devastating for the islanders themselves. Demansk could not afford that. He needed prosperous Emeralds; and a population of the Islands which, though desperate to appease their conquerors, still had the wherewithal to do so.

And, of course, partly because he would need the aura of martial triumph which such a victory would bring with it. Not the least of a would-be tyrant's job requirements was a reputation for invincibility. It was not enough for Demansk to be respected and admired for his military skills. He already had that much, from his enemies as well as his friends. What he would need in the future was their *terror*. The kind of bone-deep terror that would make the words "Demansk is coming" enough to end most battles before they began.

That kind of terror could be obtained in only one of two ways. (Or both, as Marcomann had done.) The first was to demonstrate inhuman brutality. The other was to demonstrate frightening skill at war. It was Demansk's hope—perhaps futile—that he could avoid most of the former if he could do well enough at the latter.

Olver's voice broke into his ruminations. "Father? Did you hear what I said? About the money we'll need, I mean."

"I heard. Don't worry about it, son. When the time comes, your august father will provide. And I won't have to bankrupt the family fortune to do it, either." He cleared his throat. "Though I dare say I will have to deplete it quite a bit."

Olver shrugged. "Depleting it doesn't matter, as long as we've got enough seed corn for the next year."

Demansk clapped him on the shoulder. He approved of Olver. Granted, his second-oldest son had little of Helga or Trae's quick wits and humor. But he was a *solid* boy. He always had been.

Demansk had always said he would trust Olver with his life. Now, he was about to prove it.

"Not to worry, son."

"I'm *not* worrying about it, Father," came the immediate reply.

"Just . . . wondering a bit, that's all." Before Demansk could say anything, Olver placed his own square hand atop his father's, still resting on the son's shoulder. "Don't tell me. I'd rather not know."

That night, in the privacy of his sleeping chambers, Demansk appointed his third Special Attendant. A small, wiry man, with a face like a claw hammer. Except for its narrowness, in fact, the face looked quite a bit like Willech's.

The man's name was Prit Sallivar, and he had been Demansk's closest and most trusted financial adviser for years. The family's banker, for all practical purposes.

"The Council's going to have a shitfit," he predicted. "Probably be a riot in the Assembly."

Demansk shrugged. "I don't care about the Assembly. Unless they can find a point of clear support in the Council, the 'Assembly' is just a fancy name for the 'mob of Vanbert.' Screw 'em. The Council's the key, right now. And I'm trusting you to keep it locked."

Sallivar made a face. "That's a terrible mixed metaphor. Don't let any Emerald grammarian hear you say things like that, Verice, or *you'll* be the one facing a provincial rebellion here."

Demansk chuckled. Sallivar was one of the few men close enough to him to use the Triumvir's first name. He was also one of the few who didn't hesitate to gibe at Demansk's not-always-elegant use of language. It was part of the reason Demansk trusted him. That and, of course, the fact that if Demansk fell, Prit Sallivar would be dismembered by their mutual enemies within moments thereafter.

"Use the old man, Prit." Then, scrambling the metaphor hopelessly: "He'll turn the key in the lock for you."

Sallivar's face was now truly sour. "Turn it which way?" he demanded. "Will you *please* give up the bad poetry and speak in plain and simple prose."

"Jeschonyk will keep the Council under control. He's . . . not my man, no. But he'll not wish to cross me in this. And since he's not one of Willech's creditors *or* debtors, he'll have neither a personal grudge nor any need to act impartial in the matter. And you know how well he can give that 'for the good of the Confederacy' speech of his."

"None better," allowed Sallivar. He straightened up and squared his shoulders. Stretched them, rather. It had been a long planning session.

"All right, Verice. I'll do my best. How soon?"

There was no humor on Demansk's face now. "Tomorrow," he said.

"Tomorrow?"

"Why wait?"

CHAPTER TWELVE

"I can delay it for another hour," said Thicelt tightly, peering at the vessel half a mile off from the stern of their ship. His eyes werc squinted against the sun, which gave his huge-beaked face an even fiercer look than usual. "No longer than that. The wind's not good enough to stay ahead of them before their rowers tire."

Jessep Yunkers gave the pirate ship pursuing them a last glance and turned to Helga.

"It's your decision, ma'am."

Helga hesitated, not sure what to do. Then, an oft-repeated remark of her father's came back to her.

"My father always said to rely on your First Spear's advice when you were unsure of things. So—what is it?"

Jessep's square face creased into a grin of sorts. He turned his head and studied the oncoming pirate vessel. Then, glanced at the sun and gauged its position.

"I can't see any point in waiting." He jerked a thumb at the soldiers of the hundred, who were lying down everywhere on the deck. Out of sight of the pirates in their low galley, true enough, but badly cramped. "Another hour of that, and they'll be too stiff to get to their feet easily when the time comes. Best to do it quickly."

Thicelt glanced at Helga. She nodded. Immediately, the ship's captain began bellowing orders.

Part of the crew swarmed up the rigging and began bringing down the sail. Once that was done, they would see to the backbreaking and risky work of removing the mast. That was always done when a warship was heading into battle—at least, a warship armed with a ram—or the mast would snap off at the impact.

Meanwhile, obeying the new rhythm of the hortator at his wooden drum, the oarsmen began turning the ship. To the pirates pursuing them, it would seem as if the merchant ship was making a desperate attempt to ram them.

And *desperate* was the right word for it. Unless the pirates handled their ship incredibly badly, they should have no difficulty at all avoiding the clumsier demibireme's assault. Although Helga's was a warship of sorts itself, the pirate vessel was much more maneuverable in a single ship action. Typical of the type used by the freebooters along the coast, it was a light and shallow-draft pure galley. Very wide in proportion to its length, true, in order to accommodate the huge number of rowers aboard her. But still a much handier craft than its prey.

Sure enough, before Thicelt had even finished turning his ship Helga could hear the loud jeers of the pirate crew. There must have been some two hundred men aboard that low galley. Even across the distance—still perhaps four hundred yards—their voices carried well enough.

"Stay right here where they can see you clearly when we get closer," said Jessep. "Begging your pardon, ma'am. But that'll help . . . distract them."

Helga's smile was a very crooked thing. " 'Distraction' is one way of putting it. But how are they supposed to get a good look at me? We're back in the stern, First Spear. Sorry, 'Special Attendant.' "

" 'First Spear' is just fine coming from you, ma'am. Think I prefer it some, to be honest."

Helga nodded. " 'First Spear' it stays, then, at least between you and me. But my point is—if you *really* want them to get a look at me, shouldn't I be up in the bow?"

Jessep shook his head. "That'd be suspicious, ma'am. A lady'd be either way back at the stern or . . ."

"Cowering in the hold," finished Helga, "like as not screaming her head off. Speaking of which—"

She took three quick steps and leaned over the hatch. In the semi-darkness below, she could see Polla's pale face staring up at her. Despite the paleness, which was more the product of spending days in the ship's interior than anything else, Polla didn't seem especially worried.

"It'd help if you all did some screaming," said Helga. "When the time comes. I'll give you the signal."

Polla nodded. Then, gave her own version of a crooked smile. "No problem. Won't be the first time any of us have faked it. Although there's probably no need to mention that to my, ah, husband."

Helga chuckled. Then, chuckled again, hearing Ilset's outraged hiss. "*I* never faked anything! My husband—"

"Oh, shut up, will you?" groused Polla. "If I have to listen to another paean of praise about your precious Jessep, I swear I'll . . ."

The rest faded out as Polla disappeared. Helga straightened and went back to Jessep. The middle-aged former First Spear had a *very* smug look on his face. Apparently, the injury to his head hadn't affected his hearing any.

"Okay," she said. "Now what?"

Yunkers shrugged. "You and I just stand here looking like a rich merchant and his beautiful daughter. With our personal bodyguard." He jerked his thumb over his shoulder, pointing at Lortz. Helga's personal weapons trainer, looking relaxed if none too happy, was standing near them in full weapons and armor.

"Nothing else for us to do, really," Jessep continued. "Thicelt's an excellent shiphandler, as he's made obvious by now." He nodded in the direction of one of the soldiers lying on the deck. "My nephew Uther's as good a First Spear as any you'll find, and he's led at least four boarding operations that I know about. Other than that . . ." He winced slightly.

"Other than that, there's the question of what my hot-blooded and eager young brother wants to do."

At the moment, judging from the evidence, what Trae mainly

wanted to do was curse the fates. Such, at least, was Helga's interpretation of his grimaces and gestures. The words themselves were difficult to follow, since there really weren't too many strung together in coherent clauses.

Eventually, as the string of swear words shortened, she was able to make some sense of it. Trae, it seemed, was most unhappy with the decision to end the long stern chase.

By then, he was standing in front of Helga herself and making his sentiments known.

"Dammit, Helga, I wanted to try them out! How in the name of all that's holy am I supposed to get any experience with the guns if—if—you stupid idiot!" His arms were waving about rather wildly now. "Turn the ship back around! I was just about to set the clamps!"

Yunkers hesitated, apparently reluctant to get into a fierce argument with a Demansk scion. Helga, for whom Trae was simply a younger brother, had no such compunction.

"If your precious guns are so finicky they can only be used under perfect conditions," she snarled, "then we might as well have left you behind."

As always, an attack by his older sister brought out the imp in Trae.

"You're just being nasty because these stupid pirates are getting in the way of your rut. For shame. Mother brought you up properly, too. Tried to, anyway."

"You're right," she snapped. "I want to get laid—it's been almost a year, dammit—and these freebooters are *not* what I had in mind for the purpose." She stared down her younger brother for a few seconds, *daring* him to carry the jest any further.

Not even Trae was that bold. "Okay," he muttered, reaching up and scratching his head. "Let me think . . ."

He gave the upper bank of rowers a brief study. "Oarlocks'll get in the way," she heard him mumble, "but even so . . ."

Trae turned back and looked at Thicelt. "How soon before the pirates lay alongside will you order the oars in?"

Thicelt glanced at the pirate ship. "No way to avoid them now, so any ship captain would already be starting to think in terms of repelling boarders. How much time do you need?"

"Two minutes," came Trae's immediately reply. "Three would be better."

Thicelt shook his head. "Three minutes is too long. In these seas, we'd be wallowing the gods know which way by then. Even two is pushing it. But I can manage that by keeping a third of the oars going until the last minute." Again, he glanced at the pirate ship. "Whatever you're going to do, do it quick. There are archers and slingers on that ship. They'll be starting to bombard us with missiles once they get within fifty yards."

"Fifty yards," sneered Trae. "My guns can—"

"Not on a tossing ship they can't," said Jessep softly. "This isn't like missile fire on land, young sir. You'll be lucky to hit anything until they're almost alongside."

Trae looked a bit startled. For all that he and his gunners had practiced *setting* the tripod clamps for the arquebuses, they hadn't actually fired any shots so far on the voyage. Trae had wanted to save his ammunition, since he had no way of knowing if he'd be able to replenish it in the Southron lands.

"Of course," added Jessep, "the same applies to the pirates. Most of their arrows and sling bullets will go wild also. All of this missile firing before a boarding operation is mostly show anyway."

The implied insult caused Trae's face to darken a little. Still, he was wise enough not to snarl a rejoinder. Trae understood full well that he and his beloved gunners had yet to prove themselves in action. Brash he might be, but not even Trae was cocky enough to boast about feats he hadn't accomplished yet.

"Make sure you set them up on the lower bank only," interjected Thicelt. He jerked his head toward the pirate ship, which was now not more than two hundred yards away. "As low as that galley is, all of our soldiers will still be boarding from the upper deck. No other way to do it, since that's how the special bridges are designed."

"Pain in the butt, that," growled Jessep. "Having to charge down a steep ramp—loaded with shield and armor and assegai—even leaving aside the fact that we haven't tested the damn contraptions."

He gave Thicelt a look which was not entirely filled with admiration. "Wish we had some simple old-fashioned claws."

By "claws," Helga knew, Jessep was referring to the traditional boarding ramps used by the Confederate army in their favored method of naval operation. The "claws" were nothing more complicated than wide planks, held upright and fit into prepared hinges along the rails just before action. And with spikes at the other end, which would drive into the wood of an opposing vessel when the planks were pushed over.

But there had simply been no way to adapt the demibireme to that tactic, which presupposed the large war galleys of the Vanbert regular navy. Instead, what Thicelt had done was redesign portions of the upper deck—already designed to be removed in the event of action—so that they would collapse down onto an enemy vessel alongside. He'd even added fittings for small spikes which could be inserted at the last minute. Those adaptations had not been the least of the cost to her father of getting this ship ready for her voyage.

The end result would be boarding ramps not much different from claws. In theory, at least. But like almost all soldiers, Jessep was conservative when it came to mayhem. The tried and true methods are best, and be damned to the fancy schemes of amateurs.

"They'll work," said Thicelt firmly. "We've tested them plenty of times."

Jessep left unsaid the obvious rejoinder: *not in a real battle, you haven't.* There was simply no point now in arguing about the matter. Thicelt's complicated boarding ramps would work or they wouldn't. Either way, Jessep was obviously not concerned about the outcome—*a crack Vanbert hundred against twice their number of mangy pirates? surely you jest!*—but simply the casualties. With *proper* claws, the Confederate marines would turn the pirate crew into so much ground meat. With these new-fangled things . . .

He sighed heavily. "Whatever happens will happen. And now, young sir, you'd best get to it. You don't have much time left."

Trae was gone instantly, shouting orders to his gunners waiting on the deck below. The gunners began scurrying to their newly-designated posts. Helga was a bit puzzled to see how easily they seemed to interpret Trae's orders. Most of the words her younger brother was shouting were simply obscenities.

"That much he's got right," growled Yunkers. The former First Spear grinned at Helga. "Trained soldiers pretty much know what to do anyway. You just have to cuss at 'em to keep their brains working."

Afterward, Trae and his men would be able to boast endlessly. Which, to the regret of everyone else, they did.

The pirate vessel, as Thicelt predicted, had no difficulty eluding the demibireme's ramming attempt. Then, as the one-and-a-half slid by, the pirates pulled feverishly on their oars to close the distance. The one and only benefit of the ramming attempt was that it kept most of the pirate archers and all of their slingers out of the action. There was no room on that crowded vessel, with hundreds of men working at huge oars, for more than a handful of archers to fire a few missiles. Most of which, as Jessep had foreseen, went astray anyway.

Trae waited until the pirate ship was not more than ten yards distant. By then, Thicelt had removed all the rowers and Trae's gunners had set the tripod clamps at ten places along the lower deck which gave them a clear line of fire. At Trae's command—which was nothing more than a string of particularly obscene words—the first team of gunners set their arquebuses and fired.

None of it took more than a few seconds. The gunners themselves, following Trae's previous orders, were not even aiming at individual men. In fact, they weren't shooting at "men" at all. Not directly, at any rate. Their heavy, large-bored guns were simply pointing at the side of the pirate ship. The only sense in which "aiming" applied was that they were trying to hit the wooden wall of the enemy ship at approximately the height of the rowers' benches on the other side. "Hip-high," had been Trae's specific command. But . . . with the heavy four-ounce balls fired by those two-man arquebuses, at point-blank range, anything close would do just fine.

And so it proved. The gunhandlers set their weapons, more or less "aimed," then braced for the recoil and closed their eyes when the other man of the team applied the slow match. A slightly ragged volley erupted, and one which was noisy enough to make the word "erupted" much more than a poetic allusion. It sounded like a small volcano, heard up close.

Looked like one, too. Immediately, the middle portion of the pirate ship vanished from sight, engulfed in a cloud of smoke. Helga, from her vantage point, could only see the bow and stern of the enemy. The faces of the pirates standing there, which only a moment before had been leering at her, were now so many studies in shock and confusion.

She thought that a bit odd, at first. Her former lover Adrian Gellert, after all, had been the one who first introduced gunpowder weapons to the world—using the pirates of the islands as his chosen instrument. And the Islanders had taken to the new weapons eagerly, as her father and Speaker Emeritus Jeschonyk had discovered to their dismay when the first Confederate assaults on the rebel island of Preble had been bloodily repulsed. That had been over a year ago. By now, Helga would have thought, pirates would be quite accustomed to gunpowder.

Then, seeing the rags in which the pirates on this ship were clad, she realized the truth. Like most Vanberts, Helga tended to think of "Islanders" and "pirates" as synonymous terms. But the truth was more complicated.

The Islanders could be separated into at least four distinct groups. There was the actual *Kingdom* of the Isles, ruled over by Casull the IV from his capital on the island of Chalice. Or, as he officially styled himself: "King Casull IV, Lord of the Isles, Supreme Autocrat, Chosen of the Sun God and Lemare of the Sea." Leaving aside the rhetorical flourish of the rest, the term *autocrat* was accurate enough. Except that the power of the King of the Isles, as great as it undoubtedly was, also had the historical characteristic of transience. Islander politics were even more notorious for treachery, double-dealing and palace revolts than the Confederacy's.

Then, there was—had been, rather—the smaller-scale but similar realm of Vase. The island of Vase, because it was located quite some distance from the main archipelago, had traditionally enjoyed independent status. Until Casull conquered it the year before, it had been ruled by the so-called Director of Vase. It had been in that old pirate chief's hareem that Helga had spent the most unpleasant year of her life, after she'd been sold by the pirates who captured her. The Director had been delighted to obtain a high-ranked member of the Vanbert aristocracy for one of his concubines. Even if, in practice, he hadn't been able to do much to enjoy his prize.

She grimaced, as a sudden image came back to her. A fat belly, heaving and covered with sweat, almost crushing her; and an old man's peevish voice, cursing her because *he* couldn't get an erection. He'd slapped her, that night, hard enough to leave bruises on her cheeks for days thereafter.

The ugly memory was blown away by another volley from Trae's guns. She was startled to realize that not more than a quarter of a minute had elapsed since the first. Trae really *had* trained his men well.

And he was using them intelligently, Helga thought. Trae had kept back half of his twenty two-man teams, having apparently decided that maintaining a good rate of fire was more important than the size of the volleys themselves. Now, as his teams switched places—one squad firing loaded and ready guns while the other picked up their second set of weapons—his decision proved itself. The second volley slammed into the side of the pirate ship before the cloud of smoke from the first had been dissipated by the slight breeze.

Confusion, she could remember her father telling her, *is an even better weapon against an enemy than casualties.* The pirates, she realized, had not had time to make sense out of what was happening to them before yet another volley ripped into their ranks.

Because of the smoke, she couldn't really see the casualties which were being inflicted by Trae's guns. But judging from the volume of the screams coming from amidships of the enemy vessel, as well as the dismay on the faces of those pirates she could see on the stern and bow—*they weren't gloating over their projected rapine now, the stinking bastards*—she thought the guns were tearing the enemy like a pack of predators tears a cornered greatbeast.

The unwanted image of a rapist's fat belly was replaced by another. The more slender waists of would-be rapists, sitting on benches, screaming as they stared at their shattered hip bones and ruptured intestines. Helga had seen what those lead bullets would do to a heavy pig, shot at close range. The thin planks of the pirate ship wouldn't slow them down much more than paper. If anything, she thought, the splinters the bullets would produce punching through the walls would simply double the casualties. And if pieces of broken wood sent sailing by four-ounce lead balls wouldn't do quite as much damage as the bullets themselves, they would do more than enough to put most of the men they struck half out of the action by the time the marines stormed aboard. "Half out of the action," against experienced Confederate infantrymen, was pretty much a euphemism for *dead meat.*

The first squad was back at their firing posts. Another volley, still before the cloud of smoke could vanish. Each two-man team in Trae's gunnery unit, Helga knew, had two arquebuses. With the weapons already loaded and the slow matches prepared, given the rate of fire they were showing now, that meant—

Another volley. Helga was almost shocked herself. They could manage four volleys in the first minute, before the pirate ship could even manage to close the final distance. She realized now that she'd allowed herself to be too influenced by Jessep's veteran experience. True, even with four volleys, the actual casualties inflicted would be relatively slight. She did the quick arithmetic in her head. Even assuming every bullet hit a pirate—almost certain, fired into such a packed mob, since for each one that missed another would punch through two men—then add another from splinter damage . . .

Still, only forty men hit, out of probably two hundred.

Before she could get too smug about her newfound wisdom, however, Jessep Yunkers was shouting in her ear. "A fifth of them, by the gods! I'll wager my pension on it! And before we even hit the bastards with the blades!"

She turned and stared at him. The veteran's blocky face was almost split in half with a grin. Seeing her look of confusion, Jessep shook his head.

"Y've never been in a battle, lass." He was so excited he forgot his normal *ma'am* or *young lady*, and his eastern accent was thicker than usual. "A fift' gone in th'missile volley? We don' never hope fer more than a tent', even wit' dart volleys throwed by vets." His grin turned into a jeer, aimed at the pirates. "That'll break most any'un, much less *these* scum."

She followed his gaze. The sight of the pirates on the bow and stern—the midships was *still* obscured by smoke—showed her at once that Jessep was right. Those faces were full of panic, now, not dismay.

The sight brought her thoughts back to her earlier ruminations. In addition to the pirates of the archipelago and the other large islands of Vase and Preble—"pirates" so-called; in reality they were a well-organized kingdom in their own right—there were the pirates who laired along the coast of the continent. Too far south to be under Confederate control, and too remote to be ruled more than nominally by any Southron chieftain, these were simply pirates in fact as well as in name.

Not even that, Helga realized. Most of the time, these "pirates" would survive by fishing and selling the rare hardwoods they cut from the dense forests along the continent's waist. For all their undoubted seamanship, not to mention their ferocity when easy prey showed off their coastal villages, they had little of the disciplined organization of the Islanders proper. They weren't even that closely related racially, although they had adopted many of the Islander customs and usually worshipped Islander gods. Part Islander, part Southron—not to mention a heavy admixture of slaves escaped from the Confederate plantations to the north—they were mongrels by blood as well as habit. Tough, yes; as mongrels always are. But with a "discipline" that didn't begin to compare with the Islanders proper, much less Confederate soldiery.

The fourth volley erupted. That would be it, for the moment. Helga had watched Trae's men at practice, often enough, while her younger brother trained them on the family's estate. She knew that those clumsy guns, once fired, needed at least a minute to be cleaned and reloaded. A minute, at best. After a few rounds had been fired through the barrels, they needed to be set aside to cool before they could be used again. Trae had used the best metal he could find for them, but even those precious alloys would start to weaken once the barrels got too hot.

But in this instance, it was irrelevant anyway. Thicelt was already shouting at Trae, telling him to pull his gunners out of the way of the soldiers. The men of the hundred were on their feet, crouched, ready to topple the special sections of the upper deck onto the pirate ship's rail. By now, only a three-foot gap separated the two vessels—more than short enough to allow the sections to span the distance.

The gunners scrambled aside and the soldiers yanked out the pins which held the sections in place. Then, with a shout and heaved shoulders, toppled the improvised boarding ramps onto the pirate ship.

Then—

Nothing. At their First Spear's shouted command, they simply stood by the ramps, waiting. Helga was too confused to do more than notice that they weren't even hefting their weighted darts for an initial volley.

She heard Jessep's harsh chuckle. "I told you Uther was a good First Spear. Good as I was, truth be told—sure enough at his age."

She turned her head and stared at him. Jessep's rare grin was back.

"Live and learn, ma'am. Experience always counts." He pointed with his square chin at the pirate vessel, still half obscured by smoke. "Uther's never seen gunpowder at work before, but he *has* led boarding operations onto burning ships. You don't want to lead men into a pile of smoke, you surely don't. Half your discipline'll vanish in a few heartbeats. Let Vanbert soldiers know their place—see and feel their mates at their shoulders—they'll handle anything. Let them lose their bearings, and you never know what'll happen. The only Confederate hundred I ever saw break and run did so in a dense fog."

The grin vanished, replaced by the usual block-against-block that did Jessep for a jaw. "Didn't keep 'em from being decimated afterward, o' course. Those of 'em who survived the enemy pursuit."

Now understanding, Helga nodded jerkily. Not for the first time, she was reminded of the harsh regime under which the Confederacy's soldiers lived and fought.

Another shout from Uther jerked her head back around. The smoke had cleared enough, apparently. The first wave of marines was charging across the ramp, two abreast. Even on that precarious footing, they had their shields locked and the assegais ready for that terrible underhand thrust which had made Confederate infantrymen feared for centuries.

There were four ramps, in all. The first eight men hammered into the screeching mass of pirates. Their spear thrusts were almost desultory. For the most part, the vanguard was using the force of their charge and their shields to clear some fighting room for their comrades coming behind.

The shields were well designed for the purpose. Oval in shape, covering a man from shoulder to mid-thigh, and with a metal rim and boss to bolster the laminated wood from which they were made. Between their own mass and the weight of the three lead-weighted darts clipped on the inside, the shields were just about perfect for the task of driving back a crowd.

Perfect, at least, when wielded by men trained in their use. Watching the soldiers at work, the way their shoulders hunched into the shields and their powerful legs worked like the pistons Trae had shown her in the captured steam ram, Helga suddenly understood something else for the first time.

She'd been trained in combat herself, at her insistence, and by the finest retired gladiators her father could find, Lortz being the latest of them. But her training had been, basically, in the Emerald style which was fashionable in aristocratic duels and the gladiator arenas. That style favored long swords, small round shields, with all the fancy footwork and need for room which it required.

She snorted. "It's no wonder we whipped them."

Jessep, again, showed an uncanny ability to read her mind. "True enough, la—ah, ma'am. You want a short blade for real killing. And then you do most of the killing with your shoulders and legs anyway. The spear thrust's just the finish. Easy enough, if you've gotten the strength and endurance it takes to keep a heavy shield steady at all times—and leg muscles like iron."

She remembered watching her father's soldiers at training. It had seemed a bit odd to her, at the time, the way they devoted such a relatively small amount of time to practicing spear thrusts. For the most part, the training of Confederate infantrymen seemed to be nothing more than endless running—and shield work. Time after time, she'd watched as a squad of men—always a squad, or a whole hundred; Confederate soldiers never trained as individuals—pushed a huge and heavy box full of dirt all the way across a training field. Their legs hammering like pistons, the shields steady against the obstacle. Never halting, never tiring, never stumbling.

They were doing it again now. The first wave of boarders had been joined at the front by the next two. Fully a fourth of the hundred were not using their spears at all. They were simply clearing the midships of the pirate vessel, pushing their opponents back with a solid shield wall. Their shields remaining locked, even as the men holding them threaded their way down the bench rows. Their legs drove relentlessly, never losing their footing even when the sandals stamped down on ruptured bodies instead of wood. Helga could remember watching her father train soldiers on a field littered with the carcasses of gutted pigs. She'd thought it gross, at the time.

Not to mention wasteful of perfectly valuable swine. But now, also, she understood why she'd overheard soldiers say they preferred serving under a rich officer, as long as he was competent. She'd thought, then, that they'd only been thinking of pay and bonuses. But now she realized that a man like her father could afford to train his soldiers properly, as well as provide them with the best equipment. Pay and bonus did no good to a dead soldier.

The pirates were screaming even more loudly, now that this second blow had struck them. They'd been expecting to face nothing more than the usual crew of a demibireme. Sailors, basically, who doubled as fighters only on rare occasion. Coming on top of the surprise volleys of gunfire, the shock of seeing regular Confederate marines storming across boarding ramps—*and where the hell had* those *come from?*—had unnerved them completely.

The pirates facing the marines directly weren't even fighting, except here and there. Most of them were simply trying to scramble away.

But there was no room to scramble. Two hundred men packed

aboard such a galley had left little room to begin with, even before the Confederate assault cleared the space in the middle.

"They're starting to go over the side," said Jessep. Sure enough, Helga could see at least a dozen pirates spilling into the water. A few of them from jumping, most of them simply from being knocked overboard by the sudden crush.

"Pity the poor bastards," he added. Softly, if not gently.

Helga was about to snarl something to the effect that she wanted *all* the pirates dead. The coast wasn't that far away, after all, and at least some of them would be good swimmers. But then, seeing the first fins cutting through the water not more than fifty yards away, the words died in her throat.

"These are shark waters, aren't they?" she asked.

Jessep grunted. "Famous for it." He studied the shoreline for a moment; then: "I'd say it's a good two miles. Maybe closer to three. Not too many men can swim that distance to begin with. Here . . ." He shook his head. "Not a chance."

Helga decided he was right. As they neared, she recognized the shape and markings of the fins. These were what sailors called "redsharks." Not from their own coloring, which was basically a dull gray except for the white tips of the dorsal fins, but from their handiwork. Redsharks were almost as large as the much rarer "great blues," and their gaping jaws were fringed with grappling tentacles lined on the interior with nasty little barbs.

They weren't even the same species—not even close—as most of the seabeasts which went by the generic name of "sharks." Men had been known to survive attacks by other types of sharks, even great blues. Most sharks were actually a little finicky in their tastes. They usually bit humans by mistake, thinking they were their normal prey. One bite was enough to find the taste of humans sour, and the shark went on its way.

Of course, often enough that one bite was fatal, especially with great blues. Still, many men had lived to tell the tale afterward of a great blue attack; even if, as a rule, they told the tale with a wooden leg propped up on a seaside tavern stool. But Helga had never heard of anyone surviving a redshark which sunk its teeth and tentacles into them. Redsharks were about as indiscriminate in their taste as hogs in a trough, and they weighed on average half a ton. Once a human got into their grasp, that . . . was it.

"Good," she hissed. She caught a glimpse of Jessep giving her an odd look, but paid no attention. She was engrossed with gauging the battle raging on the ship alongside.

By now, the Confederate marines had cleared the entire center of the enemy vessel and were beginning the butcher work. All of them had finished boarding. Half of the hundred was driving toward the stern, the other half toward the bow. Shields still locked—but now the assegais were flashing. And, like the legs, went back and forth like machines. Pistons, for all intents and purposes—except these pistons ended in two-foot blades sharpened to an edge which didn't *quite* match a razor's. Not quite.

"This is finished, First Spear. Isn't it?"

"Aye, ma'am. All but the killing."

She shook her head. "No reason to risk any more losses." Losses had been few enough, in truth. Here as always, Confederate training and discipline counted. But Helga could see at least five soldiers of the hundred out of action. Three of them were only wounded—and not too badly at that, she thought. They were already attending to their own wounds.

The other two . . . One of them was dead, no question about it. A skillfully wielded blade—or just a lucky one—must have come over the edge of his shield and caught his throat. Blood was still gushing out of the wound, enough to make his survival a moot point.

She wasn't sure about the other. He was lying sprawled across one of the benches, his helmet knocked askew. Might be dead, or just unconscious.

But there was no need, any longer, to risk more casualties. She might well need her hundred again, in the weeks and months to come—and there'd be no way to replace lost men down in the southern continent. At least, she'd never heard of Southrons being recruited directly into a regular Vanbert unit. Many of the barbarians served in the Confederate army, of course, but to the best of her knowledge always as members of auxiliary units.

"Call it off, First Spear," she commanded. "There's no need to lose any more of our people."

Jessep was shouting the order before she even finished. Looking at him, Helga realized he was relieved to hear her order. He'd obviously been expecting her to insist on full revenge.

Her jaws were tight. I'll get my revenge, never fear. I just don't need the hundred for it.

The instrument of her revenge was trotting toward her even now. Trae, his mouth split in a wide smile, about to utter some words of glee and self-praise.

He never got them out. "I'm not finished with you," hissed Helga. She pointed a stiff finger at the pirate ship. "Destroy that thing for me, brother."

He came to an abrupt stop a few feet away and turned his head. "What for?" he demanded. Then, seeing the Confederate soldiers begin an orderly withdrawal: "And why'd you wait so long to call them back? Another five minutes and they'd have lost—"

He broke off, seeing the expression on Helga's face. "Oh," he mumbled. "That."

He took a deep breath. "Sorry, sister. Because you never act like . . . what I mean is . . ." Another deep breath. "Never mind."

He gave the pirate ship a quick study. "Don't want to chance a grenade," he muttered, "and they're too hard to replace. Simple satchel charge should do the trick—and I've got something special I'd like to try anyway."

As always, a technical project got Trae completely engrossed. Within fifteen seconds, he was back among his gunnery crew, shouting his usual mix of profanity and orders.

It was all very quick. By the time the last Confederate marines trotted back across the ramps, carrying their dead and helping their wounded, Trae had his "special" ready. It looked like one of the other satchel charges Helga had seen, except for three flasks strapped to the side.

Very quick, though not rushed. Thicelt even had his sailors take the time to pry loose the ends of the ramps and hoist them back into position, rather than simply jettisoning them by detaching the hinges.

Then with a push of several oars, opened a space of about ten feet between the two ships.

Two of Trae's men were standing on one of the still-fixed portions of the upper deck by now, holding the "special satchel" between them. At Trae's shout, a third man lit the fuse and the two tossed the thing onto the center of the pirate galley's deck. That area was cleared, except for corpses. The pirates still alive—a good half of the crew, Helga estimated—were cowering at the bow and stern. Even after the marines retreated, they hadn't been in the least inclined to "pursue."

"Get us away from here, Sharlz!" bellowed Trae. "That's a short fuse!"

The command was pointless, really. Thicelt already had the ship under way, the hortator pounding his mallets. Their progress was slow, at first, with only the lower bank of oars working. But by the time the satchel charge blew, less than a minute after it was tossed, Helga's ship was fifty yards away and retreating rapidly. Some corner of her brain was impressed by the speed with which Thicelt had gotten the upper bank back into action.

But only a corner of her brain, and a small corner at that. Most of her mind was being washed over by a wave of sheer hatred, intermingled with horrible flashes of memories she had long suppressed. One male body after another—just pieces of bodies, really; a bare chest, a leg, a scrawny belly wet with her violation, another gap-toothed grin—slamming onto her, one after the other. She never knew how many; didn't want to know. It had lasted for three days.

At first, she was disappointed by the burst of the satchel charge. She'd been expecting to see the pirate ship simply disintegrate. Break in half, at least. But then, not more than a second later, seeing the bloom of fire wash across the ship, she understood what Trae had meant by a "special." He must have designed this satchel charge especially for use against an enemy ship.

Trae confirmed her thought immediately. "Beautiful, isn't it? There wasn't actually much powder in the thing. Just enough to set off the naphtha—some other stuff too—I had in those flasks. She'll burn down to the waterline, you watch."

Helga didn't doubt it. Neither, judging from their looks of horror and their screams, did any of the pirates still alive on the ship. Seamen fear nothing quite so much as an uncontrolled fire on a wooden vessel. Even though the waters around the burning galley were now being crisscrossed by white-tipped fins, Helga could see at least a dozen more pirates jumping overboard.

Her hatred now consumed her entirely. From the stern of the ship, she had a perfect view of the massacre. She pressed her groin against the rail, clutching the wood with hands like claws, and screamed across the waters.

"Try raping the redsharks, you fuckers! I hope—"

What she hoped, in shrieking and graphic anatomical detail, had Trae and Jessep and Lortz pale-faced within seconds. Minutes later, when she finally turned away, they were still pale.

Seeing the expressions on their faces, she snarled at them. "Tough men!" she jeered. "Try surviving three days of a gang rape, you pussies, before you think of telling me what 'tough' means."

And with that, she stalked over to the hatch and lowered herself into the hold. Muttering under her breath all the while about her need for the company of women.

Once below, she found herself spending the next ten minutes trying to quiet her wailing infant. He and Ilset's baby daughter were producing a truly incredible volume of noise.

" 'Twas the screaming did it," explained Polla apologetically. "Ours, I mean."

She gave Helga another crooked little smile. "The sound of the guns made things worse for little Yuli, but it actually seemed to steady your boy for a bit there. Like father, like son, the old saying goes."

Helga returned the smile with one that was probably just as crooked. She'd been careful, since Adrian had returned her to Demansk, to keep the identity of her baby's father a closely-held secret in the family. An unknown pirate's bastard was simply a tool for Demansk's enemies to shame him. Had it become widely known that the father of Helga's child had been Gellert himself, the repercussions might have been much worse.

But once they'd left on this voyage, she'd seen no reason to keep the secret from the new friends she was making. By the time they got back to the Confederacy—if they ever did—it would all be a moot point, anyway.

When she finally had her baby down to the point of occasional little sobs, Helga turned to Polla and whispered a few words of thanks.

Polla shrugged. "Not the first time I've had to take care of scared kids. Not the worst, neither—not by a long ways." She shook her head sadly. "I hate to see it, I really do. Children, specially babies, shouldn't be inflicted with the ills of the world."

Those words were the first thing which penetrated Helga's still-seething fury. Broke the rage, in fact, like a needle punctures a bubble.

Children, specially babies . . .

There hadn't been any children, of course, on the pirate ship. But . . . those "pirates," when all was said and done, had children of their own. Waiting for their fathers to return, back in a cluster of small fishing villages.

Helga's breath came in a little shudder. There would be no fathers returning this day. Nor any other. Helga's vengeance had destroyed those villages along with the fathers. Within weeks, she knew, as the word of the disaster spread, the nearby villages would start predating on their own. Men would come in little bands, raiding on the outskirts at first to test the rumor. Then, seeing it was true, would swarm the shattered villagers. Kill the men left—old or crippled, most of them—then sell the women and children into slavery.

Dozens of children, many of them no older than her own, had been doomed as well by Helga's vengeance. That vengeance had killed the fathers in less than an hour. It would torture their children for a lifetime.

"And so what?" she muttered, half snarling. She gave Polla a look which was almost one of appeal. But Polla only returned the look with those same soft, sad brown eyes.

"It's a pity," was all she said. "But that's the way of the world."

(((·))) (((·))) (((·)))

That night, as always, Jessep himself came down to the hold. The other senior men with "wives" aboard only visited them on occasion, but Jessep spent every night with Ilset folded into his arms.

"Folded," that is, using the term loosely. Sound carried in the hold, the partitioning cloths being no better insulators than thin linen ever is. Helga had been amused, impressed—and envious, truth to tell—at the sounds issuing from Jessep and Ilset's little partition each and every night since the voyage began. Middle-aged or no, head injury or no, Jessep Yunkers seemed to have neither difficulty nor reluctance keeping his healthy young wife entertained.

Unlike all the previous nights, however, Jessep came by her partition first. Helga heard him whisper through the cloth.

"Are you all right, ma'am?"

"I'm fine, First Spear." Then, moved by a sudden and powerful impulse: "Come in. Please."

A moment later, a bit gingerly, Jessep moved aside the cloth and stooped into her section. Helga was propped against a little pile of cushions, with her son asleep in the crook of her arm. With her right hand, she patted a space next to her.

"Sit. Please."

Jessep did as she bade him, although it was obvious that he felt very awkward in such close and casual familiarity with a noblewoman.

Helga gave him a smile which she intended to be reassuring. But, to her surprise, felt the smile dissolve into a little sob. A little sob which became wracking tears within seconds.

Now it was her turn to be enfolded in Jessep's embrace. There was nothing sexual about the contact, however. The man's strong arms reminded her of her father's, in the years now long past when she had been a child herself. And, though she'd always been a self-confident girl, there had been times when she'd needed that comfort.

"S'all right, girl," whispered Yunkers. " 'Ma'am,' I mean."

A laugh burst its way through the sobs. "Call me 'girl,' Jessep. Or 'lass' or whatever else you want. Just 'Helga' will do fine, for that matter."

She lifted her tear-blurred eyes and looked up at his blocky face. Smiling for the first time in hours.

"I'm not sure exactly how I feel about men in general, right at the moment. But I'm partial to fathers, that's for sure. And you remind me a lot of my own."

Jessep returned the smile with a little grimace. But it was a relaxed sort of wince. Even a bit of a serene one.

"Don't know as I've got his spirit. Sure as anything don't have his brains. But I'll do my best, young la—Helga."

She lowered her head and nestled it into his shoulder. "Tell me, Jessep. What do you think of vengeance?"

She felt his thick chest rise and fall, twice, while he considered his answer.

Then: "It's like this, girl. A bit of vengeance is a fine thing. Useful, now and then. But I think of it like a honing stone. You just want a little, when you need it, to keep the blade sharp. And that's it. Too much and . . . you'll wear the blade away in no time."

"I think that's good advice," she murmured. "And I think I'll take it from now on."

They said nothing further for perhaps ten minutes. Then Helga lifted her head again and gave Jessep's chest a little push. "Enough. Your Ilset will be getting fidgety."

Jessep chuckled. "She's not the jealous type, girl. And even if she were, I wouldn't have to lie anyway."

" 'Jealous' be damned!" snorted Helga. "I *know* the two of you. I should, having to listen to it every night."

Jessep flushed. Helga chuckled again. "So be off. Another ten minutes and she'll be so horny you might not survive the night. Old and decrepit as you are."

The speed with which Yunkers scurried out of her partition gave the lie to that last jibe. Not that any was needed.

Helga lay down and tried to find sleep. It wouldn't come at first, though. Jessep's advice was still rolling through her mind. Her brain seemed fixed on the image of a blade being sharpened to nothingness on a stone of hatred. After a time, the image of a blade shifted and she found herself remembering the face of Adrian's brother Esmond. A handsome face, it was. Very handsome, in fact—much more so than Adrian's, truth to tell. Even leaving aside Esmond's demigod physique, which Helga had seen more than once clad only in a loincloth, during the time she had spent as Adrian Gellert's "captured concubine."

But there was no attraction in the memory. There had always been something *wrong* about Esmond. Always, whenever he looked at her, something evil and hollow in the stare. As if he saw nothing in the woman her brother had taken for his own than just another hated Vanbert.

That's what Jessep's talking about, she realized. A splendid blade, worn down by endless honing. Such a waste.

But she didn't spend much time on the matter. By now, one thought following another, her mind was focused on the brother himself. Adrian Gellert, in whose arms she had spent many a night lying naked—and enjoying every minute of it.

New images came to her, then, of naked male body parts and a male face seen in focus—all of it and not just a leer. But there was no horror in these images. She thought she was done with that horror forever.

She hoped so. The problem she faced now was a problem she hoped she would always face, whenever she had trouble falling asleep. For which there was a simple and practical solution, even if she had found masturbation a poor substitute for the real thing, since she met Adrian Gellert.

Dammit, beloved enemy, if you're not there when I arrive—

I'll kill you. I swear I will.

She finally managed to get to sleep then, wafted away on new thoughts of vengeance. The methods by which she planned her possible murder of Adrian Gellert varied quite a bit, in their precise details. But all of them involved death from exhaustion.

CHAPTER THIRTEEN

Demansk's "tomorrow" had actually turned into four days before he was ready to strike against Governor Willech. He was learning that, in political as well as military maneuvers, logistics was always the lynchpin. It was easy to plan what amounted to a provincial coup d'etat, but actually implementing the deed required time to move the needed bodies around.

Granted, there weren't all that many bodies to move, compared to the forces involved in a major military campaign. And since most of the bodies were already in the provincial capital of Solinga, there wasn't the usual endless difficulty with fodder and supplies. But those advantages were offset by the fact that the bodies in question had minds of their own—and it was a lot harder to get officers to agree to a coup than to a straightforward military assault.

Demansk's own officers, the ones in command of the three brigades he'd brought with him to Solinga, were not the problem. Those three brigades had long been under Demansk's authority. Their officers and even the noncoms down to the First Spears of all the battalions had been personally selected by Demansk.

But, if at all possible, Demansk wanted to keep those troops on the sidelines. For political reasons, things would go much more smoothly—in the Confederate capital, if not here in Solinga—if it was local troops who carried out the purge.

And that would have the further advantage of keeping the bloodshed to a minimum. The two regiments in Solinga which were clearly loyal to Willech would be less likely to resist a coup being carried out by regiments they knew well. By now, many of the soldiers in those two regiments would have formed personal liaisons with the soldiers in the other four. They would have informal ways of getting assurance that the purge wouldn't touch their own ranks—as long as they stayed in their camps and barracks. Whereas dealing with Demansk's own troops, just arrived in the province, they would have no idea what to expect.

Which left the problem, of course, of solidifying the allegiance of the four regiments he wanted to use. Yes, three of the four commanders of those regiments were his own protégés. But a commander could not simply assume that all his officers and noncoms would follow orders, when it came to something as politically risky and irregular as a coup d'etat. So, even with those three regiments, Demansk had to take the time to have quiet private conversations with at least most of the key officers.

He did not bother trying to solidify the allegiance of the fourth regiment. He was quite certain, after meeting the commander of that unit, that the man would keep his soldiers in the barracks and out of the way. Which, for the moment, was quite good enough. Edard Noonan had all the earmarks of a politically savvy officer, the type who got his command in the first place through his efforts in the corridors of power rather than the fields of war. It was clear enough that he had sensed which way the wind was blowing. The last thing Noonan would do was try to protect a corrupt governor from a newly-elected Triumvir arriving in Solinga with the authority of the entire Council behind him.

Good enough, though Demansk. *And who knows? If Noonan proves capable in the field I may even let him keep his command.*

He turned his attention to the three officers in the room with him. It was the morning of the fourth day since he'd told Prit Sallivar to prepare for a trip to Vanbert to explain to the Council, on Demansk's behalf, just why he'd found it necessary to remove the provincial governor and assume direct control of the Emerald lands as Triumvir.

"I'll let you decide," he said, giving each of them in turn a steely gaze. At least, he *hoped* it was steely and not just menacing. Demansk was finding that as his power grew, he could no longer be as certain as he once was exactly how his expressions and mannerisms would be taken by those who saw them. Both pups and full-grown direbeasts yawned, after all. The expression was cute in the first; not, in the other.

"But," he warned, "make sure—whichever one of you is chosen for the post—that you understand clearly my conditions. The new military governor of the province will be *my* direct representative, not the Council's. So anything you do will reflect upon me, and I will take it badly if I am embarrassed."

He left the rest unsaid. Of all the men in Solinga, these three officers certainly didn't need to have the penalties for "embarrassing" Demansk spelled out in detail. They knew the details, already—had to, since they were about to carry them out.

The oldest of the officers, a trim gray-haired man named Kirn Thatcher, smiled faintly and gave a nod of his head toward the youngest.

"My vote's for Ulrich, then. He's Haggen gentry. They're an incorruptible lot of yokels, not like us decadent Vanberts proper."

That was Ulrich Bratten, whose coarse black hair and dark complexion indicated his heritage. He came from Hagga, the Confederacy's auxiliary nation in the far northeastern peninsula of the continent. Like the Roper League, Hagga retained the formal trappings of being an "independent realm," even if in practice it was simply a vassal of the Confederacy. It was not unusual at all for Haggens and Ropers to ignore the fiction altogether and simply enlist directly in the Vanbert army.

Bratten frowned. "Not sure that's such a good idea. The Emeralds have never been too fond of us Haggens. The gods know how many wars we fought with the bastards before Vanbert stifled the lot of us." He sounded vaguely distressed by the latter, as if the big and vigorous-looking young general officer regretted the passing of those lost days when Haggen and Emerald phalanxes clashed almost annually on the open plains between the two neighboring countries.

"I don't care about *that*," stated Demansk. "I'm not trying to cater to the Emeralds, just keep them contented." He ignored Thatcher's little snort of derision. It wasn't aimed at him, and he tended to share Thatcher's skepticism concerning the likelihood that the notoriously fractious Emeralds would ever be "content" about much of anything. "As long as the province is governed fairly and firmly, with no more tax-gouging and other illegal levies, that'll be good enough."

"I agree," added the third of the officers. That was Robret Crann. In age somewhere between Thatcher and Bratten, he was much heavier built than the other two general officers. He gave Thatcher a somewhat reproving glance. "I've been here longer than either Kirn or Ulrich. Personally, I've always found Emeralds easy enough to get along with. Sure, they use three words when one would do, and it always takes them an hour to get to the point. But they're not *that* impractical, when you get right down to it."

The look of reproof segued into a sly smile. "As any commander who's been swindled by an Emerald supplies provisioner can testify."

That brought a little laugh into the room from everyone, even though Thatcher's face was half-scowling. The famous metaphysical penchant of Emeralds did *not* extend to their merchants, who were stone-cold empiricists to a man.

Demansk planted his hands on his knees and straightened up on his couch. "Ulrich?"

The young officer hesitated for not more than a second. "I'll do it. Even though—" His young face, every line and angle of which practically exuded *vigor*, was not that of a happy man.

Demansk chuckled. "Relax, son. I'll be very surprised if the Island campaign is the last chance you'll ever have to prove your mettle in the field. Besides, you've already done that anyway—it's the reason you're the youngest brigade commander since . . . well, since me. And you didn't have my family connections. That promotion was won on the field, and well deserved."

He rose, took a few steps, and clapped Bratten on the shoulder.

"The truth is, the experience will be good for you. You know it as well as I do."

After a moment, Ulrich nodded. Although the rank he held was, in military terms, that of a general commanding a brigade, the formal Vanbert term for it was actually *magistrate in arms.* Above the level of battalion commander—whose rank was either "battlemaster" or simply "battalion," depending on whether the man who held the command was promoted from the ranks or received his appointment directly from the Council—the Confederacy of Vanbert drew no sharp lines between military and civil posts. Depending on the circumstances of the moment, a Vanbert leader was expected to be able to exercise competent authority in any field of political or martial endeavor.

Ulrich Bratten was one of the rare cases of a man who had risen to high command exclusively through his military ability. A fact which was explained, of course, by his ancestry. The "Confederacy" of Vanbert was theoretically a realm of equal nations, with no distinction made between the original twelve tribes and the various auxiliary nations which had been accreted to it over the centuries. The practical reality was different. With few exceptions, membership in the Council was reserved for those noblemen who could trace their ancestry back to the "First Twelve."

Of course, in the modern Confederacy, "tracing their ancestry" was a lot more complicated than it had been in former times. Here as in so many ways, Emerald philosophy and rhetoric had shaped the culture of their conquerors. The distinction between *Being* and *Becoming* had been the first to fall, once Emerald dialecticians got their hands on it.

"You'll need to hire a genealogist," murmured Robret Crann. The sly smile was back on his pudgy face. "I can recommend a very good one, by the way."

Ulrich scowled. Crann and Thatcher both enjoyed teasing the young general about his lowly origins. In Thatcher's case, the teasing had at least a solid basis. Thatcher, like Demansk, came from one of the Confederacy's long-established elite families.

Crann's claim to "noble Twelve blood," on the other hand, was stretched about as thinly as the tunic over his potbelly. If it hadn't been for his undoubted military skills, the claim would probably never have been accepted at all by the Council's Registrar, despite the size of the bribe. Everything about Robret Crann, from his penchant for gourmandizing down to his heavy accent, practically shrieked: *peasant from the east! parvenu! lowly soldier risen above his station!*

But . . . however grudgingly, the Registrar had not challenged the claim. Vanbert was practical, if nothing else. Officers like Crann were almost invariably popular with the soldiers, and nobody really wanted to irritate the army. Marcomann's dictatorship had been occasioned, among other things, by the festering resentment among his troops at the continuing prejudice against the poor easterners who filled most of its lower ranks.

"That's settled, then," said Demansk. He glanced at the hourglass on a small table in the corner of the room. "And it's time. Let's do it."

Demansk probably wouldn't have had any trouble himself smashing down Willech's door. But, since he had the largest soldier in Crann's regiment assigned to the task, he let him do it. The six-and-a-half-foot-tall giant, with the weight of full armor added to his own, went through the door like so much wet paper. He didn't even seem to break stride.

The other eight men in the squad followed on his heels, pouring into the Governor's luxurious suite like greatbeasts stampeding into a mansion. Demansk heard Willech shout something incoherent, heard a cough and a sigh, another shout—more like a shriek—from Willech, and then came into the room behind his soldiers. Doing his best to move ponderously, as suited a solemn magistrate about his duty, rather than sauntering gaily. Demansk had known Willech since they were both children romping in the corridors of Vanbert's public buildings. He'd detested the seven-year-old boy; the decades which had elapsed since had done nothing except give adult comprehension to the reasons for the detestation.

The first thing he saw, entering the room, was one of Willech's bodyguards. The regular soldier assigned the duty on a daily basis, this one. Demansk was sorry to see it, though not surprised. The soldier was lying on his back, clutching a spear wound in his belly. Blood was gushing through the fingers and spilling onto the plush red-violet carpeting. That had been the cough and sigh he'd heard.

The other bodyguard was Willech's personal one. No soldier, he, but a retired veteran of the arenas. The scar-faced ex-gladiator was standing in a corner of the room, pinned there by two squad members pressing their assegais against his ribs. His hands were raised pacifically, his sword lying on the floor not far from his feet.

Clearly enough, with the reflexes and mercenary nature of such a man, he'd made no attempt to stop the soldiers once he saw the force piling into the room. Willech be damned. Even if his master still hadn't regained his wits, judging from the continued screeching coming out of his mouth, his professional bodyguard had figured it out within a second. *A change in power. Time to find a new job.*

After a glance, Demansk ignored him. He gave another glance at Willech himself. The Governor was standing up, having apparently risen from a richly-upholstered stool spilled over behind him. The small writing desk at which he'd been working was spilled the other way.

There was nothing "hard and tight" about Willech's face now. The Governor's usually pale complexion was flushed so heavily that he seemed on the verge of outright apoplexy. His small hands were clutched into fists, which he was waving in front of him like an Emerald-style bare-handed fighter—except no real pugilist would have done it so awkwardly. So far, at least, the words coming out of his mouth were too incoherent to make any sense of. More like an animal's bay of fright and fury than a man's cry of distress.

That'll change, quick enough, thought Demansk. I'd better get the witnesses in, take advantage of that moment between pure fury and rational thought.

He turned and beckoned the two men standing in the corridor beyond. Both of them were elderly, with the stoop-shouldered appearance of scribes who had spent a lifetime hunched over state documents. The appearance was not far from the truth. The old men were actually magistrates of the city, not mere scribes. But Vanbert law, especially on a local and regional level, primarily involved the settlement of complex property claims. A magistrate on that level of the judicial pyramid spent most of his life consulting records and precedents.

Nervously, gingerly, the two entered the room. One of them gasped faintly, seeing the dying soldier on the floor. The other just looked away, his prim face contained and withdrawn. Neither of the men was there by choice. Demansk had selected them, in fact, precisely because they had the reputation for being among the few incorruptible judges in Solinga. That, and the fact that both of them were "First Twelve" by ancestry. He wanted no one claiming later that the witnesses were either bribed or, what was even worse, scatterbrained Emeralds.

The timing was perfect. Willech's words finally stumbled into something approximating coherence. Of a very profane nature, of course.

"Demansk—you fucking idiot! What do you think you're doing! I'll have you drawn and quartered, you stinking shit! I'll have you—"

He got no further. The giant soldier, whose mind was perfectly competent even if his body resembled that of a troll, strode forward and literally seized Willech by the scruff of the neck.

He even remembered his lines perfectly. "Outrageous! Public disrespect to the Triumvir!" He hauled the shrieking Willech into the center of the room and forced him to his knees, as easily as a man wrestling with a child.

"The penalty is clearly stated, sir," boomed the giant. "Do you wish the punishment applied immediately, or should I take this malefactor before the magistrates?"

"Malefactor," no less. Demansk made a note to talk to the giant in private afterward. He'd chosen the man simply for his size—he didn't even know his name—but clearly the fellow had a brain to go with the bulk. Given the new realities of Demansk's life, it could be handy having such a soldier as a personal bodyguard. The man was the sergeant of his squad, which also indicated some talent for leadership.

"No need to wait for the magistrates," said Demansk loudly. "As it happens, two are present with us." He turned slightly and gestured toward the two oldsters standing in the back of the room. "As you say, Sergeant, the penalty is clear and well known."

He'd intended to use two of his men specially prepared for the task, but decided to test this interesting ogre a little further. The sergeant had been present at the briefing, so he knew what Demansk wanted.

"Do me the service yourself, if you would."

"My pleasure, sir!" The huge soldier cast a glance at the upended writing table and made a little motion to one of his men. The squad member quickly turned the table right side up. In an instant, the giant relinquished his grip on the nape of Willech's tunic and seized his left wrist. Then, again manhandling him with ease, forced the hand flat onto the table top.

Like all squad sergeants, the man carried a short and heavy sword at his belt in addition to his assegai. The weapon was more like a large knife than a sword, really. It was primarily a ceremonial blade indicating his rank, which was carried in lieu of the three short javelins carried by front rankers. But most sergeants made sure the blade was kept sharpened in case of need.

This one was no exception. And his reflexes were excellent for such a big man. Almost instantly, he had his short sword drawn and then—*thunk!*—the heavy blade sheared through flesh and bone. The strike was clean and economical. The sergeant used his blade more like a farmwife chopping vegetables than a giant warrior wielding a sword. The four fingertips, severed at the first joint, simply rolled neatly aside. The wood of the table below was barely nicked.

It was done perfectly. The first offense penalty for publicly insulting an official was to have the entire hand removed at the wrist. Left hand if the man was right-handed, the reverse for left-handers. But the giant noncom had clearly remembered Demansk's instructions to the two men who were supposed to have done the work.

And, again, his thespianism was excellent also.

"My apologies, sir!" he boomed. "I seem to have missed."

"No matter, First Spear. That'll—"

The meaningless phrase which would have followed went unspoken. Demansk was watching Willech carefully, waiting to see if his scheme would work as he'd expected.

It did. Had Willech's hand been severed at the wrist, the man would probably have been in too much shock to have said much of anything. But simply losing the fingertips, as painful and shocking as it was in its own right, was not actually that serious an injury. Plenty of peasants and artisans suffered as much every year working in the fields and shops—and were back at work, as a rule, within a few days.

Willech was no peasant, but he was tough enough. After gawping for a moment at his severed fingertips and the blood staining the table top, he burst into another stream of profanity. These curses were uttered even more wildly than the first batch, and were only vaguely coherent.

Still, it was clear enough that they were aimed at Demansk. The Triumvir turned his head and gave the two magistrates in the back of the room a cold-eyed gaze. Both men were very pale-faced, now. One looked aside; the other down at his feet. But neither, obviously, was at all inclined to argue the matter.

When Demansk turned back, the huge sergeant was watching him. Demansk nodded slightly and the man went back on stage.

"Outrageous! Insulting the Triumvir again! And a *second* offense!"

It would all go quickly now, there was no reason to play charades any longer. As much as Demansk detested Willech, he did not enjoy watching this. Not in the least.

"The penalty for which is clear and well known also," he said firmly. "Attend to it if you would, Sergeant."

"My pleasure, sir!"

Again, the giant's hand moved much more quickly than one would expect from a creature his size. He had Willech by the scruff of the tunic again; and, with a short powerful jerk, forced his head down on the table. Willech's cheek was pressed flat to the wood. His eyes gaped; his mouth worked like a fish.

Finally, at the last instant, Willech understood just how

completely he had been manipulated. Demansk could see the comprehension in the Governor's eyes; see his mouth frantically trying to mouth new and different words.

Too late. The sergeant's sword came down again, and this was no farmwife's onion-chopping. The heavy blade missed the sergeant's own hand holding Willech by not more than half an inch. The giant knew his swordwork. The spinal cord was severed cleanly. It took two more quick blows to remove the head itself, but Willech had died instantly.

Knowing what was coming, Demansk and the other soldiers in the room had stepped aside. So the blood fountaining from Willech's neck simply gushed onto the carpet—and, with the most energetic first burst, splattered the leggings of the two magistrates standing at the back of the room. One of them simply squawked. The other stared at his bloody legs for a moment before lunging for the door. A moment later, Demansk could hear him vomiting noisily in the corridor beyond.

He gave the ex-gladiator in the corner a look. The man's face was perfectly composed, not pale in the least. Obviously, he'd figured out what was happening long before his erstwhile master.

"I'll want you to accompany the delegation which will be reporting this to the Council," Demansk rasped. "I trust your testimony will be reliable."

The former bodyguard actually managed a smile. A thin one, true, but a smile nonetheless. "Shocking, sir. Just shocking it was, the way the Governor insulted the Triumvir. And in public, too. 'T'wasn't a gray thing, not in the least."

Demansk nodded. He'd have Sallivar keep an eye on the man. But he really didn't expect any trouble from that quarter, especially after a suitably discreet bribe. And killing the man would probably cause more problems than it would solve.

Having made his decision, he turned to the next matter. "Sergeant, please see to it that the magistrates are escorted safely back to their office. And post a guard for them. There's likely to be some tumult in the streets today."

That was a delicate way of putting it, of course. A guard *for* the magistrates was just as much a guard *over* them. Sallivar would be leaving with the magistrates for Vanbert in the morning, and once on the road he'd make sure the magistrates never had a chance to talk to anyone until they reached the capital.

"Yes, sir." The sergeant started to get his men moving, but Demansk held up his hand.

"One thing also. Two, actually. First"—he pointed to Willech's head, which had rolled almost to the wall—"please take that and have it stuck on one of the spikes on the fence outside the Governor's Palace. I imagine the crowd in Solinga will be cheered by the sight."

"My pleasure, sir." Two strides and the sergeant had the grisly object off the floor. It was fortunate that he was such a big man. Willech had favored very close-cropped hair, much too short to hold. But with his enormous grip, the sergeant had no difficulty holding the skull like a normal-sized man would hold a goblet.

"And the second matter, sir?"

Demansk studied him for a moment. Then, abruptly: "Come to my quarters this evening. I'd like to speak with you further. You'll probably have to wait around a bit, I'm afraid. Things are likely to be hectic all day."

For the first time since he'd met him that morning—Crann had recommended the sergeant and his squad—Demansk saw an actual expression on the giant's face. He found the little smile rather interesting. It was not the rueful smile of a veteran acknowledging the army's inevitable "hurry-up-and-wait." There was a real gleam to the thing, as if the sergeant would enjoy whiling away a few hours watching the powers-that-were scrambling frantically out of the way of the powers-that-are.

From his accent, the man was another easterner, signed up for a twenty-five-year hitch in the army as the only alternative to poverty. Who, with no help at all from Emerald philosophers, had apparently drawn his own conclusions about the dialectic of Being and Becoming.

When he got there, Demansk's headquarters were just as much in frenzied semi-chaos as he'd expected. By the nature of things, a coup d'etat is a messier business than a straightforward battle in the open field. Even experienced and steady officers will get a little rattled and uncertain, at such a time. Partly because the tasks involved are somewhat new and different; mostly because the penalty for failure is certain to be worse than being defeated by a foreign enemy. A foreigner, at least with noble prisoners, will want ransom. A shaken but surviving old regime will settle for nothing less than heads on spikes on official fences—and *then* seize all your property for good measure.

Which, of course, was exactly what Demansk was doing himself.

"We've got most of it," said Ulrich Bratten as soon as the Triumvir came into the room which served as the nerve center for the coup. "The bulk of it was in the form of bullion in Willech's own mansion. We had to torture Willech's wife—tough bitch, that one—but we got the secret out of her."

Demansk nodded. He'd hoped the woman would have yielded without resorting to torture, but hadn't really expected it. He'd known Sandru Willech since they were both very young also—she was another child of the elite—and hadn't liked her any more than he had Willech himself. But no one had ever accused the woman of being a coward. Even as a girl, Sandru had been tough as well as nasty.

"Too bad. I would have preferred returning her to her family. You killed her afterward, yes?"

Ulrich nodded.

"So be it," said Demansk. "It's easier to explain a cremated corpse than a mutilated but living matron."

Since the thing was done, he dismissed it from his mind. "How much?"

When Ulrich told him, Demansk almost whistled with surprise. He'd known that Willech had been gouging the province mercilessly, but hadn't expected to find *that* much in the way of hidden treasure.

"The rest of it?"

Bratten shrugged. "Good chunks where you'd expect them, both in the Governor's Palace and the Treasury Office. I imagine more will turn up in his warehouses. Not much of that'll be bullion, of course, nor even coins and gems. Goods, mostly. Linens, spices, that sort of thing."

"Doesn't matter. Emeralds will deal in anything without quibble, as long as they can sell it. Speaking of which—"

Bratten jerked his head toward a door on the far wall. "Eleven of them are here already, sir. More to come, you can be sure of it. They're practically dancing in the streets out there. I told them you'd speak to them as soon as possible."

Demansk nodded and looked to Robret Crann. The older brigade commander had been the one Demansk had selected to oversee the purely military side of the coup. He'd saved aristocratic and distinguished-looking Kirn Thatcher to settle the nerves of the Vanbert nobility resident in Solinga. By now, they'd all be as jittery as a herd of greatbeasts with the smell of *predator* in the air. Demansk didn't mind the jitter—within limits, in fact, he wanted the nobility nervous and unsettled. But he didn't want the mess which an authoritative elite driven to open resistance could create.

"Things went pretty smoothly," reported Crann, "all things considered. Neither of Willech's regiments ever left their compounds, although the Fourth Jallink did mill around outside the barracks for a bit. They'll need some watching, but I don't expect any real trouble. Not after Willech's head goes up on the fence, for sure."

That was as good as could be hoped for. The resentment of the Fourth Jallink Regiment was inevitable, and expected. Willech's family were Jallink tribe themselves. But if the men of the regiment hadn't taken up arms by now, they certainly wouldn't do so once the news of Willech's execution reached them. Naturally, that would increase their resentment. But without a clear pole around which opposition could crystallize, all of those soldiers would start thinking about the risks involved if they rebelled and failed. Decimation was the traditional punishment for a unit which broke and ran on the field. The traditional penalty for units which rebelled and were crushed by the "lawful authority"—that being defined by whoever emerged triumphant, of course—was the exact opposite. One man out of ten would be left alive, to spread the word concerning the penalty for mutiny.

"All right, then," said Demansk. "In that case, I think I'll speak with the Emerald merchants right now. The sooner we can get this behind us, and get everyone's mind focused on the money they're making, the better."

Demansk always found Emerald merchants and guildmasters a bit ridiculous—although he was careful not to let any trace of his amusement show on his face. It wasn't that they weren't good at their business. Emerald merchants were as notorious as Islanders for their sharp and narrow trading practices—"acumen," they liked to call it—and, in most crafts other than weaving and papermaking, their artisans were still the best in the world. Superb jewelers and metalsmiths, for a certainty.

No, it was that same old "philosophical" penchant which made all Emeralds a bit comical to Confederates.

How many Emeralds does it take to slaughter a pig?

Eight. One to hold the beast, one to cut his throat, five—because it's a prime number and thus mystical—to convince the pig that Becoming a rasher is better than Being a swine. And the eighth, of course, to be the sophist arguing the pig's side of things.

At the moment, as it happened, the guildmaster of Solinga's shipwrights was holding forth on the significance of prime numbers. In this case, the mystical superiority of the number seven over the number five. Any resemblance to a lowly fishwife haggling in the marketplace was, of course, purely coincidental.

"It just can't be done for five thousand solingens, august Triumvir. Not a whole great ship like you're asking for, not even"—sourly, this last, since it would leave the sub-guild of decorators squealing like pigs themselves—"with such a simple and crude design." Ponderously: "Need at least seven thousand, and even at that"—more sourly—"a good thousand of it will have to be devoted to alms for the starving decorators."

Demansk decided he'd been polite enough, for long enough. "Bugger the decorators," he growled. "They can turn their skills just as easily to carving mantlepieces and headboards in the *mansions* of the *soon to be rich* merchants and tradesmen of the city as they can to carving useless sternposts for warships. I'll allow an extra five hundred just to tide them over the transition, that's all. Five thousand, five hundred per ship. That's *assuming*, of course, that you can deliver on your promise to build the size fleet I require in the time allowed. If you don't meet the schedule, the price will drop by five hundred solingens for every week you go past the deadline."

As one voice: Per week?? ABSURD!! Pardon, august and mighty (etc. etc.) Triumvir, sir, but you just don't understand—

And so it went, for another four hours. At the end, feeling more exhausted than he could ever remember feeling after a battle, Demansk tottered out of the room back into his command center. By then, he was relieved to see, Prit Sallivar had arrived.

"I held them to six thousand, two hundred," he said weakly. "With a three hundred solingen penalty per fortnight."

Sallivar pursed his lips. " 'Bout what I expected. The penalty's meaningless, of course. Those swindlers will have that fleet ready a month early—you watch—and then start squalling that they deserve a bonus. Six thousand per ship, now . . ."

Demansk watched as his banker did some complex calculations in his head. Then Prit shrugged and said: "It'll do, Verice. Not even that tight, really. Willech, the bastard, had a third again more treasure stored up than I'd estimated. We'll have a sizeable cushion." He gave Demansk a wintry smile. "Even enough to hire this bizarre new bodyguard you seem to have your heart set on. Although I hope you don't start trying to put together an entire unit of such trolls. The food bill alone would bankrupt us."

Demansk frowned, puzzled. Sallivar pointed toward the door with his thumb. "Forgotten already? Sad, what age does. The man's been waiting out there for hours."

The sergeant. Demansk had indeed forgotten all about him.

"I'll see him in my private quarters. Give me ten minutes to wash up a bit."

The sergeant seemed a bit ill at ease when he came into Demansk's salon, but not as much as the Triumvir had expected. Oddly, the giant's uneasiness seemed to increase after Demansk ordered his three regular bodyguards to leave them alone.

"I'd have thought you'd prefer not having armed men standing at your back," he said almost, but not quite, slyly. "What with old village sayings about dead men telling no tales running through your head."

The sergeant seemed to flush a bit. Then, after discreetly clearing his throat: "T'ain't thet, sir. I was na worret 'bout *thet.*"

Demansk found it interesting that the man's eastern accent was so much more pronounced now than it had been when the sergeant was, so to speak, "on stage."

The next words confirmed the guess.

"Don' think tha's a man in tha regiments—nor yars, naebit—what does no trust ya, sar. A soldier's general, yar know'd t'be. 'Tis just . . ."

The huge soldier glanced around the room nervously. " 'Tis just tha I don' know wha ta 'spect, sar. No used ta thet. Man o' my station does no speak privately with na gen'ral, naebit less na Triumvir."

His head jerked a bit, as if he was sternly reminding himself of a silent vow. When he spoke again, the thick accent was almost gone and the clean-speaking sergeant of the drama was back.

"Sorry, sir. I imagine the Triumvir would like me—me and my squad—to serve him as bodyguards. That's what my men were thinking, anyway. In the new times a-coming, you'll be having some use for a bigger guard, they're thinking."

Demansk was not surprised to discover that the sergeant had mentioned this upcoming private audience with his men—nor that the squad had apparently spent some time discussing the matter. The squad was the basic unit in the Vanbert army. Except in cases of extreme casualties, soldiers usually served their entire twenty-five-year stretch in the same squad. Half of the men in it would be related by blood, and almost all of them would come from the same village. "Squad deep" was the way Confederate veterans would refer to a man or thing which could be completely trusted.

What Demansk *did* find a bit surprising—and certainly interesting—was the actual assessment the squad had made. "New times a-coming," indeed. As an officer, even a popular one, he was and had been for years insulated from the quiet thinking which percolated through the ranks. But he'd never made the mistake which many officers made of not realizing that such thinking *was* going on.

The perspicacity of the squad, and the obvious intelligence of its sergeant, crystallized a decision he'd been weighing in his mind. As it happened, he *had* originally intended to use them as bodyguards. But he decided he had a better purpose for them.

First, though, he had to see how far he could push the matter.

"And what do you think of such 'new times' yourself, Sergeant?"

The giant stared at him for a moment. Then, sloping his shoulders like a greatbeast leaning into a load, he said softly: "'Twere—it was—a sad day for my folk when Old Marcomann died, sir. Say what they will about his so-called 'tyranny,' but it never touched me or mine. Except to lighten the taxes and give a poor man a chance. All of which went like the dew when the *sattra*—uh, noblemen and their Council got back on top of things."

The choked off word had been *sattrasacht.* An old word in the eastern dialects, it translated as "gutworms"—a type of intestinal parasite which was prevalent in poverty-striken agricultural regions of the Confederacy. It was the private term which the Confederacy's peasantry used to refer to the Vanbert aristocracy.

"Marcomann *did* leave something of a mess behind, Sergeant." Demansk's words were spoken in the tone of an observation, not a reproof.

The sergeant shrugged. Then, for the second time that day, Demansk saw the little gleam in a troll's smile.

"Yes, sir. But me and my boys figure you're a lot smarter than Old Marcomann, even if he was a great man and all."

Demansk nodded abruptly. "Done, then. I've a different job for you than bodyguard, Sergeant. I need you to keep an eye on Willech's old regiments for me, especially the Fourth Jallink. I'll give you and your squad the authority to sit in on all staff meetings, *armed,* and oversee everything they do." He stifled a yawn. "It's too late tonight to go into the details—truth is, I have to figure them out myself—but that's the gist of it."

The uncertainty was back on the giant's face. So was the accent in his voice. "Tha will no hart'ly allow no sergeant na 'is squad to do *thet,* sar."

"Three things, Sergeant. First, let's start with your name. What is it?"

The sergeant blinked. "Ma name? 'Tis Forent Nappur, sar."

"Second. I'll need you to keep that accent under control. Outside of your squad quarters, at any rate. Can you do that?"

Another blink. "Ah—yes, sir. I can do that. Sorry, sir. I'm just a bit unsettled at the moment."

Demansk waved the apology aside. "I understand. Not a problem, as long as you keep an eye on it. You know the *sattrasacht,* Forent Nappur. They'll forgive much, but never poor diction."

The sergeant choked off a little laugh. Demansk smiled, and then finished the day's work.

"And—third thing—it'll not be *sergeant* any longer. It's Forent Nappur, Special Attendant to the Triumvir, from this moment forward."

CHAPTER FOURTEEN

That explains it, said Raj. ***No wonder he's much more sophisticated than you'd expect.***

yes, chimed in Center. **the taking of hostages is common practice in iron age cultures.**

Adrian ignored them both, as he had learned to do easily enough in the many months since the odd duo had entered his mind. He kept his concentration entirely on Prelotta. Mostly, he kept his concentration on the imperative need not to burst into open laughter.

The young chief's statement was still reverberating in his mind. Adrian was trying to picture Prelotta spending five years as a boy in Vanbert, the capital city of the Confederacy. The hairdo alone . . .

Something in his tight face must have been interpreted correctly by the leader of the Reedbottom tribe. Prelotta's scarred face crinkled.

"No, no—I assure you! Not even a rash and foolhardy Southron boy was stupid enough to wear his native dress in Vanbert. Other than my pale skin and light hair, I appeared quite the normal civilized young lad."

His fingers brushed along his forehead. "Of course, the tattoos were already there, so the disguise really fooled no one. But at least I hadn't had the ceremonial scars added yet."

That made sense, Arian realized. Prelotta would have had the scars added later than usual. The normal custom among Southrons, although the specific practices varied from tribe to tribe, was to have boys tattooed at the age of four and undergo the other, more brutal, ceremonies upon reaching puberty. Prelotta had been turned over as a hostage to the Confederacy at the age of twelve, following a clash between the Southrons and the Vanberts which went badly for the tribesmen. That meant he wouldn't have been able to undergo the tribal "coming of age" ceremonies until he was seventeen.

Which, for the most part, was probably an advantage. A seventeen-year-old would have had an easier time dealing with the pain than a younger one. Except—

He winced. Prelotta, showing the perceptiveness which Adrian had come to expect from him, grinned widely. Then, grabbed his crotch in an exaggerated protective gesture.

"Yes, the circumcision was awful. I have to say—privately, of course—that you Emeralds have the right of it there. Cut the foreskin off while the newborn babe is still indignant about everything anyway."

Not for the first time, Adrian found himself liking Prelotta. Partly that was because the Reedbottom chief was far more sophisticated than any other Southron Adrian had yet encountered. But, mostly, it was simply because he'd come to like the man. Granted, Prelotta's fundamental view of the world was still that of a barbarian. But Adrian found a *thoughtful* barbarian—as rare as such were—to be less offensive than most Vanbert aristocrats. Or Emerald ones, truth be told.

Yes, Prelotta's basic view of things divided the world into nothing more complicated than takers and takees. Yes, he gave no more thought to the use of force and violence as the solution to most any problem than a direbeast. But in those respects, once you stripped away the veneer, he was really no different than most civilized noblemen. Adrian even found it a pleasure not to have a straightforward discussion of a plundering war dressed up with sophistries.

Really, the only thing Adrian still held against Prelotta was his *smell.* And even that, he suspected, was simply due to Prelotta's care in maintaining a proper outward respect for Southron custom. Left to his own devices, Adrian was almost certain that Prelotta would have joined him and the other Emeralds in their daily bath—instead of "cleaning" himself by simply slathering on another layer of oil.

Thinking of the large public baths which Adrian and his Emeralds had insisted on building as soon as they arrived in Marange brought mixed emotions.

Sadness, because his brother Esmond no longer participated in that ancient and treasured ritual of Emerald daily life. Since Esmond had recovered from the wounds Adrian inflicted on him during their duel, his brother had restricted himself exclusively to the company of the Southron tribesmen who had adopted him as one of their champions. (Esmond's defeat in the duel had not been held against him. All tribesmen except Reedbottoms considered slings a fundamentally sneaky weapon.) He exchanged fewer than twenty words a week to *any* Emerald, even the soldiers who had once been his own troops.

On the other hand, Esmond's self-imposed exile had been a blessing for Adrian, from a tactical point of view. At one time, when they served under King Casull of the Isles, Esmond had been the commander of the so-called "Sea Striker regiment of Emerald Free Companions." *Hired killers* would have been a more accurate term. Although most of the five hundred Strikers were Emerald in origin, they had taken service as mercenaries with the islanders.

All of them, with only a few exceptions, had accompanied Esmond and Adrian to Marange—as had every single member of Adrian's own unit of two hundred arquebusiers, the "Lightning Band." Counting the small horde of camp followers who had attached themselves to the two mercenary units, Adrian and Esmond had brought well over two thousand people with them to Marange.

The loyalties of the Lightning Band had never been in doubt, given a rupture between Adrian and Esmond. Adrian's brother had been quite willing to use the Band's special skills in battle. But he'd never shown any particular fondness or interest in their newfangled gunpowder gadgetry, other than for the effects they could produce. They were Adrian's men, pure and simple.

With the Strikers, the situation was more complicated. They were lightly armored infantrymen, using traditional weapons—basically, javelins and slings for missiles and short swords for close-in work. Once Esmond had established his authority among them, the Strikers had taken to him quite warmly. Esmond really was a superb battlefield commander, even leaving aside his charismatic personality. Under his command, the Strikers had won much booty and suffered relatively few casualties in the doing.

Under normal circumstances, they would surely have sided with Esmond against Adrian. But Esmond's increasing madness had driven them away. Not his cruelties, so much as his rapid adoption of Southron manners. Mercenaries or not, most of the Strikers were Emeralds—and Emeralds, in their own way, were the world's most notorious cultural conservatives. Whether or not any individual Emerald mercenary soldier had ever read any of the Emerald philosophers, he respected those who had. The fact that Esmond was a cultured man from a good Emerald family had counted for much with them. As much, truth to tell, as the fact that Esmond had been a winner in the Pan-Emerald Games.

After the duel, however, Esmond's break from Emerald customs had been rapid and extreme. As soon as he had recovered sufficiently from his wounds, Esmond had even insisted on undergoing the scarification ritual in order to become officially adopted into the Grayhills, the largest tribe of the barbarians and the one whose chief, Norrys, had just been elected as Chief of Chiefs of the loose Southron confederation. He had begun growing his hair to the length needed for the elaborate hairstyles favored by Southron warriors, and had stopped coming to the public baths altogether. Those who had spoken with him in recent weeks said he was beginning to smell as ripe as any barbarian.

That had been too much for the Strikers. Some of the Strikers were themselves Southron in origin—the Strikers, like all mercenary outfits, had people from all over the world. But even most of them had decided to give their allegiance to Adrian. Having spent some years in a largely Emerald cultural environment, most of the former barbarians had no desire to go back to a Southron lifestyle. As one of them put it to Adrian: "It's hard to give up the habit of being clean, once you've learned the trick. Dirt and grease *itch*, dammit."

So, in the end, not more than thirty Strikers had broken ranks with the others and gone with Esmond. And then all of them *except* Southrons came scampering back the next day, after discovering that Esmond expected them to undergo the same bloody rituals. The rest of the unit, at a formal vote, had decided to give their allegiance to Adrian.

Adrian had promptly appointed Esmond's former lieutenant Donnuld Grayn as the new commander of the Strikers. Grayn was a capable man, and Adrian wanted to be able to give his full attention to expanding the Lightning Band and trying to get the Southrons to adopt at least some of his new weapons and tactics.

The end result was that Adrian had almost seven hundred men under his command, and Esmond was left with nothing more than the status he could achieve for himself as a war leader among the Grayhills. It was as good a result from the rupture as could have been hoped for.

Adrian forced his mind away from Esmond. What was done was done. Or, as the famous phrase from Jopha's *Observations on Fate* put it: "The past is the one path which cannot be retraced." And before this latest little digression, he had been on the verge of reaching agreement with Prelotta.

He leaned forward on his stool, planting his elbows on his knees and lacing his fingers together. For a moment, as he collected his thoughts, he studied the rug on which both his stool and Prelotta's were resting.

It was an interesting object, as well as a decorative one. As could be expected in the quarters of a major chief, the rugs which covered the floor were very finely made. As were the tapestries which were hung on the walls of Prelotta's private tent within the pavilion.

They had been made by local weavers—Reedbottom ones, rather. Southrons had no need to import rugs. In fact, their own rugs and tapestries were one of the few manufactured items for which there was a ready market in the civilized lands to the north. That was especially true for Reedbottom products. The vivid colors which the northeastern weavers were able to obtain from various of their marsh plants were quite striking.

But what Adrian found more interesting about the rug he was studying was the design itself. Most Southron weavers favored the depiction of scenes from legend on their rugs and tapestries. Usually a scene from one of the exploits of the Southrons' mythical hero Kladdo, although often a scene depicting one or another of their multitude of gods and goddesses.

Reedbottom rugs were often different, in this even more than in their vivid coloring. As was the rug he was staring at.

A new cult had arisen among the Reedbottoms about a century earlier, founded by a man known only as Young Word. The odd name was appropriate, perhaps. The man had not lived much beyond his mid-twenties, before an irate sub-tribe had murdered him in a fit of outrage at Young Word's heretical mouthings. The execution had had the usual Southron flourish—the heretic had been disemboweled and his entrails spread across the large bush to which he'd been tied.

But his cult had grown, nevertheless—explosively so, over the past generation. His followers had seized upon the manner of his death, added it to Young Word's own remembered sermons, and created out of the mix an elaborate framework of beliefs and rituals which had proven too popular to be subjected to much in the way of persecution after the first generation. By now, from what Adrian could determine, at least a third of the Reedbottoms were adherents to the "Young Word" faith.

In fact, the cult had begun spreading beyond the Reedbottoms themselves. Although the northeastern tribe was still the center of the new creed, there were Young Word devotees scattered throughout the southern half of the continent.

The rug, placed as it was in the most prestigious place in Prelotta's tent—right under the Stool of Chieftainship—indicated that Prelotta himself was a supporter of the creed. Or, at least, did not hesitate in making his partiality to it publicly known.

not surprising, interjected Center. **prelotta's ambitions, as we**

have already ascertained, extend beyond the usual barbarian limits. there are great advantages to monotheism for such a one.

It was an odd thought, but Adrian found himself agreeing. The rug's intricate and abstract design contained a subtle message, if one considered it carefully. The Young Word cult had incorporated the image of entrails spread across branches into all their artwork. There were no "scenes," as such. Simply an intertwining of red and green strands, coiling about in a complex manner.

Complex—but not chaotic. Always, one's eyes were drawn to the center. Always, one's mind was given a reinforcement of the principal tenet of the Young Word: that all reality, all men and gods, were but manifestations of the one Fixed God. "Assan," the prophet had named that deity, using the term for the mystical ancestral spirit which was common to all Southrons.

True enough, came Raj's thought. ***In the crude material world as in the spiritual one: all things must have a center. That's the best justification for monarchy you could ask for. Way better than "I've got you by the throat today," which is about as sophisticated as political theory has ever gotten here on Hafardine. In the north as much as the south or the Islands.***

Adrian stifled his momentary urge to dispute that claim. That was his initial impulse, but . . . He'd made the mistake, once, of bragging about the subtleties of the Emerald philosopher Llawat's political theories. Raj and Center had mercilessly shredded his opinion. The gist of their argument, to which Adrian had no real counter, was that Llawat's supposedly sophisticated pyramidal schema for how a society *should* be organized amounted to nothing more than giving organized plunder an elaborate set of fancy clothes.

Just so. As usual, Raj's words carried an undertone of humor. ***"My officials and scribes and priests and accountants have you by the throat today." That's what Llawat's blather amounts to.***

Prelotta cleared his throat. It was a polite reminder to Adrian that he'd been silent for some moments and that it was perhaps time to return to the subject under discussion.

"My apologies, Chief." Adrian unlaced his fingers and spread them outward, indicating the expanse of the rug with the gesture. "I was just taken with admiration for the design."

Prelotta looked down at the rug. Then, glanced into the corner where his chiefly paraphernalia was kept. "Ah, yes. I'm partial to it myself. But I've never seen any need to be exclusive about such things. Not at the moment, certainly."

Adrian didn't need to look into the corner to understand the subtleties of the remark. Prelotta, like all Southron chiefs, had the usual symbols of authority. The ceremonial ax, indicating his power; the stool he sat upon, intricately carved and made from the horns of a greatbeast, indicating his judgement; and the clutch of birds' eggs in a basket, indicating his fecundity. There was no symbol, needless to say, celebrating his wisdom. Much less his mercy.

Later for that. So long as authority comes only from having a hand on a throat, wisdom and mercy are a moot point.

"True enough," murmured Adrian. Then he raised his head and gave Prelotta a direct gaze.

Again, he pointed to the rug. "If your weavers can do such intricate work, relying only on designs from their own heads instead of nature, I imagine they could do the same working with steel and iron."

Prelotta pursed his lips. The expression, combined with the scars, gave his face a particularly grotesque appearance.

"I should think so," he replied forcefully. "If not the weavers themselves, then certainly other members of my tribe. We *do* have blacksmiths, remember."

Adrian hesitated. "Yes, of course. But, in my experience, blacksmiths are often set in their old ways. It might perhaps be better—"

"Not *my* blacksmiths." Prelotta inclined his head toward the corner where his chiefly paraphernalia rested. "One of them made that Ax of Power, you know. The blade is quite sharp, for all the curlicues on the handle. Perfectly capable, I assure you, of removing the head of any stubborn blacksmith."

Seeing the little wince on Adrian's face, Prelotta chuckled. "You worry too much, my delicate Emerald friend. Blacksmiths are especially prone, among Reedbottoms, to belong to the Young Word. Not hidebound by tradition at all, most of them. I expect no difficulty."

The humor vanished. "But it is not your concern, in any event. Understand this, Adrian Gellert. I will not agree to your proposal *unless* you agree to train my own people in the design and manufacture of your new weapons, as well as their use. That is the one and only point on which I am not prepared to bargain."

very smart chief. Center's voice almost had a tone in it. Respect, that would have been. **he understands, where most barbarians do not, that it is the ability to make a weapon rather than use it which is the ultimate source of military power.**

Yes. Agree to it, Adrian, urged Raj. ***The long-term benefits will be even greater than the short-term. Not for the Confederacy as it is, of course, but that thing is doomed anyway.***

Adrian had had no intention of refusing. He was simply a bit skeptical about whether Prelotta's people were able to do what their chief wanted of them. But, glancing again at the rug, he decided that they might well be. And it wasn't really his problem, anyway.

"Agreed, Chief." It was his turn to clear his throat. "But in return—"

Prelotta grinned—that made for an even more grotesque face—and held up his hand.

"Please! Now that negotiations can begin, we will need refreshments." He clapped his hands loudly; an instant later, a slave appeared through the flap which separated the inner chamber of the tent from the rest of the huge pavilion.

"You will want beer, I assume."

No. You need a clear head, lad. I'd—

Adrian sent some very unkind thoughts toward Raj. "I'm not a child, damnation!" were the only ones of them which weren't obscene.

"No, thank you, Chief. Something else." Inspiration came to him. "Whatever you'll be having."

Prelotta's grin widened, and Adrian felt his stomach lurch.

"Ah. Amazing!" exclaimed the Chief. "Most people not from our tribe—Southrons as much as civilized folk—detest our favored beverage."

Thank the gods I can't actually taste anything, remarked Raj idly. ***The squeezings from swamp weeds, added to rancid milk, all of it left to stew for weeks . . .***

very nutritious, though, added Center. **assuming you survive.**

The concoction was just as awful as Adrian feared. And politeness forced him to drink three cups of it, in the long hours of haggling which followed.

In the end, however, he did survive. And at least he had the satisfaction of knowing he'd driven a good bargain, as he tottered his way back to the section of Marange which his soldiers had turned into their own quarter of the city.

It was almost nightfall when he arrived before the building which his men had erected to be his own dwelling as well as headquarters. No tent, this, but a wooden structure—and a well-built one, at that. His men might be mostly Emeralds, but many of them had served for a time in the Confederate army. They had learned the Vanbert methods of erecting real fortifications everywhere they went. And so, in the months since their arrival at Marange, they had turned their section of the sprawling port into a fortified city within a city.

Adrian was surprised to see a group of strangers lounging at ease in front of the building. And no Southrons, these, but men from the north. Vanberts, from the look of them, perhaps a dozen in all—and obviously soldiers, even without their weapons.

The youngest of them caught his eye. The man was smiling at him oddly, almost as if he knew him. Adrian couldn't remember ever meeting the fellow before, but . . . there was something about his face . . .

observe, Center said.

A grid formed over the young man's face, emphasizing the lines of contour. Next to it appeared a face Adrian remembered perfectly. The resemblance, now that Center had brought it into focus, was unmistakable.

allowing for the difference in gender, the probability is 95%± 2. unity, for all practical purposes.

"Gods," whispered Adrian. His stomach, already uneasy, began fluttering wildly. An instant later, doubling up, he vomited all over the ground.

The paroxysm of regurgitation submerged all other concerns. Not until he was finished did Adrian notice the presence of the man on one knee next to him.

"Gods, that stinks," said a cheerful young voice. "Tell me what it is later, so I can be sure to avoid the stuff. But in the meantime . . . are you done?"

Adrian nodded weakly. A pair of strong hands seized him by the armpits and hoisted him easily back onto his feet. Adrian found himself staring at the face whose resemblance to another had sent his emotions whirling.

"Are you positive?" asked the young man, now grinning. "If there's any doubt at all, best you barf it up now. My sister's waiting for you inside, and—you know this much, I'm sure—the gods help you if you puke all over *her.*"

CHAPTER FIFTEEN

Marange was the most bizarre city Helga had ever seen. It reminded her of a madhouse more than anything else. There seemed to be no rhyme or reason to the way anything was designed or constructed, outside of the immediate harbor area itself.

Docks and piers, in the nature of things, look much the same the world over. She would have said the same about buildings in general, before she encountered Marange. Granted, architectural styles varied from one nation to the next. Still, all towns and cities of her acquaintance, even the exotic islander city of Vase, had a logic to them.

Not so Marange. Although the city was technically a Southron one—the only real "city" anywhere in the southern half of the continent—its population was not more than a third Southron by birth. At least, its more-or-less permanent population. And even the Southrons dwelling there were, for the most part, outlaws and outcastes from their own barbarian society.

The inhabitants of Marange were the flotsam and jetsam of the whole world. They came from everywhere; every part of the continent, and every island. The only thing they really had in common was that, for whatever reason, they had been discarded by their own folk—or, as often as not, forced to flee for their lives.

Marange only existed at all for two reasons. The first was that, located at the highest point of the Blood River which was navigable by seagoing ships—almost 150 miles upstream from the ocean itself—it made a good and safe harbor. Whatever trade did take place between the southern barbarians and the rest of the world was channeled through Marange.

Secondly, it provided the Southrons with a gathering place for their annual intertribal assembly. That annual assembly, which took place in the autumn, was a great event for barbarian society. Its official purpose was to elect the Chief of Chiefs and settle whatever intertribal quarrels could be settled short of warfare. But it also provided them with a combination fair, trading mart, wife-seeking market, athletic contests, jousts, carnivals—and, of course, the most important time in the year for buying exotic goods brought from the civilized lands to the north.

Marange nestled against the eastern bank of the Blood River. Beyond the city's limits—insofar as it could be said to have any definite "limits"—stretched a rolling plain which provided a suitable meeting ground for the assembled barbarian tribes. During the assembly, that plain was well-nigh covered with the tents and huts erected by the tribesmen. Those temporary dwellings ranged in size and splendor from holes dug in the ground and covered with branches to the gigantic pavilions erected by the tribal chiefs.

The city itself had a similar cacophony. There was no real government ruling the place. Technically, Marange was neutral territory not allied to any tribe, and thus came under the official and direct jurisdiction of the Chief of Chiefs. But, in the real world, a Chief of Chiefs was a largely ceremonial post. The Chief of Chiefs had no residence separate from his own tribe. And, once the assembly was over, the Chief of Chiefs would depart the area and spend the rest of the year living in whatever portion of the southern continent his tribe happened to lay claim over.

As a result, the Chief of Chiefs paid no attention to Marange. For all practical purposes, the only order and authority which existed in the city was whatever its own inhabitants provided. And since they, in turn, were hardly any less tribal in their own way than the

Southrons, no one had ever really tried to exercise authority over the city as a whole. Each group of outcasts tended to congregate in its own quarter. What "order" existed was whatever they saw fit to provide—and then, only for their own.

Needless to say, this posed a perilous situation for an uninformed visitor. "Dangerous as Marange" was a saying which could be found in all the major languages of the north and the Islands.

For most visitors, however, the danger was not too great. That was for the simple reason that most visitors were northern and Islander merchants, and each of those groups had their own well-established quarters in the city. The northerners—mostly Emeralds—directly north of the harbor area; the Islanders—mostly from Vase—directly east. A merchant doing business in Marange quickly learned to establish a firm relationship with the resident "traders' associations," which would provide him both with secure lodgings and an armed escort whenever he found it necessary to take his goods inland to the fairs themselves.

Anyone else took their chances. Emeralds might try to find a refuge in the "Emerald Quarter," located in the city's southern portion. But even for an Emerald, that was chancy. The Emeralds who lived there were either half-breeds or criminals or, usually, both—and despite the vigor with which they defended their "Emerald" status, seemed no less inclined to rob and murder an Emerald than anyone else.

Outcasts from the Islands had a similar quarter, located more or less in what could be called, more or less, Marange's "downtown."

There were also, scattered here and there and intermingled with various tribal groups, portions of the city inhabited by people from the Vanbert Confederacy. These areas were even more dangerous, however. The inhabitants were not so much criminals, in the professional sense of that term which could be applied to the Emerald or Islander exiles, as they were people so destitute and desperate that they had fled the Confederacy for the shaky refuge of Marange. Runaway slaves, for the most part.

Finally—so Sharlz Thicelt discovered with a little investigation as soon as they arrived and moored at one of the piers—there was a new sector in the city. Located next to the familiar "Emerald Quarter," it was being called the "New Emerald Quarter." The distinction was apparently not a subtle one. It seemed that shortly after their arrival, one of the "new Emeralds" was robbed and murdered by a gang of Emerald criminals—and the rest of the "new Emeralds" had immediately responded by massacring every member of that gang, some dozen or so others who happened to have the misfortune to be in the area, and had then for good measure burned down a goodly chunk of the old Emerald Quarter in order to create a no-man's-land between it and the new complex of residences they were erecting on the southern outskirts of the city. Which, Thicelt was told, resembled a Confederate army camp more than anything else.

"That's our boys," announced Jessep with satisfaction, upon being told the news. "Are you ready, girl?"

Helga nodded. Not more than five minutes later, she was being escorted to her destination through the streets of Marange by Jessep's hundred as well as Trae's unit of arquebusiers—all of them scowling at every resident of the city they came upon. They were a most ferocious looking crew, and even the crowded streets and alleys of Marange opened up before them.

Needless to say, neither Helga herself nor any of the other women nestled in the center of this column were molested along the way. The only man who did have the temerity to ogle them found himself lying bloody-faced on the street seconds later.

One of Trae's men did for that. The arquebusiers had discovered early on that a gun-butt, reversed, made an excellent club in close quarters. Trae had to restrain the man from shooting his victim; and only managed to do so by appealing to the need to conserve ammunition. Helga's escort was practically bristling, like a very large dog will when he encounters strange mutts.

When they finally arrived at the New Emerald Quarter, Helga saw that it did indeed resemble a Confederate army camp. "Resembled," in fact, was too weak a term. For all practical purposes, at least in terms of its design and construction, it *was* a Confederate camp—and one of the "permanent" ones, too, not one of the hastily-erected field camps which the army would use for a single night.

"Good construction," grunted Jessep approvingly. "Too heavy on the wood—extravagant, that, not to mention a bit crude. But—"

Helga chuckled. "Half of the country around here is one great big forest. So why *not* use heavy logs? Easier than planing boards, when you get down to it."

Jessep didn't argue the point. Clear enough, the veteran would feel happier himself once they got within those reassuring walls.

Doing so took a bit of effort. The soldiers guarding the gates were none too keen to allow a large group of armed strangers into their compound—the more so once they got a look at Trae's arquebuses. They were quite familiar with the devices, obviously. Helga could see at least four arquebuses trained on them from watchtowers along the wall.

Trae was doing the negotiations instead of Jessep, since he was far more fluent in the Emerald language. His task wasn't made any easier by the fact that Helga insisted he keep her own identity a secret. Whether that was necessary or not was pure guesswork on her part. But she and her father had kept her carefully secluded since her return, especially once they realized that she was pregnant with Adrian Gellert's child. The likelihood that someone from Marange would think to take that information to the Vanbert capital, more than two thousand perilous miles away, on the off chance that someone would be willing to pay for it, was unlikely. But if a stray remark happened to reach one of the northern merchants who was returning to civilization anyway . . .

No. Best keep it a secret for as long as possible. Outside of Jessep and Trae and Thicelt, the only people here who knew that Adrian Gellert was her child's father were the women. And she trusted them to keep their mouths shut.

Eventually, the guards agreed to let in a delegation. Trae, a dozen of his soldiers, Jessep and Ilset, and Helga herself. Then, twice that number of guards insisted on escorting them to the building which Adrian used for his dwelling.

As they approached, Helga found herself more nervous than she could ever remember being in her life. Then, when she discovered that Adrian was not home—one of his officers explained that he was meeting with a Southron chief—she found herself more upset than she would have believed possible.

But she let none of it show. The officer recognized her, as it happened. His name was Donnuld Grayn, and Helga could remember him as one of the soldiers in Adrian's company during the time she had spent as Adrian's "captive."

Grayn was affability itself, once he understood who she was. Quickly, he ordered the escort to let the rest of Helga's people into the compound, and invited Helga and Jessep and Ilset to wait for Adrian in his apartments. Trae and his men waited outside, with Grayn keeping them company.

And then . . . she waited. Perched on a couch, the baby in her arms, all of her anxiety returning with a vengeance. She was too preoccupied to even notice the surroundings, or pay any attention to Ilset and Jessep's idle chitchat. She had waited for this moment—yearned for it, in truth—for well over a year. Now that it was here, she was almost gasping for breath. Her worst fears surged to the fore.

He won't even remember me. Barely, at best. By now he must have another woman. Some exotic Southron bitch. I bet he won't even—

Then, he was standing in the open door, staring at her, with Trae's grinning face visible over his shoulder.

His face was much as she remembered it, if quite a bit more pale. But his first words were . . . nothing she had ever imagined in her many daydreams of this moment. They were uttered almost desperately, and in a much thinner voice than she remembered him having.

"If I get sick all over you, please don't take it personally. It's just that I found it necessary to share a cup—several, in fact—with one of the chiefs, and the stuff is the most horrible—they make it from—*ulp*—"

He did manage not to puke on her, but it was a close thing. If she hadn't hastily lifted her feet, she would have had to wash herself afterward. And, judging from the smell, would have had to discard the sandals entirely.

"You *drank* that?" She burst into laughter and held up her baby so the boy could admire his father. "See? Don't let anybody *ever* claim you were sired by some kind of Emerald wimp."

Ashen-faced, Adrian lifted his head and smiled weakly. Then, seeing the child, his eyes grew vague and unfocused. Helga remembered that weird expression, and almost shivered. Adrian's *spirits* were communing with him.

"He *is* your son," she said, softly but firmly. "I know it, even if I can't prove it."

The color was returning to Adrian's face. His smile grew firmer. "No need, Helga. He's my child, I'm quite certain of it."

Adrian used the word *certain* in a way which Helga had never heard any other man use it. Always, as if he were—*certain*. That was those mysterious "spirits" again. Somehow, in a manner which Helga did not understand, they had examined the boy and told Adrian that he was surely his own offspring.

Jessep came over and handed Adrian a rag, which he'd obtained somewhere in the apartment. Then, with several others, began cleaning up the mess on the floor. The former First Spear was no stranger to cleaning up vomit, clearly enough.

Adrian gave him a nod of thanks and wiped his mouth. Then, his eyes moving back and forth from Helga to the baby, asked in a still stronger voice: "What's his name?"

"I don't know. I never named him. I thought that since you were the father, you'd want to have a say in the matter. And—" She took a deep breath. "I always knew I'd see you again." The last statement sounded more like a plea than a statement.

Adrian's eyes were now focused entirely on her. She remembered those bright blue eyes. Could remember drowning in them at night and warming in them at dawn. She almost uttered the word *please!*—but managed to retain enough dignity not to say it aloud.

"Me too," he whispered. "The gods only know how much I've missed you."

Now she was laughing again, and it felt like all the tension of the past year was pouring out of her in the laughter itself—like water storming through a broken dike. And Jessep was laughing, and Adrian—Ilset too, with her own baby gurgling happily.

Only the child of Adrian Gellert and Helga Demansk was silent, staring wide-eyed at this strange new apparition in his young life. Wondering, perhaps, how anything in the world could be so *blue.*

A bit later, after Adrian and Jessep had finished cleaning up, Helga shooed everyone else out of the apartment. She handed the baby to Ilset on the way out. That had been prearranged between the two of them. By now, Ilset had nursed Helga's baby as well as her own any number of times, and she would have no trouble taking care of the infant until the following morning.

"Bet you won't have to fake it, either," murmured Ilset slyly, as she passed through the door. Helga's riposte came immediately to her lips, but before she could utter it, Adrian was closing the door and had her in his embrace.

A minute or two later, Helga murmured it in his ear. "That's one advantage to a man in a savage's loincloth. I don't have to wonder if he's faking his affection."

Adrian chuckled, but said nothing. By now, Helga was delighted to note, his normally fluent language had degenerated entirely into a series of growls.

The other advantage to a loincloth, she quickly discovered, was how easily it came off. The rest of it gave her no surprises, except that it was even better than she remembered.

Trae and Thicelt left a week later. Only Jessep and the hundred remained behind. On the morning that they left, Trae was quietly taken aside by Helga and handed a sealed and bound codex.

"Give this letter to Father," she said.

Trae hefted the packet. "Letter? This weighs as much as an Emerald tome."

Helga smiled. "Well . . . I guess it is, in a way. Adrian wrote most of it. He even gave the thing a *title*, believe it or not." She shook her head fondly, the way a woman will do at the antics of a man she loves but finds often eccentric.

"A title?" Trae stared down at the package. "I won't read it, of course. But I'm curious. What's the title?"

"He called it Meditations on Successful Tyranny."

"How spiritual sounding!" chortled Trae.

Helga, remembering the "trance-haze" in which her lover had spent many hours writing the thing, knew that the jesting phrase was far more accurate than Trae imagined. Adrian had finally explained to her the nature of his "spirits." Helga didn't really understand it, not fully at least. She wasn't happy at the thought that two other disembodied intelligences were sharing Adrian's mind—certainly not when they were making love!—but she had reconciled herself to the reality. And she understood how valuable their advice would be, to her father even more than Adrian himself.

"Just make sure he gets it," she snapped. "Mind your big sister!"

PART II
THE CONQUERER

CHAPTER SIXTEEN

"It's incredible," whispered Jeschonyk. The old Triumvir, formerly Speaker Emeritus, leaned over the railing and stared out at the gigantic fleet assembling below. The balcony was on the top floor of the building which Demansk had purchased for his own residence and headquarters in Solinga, and it fronted directly on the city's huge and splendid harbor.

"Not even the ancients speak of such a fleet," he added. The whispered words carried an undertone of awe . . . and not a little in the way of fear.

Demansk decided that, within limits, augmenting that fear was to his advantage. "That's not the half of it," he said forcefully. He leaned over the railing himself and pointed to the southeast. The gesture was awkward, since he was actually pointing to someplace behind the building. "Even Solinga's famous harbor isn't big enough to hold them all. I've got as many assembling in the smaller ports of the Emeralds, further down the coast."

Then, he leaned the other way and made the same awkward gesture to the southwest. "And about half as many as this assembling in Rope. When the Roper League started whining about not getting any of the business, I threw a lot of the shipbuilding work in their direction. And they'll be provided their share of the rowers, too.

"In short," he concluded, straightening up, "what you're seeing below is only two fifths—thereabouts—of the force I'll be bringing down on King Casull's head. Which I don't expect that damn pirate will be keeping on his shoulders too much longer. Not unless bad weather saves him."

He looked down at the smaller Triumvir. Jeschonyk's face was pinched. Demansk decided that it was time to leaven fear with reassurance. Or, at least, what passed for it.

"Spit it out, Ion. You look like the proverbial greatbeast who swallowed a plow."

"That's about what my stomach feels like. We didn't expect *this,* Verice. Not even me, much less Tomsien or the Council. We've been getting reports all through the winter, of course, but I finally had to come and see for myself."

"I have not exceeded my authority," responded Demansk coldly. "And I will point out that I spent most of my own fortune equipping this fleet—without, by the by, engaging in any tax-gouging or swindling."

"Truth to tell, I'd be a lot happier if you *had.* Engaged in swindling and tax-gouging, that is. That'd be . . . business as usual. Whereas *this*"—Jeschonyk gestured with his thumb toward the harbor; then, jerked it over his shoulder—"and, what's even worse, the popularity you've gained with the Emeralds . . ."

"The economy here is booming, Ion. Simply the normal taxes, fairly applied, bring in more than all the stupid shortsighted tax-gouging and stealing ever could."

The old man's face grew more pinched still. "That's what's really bothering me, Verice. You've not simply put together a much larger military force than anyone expected, but you've also created a real provincial base for yourself. And if most Vanberts sneer at Emeralds for being a lot of limp-wristed aesthetes and faggots, I don't. I'm old enough to have fought in the last war against the Emeralds. They're as tough as anybody, as long as someone else is giving them their orders and doesn't let their incessant bickering get out of hand."

He gave the fleet a glance. "Which, clearly, you haven't. And now, if you don't mind, let's go back inside. I'm an old man, and a thirsty one."

As they walked through the open-air archway which connected the balcony with the building proper—the mild Emerald climate required little in the way of actual doors, beyond what was needed for security and privacy—Jeschonyk laid a cautioning hand on Demansk's arm.

"And I should tell you that Tomsien is more worried than anyone. You should know, if you don't already, that Tomsien's been doing his own amassing of forces. He's got an army assembling in his southern provinces that is twice the size of anything you can put together—even with such a huge fleet as this one."

Demansk nodded. "I expected as much." He went to a side table and poured them each a goblet of wine. There were no servants present. Then, after handing one of the goblets to Jeschonyk, took a sip from his own and added:

"*Good.* We'll need that army to fend off the Southrons. They'll be coming soon, Ion, don't doubt it. They're just waiting for us to be committed against the islanders. Every spy we've sent down there—you know this even better than I do, since most of them report to you first—says they're creating the largest invasion force they've ever managed to put together. That new Chief of Chiefs of theirs, Norrys, seems quite the dynamic fellow. Charismatic too, from all accounts."

Jeschonyk gave his fellow Triumvir an odd look. Part suspicion, part . . . wonder, perhaps.

"Actually," he said, clearing his throat, "my spies seem to think that it's really this sub-chief Prelotta who's the driving spirit behind it all. And *he's* the one, not Norrys, who's got that damned Emerald genius Gellert working for him. Him and his blasted new weapons."

Demansk shrugged. " 'New weapons' are all fine and dandy, Ion. But I don't place too much faith in them. In the end, it's still discipline and organization and numbers that count." He gestured toward the fleet in the harbor with his chin. "Not one of those ships, or its crews, is as handy at sea as any islander pirate. So what? The simplest way to deal with a clever opponent is just to bury him."

"There are a *lot* of Southrons, Verice," chided Jeschonyk. "'Burying them' is not as easy as it with a relative handful of islanders."

"So? That's Tomsien's problem, isn't it? And how has he funded this great army he's collected? Not using my methods, I'm sure."

Jeschonyk looked sour. "We're getting complaints and protests filed every day in Vanbert. Have been for months. He's squeezing his provinces dry, Verice. Just as you *knew* he would."

Demansk shifted his shoulders. The gesture could not quite be called a shrug. "He's set in his ways, yes. Not to mention being a greedy bastard in his own right."

"Which you counted on also. Damn you, Verice, don't pretend! You *plotted* all this—just as you plotted the fact that I'd cover it for you and be your shield."

The look that Demansk now gave Jeschonyk was icy. "And are you still? My shield, I mean."

For a moment, two of the three most powerful men in the world locked eyes. It was the older and officially most senior of them who first looked away.

"Yes," he whispered, "the gods help me." He took a couple of steps and sat down on a couch; then, sprawled wearily across it. Though not wearily enough, Demansk noted with a bit of amusement, to spill a single drop of his wine. "I feel like a midget locked in a room with two direbeasts about to go for each other's throats. Except one of the direbeasts is really a demon."

Demansk laughed. "A 'demon,' is it? Don't you think that's going a *little* too far, Ion? I'm not a cruel man, you know. I don't think anyone's ever accused me of that, not even enemies I've defeated in battle."

Jeschonyk took a long swallow of wine, then leaned over and set the goblet down on the floor. Again, without spilling a drop.

"Stop while you're ahead, Verice. Everything you say to 'reassure' me simply makes me more nervous. I *know* you're not cruel. Gods save us, you're not even particularly *ambitious.* In all respects, as close to a paragon of the old virtues as any leader we've had in Vanbert in generations. I don't count Marcomann in that, by the way. The gods know he was capable, but the only virtues he had were those of a two-legged direbeast."

Demansk sat on a nearby couch. "So what's the problem, then?"

"Stop playing with me, damnation!" Jeschonyk scowled. "I may not be a scholar, but I *have* read the classics, you know. Wasn't it Llawat who pointed out that only the virtuous can really plumb the depths of depravity?"

"Prithney," corrected Demansk. "In the third of his *Dialogues.* I just reread it last week, as it happens. And 'depravity' isn't really the right term. His point wasn't that the virtuous are depraved, simply that only the virtuous have the courage of conviction which comes from lack of depravity to carry through a project to the end—regardless of how much depravity results from it." He cleared his throat. "It's a subtle distinction, perhaps, but . . . not unimportant to me."

Jeschonyk gave him a long, considering look. "Yes, I can see where it would be. And? *Are* you prepared to carry things through to the end?"

It was Demansk's turn to look away. He suspected his own face was pinched.

He heard Jeschonyk sigh. "That's what I thought. The gods save us all."

There was silence, for a time. Then, still without looking at him, Demansk said: "Decide, Ion. You have no more choice in *that* than I do. We live in a time of decision, whether we like it or not."

He heard Jeschonyk slurping wine. Long enough, apparently, to drain the entire goblet. At least, the sound of it clinking back down on the tile floor had an empty aura about it.

Empty—but, in its own way, firm.

"Oh, I decided last year. I guess I really came up here just to make sure my decision had been the right one. Of course, that's not what I told the Council."

Hearing the old man wheeze as he levered himself back upright, Demansk looked at him again. A bit to his surprise, Jeschonyk was smiling. Almost cheerfully, in fact.

"There's this much, anyway," the senior Triumvir chuckled. "My legs and lungs may not be what they used to be, but my brain isn't rotting. At least, I can still tell the difference between a demon and a direbeast, and figure out which one of them is going to gut the other."

After a moment, the humor on Jeschonyk's face faded away, to be replaced by something which might almost be called sadness.

"There is one thing, Verice."

"Yes?"

Jeschonyk's lips twisted. "The one other part of my body that still works just fine, oddly enough, are my loins. I'm sure you know about my, ah . . . oh, let's be honest and call it my *hareem*."

Demansk nodded. "Five girls, I've been told."

"Um. Six, actually. I added another two months ago. A luscious little thing I found—ah, never mind. The point is . . ."

He lowered his head and ran fingers through his thin hair. The year before, at the siege of Preble, that hair had still been gray. Now, most of it was white.

"The point's this, Verice. My wife died years ago and my children are all full grown and long gone. Don't even see much of them any more. So those girls are really all that matters much to me, personally speaking."

He looked up, a pleading look in his eyes. "I'm an old lecher, I'll admit it, but I'm not a pervert. I've never demanded anything from them other than—well, you know. The usual. The truth is, I think they're rather fond of me. I'm certainly very fond of them. So . . ."

"I'll see to it, Ion. Whatever happens." Demansk cleared his throat. "Though—I suppose this isn't really proper, coming from a 'demon'—I can assure you that I have no intention of doing you any personal harm." A bit of exasperation came into his voice. "Why *would* I? Damn it, I'm not a casual murderer!"

Jeschonyk shrugged. "Don't make promises you can't keep, Verice. Who knows what you'll have to do? But none of it should require involving half a dozen slave girls, most of them illiterate and not one of them older than twenty." Again, his heavy sensual lips made that wry grimace. "If the word 'innocent' means anything at all in this foul world, they are indeed innocent." His voice grew so low it was almost a whisper. "So. *Please.*"

"Done. I swear it." He paused, for a moment, thinking. "Though—make sure you tell your girls, so they'll know—I'll make the arrangements through Arsule Knecht."

Jeschonyk almost choked. "*Knecht*? You've got her on your side *too*? Gods save us—she's even richer than she is crazy."

Demansk gave him a crooked smile. "Oh, she's not really a lunatic, you know. Just, ah, an enthusiast, let's call it. But she also has a larger body of household troops in the capital than anyone except Albrecht—a lot bigger than yours—and nobody really takes her seriously as a political factor." A bit harshly: "Except *me*."

Jeschonyk nodded and rose to his feet. "I'll be returning to Vanbert tomorrow. Is there anything special you'd like me to pass on to the Council for you? Other than the usual platitudes, half-truths and outright falsehoods?"

Demansk barked a laugh. "I'd miss you too much for that alone, Ion! There are times—I swear it before the Gray-Eyed Lady—when I think you are the only truly innocent man in the whole Confederacy. The only honest one, for sure."

Seeing the look of outrage on Jeschonyk's face, Demansk held up a placating hand. "Relatively speaking, of course. You *are* a legendary lecher, Ion, have no fear. And I'm using the term 'honest,' ah, in what the Emeralds would call an 'aesthetic' manner. Lyrically, if you will, not dramatically."

"Damn those limp-wristed faggots, anyway," grumbled Jeschonyk. "Can't even call an honest lie by its right name."

That evening, in the same room, Demansk met with what he had come to think of as his "inner council." These were the handful of men, each of them holding the new title of "Special Attendant to the Triumvir," who served as the fingers for his fist. The fist itself, of course, being the army.

Not all of them were there. Leaving aside Jessep Yunkers, who was—and would be for some time—with Helga in the southern continent, there were two others residing in the Confederacy capital at Vanbert. But all the key ones were present: Prit Sallivar, Forent Nappur, Sharlz Thicelt, of course; and two newer ones: a Vanbert politician distantly related to Demansk by the name of Kall Oppricht, and the Emerald merchant Jonthen Tittle—who, ironically, was distantly related to the Gellert family.

After sketching his meeting with Jeschonyk, Demansk addressed his first remarks to Oppricht. "You'll see to that, Kall? Make whatever arrangements you have to in order to make sure that Ion's girls are put under safe guard in the event . . . something happens. And while you're at it, see to the safety of Jeschonyk's entire household. Ion didn't mention them, but I know his servants have been with him a long time."

Oppricht nodded. Then, gave Prit Sallivar a quick glance. Something in the way of an appeal, it seemed, as if a subject needed to be raised which he was loath to bring up himself. Unlike Sallivar, Kall Oppricht was not an old friend of the Triumvir's.

Sallivar straightened and opened his mouth. But before he could utter a single word, Demansk was shaking his head.

"No. Absolutely not. Don't even bother raising it, Prit."

"Verice—"

The Triumvir's face was set, his jaws tight. "*No,*" he rasped. "I understand the logic, Prit. Since an assassination of Jeschonyk by my enemies—coming at the right time—would give us the best possible way to take power in Vanbert with the least possible fuss, the question is naturally posed: why not arrange it *ourselves*, and place the blame on *them*?"

"Especially since they're undoubtedly already plotting to do it," murmured Oppricht. Demansk gave him a hard look, but the politician did not flinch. He might not be an old friend of the Triumvir's, but Kall Oppricht would never have agreed to become a special attendant if he hadn't felt he understood Verice Demansk. And part of that understanding was that Triumvir Demansk was not a man who would punish an underling for speaking his mind.

"It's just a fact, sir," he said quietly but firmly. "I'd bet a large sum I could even name the ringleader—Jacreb Quain, one of Albrecht's right hand men." He nodded toward Sallivar. "Prit's equivalent. Quain would just be the paymaster, of course. The actual blood work would probably be done by thugs working for one of Albrecht's tame street gangs."

Demansk sighed, then rubbed his face wearily. "I don't doubt it, Kall. The answer is still 'no.' Some crimes simply can't be done in the name of expediency. In the end, my reputation for being good for my word is worth far more than any clever maneuver would bring us."

"I agree," said Sharlz Thicelt. Sallivar and Oppricht gave the islander a look which was half startlement, half outrage. *This—from a pirate?!*

Thicelt grinned. "Take the advice of an experienced robber on this. Honor is more important to thieves than anyone, for the good and simple reason that they do not have recourse to the law."

He shook his head with vigor, causing his heavy gold earrings to flop about alarmingly. Fortunately, Thicelt's earlobes were built on the same massive scale as his nose. "Let the suspicion spread that Triumvir Demansk is dishonest as well as ruthless, and you will turn every possible neutral into an enemy—and half your allies into neutrals. He who would be a tyrant must first of all be *trusted.* Trusted to keep his word as much as trusted to break your neck if you oppose him."

"Well said, Sharlz." This came from Forent Nappur. Oddly enough, in the months they had worked together, the former Islander pirate and the former eastern-province common soldier had become quite good friends. The friendship was all the more odd in that it had begun with a ferocious brawl in a tavern, precipitated by an exchange of racial insults. The giant Forent had won the brawl, of course. But he'd carried a good set of bruises himself, for a number of days afterward.

Demansk was not quite sure how to account for it. To some degree, it was simply the mutual respect of low-class men who had tested each other's manhood and not found it wanting. But he suspected—feared, almost—that it derived mainly from the fact that these two were really the most ruthless of his close advisers, and had formed a natural alliance.

The most ruthless, by far—despite the fact that, as again here, their advice was usually less outwardly cold-blooded than the advice Demansk got from his more cultured and upper-class lieutenants.

But that was, ultimately, the problem. Or, it would be better to say, simply the reality. However much they might be adherents to Demansk's project, such men as Prit Sallivar and Kall

Oppricht—even the Emerald Jonthen Tittle—were very much "men of the established order." All of them were wealthy, highly educated, born into good families. They could understand, abstractly, the seething fury at the injustices of Confederate society which bubbled silently in the depths of the poor millions of that society. But they didn't really *feel* it.

Neither did Demansk himself, for that matter. He was smart enough, however, to recognize its existence. And he knew, without a doubt, that neither Sharlz Thicelt nor Forent Nappur would blink an eye at the complete destruction of much of what the others still held dear. Either Thicelt or Nappur would torch a nobleman's mansion in an instant—*any* nobleman's, Vanbert or Emerald or Islander—without caring in the least that an excellent library or collection of artwork was going up in flames along with it.

Why should they? Neither one of *them* had ever been invited to partake of those pleasures of noble society. Thicelt had gone to sea as a destitute waif in the streets of Chalice at the age of six. At the same age, Nappur had been working in the fields of the hardscrabble east.

That was largely what made them so useful to Demansk, of course. Thicelt and Nappur could gain the allegiance and trust of men whom the others could barely even talk to. Such men as Nappur's network of enforcers and spies among common soldiers, who had by now imposed a subtle but iron clamp over the army. Or Thicelt's equivalent network among the sailors of the huge fleet which would transport that army to the Western Isles.

Still, they were a bit scary. Demansk was glad that both of them tended, on a personal level, to be rather phlegmatic in temperament. Even, in the case of Thicelt, flamboyantly good-humored.

It was time to bring this matter to a close. Only the Emerald had not spoken. Demansk looked at him, cocking an inquisitive eyebrow.

Jonthen Tittle shrugged. "This is really outside my area. But I tend to agree with Forent and Sharlz, Triumvir. And I can say this: a large part of the reason the merchants and guildmasters of Solinga and the other Emerald cities have been so cooperative is that they have decided you can be trusted." The smile which followed was a bit rueful. "As Sharlz said, trusted to break their necks if they are too obstreperous—just as you did last week with—"

"The man is quite healthy," interrupted Demansk, mildly. "Amazingly so, in fact, for a convicted swindler."

"Ha! Healthy, yes. You still stripped him of all his properties which, for a good Emerald merchant, is a fate worse than death."

A little chuckle swept the room. When Tittle continued, however, his smile was gone. "But you are also trusted not to break necks capriciously, or simply from personal malice. So I think Thicelt and Nappur have the right of it. Don't think for a moment that your private arrangement with Jeschonyk can remain a secret forever. If nothing else, he will certainly tell his concubines in order to prepare them in case something happens to him. And the concubines will talk to the servants, and the servants . . ."

He left the rest of it unspoken. Most of the world's elite tended to be oblivious to the fact that servants and slaves were people like anyone else—including the propensity to gossip. But none of the men in *that* room were so naïve. If they had been, they wouldn't have been there in the first place.

"It's decided, then." Demansk's tone made clear that there would be no further discussion. So, he was rather surprised to hear Sallivar clear his throat again. His financial adviser normally accepted his decisions with no demurral, once they were definitely made.

Prit held up a hand, indicating that he was not challenging the decision. "That still leaves something else unclear." He nodded toward Oppricht. "As Kall said, *others*—Albrecht's people, to be specific—are certainly plotting along those lines themselves. So, the question is: do we do anything to stop *them*?"

Demansk turned his head and stared through the open archway onto the balcony. He couldn't see the ocean itself, from his seated position—not even if it had still been daylight—but he could see the sky above it. Unusually, for this time of year on the northern coast, the sky was cloudless. Even with the lamps burning in the room, he could see the stars quite clearly.

Demansk had always liked watching the stars at night. They seemed so remote, so aloof, from the muck of earthly existence.

He could remember, once, while on campaign, standing next to Jeschonyk and staring up at the vault of the heavens. The old Speaker Emeritus was something of an astronomer; quite famous for it, in fact, even among Emerald scholars. He could remember the enthusiasm with which Ion had pointed out the various constellations and the mysterious stars which, unlike all the others, seemed to move about. "Planets," Jeschonyk had called them, insisting that they were the actual spirits of the gods themselves.

He sighed, and turned his face back to the room full of plotters. When he spoke, his voice was not much more than a murmur.

"No, Prit, we don't. Jeschonyk will either protect himself, or he won't. We will have no hand in whatever happens, but . . . whatever does, of course, you will see to it that the necessary measures are in place and ready to go."

Sallivar nodded. "I'll pass the word to Raddek and Gliev in Vanbert."

"Good enough," said Demansk. "Let's move on, then, to the next thing." With a lift in his voice, as if he were relieved to move on to a straightforward matter of military logistics: "Jonthen, I'm a bit concerned by the state of—"

They were not done until midnight. And then, politely seeing the others to the door, Demansk steeled himself for still another meeting. A pleasant enough one, to be sure, but he wondered sometimes if he'd ever get enough sleep. He seemed to have a vague memory of a time in the past when he had.

Trae was waiting patiently in a separate room. And continued waiting, out of sight, until Demansk's lieutenants had all left the building. Not that there was any secret about Trae, exactly. All of Demansk's special attendants knew of Trae's work, although only Thicelt really understood it fully. Still, Demansk was a firm believer in the axiom that one should always have a second string to one's bow. There were his special attendants; and then, there was his family. Three of his four children, at least. The two worked toward the same purpose, but they still worked separately.

Trae had little of the deference of Demansk's lieutenants. He was already scowling when he came through the door and launched immediately into his protest.

"Father, you *promised*—"

"Oh, shut up," growled Demansk. He pointed at one of the nearby tables. "Drown your sorrows in wine, if you must. Trae, it would be idiotic to risk your death or injury in this coming battle with Casull. And your precious steam ram would just get in the way, anyhow. Dammit, there's not going to be anything *fancy* about it. I will go after Casull like a man using a sledgehammer on a cornered rat. The last thing I need is complications.

"*And*," he continued forcefully, overriding Trae's protest, "I *will* need your steam ram for this other matter. As I've now explained to you at least three times."

Sullenly, Trae poured himself a goblet of wine. Even more sullenly, he flung himself onto a couch. Unlike Jeschonyk, however, he did not manage the feat without spilling some wine on his tunic. Fortunately, the garment was the utilitarian one which Trae was in the habit of wearing.

" 'This other matter,' " he quoted. Being almost, but not quite, openly derisive. For Trae, if not his sister, there were certain limits in the way one spoke to one's august Confederate sire.

"Father, that's pure speculation—and you know it as well as I do. I may be a callow youth, but I'm not dumb enough to think that a complicated plot is going to work, every step along the way, just as planned. You have *no* real idea if Albrecht's going to react—"

"Ha!" barked Demansk, cutting his son short. "Just as bad as your headstrong sister! Presuming to lecture *me* on matters of strategy and tactics."

But it was said cheerfully, and Demansk began pouring a convivial goblet for himself as he continued.

"Trae, *of course* I'm speculating. Although I think the odds that Albrecht will react the way I'm guessing are a lot better than you think. I've known the pig since he was a piglet."

He ambled over to another couch and took a seat. "The thing to remember about Drav Albrecht is that he's *impatient.* Don't ever let that smooth, sophisticated façade of his fool you. Underneath, the man is fundamentally a hothead. The past year—more than that—of leading that miserable siege of Preble will have frayed him to the limit. When he hears of my sudden triumph, and a much bigger one, over Casull . . ." Demansk took a long swallow of wine. "He won't be able to resist, Trae. Already by now, much less by late spring, he'll have everything in place to make a final assault. The casualties will be horrendous, of course, which is why he hasn't done it yet. But Albrecht doesn't really give a damn about that, not when push comes to shove."

Trae was still scowling. But, after a moment, the scowl faded a bit. "Actually, Father, I'm not really trying to second-guess you about *that* part of it. It's just that I think I understand better than you do what you can, and can't, realistically expect from my steam ram."

He waved the hand holding the goblet, managing in the process to spill some of it on the tiles. He didn't notice, of course. Demansk's youngest son combined the capacity of focusing more intently on something than anyone Demansk had ever met—while being oblivious to almost everything else around him.

"All of my new ships, for that matter—including the woodclads you're depending on to protect you from Casull's new steamships. The thing is, Father, these dazzling fancy boats Gellert designed are damn near useless in anything except good weather. And when I say 'good,' I really mean 'almost perfect.' Any kind of heavy seas, and . . . you'll be lucky if you don't sink outright." He paused, and then his innate honesty forced him to add: "Well, not with the woodclads, of course. They won't *sink* in bad weather. But you'll never be able to handle them, and the gods help you if you're near a lee shore."

Demansk started to say something, but Trae cut him off. "Yes, yes, yes—I know *you'll* be able to guarantee yourself good weather. 'Guarantee,' at least, as much as that word means anything when it comes to weather at sea." Grudgingly: "But, yes, since you're the one who's invading the Isles, you're the one who gets to decide when to do it. And I'll admit that the weather in these northern seas in late spring is about as good—and predictably so—as it ever gets."

Almost wailing, now: "But what about *me?* I'm *not* the one who'll make the decision when to use the steam ram. Albrecht'll do *that*—

and he hasn't been consulting with me lately. And the weather as far down the coast as Preble is *not* predictable, not even in the spring."

"So? The worst that happens is that you can't intervene. In which case, a lot of Islanders will get butchered—who, frankly, deserve it after the massacre of the Vanberts on Preble they carried out last year—and one of my clever schemes goes awry." Demansk shrugged. "None of my plans *depends* on your success, Trae. Although it would certainly help."

For a moment, he was scowling even more fiercely than his son. "And half of me, to be honest, almost hopes you can't intervene. Yes, it would be handy to have all those desperate—and very skilled—Islanders at my mercy. I need to get the workshops in the main archipelago running at full capacity as soon as possible after the conquest, and having thousands of refugees from Preble would be a big help. But . . ."

Trae laughed softly—softly, but quite harshly. "Once a Vanbert, always a Vanbert. They *are* a lot of sorry rebels. For which the traditional penalty is well established."

Demansk took another long swallow from his goblet. "Exactly." Still scowling: "And it's not just a matter of tradition. One of the other things I can't afford is to get too much of a reputation for mercy, either."

The scowl went away, replaced by a look of sheer weariness. "I suspect, even if all goes well, that I'm going to spend the rest of my life crushing rebellions. I don't enjoy bloodshed, Trae, but I learned long ago that often the best way to avoid an ocean of blood is to demonstrate that you are instantly willing to spill a lake's worth of it."

Trae sat up straight, finished his wine—spilling some down his chin—and set the goblet on the tiles. Then, rubbing his neck: "I wouldn't worry too much about *that*. No offense, Father"—with a crooked smile and an upraised hand—"and I'm *not* trying to teach your august self the principles of tactics, but I really don't think that before too long there's going to be anyone in the world except outright lunatics who don't understand perfectly well that only an outright lunatic would rebel against the new dispensation."

Demansk's responding smile was just as crooked. "Well. True enough, I suppose."

Trae's sour expression came back in full force. Demansk sighed. "So what *is* the problem?"

His youngest son's face, in that moment, resembled that of a five-year-old boy after being told he couldn't play that day. Demansk almost burst into laughter. He remembered that face very well.

"It's *me!* If it doesn't work out the way you plan, I'll wind up sitting on the side throughout this whole war!"

Demansk stifled the quip he was about to utter. As silly as Trae's complaint sounded to him, now that he had the perspective of decades of warfare to look back upon, he could still remember himself at that same age. Eager to prove his mettle in what, for centuries, had been the only real "rite of passage" that meant anything to Vanbert men. Even if, within a short time, he had come to understand that "honor" was a thing with real entrails, and not just a spirit. Spilled ones, usually.

So his response was entirely solemn. "Trae, I *need* you for this. I can't possibly detach enough actual warships for the purpose. Carrier ships, plenty of them, yes—to take off the refugees. I lied to Jeschonyk about those ships we're having built in Rope, by the way. I told him they were part of my own fleet. But Albrecht will be raging, be sure of it, and he won't let them go peacefully. Those ships will need to be protected, because they aren't really warships—as you and I both know. Which means your steam ram is the only thing I've got which can do the job. *Maybe.* With you in command—you're the only one I trust who can do that—and *if* you do a brilliant job of captaining it."

And now, with good cheer: "Look at it this way. If it *does* happen, you'll come back covered with glory."

Trae tried to maintain the sour expression, but it was obviously difficult. "Oh, bah. Nobody'll understand it anyway. Except a bunch of stinking Islander refugees, and who cares what *they* think."

"Not your own sailors and soldiers, boy," said Demansk forcefully. "*They'll* know—*they'll* understand. Don't think they won't."

He finished his wine, set down the goblet on the table, and ended a long day and night of plotting.

"Learn this much from your father, son. You build the respect of soldiers—real respect, not the shit that passes for it at triumphs—starting with the man next to you. Begin with the *core,* lad, and the rest will come when it comes. Without that core, it won't come at all."

And now, grinning: "As you and I both will soon be demonstrating to that foul bastard Albrecht."

CHAPTER SEVENTEEN

It took Ion Jeschonyk almost two months to return to Vanbert. Some of that was due to the simple distance—about a thousand miles, in a direct line; and much longer than that, of course, following the actual road. Still, it was a good road, even by Confederate standards. He'd made the trip *to* Solinga in less than five weeks.

But that had been in the early spring, when the weather was still foul and Jeschonyk had simply wanted to get to his destination as fast as possible. Now, with summer approaching, the countryside was blooming and beautiful. And, deep in his heart, the old man thought this would be the last chance in his life to simply wallow in the beauties of nature. He could remember doing that a lot, growing up as a boy on his family's estate. He wondered, as he had often before, what had happened to that carefree child.

So he ordered his caravan to maintain a slow pace, and stopped often—sometimes for half a day at a time, while he waded barefoot in a brook or simply sat under the shade of a tree and contemplated the meadow flowers. The soldiers escorting him didn't object, of course, much less the drivers of his own coach and the wagons carrying supplies.

By the time he finally arrived in the capital, the reports he brought for the Council were already completely obsolete. The gigantic city, with its one million inhabitants, was abuzz with word that Demansk had launched his attack on the archipelago. The news had been brought by the fast couriers employed by the Confederacy as their elite postal service. Such men could make the trip from Solinga in ten days or less.

In fact, hearing what people were saying in the markets and streets as his caravan worked its way toward his own domicile, Jeschonyk could remember seeing such a special courier galloping past the caravan just a few days past. And he realized, wryly, that his brain had still been working even while he thought it entirely at rest with the waving flowers in the fields. Because Jeschonyk had ignored the courier completely, even though it was now obvious what it *had* to have meant. And had done so, of course, because that never-sleeping part of his brain had known full well that it was better for the reality to hit the Council before Jeschonyk had to start telling his lies to them.

They wouldn't really believe him anyway, although most of them would want to. And this way, a good three fourths of the recriminations would be dispensed with. What was the point? For good or ill, the die was cast.

To his relief, there wasn't a delegation from the Council at his mansion. Under normal circumstances, there would have been representatives anxiously waiting for him, day and night, for the past two weeks. But now, he had no doubt, all the Councillors were far too preoccupied with their own plotting and scheming.

By the next morning, of course, after the news of his return reached them, half the Council would be pounding on his door. But at least he'd have one final evening of rest and repose.

"Rest and repose," in a manner of speaking. Jeschonyk was actually quite well rested, due to the leisurely way in which he'd made the return journey. And he'd been celibate for a longer stretch than any he could remember in decades. He'd not wanted to bring one of his concubines on such a politically delicate mission, and he no longer found the company of prostitutes very entertaining.

So, the old lecher barely gave his servants more than a

perfunctory response to their greetings before he marched into his private chambers. His harem already knew of his arrival, and were waiting for him on the huge bed which filled a goodly portion of the very large room which served him for a sleeping chamber. Wearing, needless to say, his favorite feminine apparel.

Which was precisely nothing. Jeschonyk had been quite truthful with Demansk. A satyr he might be, but his tastes were simple and straightforward. Granted, his pig-farming ancestors would have looked askance at the oral practices which the modern aristocracy had imported from the decadent Emeralds. But not even they could have complained about the rest of it. No outlandish perversions here—just a surprisingly vigorous old man greeting his concubines gaily and practically pouncing upon them.

They even seemed glad to see him, and to be enjoying what followed. And, who knows? They might have been.

Jeschonyk found himself wondering, an hour or so later, as he lay in their midst exhausted and sweaty. For a moment, he was even tempted to ask. But . . .

Whatever else he was, Jeschonyk was not a fool. There was no point in asking such a question. No slave concubine in her right mind, after all, was going to tell her master anything other than what she thought he wanted to hear. Especially not concubines who lived in such luxurious quarters and enjoyed such an easy life, the worst of which was simply satisfying the none-too-complicated lusts of their owner. A frequent chore, to be sure—but they had half a dozen of them to spread around the work.

Still, it made him a bit sad. He was quite fond of *them*, and not simply because of the pleasure they gave him. One of them, in particular—the oldest girl, Kata, the one who'd been with him longest.

Strange, really. She was the only Southron in his harem. Jeschonyk was generally not partial to Southron girls. The problem wasn't their appearance. Female Southrons did not sport the grotesque tattoos of the males, for one thing. And, cleaned up and shorn of those absurd hairstyles, he actually found their pale skins and light hair arousing. It was simply that the practice of female circumcision which was prevalent among the barbarians made their women, in Jeschonyk's quite extensive experience, rather unresponsive. But Kata was from the Reedbottom tribe, who—so she claimed, at least, and the evidence seemed to substantiate it—were one of the few tribes which had never adopted that particularly savage custom.

Kata was the smartest of them, that much Jeschonyk had long been sure of. And she was also the one who was most alert to his own moods. So he was not surprised to see the little frown gathering on her face, as she looked down upon him from her cross-legged position at the foot of the bed. The sight almost dispelled Jeschonyk's melancholy. Not the frown, but the posture. The view was . . . distracting. Or would have been, if Jeschonyk wasn't so completely and thoroughly satiated.

"Why are you unhappy, master? I thought we—"

"Not that, girl!" He barked a weary laugh. "You were all your usual marvelous selves, I assure you. It's—something else."

He took a slow breath and decided to get it over with. He levered himself upright—two of the girls immediately assisting him in the process—and gave Kata as solemn a look as her pose permitted.

"Things may change soon, Kata—girls. I may . . . not be here much longer." He shook his head. "No, no, I'm not going anywhere. I simply may no longer be *alive.*"

Kata's face seemed to grow even paler than usual. One of the other girls—Ursula, that was, the Emerald—emitted a little gasp.

By the gods, I think they are fond of me! A moment later, less happily: *Or, of course, it could just be that they'd miss their comforts and luxuries.*

Something in their expressions reassured him. He'd never really know, of course, but . . .

A time for decision, just as Verice says. And there's nothing that prevents me from telling the truth, except the old habits of an old liar.

"I care for you, girls. Very much. So I've made arrangements in case something happens to me. Men will come here—soldiers, probably—from Lady Knecht. Do what they say, go with them."

Several of the younger girls began babbling assurances that nothing untoward could *possibly* happen—! But not Kata. Perhaps because she was older, or smarter—or simply, like any Southron girl by the age of ten, had seen plenty of relatives hacked down in the tribes' perennial feuding.

"Can we trust them, master?"

"Yes. As long as they are from Lady Knecht. No one else, you hear?"

She bowed her head in obedience. As he had so many times before, Jeschonyk found himself admiring the clean lines of her neck and shoulders, the long blond hair spilling over her breasts, the—

"I'll be damned," he said, startled. "Once more—at my age? Come here, Kata."

He whispered just one thing that night, the rest of the noises he made being much louder. Into Kata's ear, this, so that none of the others could hear: "You have always been my favorite."

"I know," was her reply, whispered back. And there was something in those two words which let Ion Jeschonyk finally realize that, at least in her case, he no longer had to wonder.

The next morning, at daybreak, half the Council was pounding on his door. He spent the rest of the day—and the next, and the next, and the next—in a whirlpool of deceit and deception and double-dealing. Which had its own quirky pleasure, admittedly. Even at his age—perhaps *because* of his age—Jeschonyk could lie and deceive and double-deal better than anyone.

All the more so because he knew one secret that none of the other Councillors knew. Of that, he was quite sure. He had not even told Demansk that he knew.

Everyone else thought that Demansk's daughter, Helga, was still in seclusion at their distant estate in the far western province on the coast. Being a female, of course—especially a disgraced one—she was not really of much concern to the great men of Vanbert. But Jeschonyk was no fool. So he, alone, had paid spies to keep an eye on her. And he, alone, knew that she had long since departed for the south, leaving a girl who resembled her a great deal (at least at a distance) to serve as her double.

Where she had gone, exactly, Jeschonyk was not sure. Marange, according to what his spies had been able to learn. Nor did Jeschonyk have any real idea what she was doing down there.

But he could guess. He was one of the few Councillors of Vanbert who had actually *seen* the bastard. And if that blue-eyed babe with his fuzz of golden hair had been sired by a fat old islander pirate, Jeschonyk would eat his own tunic.

"So what *do* you think, damnation? Speak up, Ion!"

The half shout from one of the Councillors in the chamber broke Jeschonyk's little reverie. He looked up and saw that the shouter was one of Tomsien's allies.

Slowly, with great dignity, Triumvir Ion Jeschonyk, former Speaker Emeritus of the Confederacy of Vanbert and without question its most prestigious and respected living statesman, rose to his feet and uttered the finest lie of his life.

"Nothing to fear, my fellow Councillors! The balance of power remains intact, does it not?" He gave the man who had shouted at him a stately nod. "Despite the size of the great force Demansk has assembled—which, I remind you all, has even now set forth to rid us once and for all of the predations of piracy—Triumvir Tomsien still retains a larger force in his southern provinces. And what could possibly threaten *that* army?"

He sat down amidst scattered applause and a collective sigh of relief so loud it could have almost lifted the great rotunda of the chamber. And, while the Council proceeded to its next round of squabbles, went back to his contemplations on bastardy.

A week later, by sea, the same news came to Marange.

"That's it, then," said Helga. Adrian was already heading for the door, wanting to reach Prelotta's pavilion as soon as possible. From the room where he and Ilset made their own quarters, Jessep Yunkers was hurrying also.

"Not so fast, dammit," she growled. When Adrian turned about, looking suitably guilt-faced, Helga gave him a fierce embrace and a kiss. Fierce, but brief. She understood that this was no time for lingering affections. She simply wanted—something.

He gave her an embrace and a kiss just as fierce as her own. So, after the door closed, she was able to face the moment with something close to serenity.

"You didn't tell him, did you?"

That was Ilset's voice, coming from behind her. Helga turned and saw that Jessep's wife was standing in the doorway, her own infant in her arms and a questioning smile on her face.

"The gods, *no*," growled Helga. "If Adrian finds out I'm pregnant again, he'll *never* let me out of the wagon. Not once—you watch—in the whole coming campaign."

Ilset shook her head. "Why in the name of the gods would you *want* to? I mean—when soldiers get into their own lingo—" She made a face. "Gods, and they say women are boring!"

Helga didn't try to answer. There was no way she could explain. Not to someone like Ilset, at any rate. Nor, she suspected, to any woman she knew.

Her brother Trae would have understood, but he had long since departed. Trae, too, came from that ancient line which had never forgotten their *duty*, however much all others who claimed to be of noble blood might have done so.

She was too young to understand the absurdity of her sentiments. Her father could have explained to her how ridiculous it was to call treason "duty." Yet, all the while, he would have understood her perfectly.

Of course, Demansk *also* would have forbidden her to leave the wagon during the campaign, had he known she was pregnant. In that, if nothing else, the authoritative father was just as much a creature of custom as the rebel lover. Even if, to the world at large, the two of them were about to turn everything upside down.

CHAPTER EIGHTEEN

"Casull probably beheaded every priest in Chalice before he set out," jeered Thicelt, glancing up approvingly at the clear blue sky. "You can bet he's had them praying for bad weather for the last three months straight."

Standing next to him on the raised quarterdeck of the huge quinquireme which served as his flagship, Demansk smiled coldly. Whether or not the King of the Isles had actually executed any priests, Demansk had no doubt at all he was thoroughly disgruntled with them by now. And with his own deities, for that matter. Especially Lemare, the Goddess of the Sea.

The weather was *perfect*—had been for a week, with no sign of any change. The sea was calm, the winds just heavy enough to have made the fleet's passage down the coast and across the Western Ocean to the archipelago a matter of an easy week's voyage. Now, the largest fleet ever assembled in history was off the northeast coast of the island of Chalice. From his vantage point on the elevated quarterdeck, Demansk could see the caldera which formed the harbor of the capital, if not the city of Chalice itself. And, not too far to the west, perhaps ten or fifteen miles, the snow-covered Peak of the Sun God. The largest volcano in the archipelago was still somewhat active, although it had never erupted in historical times. There was a thin plume of smoke rising from its crest to the heavens—and rising almost straight up. Even at that altitude, obviously, the winds were light.

Demansk didn't doubt that every morning for the past many weeks the first thing King Casull IV had done, rising from his sleep, was to go out upon his balcony in the royal palace and stare up at that volcano. And then curse bitterly, seeing the same steady rise of the plume.

Half a century ago, the Confederacy had conquered and absorbed the Emeralds; and then, with that example before them, had coerced the Roper League and Hagga into accepting "auxiliary nation" status. From that moment forward, with the entire north coast of the continent under their control, there had been only three things which had kept the Confederacy from finally putting paid to the obnoxious pirates from the Western Isles.

The first was the increasing turmoil and lack of discipline among the Vanbert nobility, whose energies became more and more devoted to endless scheming and maneuvering for internal power. No one had been willing to allow any Speaker to gain enough power to amass the resources necessary to subjugate the archipelago—resources which, technically speaking, were quite easily within the reach of the Confederation. As Demansk had just proved, in a few short months.

The second was that when a leader *did* emerge who had the power to do so—Marcomann—he had been preoccupied with maintaining his own power. For all his undoubted ability, Marcomann had been guided by no vision whatsoever beyond his own aggrandizement. So he had turned the resources of the Confederacy toward a conquest of the western coast, the last area of the northern continent which still held enough territory to provide the land grants needed to win and keep the allegiance of his huge army.

Which, however shrewd a maneuver that might have been from the standpoint of keeping power, did the Confederacy no real good at all. It simply stoked the flames of internal feuding—Demansk's own father had spent most of his life preoccupied with gaining new lands in the west for his family—and just gave the pirates a fertile new area for plundering. Helga, in fact, had been seized in one of the raids on the western coast which had become so easy for the pirates in the last two decades.

The third and final factor was weather. Even for superb sailors like the Islanders and the Emeralds, bad weather could prove disastrous. For the lubberly Vanberts, one of the obstacles to devoting the resources needed to create the kind of giant fleet that Demansk had done was that a single storm could destroy it in a day. More than one Vanbert fleet, though none anywhere near as large as Demansk's, had met that fate.

Demansk had maneuvered successfully past the first two obstacles. The problem of weather he had solved in the simple and straightforward manner he had built the fleet itself. He'd simply timed his attack to coincide with the one time of year, late spring and early summer, when the weather in the northern reaches of the Western Ocean was almost invariably mild.

Still, it had been a gamble, even if one with good odds. But now that the gamble had paid off, Casull had no choice but to come out and fight a sea battle—against a fleet that was at least five times larger than anything he could assemble himself.

He couldn't simply keep the fleet in the harbor at Chalice, much as he might have wanted to. Granted, that harbor—and the city itself which rose up along the inner slopes of the caldera—was about as impregnable a fortress as any in the world. The ancient volcanic crater in which Chalice nestled still had three quarters of its circumference left. Casull could have easily blocked the narrow entrance to the harbor and bled the Vanberts for weeks, if they tried to break through.

Nor would he have had to use many men to guard the crater rim. Chalice had no walls for the simple reason that it didn't need any. The knife-edge ridges of the caldera itself were superior to any curtain wall and battlements ever constructed.

But that was also Chalice's weakness. The city was the best harbor in the world, true, but it was *only* a harbor. There was nothing—not a single path, much less a road, across the stark terrain which circled it—which connected Chalice by land with the rest of the island. The city depended on seaborne trade and fishing for everything, beginning with the food it consumed every day. Ironically, it was the worst city in the world to withstand a siege, for all that it could withstand it the best in narrow military terms.

"Right there," said Thicelt, pointing to a place farther south along the island's coast. "That's where we'll build it."

The admiral was pointing to a long and wide beach about ten miles south of the city, which curved easily and gently for another five miles or so. More than enough space, even for Demansk's gigantic fleet, to beach most of the ships. All of them, really, except the quinquiremes and the special woodclads—and what relatively few ships were needed to maintain a blockade of the harbor.

Demansk's eyes lifted beyond the beach. At a distance of not more than half a mile, a low mountain range paralleled the shore. The mountains were rocky, but still heavily forested. There was enough stone and wood there, within easy reach, for the Confederacy to build all the dwellings and breakwaters and piers it would need to turn the area into a giant-sized version of the military encampments for which its army was famous. With a harbor as good as most in the world.

Give him a summer, unmolested by the pirate ships bottled up in the harbor, and Demansk could build what amounted to a city as big as Chalice itself. A crude and primitive one, true, but more than adequate for the purpose.

That new city, of course, would also be dependent on seaborne trade for its survival. The soil in the northern third of the archipelago's main island was too rocky and sandy to make good farming land. But so what? Demansk would have control of the sea, not the Islanders. And long before winter came, with its bad weather, Chalice would have succumbed from starvation. By late autumn, under normal conditions, Chalice would be stocked full of food to carry it through the winter. But now, still in late spring, the city's larders would be almost empty.

No, the only chance King Casull had was to defeat the Vanbert fleet in an open sea battle. And with no way, even, to stage the battle in narrow waters where Casull could keep most of the Vanbert navy from swamping him.

No way, at least, in the real world. Theoretically, Casull's best move would have been to abandon Chalice without a fight and move his capital and his forces to the inner islands of the archipelago. Then, at least, he would have been in a position to fight battles in the relatively constricted—and often treacherous—waters of the various inlets which separated the islands. He could have maneuvered and retreated, as needed, to allow only a portion of Demansk's fleet to get at him at one time, always with the hope of luring his enemy's ships onto the inlets' many shoals which were not listed on any charts.

"And I'll bet he's also cursing the whole history of the Kingdom," said Thicelt, his thoughts paralleling Demansk's own. "Some other realm, maybe, the King could play a waiting game. But not with us pirates."

The heavy lips twisted into something that was halfway between a rueful smile and a jeer. "We're not good at that sort of thing, the way you Vanbert cloddies are. Easy come, easy go. Cut the King's throat and find another one."

Demansk nodded. The Islanders were notorious for their unstable politics. That was the flip side of their equally notorious egalitarianism. "Egalitarianism," at least, in the sense of personal opportunity. The Islanders' rulers were the most autocratic in the world, true—but any man could aspire to become the King, if he had the talent and the luck.

The Islanders had none of the mainland's ingrained respect for "blood lines." Any man, at least, if not woman, could rise to any station in life. And, of course, fall just as far if not farther—and even faster. As Sharlz said, one slice of the blade. Long live the new King, and toss the old one's carcass into the harbor for the sharks.

Demansk was counting on that, in fact. Even more in the long term than the short one. For his plans to work, he needed a *quick* victory here—and a relatively bloodless one. Not only for his own troops, but for the Islanders themselves. The last thing in the world he wanted was a holocaust. He needed those Islanders alive and healthy. In the short term, for the expertise which Gellert had given them in the making of the new weapons. In the long term—although this was still hazy in Demansk's mind—because he needed to infuse at least some of that egalitarianism into Vanbert itself.

That last would take decades, of course, and would not be something that Demansk himself would live to see. But, standing in the golden sunlight on the quarterdeck of his flagship, the image of his blond half-breed bastard of a grandson came to mind.

New blood. Mix it up. We've gotten stale, and corrupt, like layers of unstirred sediment.

Thicelt's voice broke into his musings, bringing his thoughts sharply back to the immediate demands of the moment.

"There they are!" the admiral barked, pointing with a rigid finger. "Casull's not going to waste any time."

Demansk followed the finger. At first, all he could see was the screen of war galleys which formed the vanguard of Casull's approaching fleet.

Impressive ships, those. They looked like so many sea serpents basking in the sun on the surface of the waters. Long, narrow, very low in the water; every line of them seemed to shriek *speed.* They looked deadly enough even without the glaring eyes and snarling teeth painted on their bows, just above the bronze rams.

The rowers on those ships were working easily, at the moment, just enough to keep Casull's ships in line and steady—the galley equivalent of a swimmer treading water. Casull's warships were making no attempt to close the final distance of half a mile which still separated the two fleets.

They were waiting for something. Demansk could guess what that was, even without Thicelt's keen eyes having spotted them already.

Then, he saw the first plume of smoke. And, a moment later, threading its way between two of the galleys, the first of Casull's steam rams. Between the distance and the wind, he still couldn't hear the sound of the engines. But he could remember what that noise was like, from his experiences with Thicelt's own steam ram at the siege of Preble. Like the heavy breathing of a monster, its claws working a treadmill which made the great paddlewheels turn.

It was nothing of the sort, of course, as Demansk had learned after capturing Thicelt's. Just a machine; more complicated than any Demansk had ever seen before, but not different in principle. Both

Thicelt and his son Trae understood quite well how the things worked, even if Demansk's own understanding was still a bit hazy beyond the level of *what will it do*?

"Four of them? Is that still the latest word from your spies?"

The moment he asked the question, Demansk silently cursed himself. That was nervousness speaking, nothing else. Thicelt had given him the latest report just the evening before, and there was no way that any more recent report from the islander's spy network on Chalice could have reached him since.

Sharlz seemed to understand that, for he made no response. Or, perhaps, it was simply that he was so intent on studying the oncoming steamships that he hadn't heard the question. Either way, Demansk was grateful.

The momentary lapse had, at least, one beneficial side effect. It enabled Demansk to suppress, quite easily, his urge to start telling his admiral how to maneuver his ships. Thicelt was the expert here, not Demansk—even more with the matter of the steamships than with the fleet as a whole. Demansk had chosen him to be the admiral of this fleet in the first place—the first Islander in history to command *any* Vanbert fleet, much less its largest—precisely because he knew that Casull would have chosen his best captain to command the first of his new steam rams.

Nothing which had happened since had led Demansk to regret that decision. Thicelt had handled the greatest fleet in history with the same ease with which, in years past, he had handled every vessel put under his command. The man was, quite simply, a superb seaman and naval officer. Even if his heavy gold earrings and shaved head and beak-nosed dark features still made him seem exotic to Demansk. Not to mention his sometimes outrageous sense of humor.

"Not yet, not yet," Thicelt was murmuring to himself. "Wait a bit, want all of them way out there where they can't retreat . . ."

That was apparently the Islander's own way of keeping his nerves steady. Probably effective, even if it was far beneath the dignity of a proper Vanbert nobleman to emulate. But Sharlz, like any Islander, didn't give a damn for that kind of "disrepute." In times past, Demansk could remember hearing Thicelt poke fun at the "steady silent calm" which Confederate nobles prized so highly. *Probably even fuck that way. Which is okay with me. No wonder I get invited into so many Vanbert beds.*

Demansk almost chuckled at the memory. It hadn't just been boasting, either, from what Trae had told him. Thicelt was apparently as skilled at seduction as he was at seamanship.

"*Now,*" Thicelt hissed. An instant later, he was waving his arm and the little corps of signal drummers on the quarterdeck began beating a new rhythm.

Demansk turned his head, looking over the stern. There, hidden behind the quinquiremes which formed the front line of Demansk's fleet, were the dozen new woodclads which Trae and Thicelt had designed for him. Their captains had obviously heard the signal, since the vessels were beginning to move forward.

Very slowly. Not only were these new ships incredibly heavy and ungainly, with the immense slabs of wood which formed their hulls—in complete contrast to the normally light construction of war galleys—but they were also powered by a relatively small number of oars. Given the nature of what they had been designed for, the woodclads had only a single bank of oars. And, while each huge oar had five men working at it, the angle was awkward also. The first bank of oars in most galleys was situated low, close to the water, giving the rowers the best possible leverage. This bank was high up, with the oars slanting down at a steep angle. The last man on the oar, on the inmost side, was forced to swing his arms over his head.

Slow. Slow, and incredibly awkward. But it shouldn't really matter. The woodclads had been designed for one purpose, and one purpose only—to serve as a counter for Casull's new steam rams. They didn't even have to *defeat* the rams, just hold them off while Demansk's fleet overwhelmed the rest of Casull's ships.

Demansk had learned enough, from his one prior experience with steam rams, to know that he could have overwhelmed them also, even with normal war galleys. Given, at least, the size of the fleet he commanded. But he would have suffered great casualties in the process, and that was the one thing he could *not* afford. Not only because he would need those soldiers later, but because he would need their loyalty as well—which, in the days and weeks and months to come, he was going to be stretching to the limit. But he thought he could manage the thing, so long as his men weren't festering with resentment at the loss of too many of their friends and comrades. Not the least of the reasons Marcomann had been so popular with his soldiers was because he gave them light casualties as well as good pay and bonuses.

"We'll find out," he murmured. Then, for a moment, felt a bit chagrined at the untoward lapse into Islander loquacity.

He saw Thicelt smiling out of the corner of his eye. "Good, good," murmured back the ex-pirate. "Why not? You'll be breaking traditions in much bigger ways, soon enough."

It was uncanny, really, the way Thicelt seemed able to read Demansk's mind. Despite the social and cultural distance which separated them—not to mention the racial and religious ones—Demansk had discovered that in many ways he found the Islander closer to him than any of his advisers. Even Prit Sallivar, whom he had known since they were both six-year-old boys.

With a little sense of shock, Demansk realized that he *liked* Sharlz Thicelt. Quite a lot, as a matter of fact. The understanding brought concern rather than pleasure. *Could he afford such a personal indulgence?*

He decided to worry about it later. The woodclads had emerged from the fleet and were taking their positions against the oncoming steam rams. Less than two hundred yards now separated the opponents.

The sidewheel paddles of one of the steam rams suddenly began churning the water. Demansk could now hear the engines—that animal-sounding *chuff-chuff* he remembered—and see heavier smoke begin pouring out of the twin tubes poking up from its turtle-shaped carapace. "Funnels," Trae called them.

"Damn," hissed Thicelt. "I was hoping they'd *all* try a ramming run. Get rid of the problem quick."

Demansk understood the logic, even if he didn't entirely share the confidence that Thicelt and Trae had in the ability of the woodclads to withstand a ram. But . . . in this area, he freely admitted, his admiral and his son were the world's two experts. Well, leaving aside that weird Emerald genius named Adrian Gellert who had designed these infernal new devices in the first place.

Within fifty yards, the steam ram was up to full speed. The paddles were whipping the water into a froth, tossing a double curl of spray ahead of the ram as it came charging forward. That also Demansk could remember from the siege of Preble—at full speed, assuming the engines buried in its bowels didn't fail, a steam ram could outrace even a war galley.

The captain of the woodclad it was aiming for apparently shared Thicelt and Trae's confidence in his vessel. Either that, or he was simply a very conscientious officer. Whatever the explanation, Demansk could see that he was following orders. Rather than trying to meet the ram head on—no way to avoid it, of course, with such a clumsy ship—he was turning his ship broadside, presenting the juiciest possible target to the ram.

For a moment, Demansk found himself wondering if that maneuver would alert the commander of the steam ram that something was amiss. But, here also, Thicelt's greater experience held true. The Islander had described to Demansk how difficult it was for the captain of a steam ram to *think* clearly, in the middle of a battle. The engines were not so many feet away from the little armored blockhouse near the bow from which the captain commanded the vessel. Between the din they produced and the poor visibility allowed by the narrow viewing slits in the blockhouse itself, Sharlz said it was like trying to fight while in a shroud. A very protective shroud, granted, but a shroud nonetheless.

And any decision to break off a final ramming drive had to be made quickly. It only took the ram a few seconds to cross the final distance—less than half a minute—before the order to reverse engines was made. That was necessary, of course. Not even one of these new warships could withstand the shock of ramming at full speed.

"Too late now," came Thicelt's soft, satisfied words. "He's committed." The admiral pointed to the woodclad's rigging. "That captain's good, too. Willem Angmer, that is. He's already got the rigging in place."

So he had. The woodclad had unusually heavy masts, very well braced. Partly that was to withstand the impact of a ram, which would normally snap off any mast which hadn't been taken down yet. Even with the heavy bracing, the only reason the woodclad's mast would survive was because of the bulk of the ship itself.

A woodclad's masts were not designed to be taken down in battle, anyway. Because the *other* reason for the heavy construction was that the masts also served as a weapon. They were Trae's design which he had worked out with Thicelt in the first days after his father brought him into his plans.

The woodclads were triple-masted vessels. The sails had been taken down well before the battle started. The great yardarms which normally held up the sails doubled as derricks. Sailors working on the deck heaved at ropes which levered up extensions onto the yardarms. At the end of each extension rested a huge clay jar, suspended by much smaller ropes. Very similar in design, except fatter in cross-section, to the containers which were used to ship oil. In fact, the things had been made by the same Solinga manufacturer who normally made the oil jars.

The end result was that when the steam ram finally struck the side of the woodclad, the jars would be hanging well out over the deck of the steam ram itself. One of them directly, and the sailors at the next closest mast were already starting to swing that jar toward it. Trae had designed the extensions with hinges which enabled them to cover an arc, not simply the area beneath the yardarms.

Demansk held his breath. The steam ram was now almost invisible to him, on the opposite side of the intervening woodclad. All he could see was the two funnels and the spray being thrown up by the paddlewheels as they reversed.

He saw the woodclad tip, and could almost feel the shudder which ran through it. The rowers on their benches, holding tightly to the oars which they had brought inboard, were shaken back and forth. The sailors at the ropes on the decks, even though they had braced for the impact also, reeled wildly. Several of the ones holding the rope which was swinging the second jar lost their footing entirely. Their jar began swinging wildly.

Demansk winced. "If that thing falls on *our* ship . . ."

Thicelt's lips were pursed. "Indeed. I think in the future we'll tell the sailors—*there it goes*!"

His outstretched finger was pointing at the other jar, the one already hanging over the steam ram. The two men assigned to the task had cut the rope holding it up. Demansk could see the jar plummeting downward. The rope which had been holding it up came whipping behind, up and out of the simple pulley through which it had been threaded.

An instant later, he lost sight of the jar. He *thought* he heard it shattering on the curved iron deck of the steam ram, but wasn't certain.

It hardly mattered. That it *had* shattered was not in doubt. Demansk could see the squad assigned to the next task already at work. The "incendiaries," Trae called them. Four of them, now standing at the rail of the woodclad and firing their odd-looking arquebuses down at the steam ram.

"Odd-looking." For a moment, Demansk found himself amused by the thought. How quickly we adjust. There was a time, not so long ago, when I would have called any firearm "odd-looking."

But he had grown accustomed to the sight of arquebuses and cannons by now, even if he didn't have his son's easy familiarity with the devices. And even Demansk could tell that these guns were never designed for normal combat. Their barrels were much too short and wide, as if they had simply been designed to fire something coarse at very close range.

Which, indeed, they had—and the word "fire" was appropriate. Demansk heard four little explosions, coming so close together they sounded almost as one, and saw what looked like four lances of flame spearing down onto the still-invisible steam ram.

Within three seconds, the ram was no longer invisible. Not exactly. The inflammable liquid with which the shattering jar had coated the steam ram—some ungodly concoction made up by Trae and his design team of apothecaries-turned-arsonists—erupted in flame. Followed, an instant later, by a huge cloud of roiling black smoke.

Again, Demansk found himself holding his breath. This was, in theory, the most dangerous part of the operation—especially if the enemy vessel's ram had become wedged in the heavy baulks which formed the woodclad's "hull."

They weren't really part of the hull. The true hulls of the woodclads were heavy in their own right, much more so than a normal warship's. But the real protection came from heavy timbers bolted on, which could be replaced after a battle.

Provided, of course, that the woodclad itself survived the battle. The problem wasn't the ramming damage. Demansk could see for himself, now, that Thicelt and Trae's estimate had been quite correct. The woodclad had obviously come through the impact with no real damage to the ship's own structure. An impact like that would have broken a normal war galley in half. Or, at the very least, hulled it enough to cause it to sink rapidly. Instead, the woodclad, after recovering from the initial jolt, was remaining level and steady. From what Demansk could see, it hadn't even sprung any leaks.

No, the real danger came from the fire which the woodclad had created on its enemy. If the Islander's ram hadn't gotten wedged, the thing should pass easily enough. Demansk could see that the woodclad's crew had taken up positions to combat any spreading of the flames onto their own ship. Except, of course, for the oarsmen nearest to it, who were now frantically using their oars to try to push off from the burning enemy ship.

If the ram was not wedged, they weren't in much danger. As much as seamen feared fire, it wasn't really likely to happen here. The heavy timbers of the woodclad's hull wouldn't take flame easily, and the sailors had already removed all of the sails and rigging which presented the worst fire hazard.

But if the ram *was* wedged . . .

A vivid image came to Demansk's mind. Trae's infernal oily concoction, spreading all over the steam ram as the jar burst. Rivulets of the horrid stuff, already starting to burn, spilling through the ventholes and the gunports—slits narrow enough to provide protection from missiles, but not from a mass of liquid. Then, in the hellish interior of the steam ram, the stacks of wood which it used to fire its furnace—and, worst of all, the gunpowder for its guns. Most of it stored more or less safely away in the powder room, to be sure, but not all of it.

He grimaced. If the woodclad was still right next to the steam ram when *that* stuff was reached by the flames . . .

"They're safe," pronounced Thicelt. Again, the pointing figure. "Look—they've made a space, and Willem's already getting the rowers working. The ram couldn't have gotten wedged."

Sure enough. Within fifteen seconds, the woodclad had moved thirty yards away from the steam ram. Demansk could now see the enemy vessel clearly. Insofar, at least, as the flames and smoke which seem to cover most of its surface allowed him to see anything.

"She's gone," said Sharlz. His voice held a trace of horror as well as satisfaction. "That'll be pure agony in there. And not really even any way to get out, except—yes, look! One of them's doing it!"

Demansk saw one of the gunports, all of which had been shuttered, swing open. An instant later, a man came spilling out, barely managing to squeeze through the narrow opening. He fell headfirst into the water. Within seconds, two more men followed him.

Thicelt was shaking his head. "Can't be many of them get out that way. The main hatch'll be impossible. By now it'll be too hot to even touch." His eyes ranged the water, narrowing as he saw the fins cutting through it here and there. "One or two of them might make it to another ship. No redsharks in these waters. But even greenies and Lemare's Maidens are nothing to share an ocean with."

Another gunport opened and two more men spilled out. By now, the woodclad was eighty yards off. A third gunport began to swing open, and Demansk saw a man crawling through.

Before he'd managed to get more than his shoulders through, however, he seemed to fly out of the gunport. As if—

The steam ram seemed to belch. Then . . . swell; then—suddenly, the entire vessel disappeared in an eruption and a cloud of smoke three times the size of the one that had already engulfed it. Even at the distance, Demansk couldn't help flinching a little. Sharlz, he noticed vaguely, didn't even try.

He held his breath. No one really *knew* what would happen if the powder magazine of a gunship exploded. If Trae and Thicelt's best estimates were accurate, even the woodclad should be safe—it was almost a hundred yards off, by now. Demansk himself, and the rest of the fleet, should be perfectly safe at a much greater distance. But—no one had any real experience with the thing, in real life.

There came another, louder, explosion. Suddenly, rising up through the cloud of smoke, came the weirdest apparition Demansk had ever seen in his life. It looked like—*what*?

"*The Lady of the Sea save us,*" whispered Thicelt. "Blew the whole shell off in one piece."

Demansk realized that what he was seeing—vanishing now back into the smoke—had been the iron armor of the enemy vessel. The bolts which held it together hadn't given way. Instead, when the magazine blew, it had simply lifted the armor off the ship itself. The shell must have guided the explosion's force mostly against the wooden hull proper.

"The rest of it just disintegrated," added Thicelt. "Must have."

Sure enough. When the smoke finally cleared away, which didn't take much more than a minute, there was nothing left. A few pieces of wooden flotsam, here and there; a couple of bobbing heads—men still alive and swimming toward the nearest Islander galleys—and . . . nothing else. The armored shell must have plummeted straight down to the bottom once it hit the water.

"Shallow waters here," murmured Thicelt. "Good divers . . . we *might* be able to salvage something."

The built-up tension erupted from Demansk in a bark of laughter. Very bad for tradition, that. But—who cared?

"Give it up, Sharlz! You're not a scruffy pirate any longer. Special Attendant and Admiral of the Fleet, remember?"

Thicelt grinned. "Old habits. Sorry." The grin vanished as fast as it came. A moment later, Thicelt was bellowing new orders.

The woodclads beetled their slow way toward the three surviving steam rams—which, for their part, had already turned broadside and were beginning to roll out their cannons. Clearly enough, no steam ram captain was going to try another ramming maneuver.

The signal drums were beating wildly now, and Demansk could hear the signals being passed along by the drummers on the nearest ships. Thicelt had set the entire fleet in motion. The regular war galleys of the Confederate navy were surging forward. No slow beetling, here. Even if they weren't as fast and maneuverable as islander galleys, Vanbert triremes—even quinquiremes—could move quickly enough.

"It's over," said Thicelt, when he finally finished with his orders.

"It's just *started,*" protested Demansk.

His admiral shook his head, the gold earrings flopping back and forth. His face was unusually solemn. "No, Triumvir. Trust me in this, as I would trust you in a land battle. Casull's only hope was that his steam rams could work a miracle—repeat what one of them did at Preble last year."

He waved a hand toward the woodclads. "But they will keep them off. Those timbers will stand up well enough even against cannon fire. And with ten against three, even as slow as they are, they'll be able to keep the steam rams hemmed in. The rest of it will just be a giant melee. Too many ships in too small a space for clever maneuvers. It'll be a Vanbert kind of sea battle—and when was the last time anyone beat you at *that*?" He snorted heavily through a heavy nose. "For that matter, when was the *first* time?"

And so it proved. Within an hour, before the sun had even started its downward descent, it was all over. One of the steam rams, either from desperation or simply because it had a fanatical captain, managed to take a woodclad with it. Ramming again, and this time with the ram wedged. Even then, most of the crew of the woodclad was saved by the bold captain of a trireme, who risked bringing his ship alongside in time to evacuate them before the magazine blew and engulfed the woodclad as well as the ram itself in the destruction.

The other two rams managed to survive, but only by keeping their distance from the woodclads who kept after them. The battle between steam rams and woodclads became something almost ridiculous, with neither side able to inflict any real damage on the other. The rams were fast enough to stay away from the woodclads, but the frantic maneuvers forced upon them to do so—two ships trying to evade nine, even if the nine were much slower—meant that they couldn't fire too many well-aimed broadsides. And even the few they got off, just as Trae and Thicelt had predicted, did little damage to the heavy timbers of their opponents.

One ram did manage, early in the battle, to get off a broadside at a passing trireme which wreaked havoc on the ship. But that was the worst blow that any of the rams managed to land in the course of the whole affair.

Most of the battle was decided the old-fashioned way—maneuverable and expertly-guided Islander galleys against much clumsier and heavier Confederate triremes. Had the odds been even close to even, the Islanders might well have triumphed. But against the numbers they actually faced, it was hopeless. The best captain in the world, commanding the best galley, simply can't maneuver when hundreds of enemy warships are covering every part of his ocean. And whenever, as was inevitable, a Confederate warship did manage to grapple with an Islander galley, it was all over within minutes. The claws came down, and the world's most ferocious close-quarter fighters stormed across. Most Islander crews surrendered immediately.

The surrenders were accepted. On that subject, Demansk had given the *clearest* orders possible—and had representatives of Forent Nappur's "Special Squads" aboard every Vanbert warship to see to it that the captains followed orders. He was determined to avoid a bloodbath, if at all possible.

Whether or not it would prove possible, of course, would depend in the end on his enemy. No soldiers in the world, not even Confederate ones—not even *Demansk's* soldiers—could be kept under discipline if their tempers rose too high. Which, given a bitter enough battle, they inevitably would.

But there, too, whatever gods there might be seemed to be partial to Demansk that day. After an hour of relatively bloodless conflict, the islander fleet suddenly began to break. Within minutes, all the surviving enemy galleys—and there were still well over a hundred of them—were pouring back toward the safety of the harbor. The two surviving steam rams, whose captains must have been superb, covered their retreat.

Doing so, in truth, was not difficult. As soon as Thicelt saw the rout, and without waiting for orders from Demansk, he gave the signal to the fleet to break off the action. In most battles, of course—certainly with a general as good as Demansk in command—the pursuit would have been undertaken with ferocity. But Demansk's strategy was political as much as military, and for his purposes here, a simple defeat was sufficient.

More than sufficient, in fact. It was ideal.

Demansk turned to Thicelt and clapped his shoulder. "My congratulations, Sharlz. You've just won the greatest sea battle ever—and I'll see to it that the historians so record the thing. And now, you're fired."

Thicelt grinned. "Such is fleeting fame." Then, sighed histrionically. "Back to that inglorious 'special attendant' business again."

Demansk nodded, matching smile to grin. " 'Fraid so. You're a diplomat now. And you know the settlement I want."

"Settlement," snorted Thicelt. "Almost as bad as Emeralds, with their 'acumen.' " He clucked his tongue, somehow managing to do it as histrionically as the sigh. "Speak plainly, august Triumvir, just as that grandfather of yours you've told me about would have done." He jerked a thumb toward Chalice. "What you want is that pig skinned. Skinned, gutted, and the meat hung up to dry."

"Just the meat, Sharlz. You can leave them the skin and the entrails." He matched Thicelt's grin with one that was almost as wide. "You watch. Within a generation, your Islanders will be calling me Verice the Merciful."

He left the quarterdeck then, heading for his cabin where others would be waiting for new orders. So he never heard Thicelt's response. The Islander, after watching Demansk's departure, turned and stared at the still-invisible city where he had been born. The "jewel in a cup," as his people called it, the beautiful—and often vicious—city which had been the center of the archipelago's culture for centuries. And which, with one of its own sons as the midwife, was about to give birth to a new world.

"No, lord," he murmured. "In a generation, they will be calling you the same thing as everyone else. Verice Demansk, the Great."

CHAPTER NINETEEN

Demansk's soldiers brought him Casull's corpse before the day was over. The King of the Isles had been aboard one of the galleys stormed by the Confederate soldiers. The crew of that galley, no doubt because the King was there himself to stiffen their spine, had not surrendered. All of them had been killed, either in the fighting or in the massacre of the wounded afterward. Casull's body had been found under a pile of corpses. The soldiers hadn't been entirely sure of his identity—none of them had ever seen Casull in person—but his garments and the accouterments of his office made it clear that, whoever he was, he was someone important. So they brought the body to Demansk.

Thicelt identified him. "That's Casull, all right." He inspected the wounds on the corpse. "Say whatever else you will, he was no coward."

Forent Nappur didn't seem impressed. "I can say the same for every man in my squad—almost every man in the army, for that matter. So why does a fucking king get special credit for doing something any peasant takes for granted?"

There was no particular heat in the words. But the anger simmering beneath them reminded Demansk, if he needed a reminder, how much bitterness and animosity the selfish and ruthless conduct of the Confederation's ruling class had stored up in the hearts of its own citizenry.

Sharlz shrugged. "A peasant doesn't have much choice, Forent. A king does. I guess that's the difference." He straightened up from the kneeling posture from which he'd been examining the corpse, and held up a hand in a little placating gesture. "But I'm not trying to start an argument. I can't say I was all that fond of Casull myself."

He glanced at Demansk and made a chucking gesture with his thumb. "Over the side?"

Demansk shook his head. "No. We'll give him an honorable burial—that's how you do it here in the islands, if I recall? Not cremation?"

Thicelt nodded. But Demansk was really watching Nappur, whose sour expression made clear that he'd personally have been inclined to toss the former king to the sharks.

Demansk understood, and sympathized, with the ex-sergeant's feelings. Still, this was something which had to be settled. In the substance of his policies, Demansk had every intention of setting old wrongs to right. He would favor the poor and downtrodden at the expense of the rich and powerful. But doing so would require, more often than not, maintaining a least a façade of respect for the established order. As long as he could harness the energy and anger of such men as Nappur, they would be of great service. Let that anger break loose unfettered, and unmuzzled . . .

He decided this was not the time and place to raise the matter. But he made a note to have a private conversation with Nappur as soon as possible. As head of the army's "internal police," Forent's attitudes—his real ones, not simply his formal agreement—would be critical.

At Thicelt's gesture, the soldiers who had brought the body picked up Casull's corpse and took it away. They'd overheard Demansk, and would bring the body to the ship's chirurgeon, who would do what was necessary to keep the body preserved until it could be buried. Most Vanberts preferred cremation to burial. But there were enough auxiliary nations and vassal states which practiced burial for a naval chirurgeon to be familiar with the basic methods of embalming. Sharlz could be relied upon to let him know if there were any special rites required by Islander customs.

He moved to the rail of his quinquireme and studied the progress of the disembarkation. By now, not long before sunset, most of the triremes had already been beached and their crews were beginning to erect the first temporary fortifications and field camps. They were moving with the speed which long custom gave them in this work—something which always astonished the Confederacy's enemies. The soldiers would work as long into the night as necessary to get the work done.

Not all of the ships and soldiers were engaged in the work. Demansk's officers had skirmishers and sentries out, ready to give warning in the unlikely event that the Islanders managed to send a ship-burning expedition over the crest of the caldera. And there were plenty of triremes still at sea, even leaving aside the great quinquiremes, to keep the defeated Islander fleet bottled up within the harbor.

Forent Nappur verbalized his own thoughts. "It's done for the day, Triumvir. Why don't you get some sleep?"

He *was* tired. He'd been up since the middle of the night, making the final preparations for the battle. And Nappur was right—there was really nothing left for him to do, until the morrow.

More than anything, however, it was the quite-evident warmth in Forent's voice which allowed Demansk to follow his advice. However much the former sergeant from the hardscrabble east detested royalty and nobility in general, that hatred clearly did not extend to Demansk himself.

It was odd, really. But, as a young man, Demansk had seen the phenomenon at work once before. Marcomann, like Demansk himself, had come from the very uppermost strata of the Confederacy's nobility. That fact seemed to have made the soldiery's adoption of him all the more fierce. *We may be scum beneath their feet, but OUR boy is as good as any of 'em. Better!*

"It's a strange world," he murmured. He and Thicelt exchanged a little smile. Sharlz, thought Demansk, was really the only one of the men around him who probably understood him fully. Perhaps that was because, as an Islander, he was an outsider to begin with.

Or, perhaps, it was simply because he was Sharlz Thicelt.

Demansk decided that he preferred the second explanation. And, as he made his way back to his cabin on the flagship, wondered if the day would ever come when he would be able to indulge in simple friendship again.

He thought not. And, not for the first time, feared for his eventual sanity. But . . . so be it. He was prepared to sacrifice everything else, after all.

By midmorning the next day, the political work which Thicelt had done prior to the attack started coming to fruit. Working secretly through cutouts, he'd been in touch with his family for months, and, through them, with others on the island. Thicelt's own family was not particularly prominent in the social hierarchy of the archipelago, but they knew a lot of people who were.

A galley set out from the harbor at Chalice, bearing a statue of Opal, the Goddess of Tranquility, on its foredeck. That was the traditional Islander method for signaling a desire for a peaceful parlay. Demansk had been expecting something of the sort, so the triremes blockading the entrance to the harbor had been given orders to let any such ship pass through unmolested.

As the Islander galley approached Demansk's flagship, however, Nappur insisted on keeping it at a distance until a boarding party could search the vessel. He admitted it was unlikely that a band of assassins was hiding in the hold, much less a load of explosives, but . . .

Thicelt didn't even argue the point, beyond making a couple of wisecracks. Nor did Demansk. The simple truth was that Verice Demansk was so critical to everything that *any* chance of an assassination attempt had to be taken seriously.

The search didn't take long. It was a small galley, with no area belowdecks except small storage spaces. Outside of the rowers—who were unarmed—and the large delegation of Island notables—most of whom were at least middle-aged, if not older—the only thing the boarding party found was a very large sack. The contents of the sack, once it was opened, proved to be of great interest. But, all the Vanbert soldiers agreed, hardly posed a threat to the Triumvir.

The officer of the boarding party brought the sack aboard the quinquireme, when he made his report to Demansk. Three of his soldiers came behind, two of them hoisting the sack between them with some obvious effort. The officer was grinning coldly; his men seemed to be smirking a little. Oddly enough, the third soldier was carrying a tarpaulin. It looked like it was probably one of the smaller sails from the trireme.

"I'd say they're lying belly-up and waving their paws, Triumvir." The officer gestured toward a bare space on the quarterdeck, and the soldier spread the little sail. Then, upending the sack, the other two dumped its contents onto it.

That explained the reason for the tarpaulin. The quarterdeck of the Triumvir's flagship was kept well-scrubbed and polished. The contents of the sack would have . . . marred it.

Thicelt was down on one knee, casually rolling the severed heads about and making a quick count. Demansk could hear him exclaiming cheerfully: " . . . three, four—ah! Prince Frand! you're looking a bit out of sorts today—five, six, seven—Royal Uncle Gander! fancy meeting you here!—eight, nine—where's . . . ah, there he is, looking as sour as ever—ten, eleven, twelve, thirteen—pardon my fingers in your ear, Queen Yora—fourteen, fifteen, sixteen—" A little hiss. "By the Lady, they didn't have to include *her.*" The count continued: "—twenty-two, twenty-three, twenty-four . . . and, twenty-*five.*"

"How many kids did he have, anyway?" asked Nappur.

Thicelt straightened up. "Seventeen in all, Forent, who survived their childhood diseases. He had several concubines, don't forget. Ten boys and six girls. The oldest boy"—his lips tightened with remembered distaste—"Prince Tenny that was, died at the siege of Preble." He pointed to the grisly pile on the tarpaulin. "All the rest of the boys are there. At least, the count's right. I didn't know all of them personally, so we'll have to double-check."

Demansk did some quick arithmetic. "And the other sixteen heads?" he asked, keeping any trace of disgust out of his voice. That would be hypocritical, leaving aside everything else. If the Islanders hadn't executed all of Casull's important relatives themselves, Demansk would have demanded it anyway. But he didn't have to like the business.

"The rest of Casull's family, those who matter. Male and female both—his wife, three uncles, a brother, two sisters, an aunt, and seven cousins. Casull relied on his family for his closest advisers and officials. I recognized all of them. And they included, for good measure, Princess Rafta. Not sure why, but probably because she was the only adult unmarried daughter. Four of his daughters are married to notables of one kind or another"—Thicelt pointed with his thumb toward the galley, his heavy lips in a half sneer—"who are probably among that pack of whipped curs, and are trying to keep their wives alive."

He scowled. "Stupid, that was. Rafta was unmarried because she was as near brainless as a person can get without having actual roots. She'd been kept secluded in the hareem her whole life."

"That leaves the youngest daughter unaccounted for," remarked Demansk. "Princess Jirri, if I remember right."

The officer who'd led the boarding party cleared his throat. "I think she's probably on the galley, Triumvir. If she's about fifteen years old, there's a girl that age—very finely dressed—in the lot. And looking about as scared as I've ever seen a girl look without breaking into actual tears."

Demansk sighed. "Well, we can put a stop to that, at least. Have the delegation brought on board, Sharlz, if you would." He gave the small crowd on the galley a quick examination. "There are too many of them to fit in my cabin, so we'll have to do the negotiations right here on deck."

He turned to the quinquireme's captain, but the man was already anticipating the order. "Bring the Triumvir's chair and desk from his cabin!" he bellowed to several of the sailors waiting on the maindeck below. "And be quick about it!"

The first thing Demansk did, when the Islander delegation crowded onto the quarterdeck, was crook his finger at the teenage girl in their midst. That she was a princess was obvious, just from the finery of her garments, leaving aside the jewelry. Whether it was her decision or someone else's, Demansk didn't know. But clearly enough the girl was prepared to die in her best outfit.

As pale-faced as a dark-complexioned Islander could get, the princess came forward. Demansk was rather impressed, actually. Her face had the tightness of someone trying desperately to show no emotion at all, but her gait was not mincing in the least.

When she came up to him, he said quietly: "No harm will come to you, girl. You have my word on it. But, now, it would be best if you waited for me in my cabin."

One of the sailors led her away. The other Islanders didn't even so much as glance in her direction. But, from the vaguely smug looks on several faces—as smug, at least, as defeated men can get—their thoughts were obvious: *A concubine for the conqueror. That's why we left her alive. Smart move.*

Demansk had considered the possibility, in fact, once he discovered that there was a surviving female relative of Casull's. Sexual possession of a defeated enemy's women was a traditional mark of conquest, after all. But he'd discarded the idea almost instantly. He intended to wound the Islanders, and grievously—but, for that very reason, would avoid rubbing salt into the wound. Wounds heal quickly enough. Humiliation festers.

His decision hadn't even been shaken by seeing the girl herself. Very pretty, she was, and Demansk was no more immune to feminine beauty than any other healthy middle-aged male. But . . . he'd been more impressed by her composure. A different idea was beginning to form in his mind. One which might advance his project considerably, although it had obvious pitfalls.

He pushed the matter aside. There would be time to think about that later, and discuss it with his advisers. For the moment, there were great bleeding wounds to inflict.

So, his voice as hard as iron, Verice Demansk began laying down his terms of surrender.

"You will be henceforth a province of the Confederacy of Vanbert, by the name of Western Isles."

The name was important, since it implied all the islands in the Western Ocean—Vase and Preble as well as the archipelago proper. And there wouldn't be any tomfoolery about "auxiliary nations" here.

"Two full regiments of Confederate troops will be stationed in the city of Chalice itself. You will be responsible for billeting and provisioning them." He nodded toward the encampment being built on the shore. "As well as providing whatever is necessary for the two brigades which will remain permanently ashore here, along with their fleet."

That was the first wound, and a big one. Maintaining soldiers was expensive, at best—especially when it included ship maintenance.

But it was also time to offer the first subtle sign that, provided there was no opposition, the occupation would be heavy on Islander purses but not crushing to their souls.

"Order among the troops will be maintained according to Vanbert law, which *will* be enforced." He gave a glance at Forent Nappur. His job, that, to make sure it happened. By law, that meant no looting, no casual beatings of innkeepers and other civilians, no rapes. In practice, the law was often ignored. But Demansk had given Nappur the clearest and firmest instructions on the matter. Clear and firm enough, in fact, that Nappur had brought impaling stakes with him on the expedition—and both he and Demansk expected that they would be used, soon enough. But not often, once the troops understood that there would be no looking the other way *here.*

"You will be required to pay, immediately, an indemnity of six million—"

All the faces began turning pale, as Demansk mercilessly continued to list the booty which he intended to squeeze out of the archipelago. The official justification he gave was "the long history of piracy and other crimes committed against the citizens of the Confederation." Which, in and of itself, was true enough—although he would be squeezing out of the Islanders, in the first month of the occupation alone, a sum larger than everything they had managed to gain from their centuries of piracy.

But the real reason was even cruder: Demansk *needed* that enormous loot to keep his soldiers happy. Every single one of his men, he had no doubt at all, had been looking forward happily to sacking Chalice. Being deprived of that pleasure would leave them disgruntled, to put it mildly, unless he could shower them with much greater wealth than they would have been able to plunder from a burning city.

"—during the first three years of the occupation, you will also be required to restitute one million—"

Several of the richer-looking delegates were moaning softly, now. The initial booty they could squeeze, to a large extent, out of the commoners on the island. But to keep handing over such huge sums, month after month after month, would bankrupt everyone in the archipelago.

Which, of course, was exactly what Demansk was planning to do. For the simple reason that a man facing bankruptcy takes a very different attitude toward a stranger who proposes a partnership than one who is awash in wealth.

Demansk needed the booty outright for his soldiers. He needed a bankrupt archipelago for his own *investments*. He was about to demonstrate that there was another way than seizing land for a conqueror to recoup his expenses. Or so, at least, he hoped. Since no conqueror in history had ever done such a thing, it remained to be seen whether it would work. If it didn't . . . Demansk himself would be bankrupt, within a few years.

By the time he was done, the expressions on the faces of the Islander delegates—some of them, at least—were mulish as well as horrified. He decided to squelch that possible resistance immediately.

"Finally, I will remind you all of something." He made a casual gesture toward the huge army encampment on the nearby shore, which was readily visible from the quarterdeck. "I can—quite easily—simply have Chalice sacked. And you know how Vanberts sack a city, since we've done it enough times." Bluntly: "Like a redshark takes a drowning man. In which case, any survivors—what few there are—will not be worrying about their lost treasure. Because they will spend the rest of their lives at work in the fields, and will have far more immediate things to worry about."

He rose from his chair, planted his hands on the table, and leaned forward. His face was bleak, cold, iron. "And if you're wondering whether I'm inclined to do it, the fact is that I'm having a very hard time *restraining* myself from doing it." In a low, almost hissing, voice: "You stinking bastards ravished my daughter and shamed my family. So go ahead and *try* to argue with me. Please."

The anger in his voice was only partly feigned. The mulish looks vanished. Most of the delegates were positively ashen-faced, now. The story of Helga's capture was well known in the islands. The captors and rapists had bragged freely about it, at the time, and most Islanders had shared in their glee at inflicting such a humiliation upon the high and mighty Confederates. And now the father of their victim had his hands on their throat, and the hands were those of a giant . . .

"Done, lord," choked the old man who seemed to be the leader of the delegation, insofar as anyone was. "It will be done."

Demansk sat back down. He decided it was time to ease up a bit. "Good," he murmured. Then, gestured toward Thicelt. "I am appointing Sharlz Thicelt, an Islander himself, to be the governor of Western Isles province. He will arrive in Chalice tomorrow. Make sure Casull's palace is prepared for him."

An Islander. The men of Chalice studied Thicelt covertly. Many of them knew him personally, at least to a degree. As a practical matter, of course, that did not reassure them much. An Islander would be even more adept at spotting attempts to circumvent the Confederacy's harsh demands than a foreigner.

Still . . . he was an Islander. The men in the delegation contained no fools among them. They could see the implications quite clearly. First, at least they would be dealing with one of their own, who would understand how to avoid needless humiliation. Second—more important—Islanders were no great respecters of station, unlike Vanberts. Yet here was the greatest of all living Vanberts, with an Islander as one of his closest subordinates.

The implications were . . . interesting.

When Demansk entered his cabin, he found the princess huddled in the corner atop his bed. Her hands were making vague little movements, as if she was trying to restrain herself from clutching her garments. Pointless, that would be, under the circumstances.

He started to scowl, but managed to keep from doing so. The girl was likely to misunderstand the expression.

"I am *not* going to rape you, child. So be at ease on that matter, at least."

She seemed to relax a bit. It was hard to tell. Again, Demansk was impressed by the girl's composure. He suspected, from things Thicelt had told him in the past, that growing up an islander princess was a harsh school in its own right.

There was a knock on the door. "Enter."

Thicelt came in, followed by three sailors returning the writing table and the chair. Sharlz waited until the sailors finished their work and were gone before saying anything.

Then, his first words were spoken in the Islander tongue, and addressed at the princess: "Relax, girl! The august Triumvir's virtue is already a thing of legend." He gave her a friendly leer. "Me, on the other hand . . . But! You are not in my hands, after all, so there's nothing to fear on that account either."

He turned to Demansk. "I assume you're going to keep her secluded, yes? Or should we have her removed while we continue our plans?"

Demansk studied the girl. The idle thought which had come to him earlier, on the deck, came back in richer color and details. *Fascinating possibility . . .*

It was worth exploring, he decided. No point in it if she isn't bright as well as good-looking.

"Come here, Jirri." He pointed to the chair at the table. The princess scuttled off the bed and hurried to do as she was instructed. Only after she had taken her seat did it occur to Demansk, belatedly, to ask if she understood his own language. Apparently so.

But to make sure, since she might simply have interpreted the gesture which accompanied the command, he asked her directly. Speaking in her own language, in which he was competent if not fluent.

"Oh yes, great lord. I speak Vanbert."

"I'm not 'great lord,' princess. The proper title is 'Triumvir.' Can you read and write?"

Jirri looked doubtful. “Not very well.”

“An Island woman,” chuckled Thicelt. “What do you expect?”

Demansk ignored him. “You can learn. Can you do arithmetic?”

The princess winced. It was the first open expression Demansk had yet seen on her face. “Not the Vanbert way.”

Demansk and Thicelt both chuckled now. “I should think not!” said Demansk. “What a miserable, clumsy thing that is. No, girl, I meant: can you use Islander numbers? The truth is, any Confederate merchant and landlord with half a brain adopted your way of doing arithmetic over a century ago. The only thing anyone uses Vanbert numbers for anymore are official documents.”

Her face cleared. “Oh yes, grea—ah, Triumvir. I’m good at numbers. My mother saw to that instruction, so that I could keep an eye out on the slaves who kept the books when I had my own house.”

Mention of the mother, whose decapitated head had “adorned” Demansk’s quarterdeck not so very long ago, caused him to wince a bit. But the girl’s face didn’t seem to echo any of that. For all that Demansk could tell, the murder of her mother—following within a day of the death of her father—didn’t seem to have affected her much at all.

For a moment, he was alarmed. If the girl was *that* indifferent to human sentiments . . .

Thicelt, as so often before, read his thoughts. “You don’t understand the reality of a royal hareem, Triumvir. Explain it to him, Jirri.”

The girl was confused. “Explain what? Uh, great lord—ah—”

Thicelt grinned. “ ‘Governor’ will do fine.” He hooked a thumb at Demansk. “What I meant was, explain to him why you don’t seem very upset at the death of your parents. Or your brothers.”

Jirri almost goggled at Demansk. “I hardly knew my father, Triumvir. And my mother’s *not* dead. She—oh. You thought she was Queen Yora. No, she was one of the King’s concubines.” After a moment’s hesitation: “To be honest, I was glad they killed Yora. I hated her, and she frightened me. I’m sure—well, almost—that she was planning to have me murdered. Her son, Prince Frand, was starting to sniff around me—even though he was my half brother—and she didn’t like it.”

Demansk rubbed his face. He'd heard tales from Helga, about the sometimes savage intrigue within hareems. And the hareem Helga had been held captive in was that of an old, tired chieftain. The hareem of a relatively young and dynamic ruler like Casull would, likely enough, resemble a nest of serpents.

"As for my brothers and half brothers," Jirri was continuing, "I either didn't know them or, the ones I did, didn't like them much. Especially Frand. I like my sisters Harra and Tlal a lot—Yuni and Fayr not so much, they're half sisters anyway—but they're all still alive too." There was a little lift in her voice, speaking that last. It seemed as if Princess Jirri had come to the conclusion that her conqueror was not a monster, after all, and so her mother and sisters could expect to stay alive.

Then, her tone grew slightly sullen. "But I don't know why they had to kill Rafta. She was a sweet-tempered thing, even if she couldn't really talk."

Demansk waved his hand. "Never mind, Jirri. I'm satisfied. And now—" He walked over to a nearby table, picked up a stylus and a blank codex, and plopped it on the table in front of her.

"What the Governor and I will now be doing, among other things, is what is called 'logistics.' A lot of that is just recording numbers—which you're going to do for us. In the Confederacy, it's called being a 'secretary.' It's quite a prestigious position, by the way, at least if you're doing it for someone important."

Jirri stared down at the stylus and codex, then looked up at Demansk. Her eyes seemed as wide as saucers.

"You want me to *do* something?" She was almost gaping. Then, a smile came to her face. And, for the first time since he'd lain eyes on her, Princess Jirri looked like what she really was—a fifteen-year-old girl.

"Oh! That sounds like *fun*."

Hours later, Jirri's eyes were starting to droop. She was clearly struggling to remain awake. Suddenly, it dawned on Demansk that the girl couldn't have gotten any sleep at all the night before.

A bit guiltily, he put a gentle hand on her shoulder. "That's enough, girl. Go to sleep. You'll have to share the bed with me tonight, I'm afraid. But I'll have something made up for tomorrow. I won't wake you, though, I don't think."

Jirri covered her mouth, yawned, and then coughed a little laugh behind her hand. "Don't think so. Everyone always teased me about how heavy a sleeper I am. But my mother says that's because I have a clear conscience."

I wish I did, lass, thought Demansk, as he watched her stumble to the bed and clamber onto it. Within seconds, she was curled against the wall and sound asleep. *But I will say that you've helped. With my conscience even more than the numbers.*

Thicelt cleared his throat. Demansk looked at him.

"The special courier ship left last night to bring word to Trae. If all works as planned, he will soon have a great accomplishment to his own name. At which point—"

Demansk grinned. "Odd, isn't it, how great minds think alike? At which point, needless to say, it will be time for my youngest son to think about getting married."

CHAPTER TWENTY

But when Trae reached Chalice, three weeks later, he was anything *but* filled with self-satisfaction at his martial exploits.

"There wasn't any fighting at *all,* Father," he complained bitterly. He upended his cup of wine, drained half of it in one gulp, and almost slammed it down on the side table—without, amazingly, spilling anything.

Sourly: "Except for killing some of my own soldiers and sailors. On three of the ships—dammit, I gave clear orders ahead of time!—the bastards started raping the women." He gave Forent Nappur, lounging on a nearby couch, a glance of approval. "Next time, if there is a next time, I'll insist on having some of *his* men along. They'd have paid attention to *them.*"

Demansk was not lounging, he was sitting upright. "So what did you do?" he asked. The question was not an idle one. In and of itself, he didn't much care about the travails of refugee women. Those who'd stayed behind on Preble would have suffered a much worse fate at the hands of Albrecht's vengeful troops, after all, when they sacked the island. But the way in which Trae handled such a challenge to his authority was . . . critical.

Trae shrugged. "What *could* I do? There were only a handful of marines on each of those ships—which, as it was, were packed full of refugees. And—fucking swine—they were the ones leading the charge anyway. All I had was the steam ram."

He grabbed the goblet, drained the rest of it—spilling some on his tunic, this time—and slammed it back down. "Ha! The marines on the first ship I ordered to cease and desist even had the gall to make obscene gestures at me."

For the first time since Trae had stalked into the Governor's Palace, an expression other than sourness came to his face. Granted, it was a young man's snarl, a bit too flamboyant to be fully effective. But . . . effective enough, Demansk thought.

"So, of course, I rammed the ship. Broke it in half! Then ordered the nearest three ships to pick up the refugees out of the water and leave the marines and the sailors to the sharks. They did it right quick, too, damned if they didn't."

The other men in the room, Demansk and Nappur and Thicelt, burst into laughter. Demansk more loudly than the others.

"Crude, crude," reproved Thicelt, still chuckling, "but I dare say it was effective."

The scowl was back on Trae's face. "I had to do it *twice*, dammit! The fleet was too big and spread out for all the ships to see what had happened to the first one."

Demansk nodded. "And the third ship?"

Trae jerked a thumb over his shoulder, pointing in the direction of the harbor below the palace. "I had the crew and marines arrested when we came ashore." With some heat: "I'd have had them—"

He broke off the angry statement. "But I'm not in charge here, so I just had them put in custody. Forent's men have them." He looked at Thicelt. "I guess you are, since you're the Governor. I think—"

Nappur's deep, growling voice went through the room like a predator's stalk. "No, he's not in charge, on this matter. I am, since it's a matter of army discipline. Those men disobeyed clear instructions from their commanding officer, given to them beforehand. You did, correct?"

Trae nodded vigorously, almost fiercely. "By the gods, yes! We spent *weeks* preparing for the expedition—months, rather. I even made a special trip to Rope to meet with the ship captains, all of them."

"Good enough," rumbled Forent. "I'll have the stakes brought out again. Haven't had to use them here since the third day of the occupation, but it won't hurt at all to have a reminder. I'll have them set up on the docks, in plain view of the whole city."

"How did the evacuation itself go?" asked Thicelt. "That must have been pure chaos."

"The gods, yes! It was a madhouse. Still"—he gave Demansk a look of admiration which any Vanbert patriarch would have basked in—"the whole thing went pretty much exactly the way Father predicted. I was surprised, to tell you the truth. I thought . . ."

He let the disrespectful notion trail off. Even—a rarity, this, to be treasured!—had a guilty look on his face.

Demansk barked a laugh. "I was *guessing*, Trae, not *predicting*. An educated and informed guess, true enough. But the whole thing was still a gamble."

Demansk rose, went to a side table, and poured himself a goblet of wine. This would be the first cup of wine he'd allowed himself since the occupation began, weeks ago. But the news of how Trae had handled the mutiny was cause enough for celebration. Demansk was struggling not to let his pride show too openly.

My son! Damn me who will, but this too was my doing. I always knew Trae had the brains—the gods know he's good-humored—but I was never sure he had the steel.

When he turned back, however, his expression was simply one of mild satisfaction. The august patriarch. Approving of his offspring, of course, but still finding it necessary to correct minor errors.

"Albrecht went berserk, didn't he, when he got the news I'd taken the archipelago? I knew he would, the stinking pig. So he ordered an all-out assault across that causeway he's been building for the past year. The kind of frontal attack that produces casualties worse than anything."

Out of the corner of his eye, he could see Forent wincing. The ex-sergeant knew exactly what Demansk was talking about.

Demansk resumed his seat. "Let me explain a little secret of siegecraft to you, Trae. The thing that usually breaks the defenders' lines, at the end, is when the men on the fortifications start panicking.

Not for themselves, but for their families. They *know* they're going to lose, you see, and so they desert their posts in order to try to find their own folks in the city. And save them—the gods alone know how—from the horrors of the ensuing sack."

Trae was watching him intently. Possibly for the first time in his life, Demansk's youngest son had not a trace of his usual cockiness. "That's what your evacuation prevented," continued Demansk. "Once the Islanders on Preble understood that there was a *chance* of saving their families—a chance which got better the more fierce a resistance they put up—most of the men would have stayed at their posts. And fought like demons."

"Truth," uttered Nappur. "There really aren't all that many cowards in the world, when the crunch comes down." He winced again. "I don't even want to think what kind of casualties Albrecht's soldiers suffered. But I'll tell you this—anyone Trae *didn't* evacuate from Preble was dead within a day. Including household pets. That would have been a massacre."

"I got off mostly women, children and old folks," agreed Trae. "Not too many men of fighting age."

"And you were expecting?" growled Thicelt. "No one's ever accused we Islanders of being pussies, you know, whatever else they say about us."

Demansk finished his wine. For a moment, he considered a second cup, but dismissed the idea. Pleased or not, he still had a titan's work ahead of him.

"Let this be a lesson to you, scion of mine. If at all possible, *always* leave your enemy with an escape route. A cornered rat is dangerous, always is. Whereas a rat huddling in a hole, after you've taken the house, is just a nuisance."

He toyed with the empty cup in his hands, for a moment. "What Albrecht *should* have done is immediately offered Preble the same kind of terms I gave the Islanders elsewhere. News of my conquest of the archipelago will have reached the defenders of Preble too. They'd *know,* then, that further resistance was hopeless."

"Why didn't he?" asked Trae. "I know you always said he wouldn't, but why not? He's not really *that* much of a hothead."

"You might be surprised. Albrecht's cool enough, most of the time. But when he gets jabbed unexpectedly, he tends to react like a maddened boar. I've never been convinced he's fully sane, frankly." Demansk placed the empty cup on the table next to his couch and pushed it aside. "But it doesn't matter, given Albrecht's ambitions. After I'd conquered the archipelago, mostly through negotiations, *he* needed a 'real victory' at Preble. If he'd settled for a negotiated surrender, he'd just look like a midget version of me. Instead, he can at least claim to be a 'real Vanbert conqueror'—and you can bet everything you own that his people in the capital are already accusing me of being false to our traditions."

"They'll be accusing you of worse than that, Triumvir," chortled Nappur. "For sure, Albrecht will try to claim that you undermined him."

Demansk shrugged. "Let him make the claim. I was careful to leave Jeschonyk a way to murk it all up politically. I didn't interfere at all—directly—with Albrecht's military command. But, as the Triumvir in charge of the new province of Western Isles—*all* of the islands—I saw fit to provide shelter for the relatives of my own new subjects."

He frowned at Trae. "Which is why, by the way, I'm personally glad you *didn't* have to attack any of Albrecht's ships. That would have made things a lot harder for Ion in the capital."

Trae's scowl was coming back, introducing itself with a snort of derision. "Them! Only two of his triremes even came around to my side of the island. The rest of his ships were supporting the assault. They took one look at me—they remember *this* steam ram, for sure, from last year—and kept their distance."

"Speaking of which," said Thicelt, "did it make it across the ocean?"

"Ha! I had to have it towed into Rope, where I left it," grumbled Trae. "Even with this mild weather, the damn thing takes on so much water in the open sea that the whole crew had to spend all its time bailing. Didn't dare keep the boilers going."

The scowl was in full bloom now. "All of which doesn't deal with *my* problem, Father! Sinking two ships of mutineers is not exactly the kind of reputation I need for—"

"Be quiet, boy." Demansk's tone was stern, almost cold. "Grow up, damn it. Who cares what kind of a reputation you have with Vanbert soldiers? I've got enough of *that* to do for the whole family—even leaving aside what Forent's men will make of it."

The giant was back to chortling. " 'So fierce was the countenance of young Trae—so terrifying the very name of Demansk itself—that Albrecht's navy recoiled and fled from his wrath.' We'll start there. By the time we get done with the mutiny, it'll sound like something out of the old ballads."

Even Trae chuckled. Demansk rose to his feet. "And what's more important—much more—is that you'll now have a reputation among the Islanders."

"We're partial to saints, y'know," drawled Sharlz. "It's a most important aspect to the creed of the Lady of the Sea. And Lemare's a far more important goddess to the common run of Islanders than the ones the former kings favored."

His face assumed an unusually solemn expression. "I'm not joking, Trae. 'Pirates' we might have been. But pirates are seamen, first of all, and no one understands better the dangers of the sea—or the blessedness of a man who rescues people from shipwreck. Which you just did on the largest scale in history."

"And now, *up,* youngest son of mine!" commanded Demansk. "You haven't got time to wallow in misery. I've got new work for you, and lots of it. First thing tomorrow morning, you're meeting a man named Marzel Therdu—he's the one who wound up in charge of Casull's armament works—along with about a dozen other Islander manufacturers. The owners of the largest foundries and smithies. As a group, they're the core of the new weapons industry Adrian Gellert created for the Islanders."

He headed for the door, with Trae following. "All of them are now destitute, of course, and their employees are even more desperate than they are. So I propose to get them all back to work, and on a larger scale than before. With you in overall charge of coordinating the work."

"We don't have much money left, Father," protested Trae. "The family's coffers are empty, as near as matters."

"Money!" jeered Demansk. "I don't need to use *my* money, Trae." He stopped in the doorway and pointed a finger back at Thicelt. "As it happens—what a coincidence—the Governor just issued a new decree. Any business in a Western Isle province which is one-third owned by a reputable citizen—which requires three generations of citizenship, so no Islander can qualify—is exempted from paying tribute. They'll still have to pay the regular taxes, of course."

Trae stared at Thicelt. Sharlz smiled seraphically. "What else could I do? My people were *starving.*"

Trae stared at his father. Who was smiling also, if not seraphically. "You see how it works? Since I'm the most reputable citizen there is—and, what a coincidence, am the only one moving immediately—I estimate that, within a year, I'll own a third of practically everything that makes money in this archipelago. I've even had fishing crews starting to approach me. Even a fruit vendor!"

"But—" Trae was frowning fiercely. "You still need *money*, Father. Immediately."

And now, Demansk's smile *was* seraphic. "To be sure. Which *I* don't have, any longer—but lots of Emerald merchants do. Especially now, when they're flush from all the money I poured into their coffers over the past year. Ropers, too. None of whom, alas—being only partial citizens or auxiliaries—can qualify for the exemption. So the Islanders provide the wherewithal and the skilled labor, the Emeralds and Ropers put up the money, I put the whole thing together." He cleared his throat. "For a modest third."

Trae was almost ogling him. "You—swindler! Um, sorry. 'August father possessed of, ah, extreme acumen.' But still . . ."

Demansk took his arm and led him into the corridor beyond. "It'll work, Trae. Okay, I'm *guessing* again—no conqueror's ever tried to do it this way before, instead of grabbing land—but I'll be surprised if, within a few years, the Demansk family's fortune isn't twice what it was at its best."

Again, he made that modest throat-clearing noise. "Olver, as you know, is the man I appointed the new governor of the Emeralds. And as it happens—what a coincidence—I've just been informed he found it necessary to decree a change in the tax laws. It seems the Emeralds were getting so rich that the sumptuary taxes were eating them alive. So, alert to the needs of his people, he decreed that any wealth accumulated in another province would be exempted from taxation beyond the usual initial levies—provided, of course, that the riches were obtained in a *legitimate* enterprise. Which—what a coincidence—requires a Vanbert partner." With a chuckle, and a nod toward the northeast, where the harbor lay: "I think half the moneylenders and merchants of Solinga and Rope are here already. The gods know, I've had enough of them clamoring for an audience with me."

They were now entering that portion of the palace which had formerly contained Casull's hareem. The giant eunuchs who once guarded the doors were gone, replaced by two Vanbert infantrymen, and the doors themselves were open instead of being barred. The men came to attention as Demansk and Trae passed through.

"This is the hareem, isn't it? I'd think you'd be more careful," said Trae with a little smirk. "You know Vanbert soldiers."

"I'm counting on it," snorted his father. "If I thought I could get away with it, I'd have already done what the conqueror of legend did—ordered all my men to marry native women. Since that would be too much of a breach with custom, I've done the next best thing. Planted thousands of single men, their purses full, in a place full of destitute and desperate women." He nodded toward the harbor again. "Of which you just brought another huge batch, most of them widows."

"Sounds like a giant whorehouse."

Demansk shrugged. "To a degree, it is. But don't forget that my new regulations apply to the soldiers also. If they *marry* their new women, they stand to create a retirement for themselves. Which, since there won't be any land grants coming from this conquest, is something that the smartest of them are already figuring out. We had eighteen marriages yesterday. By next month, I think we'll have to start conducting mass ceremonies."

They had entered the innermost chamber of the former hareem. The surroundings were plush and luxurious, if a bit garish for

Vanbert tastes. And the shallow pool at the center of the great room was completely at variance with Confederate architecture.

Trae didn't seem put off by it, though. He went over to the pool, squatted down, and dipped his hand in the water.

"Warm. They must have a heating system of some kind. They're clever, Islanders, no doubt about it. They'll make good mechanics. Better than Vanbert ones, probably."

He eyed Demansk over his shoulder. "I don't know, Father. The whole thing sounds weird to me. Wealth out of nothing. Well, not that exactly. But it's still wealth just coming out of . . . of . . ." He groped for words. "Out of money spinning around. Like that 'perpetual motion machine' the Emerald philosophers all swear is impossible."

Demansk decided it was time to bring Trae *all* the way in. "It's not impossible, Trae. In fact, it's been done many times before, and on many worlds. I didn't come up with the idea myself, although I'd been groping toward it."

He glanced at the west wall of the chamber. His own private quarters were on the opposite side of that wall, and he could visualize perfectly the writing table on which Adrian Gellert's "letter" rested. Demansk, like Trae himself, found the title *Meditations on Successful Tyranny* a bit ridiculous. But, unlike Trae, he'd read it. Done much more than read it, in fact—by now, he practically had it memorized.

"Most of it is Gellert's thinking. Helga says—"

He broke off, realizing that he would have to elaborate on the nature of Gellert's bizarre "spirits" at a later time. Something much more pressing was on the agenda at the moment.

Princess Jirri had come into the room, emerging from the door where her own quarters lay. She practically stormed into the room actually, glaring fiercely and waving a sheet of paper clutched in two little fists. Several of her fingers were stained with ink.

"Father, you have *got* to put a stop to—"

She halted abruptly, staring at Trae. Then, a moment later, her jaw dropped.

Trae rose to his feet and gave Demansk a cocked eyebrow. "'Father'? Is there something I don't know? A second wife you never told us about?" He gave Jirri a careful inspection. "She doesn't *look* like one of your offspring. Too gorgeous, for starters."

Demansk coughed. "Well. Actually, Jirri's more or less practicing, I guess you could say. I'm *about* to become her father. I don't believe I've had a chance to mention yet that you're getting married. The day after tomorrow, as it happens. The ceremony's already been prepared."

As if by cue, the sound of heavy chimes ringing somewhere in the city below wafted through the airy windows of the hareem. Through those same windows, Demansk could see the Western Ocean. The waters of the archipelago seemed especially vibrant today.

"Ah, good. I see the temples have gotten the announcement. I had to wait, of course, until you'd actually arrived."

It would be difficult to say which of the two youngsters in the room had the widest eyes, at that moment. Both pairs looked like saucers. Trae was goggling at his father; Jirri was goggling at Trae.

"You didn't warn me!" they both protested simultaneously.

"I'm not ready to get married!" added Trae.

Jirri's protest was less cosmic: "I've got ink on my hands!"

Demansk bestowed a look upon his son which was stern enough to have satisfied the All-Father himself. "There will be no discussion, Trae, and no argument. *None.* In this, if nothing else, I will stand on ancient custom. I *am* your father, and you *will* do as I say. I need this marriage to solidify everything."

He glanced at Jirri, finding it hard not to laugh at her indignation over smudged fingers. "The truth is, I even considered marrying her myself. But that would have been too much of a breach with custom, and besides, I've been thinking—never mind." Firmly: "You're perfect. As my youngest son, you're not likely to be the Demansk heir anyway. The Council will squeal with outrage, but not for long. And, in the meantime, I'll have welded the Islanders to our family inseparably."

He pointed out the window. "Listen to those chimes, Trae. That celebration's not being faked. You're not only my son, but you're the one who just rescued thousands of their kinsfolk from Preble. Wedded, the day after tomorrow, to the surviving unmarried daughter of the previous dynasty. As good a guarantee as my new subjects could ask for. So long as they obey Demansk, that same name will be their shield."

Trae stared out the window. After a moment, his shoulders slumped a little, as a man's will when he accepts something inevitable. Demansk was relieved to see the familiar wry twist come his son's lips. If nothing else, Trae would always have his sense of humor.

"Did Gellert prescribe this too?"

Demansk shook his head. "Not hardly! I don't need mysterious spirits to teach me *statecraft*, Trae. I learned the principles of that from my own grandfather."

Trae's eyes moved to Jirri. The girl was now clumsily trying to disguise her fingers. But since she only had a thin sheet of paper and a tunic which was not much thicker to hide them in, she wasn't having much success. The expression on her face was one of extreme distress. *Her first meeting with her groom! And she was filthy!*

The wry smile widened. "A practical lass, is it? Well, that's good. You'll need to be, poor thing, married to *me.*" He gave his sire a look which just bordered on derision. "Or did my scheming august father neglect to mention to you that I was a complete eccentric?"

He stepped over to her and held out his hands. "Stop fidgeting, dammit. It's silly. As good-looking as you are, girl, you'll be bearing our first child within a year—and that'll be a lot messier than a little ink. Show me the fingers."

She did as her husband-to-be commanded. Demansk, watching, thought that her instant obedience was only partly the result of Islander custom. Jirri's eyes, staring up at Trae, were still wide. But Demansk could detect the first traces of trust coming into those dark orbs.

"I'll scrub them," whispered Jirri. "Right away."

Trae clucked his tongue. "Just for a little ink? Scrape those pretty fingers raw? I don't think so, girl." He gave her a smile which was a weird cross between a comfort and a leer. "Come the night after tomorrow, I'll be wanting those fingers soft and supple, damned if I won't."

Jirri choked down a laugh. There was some embarrassment in the sound. But there was also more a trace of anticipation.

"I've got some stuff that will work a lot better than pumice and oil," continued Trae. "You should see the crap *I* get on my fingers. Ha! You *will* be seeing it, soon enough. I'll have the cleansers brought up to the palace."

And then, even Trae was at a loss for words. Demansk left them there, two youngsters staring at each other. Given the nature of the times, he thought that dirty hands were an appropriate way for a husband and wife to get introduced.

Thicelt was waiting for him in his own quarters. Not in the private chamber where Demansk slept and where he'd spent hours studying Gellert's missive, but in the great outer salon which Demansk used for meetings with his close advisers.

"They sound good, no?" asked Sharlz, gesturing with his head to the windows. "I think they've got every chime in the city ringing."

Demansk nodded. "Yes. And now comes the hardest part. Waiting."

Thicelt studied him. Then, glanced at the door to Demansk's private chamber. Sharlz had never read Gellert's treatise, but he knew about it.

"It all depends on him now, I suppose."

"Not quite." Demansk lowered himself onto a couch and stretched. He was actually looking forward to the next few days, however much his son and about-to-be daughter-in-law might be full of trepidation. A traditional celebration, with the gaiety and feasting, would be a pure pleasure. And, in truth, he really could afford to ease up for a bit.

"Not quite," he repeated. "If Gellert fails, I think I could still manage the thing. But it'd be the difference between ruling a realm and ruling a ruin."

He stared out the window. His view was not of the harbor, but of the mountains behind Chalice. Almost the exact opposite direction from the one where his and the world's fate would be largely decided in the next few weeks. But Demansk wasn't even tempted to crane his neck and look toward the south.

That wouldn't do any good at all. He'd only be staring at a wall, in any event. What Demansk needed, now more than ever, was simply a measure of serenity. And for that, his window suited him perfectly. In the center of his view was the Peak of the Sun God, rising majestically into the heavens. With, as always since Demansk had arrived at the archipelago, that steady, steady, steady plume.

"It's a good sign," pronounced Thicelt. He was speaking of the nearby chimes, of course. But Demansk, staring at silent smoke in the distance, found himself in full agreement.

PART III
THE INVADER

CHAPTER TWENTY-ONE

It's always like this, lad, said Raj. ***Don't let anyone ever feed you any crap about how much more natural it is to live in a state of barbarism.***

Adrian was about to protest that he'd never thought any such nonsense—nor, whatever other silliness they sometimes spouted, had any of the philosophers of the Grove. But, catching the little echoes which lay behind Raj's words, he said nothing. Whitehall, he realized, wasn't so much speaking to him as to himself. During the centuries in which the long-dead general's "spirit" had lived side by side with Center, the ancient battle computer had presented to Whitehall the entire panoply of human history, beginning with its origins on a far-distant planet called Earth.

Adrian had never heard of Earth until his ghostly companions told him about it. The birthplace of the human race, apparently—and, certainly, the birthplace of every stupid notion that had ever infected the species.

Did people really think there was such a thing as a "Noble Savage"? he asked, half-incredulously.

Oh, yes. At least one entire school of thought, with plenty of offshoots. Needless to say, not people who'd ever witnessed what you're seeing.

Adrian didn't really appreciate that last remark. He was having a hard enough time controlling his stomach as it was. Their column was passing through a village which had been ravaged recently by Southron cavalrymen ranging far ahead of the main army, and the leavings of their atrocities were scattered everywhere. Men tortured in the most hideous ways imaginable—the same for the women, with rape added into the bargain—children slaughtered, cottages burned.

There was not even any point to most of the butchery. Abstractly, Adrian could understand murder and rape. But why expend the time and effort to kill a peasant by flaying him alive? And why, after gang-raping his wife, impale her in such a grotesque manner? Or scatter the entrails of an infant so small that a quick sword slash would have killed him instantly?

The thing about a barbarian's life is that it's barbarous. It's not that these men are intrinsically any more evil than civilized people, it's simply that there's nothing else to serve as a counterweight. None of the cultural overlay which—sometimes, at least—a civilized society instills in its members. So when they do go on a rampage, they exhibit all the unthinking glee in cruelty that a five-year-old boy does playing with insects.

I didn't, protested Adrian. He averted his eyes from a woman's naked corpse hanging from a nearby tree. She'd been suspended upside-down and then—

He struggled fiercely for a moment, trying to keep from vomiting. *I didn't torture insects,* he repeated, protesting.

He could sense Whitehall's shrug. ***Plenty of "civilized" boys do, lad. Lots of them. But as they age, they're taught that people are not insects. Whereas for a barbarian, anyone not of "our people"—which is the same as "the" people—is usually considered no different from an animal. Except that most barbarians don't treat their animals this badly. Not even close.***

"Fucking savages," hissed Helga. She was riding next to him, at the head of the column, on her own velipad. Unlike Adrian, Helga was not trying to avoid looking at the carnage. She had a stronger stomach than he did, as he'd learned soon after making her acquaintance.

"Complete animals." She gave Adrian a look which was not filled with admiration. To put it mildly. "I hope you and Father know what you're doing," she growled. "Me, I'd rather see these bastards destroyed root and branch."

To Adrian's relief, the column was leaving the remains of the village. The road—a typically good Confederate one, even here—was reentering one of the small forests which dotted the landscape of the southernmost province of the Confederacy. This province, being one of the "marches," was relatively underpopulated. The reason for which, of course, was precisely the danger of Southron raids.

But this was a full-scale invasion, not a raid, and the villages this far from the frontier were not really alert the way the settlements near Kellinek's Wall had been. The core of the Southron army was moving very slowly—much more slowly than Confederate infantry would have done—because of their cumbersome wagons. But a good two thirds of the barbarian force came from tribes other than the Reedbottoms, and weren't hampered by Adrian's "gun-wagons." They were ranging far ahead and scattering out, following their usual customs, despite all of Adrian's protests to Chief of Chiefs Norrys. So they fell on unsuspecting villages like a sudden nightmare; a human tidal wave from a burst dam, drowning peasants caught by surprise on a flood plain.

Not that the alertness of the soldiers guarding the Wall had done them much good. The Wall had been erected by Speaker Kellinek a century earlier, and had never been designed to stop this kind of invasion. Kellinek had simply aimed to create something strong enough to deter small raids, and act as a tripwire against large ones. The job of the Wall's garrison was merely to slow down an invader long enough for the regional governor to bring up the mighty power of the regular brigades.

The Wall was really just a turf mound with a wooden palisade. Every few miles, a small garrison—not more than a hundred, usually—was stationed at a wooden fortress with a watchtower. The major weapon they possessed were a couple of ballista mounted on the towers.

Between Adrian's gunners and the numbers which Norrys

commanded, the barbarians had had no difficulty breaching the Wall. Adrian's arquebusiers had slaughtered any Confederate soldier bold enough to remain in the towers or stick himself far enough above the palisade to cast a missile. And while the Southrons had no real notion of "siege warfare," they numbered perhaps twenty thousand, in addition to the ten thousand Reedbottoms under Prelotta's authority.

The aversion of Southron warriors to menial labor did not extend to warfare. Thousands of them had readily dismounted at Norrys' command and built log-and-earthen ramps which enabled them to storm the palisade. Working with the most primitive possible tools, yes, nothing more than axes and crude shovels—but even working with such, thousands of men can erect a ramp in a few hours. Especially with Adrian's gunners providing them with covering fire.

Thereafter, given the gross disparity in numbers, the Confederate soldiers manning the Wall had been butchered. Along with, needless to say, all the civilians in the settlements which had appended themselves over the past hundred years to the fortresses.

The Wall had been overwhelmed in a single day. By the next morning, thirty thousand Southrons were pouring into the southern provinces of the Confederacy.

The only survivors, except a few who managed to flee on velipads or find hiding places in the forests, had been those overrun by the Reedbottoms. Prelotta's men treated their captives brutally, but they didn't kill them. That was at their chief's command. Which had been occasioned not by any "humanitarianism" on his part, but cold-blooded calculation. Prelotta wanted slaves, not useless corpses.

the first step forward in the rise of civilization, commented Center, **as bizarre as it may sound. enslave people instead of slaughtering them. and do it systematically.**

Adrian pondered the computer's words. Slavery was a familiar enough practice among the Southrons. But it had what you might call a "casual" nature. Most slaves were members of another tribe captured in the course of the barbarians' incessant internecine warfare. Treated savagely, at the time of capture—but then, usually within a generation, absorbed into the capturing tribe. The slaves were more in the nature of trophies and personal servants than a labor force subjected to systematic exploitation.

Prelotta, Adrian knew, intended to change that. The other Southron tribes had joined this great invasion for the customary reasons—loot, and the prospect of "martial glory." Only Prelotta was thinking further ahead than that. He intended to *occupy* this territory, and remain there after the other tribes returned south for the winter. Prelotta was thinking like a conqueror, not a raider—and for that, he needed a subject labor force.

Helga was still glaring at him. Adrian tried to think of what he might say to mollify her, but the only words which came to him were . . . best left unspoken.

This is really no different from what your father's doing in the islands, love. In principle, at least. Use a conquered land's resources and labor force to enhance your own power and wealth. Um. Granted, the methods are dissimilar. Um. To put it mildly.

The methods are what matter. A civilized conqueror—one, at least, who's willing to think like a civilized man—can substitute mercy for cruelty and forethought for rapine. So, in a generation—even less—Verice Demansk stands to rule over a realm even richer than it was, and with a subject population that is not really that discontented with its new rulers. Because they, too, are sharing in the new wealth. And even enjoying their new status, if the conqueror is a very intelligent man. Which we think Demansk is.

Then, with his usual wry humor: ***But I agree that your lady love probably doesn't want to hear it, at the moment.***

To Adrian's relief, Helga's angry expression faded and was replaced by simple sternness. "Leaving aside everything else," she grumbled, "these savages are going to be so much pig feed once Tomsien gets here with a *real* army."

She turned in her saddle and cast a sour glance back at the huge plodding column of Reedbottoms in their war wagons. "Unless this fancy scheme of yours works. I have my doubts. Savages are savages, I don't care how fancy their weapons are. No staying power, once they hit something tougher than a village of peasants."

Adrian cleared his throat. "Well . . . that's a bit uncharitable.

They're quite courageous, you know. If that weren't true, the Vanbert regulars wouldn't use them as auxiliaries." He decided it was time to point out that Helga was being a *bit* self-righteous. Pointing ahead: "Tomsien will have several thousand tribesmen under his own command, you know, in addition to his ten brigades of regulars."

Helga didn't seem much impressed. Nor, to be honest, was Adrian himself.

Ten brigades, the gods save me. Even allowing for most of them being understrength, that's still something like fifty thousand men. The biggest army ever fielded in the history of the world, leaving aside the tales in ancient legends.

You won't have to face that many, countered Raj. ***If I were in Tomsien's place—and I've been there, lad—I wouldn't be bringing more than six of those brigades. That'd be more than sufficient, under normal circumstances. Which these aren't, because of the Hussite tactics you'll be using. But Tomsien won't understand that. In fact, he probably doesn't even know about it. From what I can tell, at least, he's been incredibly lax about gathering intelligence.***

Center interjected. **always a mistake, dealing with barbarians. especially because spies are so easy to hire. one tribe will readily spy on another, and vice versa, for a small amount of money or trade goods. but tomsien suffers from the typical arrogance which afflicts empires in decline.**

Again, Adrian chewed on Raj's words. He was inclined to trust the former general's assessment. Adrian had gained a lot of experience over the past two years, but he knew full well that he wasn't and never would be Raj Whitehall's equal as a military leader. Still . . .

But why not bring all ten? I would.

It was always a little weird "hearing" a disembodied and ghostly snort of derision. But that was surely what came to his mind from Whitehall.

Stop thinking like "you." You wouldn't have been squeezing your provinces dry the way Tomsien's been doing. You've got the mind of a scholar and an artisan, not an imperialist grandee.

tomsien can't afford to strip his provinces of his troops, echoed

Center. **he'll likely have rebellions springing up all over the place. as ruthlessly as he's been ruling his provinces, he may get them anyway—even with four brigades in place to suppress them.**

He'll sure as hell get them after he's defeated in battle.

Which remark brought everything back full circle. Adrian sighed. "After he's defeated" . . . easy for Raj to say. But Whitehall was a ghost, when all was said and done. Defeating Tomsien's great army would have to be done in flesh and blood—with Adrian himself the key to it.

"I hope you and Father know what you're doing," repeated Helga, in a tone which was still surly.

"So do I," muttered Adrian Gellert, former Scholar of the Grove. "So do I."

CHAPTER TWENTY-TWO

"At least take soldiers with you," protested Kata.

Ion Jeschonyk gave his young concubine's cheek a little pat. "T'would be unseemly, girl. *Dignity,* you know? A Councillor's got to have it, at all times—to say nothing of a Speaker Emeritus and a Triumvir—or his reputation is ruined. Not even Marcomann went to Council meetings with a bodyguard."

Jeschonyk saw no reason to add: *Of course, Marcomann was a lot younger than I was, and a deadly man with a blade in his own right. Not to mention being six feet tall, with shoulders like a greatbeast.*

Kata was not going to be brushed off. Jeschonyk had suspected as much. She didn't usually accompany him as far as the front gate when he left his mansion. "I don't *care.* The city's not the same any more. The street gangs are everywhere, now—all the servants say so—bolder than ever. And—and—"

She groped for words. Kata's cloistered existence—using the term "cloistered" loosely—didn't really give her much of a clear understanding of Vanbert's politics. But even a young concubine, whose life experience since her capture from barbarians at the age of fourteen had been restricted to a wealthy nobleman's villa, could sense that the capital had become dangerous. Even for a man as powerful as Jeschonyk. Perhaps *especially* for a man like Jeschonyk.

For a moment, the old politician simply basked in the warmth of her concern. His relationship with Kata had changed, subtly, over the past few months. He'd even found himself—quite often, in fact—spending his nights alone with her, instead of in his usual orgiastic custom.

Still, she *was* a concubine. More to the point, she was young—and truly innocent of the ways of the world. So there was really no way that Jeschonyk could explain, in any words that would mean anything to her.

In truth, he barely understood it himself. Rather to his surprise, Ion Jeschonyk had discovered that in the twilight of his life he was giving thought to the future. More thought, and deeper thought, than he ever had before—and, which was especially surprising, thoughts which centered on his nation rather than he himself.

It's called a "sacrifice," sweet girl. Sometimes a nation needs one—and sometimes, whether you like it or not, you're selected for the chore.

A stray memory came to him suddenly, about the customs he'd heard were practiced by Kata's tribe.

"I never asked, now I think about it. Never cared, really. But are you a follower of the Young Word?"

Kata's expression combined puzzlement—and a trace of worry. "Yes. I haven't done the rites much, for many years now. But my clan belonged to the faith. Why?"

"Did you ever wonder why the prophet allowed himself to be murdered? From the way I heard the story, he'd been given a warning and could have fled."

Now, the worry swamped the puzzlement. "What is this you're telling me?" The subservience of a slave concubine vanished, replaced by a scolding finger which would have been the envy of any middle-aged matron of Vanbert. "Stop this nonsense! You're too old, anyway, to be a prophet!"

Jeschonyk laughed. Then, gave Kata a hug. "True enough, true enough. I certainly can't claim to have any eternal words of wisdom. Still . . . some things just have to be done, girl." He kissed her on the cheek, then pushed her away firmly. "And that's enough argument. In the event something does happen . . ."

How to say it? "Just see to it that a message gets to Verice Demansk. Tell him—oh, what, exactly? Just tell him to remember, that's all, and think about it now and again. The word is 'duty,' I believe."

He turned and passed through the gate. Then, once he reached the street beyond, set off toward the Forum of the Virtuous Matrons and the Council Hall beyond it. Moving, of course, in the stately manner which befitted a man of his stature.

He could sense Kata's eyes following him. And found it rather charming that, after more than sixty years of a life filled with struggle and travails and schemes, not turning around to meet that gaze was the hardest thing he'd ever done.

The chamber seemed almost like a madhouse. Men were screaming at each other, whispering in knots, scurrying from one clique to another. A fight even broke out at one point, with two Councillors hacking away at each other with their ceremonial short swords. Fortunately, the age and portliness of the men involved—not to mention the dullness of the blades themselves—made the thing more comical than deadly.

Still, in all his decades Jeschonyk had never seen the Council in such complete disarray and showing such a total lack of respect for decorum. In retrospect, he realized that his own insistence on maintaining traditional dignity had been pointless. He could have taken a hundred as his bodyguard, and no one would have noticed.

Of course, the guards wouldn't have let them come into the chamber itself, he mused, so what would have been the point?

Undreth sidled up to him. "The only way we're going to get order here," said the skeletal Watchman of the Door, "is to make a deal with Albrecht and his people. They've got half the Councillors—at least half—lined up with him now."

The old man gave his fellow Watchman a vicious sidelong glance. Potbellied Kirn was clustered with Albrecht himself. "He'll be no help, be sure of it."

As a last resort, the two Watchmen were supposed to establish order in an unruly Council. But, even leaving aside the question of how the two oldest men in the room could do so anyway, the fact that Kirn wasn't even pretending at neutrality made that option unworkable.

Sourly, Jeschonyk bowed to the inevitable. "Make the deal, then. I assume he'll want first speaking privileges."

"That, and no time limit," muttered Undreth. A moment later, the oldster scuttled off.

The extent to which Albrecht now controlled the Council was made clear very quickly. Within a minute after Undreth conferred with Albrecht, the chamber was returning to order. Albrecht was a superb Council politician, whatever his modest achievements as a military leader, and he had his people well organized. Whether through pre-arrangement or simply on-the-spot coercion—prearrangement, was Ion's guess—even the most unruly Councillors were taking their seats and falling into silence.

Jeschonyk saw no reason to bother with the ritual speech which normally opened a Council meeting. He'd already done a quick scan of the chamber and seen that none of Demansk's closest allies had even bothered to come. Not even Kall Oppricht, who rarely missed a Council meeting. Once silence had finally settled over the chamber, he simply nodded at Albrecht. "Councillor Albrecht, I believe, has something he would like to say."

"Indeed so!" Before Jeschonyk had even taken his seat, the leader of the opposition was standing in the middle of the floor beginning his speech.

Quite a speech it was, too. Drav Albrecht was a big man, with just enough fat to make him imposing instead of obese. He had the standard practices of Vanbert oratory down pat, and was quite an excellent speaker. The fact that the speech was sheer drivel—coming, at least, from such as he—didn't make the words seem any less grandiloquent.

—ancient traditions, now in dire peril—
—mortal danger to the liberties of the fatherland—
—one Marcomann was enough—nay, too much!—

Undreth had taken a seat just behind Jeschonyk himself. The Triumvir felt the old man's withered, arthritic hand on his shoulder.

"This is worse than I expected," hissed Undreth. "Much worse."

Jeschonyk nodded. *I should have listened more carefully to Verice. He always warned me Albrecht was impatient—impatient to the point of recklessness.*

"Leave now," he whispered to Undreth. "As Watchman, no one will think it odd. Speak to the captain of the Guard—not the one outside, but his replacement; he'll be in the guards' quarters—and tell him to summon my household troops from their barracks. Dignity be damned, Albrecht's throwing it all to the winds anyway. I'll want an escort leaving here. If Albrecht's being this rash in the chamber, you can be certain he'll have his street thugs stirred up."

Undreth made to leave, but Jeschonyk restrained him with a little tug on his robes. "And don't come back," he whispered. "Don't go to your own villa, either. Go to mine. No—better yet, go to your niece Arsule's. If there's any trouble, there'll be—never mind. I've made arrangements."

Undreth nodded and was gone. As Jeschonyk had suspected, no one really paid any attention to his departure. Between his age and the fact that, as Watchman, he was expected to periodically act as a "sentry," Undreth's absence was not taken too seriously by Jeschonyk's opponents. In truth, Undreth himself was not taken too seriously.

Albrecht's speech went on, thunderously; and, soon enough, began giving the name to the peril.

—deprived me of my rightful victory—
—collusion with the pirates—
—now his own son to marry one of the detestable creatures—
—setting himself up like the tyrants of the epic tales—
—could not be clearer—
—must act now before the monster—

This went beyond "disrespect for a public official," far beyond it. Albrecht had said nothing of Jeschonyk, as yet, but it would be only a matter of time before he started to bend his speech in that direction.

But then, to Ion's surprise, Albrecht broke off.

"And what of Tomsien, you ask? Where does he stand? Rather than speak on this matter myself, I ask that the floor be turned over to a man just come from that *honest* Triumvir's side."

Albrecht did not even bother with the formality of turning to the official chairman of the session. He simply waved a heavy hand, much like a man summons a dog.

When the "dog" rose and trotted forth, Jeschonyk sighed. *This, too, Verice foresaw. I thought he was being too gloomy.*

Jeschonyk had known, of course, that Barrett Demansk was making ties with Albrecht and his faction. But, until this moment, he had not realized that the ties had become open partisanship.

Demansk's oldest son had little of his father's innate dignity, and even less of Albrecht's practiced public demeanor. Standing in the middle of the chamber, awkwardly assuming the stance of a public speaker, he looked more like a boy playing a role in a drama than anything else.

The opening words sounded stilted, rehearsed—even ridiculous.

—great sadness—
—my own father—
—but duty to the nation—

"Blah, blah," muttered Ion. "Get to the point, you treacherous little snot, whatever it might be."

Histrionically, even more so than custom dictated, Barrett plucked a scroll from his robes and held it up.

"I have here, written before my own eyes by my father-in-law at his field headquarters where he valiantly prepares to do battle against the"—here followed a truly ludicrous list of the Southrons' faults and vices. Jeschonyk found it hard not to laugh aloud.

Bestial and filthy, certainly; and for subhuman you could at least make a good case. But cowardly and craven? Not hardly, you ambitious little twerp, or your precious father-in-law wouldn't have taken six brigades with him.

Barrett paused and took a deep breath, as if preparing himself for the climax. Then, surprised Ion again. "But rather than read it myself, I insist that Triumvir Jeschonyk do so! For he, as the senior, must take final responsibility for the actions of the Triumvirate!"

So that's it, is it? Place me squarely in the middle between Verice and Tomsien—I can just imagine the lies he told in that scroll—and try to force me to choose publicly.

This time, he really did have to struggle not to laugh. He was surprised that Albrecht was attempting such a crude maneuver. Jeschonyk was just as capable of lying through his teeth and then, a day later, officially changing his mind, as Albrecht himself. He supposed this was Albrecht's sop to whatever was left of Barrett Demansk's "principles." *Give the old man a chance to do the right thing.*

"No problem, laddie," Ion murmured to himself, as he rose and stepped forward into the center of the chamber. "You're about to see one of the world's champion liars put on a marvelous demonstration of the art."

He was rehearsing his speech even as he took the scroll and began unfolding it. Politely, Barrett stepped aside. Not so politely, Ion turned his back on him.

After I finish reading it—I know what it'll say, whatever the exact words—I'll be shocked and sorrowful, but have no choice but to agree with Tomsien that the Triumvirate failed of its purpose and must be dissolved. Due to the treachery and overweening ambition of Demansk, of course. I'll retire from public life, naturally. The shame and disgrace of it all. Blah blah blah. Tomorrow—

But it was time to read the scroll. Jeschonyk went right into it, not bothering to scan the contents ahead of time. He was as experienced and capable a public speaker as any in the Confederacy, after all.

Nor, once he got into it, were there any surprises

—great distress when I learned—
—shocking stab in the back to the august Justiciar at Preble—
—the Triumvirate now clearly seen to be a mistake—
—will remain at my post—
—deal with the barbarians first—
—full confidence in Justiciar Albrecht as new Speaker—

Jeschonyk almost choked at that part. Not in disgust, simply in disbelief. Is Albrecht a complete idiot? Can't he see that Tomsien is just using him to remove Demansk—so that he can return with ten brigades at his back, after he defeats the Southrons? What good will your street thugs do you against them, you moron?

But he was just playing a part, and so he droned on.

—restore the true traditions of our fatherland—

—but not enough—

—must also root out all treason, hidden as well as overt—

—above all—

Finally, Ion understood. He stopped his recital abruptly, stared out at nothing, and uttered the words which would make him immortal—because the men who heard them never understood they were addressed to an absent twenty-year-old slave girl.

"See? I was right to stick with duty. An escort wouldn't—"

The ceremonial sword slammed into his back just above the kidney, and drove straight through. In that, at least, as well as the good steel and sharp edge of the blade, Barrett Demansk was true to the father he was betraying. The shock drove Jeschonyk to his knees.

For a moment, he stared down at the blood spilling off the tip of the blade protruding from his belly. He recognized a mortal wound, of course, but found that he didn't really care. There were words . . .

A curse, rather. I've said what could be said to Kata.

He managed to fall on his side, so he would be looking up at his killer. Barrett was staring down at him, his murderer's hand still outstretched and his mouth half open. Like many men who nerve themselves to commit an unthinkable act, he was almost as much caught up in the shock of the moment as his victim.

Barrett swallowed; then, managed to get out his assigned words—though more in the way of a squeak than a bellow of indignant triumph. "Death to tyrants!"

"Cretin," said Jeschonyk. "The world's champion fool. Did you think—"

Albrecht's ax, hacking his throat, cut short the sentence as well as the life of the speaker. "*Death to tyrants!*"

Jeschonyk never felt the multitude of other blades which plunged into him, again and again, as Albrecht's partisans scrambled to pledge their new allegiance. Nor, thankfully, did he see the massacre perpetrated on the dozen or so other men in the chamber who had been, for years, his closest allies. Even, here and there, his friends.

The dullness of most of the ceremonial swords and axes which were being wielded in the massacre meant that men were being bludgeoned to death as much as being "cut down." When it was all over, the chamber resembled a charnel house—and of Ion Jeschonyk himself, there was less than a bad butcher would have left of a pig's carcass.

It would be said later, and grow into legend, that his entrails and ears and private parts were displayed throughout the city by Albrecht's street gangs. The legend was false, as it happens. Only the ears were so displayed, having been cut off for a trophy by one of Albrecht's toadies. The rest was simply cremated.

But it was hard to argue against such a legend. Especially when the man who spread it the most energetically would have printing presses at his disposal.

Those devices, also, were being constructed at Chalice at Verice Demansk's command. His son Trae had brought the design back with him, from Adrian Gellert, along with many others.

Hearing the tumult in the streets, followed by the bursting of the mansion's front door, the other girls cowered fearfully in a corner of their chambers. Kata did not. She knew, somehow, that the noise meant that Jeschonyk was dead. But—

She had come to trust the old man, as well as grow fond of him. So, when the soldiers came into the room and the other girls began screaming, she just hollered at them.

"Shut up, damn you!"

To the officer who seemed to be in charge:

"Where are we going?"

He seemed a bit startled. "Aren't you the cool one?" Then, with a smile: "Just keep 'em quiet, will you? It's a long way to Hagga, and I'd just as soon not be deaf when we get there."

The next few hours were as confusing as they were frightening. A hurried rush, under cover of nightfall, to a nearby villa—the richest mansion Kata had ever seen in her life. Followed by . . . nothing. Just what seemed like an endless wait, hiding in a side house while their escort fidgeted outside on the grounds of the villa.

Kata was able to keep the other girls quiet, but it became more difficult as time passed. She herself simply couldn't make any rhyme or reason out of what was happening. It didn't help her state of mind any when she realized that the officer and soldiers who had taken her and the other girls and the servants out of Jeschonyk's villa couldn't make any sense of it either.

"What does that crazy bitch think she's doing?" she overheard one of the soldiers mutter to another. The response was a shrug of resignation.

"Don't ask me. The sergeant just says we're to keep everyone here tonight, and be ready to get out of the city sometime tomorrow. Seems the Lady wants to make a speech."

"*What?* In the capital? Albrecht's goons are crawling all over the place. Is she out of her mind?"

Another resigned shrug. "What else is new? Remember that time—you ought to, it was only a few months back—she suddenly had us hauling most of the statues out of this place? In the middle of the night, as if anybody cared what she did with the stupid things?" Glumly: "Heavy they were, too. Like hoisting so many rocks."

The ensuing conversation, what little of it Kata was able to understand, seemed to revolve around the endless insanities of the guards' employer. It was not, under the circumstances, the most reassuring thing she could have heard.

But . . . there was nothing she could do, after all. So, after a time, she curled up on a couch and managed to get some sleep.

When she awoke, it was well into the morning. In itself, that was not unusual. Jeschonyk had often kept her up late into the night.

What *was* unusual was being awakened by the sound of young men shouting orders instead of an old man's caress.

She bolted upright, startled and afraid. The other girls around her had their mouths open, ready to scream.

"Be *quiet,* you ninnies!" Thinking quickly: "Those are the guards. Listen! They're getting ready to leave—and in a hurry. Get up!"

She led by example, dragooning the others into what passed for an organized group waiting by the door. When the door was opened, by the same officer who had taken them out of Jeschonyk's villa, they were ready to go.

The officer looked relieved. "Thank the gods, *some* women in the world have their heads where they belong. Come on, girls—and *hurry.* The crazy bi—ah, Lady Knecht—has stirred up the whole damn city. Her own escort had to fight their way back here."

The last two sentences were muttered over his shoulder. He was already well across the villa grounds, Kata and the girls trotting at his heels, heading toward the largest coach Kata had ever seen in her life. Also, from the looks of it, the most luxurious.

The door to the coach was flung open—by a woman's hand from the inside, not a servant's from without. That in itself was enough to convey the urgency of the moment. From what Kata could see of the woman herself, in the dark interior of the coach, she looked as if she normally expected servants to wipe her ass.

The officer practically flung them inside. Kata went last, making sure the other girls stayed reasonably calm, then clambered aboard and shut the door behind her. She barely had time to register the presence of an elderly man sitting next to the coach's owner—his skeletal face looking even more apprehensive than those of the girls—before she was flung onto the cushioned seat by the coach lurching into motion.

The same expensive-looking hand reached out and held her steady. "Not to worry, girl," came a cultured voice. "I assure you this coach is very well made"—at that moment the coach practically flew into the air, driven at a gallop over the little barrier in the gateway of the villa; Kata prayed the voice was telling the truth—"and I always employ the very finest coachmen."

She stared up at the woman. Nothing registered at first except a pair of very dark eyes, set closely together in a narrow face. The eyes seemed somewhat amused.

"I apologize for the unseemly nature of our departure." Kata's eyes widened. The woman was *obviously* from the nobility. A quick glance at the clothing was enough to tell her that much. Apologizing to slaves?

"I'm sure most people think I'm crazy to have done it," the self-assured voice continued. "Uncle Undreth here certainly does! But I simply *couldn't* leave Vanbert without letting everyone know—finally!—what I think of Drav Albrecht. And precisely which way he ought to be gutted."

Was she *crazy*?

"But enough of that." The dark eyes seemed alive with interest now, more than amusement. "Ion tells me—told me; he's dead now—"

Kata had known that must be true, but she still felt a pang of sorrow. He'd been a kindly man, and she hadn't minded satisfying his lusts. She'd have had to do the same for any master, after all, few of whom would have bothered to make sure she enjoyed herself also.

"—truly sorry, I was very fond of the old reprobate. But live for the moment, as the philosopher Yerra says, even if the Hedonist school isn't respected much these days—odd, really, since everyone *practices* his teachings at the same time they sneer at it—so let's follow the principle. As I was saying, Ion told me you're a *Reedbottom*."

Kata's brain was scrambling to catch up with the torrent of words pouring over it.

"—opportunity finally arrives to actually *talk* with one. So, girl, tell me: how exactly does Young Word reconcile this all-powerful Assan of yours with"—the cultured hand attached to the cultured voice pointed a long accusing finger out the window at the city hurtling past the coach—"all *this* shit."

Whump! Another unseen obstacle sent the coach flying. The girls shrieked; the cultured hand kept Kata steady again. The cultured voice never missed a beat.

"—All-Father, the rascal, gets away with it by blaming *other* gods.

But I can't see where the same clever trick could do your Assan much good. 'Sees all, knows all, creates all'—that doesn't seem to leave any room for *excuses,* now does it?"

Kata gaped up at her. *Yes. Assan save us. She is crazy.*

CHAPTER TWENTY-THREE

When Helga saw the first signs of a barbarian rout, she had a hard time to keep herself from cheering. As it was, she made no attempt to suppress a savage grin.

Undiplomatic, to be sure. But the hundreds of Southron cavalrymen who pounded past the huge column of the Reedbottoms and Adrian's mercenaries—heading the *other* way, as fast as they could drive their velipads loaded with booty—were too preoccupied with staying in their saddles to notice the expression on her face.

She was a bit surprised that many of them managed to stay mounted at all, much less at a full gallop. Some of the booty which the barbarians had seized in their ravaging forays was downright bizarre. One man was even trying to balance the brass headboard of a rich man's bed across his saddle.

All of them were overloaded, even for the heavy Southron mounts. If it weren't for the fact that Helga knew how that booty had been taken, she'd find the whole thing more amusing than anything else.

"Stupid as beasts, too," she hissed. "By the time they get back across the Wall, they'll have discarded half that stuff."

"Half, at least," responded Adrian. His own face looked sour. That wasn't because the Southron retreat was upsetting his plans,

Helga knew. It was simply because Adrian wasn't really any fonder of the barbarians than she was.

Well, except for that Prelotta freak, and his mangy Reedbottoms.

Helga's own opinion of the Reedbottoms, and Prelotta, lacked any of Adrian's complexity. She understood the subtlety of his Grove-trained logic, more or less; she understood much better the cold-blooded calculations which lay behind her father's schemes. But Helga's attitude toward the southern barbarians—the Reedbottoms no less than any of the others—began with their smell, and . . .

Ended there. *Stinking savages.*

A knot of horsemen was approaching the head of the column from straight ahead on the road. A large knot—perhaps fifty in all; heavily armored, and riding even larger velipads than most Southrons. And they were trotting, not galloping in headlong retreat.

Reedbottoms, then. Prelotta's tribesmen didn't share the usual Southron contempt for armor, and they transferred over to cavalry warfare their heavy infantry notions of fighting.

Before she could recognize the face of the man leading them, Helga knew it was Prelotta himself. The Reedbottom chief had led a party out yesterday to negotiate with the nearby city of Franness.

"Negotiate," she muttered.

Adrian heard the mutter, and smiled thinly. "In a manner of speaking. Much the way a footpad 'negotiates' with his victim. 'Your purse or your life.' "

Franness was the largest city in the Confederacy's southern provinces. Nothing on the order of great Vanbert itself, of course—say, fifty thousand residents to the capital's one million—but still quite a prize for a barbarian conqueror.

Helga had thought Prelotta's attempt to extort booty from them through "negotiation" was absurd. Everyone knew that Tomsien was coming, with a huge army of Confederate regulars. The barbarians could boast all they wanted, but every single time in history they'd come up against a large Vanbert force, the Southrons had gotten their heads broken.

The city notables of Franness knew that history as well as anyone. Franness was a walled city, with a *real* wall and not just a flimsy palisade. And everyone—every Confederate city notable, for sure—also knew what the penalty would be if they capitulated to the barbarians and Tomsien emerged triumphant. That, too, was a long Confederate tradition—city councils of besieged cities who surrendered before the wall was breached were subject to decimation, just as routed army units were.

That assumed, of course, that the Confederacy would recapture the city. But . . . It had never failed to do so yet.

Odd, though. Prelotta was close enough now for Helga to be able to see his expression clearly. The open, flanged helmets the Southrons favored did not obscure faces much. It was always hard for her to tell, because of the grotesque scars and tattoos, but she thought the Reedbottom chief looked rather satisfied with himself.

And so he proved.

"They refused, of course," he announced, as soon as he drew up his mount. "Even heaped the most scurrilous insults upon my head!"

Grinning while he said it. True, with the cheek scars, Prelotta's grin never seemed especially humorous to Helga. But she'd come to know the Reedbottom chief fairly well in the time since she'd arrived in Marange, and he was clearly not in a foul mood.

Adrian, as always—and in a way which continued to amaze Helga—managed exactly the right response. Her lover's innate scholarly absentmindedness, which sometimes exasperated her but of which she was basically rather fond, was something Adrian could suspend when he needed to. Those weird "spirits" of his made him just as superb a diplomat as a slinger.

"No doubt you told them you'd rape every matron in the city, by way of revenge," he drawled. "I'll warn you though, Prelotta, a good half of them will be withered crones. And the ones who are plump enough to suit you will have nasty dispositions."

Still grinning, Prelotta glanced at Helga. The glance was one of assessment, not admiration. Southron standards of female beauty, Reedbottoms even more than most, leaned very heavily toward heft. Every single one of Prelotta's three wives and eight concubines sported the rolls of neck fat which were so highly esteemed among Southron females.

"Well, yes, I did. Told them I'd rape all their daughters too." He waved his hand idly. "I might even carry out the last threat, if I can find any good-looking enough. But I think the revenge I'll take will actually horrify them even more. I'll have those precious matrons of theirs—and we'll see just how far that 'Vanbert virtue' goes!—bathe me and my chieftains in the city's baths."

Helga couldn't prevent herself from wincing—while choking down a giggle at the same time. The image of dozens of wealthy Confederate matrons, all middle-aged or older, trying to scrub the oil and grease and filth from scarred and tattooed tribesmen—all of them, savages and matrons alike, naked as the day they were born—the women even more aghast at the stench than they were at the prospect of being ravaged—

She *did* giggle. She couldn't help it, even though she knew that Prelotta's half threat to rape the notables' daughters was only half made in jest. The Reedbottoms weren't *quite* as bestial as the other Southrons, but that wasn't really saying much. If they did manage to survive Tomsien and sack Franness, there would be horrors aplenty in the city.

"But," continued Prelotta, shrugging, "the negotiation served its purpose. They know what I want now, in detail. So when I come back after we crush Tomsien, I expect there'll be no difficulty. They'll probably have all the booty stacked outside the city gates. Which will be open, of course. I *will* make Franness the capital of my new northern province, whether they like it or not."

Helga's little choked giggle had registered on Prelotta. He gave her that unsettling shark's grin.

"The truth is, I'd enjoy a bath. I've even gotten Otta and Glami here"—a quick nod toward two of his top chieftains—"to agree to join me. The rest say they'll do the same, if we survive the experience."

All eight of the Reedbottom chieftains who had accompanied Prelotta to Franness were grinning now. Helga was a bit startled. More than a bit, actually. Prelotta's sense of humor was rather good, but it was almost always of the "only half in jest" sort.

He's not kidding. He will get those savages of his into a bath.

Not for the first time, Helga found herself admitting that Adrian had been right, and she wrong. Her lover had told her that the Reedbottoms—alone of the Southron tribes—were ready to make what he called "the leap to feudalism." Which, he said, always entailed the ruling elite taking on at least the trappings of civilization.

Those "spirits" of his again. The one called "Center," more specifically. Helga knew the details, now, of Adrian's strange three-way mentality. He'd spent hours explaining it to her. Even if she didn't really understand much of it, she knew that it would be that one who would have given Adrian these notions. The other, the Raj Whitehall "person," was a strategist and a tactician. It was the "computer" who looked at human affairs the way a weaver examines a tapestry in the making. Seeing the loom itself, and not just the fabric.

Right again, damn it. Between him and my father—assuming I survive all this—I'm going to get sick and tired of hearing I told you so. Glumly: *Years and years of it, probably. Assuming, of course, they survive the next year.*

Which was still something she had her doubts about. Tomsien was said to be bringing no less than *six* brigades. Helga wasn't certain, but she couldn't think of any campaign in Confederate history which had ever brought more than five to bear on a single enemy.

Prelotta was now turning to that subject. "There's a valley not more than five miles ahead," he said, pointing over his shoulder with his thumb, "that should suit you. Can't get much sense out of these scampering Grayhills and other Jotties"—that with a sneer; "Jotties" was the slang term Reedbottoms used for other Southron tribes—"but I think Tomsien's not more than two days' march away. So we'd better move fast, if you want to make sure the laager's in place before he arrives."

One of the Reedbottom chieftains interjected: "Tomsien broke Norrys himself two days ago, in a battle somewhere to the north. The Chief of Chiefs survived, from what we heard, but he's badly wounded."

Helga was struck by the excellence of the man's diction in the Emerald tongue, even if his accent was so thick you could cut it with a knife. That was another thing Prelotta had insisted on—and forced down the throats of his underlings. He and his top subordinates continued to use their own language whenever they were discussing immediate tactics, especially under pressure. But whenever they were in Adrian's presence, Prelotta had mandated Emerald as the language of choice.

That wasn't because Adrian didn't understand their own. He was quite fluent in it, as a matter of fact. That was the doing of his "spirits" again—just as they had been the ones who explained Prelotta's thinking.

"Trappings of civilization," indeed.

Prelotta was *ambitious.* And perhaps—it remained to be seen—had the intelligence to pull it off. He certainly had the willpower. One thing was certain: the chief of the Reedbottoms was determined to transform the balance of power within the Southrons themselves. Within a generation, no more, he intended to displace the Grayhills from their long period of predominance.

Doing so, however, required giving his own tribe a new basis for wielding power. That much of Adrian's transmission of his spirits' thinking Helga had no difficulty at all in understanding. So long as the Reedbottoms remained simply populous—their numbers were at least as great as the Grayhills—they would never become anything more than the "nephews of Assan." No other tribe tried to challenge the Reedbottoms seriously on their own terrain, true enough. But past attempts by the Reedbottoms to muscle their way out of the lowlands had been repulsed just as decisively.

The hardscrabble pig farmers of Vanbert had levered their way to power by using one of the tools of civilization: disciplined organization—*government.* That was beyond the still half-savage Reedbottoms. But a powerful military based on Adrian's new gunpowder weapons wasn't. Helga had understood another of Adrian's "historical dictums" quite well, from her experience with her brother's use of firearms: *Guns spell the doom of nomad military strength. Always have; always will. Because barbarians can use guns, but they can't* make *them.*

Somewhere far back in the great column of the Reedbottom army were the wagons of the blacksmiths. Those wagons were not the least of the reasons the column moved so slowly. They were almost manufactories-on-wheels. "Wagons" so big they reminded Helga of rolling houses—which couldn't possibly have been hauled by any animals smaller than the tuskbeasts of the Reedbottoms.

"How wide is the valley?" Adrian asked.

"Maybe ten miles, north to south; a bit less, east to west." For a moment, Prelotta's face twisted into a grimace. Half a grimace, rather; the kind of face a man makes when he's having second thoughts. "Are you *sure* you don't want the high ground? There's a very nice set of hills—"

"No," said Adrian firmly. "What's the point of high ground? Tomsien doesn't have any long-range artillery, and *you're* not going to be doing any cavalry charges. And if you did, you'd be using tuskbeasts anyway—which can't handle a downhill charge any better than your first mother-in-law."

That brought a little laugh from Prelotta and all his chieftains. The mother of his senior wife—who was no lightweight herself—was so obese she could barely move.

"A broad valley is what we want," Adrian continued. He turned slightly in his saddle and pointing back toward the column. "The laager should be a mile and a half around—almost half a mile across. Any smaller than that and you're wasting wagons—not to mention that you're probably going to need the room to fit all of the Jotties looking for succor and comfort."

Another laugh, and a bigger one. Whatever Prelotta's chieftains thought of his other ambitions, his determination to make the Reedbottoms preeminent among the tribes had their full approval. And nothing would advance that project further and better than defeating a major Vanbert army for the first time in history—with Grayhills and other routed Jotties huddling for shelter under Reedbottom protection.

"So be it," commanded Prelotta. He reached out both his arms and gave his hands a little forward flip, commanding his chieftains. "See to the thing! I want this column there by nightfall."

They obeyed instantly. Strange he might be to his subordinates, in many ways, but Prelotta was a charismatic leader. Even Helga would admit as much, his stench notwithstanding.

When the chieftains were gone, the stench came nearer. A minute later, as the column lurched back into motion, Prelotta was riding next to Helga.

Instead of Adrian. That was surprising. Prelotta was always polite to her, even pleasant, but he normally didn't pay much attention to her. As a rule, even among the chiefly class, the Southron tribesmen were easier going in their treatment of women than Vanberts—leaving aside the horrid practice of female circumcision—much less Emeralds or Islanders. But they still didn't include women in their political or military councils, even if they weren't kept secluded in their private homes the way noblewomen in civilized lands usually were.

"So tell me, Helga, what's your opinion?" He had a sly little smile on his face. Helga thought it looked even more hideous than the grin. "Should I adopt the Vanbert or Emerald custom, when it comes to public bathing?"

Jesting, is it? She gave Adrian a sly smile of her own.

"Ha!" she barked. "You savages parade around in public all but naked anyway. So why in the name of the gods would you want to saddle yourself with that Emerald silliness? Separate the sexes in the baths? That means twice the number of baths—and twice the work." With a sneer: "Only the damn Emeralds, who confuse simple arithmetic with 'Mystic Number,' would come up with such foolishness."

Helga glanced at Adrian to see if she was getting a rise out of him.

Nope. Hard to do, that. Harder than with any man I've ever known.

Adrian was smiling also. "I agree, Prelotta. And the gods know I'd rather look at naked women than naked men. I've been in both, and Vanbert baths are just plain more *interesting.*"

Prelotta nodded, as solemnly as if they were discussing the fate of the world. Which, in a weird and twisted way, Helga realized, they might be.

"Done, then. I shall so instruct my people." The solemnity was fleeting; the sly little smile was back. "And no doubt that will do much to reconcile my Vanbert subjects to their new status."

Helga tried to picture a Vanbert public bath, men and women mixed together casually, crowded with virtuous matrons and . . .

Dammit, I'm going to giggle again.

CHAPTER TWENTY-FOUR

Two days later, Helga had no trouble at all to keep from giggling.

"The gods save us," she muttered. From the top of the wagon where she was perched, she had a perfect view of the Confederate army. Tomsien might not have had her father's flair for war, but he was an experienced and capable field commander. Even with a force as gigantic as this one, his Vanbert regulars were spreading out in the valley and taking up their positions smoothly and easily. It was more like watching a machine than men.

She turned her head toward Jessep, standing next to her. The ex-soldier looked as tight-faced as she suspected she did.

"Never seen it from *this* vantage point before," said Yunkers softly. "Been in the middle of it, of course. Which, I can tell you, always gives a soldier a *solid* sort of feeling."

Grimly, he watched the Confederate army continue its evolution. "From this perspective, though, it's downright scary. If your man's scheme doesn't work the way he thinks it will . . ."

He left the rest unsaid. Confederate armies were almost always harsh toward defeated opponents, even civilized ones like the Emeralds. Toward barbarians—especially ones who had plundered the southern provinces as savagely as these had just done—they would be utterly merciless.

Granted, the infantry itself wouldn't be able to butcher those who managed to flee the immediate area of the battle before being swept up. Confederate regulars would maintain their disciplined formations at all times, and, in the nature of things, a single man—especially if he's mounted—can outrun a hundred moving together.

But that was one of the principal reasons the Confederacy employed auxiliary troops. Cavalry, mostly, the bulk of them from the Southron tribes themselves. Vanbert military tradition didn't consider cavalry of much use in an actual battle. Confederate generals used their cavalry for scouting, skirmishing—and to pursue and butcher a routed foe. Which task their auxiliaries handled splendidly, and the fact that they would be butchering other Southron barbarians wouldn't bother them in the least.

Helga started to make some sour comment about savages and their innate disloyalty, but her own innate honesty kept the words from being spoken. If push came to shove after all, Jessep and his own men were quite prepared to kill other Confederates in this battle.

She eyed him sidelong, for a moment. Then, abruptly: "Does it bother you? Being on this side, I mean."

He shrugged. "Can't say it pleases me any. But . . . 'bothers' me? No, lass."

He turned away from the sight of the coming army and faced her squarely. Jessep's face seemed blockier than usual.

"There isn't much of 'loyalty' left, in a man who's served twenty-five years in the regiments. Except, maybe, loyalty to such men as led you well, in battle, and saw to your retirement if you survived. Like your father, first and foremost."

Yunkers waved his hand toward the cluster of wagons at the very center of the laager, where Adrian and Prelotta had set up the compound which served as their field headquarters. From the center of it rose a twenty-foot-tall watchtower, hastily but solidly built from lashed-together logs. "I don't work for your boyfriend, girl, or his half-tame savages. I work for your father. Same's true for my boys. *Verice Demansk* sent us down here, and told us to do whatever you wanted. For them, as me, that's good enough."

He glanced back at Tomsien's huge force, which was now

beginning its march across the valley. "Little the Confederacy ever did for me and mine, when all is said and done."

Helga couldn't keep from smiling. "Whatever I wanted, is it? Then why—"

Jessep snorted. "He was quite precise on *that* matter, girl, however loose he may have been otherwise. 'Just make sure you keep the hoyden out of any fighting herself.' Speaking of which—"

He looked down into the laager. Helga's personal bodyguard Lortz was standing not far away, staring up at Jessep and his charge perched on the wagon.

"Speaking of which, Lortz is looking none too happy. They'll be within javelin range before much longer, and the field artillery will start up even sooner. It's time you got down from here, girl, and went back to your Adrian. And *stay* in the center compound, dammit."

"As if I'll have much choice," she grumbled. "You and the hundred will be there right alongside me. The biggest—and certainly the grumpiest—governess I ever had."

But it was just a token protest. Helga took one last look at the endless files and neat formations of the coming Confederacy, and discovered that she really wasn't at all keen to meet them personally. Those locked shields looked impenetrable, and the assegais, *sharp*. She scrambled off the wagon in quite a sprightly manner, truth be told.

Once on the ground, though, she took the time to peek into the interior of the wagon through one of the gunports on the inner side. She could see into it quite easily, since the gunport was being unused. The Reedbottom warriors within the wagon were all clustered on the other side, facing the enemy.

She could see all fourteen of them. Two were at each of the five gunports, one of them with an arquebus already poking through and his partner with two more ready. Toward Helga's side of the wagon, the remaining four men of the crew had still more guns loaded and were ready to begin cleaning and reloading the used ones.

It was an impressive bit of organization in its own right, Helga had to admit. The more so since she knew this same scene would be repeated over and again, identically, in every one of the four hundred or so wagons which formed the perimeter of the laager. Before she'd come down here, she wouldn't have thought Southron barbarians could even *count* as high as fourteen—much less maintain that same number, repeatedly, as well as Vanberts maintained their own allotted forces.

In truth, most of the tribes couldn't have managed it. But the Reedbottoms had three advantages. First, they were farmers rather than herders. Reedbottom villagers were accustomed to working together throughout the year in the fields, not just during the periodic great hunts. Second, their own style of fighting, adapted to their marshy lowlands, favored heavily armored warriors wielding axes and flails in close formation. As close, at least, as those weapons permitted. Out on the open plains, the other tribes could savage them with swirling cavalry tactics and mounted missile fire. But whenever someone had to meet the Reedbottoms on their own terrain, it was another story.

Third, there was Prelotta. The Reedbottom chief was charismatic enough that he'd been able to impose a degree of discipline on his tribesmen which was unusual for barbarians. Charismatic enough—and, when necessary, brutal enough.

A fourth advantage, too, now that she thought about it. Peeking through the gunport, Helga saw that four of the crew—judging from what she could see of their tattoos and hairstyles—came from other tribes. Life was brutal for the nomads. Their incessant feuds and blood vendettas constantly shredded people from their own tribes. Whether declared official "outlaws" or simply on the run from victorious clan enemies, hundreds of them could be found roaming loose at any time in the southern half of the continent, taking what livestock they could salvage and desperately trying to find shelter somewhere.

The Reedbottoms were one of the traditional "shelters." Had been for centuries. As distasteful as their lifestyle might be to most Southrons, there had always been enough refugees trickling into the lowlands to have steadily increased the size of the "Nephew of Assan." To the point where, now, the Reedbottoms were certainly as numerous as their Grayhills rivals.

She stepped back from the gunport and examined the wagon as a whole. Then, slowly turning her head, surveyed as much of the laager as she could see. Which was all of it, except for the part obscured behind the central compound—and, of course, those parts obscured behind the masses of mounted Southron warriors from other tribes. Just as Adrian had predicted, fragments of the other tribes had come scampering to the Reedbottoms for shelter.

Chief of Chiefs Norrys himself was here, she'd heard, brought there by Adrian's brother Esmond and his own still-large force of warriors.

She scanned the area, trying to spot Esmond. She couldn't see him, but she assumed that the largest group of mounted warriors toward the eastern side of the laager—maybe a thousand in all—was where he was located. Esmond had distinguished himself in the fighting which had taken place since the breach of the Wall, by all accounts. Although Helga wondered, sarcastically, how a man "distinguishes" himself in slaughter and rapine.

But . . . perhaps she was being unfair. She'd never liked Esmond, even before his rupture with Adrian. There had been *some* fighting, after all, against sizeable Confederate garrison units in the southern provinces. From what she'd heard, Esmond had usually played the leading role in breaking those units.

He'd even, according to rumor, managed to hold off Tomsien's huge army long enough to rescue Norrys and keep the badly-wounded Chief of Chiefs from falling into Confederate hands. That had been the one and only major encounter so far between the Southrons and Tomsien—Norrys must have been seized by delusions of grandeur—and Esmond seemed to have been the one barbarian warleader who came out of the fiasco with his reputation enhanced.

The wagons which made up the laager were huge—sixteen feet long and six feet across, with a covered roof about six feet from the floor. They were drawn on wheels to match—great clumsy things, which protruded beyond the sides of the wagons themselves because they were four feet in diameter and couldn't have cleared otherwise. The wagons were not much more than two feet off the ground.

Helga couldn't really see the ground itself, under the wagons.

Once the laager was locked into position, heavy wooden shields had been lowered to prevent any enemies from crawling under the wagons. Similar shields, except taller, had been fitted into the interstices between the wagons. Like the walls of the wagons, those shields had loopholes through which guns could be fired.

In this case, guns in the hands of Adrian's own Fighting Band. The long two-man arquebuses which they favored wouldn't have fit inside the wagons. The Reedbottom gunners were armed with the crudest possible firearms, the kind which Prelotta's own blacksmiths and helpers could produce once Adrian and his experienced gunmakers showed them the trick of it. Short-barreled, with big bores—something Adrian called ".75 caliber." The weapons were incredibly inaccurate, beyond close range. But they had been designed for close-range fighting, after all, and Helga knew that if those heavy bullets did hit a man they would hammer him down. The shields used by Confederate regulars, so effective at deflecting javelins and arrows and slung stones, would be useless.

Helga shook her head, a bit ruefully. Emerald scholar or not, in his own bizarre manner Adrian had devised a method of warfare which amounted to a moving version of the Confederate army camps which had kept Vanbert's enemies at bay for centuries.

And bizarre it was, too. Adrian claimed this tactic had first been used on a planet called "Earth" somewhere back even before the times of the legends. By somebody with the peculiar name of Jan Zizka, and the Hussites. Then, of course, he'd had to explain to her what a "planet" really was. She remained skeptical. Or, perhaps, it was simply that she had fond memories of Ion Jeschonyk. It had been he, on one of his visits to her father's estate, who'd explained to Helga at the age of eight that "planets" were really the spirits of the gods. Had to be. They moved, didn't they, unlike all the other stars?

Helga also wondered how these "Hussites" would have moved their wagons. The Reedbottoms only managed it because they were one of the few tribes which had domesticated the enormous animals called "tuskbeasts." Helga had heard of them, of course, but never seen one until she came to the southern half of the continent. They reminded her of giant pigs, more than anything.

Placid enough brutes, though, at least usually. The Reedbottoms used them extensively in their agriculture. Tuskbeasts were even slower moving than greatbeasts, but with their size and strength they could dredge fields and create dykes where a smaller animal would be overmatched.

She could hear the tuskbeasts making their peculiar snorting sounds, over in the corrals which Prelotta had erected in the middle of the laager. They had been herded there after pulling the wagons into place, along with the greatbeasts which had been plundered from the countryside. Separate corrals hadn't been needed, as they would have been for velipads. Greatbeasts were cantankerous brutes, given to extreme territoriality. But not even an old bull was going to pester a tuskbeast.

"It's time to go, ma'am," urged Lortz. "Past time."

Helga didn't argue the point. Following her guard, Jessep at her side, she trotted toward the central compound several hundred yards away.

She heard a peculiar sound behind her, and started to turn around. But Jessep's firm hand on her shoulder kept her moving steadily forward.

"That's a bolt from a ballista, girl. And—trust me—this is as close as you want to hear it. Too close." A moment later: "It's starting, may the gods look kindly upon us. Though I can't think of any reason they would."

Neither could Helga. She began walking more quickly.

A new sound now, a thud. Several. She had no trouble this time figuring out what it was. That was the sound of a spear driving into wood. A very *big* spear.

She broke into a trot.

"Good girl," approved Jessep.

CHAPTER TWENTY-FIVE

By the time she reached the compound, however, she'd slowed back down to a brisk walk. She *was* the daughter of Verice Demansk, after all, even if almost no one here knew it.

Dignity, dignity.

The compound was a small laager itself, formed in the same manner as the larger one surrounding it, except the shields covering the interstices and the undercarriages were absent. It was not more than two hundred feet across, with the log tower rising from the very center.

She'd assumed Adrian would be on top of the tower, but discovered instead that he was still in their own wagon. Standing beside it, rather, maneuvering a ladder into place with the help of one of the soldiers in Helga's hundred. The hundred itself had taken up positions guarding the wagon. They would not take part in this battle at all, hopefully, unlike Adrian's men. Their job was to protect Helga, the politics of the whole thing be damned.

"Not enough room on the tower," Adrian explained. "Every damn sub-chief in the tribe is trying to fit himself up there alongside Prelotta."

He gestured at the ladder. "Come on. Let's watch it from atop our own wagon. The view won't be as good, but at this stage of the battle it doesn't really matter." He put practice to words, scrambling up ahead of Helga. Over his shoulder: "Not at any stage, really. No maneuvers, here. Just hammer back at them when they charge—and try to plug the breaches."

"Breaches," muttered Helga, as she climbed up after him. "Why don't I like the sound of that word?"

Even before she reached the top, however, a new sound arrived which perked up her spirits. The first volley of Adrian's arquebusiers, firing on the advancing Confederates. Helga knew it was Adrian's men who were shooting, not the Reedbottoms in the wagons. The long-barreled two-man arquebuses had a distinctly different sound from the squat guns of the tribesmen.

It was a very ragged volley, naturally. Adrian's men were scattered all around the laager, two teams to each interstitial shield. The men and the officers commanding them were too spread out to be given coordinated firing commands. So they had been ordered to fire as soon as the enemy in front of their own guns reached "close range"—which, for Adrian's men, was defined as fifty yards.

Still, she was impressed by how closely the guns went off. Adrian's Fighting Band, unlike the tribesmen, had quite a bit of experience using firearms in a battle. Prelotta, on the other hand, had commanded his people not to fire until the Vanbert infantry was at point-blank range—and had then added the most bloodcurdling threats regarding the way he would punish warriors who violated the rule.

Which, of course, had been half pointless. As she climbed onto the wagon top, Helga could already hear the duller *booms* of the tribesmen's guns going off. At least fifty guns, she judged.

Adrian was none too pleased, that was obvious. He was scowling fiercely, and as soon as Helga came next to him. exclaimed: "Stupid bastards! They can't hit a barn at fifty yards with those guns."

"That army's a lot wider than a barn," said Helga soothingly. "Even taller, when you figure in the depth of the ranks and the range of the bullets."

She was soothing herself, she suspected, even more than her lover. From atop the wagon, the view of the oncoming Confederate army was . . .

Impressive. Let's call it that. Since the only alternative is "terrifying" and it'd really wreck my dignity to start pissing in public.

"Terrifying" was a lot closer to the truth. To begin with, Tomsien's army was huge. Flank to flank, not counting the cavalry, the lines covered over two miles of front—much wider than the laager itself. And that was only the first two brigades, each of which was three ranks deep. Behind, separated by a space of not more than thirty yards between them, came two more blocks of brigades. In theory, thirty thousand men in all—coming relentlessly toward a force half their size. It wasn't even so much the numbers which gave that sense of irresistible power as it was the incredible degree of organization. Tens of thousands of men, marching forward into battle as if they were all cogs of a single machine.

In practice, Vanbert brigades were usually understrength. But Tomsien's would be less so than usual, because the Triumvir had had the time—and certainly the prestige and the money—to have built them up. There were at least twenty-five thousand men in that army, counting infantry regulars alone. Helga didn't have the experience to make a good assessment of Tomsien's cavalry, but she thought they had to number another five thousand at the very least.

Against them, Adrian and Prelotta had about ten thousand Reedbottoms, most of them in the wagons; a thousand or less of Adrian's Strikers—Helga saw that he was holding them in reserve not far from the central compound—and a few hundred gunners of the Fighting Band scattered throughout the laager at the shields. Beyond that—

She scanned the area. *What a menagerie.* Perhaps five or six thousand cavalrymen from all the other tribes, maybe half of them Grayhills. From what she could see at the distance, someone—probably Esmond—seemed to be bringing some degree of organization to the Grayhills clustered toward one side of the laager. But the rest of the tribesmen were just whatever routed bands had managed to find refuge with the Reedbottoms. Stragglers and deserters, for all practical purposes, who didn't look to have any more fight in them than so many whipped curs.

She glanced at Jessep, who was now standing on her other side. Oddly, the middle-aged veteran seemed to be rather relaxed.

Yunkers confirmed her impression immediately. "Tomsien's always been clumsy. Capable, mind you—but with about as much imagination as an old matron set in her ways."

"What do you mean?" she asked, frowning.

He gestured with his square chin. "What's the point of taking a battle formation like that against something like *this?* He's not facing an Emerald phalanx or a mob of barbarians. No way to outflank us—so why even try? And the saw and the wedge'll both be useless here."

She heard a massed Vanbert battle cry, followed immediately by the first real volley of Reedbottom guns going off, and jerked her head back around. Every wagon within range of the Confederates looked like a pincushion, thousands of short lead-weighted javelins having struck them in the Vanbert volley. That had been the battle cry she heard, she now realized.

"Stupid," hissed Jessep. "What in the name of the gods was Tomsien *thinking*?" He pointed a thick accusing finger. "No way a javelin is going to punch through the walls of *those* wagons. All the dumb bastard's done is create a hedge against his own men."

By "hedge," she knew, Jessep was referring to a standard tactic used by Confederates to defend their camps against assaults. Pushing branches out sideways through the walls, to impede anyone trying to scale them. Now that she thought about it, she realized that all those javelins sticking on the wagons were going to do much the same to any Vanbert soldiers trying to scale them.

True, the volley fired in response by the Reedbottoms was equally stupid. The range was still too great—although she could see that a number of Vanberts had been struck down. But, at least as long as their ammunition held out, the tribesmen could afford a few mistakes like that.

"And he's doing it again!" Jessep's hiss, this time, was more in the nature of a shriek. "What is he *thinking*?"

Sure enough. The Confederates had hurled a second volley of javelins. The wagons looked even more like pincushions than before.

She sensed Adrian turning his head toward them. When he

spoke, his voice had an odd timber to it. Helga almost shuddered; she *did* avoid her lover's eyes.

She'd heard that voice before, on occasion, and knew that Adrian's eyes would have that weird trance-haze look in them. She hated that look.

"I counted on this, Jessep."

That's a lie. A dead ancient general named Raj Whitehall counted on it.

"No one's ever tried to maneuver such a large army in the field in history. Even leaving aside the fact that it's being maneuvered against a completely new formation."

The voice was hollow, somehow. A ghost's voice rather a man's. That it was the voice of a very vigorous, self-confident and masculine sort of ghost made it all the more repellent to Helga. She'd come to love Adrian's own voice, with its undertone of whimsy and half-detached irony.

"It's sluggish, you see," the voice continued. "Bound to be. The officers can't really control it that well, from top to bottom. Too big—so big Tomsien probably can't even see all of it. So the army reacts instinctively, following routine—from the lowest filer all the way up to Tomsien himself."

Adrian placed a hand on her shoulder. That much, at least, Helga knew came from *him.* She found the touch comforting.

"Even Helga's father wouldn't have been able to do much better, at this stage. Of course, he wouldn't *keep* making the same mistakes, the way I'm sure Tomsien will."

"*The way I'm sure.*" It sounded so . . . *sure.* This time Helga did shudder; and was, again, comforted by Adrian's hand giving her shoulder a little squeeze.

She understood the meaning of that reassuring pressure, and felt herself relax a bit. *I'm still here, love. Just . . . sitting off to the side for a bit. This is Raj Whitehall's work. Got to be that way, or we might all die this day.*

She even managed to croak out a question. "What other mistake of Tomsien's do you expect?"

"Not—"

His answer was drowned out by a wave of sound. Two waves, actually, coming so close on top of each other that they smote the ears like a single thunderclap. The first, the Vanbert battle cry—the *real* cry, the full-throated one which announced an assault, not a javelin volley—followed instantly by the first *full* volley of the Reedbottom gunners sheltered inside their wagons.

Helga stared. Shocked into silence, first, by the overwhelming power of the charge itself. Ten thousand men smashing down on their enemy like a sudden tidal bore. Then, by the fact that the wave . . .

Broke. Was shattered, in fact. Hammered down, before the wave could even crest.

Another roar—all gunfire, that. The only sounds coming from the Confederate infantrymen were screams and shouts of confusion.

Another roar of gunfire. Three volleys fired in quick succession, from the three guns each crew at the porthole had ready.

From here, Helga knew, the rapidity with which the Reedbottoms could fire their volleys would decrease. Slowly, at first, as guns were exchanged for others already loaded. Then, much more rapidly, as the already-fired guns had to be cleaned and reloaded.

But she thought it would be enough. Those first three volleys had almost ruined two full brigades. Confederate tactics and armor, so effective against all previous opponents, were almost the worst imaginable under these conditions. At point-blank range, there was almost no way any of those heavy bullets could miss. They'd hit a man in the next rank, or the next, even if they missed the first.

Next to her, Jessep was almost snarling. "One of ten, I'll bet, or close to it. In the first clash, less than a minute. By the gods, that's *ruinous*. If Tomsien doesn't—"

"He won't," said the voice confidently. "No way he could, really. He doesn't have time to react himself. He probably can't even *see* what's happening."

Adrian's finger pointed. "See? The second rank's already piling forward. Having to climb over the casualties of the first, which slows them down even more. They're just as confused as Tomsien. Reacting by training and ingrained habit."

Another volley. Helga could see hundreds more infantrymen being hammered aside or down. Another volley. Hundreds more. Another volley. The same. The third rank of the two front brigades was now having to *clamber* over the corpses of their comrades. Beginning just a few yards in front of the wagons, it seemed as if the Confederates were piling up an earthwork made of their own broken and bleeding bodies.

Not even a Confederate army could sustain a frontal assault in the face of such casualties. So, beginning with the file closers and first spears, they reacted by training and instinct again. The Confederate battle formation was designed to outflank and envelop an enemy as much as overwhelm it.

No way here, of course, to use the celebrated "wedge" and "saw." The first being triangular formations designed to split apart a phalanx or barbarian mob; the second being a corresponding inverted triangle to trap them—both, together, designed to maximize the advantages of the short stabbing assegai against unwieldy long swords and pikes. The Confederate brigade formation was far more flexible than any phalanx, and could always outflank an enemy.

Sure enough. The second block of two brigades was not even trying to follow over the first. Each brigade was breaking, one to the right and one to the left, moving as quickly as such large bodies of men could move in formation. They would start hammering the laager elsewhere.

Which would—

Helga almost gasped.

"That's what I was about to say," continued the voice. "Tomsien won't be able to stop the flanking maneuver. It's too automatic, too traditional, too ingrained. Even if he was as smart as Helga's father, I doubt he could stop it. Tomsien probably won't even think to try until his next two brigades have been shredded."

For a moment, something like Adrian's own smile came to his face. And the next words were *almost* spoken in his own voice. "I could have told them, y'know? Any graduate of the Grove could. Mystic Form, and all that. How do you outflank a *circle?*"

"Damn me, lad, but you're right."

If Jessep had noticed the subtle transformation in Adrian's voice, he was ignoring it. Helga suspected the former First Spear of her father's First Regiment just plain didn't *care* whose voice was speaking from Adrian's mouth—as long as the voice knew what it was talking about.

The veteran was running fingers through his gray stubble. "You designed this formation for this, didn't you? These wagons, I mean, and this 'laager' business of yours. Designed it for one purpose, really, and one only. Destroy the largest Confederate army you could."

He left off the stubble-rubbing and pointed a finger that was almost—not quite—accusatory. "You *knew* what they'd do. Like . . . like . . . like inviting a man to attack a hot iron by spreading more of his body over it."

Whitehall's aura was back in the voice, but the words themselves were mild. Those of a man deflecting an accusation, as it were.

"I thought of it more as creating a shredder against which Tomsien would shred his own army. The biggest problem any laager has is that you can't bring all your forces to bear unless the enemy surrounds you. A problem which Tomsien will solve for me. But, yes—your analogy's very apt, Special Attendant Yunkers."

Special Attendant. The use of the title seemed to jar Jessep just a bit. Reminding him, as it were, of his new loyalties and obligations. Helga didn't doubt for a moment that Whitehall had used the title deliberately. Although, she admitted to herself, Adrian probably would have done the same. Her lover was by no means unperceptive and unsubtle, however distracted he might sometimes seem.

A sardonic little grin came to Yunker's face. "The gods save the world, what with you and Verice Demansk ganging up on it. He counted on this too, didn't he?"

Adrian shrugged. "*Counted* on it? Oh, I really doubt that, Jessep. Helga's father is far too shrewd and experienced to *count* on something. But I'm quite sure he . . . how can I put it? 'Included the likelihood in his calculations,' how's that? At the very least, I'm sure he figured I could cripple Tomsien, even if not destroy him."

Gods, have I ever heard such a cold voice? Not even cold so much as . . . empty.

But, again, she felt a little squeeze on her shoulder. And remembered something Adrian had told her once.

Center's empty, yes. Or, at any rate, filled with something which amounts to the same thing, from a human viewpoint. But Raj? He's just . . . oh, let's call it serene, why don't we? He was a man himself, once, don't forget. It's just that between his own life and everything Center's shown him, he's seen it all happen so many times before. So he looks on carnage the same way you or I might look on the ocean pounding against cliffs. That's frightening, to a child. An adult just contemplates the workings of nature.

Jessep grunted. For a time, said nothing; just watched as the grisly business unfolded. The last two brigades were starting to come into position, rolling past the third and fourth—already starting to get shredded against the farther reaches of the laager—ready to assault the Reedbottoms from the south. Bringing ever more of their men into range of those terrible guns, against which their shields provided no protection at all—and their disciplined formations provided the best possible target.

The din was almost deafening, by now. No one had ever accused Vanberts of cowardice, not once in many centuries. The battalions and the companies—the brigade structure had already collapsed, even Helga could see that, and the regiments were close to it—kept hammering themselves against the wooden walls. And were hammered back, by a much heavier hammer. Javelins and assegais against thick planks; heavy lead bullets against thin shields and armor, and softer flesh.

Never cowards. Helga could not see so much as a single squad breaking away. All the regulars were bellowing their ancient battle cries and hurling themselves into the fray. Between their own shouts—and screams—and the constant gunfire, she thought she might go deaf.

Even Jessep winced a little, now and then. That was the gunfire, to which he was not accustomed. Not, at least, in such volume. Helga didn't think the battle cries bothered him much, and he seemed completely indifferent to the screams of pain and agony.

He even, to her amazement, seemed able to think of the future in the midst of the chaos.

"How would *you* have done it, lad?"

Adrian smiled. "I wouldn't have attacked at all. The thing about a laager, Jessep, is that while it's incredibly strong it's also inflexible. More so, even, than the Emerald phalanxes. And how did you Vanberts beat the phalanxes, eh? Not by trying to match them at their own game."

"Gods, no. Can't break an Emerald phalanx head on. 'Twas never done once, that I ever heard tell, except by another phalanx." He was back to beard-scratching. "Use their rigidity against them. Force them onto broken ground, tear at 'em, pry 'em apart. Once you've done that, those great pikes of theirs weren't nothin' but a hazard to their own lives. Can't fight a man with an assegai—much less two or three of 'em at once—with an eighteen-foot long sticker. Not when you're up close, and on your own."

Adrian nodded. "Apply the same methods here, then. How would you 'pry apart' a laager?" He didn't wait for Jessep to fumble at the answer before providing it. "It's called 'field artillery,' Jessep. Not too different from those ballistas which Tomsien didn't even bother to use—not that he brought many to begin with, since he wasn't figuring on a siege—except they fire three- or four-inch iron balls instead of big spears. And you mass them up. 'Batteries,' those are called. Dozens of big guns—not too different from the bombards you've seen Trae fire—pounding away at a laager just outside the range of the laager's own guns."

Jessep grimaced. "Three and four inches in diameter? Gods, they'd punch right through those wooden walls."

"Do worse than that. Every ball will send wood splinters flying through the inside of the wagons—with nowhere much to go other than a human body."

Yunkers glanced up at the watchtower. The figure of Prelotta was plainly visible. The Reedbottom chief was accoutered in his best armor, waving a flail and exhorting his soldiers. Not that many of them could see or hear him, of course, buried as they were inside wagons resounding with gunfire. But they knew he'd be there, doing what a chief rightly does in a defensive battle. Just stand there, looking and acting fearless and resolute.

There was no sarcasm in the glance, just assessment. Prelotta *did* look fearless and resolute.

"And what if *he* figures out you're planning to betray him?" There was no admiration in his tone of voice. Rather the opposite.

Helga watched as any trace of Adrian vanished from Adrian's own face. His features looked like those of a statue, and when his voice came it might as well have come from a marble block.

This was *Center's* voice now, not even Whitehall's.

"Do not presume to judge me, Jessep Yunkers. Thousands of men will die horribly today, on this field of battle. The greatest battle in history, perhaps; certainly the greatest in a century. Most of them will be Vanberts. Many thousands more—most of them barbarians—will die on another, soon enough. And so what? Every day, every month, every year—year after year after year—as many die in every province of your precious empire, from disease and hunger and deprivation. Most of them children. Am I supposed to weep for the warriors, and not for the children? Beat my breast in anguish because I caused the death of men bearing arms? The same men whose commanders grow fat on the agony of babes?"

Yes, Center's voice—even if the words were shaped by a man grown sensitive beyond his years. A man who could put into rhetoric what a computer could only calculate.

Helga swallowed. Jessep Yunkers looked away. For a moment, he seemed to be examining the ongoing carnage. But his eyes seemed a bit glazed over, as if he was really looking at something from his own memory.

"Oh, aye," he said softly, "and haven't I seen it myself? My province is littered with the little urns. Pathetic looking, they are, perched—so many of 'em—on the hearthstones of the cottages."

When he turned back, his face seemed calm, and less blocky than usual. " 'Tis nothing, Adrian Gellert. *Special Attendant,* as you said. The gods know if there's any man can end it, it's Verice Demansk."

And now, even, some good cheer. "So. I'll leave it to you, laddie, with your quicksilver brain, to figure out how we're going to pry ourselves loose after the battle." A quick nod of his head toward

Prelotta. "He *won't* be pleased to see us go, now will he? But in the meantime—"

He jerked his head the other way. "You *have* noticed, I trust, that your splendid little plan is coming apart at the seams, here and there? Best we worry about that, eh, before we fret too much about the future."

Helga followed his gaze and gasped. Jessep was right. In three places—no, four!—Vanbert troops had finally managed to break into the laager. No matter how badly mangled and shredded, good troops *will* beat their way into a fortress, so long as their will doesn't break.

Not many, true. Most of them seemed to have done so by breaking the undershields and crawling beneath the wagons—a tactic which obviously played havoc with their own formations. But it wouldn't really take much, after all. By now, Helga had a good sense of just how brittle a laager was. Like some grades of steel, which take a razor's edge but will break under stress.

"I'd better get down there," muttered Adrian. And that *was* Adrian's voice, now. Helga wasn't sure if she was relieved or not.

She didn't have time to worry about it. Everything seemed to move much faster now. Adrian was off the wagon roof and shouting at his Fighting Band, leading some of them toward the breaches and pointing off others to cover the rest. Prelotta, on his watchtower, was bellowing loudly enough to be heard even over the gunfire. And then, pounding from the east, came hundreds—many hundreds—of Grayhills cavalrymen.

Helga recognized Esmond at their head, waving a sword and exhorting his men forward. Even with the new facial scars and tattoos, he was still a magnificent figure. Say what else you could about Esmond Gellert, he was made for desperate battles. This was his time, and he was clearly reveling in it.

Nor, to be honest, was Helga in the least sorry to see him come. Adrian was in the worst of the melees which were starting to flare up inside the laager, where Vanbert soldiers had managed a breach. Not even standing back, damn him, using his sling. She could see him right up in the front lines, with a sword in his hand.

She found herself cursing bitterly. Adrian was adept with

weapons, granted—much more so than you'd expect from such a scholarly-looking man. But he was no warrior out of legend like his brother, and he wasn't wearing even the light armor of the Fighting Band. Just . . . a sword, a helmet, a leather cuirass, and the whim of the gods.

Damn the man, anyway!

A short time later, Helga was in no position to damn anyone for recklessness. Another breach came, at the point in the laager closest to her. A few—then a dozen—then more—Vanbert regulars came crawling under the wagons. Without even thinking about it, Helga was on the ground—Jessep later claimed she'd *jumped;* but she thought he exaggerated out of exasperation—and racing toward them. Waving her sword and exhorting her hundred to follow.

Helga was an excellent runner, in very good condition—and . . . not wearing *any* kind of armor. Not so much as a helmet or a cuirass. Just a light tunic, a sword, and the whim of the gods.

Needless to say, she arrived upon the scene before any of her escort, lumbering behind her. There were perhaps thirty Vanberts inside the laager here, most of them now forming a line. She could see more coming under the wagons. Some of the Confederate soldiers were hammering at wagon doors with the short axes they carried for assault work, feverishly trying to break in so they could slaughter the bastards who'd been wreaking such havoc on them. She saw one of them hurtle back, as several rounds of gunfire from inside the wagon punched through the door.

Not sure that's wise, some still-functioning part of brain recorded. Those bullets'll do as good a job of shredding the door as an ax, fellows, and if those regulars do get into the wagon . . . rough, tough, tattooed barbarians or not, you're so much raw meat.

But that was only part of her brain, and a small part at that. Most of her brain was focused on the fact that she was standing alone, with nothing but a sword clutched in her hand, while one very large and very tough-looking and *very* mean-looking Confederate regular advanced toward her. Wearing full armor and a helmet, bearing a shield—*how in the name of the gods did he manage to drag* that *with him under a wagon?*—and holding an assegai with a lot more assurance than she was holding her sword.

Ah, just what she needed. *Two* regulars, now. No, three. None of whom seemed the least bit inclined toward anything other than hacking her to pieces.

No—*four.* The new one, judging from the sword in his hand and the quick way he steadied the others into squad formation, being their sergeant. *Oh, shit.*

Helga drew a deep breath, steadied herself, and raced through all of Lortz's training. She took the sword in a two-handed grasp—*don't even* try *that fancy Emerald swordplay against assegais, missy, not facing regulars*—set her feet—

And found herself bouncing across the packed earth of the laager ground. The first bounce on her ass, the second on her shoulders. She almost flipped upside down.

Lortz had *not* been gentle. Any more than he was, in the next few seconds, fending off the four oncoming regulars. In a bit of a daze, Helga watched the ex-gladiator put on a display of swordsmanship which would have had the mob in the arena shrieking with frenzied approval. He didn't actually kill any of them—nor even wound them badly—but she realized he wasn't trying to. Just keep them *off,* while the idiot woman he was guarding—

Rough hands seized the back of her tunic and yanked her away.

"Damn lunatic!" yelled Jessep in her ear. "Your father'd have me flayed alive—impaled—prob'ly both at the same time! What in the name of the gods—"

She ignored the rest, which Yunkers continued shouting as he dragged her back along the ground. Partly because her butt hurt—the ground was packed but had not been cleared of stones—but mostly because she was too engrossed in the scene.

Her hundred had arrived. A quick shout from First Spear Uther, and Lortz scampered nimbly away. His job was done, and done well; the professional fighter was quite happy to leave the rest to other professionals.

Wise man, she thought, wincing as another stone scraped her hindquarters and wondering whether the tunic would be salvageable.

Probably not. Jessep's pissed—really pissed—I can tell. I think he's going to drag me all the way back to the wagon.

But even that was an idle thought. Mainly, she was just fascinated to see, up close, a really excellent hundred go to work.

Tomsien's men never had a chance, really. Not only were they outnumbered better than two to one, but the crawl under the wagons had disrupted their own formation while Uther's was picture-perfect. The Confederate war machine went into action against Confederates who'd been dislodged from it. It was more like watching butchers at work than anything else. The men facing them were *trying* to form up, but Uther never gave them a chance.

Just . . . the triangular wedges went out, breaking the formations before they could jell, forcing the men into the pockets—the "saw," that—where three or four assegais could come against one. And that one, without a shield mate.

Like cutting meat. Saw, saw, saw. It was over within a minute. About the time it took Jessep to drag her to the wagon. Which, she thought glumly, had probably done a pretty good job of sawing her own buttocks.

"You could have let me up sooner," she complained, after rising painfully to her feet. She twisted her hips, bringing the damage into few.

Yep. That tunic's history. So's every position except woman-on-top, for at least a month.

"A lot sooner, dammit!"

Jessep growled. "I wouldn't trust you outside of a crib, right now."

Adrian wasn't any more sympathetic, when he found out. By then, it was late afternoon and Helga had been able to put on a fresh tunic from the wagon. The battle was over. When the final frenzied breaches had been driven off, the Confederates had quit. None of them had actually broken in a rout, except a few companies here and there. But by the time Tomsien finally called for the retreat, his army was too mangled to carry it out in an orderly manner. And since it was still hours before sundown, here in the long days of late summer,

Prelotta had ordered the wagons prepared to serve as sally ports to be moved aside. Esmond had stormed through at the head of thousands of Southron cavalrymen. His own Grayhills were primed and ready, and even the other tribesmen were now filled with triumphant vigor if not much in the way of leadership and organization. They just followed the Grayhills.

Cavalry pursuit is a ragged affair, anyway. Against a badly broken enemy, it hardly matters. The same Confederate infantrymen who, in formation and filled with confidence, could have shattered any cavalry attack, were just hunted down by the barbarians. Slaughtered left and right, by arrows in the back and sword slashes to the neck. Or simply trampled under; and, if not killed in the process, murdered later by barbarians picking over the dead and wounded for booty. An already mangled army left a trail of blood and brains and entrails for miles behind it, as it crawled off, harried every step of the way until nightfall.

It was the worst military disaster in the history of the Confederation, suffered by the greatest army it had ever fielded. Five thousand or so dead that day; another five, within a month, from wounds; perhaps a thousand or so captured—the Southrons were not much given to taking prisoners—and several thousand more simply vanished, in the way that defeated soldiers will.

When the six brigades which Tomsien had led out finally returned to the provincial capital of Harrat from whence he'd led them, their effective force was not more than a third what it had been. At best. This was an army which had suffered a terrible defeat as well as massive casualties. It would take months—a year, more like—for its leadership to restore the formations, and the discipline, and bring in the new recruits desperately needed to flesh out horribly thinned ranks.

Tomsien would not be there to do it. His body was found, late in the day, lying among the corpses of most of his staff and personal troops. With an assegai still clenched in his fist, and his shield beaten into splinters. In this, too, Tomsien had been true to his traditions.

Just as a long-dead general had known he would, and a still-living one had so calculated.

(ı·ı) (ı·ı) (ı·ı)

It would be said later, and grow into legend, that when the news of Ion Jeschonyk's death and the manner of it was brought to Verice Demansk that he cursed the gods. Each and every one of them, by name, excepting the All-Father and the Gray-Eyed Lady.

And, it would be said, when the news of Tomsien's death and the manner of it was brought to him, that Verice Demansk cursed those gods as well. Even more bitterly than he had the others. Then, ordered all his men and servants to quit his company, and not return for a day and a night.

When he reemerged from his quarters, so the legend went, he said nothing further on the subject. But the servants found that every piece of furniture in his private rooms had been broken and carved into pieces, as if by ax and sword, even the bed. And it was said that from that day forth Verice Demansk would never speak of any god in private, though he would perform the public rites and ceremonies.

There was no need for printing presses to spread this legend. The servants themselves would do so, making a handsome profit from selling the pieces of shattered furniture and shredded upholstery. For the legend was quite true, in every particular.

On the evening of the victory itself, however, Helga was not worrying about her father's possible state of mind. She had an angry lover to deal with.

"Good!" Adrian shouted. "Wish he'd dragged you all *around* the laager, while he was at it!"

Helga glared at him. Adrian glared back.

Fortunately for her, Adrian was not one to hold grudges. Within an hour, he had forgiven her. Even gave her a hug and a kiss.

"Ouch! Watch your hands, dammit!"

"Oh. Sorry." He cocked his head, giving her a sly smile. No Raj Whitehall or Center in *that* smile. "Well, that's okay. Just have to make sure you're on top."

Helga looked skeptical. "I dunno. Not the way *you* grab me when you get excited."

CHAPTER TWENTY-SIX

Adrian made his break five days later, taking advantage of the Reedbottoms' preoccupation with the pleasures of newly seized Franness. To Prelotta, he explained his unwillingness to enter the city as being due to concern for the loyalty and morale of his men. As Vanberts and Emeralds, he claimed, they would be disturbed by the atrocities committed by barbarians upon civilized folk. Adrian feared he might even lose control of them. And, even if not, unfortunate incidents were certain to occur.

Thus, while the Reedbottoms piled eagerly through the gates of Franness, Adrian and his men remained in their camp several miles outside the city. A camp which they had made, not by accident, northwest of the city.

Prelotta might even have believed him. For all his sophistication and comparatively wide experience, he hadn't actually had much contact with civilized nations since he was a boy. And then, his contact had not been with professional soldiers.

In truth, precious few of Adrian's men—or Helga's, for that matter—gave any thought at all to the conduct of the barbarian victors in Franness. Or, if they did, it was simply disgruntled envy that savages were enjoying pleasures which they weren't. "Civilized" or not, the soldiers under Adrian's command were essentially mercenaries. They took the abuses of conquerors for granted, and regarded plunder and rapine much as they did any other law of nature.

Once Prelotta and his tribesmen had installed themselves in their "new provincial capital," Adrian knew that he could escape any pursuit coming from them. Reedbottoms were slow-moving at the best of times. Not even Prelotta would be able to get an effective pursuit started with tribesmen drunk on the wine and women and wealth of Franness.

He was far more concerned about Esmond and the Grayhills. Who, if they were so moved, could easily mount a pursuit. Of course, catching up with Adrian's people—well over a thousand men now, including Helga's hundred, along with their camp followers—was one thing. *Catching* them, with only three thousand Grayhills warriors, was another matter altogether. Adrian was quite confident that, with the guns of the Fighting Band, he could beat off any such cavalry attack. But he wanted to avoid the thing altogether, if possible. Esmond could certainly inflict casualties; and, what was worse, might pin down Adrian's force long enough for Prelotta to bring up the Reedbottoms. Things would get hairy, then.

Esmond's mood was impossible to determine any longer. The two brothers had not exchanged so much as a single word in months. Indeed, they had rarely even been within eyesight of each other. To all intents and purposes, Adrian no longer felt he understood Esmond at all.

So, for days, he chewed on the matter. Finding no real help from Raj Whitehall and Center, and coming to no clear decision. Then, on the morning of the third day after the victory over Tomsien—what was becoming known as the Battle of Lurion, named after a small town in the valley—word came that the Grayhills were beginning their retreat. After participating in the initial looting of Franness, the Grayhills had apparently decided to return to the southern half of the continent.

"Seems awfully quick, doesn't it?" he asked Jessep. Frowning: "I'd expected them to stay as long as there was *anything* left to plunder. Not as if they have to worry about any Confederate army stopping them, until next year at the earliest. Not after Lurion."

Jessep's shrug expressed a simple notion: Who can possibly understand what a savage thinks?

A more coherent answer came from Raj. ***I'm willing to bet Norrys is dying from his wounds. That'll mean electing a new chief of the Grayhills, and everyone wants to get back for the dickering.***

probability 68%, ± 12, agreed Center. **the mongols broke off their conquest of europe for that same reason, when the khan ogodai died.**

Adrian vaguely remembered the name "Mongols," and a bit about their history. One of the multitude of historical episodes which Center seemed to have at its command at all times. At least half of which seemed to have taken place on this "Earth" the computer insisted was the original homeland of the human race. Skeptical at first, Adrian had come to believe the claim—simply because where *else* would human beings have managed to commit every atrocity and error conceivable. As well, he would admit, as every glory and grandeur.

Raj and Center were right. By now, Adrian's Strikers and Fighting Band had collected a fair number of Southron camp followers in addition to the people picked up in Marange. Through them, and their conversations with passing Grayhills, Adrian learned that Norrys was indeed not expected to survive much longer.

He was not surprised. On matters of this nature, at least, he had come to respect deeply the opinions of his two "spirits."

He was surprised, a bit, to hear that Esmond himself was apparently considered one of the top contenders for the chieftainship. But, there too, Raj and Center enlightened him.

Barbarians are usually less preoccupied with matters of bloodlines than civilized nations. And they take adoption seriously. With his usual wit: ***Damn well better, as miserable and painful as they make the whole process.***

yes. genghis khan did not disown his wife after she was captured and raped by enemies. nor even the son who was born thereafter, whose paternity was never certain. that son was eliminated from consideration during the succession because of

it, years later, but never penalized otherwise. the whole matter was simply treated by the mongols as a practical problem, not an issue of shame and disgrace.

Thinking of Helga's situation after her own capture by pirates, Adrian couldn't help wincing. Had her father been anyone other than Demansk, she would have been kept in real seclusion, not simply the appearance of it. Among Emeralds, truth to tell, even more than Vanberts. "Shame and disgrace." There were times when he wondered if civilization was anything more than barbarism with fancy trimmings.

Oh, it's a lot more than that, Adrian. It's just that civilization brings with it vices of its own. All of which, however, is academic at the moment. The key thing is that the Grayhills are leaving—tied up and slowed down by their great booty of livestock, to boot—and with Esmond being one of the main contenders for the chieftainship he certainly won't be prone to breaking off on any sudden chases. Now's the time. There won't be any better.

Quietly, Adrian passed the word to Donnuld Grayn to get the Strikers ready for a forced march. Helga and Jessep, of course, would handle their own men, just as he'd do the same for the Fighting Band. The camp followers wouldn't be a problem. In their own way, they were also veterans, accustomed to reacting quickly whenever their men told them to do so.

Adrian began the escape shortly after midnight, taking advantage of a clear sky and a full moon. His camp was far enough away from Franness that it couldn't be seen directly; nor, of course, would anyone be able to hear the sounds of an army on the march. Not as much noise as there was filling the streets of a city being sacked. A relatively mild sort of sack, granted, since Prelotta was making sure the city itself and its populace was not destroyed. But any kind of sack does not lend itself to maintaining sober and alert sentries.

To the disgruntlement of the Vanbert-trained veterans among his men, Adrian ordered the camp left intact instead of dismantled. Pulling apart the temporary fortress would take hours better spent creating as much distance as possible between them and Franness.

And there was always the chance that the Reedbottoms would even be fooled through a good portion of the following day, seeing, at a distance, the camp still erect and apparently occupied.

In the event, there was no pursuit. Save only a small band of Reedbottoms who caught up with them two nights later. But they were more in the nature of a delegation than anything else.

One of Prelotta's chieftains was in charge. When Adrian came up to him, after the chieftain was allowed into the camp which had been erected that night, the man did not dismount. Although he looked as if he wished he could. Reedbottoms always looked a bit awkward perched on saddles.

The chieftain's name was Rawal, and Adrian remembered him as being a rather good-natured fellow. Which, indeed, he was.

"Great Chief Prelotta says you are a fool, Adrian Gellert. But"—here, a magnanimous wave of the hand—"he does not curse you. Although I shall, since you've led me on a miserable chase. Damned velipads. Ought to roast the lot of them and be done with the stupid business."

Rawal shifted in the saddle, easing obviously stiff muscles. Then, grinning: "Thought you'd have gone straight north. That woman of yours, again. Talked you into returning her to her western homeland, didn't she? Ha! You should beat her more often."

Adrian returned the grin, willingly enough. He'd *hoped* they might make this mistake.

"Please, Rawal! You insult me. We want lands of our own—without having to quarrel over it—and the best pickings will be on the coast." He dismissed the rest with a shrug. "The woman knows the area well. She is my hunting bitch, no more."

Helga emerged from their quarters just in time to hear the last remark. Fortunately—Adrian blessed every god and goddess there was, in every pantheon he knew—she did not understand the language of the Reedbottoms very well.

Rawal glanced at her, back at Adrian, back at her, back at Adrian. Between the grin and the facial scars, Adrian thought his face might actually explode.

"No doubt. But that is not why Prelotta sent me. He asked me to deliver to you a message." Rawal's voice assumed the slight singsong of one man quoting another verbatim:

" 'Do not forget, Adrian Gellert, my lust for the matrons.' " He sat back in the saddle. "That's it. Don't ask me what it means. I have no idea. The Great Chief Prelotta is sometimes a bit odd."

And with not another word, he reined his velipad around and trotted off.

"What was that all about?" asked Helga.

Adrian translated, leaving out certain unnecessary passages involving female animals and hunting.

" 'Lust for the matrons'?" she puzzled. "What does *that* mean?"

Adrian scratched his head. "I'm not sure myself." Inwardly: *Raj? Center?*

After a moment, Whitehall's voice came. ***Interesting. Center, what was the name of that king? The one from that country named France, I think. Henry this or that. Said something—***

paris is worth a mass.

The march to the sea was a nightmare. Not dangerous, particularly, for such a large and well-organized and well-armed group of men—except for the ever-present dangers of hunger and disease. Just hideous.

The barbarian invasion had ravaged the southern provinces, saving only the larger walled towns. Then, and in many ways even worse, the rebellions and slave revolts which erupted throughout the southern Confederacy after Tomsien's disaster at Lurion ravaged them further. Landowners and nobles often escaped the barbarian bands roaming the countryside haphazardly. It was much harder for them to escape their own infuriated underlings, who not only *knew* where they lived but had a personal grudge to settle. The landscape across which Adrian and Helga and their little army marched was dotted with the burned shells of noble villas and estates—and, not infrequently, the corpses of their former owners. Who, as often as not, had been put to death in a manner whose gruesomeness would have shaken the most barbarous Southron warrior.

Nor were slaves and landless laborers the only ones with grudges to settle. After decades of increasingly extortive and corrupt rule, the Confederation was a crazy quilt of hatreds and resentments. All of which seemed to boil over at once.

Tax farmers suffered even worse casualties than landowners. If for no other reason than because the wealthiest landholders tended to be absentee owners. Their country estates could be put to the torch, but they themselves were safe—for the moment at least—behind the walls of Vanbert or the other great cities. Whereas, in the nature of things, a tax farmer needs to live close to his "crop." When the long-simmering eruption took place, tax farmers were much in the same position as a peasant standing in a field of corn—every one of whose stalks was suddenly alive, armed, and filled with bitter memories of the fate of their predecessors.

Grudges, hatreds, resentments—everywhere. In the towns, the garrisons were usually able to maintain order. Enough to suppress any major uprisings, at least, even if they could not prevent the multitude of small homicides and beatings which took place constantly. The garrisons could keep the masses from storming into the central squares; they could not possibly keep those same masses, scattered in small bands, from looting the shops and (often enough) maiming or killing the proprietors. Any money lender or pawnbroker who did not make it to the garrison barracks within a day after the news of Lurion spread was unlikely to survive another.

In the countryside, where nine out of ten members of the Confederacy still lived in the less urbanized southern provinces, the garrisons did not even attempt to maintain order. Not loyal ones, at least. Garrisons which rebelled, ironically enough, often *did* establish a certain rough "order" within the immediate region. They had to, if they were to survive themselves. A loyal regiment can expect, even if vainly, to get pay and provisions from the central authorities. Mutineers must look for their own pay.

It was sheer chaos, except for little islands and pockets of stability here and there. For the most part, outside the towns, those pockets were provided by resettled veterans. Clusters of villages, much like the ones which Jessep and his clanfolk had established on Demansk's lands. Largely populated by transplanted easterners, whose close kin ties and military experience enabled them to clamp a fist on their immediate terrain.

Invariably, such villages drove off the bands of runaway slaves which were soon roaming the countryside. Taken as a mass, those slaves probably did more damage than anything else. Not so much out of vindictiveness, once they'd settled accounts with their own masters, but simply out of desperation. A group of slaves who rise up and murder a master or burn down his estate—or both—has but one thought afterward: *flee, before the reprisal comes.*

They had no way of knowing, of course, that there was not much chance of any reprisal coming. Not soon, at least. Isolated as they were, field slaves had little understanding of the great world of Confederate politics. The one thing they *did* know for sure—branded into them over the decades with lash and stake and spear—was that any rebellion against Vanbert masters would invariably bring a quick and merciless response.

So, they fled. Immediately, and with no thought at all for how they would survive the days and weeks and months ahead. Half-naked, most of them, without food; autumn here, and winter coming.

Vanbert winters were "mild," true enough—by the standards of a nobleman in his villa, or even a yeoman farmer in his cottage. For a half-naked, starving slave on the run, it is *always* winter. "Summer" is simply that portion of winter when you might survive a little longer.

Almost every slave plantation and estate in that third of the Confederacy called the "southern provinces" erupted, within a week after Lurion. It might be better to say "burst"—like a sudden ulcerous wound, spilling toxins within the body politic. Tens and tens of thousands of slaves roaming everywhere, like so many locusts. Except these locusts had hands; and brains, which, however uneducated, were no less shrewd than any other human brain. They plundered where they could; robbed where they couldn't; thieved at all times.

They had no choice, whatever their own inclinations might have been. There was no work. The estates were shattered, the towns were closed, and the villages of freemen attacked them on sight. If the villagers were transplanted easterners, the attacks would be carried through with pogromist fury. Easterners hated slavery, because it had ruined them—and, as is almost always the case in history, made no sharp distinction between the slaveowner and the slave. Except that it's usually a lot easier to lynch a slave.

Every day, Adrian and Helga's army marched through horror. Ruin and destruction everywhere. Rich farmlands now watered with blood; and a fruitless watering, to boot, because the crops in the fields were either ruined or left untended.

Helga was aghast. It was like seeing an entire nation subjected to gang-rape.

"*This* is what Father wanted?" she wept, one day. "And you also?"

There was no way to answer, really. Explain, certainly—that Adrian could have done at length, and with all of Center's encyclopedic knowledge of human history to document his argument. But *answer*?

He settled on the simple truth. "Yes," he said. "This is what we wanted. Because a boil cannot heal until it is lanced. A long-gaping, cankerous wound cannot close until it is cauterized."

She avoided him for days thereafter, insofar as she could in the cramped quarters of the marching column and the field camps. Until, three weeks after the march began, the column came over the crest of a hill and saw the sea beyond. The sea and, standing like a burnt shell before it, what had once been the great western villa of the family Demansk.

The ruined villa seemed to steady Helga. As if she found comfort in the fact that, whatever else, her father had not spared himself from the bleeding. And then, steadiness shifted into hope, as she saw that Trae's villa and the workshop on their side of the river was still standing and intact.

Rather more than that, actually. It seemed to be a veritable hive of activity. As they drew nearer, she could see that two ships were moored at the pier. One of them she even recognized—the same demibireme which had carried her to Marange earlier in the year.

"There's an army camp not far away, too," said Adrian, pointing. His own hopes had raised, seeing Helga's face. "There, you see? A bit off, next to the woods."

(•) (•) (•)

Trae himself was there, with not less than a battalion of Demansk's regulars. Fresh from their triumphs in the islands, and not the least bit intimidated by rampaging slaves or lynch-minded villagers or rumors of Southron hordes.

Especially not by rampaging slaves. Of which, as it turned out, there had been none.

Eddo J'kot, the former majordomo of the mansion—a slave himself, technically speaking—was most apologetic about the whole thing.

"Couldn't be helped, missy!" he practically wailed. "Th'master himself give me the instructions. 'Make sure it's burned, Eddo! And no saving the furniture.'"

The stoop-shouldered, elderly slave wiped his nose with a sleeve. A rather fine fabric it was, too. "Y'father's the odd one, sometimes, though I shouldna say it. But those were his orders. He made me repeat them to him. Twice."

J'kot glared at a nearby slave. A burly fellow whose name Helga couldn't remember, although she recognized his face. One of the estate's slave underbosses.

"'Twas him did the deed. Led the rascal in himself, he did, a torch in's hand."

The burly one grinned. "Master gave me my own set of orders. Made me repeat them twice, too. 'Make sure it's burnt proper,' he said. And what are you complaining about, old man? I *did* let you get out all the mementos first."

Helga couldn't keep herself from bursting into laughter. "You mean it was all a *fake*?"

The underboss frowned. Worried, as much as disapproving. "Fake?" he demanded, waving a thick hand at what was left of the mansion across the river. " 'Tis burnt to the ground, right 'n proper! Don' you be telling your father I slacked off, now, missy! T'would be a falsehood and a lie! You'll get me in trouble deep. 'E's a goodly master, Verice Demansk is, but he's not one to tolerate disobedience."

That just made her laugh harder. When she finally finished, she seemed in good cheer for the first time in weeks. Adrian sighed with relief.

Trae was grinning himself. "It's just a building, sister. The *people* on the estate are fine. The villagers up north have been promised there won't be any slaves trespassing, and the slaves themselves will get the lands. Father promised it to them. So they've kept everything up. Even drove off three bands of foreign slaves themselves, not calling out the villages."

He nodded toward the burnt shell that had once been one of the finest edifices in the Confederation. "Father lost the symbol, which he'll use as he needs. For the rest, this area will be as good as ever, next year. Better, most like."

He gave the underboss a sly smile. "Though Trippa here might not be so happy, soon enough, when he realizes he's out of a job. The sla—ah, freedmen—are working the fields harder than ever, now, and I dare say they'll not take kindly to any more 'bossing.' "

That didn't seem to fret Trippa any. "I'll get two and a half shares of the land myself. Master promised."

A whimsical thought came from Raj. ***I dare say even Center will admit something in the universe is new. We may be witnessing the only episode in history of feudalism come and gone before it can settle in.***

not entirely new. something not too different happened on— Here the computer wandered into the details of an episode which had apparently occurred on some planet Adrian had never heard of, but he paid little attention. He was too busy admiring Helga's cheeks. The dimples were back.

—but, crudely, you are correct. given the rapidity with which Demansk will get an industrial revolution under way, this smug underboss here will be lucky if he enjoys a decade of pseudo-nobility. though, if he's energetic and capable, he might well leverage his way into a new rising gentry class.

Adrian understood the logic, well enough; but, again, didn't really care. Not at the moment, for certainty. The dimples were facing his way.

"So what next, O great master schemer?" *Yes! There was even a lilt in her voice.*

Trae answered for him. "You—everyone, including all the camp followers—take ship to Solinga. You and Adrian and his gunsmiths, immediately. The others can follow in later ships. Father's there already. He wants to drive on to the capital as soon as possible, but he wants Adrian with him to oversee the siege guns. I'm really the only other one could do it, and I've got to get back to Chalice."

He gave Adrian a look that was half apologetic. "My brother Olver's the governor of Emerald province and that won't change right away. But we need to get you installed in his place as soon as possible."

Adrian's mind seemed blank. What in the name of the gods was he talking about?

"The new proclamation," Trae explained. Then, seeing the confusion still on Adrian's face, found it necessary to explain the explanation. "The newest, I should say. Father's being making a lot of them. The proclamation that extends the rights of the core provinces to the rest of the Confederation. Everyone's a citizen now. A full citizen, with all the rights, not this half-and-half business. Even the members of the auxiliary nations, if they choose. As soon as they make a public sacrifice at the nearest temple of the All-Father, and get it officially recorded by the temple scribe. And, um, goes without saying, take an oath to support the lawful Triumvirate."

Adrian was still trying to catch up. The running commentary from his inner ghosts was more confusing than a help.

—brilliant move. He'll have the Emeralds and the Islands welded to him solid. The Ropers and the Haggen, too, as soon as they realize—

—on hrapti also. here, with this quality of leadership, the probability is even higher. 84%, ± 3. and—

—core of the new industrial base. Who cares about the capital? Just a mob and a pack of bureaucrats, let 'em fester in their own juices. Within a year—

—key now are the eastern provinces. if demansk—

—gaining twice what they lose—

—probability lower, but still 74%, ± 6—

"Shut *up,*" he hissed. "Sorry, Trae. I was, ah, talking to myself and didn't want to hear it."

Helga seemed to choke down a laugh. Trae just looked puzzled.

Adrian took a slow breath. "Start from the beginning. Are you saying you—your Father, rather—wants *me* to become the new governor of the Emeralds?"

Trae bobbed his head, like a schoolmaster encouraging a none-too-bright schoolboy reciting his lessons.

"That's insane! There's a price on my head in the Confederacy!"

Trae managed to look mildly embarrassed. "Well. Not any longer. Turns out the whole thing was a mistake on the part of the Justiciar who was in charge at the time of the investigation into the Redvers rebellion. Turns out—amazing, really—the Justiciar himself was in league with the traitors and cast the blame elsewhere to protect himself. That was Albrecht's man Jacreb Quain, in case you'd forgotten. When Father found out—did I mention that he's got the most amazingly capable man running his own new police force?—he was purely furious."

Trae was leading them toward the workshop, Helga's arm in one hand and Adrian's in the other.

"The police chief's an Islander, believe it or not. In fact, he was supposed to have been one of the chief conspirators leading the rebellion on Preble. Man by the name of Enry Sharbonow. Thicelt recommended him to Father, and once Father discovered that Enry—like you, of course—had been one of the loyalists playing a double game to undermine the traitors, he had the records corrected. Um. Actually, I believe he had them expunged altogether. Anyway—"

"How can Father *trust* such people?" protested Helga. "They're—they're—" An apologetic glance at Adrian. "Well, not you, of course. But—"

Trae shook his head. "I don't think 'trust' particularly enters into it, sister. Except trust them to do their job. Father does still have the only large and *triumphant* army in the Confederacy, y'know? Four brigades worth—more than that, and building."

He gave Helga an odd look. "And, um, he has his own way of testing whether they can be trusted at the job. In the case of Enry, he set him the task of tracking down every member of the pirate crew that, ah, despoiled you. They keep good records, you know, the Islanders. I doubt if Enry missed more than a handful."

Helga stared at him. Her expression was . . . mixed. Satisfaction, anger; the gods knew what else.

"I told you to tell him I'd already taken my own revenge."

Trae looked uncomfortable. "I did. But—well. Actually. I don't think 'revenge' is quite the right word, sister. I think Father just felt he needed to make another point to his new Islander subjects. No indiscriminate reprisals; no general violence; work your butts off for me and I'll see to it you share in the rewards. But don't *ever* mess with me or mine again."

He cleared his throat. "I dare say he made it rather effectively. All of them were executed on the piers at Chalice, in plain view of the whole populace. The city rises up from the harbor like an amphitheater, you know. Beautiful place, by the way. Nothing fancy. Cut their throats and pitched the bodies to the scavengers. Father did the first three or four himself—the captain and his lieutenants—then left the rest to Forent and his boys."

Adrian's head felt like it was whirling. So, from what he could tell, did Helga's.

"And what else is new?" he croaked.

Trae frowned. "What else? Let's see. Oh, yeah. I'm the new Governor of Western Isles. Father wants Sharlz back in the fleet, keep it under tight control. That's why—"

"And what *else* is new?" demanded Helga, almost snarling.

Trae gave her a reproachful look. "I was just getting to that." They had reached the side door to the work shed. Trae swung it open. Standing beyond, facing them, just inside, her very fine apparel looking out of place, stood a very young and very pretty girl. Watching them nervously and making an obvious effort to keep from wringing her hands.

"Meet my wife. Oh. Did I mention she's a princess?"

PART IV
THE DICTATOR

CHAPTER TWENTY-SEVEN

Demansk went down to the docks to meet them, when word came that their ship had arrived. It was a short distance, after all, and he got little enough in the way of exercise as it was. Most of his life, it seemed, would henceforth be spent sitting on chairs giving orders.

More important, he thought it was imperative to "legitimize" Adrian immediately. Demansk's propagandists had been working day and night toward that end, to be sure. In that work, as well as ferreting out rapists—not to mention organizing treasonous insurrections—Enry Sharbonow had been invaluable. Although he was an Islander himself, the man was a cosmopolitan sophisticate, equally at home in the salons of the Emeralds. Using the new printing presses and the old methods of paying rumormongers, he and his men had spread the word that Adrian Gellert had all along been an agent of Demansk's. Working tirelessly, it seemed, to advance the interests of the Confederacy and rescue Demansk's daughter from captivity.

A nice touch, that last. Not least of all because it allowed Enry to slide through the rumor that Adrian and Helga had been secretly married long since. The maiden—well, best not dwell on that—rescued from durance vile, smitten by her hero, etc., etc., he likewise, etc., etc., a wedding in a cellar while he rescued her from Vase under the guise of helping King Casull conquer it—best not dwell on that, either—and etc., etc.

Utter nonsense, which no Emerald in his right mind would accept for a moment. Emerald men did *not* "get smitten" by women. But . . .

The Emeralds were not quite in their right mind, these days. For the first time in history a Vanbert politician was wildly popular with the Emeralds, and in all classes of that society. Anything connected with the name "Demansk" would be accepted as good coin—publicly, at least, which was all Enry or Demansk cared about. The more so since, in this case, the "hero" just happened to be an Emerald himself, and of a well-known and respected family of Solinga at that.

Which not only made their awkward bastard legitimate after the fact, but—hardly a coincidence—enabled Sharbonow to pass off his own treasonous history as being that of Gellert's agent on Preble. The fact that the latter claim was pure gibberish didn't seem to bother anyone either. Not in the northern provinces, at least. And after watching several dozen former pirates bobbing facedown in the harbor waters of Chalice, scavengers and sharks drawn by the blood tearing at their corpses, no Islander in his right mind was going to question much of anything said by Enry Sharbonow.

Albrecht and his faction, from behind the safety of Vanbert's great walls, pointed to all these claims as further proof of Demansk's treachery and duplicity. All of the members of the Confederate aristocracy who were siding with him—which was most of them, at least of the "First Twelve"—were in full agreement. So, of course, was the great mob of the capital's underclass. Who were being showered with favors and festivals by Albrecht, and being disciplined where necessary by Albrecht's street gangs.

Demansk was not really concerned about Vanbert itself, for the moment. He had a different answer to the capital's opinion than printing presses. His son Trae, taking the name from Gellert himself, called them "bombards"—and they fired not broadsheets, but 64-pound balls.

The printing presses would still have their place in the coming civil war, though, and a great one. Because what Demansk *was* concerned about, deeply and immediately, were the eastern provinces. They held the balance of power now. Demansk had the north and the islands. Albrecht had the capital and the center. The south and the west had dissolved into such chaos that they were irrelevant. That left the east—the source, now as for centuries, of most of the Confederacy's military strength.

But he and his escort had reached the docks now, and Demansk broke off his ruminations on strategy and tactics. All of those figured in his decision to come down to meet the ship now being moored to the pier, to be sure. But, mostly, he'd come down because he wanted to see his daughter.

"Well, she looks healthy, that's for sure," commented Nappur as he watched the pretty, buxom girl mincing her way down the gangplank with a babe in her arms. His tone was full of approval. Easterners, like Southrons, preferred their women with some heft to them. "I thought she'd look a bit older, though."

Demansk chuckled. "That's Ilset Yunkers, Forent. Jessep's wife. Helga—"

A second woman appeared and began striding down the gangplank. Tall, broad-shouldered, her legs—far too much of them displayed in a tunic which suited a warrior, not a lady—well-shaped but definitely on the muscular side. Demansk sighed. The fact that she bore a sword—and a real one, requiring a baldric—didn't help matters in the least.

The giant Forent's eyes were almost bulging. "Is *that*—" he choked.

"Indeed, so."

Enry Sharbonow was standing to Demansk's left. His own eyes weren't bulging, no. But they were squinted. "Got our work cut out for us," Demansk heard him mutter.

A young man started down the gangplank. No taller than Helga; a bit more broad-shouldered, perhaps; and reedy-looking rather than muscular. He was carrying no weapon of any sort. He *did,* at least, have a gorgeous head of corn-gold hair.

Demansk sighed. He'd never seen Gellert before, but he'd had him described. He almost winced, waiting for Sharbonow's—inevitable—next words.

"Let me see if I understand the story right. Best I do, since I'm the one who's been spreading it. *He* is supposed to have rescued *her*?"

"He's said to be quite an accomplished slinger," grumbled Demansk. "Just *lie,* dammit."

"Oh, certainly, certainly. No problem, Triumvir. But . . ." Even Enry seemed at a loss, for a moment. "Emeralds don't get smitten by women to begin with, much less . . ."

Demansk ignored the rest. Helga had spotted him and was racing up. In bounding leaps, like an athlete of the Five Year Games, each great stride bringing yet another mutter of despair from Sharbonow.

When she seized her father in a hug and began jiggling him up and down in glee and pleasure—his feet were off the ground, most of the time—Sharbonow's muttering became nonstop.

But Demansk ignored it all. Sharbonow would figure out a way to tell the lies. And, in the meantime, it was one of the great moments of his life.

"You're getting married a few days from now. In a great ceremony at the shrine of the Gray-Eyed Lady of the Stars." Demansk drained his cup. "Remarried, I should say. The priests have agreed that your, ah, secret wedding in the cellar on Vase doesn't preclude a more formal ceremony." He blithely ignored the blank looks on the faces of his daughter and soon-to-be-even-if-he-already-was son-in-law. "Do be sure to get the details from Enry regarding the, ah, earlier wedding. No reason to confuse the priests at this point, seeing as how they're being so cooperative."

He set the cup down on the side table next to him and glanced around the salon. Eyeing, in turn, the other men in the room—Trae, Forent, Prit Sallivar and Enry Sharbonow.

Not a chance. The sole surviving Triumvir could not get one of his cohorts—not even his own son—to meet his gaze.

No help for it. Got to do it myself.

"I'd have preferred to have the wedding tomorrow. But . . ."

He cleared his throat. "But it'll be a double wedding, as it happens, and the lady who will figure in the second wedding hasn't arrived yet. She's on her way here, from her estate in Hagga where she took refuge after Albrecht's massacres in the capital. I'm not quite sure when she'll get here. I received a letter yesterday from the commander of her escort saying that the journey would take a bit longer than expected. It seems the noble lady, ah, insisted on bringing along several wagonloads of art treasures. Twenty wagonloads, to be precise. Marble sculptures, mostly. And, ah—unusual, this—apparently quite a few wooden ones. Reedbottom carvings, as it happens. Seems that new cult of theirs—what's it called? the 'Young Word'?—is given to religious icons."

"Sculptures?" choked Helga. "Icons?" Her eyes widened. "We're in the middle of the worst civil war in history and some noblewoman is hauling useless crap through the countryside? To a *wedding*? What kind of lunatic—"

She broke off and rolled her eyes to the ceiling. "Oh, the gods. Don't tell me. *Twenty* wagonloads? There's only one woman in the Confederacy rich enough for that. Not to mention crazy enough!"

Demansk thought it was time to pour himself another cup of wine. A full one.

"Well. Yes." He attempted a look of stern fatherly reproof. "Though I believe the proper term for a lady of her station is 'eccentric.' Not, ah, 'crazy.' " The patriarchal cluck of the tongue which followed sounded hollow, even to Demansk. "She's hardly a peasant crone, Daughter. About as respectable and wealthy a widowed matron as exists, anywhere in the land."

Helga chuckled. "To say the least. Wealthy, that is. I'm not sure how many of the Councillors—not to mention their wives—would call Arsule Knecht 'respectable.' "

To Demansk's relief, Prit Sallivar came to the rescue. "None at all, these days. Not in the capital, at any rate. The morning after Ion Jeschonyk and the others were massacred, Lady Knecht mounted a speakers' platform in the Forum of the Virtuous Matrons and denounced Albrecht for a murderer and a traitor. She barely escaped from the city with her life. Wouldn't have, if she hadn't taken the precaution to bring her household troops—and if her husband hadn't been one of the few to maintain his troops up to the legal limit."

And now Enry Sharbonow sallied forth. "And if the lady herself hadn't had the foresight to *keep* those forces up to strength, in the years since her husband died." He straightened up in his chair. Unlike most of Demansk's close counselors, though not Demansk himself, the Islander preferred chairs to couches. "I've met the lady, as it happens. Several times, the last of them quite recently. She's really not the, ah—" He groped for words.

"Try 'lunatic,' " suggested Helga. "As I recall, that's usually the term I heard people use."

Sharbonow's frown was quite fierce. "A slander! Slander, I say. I admit the woman has her, ah, eccentricities, but—"

Helga waved her hand. "Never mind, never mind. It's not as if I care. I'm just curious. Who here in Solinga is crazy enough to marry her?"

Dead silence fell upon the room. All of Demansk's counselors were studying the tapestries on the walls. Except Trae, who seemed utterly engrossed in the ceiling. Which, as it happened, had not so much as a single fresco painted upon it.

Treacherous bastards. Demansk sighed, drained half his goblet in one long swallow, and set it firmly down upon the table. *Most powerful man since Marcomann. Courage!*

"I am," he announced.

He was prepared for a ferocious brawl. After Helga stopped laughing, at least. But, to his surprise, his past-and-future son-in-law intervened.

Until that moment, Adrian Gellert had said nothing since he arrived, beyond a few murmured words of polite greeting. So far, at least, Demansk was rather mystified by the man. For someone who'd had such an incredible impact on the world, his daughter's lover seemed more like a distracted Emerald scholar than anything else. The kind of man you wouldn't trust to walk across a small town without getting lost on the way.

"It's a good move," he said firmly. "Might even prove to be a brilliant one."

Helga choked off her laughter and goggled at him. "You have *got* to be kidding! You've never met her, Adrian. You have no idea—" Another choked-off laugh. "For as long as I can remember, every nobleman in Vanbert has made fun of her. You don't want to know what the matrons say! Especially the time—"

"Who cares what they think?" demanded Adrian. "Helga, don't you understand *yet*?" He pointed a finger out the window of the airy salon. The southern window, that was. A thousand miles beyond it lay the great capital of the world's greatest empire. "You're talking about the aristocracy, which is *finished*."

His eyes swiveled toward Demansk. Incredibly blue, those eyes were. But what struck Demansk far more was the weird sense that something lurked within them. Something wise as well as pitiless. As if a scholar was inhabited by . . .

Helga's "spirits." The gods save us, she was right. And maybe that's what will do it, since the gods have gone away.

"Not, at least, in their present form," Gellert continued. "We haven't spoken yet, sir, but I imagine you've already given some thought— Well, that's for later. I think of it as the nobility of the pen, rather than the spear."

He turned back to Helga. "What matters—this is what your father understands and you don't—is what the *gentry* thinks. Because you can destroy—cripple, anyway—a small elite. You can't destroy a numerous class of gentrymen. Not, at least, without destroying most of your educated populace. And try building an efficient and civilized realm without *them*. It could be done, but not without paying a bitter price."

Demansk felt the tension in his shoulders ease. Took another drink from his goblet—a sip, this time—and leaned back in his own chair.

Helga was right, bless her. By whatever gods might still exist, I'll forgive her all her trespasses. Just for having had the sense to fall in love with the right man.

Then, half ruefully: *Might even add five years to my lifespan, letting her quarrel with him instead of me.*

"The *gentry*," Adrian reemphasized. "They're the key. One of them, at any rate. And what's the old saying about the Vanbert gentry? There's nothing they adore more than a crazy aristocrat—who does all the things they'd never dream of doing, and provides them with half their gossip, to boot. Provided, of course, that the aristocrat is a *real* one. The crust of the upper crust, as it were."

He glanced at Demansk, then Sallivar. "I'm not personally familiar with the lady, but I get the sense—"

"Gods, you're *serious,*" exclaimed Helga. She shook her head, as if to clear it. Then, for the first time, seemed to finally consider the question as something other than a joke.

"Oh, she's that, all right. Adrian, you have no idea. Not only is Arsule Knecht the wealthiest woman in the Confederacy—was, at least, before all this—"

"Still is," said Sallivar firmly. "She's really *not* 'crazy,' Helga. In some ways, she's saner than most. She took the precaution, over the past several months, to move almost all of her portable assets and wealth to her estates in Hagga. She's closely connected to the Haggen aristocracy, you know, on her mother's side. And since she's showered the Haggen with philanthropic enterprises for decades—she grew up there, on her mother's family estates—they think most highly of her."

Now that he was confident of the subject, Prit took the time to rise and refill his goblet. "As for her lands, she also had the good sense to keep them scattered all over the Confederacy. A big chunk in Hagga, another one in the east—still stable, you know?—relatively, at least." Easing back onto his couch, he shrugged. "She'll lose much of it, of course—either through . . . Well, never mind. We can discuss that later."

Very firmly: "But it doesn't matter. She'll still come through all this the richest woman in the world. The richest *person,* for that matter. At least"—here, his confidence seemed to desert him a bit—"until your father's investments begin to return a profit."

"So *that's* it," said Helga. She gave her father a look which was not so much accusatory as speculative. "You're bankrupt, aren't you? Finer trappings than ever—and the coffers empty."

Demansk grimaced. "Crudely put, but—yes. Though 'bankrupt' isn't really the right word—no, I'm not glossing over anything!—

because I'm actually wealthier than ever. But there's almost no *cash* left, Helga. And I've got a civil war to win—and quickly, before the Southrons return—and soldiers won't fight for promises. Much less some newfangled nonsense called 'stocks.' "

Sallivar smiled. "I believe your father neglected to mention that Lady Knecht is bringing *thirty* wagons with her. Only twenty of which are laden down with, ah, her enthusiasms."

"Wouldn't even put it that way," rumbled Nappur. "I spoke to her myself, when Prit and Enry and I went to Hagga to make the final negotiations." The giant ex-trooper's face was cheerfully grim. "I dare say she's even more enthusiastic on the subject of gutting Albrecht than she is her patronage of the arts. Right at the moment, for damn sure. Old Undreth's her uncle, you know—he's the Watchman who escaped the massacre at the Council—and he went into exile with her. Right horrid stories he's been telling her since. And none of them lies."

"She always despised Albrecht anyway, Helga," said Demansk. "I can remember, one time when we visited Arsule years ago—she *was* a friend of your mother's, you might consider that also—" He smiled at the memory of a long-ago conversation at a dinner table. "A very poetic—her rhetoric's excellent—and very detailed comparison of the virtues of Drav Albrecht and one of her pigs. The pig came off the winner, hands down."

But Helga wasn't really paying attention. Her eyes were a bit unfocused, as a person's get when they're trying to do calculations in their head. "Ten wagons full of cash? How big are the wagons?"

Firmly, in one voice, Sallivar and Nappur and Sharbonow together: "*Big.*"

Helga grinned. "I take back anything bad I ever said about the lady. Shocking, the way these slanders spread!"

Enry looked smug. "Wait'll you see the counteroffensive. *I've* got printing presses." He began counting off his fingers. "Patron of the arts and philosophies—that'll go down well *here,* among Emeralds—"

"Especially since half those wagonloads are sculptures we swiped from the Emeralds in the first place, now being restored." That from Demansk, who was beginning to feel a little smug himself.

"Indeed so. Then, benefactress of the poor. The rest of the nobility, most of them, never paid this much attention. But the fact is—gods, it's even *true*, and isn't that a change?—she's been the primary support of the Temple of Jassine for years."

Helga was startled. Jassine was the Goddess of Mercy. But, for all the official respect paid to her, not one whose temples were frequented by the nobility. "I didn't know that."

"She never made it public," explained Sallivar. "She's still not happy about changing that, but . . . she agreed, after a protracted argument."

Enry was counting off a third finger. "Then, there's her public denunciation of Albrecht after the massacre. A good third of the aristocracy was appalled by the deed, y'know. Ion Jeschonyk was popular to begin with, and now he's a veritable martyr." He cleared his throat. "Along with courageous Tomsien, of course."

Hastening past *that* subject: "But she's the only one had the, ah, balls to denounce Albrecht in public. In the capital, at least. So that makes her a heroine, as well."

All his fingers were up now, and Enry was clearly prepared to count them all. He was an enthusiast as well as master of propaganda.

But Demansk cut him off. "Enough, for the moment. We can talk political tactics later. Right now . . ."

His eyes fell on Adrian. The blue eyes, he realized, had never left his own face. For minutes, now, that oddly *deep* gaze had been studying Demansk to the exclusion of everything.

"If you'd all do me the favor—you too, Helga—I'd like to spend some time alone with my new son-in-law. We need to become better acquainted, I think."

A deep gaze. As if, somewhere inside, a man very much like Demansk himself was staring back at him. Blue eyes, bright with youth, which still seemed somehow shadowed. Not by grief, or remorse, or anguish. Simply by . . . knowledge.

"Leave now," commanded the Triumvir. "I need this time alone."

Arsule Knecht arrived three days later. The dual wedding was held the following afternoon.

It seemed as if the whole city of Solinga turned out to watch. Along with, according to Sharbonow, half the Emeralds from the surrounding countryside.

And why not? Whatever else happened, for better or worse, the old days of Emerald humiliation were over. Either Verice Demansk would triumph, and the Emeralds would be able to recast the Confederacy much more to their liking. Or he would go down in defeat, in which case no Emerald doubted at all that Drav Albrecht would inflict much worse than humiliation upon them.

So, rejoice in the day and celebrate the weddings. And then, on the morn, pour back into the new shops where their lord and master's son and son-in-law were forging the instruments that might save the Emeralds as well as enrich them.

For Demansk himself, the morn seemed a long ways off. The night bid fair to stretch on endlessly.

He and Arsule were alone, the ceremonies finally over. Alone, in the chambers which she would share with him—officially, at least—and sitting across from each other in the salon. He, on a chair; she, lounging in proper style on a couch. He, groping for words; she—

Not.

"Oh, stop ogling me, Verice. Or, at least, don't do it the way a boy ogles the great-great-aunt of the family he's just met for the first time. The one with the ogre's appetite."

She sniffed. "If I didn't know better, I'd swear you were meeting me for the first time." She glanced down at her robes. "Or have you forgotten how many times you and I and Druzla shared a bath together?"

As it happened, Demansk was remembering one of those occasions quite vividly. It had been a rather awkward moment, he recalled. Arsule had been telling Druzla, with great enthusiasm, of her latest artistic discovery. Enthusiasm, with Arsule, was always accompanied by many gestures and a considerable amount of bodily movement. Which, since she'd been toweling herself off at the time, had exposed to full view every portion of her extravagantly female form.

Awkward. Fortunately, the bathhouse was dim and the waters dark, so Demansk's wife hadn't noticed his fierce erection. Not until a bit later, when Arsule had left, by which time he had a perfectly respectable explanation and use for it. Druzla had certainly not complained.

"Thought so," chuckled Arsule. "You remember that one time? I don't think Druzla did—I made sure to get out of there quickly—"

"Not *that* quickly," he grumbled. "You and your damned hobbies. Not to mention the indiscreet way you dry yourself off."

She smiled. "It's the way I am." The smile began to fade. "And what now, Verice? How do you want it?"

He swallowed, with a bit more difficulty than he would have expected. "It's a marriage of state and necessity, Arsule. I'm not—not—"

"What?" she demanded, an eyebrow arched. "Not a rapist? By law, a husband can't rape his wife anyway. Anything he does, anytime he does it, is quite proper."

" 'Proper' be damned," he snapped. "There was never a time—not once—that Druzla had to be forced—"

"Oh, stop it! Think I don't know that already? She was a good friend, Verice. There was little we didn't discuss, one time or another."

She ran her hands down the robe. It was difficult to be certain, due to the rich and heavy fabric, but Demansk thought the flesh beneath still seemed as firm as the flesh he remembered seeing in years gone by. Close, anyway. Arsule was heavily built, yes; but neither flabby nor obese.

Arsule chuckled again. "As always. 'Verice the Virtuous.' How I sometimes envied Druzla. My own husband was a pleasant enough man, but—gods!—he was a whoremonger. You never even kept any concubines, did you?"

He shook his head. "I've been a soldier most of my life, Arsule. Most such take advantage of the opportunity. I . . . didn't. Maybe it was simply because there was too much of it."

"Like a man who abstains at a feast, from watching others gorge themselves sick?"

"Something like that."

Now, it was more of a laugh than a chuckle. "Gods, isn't that just like the man?" She gave him a very dark-eyed look. "So. Tell me, then. When *was* the last time you got laid, Verice Demansk?"

He tried to find the answer, but his mind was blank. Or, rather, seemed too focused on a woman present to remember women past.

"Thought so. Well, you decide for yourself. But let me tell you what *I* want."

She looked away. Unusually, for Arsule, seeming uncertain and almost shy. When she spoke, her voice was soft. "I didn't agree to this simply for reasons of state and necessity, Verice. I never had any use for gigolos, either, so . . . It's been a long time. As I told you once, I believe, after Toman died I even stopped my own adulteries. Well, almost." Her lips shaped a wry smile. "And even that little self-indulgence is precluded henceforth, needless to say. What the widow—even wife—of a Councillor can get away with is one thing. The wife of a dictator . . . nothing."

She brought her eyes back. They seemed black, now, no longer simply dark. "I always liked you, Verice—quite a bit—even if you were rude, now and then, about my hobbies. And I always thought you were quite handsome." Almost pleadingly: "I'm too old to bear any more children, so you needn't fear complications in the inheritance. I think your children even like me. Trae, anyway. So—"

"Not worried about that," rasped Demansk. His throat was dry. "I'm planning to adopt a custom my son-in-law told me about—"

So dry, he had to stop and clear it. "Ah, never mind. Official adoption, leave it at that for the moment. It's got nothing to do with the inheritance, Arsule, it's just that—that—"

Arsule clapped a hand to her cheek. "By the gods! You didn't even *think* about it! So damn busy plotting and scheming and calculating everything else—"

Then, burst into laughter. "Some tyrant you turn out to be! The one time it'd do me the most good!"

When the laughter stopped, the eyes were still dark. But, also, very warm.

"Oh, give it a rest. Let *me* do the planning and plotting and scheming, at least in our own chambers. And the dictating." She patted the couch next to her, very firmly.

"Come *here,* husband. Right now. Your wife is filled with lust."

CHAPTER TWENTY-EIGHT

Demansk saw little of Arsule over the next three weeks, except late at night. He was far too busy organizing the campaign against Albrecht and the upcoming emergency session of the "legitimate Council," which was to take place in Solinga by the end of the month. The month in question was the one Vanberts called Dura, the last day of which marked the traditional onset of winter. Emeralds, naturally, had *two* different names for the same month, not being able to agree with each other even on a common calendar.

That was the least of the reasons Demansk had to curse Emeralds, however. They gave him more than enough grief on other subjects. *Every* other subject, it seemed like.

Luckily, he was able to pass most of that grief onto his son-in-law. Among Adrian Gellert's many other talents, his strange "inner spirits" also gave him superlative diplomatic skills. Which, dealing with squabbling Emerald merchants and manufacturers and politicians, mainly took the form of couching his words in a dialectic which, after the fact, could be interpreted in at least five different ways—no less than three of which were guaranteed to be mutually exclusive.

Of Trae he saw even less. His youngest son was closeted with Gellert every hour that Gellert was not confusing petitioners. Gellert himself was overseeing the manufacture of the great siege guns which Demansk needed to reduce the walls of Vanbert. Those were being built right here in Solinga. But it would be Trae's job, upon his return to Chalice, to see to it that the large quantity of field guns which Demansk would need for his subsequent campaign against the Southron invaders was ready by next spring.

Of Helga, he saw even less. Much to Demansk's approval—even glee—Helga's husband had invoked ancient custom and ordered her seclusion in their mansion in Solinga.

Quite outraged, he'd been, when she finally confessed the truth.

"You were *pregnant*!? Bad enough you charged up in the first place! But—*pregnant*?!" Demansk, present at the time, thought Adrian's stomping up and down in the salon of their mansion was a *tad* undignified. Not to mention the rather wild waving of his arms. But, then, he was an Emerald. One had to make allowances.

"Jessep says you *jumped* off the wagon!"

"Did not! Well—I don't think. Couldn't have! It was a good eight feet off the ground. I'm sure—"

"Silence, woman!" The ensuing pointing of the finger to the private quarters was excellent, Demansk thought. Quite up to Vanbert patriarchal standards of the old school. Admittedly, the fact that he had to physically manhandle Helga thither—which was no easy task, and gave him a black eye in the doing—detracted somewhat from the august majesty of the occasion.

When Adrian returned, nursing his wounds, Demansk cleared his throat and said: "You realize you won't be able to *keep* her there."

"Sure I can! Well, for a few weeks, anyway. After that, she'll be too gravid to climb the walls of the villa." With the eye still open, he peered through the spacious archway which connected the salon with the patio and the grounds beyond. "Um. I think."

Demansk was already reaching for his purse. Thanks to Arsule, it was bulging again. "No," scowled his son-in-law, "I am *not* going to place a wager on it."

He did see Arsule at night, however. Without fail.

Demansk didn't really take her threats if he did otherwise seriously. He'd come to understand Arsule well enough to know that she really wasn't attracted to gigolos. And, even if she were, no gigolo in Solinga—anywhere in the continent—would be insane enough to cuckold Demansk. The story of the pirates bobbing in the harbor was now as well known everywhere as it was in Chalice. And the name *Enry Sharbonow, Special Attendant to the Triumvir,* was more often than not spoken in whispers.

The threat of embarrassing him politically was a more serious business. Even without meaning to, Arsule embarrassed him politically often enough as it was. The idea of her *trying* to do so was . . . awesome.

Mainly, however, he spent every night with her because he enjoyed it. Immensely, truth be told. For all practical purposes, Verice Demansk had been celibate since his wife died. He hadn't realized how much he missed the company of a passionate woman until another one was sharing his bed. And if he didn't feel the same warmth toward Arsule that he had toward Druzla, well . . .

He reminded himself firmly that it had taken several years of marriage before he and Druzla became truly intimate. That too, after all, had been a marriage arranged for political reasons. He'd hardly even known Druzla before the wedding. And, in his more honest moments, he admitted that for all the passion of her love-making, his former wife had been rather unimaginative about it all. Whereas Arsule was anything *but.* She'd managed to surprise Demansk more than once—even shock his somewhat staid Vanbert soul—in the nights after their wedding.

Not, he would admit in his *most* honest moments, that his sense of shock had ever prevented him from enjoying what followed. Even relishing it, more often than not.

Oddest of all, perhaps, was that he woke up every morning feeling refreshed and alert, even though he was getting less sleep than ever. He would spend a few minutes enjoying the lassitude, enjoying the sight and feel of Arsule's naked and voluptuous form enveloping him—she was a cuddly sort of sleeper—before prying himself loose and rising to the tasks of the day. Occasionally, that awakened Arsule, in which case she would demand that he return to bed for a time. A very pleasurable time. But, not usually. Unlike Demansk, she was a heavy sleeper; and, unlike Demansk, was not accustomed to rising with the sun.

In truth, the marriage was turning out to be a blessing, in many ways; and less of a nuisance than he'd expected.

Not *that* much less. He'd been prepared for Arsule's loquacious tongue; for her obsession with the arts; even for her sometimes salacious sense of humor. What he *hadn't* been prepared for was the energetic way she threw herself into the politics of the time. Which, given Arsule's measure of energy, could be downright frightening at times.

"No! No, no no! Damnation, Arsule, I can *not* extend the emancipation to *all* the slaves. If I even breathed a word to that effect—damn you, woman, if *you* even breathe it!—every nobleman who's rallied to me—half the gentry too!—would race back to Albrecht. Are you *mad*?"

The most infuriating thing about Arsule, he often thought, was the way she responded to his chastisement with nothing more than serenity. The worst kind of serenity, too—the sort a mother bestows on a headstrong and foolish child.

"But it's so *silly,* Verice. You know as well as I do that once you uproot slavery in half the continent it's bound to collapse everywhere else. Within a generation, I'd say—probably even faster, once your beloved new factories start serving as a beacon for runaway slaves. You know as well as I do—"

"That's not the *point.* What I know and you know is one thing. What we rub the aristocracy's face in is another."

"—and the same goes for this nonsense you've been telling them about—what do you call it? Sharecropping?" She threw back her head. "Ha! Why in the world would any freedman agree to become a sharecropper when all he has to do is pack up his family and head for the nearest town? Where *now*—thanks to you—there'll be work for him."

"Plenty of 'em will," replied Demansk sulkily. "You watch." *Long enough to let me get away with it,* he added to himself mentally. But he saw no reason to say that aloud.

Since Arsule, naturally, said it for him.

"Oh, sure. For a few years, yes. At least those ex-slaves with no previous skills—which, don't forget, many of them have because they're war captives." She waved her hand airily. Despite the heat of the moment, Demansk found the gesture a bit enchanting. Arsule really did have very lovely hands—and adept ones, to boot.

"But so what? Unless you're going to reimpose the same slave laws under a new guise—which you are *not,* I trust?" This with a frown which intimidated even Demansk; he shook his head quickly.

"—then as soon as *any* significant portion of the freedmen start abandoning the land, the rest of them will start driving up their share of the arrangement. You know that as well as I do!"

"I'm counting on it," he growled. "The faster the gentry and the nobility—what's left of them, after we're done—start thinking of other ways to secure their fortunes than stupid land deals and tax-farming, the better. Nothing will stop *them* from looking to the cities either, you know."

She studied him for a moment, then shook her head fondly. "Ah, Verice. I sometimes think you're enchanted with maneuvers for their sake. Well—so be it. I certainly won't embarrass you in public on the subject, of course. I know my wifely place."

He almost choked, hearing that last. *Now there would be a miracle . . .*

True, in the days thereafter, Arsule had breathed not a word in public of her opinion on the subject of the much-discussed "Emancipation Proclamation." Unfortunately, Arsule had a very strict definition of the term "public," which did not include her "private" soirees and salons—not one of which failed to draw less than a mob.

Strangely enough, however, neither Prit Sallivar nor Enry Sharbonow nor any of Demansk's other close advisers shared his disquiet over Arsule's conduct.

"Relax, Verice," said Sallivar. "You don't understand—Arsule makes *you* look good."

"To put it mildly," chuckled Sharbonow. "She's a marvel with the gentry, especially. They and their wives flock to her salons in hordes—imagine! them! sharing an evening with the Premier Lady of the Land!—and then scurry away at the end of the night chattering to each other about that *insane* noblewoman—and isn't it a *blessing* she has such a sensible husband to keep her under restraint."

Demansk did choke, hearing that. As it happened—at her insistence, dammit—he *had* restrained her the night before. Quite literally, with velvet ropes she'd obtained for the purpose. Arsule could be . . . exotic, at times.

After clearing his throat, he said: "Well, I suppose. But it's a different story with the noblemen. Sure as hell *their* wives. They know damn good and well that a woman in her position has far more influence in the real world than the fine patriarchal principles of our ancestors allowed for. Even in the old days, much less now."

Sharbonow shrugged. "Yes, true. And, so what?" He gave Demansk a sidelong glance, as if estimating the limits he dared push a matter. Then, apparently, decided the limits were extensive. "Triumvir, I think you're allowing yourself to be overly influenced by the aristocracy's attitudes. Not surprising, really, since you've been spending so much time with them lately. And correctly so, let me add, since it's essential that the upcoming emergency Council meeting goes smoothly. But—"

"Oh, stop being such a damned diplomat, Enry," grumbled Sallivar. "Verice, you're getting spooked! Who gives a shit what the noblemen *really* think? Most of them have rallied to Albrecht anyway—and the ones who've taken refuge here under your wing are not about to challenge you. Not as long as you leave them a hole in the corner—and when have you ever failed to do that?"

"Not this time, for sure," chimed in Kall Oppricht from his seat in the corner. "That proclamation you made last week—the one qualifying the universal citizenship—was a genuine stroke of genius. I thought you were making a mistake at the time, risking all the good will you've built up with the Emeralds and the Islanders—not to mention the Haggen and Ropers—but . . . not so. They don't even seem to be grumbling, and in the meantime—"

He started chortling. "I swear by the gods, I must have had no less than *fifty* gentrymen approach me by now. Each and every one of them avidly trying to get a recommendation from me for a good Emerald or Roper or Haggen—even Islander!—ah, what's that new term you favor?"

" 'Businessman,' " replied Demansk.

"Yes, that." He made a little face. "Crude word, I've got to say. They don't *call* it that, of course—most gentry prefer 'reputable tradesman or merchant.' But, call it what you will, they've got money to invest—scared shitless their lands won't be worth much of anything by next year—not the vaguest idea in the world *how* to make an investment in manufacturing or trade turn a profit—and plenty of non-citizens eager to leap-frog the five-year waiting period you decreed."

Demansk nodded toward Gellert, sitting in a different corner. "Credit where credit's due. It was Adrian's idea." As always, he made no mention of his son-in-law's peculiar triple personality. In fact, Demansk suspected the idea had originated from the one called "Center." But only he and Helga—and Trae now, too, of course—knew of that secret. Or ever would, except possibly Olver. Here, as elsewhere, Demansk would use his family as the second string to his bow.

Olver himself spoke next—to Adrian, not his father. "Weren't you worried the Emeralds would have a fit? After Father had promised them immediate citizenship?"

Gellert shook his head. "Not really. I was a bit concerned about how the Ropers and Haggen would react. But since they enjoy auxiliary nation status already, I didn't think they'd care that much. The Islanders, of course, aren't about to throw a public tantrum. Not with two regiments in Chalice and another two brigades sitting on the beach a few miles away. The Emeralds . . ."

Demansk wondered if he was the only one in the room who found the smile which came to his son-in-law's face far too ironic for a man still in his early twenties.

"I'm not sure anyone not an Emerald can ever quite understand the way we lunatics think. You remember the joke about why it takes eight Emeralds to slaughter a pig?"

Everyone nodded, several of them grinning.

"Ah—but you don't *really* understand it. Emeralds find that joke funny too, you know—because of the *eighth* man in the story. The sophist who argues the pig's side of things."

He shrugged. "It's hard to explain. Let's just say that Emeralds appreciate a good maneuver for its own sake." He inclined his head toward Demansk. "Most of them understand well enough what the Triumvir's doing. Giving the Vanbert upper crust a hole in the corner, if you will. *You've got five years to find yourselves a partner who needs your blessing to get rich. After that, you'll have to face the grasping, greedy—and very capable—bastards on your own. Because, five years from now, their citizenship will be as good as yours.*"

"Crude, crude," chided Oppricht. "Almost as bad as 'businessman.' But—accurate."

Accurate, it was. Every move Demansk made leading up to the emergency Council meeting was designed for the same purpose: turn the world upside down, mix it up, break all the old crusted and rancid layers—while still leaving everyone a hole in the corner.

For the slaves, immediate emancipation for those under Albrecht's rule and at least the hope of eventual emancipation for all others. So much for theory. In practice, Demansk was also creating the economic conditions which would dissolve slavery like so much acid.

For the slaveowners, enough of an illusion that—if loyal to the "legitimate Council"—they could retain their slaves; combined with enough uncertainty to start them thinking about alternatives. So much for theory. In practice, Demansk was also providing them with the alternatives. Sharecropping for some; investments in new enterprises, for others; and—though he hadn't really unveiled this yet, and wouldn't for some time—the prospect for the rising generations of gentrymen to become well-salaried public servants doing useful work instead of a class of drones and tax-farmers, good for nothing except fighting wars.

For the people of the subject nations, he was offering full citizenship. Delayed for five years, true enough—only those who could demonstrate a citizen "sponsor" could skip the waiting period. Still, it was a clear and definite end to what had seemed the endless prospect of Vanbert's iron heel. So much for theory. In practice, most of those folk would not find their lives changing much—and, when it did, often for the worse. For all the aristocratic sneer behind it, the dictum of the old Emerald political philosopher Llawat had more than a grain of truth in it: "Freedom is simply the freedom to starve."

In the name of "justice," Demansk was unleashing much injustice into the world, and knew it perfectly well. But he was not trying to create "justice," in the end. That task was quite beyond his power, great as it was. Justice would have to take care of itself, in the years to come. What Demansk *could* do was shatter a world which made justice impossible.

Finally, there was his masterstroke. The same "silly" Emancipation Proclamation which Arsule derided because it freed those Demansk could not free and kept enslaved those he could, was the thing—so he thought, at least—which would win him a civil war.

Arsule was a brilliant woman, in many ways. She was certainly capable of grasping things which were normally beyond the imagination of her class. But, ultimately, she was a noblewoman from the top of her glossy black-and-white hair to the soles of her well-manicured and lotioned feet. Hers was a world of bright conversations, and art, and philosophy. She simply didn't understand—couldn't understand—the way the world looked to the men who, when all was said and done, would thrust Demansk to power and keep him there.

Jessep Yunkers; Forent Nappur—and all the men of that hardscrabble, bitter commonality, especially that of the eastern provinces. Men who, generation after generation, had spent the prime of their lives wearing a helmet and hefting a spear in the service of the nobility—the same nobility which, generation after generation, had driven them off their land and replaced them with slave labor on their great plantations.

What Arsule did not understand was that freedom *of* the slaves also meant freedom *from* the slaves. And so, what would the soldiers who filled the ranks of Albrecht's army gathering in Vanbert do? When they discovered, by means of Sharbonow's endless supply of leaflets—the papermakers of Solinga were, not accidentally, one of the most prized catches for "sponsors"—that if their enemy triumphed, they could seize back their land *now*. Whereas if their commander triumphed, they . . . could look forward to serving out their term, in the *hope* that the gracious lord might deign to give them a good retirement bonus.

To Demansk's surprise, the high priest of the Temple of Jassine had grasped it perfectly. "Do you understand what will happen to the slaves of the east?" he had demanded.

"Yes. They will be driven out, by spear and fire. Murdered outright, any who put up resistance. And the rest—cast into the wilderness, left to starve and roam. Do you have an alternative, Priest?"

The old man had looked away, for a time, studying the image of his goddess.

"Part of one, yes."

And so, on the next day—the very eve of the Council meeting—Demansk issued a new proclamation. In light of the misery stalking the land, and out of his deep sense of pity, the Triumvir decreed that anyone who made a donation to the cult of Jassine—properly notarized, of course—would be given twice that amount in the form of a tax forbearance the following year. And, in the case of non-citizens, a reduction in the time needed to qualify for citizenship, the amount of time determined according to a formula whose construction pleased Demansk's bureaucrats no end.

"Piss on it," he'd growled afterward to Sallivar. "You know as well as I do that the damn bureaucrats would filch three quarters of the tax collected anyway. I'd rather trust Jassine's priests to provide food and shelter for ex-slaves than *that* lot."

Sallivar hadn't argued the point. In fact, he'd even used it to urge Demansk—again, and for the sake of peace at home if nothing else—to give his blessing to Arsule's increasingly strident demand for the formation of what she called a "new and greater Grove."

"Sure, and the youngsters will learn some foolishness. But at least we'd have a generation of public servants who'd be educated enough to catch each other stealing."

"Done."

Arsule was suitably pleased with her husband. The night before the Council meeting, she kept him up very late indeed.

"I have *got* to get some sleep."

"Oh, damnation, I suppose so." The long fingers stroked his chest, seeming to revel in the sweat. "It's just . . . I am growing *very* fond of you, Verice. You excite me, always do."

"I'm almost a corpse," he croaked. "*Please* don't tell me you've decided to experiment with necrophilia."

She gurgled a laugh into his neck. "I draw the line *somewhere,* you know. Speaking of which, I got rid of the ropes. I wanted to try it out, but . . . the truth is, I don't *like* being immobilized."

"Pity. At least with your hands tied—will you *stop* that?"

"Oh—phft! Sleep, sleep, sleep, all you think about any more."

"That's a foul and damnable lie," he wheezed, "and you know it—you of all people." He managed to lever himself up on an elbow and gaze down on her.

"Truth is, girl, I'm growing very fond of you myself. In between wanting to strangle you, anyway." Hastily: "No, that's not a suggestion."

She smiled lazily. "Oh, good. In that case—yes, yes, tomorrow night, of course, not now—I want to try something out of this marvelous book Sharlz gave me the other day. You know, they may be just barely this side of barbarism, but the islanders *do* have some interesting customs. For instance . . ."

By the time she finished explaining the "for instance," Demansk was lying flat on his back and staring at the ceiling. The look on his face wasn't *quite* one of sheer despair. Despair there was, to be sure, and in goodly measure. But there was also—

"Gods, I love that little gleam in your eyes. Don't lie, Verice!"

"Can't," he croaked. "I'm saving all my lies for the morning—which is now not more than three hours away. I have *got* to get some sleep."

"Oh, all right."

She left off anything but cuddling then; which, as always, got Demansk to sleep quickly and easily. But when he rose at sunrise, he found to his surprise that Arsule was awake also.

"Think of it this way, Verice," she murmured as he began clothing himself. "This is probably the first Council meeting you've ever attended which will seem like a restful occasion."

His lips quirked. "An exaggeration, woman. But . . . not without some merit."

He came up to the bed, stroked her cheek, and turned to leave. But a hand on his tunic turned him back.

"Come home in triumph, Verice Demansk. Your Vanbert wife demands it."

"And if I do?"

Throughout the day, the ensuing smile kept flashing into his brain—sometimes at the most awkward moment. But return in triumph he did, even if it was late in the evening; and, as he returned, the smile seemed to draw him like one of Gellert's bizarre new "magnets."

"Done, woman," he announced, entering the bedroom. "Triumph indeed. All proclamations ratified by the *legitimate* Council—which, of course, used the occasion to declare itself such. A new Triumvirate elected. They didn't even choke much at Forent Nappur, though I think one or two of them may die of apoplexy in the next few days contemplating his 'Registry.' Not at all, at Prit Sallivar—ha! Compared to Forent, Prit looks like a blueblood."

Arsule laughed. "What a trio! You, a gentryman, and a plain and simple peasant. Where it all began, after all, so why not?"

"Just what I said, when someone—that verminous little Wrachet—whined that Forent's Registry seemed illegible." He snorted. "It damn well *should.* Enry hired the best forger in Solinga to draw it up."

"And you?"

He preened histrionically. "As I foretold. 'First among equals,' of course—no more, no more. But they did *insist*—the vote was unanimous, believe it or not—that I take on a special title." Relaxed, more seriously: "Better that, of course, than plain and simple 'dictator.' "

"So? What was it? Adrian's proposed 'Principal'?"

"No, no—too damn Emerald foppish. These are solid Vanberts, remember. Decadent, to be sure. But this once, at least, they held their breath and seized their ancestors."

He hopped onto the bed—and a goodly portion of Arsule as well. " 'Paramount,' woman! And don't you forget it!"

"Oh, marvelous!" she cried, drawing him down the rest of the way. "Exactly what the book calls for!"

CHAPTER TWENTY-NINE

Don't be an idiot, Adrian, said Raj Whitehall. ***He's going to kill his oldest son, the first of his babies who came into the world and whom he can still remember cradling in joy and wonder. Of course he wants his daughter at his side.***

The quiet thought jolted Adrian out of his gathering storm of protest. For a moment, he stared at Demansk—and, for the first time since Demansk had advanced his proposal, noticed the tightness in the man's face. His father-in-law was such a formidable person that even his closest friends and allies and relatives tended to forget that he was made of flesh and blood.

Except Arsule. And you can thank whatever gods there are that she shares his bed every night. If we do manage to keep this man sane, in the years to come, she'll play the largest role in the doing. And the gods help the world if we don't.

Adrian remembered the old Emerald saying: "Whom the gods would cast down into madness, they first raise on high."

you can find that saying, in one variation or another, on all planets and in all times, added Center. **it's the derivative of another famous old saw: power corrupts; absolute power corrupts absolutely. what people often fail to understand, however, is that the rot strikes at a man's intellect much faster than it does at his**

morals. gigo, a later time would call it: garbage in, garbage out. a man with the power to punish anyone never hears anything except what he wants to hear. or, what's worse, what his subordinates think he wants to hear—and they don't dare ask him what it is. such, at least, is the tendency—and it is very hard to counter.

Adrian sighed. "Yes, Father, of course. Helga can come on the campaign with us. And the children too. Jessep's already told me he's bringing Ilset—who's got another new baby of her own, you know. So if Helga needs a wet nurse, we'll have one she trusts at hand."

He was *not* happy about it. Adrian knew perfectly well how difficult it would be to keep Helga far out of any danger. The damned woman—

"Damn girl," chuckled Demansk. But the tone had a certain warmth in it, and the harsh lines in his face seemed to be fading a bit. "I know she'll drive us both half insane, but . . ."

Quietly: "I think I might go insane altogether, if she weren't with me along with Olver. This is going to be . . . difficult." He placed a hand on Adrian's shoulder and gave it a little squeeze. "I thank you for this, son."

Adrian nodded. He tried to think of something to say, but couldn't. At some point, he knew, he was going to have to raise openly and straightforwardly with Demansk the dangers of the future. But—

Not now. Let the man finish the job of becoming a tyrant—the task of a titan already—before you start nattering at him about all the ways he should start unraveling his work. That'll be the last thing he wants to hear at the moment, any more than a man feverishly building a dyke to contain flood waters wants someone prattling in his ear about the danger of future droughts.

"I don't imagine you'll have any trouble getting her ready," said Demansk. The chuckle this time was full of warmth. "Even though the expedition leaves tomorrow."

"Not hardly," said Adrian sourly. "Just remove the bolts and chains and armed guards and hexes and amulets and fetishes and—if that stupid spell had worked right—the demons that were supposed to have been keeping her locked safely away in her chambers."

Demansk laughed. "Which spell was it? Druzla probably tried it herself, years gone by. Didn't work, of course."

He lifted the hand of comfort and thanks from Adrian's shoulder and gave it a hearty clap. *Exactly* the kind of hearty clap on the shoulder which fathers-in-law have given sons-in-law throughout the ages. *Well, boy, she's all yours now. Have fun. I'm going to get some rest.*

"Tomorrow morning, then," he added as he turned away. "I'll have Jessep and Uther keep an eye on her, Adrian, I swear. And by the time the siege has settled in, you'll have arrived yourself with the guns and the rest of the train."

The last remark had, at least, the virtue of distracting Adrian from his worries over Helga. Fine for his father-in-law to talk serenely about a "siege train." Since Adrian—not he—was in charge of actually *getting* the thing to the siege.

"Train." Ha! Remind me again, Center, what a train is supposed to look like.

Now and then, Center had flashes of something close to a sense of humor. He gave Adrian, first, an image of a mechanical behemoth snorting its smooth way across a countryside. Then, the piled-up jumble of a trainwreck.

Yeah, what I thought.

Luckily for Adrian, Center's quasi sense of humor manifested itself but rarely. So, in the weeks which followed, as he struggled and strained and cursed and beat his breast in despair trying to keep huge and ungainly cannons moving—slowly, slowly—across a ravaged countryside in the middle of winter, he was at least not forced to grit his teeth at the computer's witticisms.

Raj Whitehall, of course, was a different matter. Yes, true enough, the former general was also a fount of excellent advice. But Adrian could have done without the jests and wisecracks—much less the disquisitions on the ironies of military life.

—never fails either. Just when the risk of an epidemic ravaging your troops has passed with warm weather, it comes right back again with the hard soil of winter. Nothing soldiers hate worse than

digging latrines in winter—grouse about, anyway—but if you don't—

—lucky at that your winters are so mild. On—

And so it went, week after week. Excellent advice, yes; which got Adrian out of many a jam. Complete with commentary.

—can't do that, lad, I'm giving you fair warning. You'll have a mutiny within a week—

—logs as paving. Pile 'em straight down through the muck. It'll work, trust me. I did it during—

—and the time the only good surgeon got too drunk to work, right in the middle of a battle. Let that be a lesson to you, lad. Always—

On and on, week after week. By the time Adrian crested the hill overlooking Vanbert, the siege train coming up behind him, he was desperately trying to figure out a way he could make both Whitehall and Center materialize in front of him. So he could strangle the first and turn the great guns on the other.

His thoughts, of course, were no secret to his would-be victims. Center did not deign to comment. And all Raj had to say, when the sight of the enormous city finally loomed before them, was: ***A good job, lad. Lost only two of the guns along the way, got here in plenty of time—and even managed not to murder anyone, corporeal or otherwise.***

That praise was modest compared to the accolades which Demansk heaped upon him. Adrian lost count of the number of times his father-in-law used the word "brilliant" to refer to Adrian's exploit at his staff meetings. "Daring" and "dashing" were tossed around freely also. Not that Adrian could, for the life of him, understand how even an Emerald—much less a stodgy Confederate—could possibly apply such terms to an enterprise that had consisted, for the most part, of sheer drudgery.

But . . . Adrian didn't really need Raj and Center's commentary to explain it to him. Sieges are a miserable business, under the best of circumstances—which a siege undertaken in winter most certainly was *not*. Even with their confidence in eventual victory, the morale of

Demansk's own soldiers was none too high at the moment. Having Adrian finally show up with the great guns—*impressive,* they were, to the besiegers who gawked at them as they were hauled into position—gave an enormous boost to their spirits.

And, of course, correspondingly depressed the spirits of the defenders. By now, the arquebusiers whom Adrian and Trae had trained and Demansk had brought with him had inflicted misery enough on the soldiers manning the walls of Vanbert. To see what even unsophisticates such as themselves could immediately recognize as giant versions of arquebuses, training their huge muzzles toward them . . .

Finally, Adrian realized, his father-in-law was—as always—seeing to it that the "second string" to his bow was kept taut and ready. Now, as before and in the long years to come, Verice Demansk would be leaning heavily on his family. And if he was about to lose a son, he was reminding everyone that he had gained a son-in-law capable of replacing him. Reminding himself, perhaps, more than anyone.

"Let's do it," Demansk ordered. His face was drawn and tight, looking like a mask in the lamplight of the command bunker, but showed no emotion otherwise. "Send in the propaganda teams and the spies tonight, Forent. By now, that wall is like a sieve. For small groups of men, anyway."

Nappur nodded. Adrian was a bit surprised that the giant seemed so placid at the prospect of trying to infiltrate hundreds of men into a city which was supposedly, after all, "under siege." But Raj enlightened him immediately.

Forget the imagery, lad. What's the axiom of your philosopher—can't remember his name at the moment—about not mistaking the portrait for the man? Same's true with a siege. Precious few sieges are really all that tight, especially with a city as enormous as Vanbert. Keep out massed assaults, yes. Keep out spies, deserters—both ways—traders, hell, even housewives looking for husbands and vice versa—not a chance.

Demansk turned to Adrian next. "We'll give the proclamation

two days to eat away at Albrecht's troops. Morning of the third, I'll want to start the barrage. Can you manage it?"

On that subject, Adrian had no questions at all. "Yes, easily. I could start by tomorrow night, if you wanted."

Demansk shook his head. "No, the proclamation gives the troops two full days to decide, and I'll stick to it. Whatever I might gain in the way of a tactical surprise wouldn't be worth the political damage. 'Verice Demansk is good for his word.' That's gotten us this far, it'll take us the rest of the way."

And so it proved. To Adrian's immense disgust—combined with relief, admittedly—the siege guns never went into action at all. By noon of the second day, mutinies began erupting among Albrecht's troops. By midafternoon, half the garrison of Vanbert was in full revolt. By late afternoon, the revolt was completely out of control. The gates of the city were being thrown open from within. Civilians began pouring out to plead for mercy and soldiers began pouring out to make a formal surrender—before, still carrying their weapons as Demansk had promised them, they began their own long march back to the eastern provinces from which they came.

Most of the soldiers, at least. Those who had decided to take advantage of Demansk's proclamation that the land of all noblemen under Albrecht's banner—which was a good half of them, taken as a whole, and almost three quarters of those whose estates lay in the east—was forfeit to the state. Which, in its mercy and justice, would allow any yeoman of the rebellious provinces to claim for his own. And would ask no questions regarding the status of their military service.

Enry Sharbonow had even printed up samples of the legal form which would be required to substantiate the new land tenure. A very simple and straightforward form, quite unlike the typical official document of the Confederacy. Even a half-literate foot soldier could study the thing and see how easy it was, and explain it to his fellows who could not read at all. *Just grab it and get nine other people to say you're a good and proper fellow. And that's—IT. Okay, guys—we all know each other and there's ten of us. Let's go. Squad deep.*

So, three brigades' worth of soldiers began a disorganized race back to their homeland, each and every one of them bound and determined to carve out for himself a farm he could live on and raise a family. And the gods save anyone who got in their way.

Not all of the soldiers, however. Quite a few, either because they were more short-sighted, filled with a more immediate greed, less ambitious, lazier—it was a *long* way back to the eastern provinces—decided they'd rather keep enjoying the pleasures of the capital, or, simply, were too unpleasant to have nine people ready to vouch for them, decided to take advantage of Demansk's *other* offer.

And a full land share taken from their estates—or half its equivalent immediately, in cash—to anyone who brings before Verice Demansk, Paramount Triumvir, the heads of any rebellious nobleman. The features must be recognizable.

A separate leaflet—a bound-together cheap little codex, actually—specifically listed the names. That was more in the way of a formality than anything else, however. Forent saw to it that his infiltrators distributed hundreds of those, as well, but precious few people within the city bothered to study the list. After ruling the roost in Vanbert for so many months, Albrecht and his cohorts were quite well known to the populace and its garrison.

Besides, the principal leaflet—distributed in thousands of copies—had the real prizes listed on it.

Double shares for any member of Albrecht's false and traitorous so-called 'Council.' Triple shares for Drav Albrecht himself and his principal conspirators.

That was a short list. Six names, beginning with Jacreb Quain and ending with: *Barrett Demansk.*

Demansk kept his troops out of the city for the first two days of the massacre. Albrecht's street gangs, of course, were doing most of Demansk's dirty work for him. They were the ones who had the easiest access to Albrecht and his cohorts, the ingrained habits of thuggery to fall back upon, and could most easily intimidate the populace into revealing the hidey-holes of those noblemen who managed to escape the initial slaughter. But, in the nature of things, would also be the most uneasy at the presence of regular soldiers in the city.

On the morning of the third day, by which time most of the heads had been collected in any event, Demansk—in his justice and mercy—heeded the pleas of the city's everyday citizens to put a stop to the brigandage and mayhem which the street gangs had also unleashed on the capital.

So, a new proclamation was issued—and four brigades of regular troops stormed into the city to enforce it. Or, to put things crudely but more truthfully, cash in on it.

The Paramount Triumvir is distressed to discover that criminal elements are running amok in the capital. Therefore he has decreed that any soldier who brings him the head of such a criminal will be entitled to whatever property the criminal possesses. Features must be recognizable.

A new set of codexes was distributed—not many; Enry's portable printing presses were temperamental gadgets—which provided a long list of the names of criminals. The list was even fairly accurate and up to date, since everyone who had turned in a nobleman's head had been required to sign or mark a receipt. True, many of the names on the receipts were fictitious; but an amazing number of street gang members had given their own.

And, again, it hardly mattered. The populace of Vanbert, which had suffered the swaggering abuses of the city's gangs for decades—and never more so than in the past months—were even more adept at leading soldiers to the hidey-holes of criminals than the criminals had been at ferreting out noblemen. Within the first hour, in fact, the transaction became more-or-less standardized. *Show us where the bastards are and we'll cut you in—a tenth of whatever the squad gets.*

That was perhaps the brightest side of the affair. At least thirty-two marriages came out of those impromptu liaisons between squads and civilians—along with more than twenty adoptions. One street urchin was even, officially, adopted by an entire squad. Which they thought was eminently reasonable and fair, since the shrewd and plucky lad had led them to no less than thirteen hidey-holes. (And never you mind how the boy knew about 'em. How many *real* crimes could he have committed, anyway, at the age of nine?)

There was a much darker side to it, of course, as Demansk had known full well there would be. Not all of the "criminals" who were pointed out to the soldiers were anything of the sort. It was easy enough, in the chaos and carnage of the moment, for someone to settle an old score or grudge by simply making the claim. Soldiers were not given to asking too many questions, after all, under such circumstances. Unless others—neighbors, friends, relatives—put up a fierce argument on the spot, most squads were ready enough to chop off a head on anybody's say-so. Although, now and again, it did happen that, once convinced a "criminal" was innocent, the soldiers cheerfully decapitated his accuser and brought *that* head before the Paramount Triumvir.

And . . . got paid. Demansk was asking no questions. He had not asked any, since the third hour of the slaughter, on the first day, when the head of his son was presented to him.

Helga hissed, faintly, and her hand on her father's shoulder tightened. Olver, standing nearby, looked away and grew wet-eyed. Adrian gave a moment's thanks that Trae was across an ocean in Chalice. But, so far as Adrian could tell—even with the visual acuity Center gave him—Demansk's expression never changed at all.

A face made of iron, that was. Had been, and would be, throughout the crushing of Vanbert. And his voice, as level and even as a road made of stone.

"Yes, I recognize him. Pay the man. Cash or future land grant, whichever he prefers. Next."

How can he do it? Is he already insane?

There was no humor at all in Whitehall's response. ***Steady, boy. Come this spring, you'll have to do the same. Not until you examine yourself after Esmond's death will you be able to answer that question—or even ask it in the first place.***

Adrian would never know the answer, really. In some ways, he was and would always remain too different a man from his father-in-law. An Emerald scholar, ultimately, reared by a merchant father and trained by philosophers; where Verice Demansk was, ultimately, the boy shaped by the harsh Confederate grandfather.

Arsule had enabled Demansk to pass through the ordeal. Not she, really, so much as what she brought with her when she arrived at the siege the day before the garrison broke.

"I told you to stay in Solinga," grated Demansk.

"Oh, Verice, give it a rest." Arsule plumped herself down on the cot which served Demansk for a bed in his command bunker. Then, winced. "Gods, you *sleep* on this thing?" she muttered. "How are we going to manage—"

She broke off *that* train of thought, after a glance at Demansk's angry face. Sighing: "Give it a rest, I say. *You* of all men in the world don't have to maintain your august image. You know it as well as I do. Besides—"

Arsule was quite shrewd enough to have figured out that her graceful hands, in motion, soothed the savage patriarch. So, with a particular flourish, she accompanied her next words with many a gesture.

"Besides, Jonthen Tittle's doing a splendid job of serving the Emeralds as a deputy governor while Adrian's down here with you. The province is quite peaceful and steady, I assure."

Her husband's face was still angry. The hands picked up their tempo, one of them making a come-hither gesture. Not toward Demansk, but toward a figure standing nervously in the crude wooden frame of the doorway.

"Besides, I thought you would need Kata here. So I brought her with me."

Demansk swiveled his head and gazed at the slave girl, rather like a cannon gazes on its target. For a moment, the fair-skinned former concubine of Ion Jeschonyk looked as white as a sheet. And was obviously on the verge of bolting in sheer terror.

But the Paramount Triumvir's angry expression broke, before the girl's fears crested. Demansk's face seemed to cave in, for a moment; then, the way a man rebuilds something precious which has been broken, slowly came back to itself.

In the end, the Demansk who glanced back and forth from slave to wife was the man the wife had come here to salvage. He even managed something that might be called a smile.

"Yes. Thank you. She will be of help."

A real smile, now. "As for the cot, it was never *designed* for the purpose you're contemplating. Nor would I be in any mood for it, to be honest. But . . . in a few days, I expect we'll be in more, ah, appropriate quarters."

He turned back to Kata. "Remind me again, girl. The exact words."

Kata cleared her throat. Then, in a little singsong, did her best to give a girl's soprano the rasp of a man grown old from a life filled with duplicity, deceit, and debauchery.

"Just tell him to remember, that's all, and think about it now and again. The word is 'duty,' I believe."

In the days which followed, Adrian wondered from time to time why Demansk had included a slave girl in the small coterie which surrounded him during his ordeal. Not simply included her but even gave her a place next to his own child. Both of them standing just behind him, as he sat dispensing blood in the name of justice. The daughter's hand on one shoulder, the slave's on the other. She was not his concubine, after all, of that much Adrian was quite certain.

Center could have explained it to him. But, for whatever reasons impel a computer's inhuman mentality, chose not to.

It was an old custom. Recreated here on Hafardine independently, to be sure, but drawing its roots from ancient times and places. The Romans, too, had used the trick. Not, perhaps, to any great purpose—but who was to say how crazed their great ones might have become otherwise?

Always a slave, riding with the conqueror in his chariot at the triumph, to whisper in his ear: *this, too, shall pass.*

And if Kata whispered nothing, the hand did as well. Perhaps better. The hand, after all, served to remind the shoulder bearing the world's grief as well as its brutality, that triumphs produce many forms of madness—but all triumphs fade. Perhaps madness can, too.

PART V
THE MAN ALONE

CHAPTER THIRTY

Helga turned away from the city lying below the hillside, sighing quietly. Franness was a beautiful town, especially now with the spring in full bloom. Like a pearl-and-red gemstone, tile roofs atop whitewashed walls, cupped in a low valley draped in green and all the colors of the flowers. Nor, from what she could tell at the distance, had the long months of the barbarian occupation produced any noticeable damage.

But the sight brought her no pleasure, and even less in the way of comfort.

Most of all, I miss Jessep. Even more, I think, than I miss my husband or my own father. Both of whom are right here—

She glanced down the back slope of the hill, where the army of the Paramount Triumvir was erecting its field fortifications. Very extensive, those fortifications were; as they needed to be, given the size of the army.

—but might as well be on one of those "planets" Adrian insists the moving stars really are. Maybe he's right, who knows? Big balls of rock or spirits of the gods, it hardly matters to me. Either one of them is untouchable.

Gloomily, she studied the army camp without really noticing any of its details. Her mind was still focused inward, awash in memories of Jessep's warm presence and Ilset's frequent gaiety. But Jessep and Ilset were gone, now. The Paramount had ordered his Special Attendant to the eastern provinces, to give Forent Nappur what aid he could in bringing that region out of a state of chaos. They were low-born easterners themselves. If anyone could cajole or convince or swindle—or just break the heads, where needed—of those headstrong commoners recapturing their yeomanry, it would be men like them.

Helga understood the logic of her father's command. Just as she understood the logic of everything he did these days. But she didn't have to like it, or the way that logic was turning her father into a grim and forbidding presence—and had deprived her of a substitute in Jessep. Much less the way it had turned her own husband into someone who, for all that he moved and talked and walked about—even made love to her, now and then—reminded her more of a statue than anything else.

A voice startled her. "Oh, give it a rest, girl. Men are men, it's the way it is."

Arsule was huffing her way up the trail. Just behind her, walking with far greater ease, was Jeschonyk's former concubine Kata. Arsule had more or less adopted the slave girl, unofficially—and had already announced she *would* adopt her, once her husband had the good sense to extend the emancipation throughout the Confederacy. Or, at least, make manumission something feasible, instead of the tortuous legal process which had so far stymied even the wife of the Paramount.

Arsule reached the crest and took a few triumphant breaths. Then, slapped a hand on her rump. "There's advantages to having a meaty ass—your father damn well dotes on it—but rigorous exercise is not one of them. However, I thought this would be a good time for us to talk. Which we need to—and you, I think, much more than me."

She fluttered her fingers toward the army camp. "Forget all that, would you? Nothing you can do about it, and all this fretting and glumming you've been doing is not good. Not for you, not for anyone else."

"There's no such word as 'glumming'," replied Helga, a bit sullenly.

"Of course, there is. I just used it, didn't I?" Arsule gave her that sideways cock of the head which Helga still found a bit weird. After all these months of close proximity, Helga had gotten accustomed to Arsule's multitude of mannerisms, quirks and eccentricities. But only . . . more or less.

"Fussing over the decline of the menfolk, are we? And just what did you *expect* would happen, silly girl? They're not actually monsters, you know; it'd be easier for them if they were. Just men trying to play the part, and getting worn down by it in the process. Especially when it goes on, month after month, with no end in sight."

She straightened her head with a jerky, bird-like motion. "Oh, to be sure, this nasty business here will be settled soon enough. But there'll be something else come along right after, you can bet on it. The eastern provinces will dissolve into sheer anarchy; there'll be another rampage of starving ex-slaves somewhere in the west—or here, more likely. Plague, pestilence, that's guaranteed. Another pathetic uprising by some piece of the aristocracy still intact. Easy enough to crush, of course, but crushing doesn't really come all that easily to our sort of men. Praise whatever gods may be. Which," she said firmly, "brings me to the subject at hand."

She beckoned Kata forward. Helga was shaking her head, trying to follow the—as usual—convoluted route which Arsule's thoughts always seemed to take.

"What are you *talking* about?"

Arsule's eyes widened, as a polite person's will do when someone asks them a particularly inane question.

"Religion. What else? You and I are going to become fanatics. Well . . . devout converts, anyway, if not outright fanatics. Not overnight, of course. Men aren't *that* stupid. And we happen to be cursed by an especially shrewd pair of them, to boot. So we'll have to ease our way into the thing."

She waved her hand, forestalling Helga's little splutter of—

Protest? Disbelief? Reacting to Arsule, it was always hard to say.

"But that's for later. Tactics can wait. Right now, you and I have to decide which flavor we'll pick. You take one, I'll take the other. Between us, we'll drive my husband and yours so mad with aggravation they'll forget their other woes. You watch."

Helga wasn't even spluttering, now. Just gaping at Arsule as if she was faced with a lunatic.

"Oh, close your mouth. You look silly." Arsule took a deep breath. "No, I am *not* insane. Most everyone thinks I am, of course. But I'm always a bit puzzled why they never seem to notice that I'm about the only woman in the world who almost always gets what she wants."

Helga's jaw snapped shut. She squinted at Arsule suspiciously.

Now that she actually *thought* about it—

"It's an *act*?"

Again, the fluttering fingers. "Oh, who knows? Act a part long enough, and it's hard to tell any more where the person leaves off and the act begins. *Which,* my dear girl, is precisely the danger we face today. Not with us, but—"

She pointed a finger toward the army camp. "Those two. And their cohorts and conspirators, of course. But if we can keep Verice and Adrian *this* side of their act, we'll have done well enough. That much, at least, you can rely on men for. Keep them in line, and they'll right quick do the same for their underlings."

She swiveled her head and beamed at Kata. "So. Which flavor do you want? Personally, I recommend that you take up the 'Young Word.' It's a far more passionate creed than the cult of Jassine, so I think it'd suit you better. And I'm probably too old anyway for all the rigorous debates you'll have to sit through, after you milk Kata for all she's worth and then hire a dozen or so of the best Emerald philosophers to give it all a respectable polish and proper terminology. Whereas—"

Now she was beaming at Helga. "I think the cult of Jassine suits me to perfection. It's a small cult, neglected, praised in theory but scorned in practice. In short, exactly the kind of project I've taken up with, oh, must be a hundred unknown artists I've championed over the years. A good two thirds of whom, by now, are rich and famous."

Helga was not often speechless. But this was one of the times. Arsule drove on in her inimitable manner. Silence didn't deter the woman's torrent of words any more than loud conversation could. Or, thought Helga wildly, a volcano could.

"Between you and me—our patronage, I should say; we mustn't

be immodest and claim *everything*; prophets and sages and scholars do have their place, after all—we'll have driven that nasty Wodep and all the rest of the sorry louts into semi-oblivion within a decade. Our husbands will shut us up in seclusion, naturally, now and then—gods, we'll drive them insane, it'll be such fun—but who cares? Toman used to do that with me every couple of years or so. Never lasted more than a few months, though. Actually, I found it rather restful. Then, of course, you and I will have to fight it out. But I don't foresee that being a major problem, either. If we've done our job properly—main thing is getting the very best philosophers to parse the rhetoric—we should manage a suitable compromise. Kata thinks so, anyway."

Shyly, the blonde slave smiled at Helga. "It's the saints, you see. The Young Word himself talked about them."

She closed her mouth. Helga's half glare, half goggle intimidated her in a way it couldn't Arsule.

"Don't let her intimidate you, Kata," snapped Arsule, "even if she is wearing that silly sword."

At last, something Helga could grapple with. "You don't 'wear' a sword, Arsule! You 'bear' one."

Arsule sniffed. "Men 'bear' a sword, girl. *You* wear one, whether you like it or not. It's past time—you've got two children now!—you stopped this foolishness. And why do you insist on it, anyway? It's *boring*."

Helga choked on a laugh. However different they might be in almost every other respect—birth and breeding, just for starters—in this, at least, Arsule and Ilset were much alike. She could remember Ilset saying to her, once: *Why in the name of the gods would you want to? I mean—when soldiers get into their own lingo—gods, and they say women are boring!*

"So!" pronounced Arsule. "Are you willing to stop being lazy and go to *work?* I warn you, girl, if you keep lounging about much longer your brain will get as heavy as my ass. And a lot fatter! At least my butt gets some exercise, which your brain certainly doesn't."

Helga's mounting irritation was suddenly broken. Not by Arsule's frown and torrent of words, but by the look of half terror/half excitement on Kata's face.

Gods, the girl's looking forward to it. A slave. An illiterate barbarian, to boot.

She looked down at the army camp. Tomorrow morning, the siege of Franness would begin. She could see that Adrian already had the handful of big siege guns at the gate, ready to be hauled out on the morrow. And, turning her head, she could see that the berms where those guns would be positioned were already finished and being guarded by several battalions.

And what do I have to do with all that?

Nothing.

Gods, she's right. I'm bored stiff. No wonder Adrian doesn't listen much to me anymore. I haven't got anything to say except what he already knows.

"What are 'saints'?" she asked.

Kata launched into a somewhat incoherent explanation, which was not helped any by the fact—soon obvious even to Helga—that the Reedbottom originators of the Young Word creed had all the usual sense of "logic" typical of barbarians anywhere. As sloppy as a pig trough.

"Never mind," she said at length. "Come back with me to the camp and we can talk about it more this afternoon. Maybe I'll be able to follow things better with a cup or two of wine. Adrian will be busy all day anyway."

To Arsule: "So let me understand you. You're thinking that *Jassine* . . . but what about her priests?"

"Priests! They're all dependent on the state purse anyway, Helga—the cult of Jassine more than any of them. They'll trot into line, watch if they don't." More charitably: "Besides, Jassine's priests tend to be a fairly self-effacing sort, as priests go. Some of them are even quite pleasant fellows. I know, I've been spending a fair amount of time with them lately."

Arsule started to add something else, but closed her mouth. Which was something of a miracle in its own right.

Helga chuckled. She could just imagine what Arsule had been about to say. *While you've been idling about contemplating your miseries.*

"Oh, why not? If nothing else, it'll give me something to *do.*" She placed a hand on Kata's shoulder and turned her back toward the trail. "Come on, girl. You can keep talking. That might slow us down enough to allow my blessed stepmother to keep up."

Behind her back, she heard Arsule sniff. "Hmph. Technically, I'm your *mother.* All the laws say so! Do try to show a certain modicum of respect, will you?"

There came another rapid set of sounds, ending with a *thump.* Helga turned around and saw that Arsule must have slipped.

"I admit it's sometimes a bit difficult," Arsule grumbled, as Helga helped her back onto her feet. "But, as I said, having a hefty ass helps. Matrons would be lost without it."

She gave Helga a half smile/half leer, and then swatted her on her own rump. "Gods, your butt's almost as solid as a man's. But don't worry, girl. By the time you need it, you'll have a proper ass."

As they resumed their downward progress, Arsule's voice provided a steady accompaniment. "All those hours, just sitting on couches . . . the only exercise trying to keep philosophers from each other's throats . . . good thing they're such a weedy and wheezing bunch, for a girl as strong as you it'll be easy . . . remind them of the grisly fate of a certain band of pirates, now and then, that'll help . . ."

Late that night, after Adrian returned to their quarters to get a few hours' rest before the trials of the morning, Helga insisted on making love. Adrian was willing enough, for all his tension. He didn't have all that much choice anyway, since—for the first time in weeks—Helga was being aggressive about it.

Afterward, as they lay in each other's arms, contently exhausted, Helga began casually mentioning some parts of her day's conversation with Kata.

Adrian was more-or-less oblivious to it, at first. But, after a while, his scholarly instincts were aroused, as Helga had known they would be.

She could see him frowning in the dim light thrown out by the small lamp in the bunker, as he stared up at the wooden logs which formed the rough ceiling.

"Doesn't make sense, Helga. Blithering barbarians! How can a man be both a prophet *and* the manifestation of a god at the same time? One or the other, fine, but not *both.*"

"Well, it didn't make a lot of sense to me either. But Kata says—"

After a while, Adrian's lips quirked wryly and he gave his head a little shake. "Gods, what a tangled mess. As much rhyme and reason as a bramble bush. But . . . for a moment there . . . Heh. If I didn't know better, I'd swear I was listening to one of the Hallert school."

"Hallert? Who are they?"

" 'Him,' not they. Hallert's been dead for, oh, must be a century and a half, now. He was one of the founders of the Numerology School, which is still very prominent in the Grove. Hallert himself broke away, though, early on. He got obsessed with geometry instead of sticking with straight Number and Form. The convoluted stuff he came up with! I can still remember the headaches it gave me as a student. One of my tutors belonged to his school of thought."

Helga rolled her head into his neck. "What was his name?" she murmured. "The tutor, I mean."

"Schott. Kerin Schott. Nice enough old gent, mind you. Still pretty spry, too—at least, he was several years ago. Smart old man, no doubt about it. But, gods, what an obsessive maniac. Show him anything in the world, and he'd immediately try to figure out how it was all a manifestation of geometry."

"Really? How odd." She planted a wet kiss on the neck. "Introduce me to him, why don't you? When we get back to Solinga. I've always found geometry a bit interesting myself."

Adrian gave her shoulder a warm squeeze. "Certainly, love, if that's what you want. Though, I'm warning you . . ."

But he fell asleep before he could do more than start warming up to the warning. Which, the more she heard, warmed Helga herself.

Fit a saint into the kaleidoscope, no sweat. I'll bet that old man eats kaleidoscopes for breakfast. If I can just get him interested in the problem . . .

CHAPTER THIRTY-ONE

The sounds now coming from behind the walls of Franness were those of gunfire—and velipads squealing with pain and fright, and men shouting in anger. The kind of bitter rage that comes from betrayal, not the simple fury of battle.

We've underestimated Prelotta all along, Raj Whitehall admitted. ***What a brilliant bastard. The number of barbarian warlords who can understand the difference between a defeat and a partial victory—which is all he can hope for now—are as rare as hens' teeth. Even rarer are the ones who can calculate it beforehand. Which he obviously did.***

For a moment, Adrian was distracted by an idle question. *What are "hens"?* But the meaning of the expression was obvious from the context, and he was doing his level best to keep his thoughts concentrated. That was hard enough, under the circumstances.

yes. that is why he built those new fortifications. i was wrong.

That admission of error, coming from Center, almost amused Adrian enough to break through the bleak shell which had surrounded him for days. Center had stated—with his customary "stochastic certainty"—that the purpose of the new outer wall which Prelotta had built on the northern side of Franness had been . . . nothing, really. Just the ignorance of a barbarian chief, fumbling with the concept of siege warfare for the first time. One wall good, two walls better. "Probability 68%, ± 17."

The *real* purpose of the wall was now obvious. Adrian didn't know whether to bless Prelotta or curse him.

Inside that new outer wall—but kept out of the city proper—were the thousands of Southron cavalrymen, mostly Grayhills, who had been driven by Demansk's relentless campaign this spring to seek shelter from the storm. The only real shelter, of course, being the major walled city in the south under Southron control.

Franness, still the "new provincial capital" of the Reedbottoms—and with Prelotta himself, according to all spy reports, still resident. Along with most of the ten thousand men he had brought north with him the year before.

Thousands of Reedbottom warriors, trained and equipped to fight with the new guns. Well-equipped, in fact. In the months since he had taken the city, according to the spies, Prelotta had built up a significant arms industry around his initial core of blacksmiths. Whatever the other Vanberts of Franness might think of their new barbarian overlord, the metalworkers and apothecaries were quite pleased with him. They were more prosperous than ever.

But now, the Reedbottoms would be fighting from behind the very solid inner walls of the city. Prelotta had been smart enough to understand that the laager tactic which had worked so well against Tomsien would be suicide against Demansk. The Reedbottom chief, both Adrian and Demansk were positive, had his own corps of spies. They would have described to him, by now, how murderous the field guns which Trae had built over the winter in Chalice were proving to be against anyone who came against the Paramount.

Demansk had already crushed the only significant noblemen's revolt against him, just a few weeks earlier, using those guns. He would have crushed them anyway, using his three brigades of well-paid and disciplined Confederate regulars against the ragged "brigade" which the noblemen had manage to assemble in opposition. But he hadn't bothered. He'd simply had Adrian fire several volleys from the field guns, before the rebels could come within three hundred yards. At that range, against massed infantry, the skittering iron balls had wreaked havoc. A final volley of canister had ended the affair entirely.

The Southron cavalrymen whom Demansk had been hammering since then were not as susceptible to the weapons, of course. But they could not stand against them, either. And so, week after week, Demansk had harried the barbarians and driven them steadily out of the Confederate lands they had been ravaging again this spring.

According to Demansk's spies, the other tribal chiefs had pleaded—demanded, in the case of Esmond, who had been elected the new chief of the Grayhills—that Prelotta lead his men out of Franness and set up the laager again. But Prelotta, no fool, had understood perfectly well that the same wooden walls which had shrugged off javelins would be a death trap facing cannonballs. So, stubbornly, he had remained within the walls of his new capital—while inviting the other tribes to join him there in a certain-to-be-victorious defensive battle against the oncoming Vanberts.

Join him they had, even the Grayhills under Esmond. But Prelotta had never allowed them beyond the *first* wall. Claiming, according to the spies, that the city was too crowded and rife with disease already to accommodate ten thousand more warriors. So, for a week now, Esmond and his six thousand Grayhills and the thousands of men from the other tribes had been trapped within Franness' "outer pocket."

A large pocket, true. Prelotta had not stinted on the work, using his own warriors as well as dragooned civilian labor to build an outer wall which extended four hundred yards beyond the city itself and stretched for almost two miles, across its entire northern length and curving a good way down the western side.

It was a crude wall, of course, nothing else had been possible in the months available. But, to barbarians, it must have looked impressive.

Now . . .

A dozen volleys from Adrian's four big siege guns had reduced a whole stretch of it to rubble. Rubble which would pose little difficulty to Demansk's brigades of infantrymen, when they stormed across it, but would be a death trap for cavalry. On those broken mounds of stone—even in the cramped space of the outer pocket—Southron tactics would be useless. Not even arrogant and cocksure Grayhills were foolish enough to think they could stand against Vanbert regulars in a toe-to-toe slugging match in a box.

Once they realized that, the Grayhills and other tribesmen had begun shrieking for Prelotta to allow them behind the much more substantial walls of the inner city. He had ignored their pleas, and now—when the pleas had turned to demands and men began trying to scale the wall—was answering them with gunfire.

Trapped. Barbarian cavalrymen had no more chance of scaling the inner wall of Franness—not against thousands of Reedbottoms firing down on them with their stubby guns—than they had of facing Demansk's infantry inside the outer pocket.

In short, Prelotta's foresight and ruthlessness had produced a situation where, by nightfall, the preeminence of the Reedbottoms over the Grayhills would be established for the first time. And, in all likelihood, for generations to come. Precious few Grayhills warriors would return from what, at its onset, they had expected to be one of the great plundering raids of memory.

All that, of course, assumed that Prelotta himself would survive the aftermath. But . . .

He's gambling there too. Gambling on Demansk—and gambling on you, most of all. Which are not bad odds, when you think about it.

Adrian shook his head. He would have time later to deal with that question. At the moment . . .

The sally ports in the outer wall were swinging open. Those of them, that is, which Adrian's siege guns hadn't already splintered.

All the sally ports that Adrian could see, all down the wall.

Esmond's doing all that's left to him. A great massed cavalry attack. Hit Demansk's brigades as hard as possible, hoping to clear the way for a retreat back to the south. If he can escape this immediate encirclement, he'll at least manage to get his men out of here. It's a good move—best he's got, anyway—by a brave and resourceful commander. And I salute him for it.

Then, quietly: ***I'm sorry, lad. But it's time.***

Adrian took a deep breath and nodded. If the officers standing around him waiting for orders thought there was anything odd about a man nodding to himself, they gave no sign of it. By now, they were accustomed to Adrian and his often peculiar mannerisms and temporary distractions.

They weren't even bothered by it. Adrian Gellert was almost as eccentric as his father-in-law's new wife, true enough. And so what? Demansk was Paramount, after all. And while his son-in-law was perhaps a bit crazed, what did it matter? The gods knew he was capable enough with his guns. Besides, he was an Emerald anyway. They're all a bit crazed.

Time. Oh, brother, I am sorry for it. I wish—

No point in that. The father-in-law had sacrificed the son; Adrian would have to do the same with the brother. So it was.

The shell came back around him, tight, solid, cold.

"All right, men." He clapped his hands once. "You know what to do. Same drill as before. We'll just be receiving the sorry bastards a little quicker, that's all. But since velipads make a bigger target, who cares?"

He managed a predatory grin of sorts. A rictus, anyway. The officers around him responded with their own.

"Round shot until they're within three hundred yards, remember. And—don't think I won't be watching—the gods help whatever crew moves to case shot any sooner."

He turned his head, his eyes ranging up and down the long ranks of the regular brigades standing some yards behind the field guns. There was no real point to that examination, since Adrian knew full well that Demansk had his infantrymen properly positioned. But he thought it might help steady his gunners if they thought Adrian was satisfied.

Which, needless to say, he was. Adrian and his father-in-law had spent time, over the winter, deciding how best to adapt Confederate tactics to incorporate field guns. And then, since the campaign began this spring, had had more than one occasion to test it in practice.

Easy, really. Unlike the Emerald phalanxes, the Confederate brigade formations had always been designed for flexible field tactics. It was simple enough, for men accustomed to the wedge and saw in the heat of battle, to learn how to quickly open lanes through which the field guns could be withdrawn once the enemy got near. Then, close back up again in time to receive the charge with shields locked and assegais ready. And, as the charge recoiled, reopen the lanes so the deadly guns could resume their work.

After the battle where the noble rebels had been destroyed, the Vanbert regulars had become quite the enthusiasts of field guns. They'd suffered practically no casualties at all—and been rewarded with the typically fulsome loot of aristocrats gone down to ruin. In this battle, they could be counted on to do their job.

Adrian clapped his hands again, twice. Not so much by way of command, but simply to emphasize his satisfaction and confidence in a bright and rosy future.

"That's it. Let's go!"

The officers trotted off, in both directions, down the ranks toward their batteries. Adrian moved forward a few paces to stand next to the officer in command of the battery at the very center of the Confederate army. That battery was facing the largest of the sally ports. The one which, Adrian was almost certain, his brother himself would come charging through. Say whatever else you would about Esmond Gellert, he was not one to skulk while he drove others forward. He would die, as he had lived, a leader of men.

"Ready, sir," murmured the officer. Adrian simply nodded.

A great whoop came from the outer walls of Franness. And then, a moment later, the first contingents of the Southron cavalry pounded through. They were more of a disorganized mob than a formation, but with their numbers and their barbarian energy, looked formidable enough. Charging cavalry always looks formidable, and Adrian had no doubt at all Esmond had been whipping up his men to the heights of fury and determination. He was good at that.

"The cairns mark eight hundred yards, sir."

That was the officer's own nervousness. Adrian stifled the

impulse to snarl in reply: *Yes, I know. You dimwit, I'm the one who ordered the cairns placed there last night in the first place. Just as I had the second line of cairns placed at the three hundred mark. Is there something you'd like to explain to me about how to eat, too?*

But . . . he stifled it. He just stood there, silent, unmoving, his hands clasped behind his back. And watched as the Southrons stormed forward toward the killing zone.

They had a ways to go. Demansk, following Adrian's recommendation, had drawn up two brigades of his regulars about twelve hundred yards beyond the outer wall of Franness. The river which bisected the city protected his left flank—and also, of course, kept the Southrons from being able to seek any escape in that direction.

Did Prelotta have that in mind also, when he built the pocket where he did? Probably. He's cold-blooded enough.

There was space open to the right of the Vanbert lines, which led toward the sanctuary of the southern continent across Kellinek's Wall. But the wall was over a hundred miles distant, and Demansk had drawn his third brigade across that line of retreat, not more than a mile away. With most of his auxiliary cavalry there, covering its flanks.

So there would be no advantage to Esmond to attempt an immediate break to the south. True, he'd been fighting one brigade instead of two—but he'd have to withstand the withering fire of the field guns anyway. Hitting him on the flank instead of the front, and with no real prospect of escaping the fire quickly. A single Confederate brigade would not be that much easier to break than two of them, especially not with auxiliary cavalry in support.

No, best to hit the core of Demansk's strength head on. Esmond could either break it or he couldn't. What he couldn't do at all was hope to sidestep it.

"About a thousand yards, sir." Again, Adrian bit down on a harsh response. *My eyesight's probably three times as good as yours. Shut up!*

It was all moving very fast, now. Even massed in thousands, mounted barbarians could cover ground very quickly in a charge.

Adrian's eyes matched the first rows of cavalrymen against the cairns. He thought, for a moment, to catch a glimpse of a particularly tall and powerful looking man in their midst. Esmond?

Not time for that now. The cairns—

He opened his mouth, but the officer was already shouting.

"Fire! Fire! Fire, you stinking sots!"

The entire scene vanished behind billowing clouds of smoke. The first volley had gone off splendidly. Not ragged at all.

There was no way to tell what effect it had had, however, nor had Adrian expected to be able to tell. He and his gunners were familiar enough, by now, with the great drawback to gunpowder weapons: *first volley, and you fight half blind thereafter; pray for a good breeze, if you think you're winning.*

Under these conditions, Adrian didn't try to halt the gunfire while he waited for gaps to appear in the smoke. No reason to, really. He and his artillerymen had had more than enough time to sight their guns before the battle. And since there was no danger of running out of powder and shot, the worst that could happen was a wasted volley. Which, since it would help shore up the morale of the Confederates, wouldn't be a waste in any event.

"Fire! Fire! I want grazing shots, you bastards! Or I'll have you whipped!"

Adrian made a silent promise that he would ease this particular officer out of his post. Make him a quartermaster or something. *Any* post that wouldn't subject good men to an idiot commander. How the hell were his gunners supposed to make grazing shots at a target they couldn't see? And how would the officer who made the threats even know himself?

The volleys were getting a bit ragged now, as the better crews began pulling ahead in their rate of fire. Adrian had time to consider a problem he hadn't previously, and wonder whether he ought to demote *himself* to a quartermaster. There was really very little breeze at all. The smoke clouds hadn't had a single gap yet that he'd spotted. So how exactly was *he* going to make good his threat to punish any crew which began using case shot before the enemy had reached the three-hundred-yard mark?

Awkward. In fact, the officer of this battery was already starting to give him the eye. Wanting, of course, to order his crews to move to case shot, but not daring to do so until he could see that the talismanic cairns had been reached.

And how to gauge *that?*

observe. A strange kind of grid appeared in Adrian's mind, one he'd never seen Center use before. Not so much a grid, as a . . .

echolocation. certain nocturnal animals—not here on your planet—use it quite successfully. and there are no doubt some marine animals here which do so as well.

Adrian realized that he was "seeing" with his ears. Not really seeing so much as calculating, from the sounds, the closeness of the enemy. It was a very blurry kind of "vision," of course, but—

Good enough. There really isn't anything magical about three hundred yards, after all. I'd say that's close enough, Adrian—nothing else, it'll make your men feel better.

He nodded and began shouting. "Case shot! Switch to case shot!" He saw the relief flooding the officer's face, and, a moment later, the crews of the battery switch over to canister. He turned and made vehement gestures to the small group of runners Demansk had insisted on providing him—realizing, as he did so, that once again his experienced father-in-law had understood something he hadn't.

Other crews, of course, wouldn't be able to hear the command—not above the din the guns themselves were making. But the runners would notify them quickly enough. They were already sprinting down the lines.

Nothing ever works quite the way you figured it in a battle, son. Or any kind of fight, for that matter. That's why I always like to have a second string to my bow.

A few seconds later, such being the whims of fortune, Demansk's foresight proved unnecessary. A sudden breeze cleared great swaths from the smoke clouds. Once again, Adrian could see the battlefield.

Enough of it, anyway. And the portion just in front of him was quite visible.

Carnage everywhere. The first volley of canister had gone off just about at the right moment, hitting an enemy already ravaged by round shot skittering and bouncing across the ground. Each one of Adrian's four-pounder field guns—six to a battery, and ten batteries down the line—fired dozens of arquebus-sized balls with each discharge of case shot. As wildly inaccurate as they were, even at a hundred yards much less three hundred, they were bound to hit *something.* Enough of the balls, at least.

Broke the charge. Look. There's Esmond. You can see him now, trying to rally them.

Sure enough. Even without Center's help, Adrian would have recognized his brother at the distance. If for no other reason, because his head was uncovered. Whether because his helmet had been sent flying by a bullet, or because Esmond himself had taken it off. More likely the latter, thought Adrian. It was the sort of gesture Esmond would make, at a time like this.

He took a last look at that glorious crown of golden hair, making no attempt to recognize the features beneath it. So would he choose to remember a man whom he had once called *brother.* Gold, shining in the sun; not tattoos and scars across a face grown scarred already with hate and fury.

He stepped forward and seized the officer's shoulder with a firm hand. Then, having the man's attention, pointed across the field.

"Him, you see? Yes? I want him down. Now. All guns trained on him. Maintain case shot."

It was a well-trained crew, whatever the qualities of the officer. Within moments, the command was carried out. Smoke clouds filled the air.

When they cleared, the gold was gone.

Three volleys later, the Southrons were in full retreat. Some, pouring back into the pocket behind the wall. Others, and most of them—the pocket was a death trap—desperately trying to thread an escape route between the guns and Demansk and the third brigade drawn up to block their route.

Some of them would make it. Most wouldn't. And, once again, Confederate regulars had not even had to bloody their assegais. They would later, in just a bit, as they stormed over whoever was left huddling in the pocket. But that would be more of a massacre than a battle, against an enemy completely disorganized and broken in spirit. Their casualties would be very light.

Already, the first cheers were going up. Adrian's heart felt like a lump of lead. But he realized that this day, if not already, he had cemented his position within the hearts of Vanbert's regulars.

Our golden boy, by the gods! Our good luck charm! Even if he is a crazy Emerald!

Play it out to the end, lad. You father-in-law needs it and you owe those spearmen that much anyway. And perhaps Esmond also.

Adrian turned to face the serried ranks, removed his helmet, and bowed toward his father-in-law's men. Then, turning slightly each time, bowing again and again, as he gave each regiment its due.

A golden head acknowledging stalwart hearts. Power recognizing its source. Tyranny triumphant, returning the favor.

CHAPTER THIRTY-TWO

Demansk found Adrian squatting next to a corpse lying on the battlefield. The corpse was a mass of blood and torn flesh, looking as if it had caught an entire load of canister itself. Other than being the body of a large man, there was no way to recognize anything else about it.

Except—

As he drew closer, Demansk spotted a piece of the scalp. He didn't have to remove his son-in-law's helmet to know that the color would match the bright corn-gold of Adrian's own hair.

Adrian hadn't seen him yet. The young man was simply staring across the field, looking at the river which flowed sluggishly through Franness. His eyes seemed unfocused, which, Demansk didn't doubt at all, they were in actual fact. He knew that stare; had done it himself more times than he could remember.

The sight, along with that of a face drawn far more tightly than a young man's should be, brought a decision. Demansk had been weighing Adrian's advice; hesitant, matching his son-in-law's proven shrewdness against old Vanbert wisdom—also proven, time after time; not being able to decide.

Enough. I don't trust that old bloodlust. Less, now, than ever. Do I really need to prove to anyone, any longer, that I'll wade through a river of gore?

Adrian had noticed him, finally. The golden head was turning his way.

And there's this, too. That actor Arsule told me about yesterday, the one who played a part for so long that he forgot who he was. For all the damn chatter, it's amazing how often she hits something. Whether she means to or not, who knows? But—

Enough. Enough!

"All right, Adrian. We'll try it your way. Be ready by nightfall." Demansk glanced toward Franness. "As you predicted, Prelotta's men didn't fire on us while we scoured the rest out of the pocket. So I guess that counts for something. If he sends out for a parley—what's the signal again—?"

"With Reedbottoms, it'll be a bushel of reeds, carried by two old women." The voice, like the face, was harsh beyond its years. "That's the usual practice, anyway. How Prelotta will manage it, here, I don't know. But it'll be something similar."

Demansk nodded. "If he wants a parley, I'll give him one. You'll be my envoy. And—"

He paused, took a deep breath.

Just do it, tyrant. If I have to look at another mound of corpses . . . sooner or later, I'll stop seeing them as human bodies. Sometimes I feel as if I'm there already.

"You have my permission—authority—to negotiate as you choose. As long as it's within the boundaries we discussed, I'll leave the details to you."

When Prelotta did send out for a parley, Demansk couldn't help but smile. Whatever else—even under these circumstances—the barbarian had a sense of humor. There was something just plain comical about two proper Vanbert matrons mincing their way across a bloody field, looking simultaneously nauseated and scared out of their wits, carrying between them a big bundle of official documents. Tax records, from the look of them. Nothing else was that bulky and voluminous.

Adrian returned a day and a half later.

"The sticking point, from your point of view, will be Franness. He's agreed to all the rest. Auxiliary nation status for the Reedbottoms—your vassals, he knows it, with a face-saving veneer. The Reedbottoms to tear down Kallinek's Wall and build Demansk's Wall two hundred miles to the south, covering the territory not already shielded by the Reedbottoms themselves. No hindrance to the movement of Confederate troops anywhere this side of the new wall. That includes moving through Reedbottom territory, although I agreed to Prelotta's demand that we have to give them a week's notice."

Demansk nodded. "No problem, that. I'd give them a month, anyway—pure misery for people, forcing them to billet armies without sufficient time to provision—unless we have to go to war with the Reedbottoms. In which case, of course, I won't give them any notice at all. We'll come back to Franness later. What else?"

"He keeps his guns, and his gunmaking industry. But he agrees not to make any field guns or siege guns, although he insisted on having the right to purchase a few from us. Which I gave him. May as well. He'll start a secret industry anyway, and there's more than enough swampy badlands in Reedbottom territory to hide it. If we let him buy a few, maybe he won't drive the secret industry that far."

Again, Demansk nodded. "I don't care about that. He'll never be able to match our production anyway. Truth is, he'll need some big guns soon enough. The rest of the Southrons are *not* going to be happy with him."

For the first time Demansk could remember in weeks, the smile on his son-in-law's face seemed genuine. "To put it mildly. Especially when they find out that we've agreed to *his* definition of where the territory of the Reedbottoms ends—which is going to come as a big surprise to the Grayhills, I can assure you."

"Good," grunted Demansk. "Keep him busy the rest of his life fighting off the damn savages, instead of us having to do it. And hope that his successor isn't as capable as he is. Or—"

He waved his hand. "But that's for someone else to worry about, half a century from now. We can't solve every problem. Did he also agree to provide assistance for the, ah, 'settlers'?"

Adrian's smile widened. Demansk felt his own heart lighten a bit. *Damn, I like this young man. He's almost managed to crowd Barrett's memory out. Far enough, anyway, that it doesn't ache all the time.*

"Oh, by all means. Prelotta will be *delighted* to assist us in relocating the 'new settlers' to that big chunk of land we're taking for ourselves in the southern continent. Why not? If we fill up the territory between Kallinek's Wall and Demansk's Wall, it means *we'll* have to keep troops along the new wall to defend the new settlements. Leaves him free to use his own forces to keep encroaching on his neighbors."

"He had no problem with the status of the, ah, 'new settlers'? Most Vanberts would."

Adrian shook his head. "He could care less that they're all a bunch of ex-slaves. He's *smart,* Father. Smart enough, I'm sure, to understand that many of them will give up farming, soon enough—tough business, that, carving a farm out of wilderness—and start drifting into Reedbottom territory. Even the least-skilled freedman will know how to do something that barbarians don't. The Reedbottoms just wind up absorbing some new members into their tribe, which they've been doing for centuries anyway, and get another boost. On things like this, they're . . ."

He let the words trail off. Demansk filled them in for him.

"Better than us. Oh, yes, son, let's not deny it. There was a time, you know—back when the 'First Twelve' were just a bunch of ambitious pig farmers—when we Vanberts knew how to do the same. Of course, they weren't the 'First Twelve' then, either."

He ran fingers through his beard. "All right. That leaves Franness. And I assume he wants the surrounding territory included as well. Create a solid stretch of Reedbottom territory that extends into the northern continent as well as the southern. And gives him a city he can call a 'capital' while keeping a straight face."

Adrian hesitated. Clearly enough, he was half expecting an eruption.

"Spit it out, Adrian. Knowing Prelotta, I'd figured out already he'd be brazen. I promise not to do more than curse *him* for five minutes or so. Not you."

Adrian told him. Demansk cursed for five minutes or so. But, true to his promise, did not heap any of the curses onto Adrian's head. Although he did, more than once, give his—his—*idiot son-in-law!*—a ferocious glare.

But, when it was all over, Demansk ceased stomping around and sat back down on the stool in his command bunker.

"All right," he rasped. "Since you already agreed, I'd be undermining family solidarity if I overruled you. Of all things, I can afford *that* least of all."

A deep breath. "Done."

The smile came back on Adrian's face. A bit gingerly, at first, as if it was testing the waters. But, soon enough, in full bloom.

"If it makes you feel any better, Father, I'm really *not* being a sentimentalist about the whole thing. Sure, I suppose I still feel a tad uncomfortable about the way I 'betrayed' Prelotta last year. But not much—and Prelotta himself seems to have laughed the whole thing off. I'm really thinking much more in terms of the future. Let Prelotta have a capital—a real *city,* with its baths and fleshpots; for that matter, its libraries—and you watch how long that 'barbarian vigor' will last."

Demansk grunted. Abstractly, he understood the logic. But, deep in his Vanbert bones—which were as concrete as bones always are—the logic grated on him. Conquerors *took* cities, damnation, they didn't give them away!

"Look at it this way, Father. You'll be mollifying all the matrons of Franness whom Prelotta forced to bathe him and his chiefs. Giving them a certain status after the fact. One thing to be forced to bathe filthy barbarians; another, to have done it for a proper vassal lord and his nobles."

Seeing Demansk's eyes widen, he chuckled. "Oh, yes. He carried out the threat. Apparently, in fact, he forced *all* the matrons of the city to do it."

Demansk's eyed widened further. He was trying to picture . . .

"How did he fit them all *in?* Not even Vanbert has public baths big enough."

"In relays, according to the story I heard—all three versions of it, in fact. He must have ended up the cleanest man who ever lived. Not a single matron of the city tried to escape the obligation, since the alternative he gave them was to have their daughters raped. Or the matrons themselves, according to one version."

Demansk put on a very histrionic frown of disapproval. "Shameful! If the matrons had been properly virtuous, they could have killed the bastard from overwork." This was followed by an equally histrionic sigh. "But such, I'm afraid, is the reality of the times."

He planted his hands on his knees and rose. "Done, as I said. And, who knows, you may even be right about the end result. But that's the future. Right now the question is: which one of us gets to handle the outraged delegation from the *proper* citizens of Franness? Been Vanberts for a hundred and fifty years, you know. They are *not* going to be happy at their new status."

But Adrian's smile didn't waver in the least. "Oh, you should, Father. Absolutely. It won't be hard to handle. Not for you, as Paramount. It occurs to me . . ."

And so it proved. Demansk listened to the voluble protests expressed by the delegation—who seemed to consist of every single member of the city's former council of notables—for not more than ten minutes. Then:

"Well, if you insist, I'll take Franness back into the Confederacy. But I was just trying to be merciful. As Prelotta's subjects, you've done nothing wrong." Here came a frown so histrionic it might have caused any actor to die from envy. "But as *my* citizens, I note that you surrendered the city to barbarians without so much as a single breach having been made in the wall—and them with no siege train worth talking about! Under the stern and ancient law of our forefathers—and that much has *not* changed—I have no alternative but to decree the decimation—"

But, by then, of course, wiser heads were beginning to prevail. Notable after notable recalling various virtues of Chief—no, *King*—Prelotta; others commenting wisely on the need not to embarrass the Paramount by having him rescind a decision already made public; still others suddenly noticing the trade possibilities, what with

Franness—because of its new status, of course—being the natural provisioning center for, ah, settlers on their way to their new farmlands. One old notable, who apparently had some Emerald blood in his family tree, even began opining on the significance of the distinction between Being and Becoming.

Two nights later, King Prelotta threw a great feast for the Confederate grandees who came to pay their first official visit on Vanbert's new auxiliary nation. Paramount Triumvir Verice Demansk headed the list of guests, along with a splendid pantheon of his closest associates and relatives. No mention was made, of course, of the regiment of regulars who accompanied him into Franness; nor, needless to say, of the fact that the siege guns—still in place—were kept trained on the gates of the city throughout; nor, even, of the odd custom of the Triumvir of having his food tasted first by the King himself.

All considerations given, the event went quite smoothly. Things were helped along immensely by the fact that King Prelotta and every single one of his chiefs—barons, rather; in the new "northern province" they held that title—showed up at the feast fresh from the baths.

They were helped even more, however, by the unexpected cordiality—even, one might say, friendship—displayed by the Paramount's daughter Helga toward the new King. The young lady's prestige among the Reedbottoms was doubled by virtue of her marriage to the man who was not only Governor of the Emeralds but also, as it happens, was *not* at the feast—since he was standing outside the city alongside the siege guns. (With, according to rumor, a lit match in his hand—a rumor which Prelotta's spies later reported was quite false. Yes, the match was lit, and smoldering in its tub. But his spies assured the King that Adrian Gellert had spent the entire evening in casual conversation with his gunners. At least five feet away.)

Arsule was at the feast also. Demansk having tried, but failed, to keep her away on the grounds of her own safety.

"Give it a rest! You're just afraid I'll annoy the Reedbottoms with my prattle. Ha. Much time *you've* spent in the company of barbarians. *I* speak from experience, Verice. Nothing savages enjoy more than a good conversation."

Whether she was right or not would never be determined. Other than exchanging a few pleasantries with Prelotta and his top barons, Arsule spent the entire evening in close company with Franness' small number of priests devoted to the cult of Jassine. Much to Demansk's relief at the time.

And distress the next day. Arsule badgered him for hours.

"—just terrible! And no way to fix it in Franness itself. Place is hopeless now, with those savages running it. Verice, I *insist* that you fund a new temple in this new city you're determined to found on the isthmus. And don't try to fool *me* with that 'keep an eye on the new border,' nonsense, either! I know perfectly well you're scheming to build a new capital for the Confederacy. Which is probably a good idea, I admit, since Vanbert's become such a boorish place. Yes, yes, it was a splendid notion to kill off half the noblemen and ruin their families in the process—for *you,* the scheming politician. But for *me,* a patron of the arts, it was a disaster. Only thing for it now is to start all over again someplace new. The isthmus will suit me fine. What with that great canal you're planning to build—"

Can I keep any secrets from this cursed woman? Demansk asked himself sourly.

"—also a good idea, since it'll bring trade from the islands somewhere other than into the hands of those damned rapacious Emeralds, who are the greediest folk in the world as well as probably the smartest—but, what's more to the point, will also bring Islander artists too. A whole new territory for me to conquer. As it were. *So.* To get to the point—"

Please!

"—new temple for Jassine is *essential.* Furthermore—"

"I agree, Arsule, I agree!" The smug look on her face alerted him. "Ah . . . exactly how *big* a temple are we—"

"Well, that's just the point. If you hadn't interrupted! Since this will be the temple in the new *capital*, well—naturally!—it'll have to be of a size and splendor to match. Be a terrible stain on your reputation if it weren't." Sweetly: "Which you can *hardly* afford now, dearest, seeing as how the only legitimacy you have is based on intestines. Yours and your enemies. In rather different ways, if you see what I mean. *Nothing* could enhance your reputation more than founding such a magnificent—"

"Enough! I agree!" Gloomily: "I suppose you'll want me to pay for the priests also. Fine. As long as they don't get extravagant."

"Priests of *Jassine?* Don't be ridiculous, Verice. The most abstemious bunch imaginable." She paused for a moment. Demansk began to heave a sigh of relief.

Short, truncated sigh.

"Of course, while their *own* needs are modest, they will need help in their *charitable* works. Quite a bit, too, seeing as how you've bankrupted and ruined half the population. Yes, yes, all in a good cause—no doubt. Still, facts are facts, and the fact is that you could walk from here to Vanbert on the corpses of emaciated children."

That was an exaggeration—rather a gross one, in fact—but . . .

There was enough truth in it to make him wince. Demansk sighed, not with relief, and resigned himself to a long day. Arsule, clearly enough, was just getting started.

Adrian enjoyed the next day, himself—and several thereafter. Helga was in very good spirits. So was he, for that matter. Since they had no particular duties to distract them until the Paramount decided to return to the capital, they spent much of their time in bed.

When they finally did leave Franness, almost a week later, Adrian was in a better mood than he'd been . . . in a very long time. And he was pleased—though he was not foolish enough to say so—that Helga had chosen not to wear her sword while she rode alongside him.

He was not entirely pleased by the gaggle of barbarians who were plodding along behind their wagon. But Helga explained that it was a favor she had agreed to do for Prelotta which, since it was a small thing, she'd seen no reason to decline.

Before Adrian could ask exactly who they were, Helga drove on to another subject.

"This notion you have—heh; or should I say Center and Raj?—Father was telling me about it. Dissolving the Assembly entirely and replacing it with local, what did he say you'd called them?"

"Speakers' Houses."

"Yes, that. Interesting idea. Father thinks you're probably crazy, but then he admitted he always think that when he first hears your ideas so maybe you're not. But *I* don't understand it."

"The Assembly's nothing but a source of trouble, Helga. Might have made sense, back when Vanbert was a small nation. But today? There's simply no way that the commoners can have their voice heard in a single 'popular assembly' in the capital. Even if they're literate, which most of them aren't, they can't afford to make the trip. So, in the real world, the Assembly's just become a place where ambitious politicians can bring mob pressure to bear. Capital loafers, to boot, not farmers."

Helga waved her hand impatiently. "I understand all that! Don't disagree, either—nor does Father. It's the *other* business. Why the new 'Speakers' Houses'?" Her eyes widened. "And why—especially—this bizarre idea of giving *them,* rather than the Council, the exclusive right to approve new taxes. That's crazy, Adrian! If you let—"

By now, Adrian was well into the spirit of the argument. "Don't be silly," he growled. "The Council's *always* going to draw the central powers of the nation into it. Bound to happen. If, in addition, you let *them* decide on taxes—much less administer the collection!—you'll be right back into the soup. The same crap will happen all over again. I think of it—okay, okay, Raj and Center call it—'separation of powers.' "

The argument went on for most of the day. By the end, Helga was not convinced of the merits of the idea. But she was willing to allow that it would probably, if nothing else, keep her father sane.

"Not him I'm worried about," Adrian said quietly. "Verice Demansk will remain sane, whatever else. So, in all likelihood, will *his* successor. But after that? The third Paramount—much less fourth, fifth and sixth?"

He shook his head. "A tyrant is one thing, Helga. The world can survive that—even prosper from it. A state of tyranny is something else again. So, anything we can do *now*, however modest, which starts undermining the logic of what your Father's done—and I helped him do it, mind you, and don't regret it—is all to the good. Will this idea of mine work? Who knows? But it's worth a try."

Helga thought about it, for a time, as they prepared their portion of the army's camp. Then, as evening fell, announced that she would support Adrian in the matter.

"As you said, why not give it a try?"

But Adrian was only half-listening to her. He was watching the Reedbottoms who had accompanied them, preparing their own bedding—but interrupting the work just at sundown in order to engage in a peculiar little ceremony.

Odd, he thought. Is that caterwauling prayer? Reminds me a bit of—but not to this extent—still—

A sudden suspicion came to him. "Helga, these people Prelotta asked you to bring with us back to Vanbert. I never heard of such a thing, but are they Young Word *priests*?"

Helga seemed to redden a bit. Hard to tell, though. It might just have been the sunset.

"Well. Yes and no. They're a special kind of priest, not like the ones you and I are familiar with."

"What are they called?"

"Uh, what's the word? Oh, yes. 'Missionaries,' I think."

EPILOGUE

Demansk, leaning on the balustrade, admired the sunset. In the three years since he'd transferred his capital—in practice, if not in legal theory—to the new city he was having built on the isthmus, he'd come to appreciate the place more. The weather was still too hot and muggy for his tastes, but the sunsets were frequently gorgeous. Granted, he'd been able to enjoy the sight of the sun setting over the ocean on his old estate. But the typically clear skies there didn't produce the same magnificent color patterns.

Hearing someone padding up behind him, Demansk shifted the weight on his elbows and craned his head around.

It was Thicelt, not to his surprise. The big Islander was Demansk's only close associate who actually "padded" when he walked. The old habits of a robber, Demansk wryly suspected.

"So?" demanded Sharlz, waving a hand at the sunset. "Have you finally become reconciled to admiring sunsets instead of sunrises?"

Demansk smiled. He'd *still* have preferred founding this city on the eastern side of the isthmus. But . . . that would be a little too near the Reedbottoms. Here, the Confederacy was close enough to crush them if necessary, not so close that the Reedbottoms could overwhelm the new capital with a sudden attack.

He left all that unsaid, however. Thicelt's words, though the admiral had not intended them to do so, gave Demansk the opening he needed.

"As it happens, 'sunsets and sunrises' are the reason I summoned you all here."

Thicelt's face grew still then, even solemn. "Ah." He glanced at Demansk's oldest son—oldest living son—who was seated at the huge table on the balcony, chatting amiably with his sister. Helga had the third of her children, a baby girl, perched in her lap.

"Ah," he repeated. "Have you discussed the matter with Olver?"

Demansk was pleased, even delighted, to see that Thicelt's quick wits had not slowed down any since he'd seen him last. Sharlz had been gone for over a year. At Demansk's command, Thicelt had led a fleet on a circumnavigation of the entire continent.

A very slow voyage, that had been. Thicelt had spent considerable time in every significant port. Laying over to take on provisions and allow his crews shore leave, officially. In reality, to drive home—none too subtly—the immense power at the disposal of the new regime of the Confederacy.

He'd also, of course, taken the opportunity to crush every nest of pirates along the way. And—this had been the most time-consuming part of his expedition—he had founded no less than nine new cities at strategic places he'd selected as he went. Two of them on the western coast of the southern continent; five along its southern coast; and two more on the small new archipelago he'd discovered a few hundred miles off the east coast.

Again, being none too subtle. All of them had been given the name of "Demansk," in one variety or another. Sharlz had used local dialects—Demansk City; Demanskburg; Demanskville; Demansk Town—everywhere except in the new archipelago, which was uninhabited. There, founding the two new cities which would stare down the Reedbottoms, Thicelt had eschewed subtlety altogether. He'd simply called one city "Demansk" and the other . . . "Demansk Too." The pun didn't work in the language of the Confederacy, but it did in the tongue of the Reedbottoms—for whom the word "also" was a homonym for "two."

So, Thicelt had been gone during the entire period when

Demansk had slowly come to the decision he would implement today. Had never exchanged so much as a single word on the subject with his ruler and sovereign-in-all-but-name. Still, he'd understood immediately, simply by a subtle reference to "sunsets and sunrises."

Gods, I've missed him. Especially now, when I can relax enough—I think—to enjoy a simple friendship.

"You'll be stationed here for quite a while, in the next period," Demansk mused. "Come visit, will you, Sharlz?"

Thicelt eyed him for a moment. Then, obviously realizing that this was a friend's request and not a tyrant's command, simply nodded. "It would be my pleasure, Verice. Although . . ."

Demansk chuckled. "Yes, yes. I can well imagine that organizing a circumnavigation of the entire globe will consume much of your time. Most of it, even though the expedition is still at least two years off."

He swiveled his head and studied Olver. "Yes, I've spoken to him. Quite some time ago, in fact—he was the first one I approached." Firmly: "There'll be no problem."

Thicelt rubbed his nose. "Didn't expect there would be. Olver's . . . ah, what's the word?"

For a moment, Demansk's face grew stiff. It still hurt, even after three years. "The opposite of Barrett, we can say."

Thicelt gave his head a little shake. "That's simply a negation, Verice. Unfair to both sons, truth be told, Olver even more than Barrett. Olver is . . . steady. To the point of saintliness, I sometimes think. He'd have made a good priest for Jassine."

Demansk barked a laugh. "Please! Do *not* mention that around Arsule. She gives me enough grief as it is on the subject of her favorite project."

He cast a sour glance toward the city on his left. There, in the very middle of it, the gigantic temple of the cult of Jassine was rising.

Still rising. Demansk was beginning to entertain dark suspicions that Arsule intended to keep the construction going until the peak of the temple overtopped even Demansk's palace—which had the head start of being perched on a bluff overlooking the city.

Thicelt cleared his throat. "Speaking of your gracious wife, are you—"

"She'll be allowed out of seclusion for the evening," growled Demansk. His eyes ranged the walls surrounding the palace, much as a general's survey an army camp. "No more, though. I don't dare let her out of her quarters onto the grounds itself for longer than that. Not unsupervised—and except for me, I can't trust *anyone* to keep an eye on her. The last time I let her onto the grounds, she and her damned priests started communicating with mirrors."

Thicelt started chuckling heavily. "Oh, Verice—give it up. Especially with Trae here for—what's it going to be? three months?—you don't have a chance. The boy dotes on his stepmother, you know he does. You think Trae can't figure out something which will undo all your strenuous efforts to keep her under control?"

Thicelt cleared his throat. "Have I mentioned Trae's latest enthusiasm? Something he got from Adrian during your son-in-law's last visit to Chalice. I don't really understand the principles that well, but here's . . ."

A few minutes later, Demansk was scowling at a sunset whose colors he no longer found splendid in the least.

Darkness, darkness, everywhere.

Radio?!

When Arsule made her entrance, however, just in time for the feast which was being prepared on the balcony, Demansk found his gloom lifting. Despite himself, Arsule always had that effect on him. Especially when her dark eyes sparkled so, as she gave him a sultry glance.

Whenever Demansk imposed his authority over her—which happened at least twice a year—Arsule immediately retaliated by locking the doors to her private quarters. Demansk could, of course, have ordered those doors broken down by his soldiery. But . . . leaving aside everything else, that would be *so* undignified.

Besides—also predictably—the doors never stayed locked for more than a few weeks. No matter how often they clashed, the fact was that Arsule and Demansk had grown very intimate over the past three years. As intimate, he would now admit even to himself—more intimate, in some ways—as he had ever been with Druzla. And . . .

The feast was starting. The Paramount Triumvir, master of the world, took his seat next to his wife at the head of the huge table. In every aspect, from his stern visage to his ponderous way of moving, he exuded the dignity one expects from such an august personage. All of which was actually quite at odds with the thought uppermost in his mind.

I'm getting laid tonight.

Under the table, unseen by anyone because of the rich cloth spilling over the edge, Arsule's slim fingers stroked his inner thigh.

Oh, yes indeed.

When the meal was finished, Demansk rose. Silence fell over the table. He gave the crowd gathered there a long and slow examination.

All my family.

His eyes fell on a slim and very pretty blonde young woman, seated not far down the table to his left. She was erect in her chair, very stiff, and looked nervous. Not surprising, of course, since it was the first time she had ever participated in such an affair.

Kata too, now that Arsule finally got the adoption through the bureaucratic maze. His lips quirked a little. He had no doubt at all that Arsule's present warmth was due to the adoption. Demansk himself, at the end, had settled the issue. Amazing, really, what the banishment of one obstreperous official to a remote post had on the efficiency of all others.

There was some sadness, seeing Kata at the table. It reminded him of Ion, whom he was coming to miss all the more as time went by. But not much. Whatever else, Demansk would be able to face Jeschonyk's shade in the afterlife.

Close advisers, most of them. Many of them, I think, now friends as well. Hard to tell, of course, with any except Sharlz.

Prit was there, naturally. As the highest financial official of the Confederacy, Sallivar was resident in the new capital.

So were Forent Nappur and Jessep Yunkers, who were also

sitting at the table. Demansk would allow the Council at Vanbert to retain their illusions of still being the "seat of power." His son Olver, who now resided in Vanbert, was always present at the Council to give his father's view on things. And while Olver had come to this gathering, Kall Oppricht had remained behind. To keep on eye on things, so to speak.

More to the point, Enry Sharbonow was there with him, *really* keeping an eye on things.

But when it came to the two real sources of Demansk's power—money and the assegais of his regiments—there would be no pretense. As the Emeralds would say, the Form of power remained in Vanbert. The Substance . . . elsewhere.

Demansk's eyes ranged all the way down the long table on the balcony of the palace—the size of a galley on the ocean—taking note of all the officials and notables gathered for the occasion. Their faces were quite well illuminated by the new gas lamps which Adrian had designed and which had first been introduced, outside of Adrian's own palace in Solinga, in Demansk's new capital.

It was . . . impressive.

He had everyone's attention. It was time to do the thing. And, now that it was, Demansk was immensely relieved to recognize the emotion that swept through him.

Relief itself. *I have not gone mad, after all.*

"It is time to make a change," he said. Loud enough to be heard easily, but eschewing all traditional histrionics. In that, too, he had created a new style of rulership. Demansk was tired of drama.

"I am nearing sixty." He gave his belly a little pat. Rather a self-satisfied one, truth be told. There still wasn't much fat there. Despite his sedentary existence, Demansk maintained enough of his old exercise regimen to stay in good shape. Arsule certainly—

Feeling the heat building in his loins, Demansk pushed the idle thought aside. The official robes of office he was wearing were lightweight, as was necessary in the climate of the isthmus. An erection would be quite noticeable, to those seated nearby, and not even Demansk's new style of public rhetoric was *that* informal.

So, he pushed on firmly to the subject at hand. "Time, in short, for me to start thinking of retirement."

A little stir went around the table. Not much of one, however. Although few of the people at the table had discussed the matter explicitly with Demansk—only four, really; Demansk's own children—he hadn't expected anyone to be that surprised.

And, here too, he realized, his relief was well-founded. It came as a little surprise to recognize that perhaps he alone, of all those closest to him, had ever really worried about Demansk maintaining his sanity.

Well . . . leaving aside Arsule's frequent pronouncements on the subject. *Private* pronouncements, of course—but Arsule's definition of "private" hadn't changed in the least over the years, even as her salons and soirees and gala events had trebled and quadrupled in size.

He was startled to feel her hand slide into his, the fingers wrapping around his palm and knuckles and giving them a little squeeze. *In public? How undignified! Was she mad?*

Probably. But he did not spurn the fingers—even gave them a little responding squeeze of his own. It was a mad world, after all, and Demansk's own definition of sanity had undergone a certain transformation over the world.

Besides, I adore the woman—not that I'd ever say that except privately. And my definition of "private" is—my thoughts alone.

Arsule's thumb, hidden in his palm, began making a little movement which was so far removed from the concept of "august dignity" that it boggled the mind.

Although, I don't think I'm fooling Arsule any. The thumb moved, moved. *Which is probably just as well. Best exercise I get.*

He cleared his throat noisily. "As I was saying, it's time for a change. The beginnings of one, at any rate."

From there, his speech took on a more formal aspect. For some time, Demansk orated—hoping he wasn't simply "droning"—on the principles of rule. As exemplified in practice—good and bad—by the experience of the Confederacy; as illustrated in theory—good and bad—by the philosophers of the Emeralds. Perhaps more to the point, as deduced by Demansk himself from a lifetime of experience.

He saw no reason to add: *a thousand lifetimes, actually, since I've spent more hours than I can remember talking to Adrian about it and, through him, his "spirits."*

"—for which reason, until our populace enjoys the wealth and literacy which could make the Speakers' Houses—and the Council, of course—something which truly embodied and represented their desires and interests, it seems best to stabilize the current regime. Which in turn—"

Hours and hours and hours. Sometimes in face-to-face conversation—as weird an experience as any in Demansk's life, talking to one man who was actually three.

"—no desire, *none whatsoever,* to repeat the endless cycle of factional maneuvering for the mere sake of a year's worth of self-aggrandizement—to call it by its right name, plunder of the public treasury, as often as not—by gaining election to the Speakership—"

No, not that, really. Demansk had come to understand that while two spirits inhabited his son-in-law, they did not *possess* him. Any more than Demansk's own closest advisers "possessed" *him.* Adrian Gellert's mind was enhanced, surely. His soul remained his alone.

"—hence the reintroduction of the hereditary principle seems called for, although—"

He gave a quick glance at his daughter, seated just four chairs to his right. And, slightly behind her, the stools and attendants which kept her offspring in something vaguely resembling "order" at a public event. Three of them, now—with, judging from the swell of her midriff, yet another soon to join the world.

Sure as anything, no spirits did that.

As he droned on—orated, rather—Demansk had to repress a grin. He had no doubt his grandfather would have fiercely disapproved most of what Demansk was doing, not least of all the way he was favoring an Emerald son-in-law. But on one subject, at least, the stern old man would have grudgingly given Adrian Gellert his approval. *Keep 'em barefoot and pregnant, whatever you do. Barefoot, you can negotiate, now and then.*

"—so, to conclude, I propose a modification which, I think, will give us, dealing with present circumstances, the best of all possible worlds."

He was tempted to add: *as shown to me by a machine which* knows *all possible worlds.* But he left it unsaid. For almost all of the people gathered around this table, as well-educated and sophisticated as most of them were, the explanation would have been indistinguishable from "magic." Given that Demansk had not yet seen fit to eliminate the laws outlawing magic, that would be . . . awkward.

He was nearing the end of his speech, which was going to probably be awkward enough.

"—each Triumvirate, therefore, to become a cycle. A training ground, as it were, the senior Triumvirs—with the approval of the others—adopting their own successors. Neither relying on the vagaries of fate—"

As always, the memory of Barrett ached. Not so much, true, yet never absent. But Demansk had long since realized that particular ache was the surest sign he was still sane.

"—nor the whims of factional strife—"

Drone, drone—*wrap it up, damnation.*

"So, in conclusion, I take this occasion to announce my own successor. A choice which, I might mention, has the full approval of both of my fellow Triumvirs as well as"—here, his voice grew stern: the patriarch in full glory—"my own magnificent sons."

And . . . that's enough. There'll be endless time for all the squabbling. I'm tired of drama. Have been for a long time.

He simply pointed to Adrian, seated three chairs to his right. With no one between him and Demansk except Olver and Trae.

"Him." And sat down.

Three things happened simultaneously.

Dead silence fell over the small crowd. Except—

Olver and Trae both shot to their feet, holding up their goblets of wine and calling for a toast.

Arsule leaned over and whispered into his ear: "I thought you'd sworn off drama and histrionics."

⁂

The fourth thing which happened, of course, was a given. Far down the table, one of the officials from—Demansk couldn't quite remember which branch of the bureaucracy; some post in the Registry—rose to his feet and began speaking.

"—fully agree with the political insights of the Paramount—"

Again, a whisper from Arsule: "I *told* you to have the whole lot of them executed. Exile just one of them! Ha! Like trying to drown a redshark."

"—still, a well-nigh insuperable problem. Difficult, at the very least. As the Paramount's *son,* of course, the august Gellert will have no choice but to divorce his wife, she now being his sister. But—"

Adrian choked on his goblet of wine. Helga sat up straight in her chair and bestowed upon the far distant bureaucrat a glare of fury that would have wilted anyone except—

"I'm telling you, Verice," whispered Arsule, "they're not really human. Trust me! According to the high priest of Jassine, bureaucrats are actually—"

"—leave the legal problem of the status of the children to be decided. By rigorous interpretation of existing law, of course, exposure on a rock is the only—"

What followed next confirmed for Verice Demansk, anew, the wisdom of always having two strings for his bow. His daughter had long since given up the practice of bearing a sword in public. But—no fool, she—Lortz was always nearby, ready to hand it to her.

The official from the Registry did manage to escape from the palace grounds with nothing worse than a minor flesh wound. But it was a close thing; and, the guards who witnessed the events all agreed, was saved only by his pursuer's quite evident state of pregnancy.

When Helga stalked back on to the balcony, she returned the sword to Lortz. Then, glared at the crowd in general. Then, at Adrian.

To the first, she said nothing. Words would have been, indeed, superfluous.

To Adrian, hissed: "Go ahead. Say *anything* about the responsibilities of pregnant women."

Adrian, confirming again Demansk's judgement of his successor, maintained the silence of a sage.

For once, Arsule agreed with her tyrant husband. "Well, at least *he's* not crazy."

AFTERWORD

How It All Came About

by David Drake

Many years ago I wrote plot outlines for what became The General series. I used the career of the 6th century a.d. Byzantine general Belisarius as the template for my hero, Raj Whitehall, but I gave him the support of a supercomputer and a purpose greater than that of satisfying the megalomania of his master Justinian. Steve Stirling very ably turned the four outlines into five fat novels.

Jim Baen liked the result (so did I and so have quite a number of readers) and suggested I plot a series of single-shot spin-offs utilizing other historical templates. I did so, though I'm afraid with less success. *The Green Planet* was probably a bad idea (no, it wasn't my idea but I acquiesced); it's unlikely ever to be turned into a novel. *The Chosen*, based on what I considered the reality of Steve's Draka universe, had unexpected practical problems. The result is a good book, but getting to that point wasn't a process either Steve or I would willingly undergo again.

That left two first-rate outlines, one based on an Ancient Egyptian model and the other on the fall of the Roman Republic. The latter was particularly complex; Steve, Jim, and I agreed that it should be split into two novels (as had happened with the third outline of the Belisarius series) to make up for my failure with *The Green Planet.*

Unfortunately there were more glitches. Steve ran into physical problems. The first half of the outline, published as *The Reformer*, was a lot shorter than anybody had expected, and Steve then decided he wouldn't be able to finish the series on a practical timeline. Eric Flint cheerfully stepped in (well, he was more cheerful about the situation than I was) and took up the slack.

The Tyrant is therefore the sequel to *The Reformer*. Eric had a very difficult task in integrating the existing novel with his own, in addition to following the remaining half of the outline and creating a self-standing novel at the same time. I'm extremely pleased with the way he handled it. Those of you who read both halves will be interested in the way two different, able writers have handled the same material.

The material itself is a subject that I've pondered for all my adult life. The collapse of the Roman Republic looks simple when you simply follow a schematic of the events: Marius and Sulla, victorious generals, fought for leadership of the state. Sulla won, returned the government to what he considered its ideal form, and died. Reckless adventurers, in particular Cataline (who was put down by the heroic efforts of Cicero), attempted to gain power by force but for a time were prevented.

Then Caesar and Pompey, successful generals in the mold of Marius and Sulla, fought for the throne—first through gangs of thugs in the city, then with armies across the entire empire and beyond. Caesar won, and despite his immediate assassination, his victory had doomed the Republic and even the semblance of democracy in Rome.

As I said—simple. And almost entirely untrue.

In large measure the simplicity is what makes it false. Marius and Sulla were only two actors in an enormously complex struggle which involved many parties within the Roman polity and even more outside it. The rights of the elites of the Italian states (the *Socii*, allies), foreign enemies who used resentment of Roman rule to gain support within the outlying provinces (Mithridates VI was the most prominent but by no means the only example), local resistance movements aided by one or another Roman party (Sertorius and others), piracy on a scale unequaled by illegal enterprise until the appearance of modern drug cartels, and a massive slave revolt were all major factors.

That was just the prelude. The Civil War, the climactic struggle that gave us genuine works of art in the form of Lucan's epic *de Bello Civile* and Caesar's prose dispatches collected under the same title, was just as complex. After the fact it's easy to assume that—for example—Clodius was in command of Caesar's street gangs in Rome. Caesar wouldn't have claimed that, and Clodius would have denied it hotly: his blood went back to Attus Clausus at the beginning of the Republic, and he was very much a player in his own right.

The same is true of scores of others, great men or would-be great men, whose names are forgotten now except by experts on the period. Alliances were circumstantial and unstable (look at the Northern Alliance in Afghanistan for a contemporary model of the situation). Every man had his own vision, and almost every one was out for himself. The Roman conquest of the Near East with its enormous wealth had made the potential prizes (for the infantryman no less than for the warlord) so great that greed generally overwhelmed honor.

Oddly enough, Caesar himself was one of the few who actually tried to save the state. He saw that the old system was dead: the government suitable for a city-state couldn't effectively rule an enormous empire, especially given the difficulties of communicating over the distances involved. The system he tried to put in place required that all parties recognize that it was the best possible compromise.

None of them did. Greed and fanaticism won, leaving Caesar dead on the floor of the Senate house.

Caesar's system might not have worked anyway. He was a very smart man and perhaps a wise one, but he wasn't a saint. At the time of his murder he was planning another military expedition, this time into Mesopotamia. Perhaps he meant it as a way to occupy the tens of thousands of soldiers who were too dangerous to demobilize, but it could as easily have been because Caesar himself had no real plan except war till Rome's armies had marched to the ends of the earth.

Regardless, Caesar's attempt to turn the Roman Republic into a moderate autocracy was never tried. At his death, another—even messier, even bloodier—civil war convulsed the Roman world for fifteen years. At its conclusion, Augustus—Octavian—reigned supreme in a fashion no one could call moderate.

One of Caesar's last acts was to send away his German bodyguard, saying that a Roman official didn't need foreigners to protect him against his own people. That was a mistake Augustus never made.

And Augustus died in bed.

—David Drake
david-drake.com

•